THE MANGY PARROT

THE MANGY PARROT

THE LIFE AND TIMES OF PERIQUILLO SARNIENTO,
WRITTEN BY HIMSELF FOR HIS CHILDREN

José Joaquín Fernández de Lizardi,
"El Pensador Mexicano"

TRANSLATED BY DAVID FRYE
Introduction by Nancy Vogeley

First edition, 1816
This translation is based on the third edition
(5 volumes, 1830–1831)
and fourth edition (4 volumes, 1842)

Hackett Publishing Company
Indianapolis/Cambridge

Copyright © 2004 by Hackett Publishing Company, Inc.

Printed in the United States of America

10 09 08 07 06 05 04   1 2 3 4 5 6 7

For further information, please address
Hackett Publishing Company, Inc.
P. O. Box 44937
Indianapolis, IN 46244–0937

www.hackettpublishing.com

 This translation was supported in part by an award from the
National Endowment for the Arts.

Cover image is *Terulia de pulquería* by José Augustín Arrieta, 1851. Reprinted by
permission of El Museo Andrés Blastien.
Cover design by Abigail Coyle
Interior design by Meera Dash
Composition by William Hartman
Printed at Sheridan Books, Inc.

Library of Congress Cataloging-in-Publication Data

Fernández de Lizardi, José Joaquín, 1776–1827.
    [Periquillo Sarniento. English]
    The mangy parrot : the life and times of Periquillo Sarniento : written
        by himself for his children / José Joaquín Fernández de Lizardi ;
        translated by David Frye.
            p. cm.
    Includes bibliographical references.
    ISBN 0-87220-669-6 (cloth) — 0-87220-735-8 (paper)
        I. Title.

    PQ7297.F37P313 2004
    863'.5—dc22

                                                    2003056894

∞

. . . No one should believe that this portrait is of himself, but rather that there are many devils that look very like one another. Whoever has dirt on his face would be better served spending his time washing himself, than criticizing and scrutinizing my thoughts, my locutions, my ideas, or any other defects of my work.

TORRES Villarroel, Prologue to *Barca de Aqueronte*
(The Boat of Acheron), 1744

CONTENTS

INTRODUCTION

Satire and Decolonization

When José Joaquín Fernández de Lizardi published his masterwork, *El Periquillo Sarniento*, in 1816 in Mexico City, he was making a clean break with three centuries of colonial practice. Through the long years of Spanish rule, not even the most creative of writers in the colonies had produced a novel—and this in spite of the fact that the novel was a favored genre in Spain itself in the 16th and 17th centuries.[1] Literary historians have long speculated about the reason for this discrepancy. Some have argued that American writers shied away from the novel due to the Inquisition, which denounced fiction for uselessly stimulating readers' imaginations and banned the novels from the colonies, the weaker peoples of which it would have harmed; yet the fact that the classic Spanish novels were exported to the Spanish Americas and avidly read there—not only *Don Quijote*, but also such fictions as the romances of chivalry, *Guzmán de Alfarache* and *El buscón*—belies this theory. Others have argued that American realities were so marvelous in themselves that colonial writers had no need to invent stories.

A very different explanation for the absence of the novel in Spain's colonies, or indeed of any mirroring prose technique, can be found in a definition of satire that Lizardi himself wrote for an unpublished collection of poetry dated December 3, 1822:[2]

> A satire is a poem that rebukes vices by ridiculing them, insofar as it deals only with the vices themselves and not the persons—which is what we endeavor to do, following Martial's advice: *Parcere personis, dicere de vitiis.* Book X, Ep. 33. A satire is pleasing to readers and, according to one Spanish writer, it is even more so than a panegyric poem; the reason he gives is that satire is always true and devoid of the flattery and hyperbole which (generally speaking) adorn praise, so that satire enters the readers' minds more easily.
>
> There have been many famous poets who have written in this style in every era. Outstanding examples among the ancients are Horace, Juvenal, and Persius; among modern poets: Quevedo, Góngora, Moreto, Gracián, and so forth, among the Spanish; the inimitable Dante, among the Italians; Régnier, among the French; and so on elsewhere, for it would seem pedantic to list

---

[1] Literary historians are generally agreed that the *Periquillo* is the first novel to appear in Spanish America, indeed in Mexico. A few scholars, however, have argued that other prose works, produced earlier, deserve this distinction. For further discussion of this matter and other assertions I make throughout the remainder of this essay, see my *Lizardi and the Birth of the Novel in Spanish America*.

[2] I have edited this previously unknown collection, together with a study of manuscript writing at that moment in Mexico: *La literatura manuscrita: Un manuscrito inédito de poesías de José Joaquín Fernández de Lizardi* (México: UNAM, Bancroft Library, 2003).

even just the ones who have come to my attention, and what I have already said is enough to prove my point.[3]

Of course there will be some people who, knowing nothing about what I have just mentioned, will want to try to give a malign interpretation to some of my writings; there will also be some who say that my pen flows on too long about these matters; and finally, there will be some who, treating what they don't understand as a mystery, will be shocked that my works have been permitted to be published. To the first of these, I say: learn before you talk, and understand that heretics also know how to interpret the Holy Scriptures to suit their whims. To the second ones, I say: compare my satires with those of Quevedo, Moreto, and others, and see whether those poets' works are more honest than mine. And to the last, who are so put out (which makes me fear that, seeing their own portraits in my writings, they complain as if they have been wounded), I say: if nobody asks you, you don't have to give your names; just sit back and let things take their course, which is the prudent thing to do, and enjoy the following tale.[4]

Poetry was the operative literary mode in the colonies throughout the years of colonial rule, and only two forms were to be found there: the *elogios*, or celebratory verse associated with viceregal celebration and mourning, and satire. Of the two, Lizardi found that only satire told the truth. As a colonial who was opening up things that others preferred to hide, Lizardi took pains to establish a literary lineage for satire in which he could safely position himself; thus he mentioned the national poets of

---

[3] Horace (65–68 B.C.); Juvenal (60?–140); Persius (34–62); Francisco de Quevedo (1580–1645); Luis de Góngora (1561–1627); Agustín Moreto (1618–1669); Baltasar Gracián (1601–1658); Dante Alighieri (1265–1321); Mathurin Régnier (1573–1613).

[4] "La satira es un Poëma, que reprehende los vicios ridiculizandolos, y siempre que toque solo á estos, y no á la personas, que es lo que procuramos, sigueiendo el consejo de Marcial: *Parcere personis, dicere de vittis.* Ep. 3 del lib X. [La satira] es agradable á los lectores, y segun un Escritor español, lo es aún mas que el Poëma panegirico, y dá por razon: que como la Satira siempre es verdadera, y carece de la lisonja, ó hiperboles, de que (por lo regular) se vistan los elogios, de hay [alli] es, que se introduce con mas facilidad en el entendimiento.

"Muchos, y celebres, han sido en todos tiempos los Poëtas, que han escrito en este estilo: entre los antiguos sobresalieron Horacio, Juvenal, y Persio. Entre los modernos, Quevedo, Gongora, Moreto, Gracian, && entre los Españoles, el singular Dante entre los Italianos, Regnier entre los Franceses, y asi en otras partes, que pareciera pedantisimo poner en lista aún solo los que han llegado á mi noticia; y para lo que intenta persuadir basta lo dicho.

"No falta quien, en ayunas de todo esto quiera interpretar siniestramente el sentido de algunos de mis papeles; no falta tampoco quien diga, que mi pluma corre demasiadamente en la materia; y no falta, por fin, quien haciendo misterio de lo que ignora, se espanta de que se permitan publicar mis producciones. A los primeros digo: Que se instruyan antes de hablar, y que sepan, que tambien los hereges saben interpretar a su antojo las Santas Escrituras. A los segundos digo: que cotejen mis satiras con las de Quevedo, Moreto, y otros, y vean si las de estos les exceden en honestidad: y á los ultimos, que se mosquean tanto, (por cuanto temo, que viendose retratados en los papeles, se quejan como adoloridos) les digo, que si no les preguntan, no digan como se llaman, que dexen correr la bola, que es prudencia, y se diviertan con el siguiendo Cuentecillo. . . ."

Spain, Italy, and France, finding in their satire the justification for his own criticism of local wrongs and the rationale for his portrayal of national peculiarities.

Although he focused on poetry in this definition of satire, his sense of the term is loose. For Lizardi, "poetry" refers not to a genre, but rather to the rules and expectations for colonial literary production. His recognition of satire as an alternative to adulatory poetry was a recuperative strike in his colonial world at that moment, legitimating varieties of discourse on which officials had frowned. The literary terminology of "genre," as we are accustomed to using it today to contrast "poetry" and "prose," seems, therefore, to have been of little concern to Lizardi. His choice to write as a satirist, or poetaster in the case of most of his "poetry," reflects his preference for critical and popular literature, and it reflects as well the climate of rebellion around him as the colony fought a war that resulted ultimately in independence from Spain. Fiction, which he employed in the *Periquillo*, his other novels, his works of theater, and in several of his newspaper essays, was an extension of this satirical preference.

This authorial definition of satire is a useful starting point for a discussion of the *Periquillo*. In the definition, Lizardi displayed the memory of Mexico's past and great self-awareness. He apparently understood how the heavy weight of politics determined what writers could produce—in remote times and in his own day, when colonial strictures still prevailed. Colonial literature either catered to the governing elite or escaped the pressures of patronage and permission-solicitation by seeking to have its honesty be "agreeable" to, one supposes, readers outside that small circle. He does not associate it with the pleasure of comedy or humor, nor does he suggest that satire, the truth-telling mode, was often the low product of popular song, anonymous subversion, and the scurrilous attacks of the powerless. For him, satire's agreeableness was a function of its rational appeal to honesty (by "honesty," one understands exposure of the lies told by the other kind of poetry, subject matter that revealed previously ignored realities, and explicit language).

Many colonial attitudes toward satire are packed into this definition. "Satire" was a term used by colonial authorities to describe the slander and vilification that were directed at them, and which they tried to control by Inquisition decrees and police efforts. The Church, too, weighed in on satire and how criticism was to be handled. It cautioned that moral failures and portrayal of such errors in pious literature such as the catechism had to distinguish between the sin and the sinner, insisting that only the sin was being attacked and no harm was intended to the person; a satirist had to have a pure heart and avoid any impression of vengefulness. In European countries, other than Spain, that were beginning to transmit knowledge of their cultures to Mexico, satirists such as Molière were using caricature that exaggerated the sin and the sinner for comic effect and society's correction; there, satire was justified. Consequently, Lizardi would have received these various attitudes toward the literary tool he chose to employ in the *Periquillo*; and it seems he understood that his use of satire in the Mexican context had to be restrained for still another reason. After independence, Mexicans would have to come together in a harmonious family. The hatreds occasioned by the independence war would have to be healed. Thus his humorous criticism of persons and conditions, although direct enough to be recognizable, is usually not cruel; instead, the reader's smile or laughter often results from Lizardi's penetration and revelation of society's deceptions, from his clever turn of phrase.

Although, in his definition of satire, Lizardi invoked European traditions as protection against those who might take offense at seeing themselves portrayed in his depictions, the specific Mexican circumstances of the novel and his other work give the lie to the pretense that he belongs to the Spanish (or any other European) tradition, and tacitly establish his Mexican identity and the beginnings of a new Mexican literature. He only borrowed his national consciousness, he said, from European writers whose subject matter grew out of their particular geographical and historical identities. Additionally, his meditation on satire importantly extended to an awareness of who his Mexican reading public might be. In imagining the three categories into which his readers might fall according to their reactions, he revealed sensitivities as to not only his work's reception, but also the censorship and system of permissions still used in the first decades of Mexico's 19th century, which limited writers and trained readers. He particularly worried about the accusations that professional intellectuals might level at him. In the imperative, "[K]now that even heretics know how to interpret the Holy Scriptures," he argued that laymen and persons educated according to untraditional standards could have access to sacred books. Thus in anticipating the criticism of professional writers, he revealed his own insecurities as a self-educated writer who was daring to enter the Mexican print world, formerly controlled by Spanish professionals and loyalists. His use of the plurality of "heretics" suggests that many Mexicans were heretics, variously stepping beyond their assigned inferior station and submissiveness to compete with and attack established authority. Mexico's independence war was only the most obvious example of colonial rebellion.

The war, which began in 1810 with Miguel Hidalgo's *Grito de Dolores*[5] and ended in 1821 with Mexico's independence from Spain, was a complex of battle issues and alliances. Mexicans fought against Spaniards, but they also fought one another. Royalists and insurgents changed sides; liberty with religious freedoms was not the same campaign in Mexico that it was in other parts of Spanish America where independence wars were waged; Spain was alternately identified with the liberal constitutionalism of the Cortes de Cádiz, and with the monarchy of Fernando VII. When the Congress of Vienna in 1814 and 1815 ended the Napoleonic presence in Europe and restored Fernando to his throne, conservative Spaniards, but also liberals who hoped for modernizing reforms, at first welcomed him, but then soon revolted against his harsh rule. The freedom given to Mexico's presses in 1812 was terminated. Yet the brief period of debate the free press permitted seems to have set ordinary Mexicans to thinking for themselves about a national future. The many newspapers and political pamphlets published from 1812–1814 and then again after 1820 accustomed Mexicans to writing and reading their own literature. They began

---

[5] Miguel Hidalgo y Costilla (1753–1811), priest of the town of Dolores, began the war of independence at five in the morning of September 16, 1810, with the "Grito" (shout or cry): "¡Viva la Independencia! ¡Viva la América! ¡Muera el mal gobierno!" (Long live independence! Long live America! Death to bad government!). This rallying cry is repeated on this same date every year, to commemorate Mexican independence and the birth of the nation.

to examine their own needs and to reject the lessons Spanish governmental and Church representatives had taught. They learned to tolerate different points of view in a way that suggested orthodoxy was yielding to heterodoxy. The new books that were being imported as a result of port officials' laxness and changing political loyalties encouraged rereadings of sacred texts, and access to prohibited works.

In the phrase "even heretics know how to interpret Holy Scripture," it is significant that Lizardi employed religious language to describe his secular writing. Ostensibly, he was drawing a comparison between his critics, who he said "give a malign interpretation" to what he wrote, and "heretics," a term that in that late-colonial period was understood to refer to the Protestant reformers who put their own spin on the holy text of the Bible. His use of the metaphor is awkward and slippery, however; and it can easily be read as comparing his own satire with the "heretical" rethinking of canonical Writ. Without mentioning Martin Luther, Lizardi seems to have been comparing his own unauthorized access to books and his advance into Mexico's print world with the translation work done by Luther, which led to alternative belief and divisions in Christian Europe. As a public writer, he had neither the Church nor the colonial government to back him up, and his run-ins with both of those gatekeepers of orthodoxy certainly lent him a heretical air.

In his focus on his critics' varying responses to his writing—largely based on their ignorance and misunderstanding of their increasing need to assume responsibility for judgment in reading the new material printers were making available, once Inquisition authorities no longer verified "truths"—Lizardi gave evidence that he had thought about how ordinary Mexican readers might venture into the book world, from which they had previously been excluded. He said that these readers would prefer satire because they could understand it more easily. Satire does not have the obfuscation that praise and hyperbole do. Here he diagnosed the special needs of the colonial reader. Conditioned to stay away from books that he was told were the prerogative of specialists, and put off by the language of books he had attempted to penetrate, the colonial reader needed a new kind of literature—one that Lizardi would provide.

I

Many modern-day critics subsume the *Periquillo* into a literature variety called "the picaresque."[6] The list of those critical authorities who do so is long and impressive: Luis Urbina, Pedro Henríquez Ureña, Arturo Torres-Ríoseco, Fernando Alegría, María Casas de Faunce, Katherine Anne Porter, and Jefferson Rea Spell. The colonial censor, José Mariano Beristáin de Souza, when he first read Lizardi's novel in 1816, helped to determine this classification with a Peninsular literary category when he compared it with Mateo Alemán's *Guzmán de Alfarache*. This novel from Spain's Golden Age (1550–1650) is commonly regarded as a model for the picaresque genre, and formalist critics and comparatist historians trace that pattern in books as remote from one another as *Moll Flanders* and *The Adventures of Huckleberry Finn*.

---

[6] A useful study is Peter Dunn's *Spanish Picaresque Fiction: A New Literary History* (Ithaca: Cornell University Press, 1993).

They use a checklist to see whether a novel conforms to the Spanish form (a first-person narrator, usually from the underclass; a chain of events in which the *pícaro* meets various social types whose immoralities represent the pathology of the whole society; an open-ended conclusion; black humor; and so on); and, if it does, they then usually remove the novel from its roots and place it in the prestigious body of writing called *Weltliteratur.*[7]

However, when one goes back to the literary histories of the 19th century, which were beginning to formulate a Spanish national canon and standardize the teaching of these approved texts to young readers, one does not find the picaresque genre emerging until mid-century. Even then, one reads of how the authors of those histories debated as to whether "the literature of roguery" or "the literature of beggary" best described the category they were inventing.[8] Recently, though, studies such as those of Anne Cruz,[9] which understand the picaresque as "discourses of poverty," are in the process of examining past literary practices and asking how and why that underclass world was objectified by writers, prettified by their Baroque language, and then made respectable by critical elevation to the canon.

Thus, I will argue that to include the *Periquillo* in a European-based line of literary development is misleading; the displacement robs the book of its Mexican originality and avoids serious consideration of its low viewpoint. In Lizardi's day, "satire," with its origins in classical literature and the vernacular national poetry Lizardi listed (but also in the counter-discourses already around Mexicans), would have absorbed discussions of what has come to be associated with the picaresque literary mode. Lizardi's readers would have had a different set of expectations for their reading. That is why Lizardi's discussion of satire is so useful in helping to establish just what those colonial expectations—based on the parameters set by politics—were at that moment of decolonization. Satire then was not the light touch that today we often associate with literary irony, but rather the full blast of words that opened up a wrong to public view and shame.[10]

Contemporary newspapers like the *Diario de México* reveal conflicting attitudes toward "the novel." There, the novel is contrasted with the earlier romances of chivalry, the stories of which had been invented; they were fantasies that were based on untruth and that strained the reader's credulity. The novel, then, in its first forms,

---

[7] See the influential work of Claudio Guillén in *Literature as System: Essays toward the Theory of Literary History* (Princeton: Princeton University Press, 1971), particularly Chapters 3 and 5.

[8] Antonio Alcalá Galiano, *Literatura española siglo XIX : De Moratín a Rivas.* Trad., edición de Vicente Llorens. (Madrid: Alianza Editorial, 1969); Frank W. Chandler, *The Literature of Roguery.* 2 vols. (Boston, New York: Houghton, Mifflin, 1907).

[9] *Discourses of Poverty: Social Reform and the Picaresque in Early Modern Spain.* (Toronto: University of Toronto Press, 1989).

[10] Two proofs that Lizardi was concerned with satire at the time he wrote the *Periquillo* are (1) his early discussion, in the novel, of satire and his concern that his readers would denounce his contemporary critique of Mexican life, vilifying him as "a mordant satirist," and (2) his publication in 1816 of a newspaper, *Las sombras de Heráclito y Demócrito,* in which satire was an important topic. Here and throughout the rest of this essay, I draw on the accessible paperback edition of the *Periquillo,* edited by Jefferson Rea Spell, first published by Porrúa in Mexico City in 1959 in the "Sepan Cuantos" series, and in print ever since.

such as *Don Quijote* and *Guzmán de Alfarache*, parodied the chivalric romance by showing how its fantasies were foolish and its ideals were usually confounded by earthly realities. Thus the novel's realism, a kind of demythification, was admired. But the novel could also be suspected of falsehood, since its stories were made up; and writers of the 18th century who conformed to neoclassical aesthetic preferences, usually hid their narrative fictions behind labels such as a "life," "dreams" or "reveries," "letters," "confessions," or "histories." Mexicans in particular were caught between conflicting attitudes toward the novel, reflecting, to a large degree, their political loyalties. Mexicans with French tastes looked down on the novel. Yet Mexicans with Spanish ties took pride in the novel's roots in Spain, and spoke admiringly of *Don Quijote.* Mexicans read avidly the Spanish translations of novels by authors such as Daniel Defoe and Henry Fielding, which Inquisition censors approved of and the importation of which into Mexico they permitted; Mexicans read with enthusiasm the narrativized essays of Spaniards such as Diego de Torres Villarroel and P. Francisco Isla.[11]

Novels were likened to histories in supposedly being based on real events and certain geography. However, this worried Mexicans who wondered whether they could rely on the accuracy of the histories that had told of their conquest. When they began to compare the new histories that praised the accomplishments of Mexican Indian peoples, written by men like P. Francisco Xavier Clavijero, with the accounts of Spanish victories over barbarian peoples, produced earlier by the Spaniards Hernán Cortés, Bernal Díaz de Castillo, and Antonio de Solís, they found discrepancies.[12] Thus Mexicans in the first decades of the 19th century began to question the reliability of "history" and were coming around to the possibility that perhaps invented narratives—novels—revealed truth more fully and convincingly.

II

It is against this background, then, that in 1816 Lizardi published the *Periquillo.* Emerging in the midst of the warfare, the novel found a publisher—Alejandro Valdés—and enthusiastic readers for several reasons, the most important of which was its satiric pedigree. Although satire licenses the representation of ugliness and baseness in a way that might appeal to prurience, a moral stance holds out a criterion for improvement. Although sniggering laughter might result from seeing a proud nobleman humbled, on reflection the vice satirized might also be found in the reader's self. Although the novel dramatized a young man's fall to crime, the book's ending stressed his repentance, his rehabilitation to decency, and the moral lessons to be learned from such an experience. This double vision of sin and redemption, wild abandon and censure, disorder and order, which satire usually insisted upon then, structures the *Periquillo's* story.

---

[11] Defoe (1660–1731) and Fielding (1707–1754), English novelists; Torres Villarroel (1693–1770) and Isla (1703–1781), Spanish writers.

[12] Clavijero (1731–1787), Mexican Jesuit historian; Cortés (1485–1547), Spanish conquistador and letter writer; Díaz de Castillo (1492–1581?), Spanish soldier with Cortés and historian; Solís (1610–1686), Spanish chronicler of the Indies.

Pedro Sarmiento, who is given the ridiculous name Periquillo Sarniento (Itching Parrot) by his classmates, is the book's hero. "Perico" is a diminutive form of Pedro, but it also can refer to any unimportant person; another of its meanings is "parrot" or "parakeet." "Periquillo" further adds to the diminutive and debases the respectable name. Similarly, "Sarniento" takes "Sarmiento" and converts it into "mangy" or "lousy." The son of *criollo* parents (Mexican-born Spaniards whose cultural leanings were toward Spain and whose political loyalties were usually to the ruling class), he is educated according to the standards of his day: that is, his teachers, themselves badly educated, only teach their pupils to spout useless Latin, superficial logical proofs, and misunderstood scientific terminology, without giving them any practical knowledge of the world in which they actually live. His parents, though they have a respectable Spanish surname, have little money, and so Pedro's father seeks to have his son learn a trade that will sustain him in adulthood. But Pedro's proud mother resists the notion that her son must work to earn his living. The boy then unsuccessfully studies theology and begins religious studies, preparatory to becoming a priest.

However, once his father dies and he wastes the little inheritance he has gotten, Pedro descends to a life of debauchery and crime. Imprisoned, first for his minor crimes, in a Mexico City jail, he is later sent to Manila, where Mexico banished its hardened offenders. This interlude, along with a few chapters in which Pedro is shipwrecked and marooned on a Pacific island on his way home, are the only departures from a story set in contemporary Mexico. Lizardi ends his book with further evidence of its topicality, by having his fictional counterpart say that he has written it in 1813 in the midst of the war. Although there he states that he could elaborate on the causes of this war to decide which of the parties—the Spanish government or the Americans who want independence—is to blame for the war, he refrains from this analysis, he says, for fear of compromising his readers. And, further avoiding the questions of historical cause and blame, he ends this comment by describing the effects of civil war, which is what this war has become in Mexico: "Rage, vengeance, and cruelty, inseparable from any war, are nourished in those citizens who take up arms to destroy their fellows."[13]

This atmosphere of mutual hatred and cruelty, which prevailed in Mexico at that time, permeates Lizardi's novel. Pedro and his companions cheat innocent victims, but they also prey on one another. They disregard society's rules but also suppress innate feelings of human sympathy. Pedro repays his father's kindness with deceit and, when he marries during his lowlife escapades, does not do so out of love. He betrays a Chinese man who has shown him favors. Only toward the book's end, when Pedro reflects and learns the lesson of gratitude as he attains maturity and approaches death, does his character change. Throughout the book, Lizardi's language furthers this sense of Mexico's turn toward inhumanity. In the flippant tone, insulting exchanges, and low humor sometimes connected to bodily functions, the author conveys this climate. In the story, and also in the language with which it is

---

[13] "La ira, la venganza y la crueldad, inseparables de toda guerra, se ceban en los mismos ciudadanos que se arman para destruirse mutuamente" (452).

told, he deconstructs the myths by which decent society lived and expresses the bitterness of coming to grips with harsh truths.

The novel, which was published in installments on Tuesdays and Fridays beginning in February 1816, was immediately popular. Although the whole novel was only published in 1830 and 1831, after Lizardi's death in 1826 (because the last part, which dealt with slavery, had been suppressed by the censors, owing to the fact that, they said, it placed into question a practice that the Spanish government had already approved of), Mexicans eagerly bought the chapters as they came out and discussed Lizardi's characters, as if they were real people, in the other popular literature permitted at that time (newspapers, pamphletry, and so on). It is true that educated critics reproached Lizardi for his use of substandard language in the pages of a book for decent people, and asked why his characters were unremittingly low. Lizardi replied that kings were unavailable in the colonial world and posed the question: besides, what other types of people would a dissolute youth normally associate with?

Lizardi's critics also attacked the book on the basis of the author's lack of a formal education. They claimed to see in the novel's intellectual frame the scattered reading of an autodidact. Born in 1776 in Mexico City to *criollo* parents who resembled those he portrayed in his novel, Lizardi had the same type of elementary and advanced education also depicted there. When his mother died and his father remarried, Lizardi seems to have become a wayward boy; in 1794, his father denounced his son to the Inquisition for possessing a deck of cards with off-color meaning. In 1798, when his father died, Lizardi left his studies at the Colegio de San Ildefonso; from then on until 1808, when an early poem of his was published in the *Diario de México*, his life is a mystery. It is thought that he drifted during that ten-year period, learning of the *demi-monde* he would depict later in the *Periquillo* and another of his novels, *Don Catrín de la Fachenda*. He married in 1805 or 1806, but that is the only hard fact emerging from those years. Paul Radin, who has studied Lizardi's life, claims that in 1810, Lizardi had his own printing press and earned his living as a maverick publisher, cut off from conventional publishing. Once the independence war started in September 1810, Lizardi was discovered to have been in Taxco, acting as *subdelegado* for the Spanish government. When, however, he turned over arms and ammunition to the insurgents, official authorities jailed him. Lizardi, in his defense, said that he had done so to protect the townspeople from possible violence. Yet the authorities did not believe him, and he remained in jail until early 1811. Lizardi never clarified this episode, nor did he ever firmly declare his political sympathies. When, toward the end of his life, he applied for a pension for service to the independence cause, friends and enemies argued over his real loyalties.

It is thought that Lizardi wrote his first novel, the *Periquillo*, because colonial censorship blocked the direct criticism his newspapers and political pamphlets had permitted and forced him to find another way to earn a living. By 1816, Fernando VII had returned to the Spanish throne, imposing tight controls on press freedom throughout the empire. So Lizardi had to discontinue the political journalism he had begun with his *El Pensador Mexicano* (The Mexican Thinker), a weekly newspaper that ran from October 1812 until 1814. Between 1816 and 1819, during the final years of Mexico's independence war that lasted until 1821, Lizardo wrote three other novels—*La Quijotita y su prima* (1818), *Noches tristes y día alegre* (1818), and *Don Catrín de la Fachenda* (probably written around 1819, though not published until 1832). During his lifetime, Lizardi wrote almost 300 political pamphlets, edited and wrote a dozen newspapers almost in their entirety, and produced a collection of fables, almanacs, theater, and poetry. His writings triggered debate among his fellow Mexicans, and many of his pamphlets are responses to attacks by his critics. He supported Agustín de Iturbide in Mexico's first government after independence; indeed, Lizardi served as editor and publisher of Iturbide's portable press as it moved into Mexico City from the provinces. (Later, however, he criticized his employer when Iturbide proclaimed himself emperor and tried to start a new imperial dynasty.) From February 22, 1822, until December 1823, Lizardi was excommunicated for having written a pamphlet that was understood to defend Freemasonry, an underground movement that attracted many Mexican intellectuals. When he died of tuberculosis in 1827, he was worn out. Perhaps because he was not formally educated, as Mexico's other intellectuals were, and earned his living by his writing, which depended on its appeal to a newly self-conscious middle class, he was scorned by many professionals of his day for invading their territory and vulgarizing their discussion of law, history, morals, and so forth, for consumption by that class.

III

The theory that Lizardi turned to novel-writing so as to disguise his criticism and earn a living during the period when censors were monitoring public utterances for what they considered to be attacks on the colonial authorities may be partly true. But critics' use of the term "pot-boilers" to describe his novels suggests that the novels are only longer versions of his political journalism, into which he stuffed heterogeneously all the entertainment, moralism, and erudition he could sell. These critics particularly lament the *Periquillo's* many digressions, which, they argue, detract from the basic picaresque story of a rogue. Wanting to classify the novel according to the picaresque line of development, they focus on the story of wickedness and regard everything else as extraneous. One edition of the *Periquillo* even printed the digressions in italics so that readers could skip those passages.

However, such reductionism strips the novel of its artistry. It fails to account for how Lizardi used the novel form to explore the complexity of his moment in history, and to gather his own response to the dilemma Mexico's independence war posed to him and his generation of Americans. The novel's satire permitted him some leeway to acknowledge the corruption he saw around him in Mexico. The picture of a just society, fictionalized as part of the *Periquillo's* story in the interlude on the Pacific island, allowed him to draw a blueprint for possible reform; its system of law and order, in which everyone worked to contribute to the economy, privileges of birth did not exist, and religion's representatives were often made useless, was—point by point—a parallel world to Mexico's.

Nevertheless, it is in the story of the delinquent boy who becomes Periquillo Sarniento that Lizardi demonstrated his greatest creativity. The youth's disregard for parental authority and advice represented the Mexican experience. His descent to a disordered life of crime, in which he drifted from easy deceit to serious infractions of robbery and murder, made apparent Mexico's crimes of parricide and fratricide. The reader at first sympathizes with Periquillo's adolescent fling, but soon realizes the seriousness of his departure from traditional morality; as Periquillo learns from his experience of deviance and finds his way back to parental status, when he in turn, becomes a father and teaches his children, readers of his life story could question the novel's applicability to their own circumstances. Mexico had thrown off the advice and protections of a mature adult; in defying the king, Spain (*la madre patria*), and the appeals of higher Church authorities to obedience, Mexicans had, like adolescents seeking to become adults, challenged paternalism and all of the lessons the colony had historically learned that kept it dependent. The country now had to rely on its own consideration of self and the experiences that had brought it to this moment. The youth Pedro makes mistakes. Once free and forced to survive on his own, he unthinkingly imitates the charlatans and thieves who populate the Mexican world; he listens to the advice of so-called friends who are as unprincipled as he. His encounters with the blacks and Indian peoples from the lower social classes—persons usually scorned by decent society and seldom depicted in the literature of the period—teach him valuable lessons; although they speak Spanish imperfectly and sometimes behave brutishly, they often display an honesty that the upper classes do not possess.

Thus the novel, in the adolescent perspective that comprises most of the text, is at once a critique of paternalism and, in the story's resolution based on the rightness of fatherly wisdom, an affirmation of such a system. This double message undoubtedly traced Lizardi's personal attempt to resolve his generation's dilemma: Lizardi could neither bless the independence movement, which in its rebellion threatened to end any semblance of law and order in the colony; nor could he totally support continuance of a government based on the legal metaphor of a father's claim over a son. In dramatizing the youth's experience with freedom, he explored the colony's probably mixed experience of decolonization. Even in Periquillo's passage through his picaresque adventures, the characters he meets are neither totally good nor totally bad; neither totally wise nor totally foolish. For example, Januario, a friend who leads him astray, accurately observes that "the world is full of thieves. The thing is that some people steal while keeping the appearances of being just, while others [steal despite the fact that they don't have the protection of those appearances]."[14] Because virtue and vice were being redefined at that historical moment, Lizardi chose to write a novel in which the two parts seemed to be separate, but, after closer examination, were really merged.

Certainly this adolescent story that imitated the Mexican experience of decolonization is central to understanding the novel's meaning. Attendant to that political reading, however, are interpretations of other dimensions of Mexico's changing history. The society was changing from one built on old-fashioned Spanish distinctions

---

[14] "El mundo está lleno de ladrones . . . unos roban con apariencia de justicia, y otros sin ellas" (152).

of aristocratic station to one constructed according to new commercial ties. In fact, as Spanish restrictions on trade were being lifted and "contraband" business was becoming honest economic activity, Mexicans were drawn to that new means of earning a living and that connection with the modern world. But the notions associated with commerce were not universally accepted. The risk, greed, and self-interest (if not selfishness) implicit in the new economic philosophies repelled many. The luxury and materialism they promoted spelled the end of Christian idealism; connections with Protestant capitalist countries such as England filled many Mexican Catholics with fear. Lizardi explores these challenges to traditional Mexican thought in the speeches of many of the characters.

The Utopian picture he paints of life on the island is only one of the many digressions from the rogue's story that Lizardi includes in his novel. The completeness with which that world is described, and the seriousness of the moral asides and flights of erudition, contrast with the ironic tone of the novel's satire and make clear that the two parts of the novel must be considered if Lizardi's whole message is to be understood. The digressions are an essential part of the novel. In them, Lizardi documented his reading and thus advertised the intellectual sources for his thinking. In the formality of several of the characters' speeches and in his own editorial comments (inserted textually or in footnotes), Lizardi balanced the book's many varieties of informal language. In the clear prose of the digressions, he indicted the colonial language circumlocutions that had impeded the formation of real Mexican thought. Indeed, the sheer length of the novel proves the complexity of Lizardi's thinking; the book's employ of many characters and situations reproduces the conflicts and uncertainties of the author's mental world. Lizardi introduced his novel in the guise of satire, which might only have allowed him criticism and comedy; but he went beyond satire's limitations in his effort to think through implications of Mexico's choices and provide answers to its problems.

IV

Today the *Periquillo* is universally honored as Mexico's national book. Literary historians in Mexico and throughout Spanish America mention its foundational importance at a time when the Spanish American colonies were engaged in a fight for their independence and then political consolidation. They celebrate the novel's arrival in the Americas and Lizardi's efforts to capture the separate language and customs that military victory would confirm. Throughout the 19th century, it seems that the novel continued to be a success. After its initial publication in 1816, editions of the *Periquillo* appeared in 1825, 1830–1831, 1842 (two printings), 1865, 1884 (two printings), 1896, 1897, 1903, 1908, and 1909. These many editions attest to the wide circulation of the story. Additionally, in 1866, seven *calendarios* (mini-almanacs, thirty-two pages long) were published that printed excerpts from the *Periquillo*, as well as from Lizardi's other novels, fables, and newspaper writing. These cheap paperbacks spread the story beyond the circle of more well-to-do readers, who could afford to buy more expensive editions. In 1879, a newspaper, evoking Lizardi in its title *La sombra de Lizardi,* published several articles that the government found objectionable and censored.[15] Between 1895 and 1896 an anonymous writer who called himself "Un Devoto del Pensador Mexicano" published a novel that he called *Perucho, nieto de Periquillo.* In it, he borrowed from Lizardi's work to show parallels between the early 19th century and its colonial tyranny, and the late 19th-century despotism and foreign ownership, rampant under Maximilian and then under Porfirio Díaz. The literary recycling in this later novel, published in installments in a Mexico City newspaper, shows the vitality of the *Periquillo*, almost one hundred years later, in the Mexican literary imagination.[16] It suggests that Devoto did not read Lizardi's novel in line with the European picaresque, but instead saw its satire as a model for interrupting official literature and alluding to a historic pattern of collusion by the Mexican elite with outsiders.

Ignacio Altamirano, a prominent novelist and critic in Mexico in the 19th century, points to a factor in understanding Lizardi's literary reputation then. Altamirano called Lizardi "an apostle of the people, and for that reason they love him tenderly and they venerate his memory, like the memory of a dear friend. . . . He suffered a great deal, he ate the bread of the people watered with the tears of misery. He went to his grave, obscure and poor, but with the holy aureole of the martyrs of liberty and progress." Altamirano's words reveal Mexicans' connection with the author, rather than with his book—an important fact because it tells that Mexicans were not associating the text with past or foreign elements in Mexican culture, but instead with present-day realities, the voice behind the book's words, and the recognizably Mexican human beings whom they saw in the book's pages. Lizardi's popularity depended on the fact that Mexicans claimed the book as something made by a real Mexican, as a contact with a friend, and as a means by which they could relate to their countrymen. Ignored was any linkage to a European culture or a literate tradition. Altamirano's effusion also helps linguists to understand why the *Periquillo's* language might have entered the Mexican folk repertoire; Lizardi's satiric stance was like their outsider status in the Mexican nation. How the book's language was transmitted to the people's oral culture, however, is still largely a mystery.

Altamirano's assessment of Lizardi's connections with "the people" shows how the national artistic and intellectual class was beginning to distance itself from the popularity that Lizardi's novel represented. In the first decades of the 20th century, two members of Mexico's prestigious Ateneo de la Juventud, Alfonso Reyes and Carlos González Peña, continued to categorize Lizardi as a popular writer. Reyes stated that "The *romance of the Periquillo* . . . is loved without being read—much less enjoyed." González Peña said: "Four generations have kept silent about or disguised the truth, and the truth must be told: the *Pensador* [Lizardi] was a bad novelist who does not deserve the destiny of immortality for his intrinsic value, for his literary representation in our art. His importance is only historic; he has been a precursor and a rebel.

---

[15] Published by Clemente Osio on March 2. I do not know how many issues were published, since I have only seen a reference to the paper in María del Carmen Reyna, *La prensa censurada durante el siglo XIX* (México: SepSetentas, 1976), 188.

[16] See my article, "Intertextuality Defined in Terms of 19th-Century Nationalism: *Perucho, nieto de Periquillo.*" *Bulletin of Hispanic Studies* 71 (1994): 485–97.

He brought with him to the field of letters a new genre." Mariano Azuela, the most famous of the novelists who set their stories in the contemporary revolution of 1910, also discredited Lizardi's fiction, finding the *Periquillo* tedious to read and technically crude, like village art.

These judgments say as much about the critics who damned Lizardi with faint praise as about the realities of the book's reception in the 19th and 20th centuries. That story of conflicting class values is still to be told, as the many editions of the *Periquillo*, already listed, attest to. Someone was reading all those copies, and Altamirano's description of Lizardi's life in the imaginations of the common people does not tell the whole story. His suggestion that the book and the memory of its author lived on in the people's oral culture must be balanced by the evidence we have seen, in *Perucho* and *La sombra de Lizardi*, that literate Mexicans, too, remembered the book long after its initial printing; writers thought it capable of suggesting satire pertinent to their own circumstances, and readers apparently understood that invoking Lizardi meant standing outside the boundaries of official literature and criticizing its hypocrisies.

Still one more proof that Lizardi lived on in Mexican imagination throughout the 19th century must be noted. At the end of the 19th century, Mexico City's illustrator and engraver, José Guadalupe Posada, often drew on the imagery of Lizardi's novels for his broadsides. Combining pictures and words (the picture was usually at the top of the paper and the prose or poetry at the bottom), these broadsides criticized conditions under the *Porfiriato*.[17] Though the pictures were usually caricatures, such as *calaveras* (human skeletons) imitating people, sometimes they were realistic in portraying something that had just happened, such as the suicide of an avaricious banker, or a bull goring a bullfighter.

Patrick Frank[18] quotes from one 1902 broadside, illustrated by Posada, in which the comic character, the coward Don Chepito, recalls the *Periquillo* when he brags: "I have always been a brave military man myself, and such a hero that I have defeated valiant battalions of bugs, fleas, and lice on the field of my bed. Citizens! Long live the homeland of Periquillo Sarnoso."[19] Posada illustrated a newspaper called "El Periquillo Sarniento," which was published in Mexico City between 1902 and 1903; also in 1903, Posada illustrated schoolbook editions of the *Periquillo* and

---

[17] "Porfiriato" refers to the regime of Porfirio Díaz (1876–1910), a period of modernization in Mexico. Ostensibly, the historic powers of the Catholic Church were curtailed as liberals who professed the European philosophy of positivism and appeared to be the intellectuals behind the regime sought means of progress. However, the Church *de facto* operated to maintain behind-the-scenes controls, Mexican landowners continued feudal practices, and U.S. investment bought up Indian lands and mineral rights. Dissatisfaction with the *Porfiriato* provoked the Revolution of 1910.

[18] "Un discurso sin igual de D. Chepe el retozón, Respecto a los Reservistas Que Hay en aquesta Nacion," *Posada's Broadsides, Mexican Popular Imagery (1890–1910)*. (Albuquerque: University of New Mexico Press, 1998) 200–1; see also *Posada's Mexico*, ed. Ron Tyler (Washington and Fort Worth: Library of Congress and Amon Carter Museum of Western Art, 1979).

[19] "Yo siempre fui militar bravisimo y cual un héroe me he batido con valientes batallones . . . de chinches, pulgas y piojos en el campo de mi cama. ¡Ciudadanos! ¡Viva la patria de Periquillo Sarnoso" (200–1).

La Quijotita. Posada made much use of another of Lizardi's novels, *Don Catrín*, for his caricatures of the *catrín* (dandy or fop, representing a social class whose pretensions to elegance were undercut by poverty and easy morality). Thus, throughout most of the 19th century, the *Periquillo* and *Don Catrín* seem to have survived at the level of satire and criticism—in pieces often dismissed as "popular," and which, supposedly having no aesthetic value, did not deserve to be called "literature." At some point in the late 19th and early 20th centuries, Mexico's culture was splitting into divisions along class lines that enabled critics like Reyes and González Peña to assume a loftier pose.

Studies of "literature," in focusing on printed material and canonical authors recognized as having contributed to a belle-lettristic tradition, have generally excluded the evidence of alternative cultural forms. It is only lately that colonial studies have begun to look for and reevaluate manuscripts, non-literary writing, and surviving oral forms relative to those years of Mexico's history. There has yet to be a parallel development to retrieve the mass of political newspapers, broadsides, school printings, and so on, from Mexico's 19th century. Indeed, it is instructive to introduce Posada in tracing Mexico's memory of Lizardi, and to compare the novelist and the artist. Although, in its first edition, the *Periquillo* was printed on the good paper of the day, with costly illustrations by a skilled engraver, the fact that it came out in installments tells that Lizardi aimed for a wide readership. Later, Lizardi's novels, like Posada's broadsides, were often sold in cheap printings on bad paper to as many customers as possible. Both made use of non-standard literary sources drawn from the world around them. The visual aspect of Posada's illustrations of a printed text (a *corrido* is a long poem that often narrated a sensational news item, a political rumor, the sorrowful stories of men and women, etc.) is similar to Lizardi's technique of using the story of his fictional hero to dramatize the messages contained in his moralizing digressions. Although Posada's portion of the broadside was calculated to communicate the text's message to illiterates (and perhaps also to literate Mexicans who hurried by the street corners where the broadsides were posted and did not take the time to read), Lizardi's narrative worked a bit differently. Lizardi's story of Periquillo Sarniento draws the reader along and evokes a mental image that points beyond to the novel's non-narrative parts, contained only in non-referential words. Some of the consumers of Lizardi's novel would have been readers only minimally, but the frequent cautions Lizardi scattered throughout his novels of how to read—enjoying the story, but then pausing to reflect on its meaning—demonstrate his special awareness of his readers' interpretive limitations. Many readers were unsophisticated, recently won to reading by the print explosion around them. Others, hardened to what a book might offer by years of reading colonial literature, needed shocking language to wake them up from their lethargic acceptance of convention, moralizing restatements of the plot to help them understand Lizardi's message, and humor to soften the devastating criticism of the ills around them.

By relegating Lizardi to popular status, Altamirano, Reyes, González Peña, and Azuela succeeded in erasing him as a viable literary model for later national writers. Perhaps they were not entirely to blame, however. In 1886, Manuel Sánchez Mármol, a critic and himself a novelist, wrote, "Mexico is a country without a literature,"[20] apparently forgetting about Lizardi in the new enthusiasm for literary realism. In the climate of late 19th-century *porfirismo*, French novelists such as the Goncourt brothers and even the Spanish writer José María de Pereda seemed to provide more acceptable narrative models to the official positivists. Discussing the 1884 novel by Arcadio Zentella Priego, *Perico* (the title of which, he claimed, meant "nobody" and had nothing to do with Lizardi's *Periquillo*), another critic, Manuel Antonio Romero, said that realism should avoid any contrived situation that might force a Catholic or Roman lesson. It appears that Lizardi's technique was remembered as too satiric, too manipulative of invention to be useful to later writers. Critics who favored realism wanted matter-of-fact description without the language humor or moralizing digressions thought to be typical of the *Periquillo*. In his essay for the 1950 edition of *Perico*, Romero discusses Zentella's importance for the appearance of later writers of *la novela social*, such as Sánchez Mármol, José López Portillo y Rojas, Federico Gamboa, and Heriberto Frías. Romero says that these novelists said only what was true, in a sober manner. Further—although Romero does not go on to say this—in indicting the exploitation by landowners in rural areas and the injustices of Mexico's legal system, they exposed a side of Mexican life that Lizardi's novel, situated in Mexico City and seemingly limited in its criticism to the vices of individuals, did not take on (xiii–xxii).[21]

These novelists, as well as Alfonso Reyes, who, instead of cultural *mexicanismo*, advocated *americanismo* and Mexican embrace of what he called a universal Hellenism, turned Mexicans away from remembering their specific national past. However, González Peña, who in 1928 wrote one of the first summaries of Mexico's literary history, *Historia de la literatura mexicana*, must have contributed most to the relegation of Lizardi and the *Periquillo* to the periphery of Mexico's canon; his period classifications pushed Lizardi into the past and tended to dismiss him as a journalist and political hack. Today schoolchildren mechanically learn of Lizardi's book—its title, author, and date of publication—and perhaps read watered-down excerpts; but as adults, they usually fail to read the whole book. Linguistic scholars treat the text solely as source material for their studies of vocabulary and turns of phrase used by Mexicans in the period. Historians, reading literally, dip only into those parts that seem to provide the period documentation they want. Perhaps for present-day political reasons, the colonial and independence periods are overlooked in discussions of Mexico's literary past. More important than the independence war of 1810–1821 is the social revolution of 1910–1921. Mexican readers, then, in taking their nationhood for granted and focusing instead on the class war that the novel of the Mexican revolution seems to explore, have held up later literature as important and ignored

---

[20] "México es un país sin literatura." This statement appears in the 1950 edition of Arcadio Zentella Priego's *Perico* (Mérida: Club Yucatense "Club del Libro"), 171.

[21] Zentella Priego (1844–1920); Sánchez Mármol (1839–1912); López Portillo y Rojas (1850–1923); Gamboa (1864–1939); Frías (1870–1925). Ralph E. Warner in *Historia de la novela mexicana en el siglo XIX* (México: Antigua Librería Robredo, 1953) discusses the author and his novel (91–92). However, the *Enciclopedia de México* (México, 1977) does not include either Zentella Priego or Romero in its coverage.

the literature of Mexico's earlier period. Carlos Fuentes, perhaps the most preeminent of Mexico's novelists today, has yet to mention Lizardi as a novelistic precursor, preferring to refer instead to foreign writers like Jane Austen and James Joyce.[22]

However, the balance has lately begun to shift. In 1940, Agustín Yáñez stirred interest in the *Periquillo* when he wrote that Periquillo Sarniento was a national type, the *pelado* (skinned or plucked person), who was at the mercy of social forces; like the *gaucho* in Argentina, the *pelado* had entered bookish culture to become a symbol of national traits. Yáñez's interpretation of Lizardi's character reflected analyses of the national ethos that were being done in the 1930s by Samuel Ramos, and later by Octavio Paz.[23] In the 1960s, a team of researchers at UNAM (Mexico's national university) began to compile and publish all the works of Lizardi; that effort, under the direction of María Rosa Palazón Mayoral, now runs to fourteen volumes and has enabled scholars to study the writer more fully. More recently, Noël Salomon and Jean Franco have reexamined the *Periquillo*, taking seriously its artistry. In my own work, I have explored the novel's connections with the topics and range of discourses of the *Diario de México*. In my book-length study of Lizardi's four novels, I have attempted to go beyond the literal readings of historians and to analyze Lizardi's creativity in writing the first Spanish American novel.

A chance for the *Periquillo* to cross the Río Grande and assume importance in translated form in the United States came at an unfortunate time. When, in 1942, Doubleday, Doran published *The Itching Parrot*, the translation—done by Eugene Pressly, then Katherine Anne Porter's husband, and edited by her—quickly fell into oblivion. The world was at war, and other artistic and intellectual issues soon eclipsed a book that seemed to be nothing but irrelevant history. Although Lionel Trilling and Bertram Wolfe reviewed it, their judgments were not enthusiastic; Trilling called the book "a bore." Publishing demands had forced Porter to omit Lizardi's long digressions, reducing the story to what she claimed was a rogue's "picaresque" story. Trilling, however, was perceptive enough to recognize that the cuts eliminated what he called "the power of mind" that he guessed the original version possessed.

David Frye's new translation, then, which updates the Pressly/Porter language and, in this edition, reproduces Lizardi's whole text, is a major contribution to the body of world literature that is read in the United States. I say "world literature," rather than just "Mexican," because the experience of linguistic and literary decolonization, which the novel records, is a universal phenomenon. Lizardi operated within the confines of his historical period (as do all writers), choosing what he could express from the options available to him. Satire permitted him the honest expression he wanted. Indeed, that satiric play needs to be understood so as to appreciate the value of Spanish America's first experiment with the novel. If later novelists who aspired to a different kind of art and academic critics misread Lizardi's novel,

---

22 See the essays in *Myself with Others* (New York: Farrar, Straus & Giroux, 1981).

23 Samuel Ramos, *Profile of Man and Culture in Mexico*. Translated by Peter G. Earle, introduction by Thomas B. Irving (Austin: University of Texas Press, 1975); Octavio Paz, *Labyrinth of Solitude and The Other Mexico*. Translated by Lysander Kemp, Yara Milos, and Rachel Phillips Belash (New York: Grove, 1985); Yáñez (1904–1980); Ramos (1897–1959); Paz (1914–1998).

forcing it into a category where it did not belong or forgetting it altogether, reexamination may help to validate the book and the literature of this historical period. Rereading the *Periquillo* will provide a salutary exercise in establishing connections between the various episodes of Mexico's literary development and thus recognizing interrelationships that have not always been apparent. That exercise will take us far toward seeing more clearly the history of Mexican literature.

Nancy Vogeley
Professor Emeritus, University of San Francisco

List of Recommended Readings in English

Anna, Timothy. *Forging Mexico, 1821–1835*. Lincoln: University of Nebraska Press, 1998.

Brading, David. *Origins of Mexican Nationalism*. Cambridge: Cambridge University Press, 1985.

———. *The First America: The Spanish Monarchy, Creole Patriots, and the Liberal State, 1492–1867*. New York: Cambridge University Press, 1991.

Brushwood, John S. *Mexico in Its Novel: A Nation's Search for Identity*. Austin: University of Texas Press, 1966.

Cockcroft, James D. *Mexico: Class Formation, Capital Accumulation, and the State*. New York: Monthly Review Press, 1983.

di Tella, Torcuato. *National Popular Politics in Early Independent Mexico, 1820–1847*. Albuquerque: University of New Mexico Press, 1996.

Foster, David William. *Mexican Literature: A Bibliography of Secondary Sources*. Metuchen, London: Scarecrow Press, 1981.

———. ed. *Mexican Literature: A History*. Austin: University of Texas Press, 1996.

Franco, Jean. *An Introduction to Spanish American Literature*. London: Cambridge University Press, 1969.

Gómez Quiñones, Juan. *Mexican Nationalist Formation: Political Discourse, Policy, and Dissidence*. Encino: Floricanto Press, 1992.

González Peña, Carlos. *History of Mexican Literature*. Translated by Gusta Barfield Nance and Florence Johnson Dunstan. Dallas: Southern Methodist Press, 1968.

Hamill, Hugh M., Jr. *The Hidalgo Revolt: Prelude to Mexican Independence*. Gainesville: University of Florida Press, 1966.

Hamnett, Brian R. *A Concise History of Mexico*. Cambridge: Cambridge University Press, 1999.

Johnson, Julie Greer. *Satire in Colonial Spanish America: Turning the New World Upside Down*. Austin: University of Texas Press, 1993.

Kandell, Jonathan. *La Capital: The Biography of Mexico City*. New York: Random House, 1988.

Meyer, Michael C., and William H. Beezley. *The Oxford History of Mexico*. New York: Oxford University Press, 2000.

Radin, Paul, ed. *An Annotated Bibliography of the Poems and Pamphlets of J. J. Fernández de Lizardi: The First Period (1808–1819)*. San Francisco: California State Library, 1940.

————. "An Annotated Bibliography of the Poems and Pamphlets of Fernández de Lizardi (1824–1827)." *Hispanic American Historical Review* 26 (May 1946): 284–291.

————. *The Opponents and Friends of Lizardi.* Mexican History Series, No. 2 - Part II. (San Francisco: California State Library, 1939.)

Solé, Carlos, and María Isabel Abreu, eds. *Latin American Writers.* 3 vols. New York: Charles Scribners & Sons, 1989. Supplement I. Carlos Solé and Klaus Müller-Bergh, eds. New York: Scribners, 2002.

Spell, Jefferson Rea. "The Life and Works of José Joaquín Fernández de Lizardi." Dissertation, Philadelphia: University of Pennsylvania, 1931.

Torres Ríoseco, Arturo. *The Epic of Latin American Literature.* Berkeley: University of California Press, 1964.

Vogeley, Nancy. *Lizardi and the Birth of the Novel in Spanish America.* Gainesville: University Press of Florida, 2001.

Zea, Leopoldo. *Positivism in Mexico.* Translated by Josephine H. Schulte. Austin: University of Texas Press, 1974.

TRANSLATOR'S NOTE

On Translating the Parrot

It was on November 15, 1776, just months after the struggling British colonies of North America had declared their independence from Europe, that José Joaquín Fernández de Lizardi was born in the richest and largest city on the continent. Today we call it Mexico City, but for Lizardi it was simply Mexico, and in his writing, Mexico refers always to the city that he calls "the capital of North America." When Lizardi wrote the novel for which he is best known today, Mexico had been the opulent capital of the Spanish colony known as the Kingdom of New Spain for nearly three centuries, and the spectacular capital of the Aztec realm for two centuries before that; the upstart city of New York was only beginning to catch up in size and wealth. Yet when *The Mangy Parrot* was snatched fresh from the printer in twice-weekly installments over the first half of 1816, it was the first time that the public of Mexico had seen their own city depicted in fiction. For these readers, it was a fresh and entirely *novel* experience to read fictional adventures set in the recognizable haunts and byways of their beloved town. Lizardi deliberately heightened this experience by populating his book with every social type of the city and the surrounding countryside, and by filling the text with an exuberance of popular speech, from the accents of the Indian laborers and country farmers who came to the city to sell, trade, and marvel, to the current slang of the town's "dissolute" youth.

Lizardi was emblematic of the generation of intellectuals, artists, and writers who led Mexico into the modern era. His own life history resonated with the ambivalences and outright contradictions of a world torn between colonial rule and independence. His writings—four novels, several fables, two plays, dozens of poems, over 250 articles and pamphlets—are important in three ways: as artistic expressions in themselves; as texts that contributed in vital ways to the intellectual life of Mexico early in its independence; and as windows into the daily life of that period. Of Lizardi's many published works, *The Mangy Parrot* remains the most important. It typifies the dual impulse of his writing: to entertain and to edify. It is also a lively, comic novel that captures much of the reality of Mexico in 1816. It can be read as a nation-building novel, written at a critical moment in the transition of Mexico (and Latin America) from colony to independence. Jean Franco has characterized the novel as "a ferocious indictment of Spanish administration in Mexico: ignorance, superstition and corruption are seen to be its most notable characteristics."[1] As Antonio Benítez-Rojo writes, citing Benedict Anderson's use of *The Mangy Parrot* as an exemplar of the anti-colonial novel, "the illusion of accompanying Periquillo along the roads and through the villages and towns of the viceroyalty helped awaken in the novel's readers the desire for nationness." Lizardi's last novel, *Don Catrín de la Fachenda*, "is artistically superior to *El Periquillo Sarniento*," Benítez-Rojo continues, "yet for all its

---

[1] Jean Franco, *An Introduction to Spanish-American Literature* (Cambridge: Cambridge University Press, 1969), p. 34; cited in Benedict Anderson, *Imagined Communities: Reflections on the Origin and Spread of Nationalism*, revised edition (London: Verso, 1991), p. 29.

defects, the latter, because of its great vitality, is a major work of Mexican literature."[2] Finally, within the world of the Latin American novel, *The Mangy Parrot* has
the virtue of being the first. This was a fact that Lizardi himself noted with under-
standable pride:

> I am far from believing that I have written a masterpiece that is free from
> defects: it has many that I recognize, and must have others still that I have not
> noticed; but it also has one undeniable distinction, which is that of being the
> first novel that has been written in this country by an American in three hun-
> dred years.[3]

A pioneering Mexican journalist in an era of rebellion against Spanish rule, Lizardi
turned to writing fiction when the colonial regime shut down his newspaper, *El Pensador Mexicano* (*The Mexican Thinker*). There is a certain similarity between *The
Mangy Parrot* and the typical newspaper of Lizardi's day: both are highly opinion-
ated, replete with dialogues on moral questions, chock-full of classical allusions, and
interspersed with information about every topic the writer finds of interest, from
economics to astronomy. It is tempting to view this novel as an end-run around the
censor; a journal of opinion by other means. For a while in the early 20th century, as
Nancy Vogeley details in her introduction to this translation, it was fashionable for
Mexican writers to dismiss *The Mangy Parrot* as a crude mishmash by an untrained
popular writer with a tin ear, and it is undeniable that he was not a great stylist in the
modernist sense—there are no rolling waves of polished prose here. Indeed, when
Lizardi writes himself in as a character toward the end of his own novel, he disarm-
ingly confesses "that by my natural inclination, I don't have the patience to read
much, write, erase, correct, nor consult my own writings at a slow pace." He could
hardly have done any differently, to be able to write and publish this massive work
within the space of half a year, a speed dictated by his need to keep his family
clothed and fed.

   Yet in translating the novel, I have become familiar with a different, less often
remarked side of Lizardi's writing: he was, like most great writers, intoxicated with
language. He luxuriated in his tremendous vocabulary; he reveled in the slang and the
obscure gambling terms of his underworld characters even as he pretended to criticize
them; when they took to sea, he threw in every nautical term he knew; his priests
bandy about the abstract language of theology, his lawyers and notaries delve into the
technical language of the law, his pharmacists and doctors confound their patients
with their Latinate medical terms. True, he did not polish his writing, and at times he
puts an entire two-page editorial in the mouth of a character (to whom the other characters listen in rapt attention—an editorialist's fantasy, no doubt!), but when he came
to straightforward dialogue, he had a keen ear for the accents and the turns of phrase

---

[2] "José Joaquín Fernández de Lizardi and the Emergence of the Spanish American Novel as
National Project," p. 335; 336.

[3] Cited in Jefferson Rea Spell, *Bridging the Gap* (México: Editorial Libros de México, 1971), p.
267. My translation.

that brought his characters to life. There is an exuberant love of life and language that is the very heart of this novel, and that is what has made it such a pleasure to translate—and I hope that this vitality will also make it a pleasure to read.

Within this exuberance of language, *The Mangy Parrot*, like any literary text, encompasses many layers or dimensions of meaning, and the first question I had to address before I began to translate it was which dimension to emphasize. One legitimate approach to a historic text such as this would have been to use the English or American vocabulary from the literature of the 1810s, emphasizing the work's age (or its quaintness, as the case may be). My decision was rather different: what I wanted to do was to convey something of the experience that the novel's first readers had when they picked up the book as it was issued in Mexico in 1816. I wanted to emphasize not its age, but its vitality, freshness, and novelty.

In so doing, I tried to negotiate the straits between maintaining a sense of distance (to keep the reader in mind of the fact that Lizardi, after all, lived in a different world—not only because it was Mexico, but just as importantly, because it was another century) while making the dialogue as fresh and natural as it would have sounded to Lizardi's contemporaries. My goal was to remain faithful to the original while I put it into English; above all, I attempted to reproduce the tone of the original. I tried to translate stilted prose into stilted prose, formal prose into formal prose, rhymed verse into rhymed verse (a departure from my usual practice with translating poetry, but one that I think makes sense in the case of Lizardi's doggerel), and colloquial turns of phrase into colloquialisms. The didactic and moralizing digressions remain didactic and moralizing, but when Lizardi quotes people talking with each other, I have done my best to make them express themselves in words that sound like something a real person might actually say, because that is precisely what Lizardi did (to the scandal of some critics and the delight of his readers) nearly two hundred years ago.

I have rendered the title of the novel not as *The Itching Parrot* (as in the first, abridged English translation of the novel) but *The Mangy Parrot*. The former title, though commonly used in English citations, conveys little meaning. "Mangy" is both a more precise translation of *sarniento* and a better reflection of the slightly disreputable connotations of the word, and of the narrator.

The Mexico that Periquillo displays for us is, in today's terminology, multicultural and multiethnic. In the pages of the novel, Indians rub shoulders with blacks, whites, mestizos (people of part-Indian, part-Spanish ancestry), and "*lobos* and mulattos" (people of part-African descent, in the vocabulary of the time). When read in the context of modern Mexico—with its official ideology that exalts the mestizo as the national type of the country, denies racism, and scarcely acknowledges the importance of Africans in the population of colonial New Spain—Periquillo comes across as shockingly candid in his racial and ethnic observations. Equally striking is the fact that he evidently has no word to talk about "race," other than the rather vague term "quality," and he rarely discusses even that. On the other hand, he has an extensive and unvarying vocabulary to refer to the different types of people that compose his Mexico. Because of the manifest importance of these terms to Lizardi's understanding of his world, I endeavored to adopt a single, invarying English term to translate each of his words and phrases relating to social categories, in contrast to my general approach of duplicating his exuberant vocabulary by varying my translations of his phrases.

In the novel, sophisticated city folk disparage the simple-mindedness of people from the countryside, whose speech patterns carry the characteristic rhythms and pronunciations of rural Mexico; these people are always called *payos*—"bumpkins" in my translation, though *hicks, yokels, rustics,* or *hayseeds* would have worked as well (terms that prove the anti-rural prejudices of Lizardi's Mexico have their counterparts in the U.S.). Indians are likely to mix their Spanish with "Mexican" (*mexicano*), the language of the Aztecs that is known today as Nahuatl. Though Periquillo notes the color of the people he deals with, he is much more interested in the social hierarchy of his city and where people fit within it. Hierarchy is everywhere: employees have *jefes* ("bosses"); slaves have *amos* ("masters"); apprentices have *maestros* (*"maestros"*: though the normal English translation in this sense would be "masters," I retain the Spanish because Lizardi makes a point of distinguishing between the slave's *amo* and the apprentice's *maestro*, which can also mean both master craftsman and teacher). In the religious realm—Catholicism is, of course, the only religion here—laymen yield to the wisdom of the *clero* ("clergy"), and *curas* ("parish priests") hire *vicarios* ("curates")—assistant priests who do their heavy lifting for them. Above all, *los pobres* ("the poor") and *los plebeyos* ("the plebeians") submit to *los ricos* ("the rich"), and *los títulos* ("the titled nobility") tower over the merely wealthy.

The members of that titled nobility—the counts and marquises who numbered only a few dozen in a city of over 100,000 people—are one of Periquillo's constant preoccupations. He talks about them, listens to stories about them, and even gets away with pretending to be one of them for a few months; but all the while, in his persona as a repentant sinner making his deathbed confession, he disparages the artificial nobility that titles confer on these gentleman in favor of the true nobility of character of the sort of man that he calls an *hombre de bien*. The *hombre de bien* is one of Lizardi's main social concepts, and in his conception of the world, this man represents the height of morality. It is not a very easy term to translate, though. "Good man" would be literally correct but rather thin; "honest man" is better, but not always adequate; "true gentleman" comes closer, but also puts words in Lizardi's mouth; "upright citizen" is perhaps the closest to what he means, but sounds somehow anachronistic for Lizardi's times. What Lizardi-Periquillo means by the term is summed up in the narrator's last will and testament, where (in what reads like a precursor to the Scout Oath) he charges his children to be "humble, thoughtful, friendly, kind, courteous, honorable, truthful, simple, sensible, and *hombres de bien* in every way." The best two-word phrase that I could find to encapsulate these qualities was "upright man," and that is how I have translated *hombre de bien* wherever it occurs. Yet at the same time, I have to acknowledge that the translation is inadequate, especially insofar as it ignores the other connotations the term had outside of Lizardi's work, for many people of his time seemed to think of the *hombre de bien* as simply a wealthy person, as Lizardi remarks in footnote 3 to Chapter 23:

> Some people confuse the idea of *hombría de bien* [i.e., of being an *hombre de bien*] with that of luxury and money, and in their opinion the term *hombre de*

bien (upright man) equals rich or semi-rich, while they judge that *poor* is the equivalent of rogue; so, reasoning from these false premises, they are likely to deduce such nonsense as this: Pedro is rich, he has money, he dresses decently; therefore, he is an upright man. . . . [But instead,] behaving in accordance with healthy morals is the surest witness for determining true *hombría de bien*.

By praising the *hombre de bien* over and above the counts and marquises, Lizardi was (I would argue) making a case for the moral superiority of the middle class over the titled nobility. I would further note that Lizardi was himself a product of the middle class, and he was writing for that class; but I also must note that he had no vocabulary for talking about it, or indeed for conceiving it, *as* a class. It is notable that, while his narrator frequently talks about rich and poor, he has no term for those who are in between the extremes of wealth and poverty. It is striking how often the *hombres de bien* (such as Periquillo's father) describe themselves as "poor," even though they are never confused with the social group who are collectively called "the poor." The difference is that *hombre de bien* is poor only in the sense that he must always continue to work for his living and to support his family; he can never sit back to live from his inherited wealth; but on the other hand, he is not *miserable* (destitute, poverty-stricken), and he always strives and usually manages to remain *decente* (decent)—that is, clean and tidy, but not ostentatiously wealthy.

Finally, it should be noted that *hombres de bien* are always men; always male. For Lizardi, the difference between men and women was irreducible. A man can *become* honorable and *become* an *hombre de bien* by what he does (keep his word, work for a living, support his family, confess, reform). A woman, on the other hand, must *retain* her honor, as defined within the Catholic system of sex and sin, and there is no apparent means for her to regain honor once she has lost it by having sex outside of marriage. For a woman, then, there is no category of *mujer de bien*, but rather, the corresponding term to *hombre de bien* is *mujer prudente* or prudent woman: the woman who puts her honor (that is, her chastity) above all else.

The unilateralism of Lizardi's moral understanding of women takes its toll on his portrayal of them in the novel. The entire plot of the novel revolves around men's ability to transform themselves over time—to go forward from being a rogue and a scoundrel, either by reforming and becoming an *hombre de bien*, or by descending into depraved criminality. Women, on the other hand, have only two states, honorable or shameless, and only a few of his female characters (Periquillo's mistress Luisa, for example) show hints of life beyond this one-dimensional scheme. The limits that this aspect of his morality placed on Lizardi's moral imagination become apparent in the final chapters when, in quick succession, two male characters in their late thirties marry young women (or girls) just barely past puberty, and no one bats an eye at this dubious practice. As noted, *The Mangy Parrot* is often seen as a nation-building novel, and indeed its male-oriented plot is a mirror for early Mexican nationalism, which, like so many other nationalisms the world over, focused on male struggles, desires, and accomplishments while too often writing women out of the picture. In this, too, Lizardi and his novel reflected the tenor of his times.

The Author

José Joaquín Fernández de Lizardi was born in Mexico City in 1776 to professional-class parents of moderate means. His mother was the daughter of a bookseller in the city of Puebla, just east of Mexico City; his father was a physician who for some time supported his family by writing. His father's illness in 1798 and subsequent death forced young Lizardi to leave his studies in the Colegio de San Ildefonso at the University of Mexico, and to enter the civil service as a minor magistrate in the Taxco-Acapulco region. He married there in 1805, and the necessity of providing for a growing family led him to supplement his meager income by writing.[4]

Lizardi began his literary career in 1808 with the publication of a poem in honor of Fernando VII—a patriotic stance for a Mexican intellectual to take in the year of the Napoleonic invasion of Spain, and one in line with Lizardi's later proto-nationalist views. At the beginning of Mexico's wars of independence in November 1810, Morelos' insurgent forces fought their way into Taxco, where Lizardi was heading the local government as acting *Subdelegado* (the highest provincial government position in the colonial system). In the face of an initial insurgent victory, Lizardi appears to have played both sides. On the one hand, he received the insurgents as friends and turned over the city's armory to them; on the other, he informed the viceroyalty of rebel movements. Judged in the context of his later writings, his actions do not appear hypocritical: he was always supportive of the intellectual aims and reformist politics of the insurgents, but was equally opposed to war and bloodshed. By peacefully capitulating, he aimed, above all, to avoid loss of life in the city then under his command. Following the royalist recapture of Taxco in January 1811, Lizardi was taken prisoner as a rebel sympathizer and sent with the other prisoners of war to Mexico City. There he appealed successfully to the viceroy, arguing that he had acted only to protect Taxco and its citizens from harm.

Though freed, Lizardi lost his position and his confiscated goods. To support his family, now living in the colonial capital, it appears that he turned to literature. Over the following year, he published more than twenty lightly satirical poems in broadsheets and pamphlets. Then, on October 5, 1812, the footdragging colonial authorities finally published the decree by which the liberal Cortes of Cádiz had established a limited freedom of the press in Spain and its empire some two years earlier. Lizardi jumped at the opportunity that had suddenly opened, and a mere four days later he put out the first issue of his periodical *El Pensador Mexicano* ("The Mexican Thinker," a title he adopted as his own pseudonym).

In his periodical work, Lizardi turned from light social criticism to direct commentary on the political problems of the day, with attacks on the autocratic tendencies of the viceregal government and support for the liberal aspirations represented by the Cortes in Spain. His articles clearly demonstrate the hold that Enlightenment

---

[4] The primary work on the life of Lizardi is Jefferson Rea Spell's *The Life and Works of José Joaquín Fernández de Lizardi* (Philadelphia, 1931), reprinted in his *Bridging the Gap: Articles on Mexican Literature* (México: Editorial Libros de México, 1971, pp. 99–141). I have relied heavily on Spell's work for this brief biography.

ideas, derived from clandestine readings of the forbidden Voltaire, Rousseau, and Diderot, had on his imagination. These ideas would later achieve novelistic form in *El Periquillo Sarniento*; but first they were to land Lizardi in prison.

The ninth issue of the paper, in December 1812, contained a direct attack on the viceroy; the result was arrest and detention for Lizardi. He continued to issue *El Pensador Mexicano* even from prison, but to the dismay of his pro-independence followers, he suppressed his sympathies for the insurgents, muted his critiques of the system that had imprisoned him, and even published lavish praises of a new viceroy who he hoped (correctly) would free him after seven months in his cell. Lizardi continued to write and publish his periodicals for the next two years, though increased attention from royalist censors and the Inquisition still muted his critical tone.

After the Spanish Cortes were overthrown in 1814, and with them the liberal constitution and the freedom of the press they had proclaimed, Lizardi turned from journalism to literature as a means of expressing his social criticism. This social and political conjuncture, then, was the genesis of Lizardi's first novel, which is commonly recognized as the first Mexican and indeed the first Latin American novel. Like Lizardi's periodicals, the publication of *El Periquillo* (sold chapter-by-chapter in weekly installments throughout 1816) was eventually halted by censorship. The first three volumes slipped past the censor, as Lizardi had hoped they would in their fictionalized guise, but Lizardi's direct attack on the institution of slavery in the fourth volume was enough to have the publication stopped. The final sixteen chapters of *El Periquillo* were only published in 1830–1831, after Lizardi's death and a decade following Mexican independence. Lizardi's other works of fiction appeared, also by installments, during the years of renewed royalist repression that lasted until 1820: *Fábulas* (a collection of "fables," 1817), *Noches tristes* (novel, 1818), *La Quijotita y su prima* (novel, 1818–1819), and *Don Catrín de la Fachenda* (completed 1820, published 1832).

With the re-establishment of the liberal constitution in 1820, Lizardi returned to journalism, only to be attacked, imprisoned, and censored again—by royalists, until the independence of Mexico in 1821; by centralists opposed to his federalist leanings after independence; and, throughout, by clerics opposed to his Masonic leanings. He died of tuberculosis in 1827, at the age of 50. Because of his family's extreme poverty he was buried in an anonymous grave, without the epitaph he had hoped would be engraved on his tombstone: "Here lie the ashes of the Mexican Thinker, who did the best he could for his country."

Following Lizardi's death, his novels were reissued in complete form, some for the first time, between 1830 and 1832. They have remained in print, in multiple editions, ever since.

The Novel

The Mangy Parrot is framed as the deathbed confessions of its namesake hero, Pedro "Periquillo" Sarmiento, who recounts an improbable number of misadventures that took him across the city and through all the social classes of Mexico, from his good birth and miseducation through his endless attempts to make an unearned living in the final decades before New Spain gained its independence. Throughout this narrative, Lizardi uses the voice of his elderly and repentant narrator and alter-ego to lambaste the social conditions that led to his wasted life. In this, the novelist mimics the role of the early 19th-century journalist, more interested in arguing opinions than relating mundane incidents. The marriage of slapstick humor with moralizing social commentary, established in *El Periquillo*, remained a constant in the Mexican novels that followed on its heels throughout the 19th century.[5] At the same time, as critics have noted, Lizardi's interest in depicting the realities and reproducing the speech of Mexicans from all social classes makes his novel a bridge between the inherited literary forms that go into its overt structure and the *costumbrista* novels of the 19th century.

The first two chapters set the novel's tone, as Pedro (better known by the diminutive Perico) tells of his early life, from his birth in Mexico "between 1771 and 1773" through his first, disastrous experiences in primary school, at the end of which he receives the nickname "el Periquillo Sarniento" ("the Mangy Parrot"), by which he will be known for the rest of his life. Lizardi uses these experiences as occasions to satirize the superstitions, child-rearing practices, and poor educational standards of colonial Mexico. This pattern holds for the remaining fifty chapters of the novel: Periquillo adopts one way of life after another in a variety of settings that add up to a social map of Mexico in the early 1800s, encountering both scoundrels and well-intentioned people at every step along the way, and commenting throughout on their moral failings and foibles.

His life journey takes him in turn to the university, a country estate, a theology school, and a monastery, where the hard life of a novitiate dissuades him from entering the religious orders. His father dies—an occasion for reviewing the funeral customs of Mexico at the time—and he quickly dissipates his meager inheritance. He becomes a professional gambler, then is beaten severely by a victim of his card tricks, giving us an opportunity to see a colonial hospital. A companion robs a house and Periquillo is picked up as an accessory, giving us a view of the inside of a jail.

Released, Periquillo is apprenticed in quick succession to a scribe, a barber-surgeon, and a pharmacist; he takes to the road, using his rudimentary knowledge of drugs to become a charlatan doctor. Accused of thievery, he flees back to Mexico City; winning the lottery, he takes up life as a gentleman. We see him take a mistress, then dismiss her so that he can make a more favorable marriage. After he loses his fortune at cards and his wife dies in poverty, he chances to find his former mistress, now married; her jealous husband attacks and nearly kills Periquillo.

After recovering, Periquillo becomes (again, in quick succession) a sexton's helper, a "blind" beggar, and (with the help of a former acquaintance) a civil servant in a small town. Here he is jailed at the insistence of the corrupt town priest, sentenced

---

5   Antonio Benítez-Rojo, "José Joaquín Fernández de Lizardi and the Emergence of the Spanish American Novel as National Project," *Modern Language Quarterly* 57(2): pp. 334–35. Agustín Yáñez justifies this often-criticized "moralizing" tendency in Lizardi as "a constant in the artistic production of Mexico . . . and moreover, it is a constant in Mexican life" ("El Pensador Mexicano," in Cedomil Goic, ed., *Historia y crítica de la literatura hispanoamericana*, t. I, *Época colonial*, Barcelona: Grijalbo, 1988, pp. 428–29; my translation).

to eight years of military service, and sent through the port of Acapulco to Manila. Here a colonel takes Periquillo on as his adjutant, and comes close to reforming him. In one conversation between the two, the colonel blames the social problems of "the Indies" (that is, Mexico) on the easy wealth of its silver-mining economy, and he compares these problems with the moral dissolution of a hypothetical young man who inherits his money and so never bothers to learn how to earn it. As he speaks, the reader realizes that the hypothetical young man is Periquillo himself, and therefore that Lizardi saw Periquillo's life as, to some degree, an allegory for the moral decline of his beloved Mexico.

After his years in service in Manila, Periquillo returns to Mexico. On the way back, he is shipwrecked for a few months on a utopian island in the north Pacific (an interval possibly inspired by the episode of Sancho Panza's governorship of a fictional island in *Don Quixote*, a book that Lizardi cites several times in the final chapters), giving Lizardi the opportunity to comment on Mexican society from the outside. Here he is befriended by a noble Chinese who becomes his traveling companion and takes him back to his homeland, but he abuses the noble's trust and returns to a life of poverty. He wanders from the city of Mexico and falls in with a gang of former companions, now highwaymen, who keep him with them in their mountain lair for several weeks. Only after a deadly disaster among these thieves does he sincerely repent of his ways. His honest confessor—another old companion, who took the right path—finds him a job in a small town just south of the city. Reformed now, he prospers and is surrounded by good friends, including Lizardi, who writes himself into his text as Periquillo's literary executor, until his peaceful death of "old age" in 1813 (when he would have been about 42!), just as the wars of independence are flaring.

A Note on Money

Much of the novel deals with Periquillo's money problems, so it may be worthwhile to mention the coins at issue. The basic coin of colonial Mexico was the *peso*, a silver coin weighing approximately one ounce. The peso was divided into eight *reales*—sometimes divided literally, by snapping a peso into eight bits, though the *real* (pronounced "ray-all," with two syllables) was also produced as a silver coin in its own right. There were also half-real and quarter-real pieces. When these terms are used metaphorically in the novel to refer to small amounts of money, I sometimes translate them as "dime" or "penny."

Other forms of cash mentioned in the text are: the silver mark (*marco*), which was a half-pound bar of silver, equal to eight pesos; the ounce of gold (*onza*), a gold coin worth 40 pesos; the *peseta*, worth two reales or one-quarter peso; the doubloon (*doblón*), an old gold coin worth between 5 and 40 pesos, and used in this novel only in a metaphoric sense; and the "moneys of account," *granos* and *maravedís*, tiny fractions of the peso that were used only for accounting purposes, not as actual coins. (Lizardi also mentions the *talega*, worth 1,000 pesos, and the *tomín*, which in Mexico was synonymous with the real; I have simplified by converting these into pesos and reales.)

It is impossible to give modern equivalents for what the peso was worth in Lizardi's time, because much of what we buy with cash today simply did not exist in 1816. The Mexican peso was one of the most widely accepted currencies in the world from the 1700s into the early 1800s; the U.S. dollar was modeled on it, and throughout this period, one peso was worth slightly more than one dollar. As a rough guide of values at the time, consider these figures: one real would purchase between 5 and 10 pounds of corn (the basic staple) in Mexico City during most of this period; a domestic servant might be paid 12 reales (one and a half pesos) a month, in addition to room and board; one and a half reales a day, or 50 pesos a year, was a standard wage for a day laborer or farm hand; 100 pesos was a common annual salary for a poor rural school teacher, and would have been a substantial sum to carry around on the street; 400 pesos was a very respectable annual salary for a notary or an assistant priest; 2,000 pesos would have been just enough capital to keep a shopkeeper afloat; and 20,000 pesos would have been a minor fortune, enough to purchase a small hacienda.

The Text

Numerous differences exist among the various editions of *El Periquillo*, though these variations have little effect on the meaning of the text. For this translation, I have mainly followed the most widely available version, edited by Jefferson Rea Spell (Mexico: Editorial Porrúa, 1949), which in turn is based primarily on the fourth edition of the novel (1842). I have also drawn on the third edition (the first to publish the entire manuscript of the novel, 1830–1831), as edited and annotated by Carmen Ruiz Barrionuevo (Madrid: Ediciones Cátedra, 1997).

As in Spell's edition of the novel, the footnotes added by the editor of the 1842 edition are followed by "–E." I have added a few clarifications in brackets to these notes and to Lizardi's. My translator's footnotes are also bracketed, and followed by "–Tr." References to Spell in the bracketed footnotes are to Jefferson Rea Spell, *Bridging the Gap: Articles on Mexican Literature* (Mexico: Editoral de Libros, 1971), and particularly to the indispensable articles "The Intellectual Background of Lizardi as Reflected in *El Periquillo Sarniento*" and "The Historical and Social Background of *El Periquillo*." References to Ruiz Barrionuevo are to the notes in her edition of *El Periquillo*.

David Frye
Ann Arbor, Michigan
2003

THE MANGY PARROT

The Life and Times of Periquillo Sarniento,
Written by Himself for His Children

My dear Sirs: As I tried to bring to light this Life of the Mangy Parrot, El Periquillo Sarniento, one of the thorniest problems I encountered was that of selecting the person to whom I might dedicate it, for I have seen an endless number of books, some of little merit, others of great, adorned with opening dedications. The long continuation of this custom made me think that there must be some good in it, for all these other authors have managed to select patrons or sponsors to whom they could dedicate their pieces, believing that by doing so they would necessarily reap some profit.

I became more convinced of this idea when I read in an old book[1] that some authors have managed to come to agreements whereby they would dedicate their work to a certain fellow, and he would give them a specified amount of money; one dedicated his book to a potentate, and then consecrated it to a second one under a different title; Thomas Fuller, the famous English historian, divided his works into many volumes, and solicited a different magnate to sponsor each of them; others have dedicated their productions to themselves; and, finally, others have allowed the printer to dedicate their works for them.

In view of this, I said to a friend, "No, my work cannot go without a dedication; no, no, not as long as King Carlos lives. What would the public say about me, unless it saw on page one of my little work that His Excellency, His Lordship, or at least Mr. Somebody had taken it under his wings? Besides, there's got to be some benefit in dedicating a book to a great or rich man; for who would be so shameless as to let someone dedicate a work to him; dust off his grandparents' bones; come up with testimonials to his ancestors; trace his genealogies; tie them in with the Pelayos and Guzmans; mix his blood with the blood of the Three Kings of Orient; expound on his knowledge, whether or not he has any; praise his virtues, both known and imagined; separate him utterly from the common mass of men; and deify him in the blink of an eye? And finally," I continued to my friend, "who would be so shiftless as to see himself buttered up and down *ante faciem populi*,[2] and in capital letters to boot, yet be so miserly that he wouldn't subsidize my printing costs, or find me a decent job, or—if worse comes to worst—show me his gratitude with just a dozen ounces of gold so I could buy myself a cloak? Isn't that the least I'd deserve for the arduous task of immortalizing a patron's name?"

"But to whom are you thinking of dedicating your work?" my friend asked me.

"To any gentleman I thought might dare to pay for the cost of printing it."

"And how much might that amount to?" he said.

"Four thousand, one hundred some-odd pesos, more or less, more or less."

"Santa Barbara!" my friend exclaimed in some alarm. "That's how much four tiny quarto volumes cost?"

---

[1] [The book is Johann Burkhard Mencke, *De charlataneria eruditorum declamationes duae* (1715; *The Charlatanry of the Learned,* NY, 1937), translated into Spanish as *Declamaciones contra la charlatanería de los eruditos* (Madrid, 1787). See Jefferson Rea Spell, *Bridging the Gap: Articles on Mexican Literature* (Mexico, 1971), p. 150. –Tr.]

[2] In view of everyone.

"Yes, my friend," I said, "and that is one of the most formidable obstacles that have faced American talents and have kept them from having the success they deserve in the literary theater. The costs you have to cover in this kingdom if you want to print a thick volume are so high, they keep most people from taking on such projects, considering how exposed they would be—not merely to receiving no reward for their toil, but perhaps to losing all their money; thus, many jewels that might profit the public and bring honor to their authors, instead remain on the shelf, unpublished. This misfortune means that there are no exports of printed works from here; for just imagine: once my little work is printed and bound, it will certainly cost eight or ten pesos at the least; so even if it was a worthy book, how would I dare send a boxful to Spain, knowing that as expensive as it is here, it will necessarily be far too expensive over there? Because, if you start with ten pesos of printing costs, and add another two or three in shipping, rights, and commissions, it would have to go for thirteen pesos or more; to make any money in this business, you would have to sell it for fifteen or sixteen pesos a copy, and then who would buy it there?"

"God help me!" said my friend. "That is true; but that should also dissuade you from soliciting a patron. Who would want to risk his money so that you could print your work? Come on, don't be a fool, put it away or burn it, and don't expect to find a protector, because you'll lose your mind first. I can see you now, spending the money you don't have on making a clean copy of your notebooks; you have your eye on dedicating it to Count H., thinking that—since he is a count, since he is rich, since he is liberal, since he can spend 4,000 pesos on his carriage, 500 on a horse, 1,000 on a ball, and whatever he wants on the gaming tables—he will graciously accept your offering, thank you for it, offer you his protection, pay for your printing, or at the least, give you a fine present, as you said.

"Trusting him, you go home, trace his ancestry, investigate his origins, search in Moreri's dictionary[3] for a great house that has some vague connection with his family name; you stick his name in, whether it fits there or not, you take down a thousand testimonials about his parents, you make him descend from the Visigoths, and you get it into his head that he is of royal blood and very close kin of the Sigericos, Turismundos, Theudiselos, and Athanagildos; fortunately, he didn't know them, and nobody's going to go investigate it. Finally, and to put it in the clearest terms possible, you work as hard as you can to give him a first-class bootlicking; and with your dedication in hand, you go there, frowning gravely, and lay it at his feet. Then the gentleman, who sees the bushel of paper that you've written, and who would give any amount of money just to keep from having to read it if someone tried to make him, laughs at your simple-mindedness. If he's in a bad mood, he won't allow you in to see him, or will toss you out with a curse as soon as he fathoms your designs; but if he's feeling good, he'll thank you and tell you to do

---

[3] [French writer Luis Moreri published his *Grand dictionnaire historique* in Lyon, 1674 (*The Great Historical, Geographical, and Poetical Dictionary*, London, 1694); one of several Spanish translations, *El gran diccionario histórico o Miscelánea curiosa de la historia sagrada y profana*, was published in Paris in 1753. –Tr.]

whatever you'd like with the dedication; but with all this business of the insurgents, and the war, and current crisis, and so on, he really can't be of any help to you at the moment.

"You leave him there, feeling gloomy but not yet in despair. You go accost Marquis K. with the same business, and the same thing happens to you; you approach wealthy Mr. G., and more of the same; you solicit Canon T., and ditto; until you are tired of wandering through the whole alphabet and working fruitlessly on a thousand dedications, and, bored and despairing, you hand your poor work off to some oil-and-vinegar shop. It's a waste of time, my boy; we poor folk shouldn't be writers, nor try to take on any task that costs money."

I listened crestfallen to my friend, all sad and confused; as soon as he finished, I fetched a sigh from the deepest corner of my breast and said, "Dear brother of my soul! You've told it to me straight, but at the same time you've given me great sorrow. Yes, you've pulled the wool from my eyes, and made me see a pack of truths that unfortunately cannot be denied; worst of all, the upshot of it is that I'm going to lose all my work; for though I'm so slow-witted that you can't expect me to have done anything sublime, just humble and trivial stuff, believe me, this book has cost me some toil, especially since I'm a clumsy oaf and have had to shape it without the right tools."

"I suppose you're referring to your lack of books."

"That's just what I'm referring to; you see how doing this has multiplied my exertions; and it would truly hurt if—after so many sleepless nights, after running here and there searching for books to borrow, after having to consult this, investigate that, write and erase the other, and so on, just when I was hoping to support my poor folks in some fashion or other with my book—if it should remain with me, stillborn, for lack of protection. . . . The devil take it all! I would have been better off if they had given me thirty purges and twenty enemas. . . .

"Quiet," my friend told me, "because I can suggest a group of patrons to you who will surely pay for your printing."

"Tell me, man! Who are they?" I asked, quite delighted.

"The readers," my friend replied. "Who rightly deserves to have your work dedicated to them, more than those who spend their own money to read it? They are the ones who pay for the printing, so they are your surest patrons. So cheer up, don't be a fool, dedicate your book to them, and your worries are over."

I thanked my friend; he left; I took his advice; and from that moment forth, I resolved to dedicate this Life of the world-famous Mangy Parrot to you, my dear readers; and that is what I now do.

But following established dedicatory usage, and in my role as your grateful or ingratiating client, I should offer you the most admiring tributes, in the safe knowledge that your modesty will not be offended.

Entering upon the vast field of your credits and virtues, what can I say of your illustrious lineage, other than that it is the most ancient and happiest in its origins, for you descend from no less than the first monarch of the universe?

What can I say of your glorious deeds, other than that they are beyond my knowledge or comprehension?

What can I say of your titles and honorifics, except that you are, or might be, not merely *you there* or *hey you*, but *Your Graces, Your Lordships, Most Reverend Sirs, Your Excellencies*, and for all I know, *Your Eminencies, Your Serenities, Your Highnesses*, and *Your Majesties?* Who could properly praise your worth? Who could even begin to outline your virtue and your knowledge? Who, finally, could enumerate the resounding family names of your illustrious houses, and all the eagles, tigers, lions, cats, and dogs that fill the quarters of your coats of arms?

I know quite well that you descend from an ingrate, and that you are related by kinship with the fratricidal Cains, the idolatrous Nebuchadnezzars, the prostituting Delilahs, the sacrilegious Balthasars, the accursed Hams, the traitorous Judases, the perfidious Sinons, the thieving Cacuses, the heretical Ariuses,[4] and a host of roguish ladies and gents who have lived, past and present, in the same world as ourselves.

I know that perhaps some of you are plebeians, Indians, mulattos, blacks, criminals, fools, and idiots.

But far be it from me to remind you of any of this, as I try to win your benevolence and affection for the work that I am dedicating to you; nor would I think of departing one inch from the path that has been so well trodden by my teachers, the Dedicators, whom I observe cultivating their ignorance of the vices and defects of their patrons, and remembering only their virtues and glory, so that they can repeat and exaggerate them.

That, oh most Excellent Readers!, is exactly what I now do, as I dedicated this small book to you, offering it as a fitting tribute to your noble (money's) worth.

Please be so good, then, as to accept it favorably, each one of you buying six or seven chapters a day,[5] and taking out five or six subscriptions at least, even if you later curse yourself to Barabbas for having wasted your money on something so tiresome and tedious; even though you criticize me up and down, even if you cut up my books to make napkins or paper cones; because, so long as you pay for the printing cost with just a pinch to spare, I will never regret having followed my friend's advice; rather, from hence forth, and from forth hence, I select and elect you to be my patrons and benefactors for each and every hodgepodge I come up with, showering you with praises as I do now, and praying that God keep you many years and give you lots of money, and that He allow you to spend it for the benefit of authors, printers, stationers, booksellers, binders, and all the others who depend upon your taste.

My dear Sirs . . . (etc.)

I remain yours . . . (etc.)

THE THINKER

---

4 [Cain, Nebuchadnezzar, Delilah, Balthasar (or Belshazzar), Ham, and Judas are Biblical figures. Sinon was the Greek who built the Trojan Horse in the *Odyssey.* Cacus was a giant who stole cattle from Hercules in Greek myth. The historical figure Arius (250–336) was the Greek theologian who authored the Arian heresy. –Tr.]

5 The first edition of the book came out chapter by chapter. –E. [It was published at a rate of two chapters per week and sold to subscribers. –Tr.]

Prologue by the Mangy Parrot

If I am writing my life story, it is only with the worthy object of having my children learn the matters about which I tell them.

It is my wish that these notebooks not leave their hands, and I have urged them to keep my wish; but, as I cannot know whether they will obey me, or whether they will get it into their heads to run around loaning them to one person after another, I find myself obliged (to keep others from gnawing on my rotting bones, or bearing false witness against me) to write a sort of *Prologue*, all by myself, since I wouldn't trust anyone else to do it; because prologues serve as muzzles for the stupid and the wicked, and at the same time (as someone or other once said), they are a preventive medicine for books; and in view of this, let me say: this little book is not for the wise, for they have no need of my poor lessons; but it may prove useful to lads who perhaps lack better works from which to learn, or also to young people (or even not so young) who enjoy reading light novels and comedies; and since they might run out of novels to read, or might some day find themselves without any at hand, they can still enjoy themselves and pass the time by reading about my misspent life.

I am recounting it so that I can point out to my children some of the rocky shores against which youth are too frequently dashed, when they do not know how to guide themselves, or when they scorn the advice of more seasoned pilots.

If I reveal my vices to them, it is not to boast about my picking them up, but to teach them to avoid doing the same, by depicting their foibles; likewise, when I recount some good act or other that I have performed, it is not to win their applause, but to instill in them a love for virtue.

For similar reasons, I present for their view and contemplation the vices and virtues of other people I have met; and it should be understood that almost all these passages are true and that nothing about them has been feigned or dissimulated, except for their names, which I have tried to disguise out of respect for their relatives, who are still alive today.

But no one should think, on account of this, that I have portrayed him; please pretend that nothing that I speak of has ever happened, and that it is all a fiction drawn from my fantasy; I will gladly pardon anyone who doubts that I tell the truth, as long as they do not slander me as a mordant satirist. If you find any spicy satire in my small book, I only mean it to lash at vice itself, leaving people untouched, as my friend Martial says:

> *Hunc servare modum nostri novere libelli.*
> *Parcere personis, dicere de vitiis.*[6]

So there's no reason to think, when I'm speaking of some vice, that I am portraying a particular person, or even thinking about it, because the only thought in my mind is that absolutely anyone who has that vice should detest it, and so far, I haven't found anything reprehensible about such a practice or desire. Especially since I am not

---

[6] [Marcus Valerius Martialis, *Epigrams* X.33, vv. 9–10. –Tr.]

writing for everybody, just for my own children, who concern me the most, and whom I have an obligation to teach.

But even if everyone were to read my book, nobody has any call to get offended when they see their own vices depicted here, nor to attribute to my malice what in reality is their own depravity.

This habit of criticizing, or better said, of grumbling about authors is very ancient, and has always been practiced by the wicked. Father St. Jerome complained about it when he said, regarding the aspersions cast by Onaso: "If I am talking about people whose noses have rotted off and who talk with a nasal twang, why do you go and complain about it, saying that I said it about you?"

Likewise, I say: if, in this small book of mine, I speak of *bad* judges, *criminal* notaries, *trouble-making* lawyers, *shiftless* doctors, *indolent* family fathers, and so on, why should all the judges, notaries, barristers, doctors, and the rest jump right up and claim that I'm maligning them and their abilities? That would be unjust and foolish; if you complain, it must be because something hit a nerve, and in that case you'll be better off if you don't let on than if you confess, unless someone asks you why you're limping.

I started off in the beginning by mixing a few sentences and verses in Latin into my work; and although I've given you the translations into our language, I've tried to skimp on them in the rest of the book, because I asked Mr. Muratori[7] about this question, and he told me that Latin tags are stumbling blocks in books for readers who don't understand them.

The method and style that I follow when I write are what comes naturally to me, and what cost me the least trouble, for I am convinced that the best eloquence is whatever persuades the best and conforms most naturally to the type of work one is writing.

I have no doubt that, between my meager talent and having written this book almost without lifting pen from paper, it will be filled with a thousand flaws, which will give the less-scrupulous critics plenty of practice material. If that proves to be the case, I promise to listen to the wise with resignation and thank them for their lessons, in spite of my self-love, which would rather I didn't put out any book at all unless it deserved the widest possible praise; though this bitter blow is softened somewhat by the knowledge that there are few works in the literary world without some blemish, even in their most resplendent passages. On the surface of the brightest globe in the sky, the one that gives us life, astronomers have discovered spots.

Finally, I have one consolation, which is that my writings will please precisely my children, for whom I created them in the first place; if the book does not suit everyone else, I will feel that it has not matched my desires, and will say to each of my readers what Ovid told his friend Pison: "If my writings do not deserve your praise,

---

[7] [Ludovico Antonio Muratori (1672–1750), Italian historian and archaeologist; according to Spell (p. 151), Lizardi is quoting from the Spanish translation of Muratori's *Delle riflessioni sopra il buon gusto nelle scienze e nelle arte* (Venice, 1708): *Reflexiones sobre el buen gusto en las ciencias y en las artes* (Madrid, 1782), pp. 75–76. –Tr.]

at least I hoped that they would be worthy of it. I flatter myself for this good intention, not for my work."

> *Quod si digna tua minus est mea pagina laude*
> *At voluisse sat est: animum, non camina, jacto.*[8]

General Note for the Readers

We well understand that it goes against common usage to add an adornment of notes and texts to a novelistic work such as this one, in which action should predominate over explanations of morality, and which is, moreover, incompatible with great erudition; yet, since it was our author's idea not merely to retell his life story, but to instruct his children insofar as he could, he undertook rather a few digressions, whenever he found an opportune chance in the course of his work; though (in my opinion) these digressions are not overly repetitious, disconnected, or vexatious.

I tend to agree with his way of thinking, and, in honor of the friendship in which I held him, I have seen to it that it is illustrated with a few texts that I think concur with his own intentions. At the same time, to save the less-educated readers from the stumbling blocks of Latin tags, as he has noted, I have left the Spanish translation in its place; sometimes I put the original text among the notes; other times, I omit the text and include only the citation; and sometimes I omit both altogether. In this way, the reader who only knows Spanish will be able to follow the reading uninterrupted, and the reader who has Latin will perhaps be pleased to read the same in the original language.

Periquillo, despite his economy of words, nonetheless corroborates his opinions with the teachings of the pagan poets and philosophers.

In exercising the authority he gave me to correct, add, or subtract whatever I thought necessary in his book, I could have suppressed all of these texts and authorities; but while I was battling with my doubts about what I ought to do, I read a paragraph by the erudite scholar Jamin that seemed quite to the point, which says:

> I have taken my reflections from those of the profane philosophers, and have not omitted the poets' testimony, for I am convinced that theirs, . . . albeit sensualist in general, established the severity of their customs more forcefully and conclusively than that of the philosophers, of whom there is reason to suspect that only their vanity has moved them to establish the austerity of the maxims that lay at the heart of a superstitious religion, which at the same time gave rein to every passion. Indeed, when one hears a sensualist writer praise the purity of the ancients' customs, it will be obvious that only the force of truth has wrested such brilliant testimony from his mouth.

---

[8] [The lines are from an unknown Roman author, not Ovid: "Laus Pisonis," vv. 214–5. –Tr.]

Thus says our noted authority, in paragraph XX of the preface to his book entitled *The Fruits of My Reading*.[9] Now, I say: if a young sensualist man, or a vice-clotted old man, sees his vices reproached, and the opposing virtues praised, not by anchorites and hermits in the desert, but by men who lack perfect religion, solid virtue, and the light of the Gospel, won't they necessarily form a very favorable view of the moral virtues? Isn't it conceivable that they will be ashamed to see their vices reprehended and ridiculed, not by the Pauls, Chrysostoms, Augustines, and other fathers and doctors of the Church, but by the Horaces, Juvenals, Senecas, Plutarchs, and other such blind men of pagan antiquity? And shouldn't the love of sound morals or the abhorrence of vice that might be produced by the testimony of the gentile authors be of laudable interest, both to our readers and to society itself? So it seems, at least to me, and therefore I have not wished to delete the authorities of which we speak.

---

[9] [Nicolas Jamin, French Benedictine ascetic and author, *Le fruit de mes lectures ou Pensées extraites des Anciens Profanes* (Paris, 1775); Lizardi quotes from the Spanish translation, *Máximas y sentencias políticas* (Madrid, 1795), p. xvii. –Tr.]

CHAPTER 1

PERIQUILLO BEGINS BY WRITING WHY HE HAS LEFT THESE
NOTEBOOKS TO HIS CHILDREN; HE DESCRIBES HIS PARENTS, HIS
COUNTRY, HIS BIRTH, AND OTHER CHILDHOOD INCIDENTS

Flat on my back for many months now, struggling against both illness and doctors, and waiting with resignation for the day when, in accordance with the plans of Divine Providence, you will have to close my eyes, dear children, I have thought to write down the not uncommon events of my life, so that you will beware of and guard against the many perils that may befall and even harm a man in the course of his days.

It is my hope that, by reading this, you will learn to avoid many of the mistakes you will find admitted here by myself and others, and, forewarned by my example, that you will escape the suffering I have endured through my own fault. Be satisfied that it is better to learn from another's disappointments than to feel them falling on your own head.

I earnestly beseech that you not be scandalized by my youthful waywardness, which I will recount in all frankness and with some embarrassment, for my desire is to instruct you and to lead you away from the many pitfalls I encountered in my youth, to which you are now exposed.

You should not think that reading my life story will be a tiresome chore. As I am well aware that variety delights the mind, I will be sure to avoid the monotonously even sort of tone that enrages readers. Therefore, you will find me at times as serious and sententious as Cato, and at other times as light and foolish as Bertoldo.[1] You will read bits of erudition and scraps of eloquence in my writings, and then you will see a popular style that mixes in the sayings and foolishness of the common folk.

I also promise to give you all this without any affectation or pedantry, but just as it comes into my head, and from there straight onto the paper, a method that seems to me the most analogous to our natural fickleness.

Finally, I request that these notebooks not leave your hands, so that they will not become the objects of slander by fools or knaves. However, should you ever succumb to the temptation of lending them out, I beg you never to loan them to such fellows; nor to hypocritical old women, nor to enterprising priests who like to do business with their parishioners both living and dead, nor to bungling doctors and lawyers, nor to thieving notaries, agents, court reporters, and solicitors, nor to swindling merchants, nor to executors who end up with the inheritance, nor to fathers and mothers who are inattentive to their families' education, nor to foolish and superstitious churchgoing women, nor to venal judges, nor to rascally constables, nor to dictatorial jailers, nor to half-baked scribblers and poets like myself, nor to officers and soldiers who are all boast and bluster, nor to rich, proud, stubborn misers who tyrannize other men, nor to men who are poor due to their own laziness, uselessness, or bad behavior,

---

[1] [Here, the narrator (Periquillo) contrasts Cato the Censor, the classical Roman orator, with Bertoldo, the buffoonish hero of an early 17th-century Italian comic novel that saw several translations and adaptations into Spanish in the 18th century. –Tr.]

nor to feigning beggars. Nor should you loan them to the girls who hire themselves out, nor to the young women who run away, nor to the old women who paint their faces, nor . . . but the list grows long. Suffice it to say, you should never loan them for one minute to any who you think would see themselves described in what they read: for despite what I have written in the prologue, the moment they see their inner selves portrayed by my pen, the second they read some opinion that seems new to them or that does not conform to their own depraved imaginings, in that very instant they will call me a fool, will pretend to be scandalized by my arguments, and some of them will even argue that I am a heretic and will try to have me arrested as such, even after I have turned to dust. Such is the power of malevolence, of prejudice, of ignorance!

Therefore, either read my notebooks only for yourselves, or—if you must lend them out—do so only to men of true good will, for although in their frailty they may stray at times, such men will recognize truth when they see it without feeling personally affronted, noting that I speak of no one in particular, but rather of all who overstep the bounds of justice. But if the former sorts do, in the end, read my book, when they grow cross or begin to mock it, you can just tell them this, in full confidence that it will scare them off: "What are you getting excited about? Why are you sneering, if, changing the names, the story of this disorderly man's life is your own?"[2]

My children, after my death, you will read these scribblings for the first time. Direct then your prayers for me to the throne of all mercy; let my mad acts be a lesson to you; never let yourselves be seduced by the falsity of men; learn the maxims I am teaching you, remembering that I learned them myself at the cost of hard experience; never praise my work, for I have undertaken most of it with the aim of improving you; and, when you have absorbed these warnings, begin to read.

My Country, Parents, Birth, and Early Education

I was born in the city of Mexico, the capital of North America, in New Spain.[3] Never could my mouth sing sufficient praise in honor of my dear country; but since it is mine, such praise would be ever suspect. Those who live there, and the foreigners who have seen it, can give more believable panegyrics, for they are not constrained by partiality, whose magnifying lens can at times hide defects while enlarging the advantages of a country, even to those born there. Leaving, therefore, the description of Mexico to impartial observers, I will say: I was born in this rich and prosperous city between 1771 and 1773, to parents who were neither wealthy nor mired in poverty; who were pure of blood, a purity that gleamed and was better known for their virtuous behavior.[4] Oh, if only children would always follow their parents' good examples!

---

[2] ". . . . Quid rides? / mutato nomine de te fabella narratur." [Horace, Satires I.1, 69–70. –Tr.]

[3] [Throughout the novel, "Mexico" refers exclusively to the capital, which today we call Mexico City. The colonial kingdom of New Spain corresponded more or less to the modern country of Mexico, which became independent five years after *Periquillo* was first published. –Tr.]

[4] [Pure of blood (*de limpia sangre*): this phrase was applied in colonial Spanish law to "Old Christian" families—that is, to those with no Jewish, Arabic, or African ancestry. –Tr.]

After I was born, following the baths and other necessities of the hour, my aunts and grandmothers and other old-fashioned ladies wanted to bind my hands and wrap me up as tight as a bottle-rocket. They argued that if they were to leave my hands unbound, I would likely frighten myself; they said I would grow up to be free with my fists; and finally—this was their weightiest, most incontrovertible argument—they said that this was how they had been raised, and was therefore the best and the safest way to follow, and that no one should think of arguing against them, because old folks are wiser than the people of today, and since they had bound their own children's hands, their example had to be followed blindly.

They then drew from a basket a length of ribbon that they called an *amulet sash*, adorned with *deer's-eye seeds, azabache hand charms, crocodile teeth,* and other such trinkets, so as to dress me up with these relics of superstitious paganism on the same day that had been set aside for my godparents to profess, on my behalf, my faith in the holy religion of Christ.[5]

Lord help me, how my father had to fight against the old ladies' prejudices! He wasted so much saliva convincing them that it was a pernicious and absurd flight of fancy to bind and tie the hands of babies! And he had to work so hard to persuade these sweet foolish women that jet, bone, stone, and other suchlike and unlike amulets have no power whatsoever against wind-sickness, anger, evil eye, and similar claptrap!

His Honor told me this story many times, along with how he eventually triumphed over them all, so that, like it or not, they refrained from imprisoning me, and merely decked me out with a rosary, a holy cross, a reliquary, and the four Gospels; and then, he tried to baptize me.

My parents had already found me godparents who were far from poor, and were naively convinced that this couple would take care of me in case I were orphaned.

My poor old folks had less knowledge of the world than I have acquired myself, for in my long experience, the majority of godparents know nothing of the obligations they are taking on toward their godchildren, so that they think themselves grand to give them half a *real* when they see them; and if the children's parents die, they think of them as seldom as if they had never met. True enough, there are godparents who fulfill their obligations to the letter, and even surpass their godchildren's parents in giving them shelter and education. Praised be such godparents!

As it happened, my own godparents, rich as they were, did me as much good as if I had never seen them; as good a reason as any for me never to think of them again. Indeed, they were so miserly, indolent, and stupid that, given how little I ever owed them from infancy onward, you might have thought my parents had picked them from the most wretched poorhouse in town. I abhor such godparents; even more, I abhor those parents who "do business with the Sacrament of baptism"

---

[5] [The items that Lizardi mocks here as superstitious relics (*faja de dijes, ojos de venado, manitas de azabache, colmillos de caimán*) are still common protections against the folk illnesses of wind (*aire*), anger (*coraje* or *rabia*), and evil eye (*mal de ojo*) in many Mexican communities. *Ojo de venado* is the eye-like seed of the plant known in English as "cowhage"; *azabache* is jet, a black mineral that can be carved into the shape of charms. –Tr.]

by not searching out virtuous and honorable godparents, going rather after the rich or well connected, whether in the crude hope that they will get some trifle from them, or because they are foolishly convinced that perhaps, due to some unforeseen contingency in the public order or disorder, they will be useful to their children after their deaths. Pardon me, dear offspring, for these digressions, which spill naturally from my pen and will do so more often than you might like in the course of this work.

They did baptize me in the end, giving me the name of Pedro, followed (as is the custom) by my father's surname, which was Sarmiento.

My mother was beautiful, and my father loved her to distraction; because of this, together with the arguments of my discreet aunts, it was unanimously decided that I be given a wet nurse, or *chichigua* as we say here.

Dear children! If you ever get married and have children of your own, never leave them to the mercenary care of that class of people. In the first place, they are slovenly as a rule, and the moment their attention wanders, they are likely to cause the children to get sick; since they don't love them but only feed them out of monetary interest, they take no care to avoid getting angry or eating a thousand things that damage their health, and consequently that of the infants who are put in their care; and they commit other harmful excesses, which I refrain from recounting in respect of your modesty. Second, it is a scandal against nature for a rational mother to do what no ass, no cat, no dog, nor any female animal devoid of reason would do.

Which of these females would leave its children in the care of some other brute, or even of man himself? Why, then, should man, endowed with reason, ride roughshod over the laws of nature and abandon his children to the rented arms of the first Indian, black, or white woman, be she healthy or sick, good or depraved in her manners, since the parents ask no further questions once they find that she has milk to give, to the outrage of the dog, the cat, the ass, and all the other irrational mothers?

Oh, if those poor infants of whom I speak were endowed with reason, then the minute the innocent babes found themselves abandoned by their mothers they would wail with sorrow: "Cruel women, how can you be so insolent and shameless as to call yourselves mothers? Do you have any inkling of a mother's great dignity? Are you aware of the tokens by which she is known? Have you ever remarked the lengths to which a hen goes to preserve her chicks? Oh, no! You conceived us out of lust, you gave birth to us out of necessity, you call us your children out of habit, you comfort us now and then out of obligation, and you abandon us out of an excess of self-love or detestable lechery. Yes, we are ashamed to say it; but be honest, if you dare, about the reasons why you find us tiresome. Except in grave cases in which your health is at risk, and which ought to be certified by a doctor who is knowledgeable, virtuous, and not bent to your will, tell us: were you moved to abandon us by any motive more pardonable than the desire not to get sick and ruin your own beauty? To be sure, these and none other were your criminal pretexts, cruel mothers, unworthy of that beloved name. We have found out how much love you have for us, we know now that you suffered us in your bellies only because you had to, and now we find ourselves relieved of any need to feel grateful, for just as soon as you can, you toss us into the arms of a strange woman, as not even the most horrific beast would do." So would the poor little ones argue if they had use of their reason and their tongues.

I thus ended up in the care, or lack thereof, of my *chichigua*, who surely lacked a good nature—that is, a well-formed spirit. For, if it is true that the first foods we are fed make us take on some of the properties of the women who give them to us, so that a child raised by a nanny goat is all too likely to turn out mischievous and jumpy, as others have noted; if this is true, I say, then my first wet nurse must have had a wicked disposition, to judge from how ill tempered I turned out. And all the more so, considering that it wasn't just one woman who gave me her breast, but rather one today, another tomorrow, yet another the day after tomorrow; and each of them, more often than not, was worse than the last: because if she wasn't a drunk, she was a glutton; if not a glutton, syphilitic; if she did not have this disease, she had some other; and if she was healthy, she would suddenly turn up pregnant; and this is only so far as the diseases of the body go, because as for diseases of the soul, it would be a rare one who could get a clean bill of health. If mothers would only notice at least these results of their abandonment, they would perhaps be not quite so slothful with their children.

Not only did my parents manage to make me ill tempered by their neglect, they also made me sickly by their care. My wet nurses began to weaken my health, and to make me proud, pretentious, and impertinent with their carelessness and untidiness; my parents finished off the job with their excessive and misdirected care and tenderness. For as soon as they had gotten me off the breast—which cost more than a little trouble—they set about raising me to be pampered, delicate, and lacking all direction or moderation.

It is essential that you know, my children (in case I have not told you so before) that my father was a man of good judgment and not the least bit vulgar, and as such, he always opposed my mother's silly notions. But sometimes (not to say most of the time) he would relent when he saw that she was growing distressed or upset, and this is why my rearing swung between good and bad, to the detriment not only of my moral education, but of my physical constitution as well.

All I had to do was show a desire for something, and my mother would put herself out to get it into my hands, justly or unjustly. Let's say I wanted her rosary, her sewing thimble, a piece of candy that some other child in the house was holding, or anything of the sort; I had to get it that very instant, or else; for otherwise I would deafen the whole neighborhood with my screams. And since they taught me that they would give me anything I wanted to keep me from crying, I would cry for whatever caught my eye, just to get it right away.

If some maidservant bothered me, my mother would have her punished in order to satisfy me; and this did nothing but teach me to be proud and vengeful.

They fed me whatever and whenever I wanted to eat, no matter the hour, without any rule or order in the quality or quantity of my food; and with this pretty method, within a few months, they managed to make me diarrhetic, potbellied, and pasty-faced.

Apart from this, I slept until ungodly hours; and when they got me out of bed, they would dress me from head to foot, wrapping me up like a tamale, so that (I am told) I never got out of bed without my shoes on, and never left my musty little corner without my head bound up. And more: although my parents were poor, they were not so poor that they could not afford little glass windows in their house; and since they had windows, I was never allowed to go out onto the balcony or the passageway, except by some rare accident, and that only late in the day. They skimped terribly on my baths, and when they did bathe me once in a blue moon, it was in a tightly closed room, and with steaming hot water.

Such was my early physical education. What could possibly result from worrying about so many things at the same time, other than raising me to be weak and sickly? Since they almost never offered me clean air, my body never grew accustomed to receiving its healthy impressions, so I would succumb to it at the slightest lapse, and at the age of two or three I was constantly coming down with colds and catarrhs, stunting my growth. Oh, mothers have no idea how much harm they do their children by following these methods. They should accustom their children to eating as little as possible, and give them foods that are easy to digest, in line with the tender resilience of their stomachs. They should familiarize them with fresh air and the outdoors; make them rise at a regular hour; have them go barefoot and without scarves or wraps on their heads; dress them without binding them up, so that their fluids can flow unhindered; allow them to play whenever they want, and in the fresh air whenever possible, so that their little muscles can grow stronger and more agile; and finally, bathe them often, and in cold water if possible, or lukewarm at most. It is incredible how much children would benefit from this plan of living. All the knowledgeable doctors recommend it; and in Mexico, we can now see it being practiced by many wealthy and broad-minded gentlemen; and in the streets, we now see crowds of children of both sexes dressed quite simply, with their heads exposed and no more wrappings on their legs than their little skirts or loose trousers. May God grant that this method become widespread, so that all young children might grow into robust adults who are therefore useful to society!

My poor, dear mother had one other silly notion: to fill my imagination with monsters and bogeymen, which she used to intimidate me whenever she was angry and I refused to keep quiet, go to sleep, or something of the sort. This corrupt practice gave me a cowardly and effeminate spirit, so that even at the age of eight or ten, I couldn't hear any little noise at night without being frightened, nor see any shadow, nor attend a funeral, nor enter a dark room, because everything filled me with terror. Even though I no longer believed in the bogeyman, I was still convinced that the dead appeared to the living all the time, that demons jumped out to scratch us and squeeze our necks with their tails whenever they felt like it, that there were shades that attacked us, that souls in torment wandered around begging us to pray for them; and I believed in other absurdities of the sort more than in the articles of the faith. All thanks to a gaggle of old women who, either as maidservants or as visitors, endeavored to entertain the little boy with their tales of ghosts, visions, and intolerable apparitions! Oh, how those old women damaged me! What a harmful concept I formed of the divine, and what an advantageous and respectable attitude toward the demons and the dead! If you should marry, my children, never let your own children become familiar with these superstitious old women (may I see them burnt with all their frauds and fairy tales in my lifetime). And do not permit them to share the society and conversation of stupid people, who, far from teaching them anything useful, will imbue them with a thousand errors and idiocies, which stick more tightly to our imaginations than ticks; for children pick up ideas of good and bad with great tenacity at their age, while, once they are adults, not even sage books and teachers suffice to erase the impressions made by the first errors that nurtured their spirits.

This is the reason why we see men, every day, whom we respect for their authority or character, and in whom we recognize a fair amount of talent and education, who we nevertheless find capriciously faithful to some ridiculous superstition; and worse, they clutch it more tightly than covetous Croesus did his treasure. They tend thus to die embracing their antiquated ignorance; this being rather natural, as Horace said: "The jar long retains the smell of the first fragrance that imbued it when it was new."

My father was, as I have said, a very judicious and very prudent man; he was always disturbed by these foolish stories; he was absolutely opposed to them; but he loved my mother to distraction, and his excessive love was why, not to cause her grief, he suffered and tolerated, despite himself, almost all her extravagant ideas and, without any bad intentions, allowed my mother and my aunts to conspire to harm me. And, God help me, how coddled and spoiled they made me! What, deny me anything I wanted, even if it was illicit for my age or harmful to my health? Impossible. Scold me for my childish rudeness? Not a chance. Restrain the first impulses of my passions? Never. Just the opposite: my vengeful acts, my gluttony, my stubbornness, and all my foolishness were passed off as amusing actions proper to my age, as if early childhood were not the best age for imprinting us with ideas of virtue and honor.

Everyone forgave my waywardness and sanctioned my crude errors with that ancient and too often-repeated chorus: "Leave him be; he's just a boy; it is natural at his age; he doesn't know what he is doing; how can he start where we finished?" and so on. With this indulgence, my mother perverted me even more, and my father had to yield to her inappropriate tenderness. How wrong men are to let their wives overrule them, especially regarding the rearing and education of their children!

Finally, this was how I lived in my home for my first six years in this world. That is, I lived like a mere animal, not knowing what I should know, while learning too much of what I was better off not learning.

The time then came for me to leave the house for a short while; I mean, they sent me to school, and there I again managed not to learn what I needed to know, while learning, as always, what I should never have known, and all because of my mother's unthinking disposition; but the events of this era I will leave to the following chapter.

CHAPTER 2

My father sulked a bit, my mother pouted, and I ranted and raved, cried and screamed; but nothing could make my father revoke his decree. They marched me off to school, whether I liked it or not.

The teacher was quite the upright man, but he lacked the sufficient prerequisites for the job. In the first place, he was poor, and had undertaken this profession merely out of necessity, without regard to his abilities or inclination; little wonder he was so upset and even ashamed of his fate.

Men believe (I do not know why) that boys, being boys, neither care about listening in on their conversations, nor understand them; and putting their faith in this error, they carelessly say many things in front of the boys that later come back to haunt them, and only then do they realize that children are curious, snooping, and observant.

I was one of them, and I fulfilled my duty to the letter. My teacher had me sit right next to him, whether at my father's own recommendation or because I was the best dressed among his pupils. I do not know what it is about a good exterior that it is so respected, even in boys.

Sitting in such immediacy to him, I never missed a word he exchanged with his friends. Once I heard him say in conversation with them, "Only my blasted poverty could have made me a schoolmaster. I have no life with all these damnable boys—they're so mischievous, and so stupid! No matter how hard I look, I can't find one good worker among them. Oh, drat this blasted job! On top of that, being a schoolteacher is the ultimate trick the Devil can play on us!" So argued my good teacher, and by his words you will recognize the innocence of his heart, his lack of talent, and the low opinion he had formed of an occupation that is so noble and laudable in itself; for teaching and giving direction to youth is a calling of the highest dignity, which is why kings and governments have showered wise instructors with honors and privileges. But as my poor teacher was unaware of all this, little wonder he should form such a low opinion of such an honorable profession.

In the second place, as I have said, he did not have the right disposition or temper for teaching. His heart was too sensitive; he loathed causing anyone pain; and this soft temperament caused him to be too indulgent with his students. It was rare for him to scold them harshly, and even rarer for him to punish them. His decrees left the rod and the ruler with little work to do; so the boys were in their glory, and I among them, for we could do whatever we pleased with impunity.

You see, my children, although this man was good in himself, he was awful as a teacher and head of household; for just as you should not hover over young children all day with whip in hand like a prison warden, neither should you ease up on them completely. It is fine if punishment is only employed every once in a while, if it is moderate, if it does not look like vengeance, if it is proportionate to the crime, and if it is only resorted to after every sweet and kind means of seeking reform has been tried; but if such means do not work, it is perfectly fine to use harsher methods, depending on the child's age, evil intent, and condition. I do not mean that parents and teachers should be tyrants, but neither should they pamper and indulge their children or pupils. As Plato said, "children's passions should not always be restrained with severity, nor should they be habitually petted and caressed."[1] Wisdom consists in finding the medium between these extremes.

Then again, my teacher lacked any of the talent needed for his job. At most he could read and write well enough to understand and be understood, but not well enough to teach. Not everyone who reads knows how to read. There are as many ways to read as there are styles of writing. Cicero's orations cannot be read like the *Annals* of Tacitus, nor Pliny's *Panegyric* like the comedies of Moreto. I mean that a reader has to be able to distinguish among writing styles, in order to animate his reading through his tone of voice; he will then demonstrate that he understands what he is reading, and that he knows how to read.

Many people believe that reading well consists in reading quickly, and following this method, they spout a thousand absurdities. Others think (and they are in the majority) that if you read by following the correct spelling of what is written, it will turn out perfectly. Others read like this, but listening to themselves, and pausing in a way that annoys all their listeners. Others, finally, read every sort of writing with a lot of affectation, but in a monotonous tone that tires the listener. These are the most common ways of reading, my children, and as you experience what I am saying, you will realize that good readers are not as common as you might think.

When you hear someone read a sermon as if he is preaching, a story as if he is recounting it, a comedy as if he is acting in it, and so on, so that if you closed your eyes you would think you were hearing a preacher in the pulpit, an individual on the witness stand, a comedian in the theater, and so on, then you can say, "This fellow can read well." But if you hear someone reading in a sing-song voice, or garbling the words, or disregarding the lines, or in an unchanging modulation so that he reads Young's *Night Thoughts* in the same tone of voice as the catechism, then you can say without hesitation, "This fellow has no idea how to read," as I say now about my first teacher.[2] Listen, he was one of them who read by spelling things out—"C, A, T: *cat*. C, I, T, Y: *kitty*"—so what could you expect?

And if he read like this, how well could he write? That much worse, and there was no way it could have been otherwise; for you can never build a solid structure on flimsy foundations.

It is true that he knew a smattering about that part of writing known as *calligraphy*, for he knew about lines, serifs, flourishes, proportions, distances, and so on; in a word, he painted pretty letters; but as for *orthography*, he did not know a thing. He adorned his writing with periods, commas, question marks, and other punctuation

---

[1] Plato, *On Laws*, book VII.

[2] [Edward Young's poem *The Complaint, or Night Thoughts* (1742) had been translated into Spanish, and was a favorite of Lizardi's. –Tr.]

signs, but without any order, method, or knowledge; so some of his things came out so ridiculous that he would have been better off not writing a single comma. If you try to do something you don't understand, you might pull it off the first time, like the donkey who played the flute by accident; but most of the time you will spoil everything you touch. This is what happened to my teacher in this matter, for where he should have put a colon, he put a comma; where he needed a comma, he left it out; and where he needed a colon, he usually put a period. Reason enough to realize straight away that he muddled everything he wrote; it would have been bad enough if his miserable punctuation had only resulted in absurdities, but at times he turned out scandalous blasphemies.

He had a lovely image of the Virgin of the Immaculate Conception, and at its foot he placed a quatrain that should have read thus:

> For of our heavenly Father
> Was Mary the favored daughter:
> Only she could be conceived
> Without original sin.

But the wretched man muddled his placement of punctuation marks from one end to the other, as was his custom, and made a devil of a mess, for which he would have deserved to be gagged if he had understood what he was doing, because he wrote:

> For of our heavenly Father,
> Was Mary the favored daughter?
> Only she? Could be, conceived
> Without: original sin.

You can see, children, how likely someone is to write a thousand foolish things if he lacks training in orthography, and how important it is for you not to neglect this point with your own children.

It is a pity how little effort is put into this branch of learning in our kingdom. A thousand gross barbarisms are written publicly every day, in the candle shops, chocolate stands, kiosks, the bills posted on street corners, and even in the posters at the Coliseo.[3] It is common to see a letter capitalized in the middle of a noun or verb, one letter switched for another, and so on. Such as: *Famous ChocoLates, Royel Sigars, The Barber of Cevvill, Proude Bakkery,* and similar infelicities, which display not only the ignorance of the writers from a mile away, but the neglect of the authorities in this area.

What a miserable impression the foreign visitor must form of our state of enlightenment, when he sees that such shabbiness is permitted to appear in writing, not just in some village, but in no less than Mexico, the capital of the Northern Indies, in full view and with the forbearance of so many respectable authorities and of such a large

---

[3] [Coliseo: the main theater in Mexico City at the time, located on the street now known as Bolívar. –Tr.]

number of educated men from every field! What could he say, what idea could he form, other than that the common people (and this, only if he is being equitable) are terribly vulgar and ignorant, and that their enlightenment is being utterly neglected by those who should be educating them?

It is to be wished that writing these public barbarisms, which contribute more than a little to damaging our reputation, should be outlawed.[4]

As you might imagine, what could I have learned under such a talented teacher? Nothing, of course. I spent one year in his company, and in that year I learned to read "fluently," as my simple-minded tutor liked to say, though I was really reading at full gallop; because, as he never paused for any such childishness as teaching us to read with punctuation, we jumped right over the periods, parentheses, exclamation points, and other such details as lightly as cats; and for this, my teacher and his fellows congratulated us.

I also forgot, in just a few days, the few scattered maxims of good breeding that my father had taught me while I was in the midst of being spoiled by my mother; but in exchange for the little that I forgot, I learned other little pleasantries, such as how to be shameless, bad-mannered, argumentative, sly, loudmouthed, and mischievous.

This school was not only poor, but poorly run, so that only very common boys attended it. In their company and with their examples, helped along by my teacher's neglect and my good disposition toward being bad, I turned out very well educated in all the arts I have mentioned. One of them was the custom of giving nicknames not only to my schoolmates, but to everyone I knew in my neighborhood, even the most respectable old people. A bad habit, unworthy of anyone of good birth! But this vice has been introduced into almost every school, college, barracks, and other public institution; and it is so common in the villages that no one there could escape having a nickname behind their back. At my school, we forgot our own given names because we only called ourselves by the insulting ones that we made up for each other. One boy was known as Squinty, another was Hunchback; this one was Sleepy, the other was Wasted. There was one who happily answered to Crazy, another to Donkey, a third to Turkey, and so on down the line.

With so many godparents around, I could not escape my christening. When I went off to school, I wore a green waistcoat and yellow pants. These colors, and the fact that my teacher sometimes affectionately called me not Pedro but Pedrillo, furnished my friends with my nickname: *Periquillo*, or Little Parrot. But I still needed some kind of adjective to distinguish me from another Parrot we already had. This adjective or surname was not long in coming: I came down with a case of *sarna*, or mange, and the boys had no sooner noticed it than they remembered my true surname, Sarmiento, and turned it into the resounding title of *Sarniento*, Mangy. So

---

[4] All over the world, good taste has complained of the injuries brought on by barbarity. Speaking on this subject, Don Antonio Ponz, in his *Viaje fuera de España* [Madrid, 1785], commenting on similar barbarisms that he had seen written publicly in his own country, celebrated the policies of many European cities where he had seen public signs written with great orthographic exactitude and in elaborate calligraphy. He offered his fellow countrymen these models of enlightenment in the hope that they would imitate them; the same hope inspires these remarks.

here you have me, known not just at school and as a child, but full-grown and far and wide, as Periquillo Sarniento, the Mangy Parrot.

It caused me no concern at the time, for I was content to repay my nicknamers by making up as many sobriquets for them as I could. But when, in the course of my life, I began to see what a hateful and unsightly thing it is to have nickname, I berated myself, condemned the vice, and showered curses on those boys: but it was too late.

Nonetheless, you should take advantage of these lessons, and never allow your own children to give themselves nicknames. Warn them that, if nothing else, this rude habit implies low birth and a coarse education—I say "if nothing else" because if it is not just done as a pun and a joke, if the nicknames are hurtful in themselves or are given with the aim of hurting, then they demonstrate that the one who makes them up or uses them has a lowly or corrupted soul, and the so-called joke is sinful, with the gravity of the sin depending on the spirit in which the names are used.

Among the Romans, the custom was to give each other bynames denoting their physical defects; but what was then a custom adopted to immortalize the memory of a hero, is a rude habit among us today. The laws of Castile impose serious penalties on anyone who harms another with words, and Christ himself says that "whosoever shall say to his brother, Thou fool, shall be in danger of hell fire."[5]

And if we should abstain from this vice even with our equals, how should we act toward our superiors in age, wisdom, and authority? Yet despite this, is there any superior, no matter his class or character, who has not been given a nickname in the village or community he governs? This is bold impudence, for we should respect them both in public and in private.

Merely being old should be motive enough to win our respect. Gray hairs give their owners a certain authority over the young. This truth is so well known and so ancient that already in Leviticus we read, "Rise up before the hoary head, and honor the person of the aged man."[6] Even the pagans themselves could not conceal justice in this regard; Juvenal tells us, "There was a time when it was held to be a capital crime for a young man not to rise in the presence of an old man, or a child in the presence of a bearded man."[7] Among the Lacedaemonians, the law was "that children must publicly revere their elders, and yield way to them on all occasions."

What would these ancients say if they could see the boys of today making fun of poor old men, thanks to their weary age? Forty-two boys perished in the arms and teeth of two bears. Why? Because they had made fun of the prophet Elisha, shouting "Bald head!" at him.[8] How wonderful it would be, if there were always a pair of

---

[5] [Matthew 5:22. In this translation, biblical quotations follow the authorized Catholic (Douay) version, except that names are generally given in the more common King James Version (e.g., Bathsheba, rather than Bethsabee). When there are differences in the numbering of chapters and verses, the KJV numbering is noted in parentheses. One of Lizardi's favorite books, Ecclesiasticus, is included in the Catholic bible but considered apocryphal in many Protestant traditions. –Tr.]

[6] [Leviticus 19:32. –Tr.]

[7] Satire XIII.

[8] [II Kings 2:23–24. –Tr.]

bears at hand to punish the insolence of all the spoiled, impudent boys we raise among us!

Quite apart from the old, fun should never be made of the simple-minded or the insane for any reason. The spiritual defect of these unhappy creatures should make us give thanks to the Creator for freeing us from the same fate; it should restrain our pride, causing us to reflect that tomorrow or the day after, we might well suffer the same disorder, as we are made of the same flesh; and finally, it should rouse our compassion toward them: for the wretched carry, in their very wretchedness, a letter of recommendation from God to their fellows. See, then, how cruel it is to make fun of any of these poor beings, rather than pity them and aid them as we ought. Learn this well, so that you may use it to inspire your own children; and do not think my digressions annoying.

Returning to my progress at school, I must say there was none; and things would have remained that way if an unforeseen accident had not freed me from my teacher. As it happened, one day a priest entered with a child he was entrusting to my teacher's care. After they had chatted, the priest was leaving when his eyes fell on the quatrain I mentioned earlier. He looked at it closely; took out his spectacles and read it again; tried to clean off the question marks and commas, thinking they must be flyspecks; and when he was satisfied that they were firmly painted characters, asked, "Who wrote this?"

To which my teacher responded that he had written it himself in his own handwriting. The ecclesiastic grew indignant, asking him, "And just what, sir, did you mean by what you have written here?"

"Father, I, well," my teacher stuttered in reply, "I meant to say this: that the most holy Virgin Mary was conceived in original grace, for she was the favored daughter of God the Father."

"Well, my friend," the cleric responded, "maybe that is what you meant to say, but the way it reads here it is a scandalous blunder. However, since it is just a consequence of your bad orthography, take the pen from the inkwell, and all the cotton you have, and erase this perversely written poem right now before I go. And if you do not know how to use punctuation marks, you should never draw them; better off trusting your letters and everything else you write to the discretion of your readers, without a drop of punctuation in them, than to write blasphemies like this because you do not know what you are doing."

My poor teacher, all embarrassed and filled with shame, erased the fatal verse in front of the priest and all of us. After he had concluded his tacit retraction, the ecclesiastic continued, "I am taking my nephew with me, for he is blind because of his age; and you are just as blind because of your ignorance; and as you have heard, when the blind leads the blind, they both end up falling over the precipice. You have a good heart and good manners, sir, but these qualities are not sufficient in themselves to make men good fathers, good tutors, or good teachers of the young. The necessary requirements for these occupations are *knowledge, judgment, virtue,* and *aptitude.* All you have is virtue, and that by itself will make you a good errand boy for nuns, or a good sexton, but not an educator of boys. Therefore, you will have to seek some other position, for if I see this school open again, I will let the teaching inspector know, so that he will confiscate your license, if indeed you have one. Goodbye."

Just imagine how this panegyric left my teacher feeling. As soon as the priest left, he sat down and lay his head on his arms, full of confusion and profoundly quiet.

That day we had no writing exercises, no lessons, no prayers, no catechism, not a bit of work. We shared in his grief and mourned his sadness as best we could, for we set aside our exercises and books and did not dare raise our voices at all. Of course, just to keep in shape, we played and talked in whispers until the stroke of noon; and as that hour began to ring, my teacher came to. He prayed with us, and after giving us his blessing, said in a very tender voice, "My children, I will not attempt to carry on in a position that not only keeps me poorly fed but takes away my appetite. You have just seen my run-in with the priest. God forgive him for the hard time he gave me; but I will not leave myself open to a second round, so do not come back this afternoon. Tell your parents that I am sick and have closed down the school. So, my children, good luck to you all, and pray for me."

We continued to grieve for a while, and our eyes continued to show our sorrow, for we indeed felt sorry for our teacher—since, fools though we might be, we knew we could not find a softer teacher if we had one made to order of butter or marzipan. But, in the end, we left.

When each boy got home, he must have done what I did, which was to tell the whole story from start to finish, down to my teacher's resolution to close down the school.

Upon hearing this news, my father had to seek a new teacher for me. After five days, he found one, brought me to his school, and handed me over to his terrible rule.

How unstable is fortune in this life! Scarcely does she smile at us for one day, when she frowns upon us for months on end. Lord help me, but did I ever learn this truth when I changed schools! In an instant, I went from a paradise to a hell, from the care of an angel to that of a tormenting devil. My world turned upside down.

This new teacher of mine was tall, gaunt, gray-haired, rather bilious, and melancholy; a full-fledged, upright man proud of his reading, famous for his penmanship, skillful at arithmetic, and quite a fair student. But all his good qualities were tarnished by his temperament, which was gloomy and harsh.

He was all too efficient and exacting. He had very few students, and he considered each one of them the sole object of his institute. A beautiful sentiment, had he known how to carry it out judiciously! But where good judgment is lacking, some sin to one extreme and others to the other. My first teacher was excessively compassionate and obliging; my second was excessively severe and exacting. The first spoiled us; the second did not let us get away with anything. The former pampered us without reserve; the latter tortured us without pity.

Such was my new tutor, from whose lips all laughter had been forever banished, and whose sallow visage displayed the severity of an Areopagite. He was a follower of that cruel and vulgar maxim, "Letters are learned with blood," and under this system, it was a rare day that he did not torment us. The whip, the cane, the dunce cap, and all the instruments of punishment were in constant motion against us; and I, being full of vices, suffered from them more than any of my classmates.

If my first teacher was unfit because he was overindulgent, this one was even less fit because he was a tyrant. If the former would have made a good errand boy for nuns, the latter would have made a better coachman, or sweatshop overseer.

It is a gross error to think that fear can make us advance in childhood, if it is excessive. Pliny rightly stated that "fear is a very unfaithful teacher." When someone undertakes something under threat of fear or terror, it is a miracle if he succeeds; the troubled spirit, as Cicero said, is unsuited to fulfilling its functions. So it was with me. When I went or was taken to school, I arrived already filled with an imponderable fear; my trembling hand and stammering tongue could neither write a well-formed line nor articulate a word in its place. I mixed up everything, not for lack of will and work, but for an excess of fear. My errors were followed by whippings, the whippings by more fear, and more fear made my hand and tongue more clumsy, which only yielded me more punishment.

I lived in this horrific circle of errors and punishment for two months, under the domination of that infernal satrap. Throughout this time, my mother, urged on by my complaints, implored my father to change schools for me. What grief she suffered! How many tears she shed! But my father was unyielding, convinced that it was all because of her pampering; and in this he did not want to acquiesce to her, until by fortune a friar came visiting one day who already knew of my new teacher's fine stew, and volunteered to speak of his cruelties. My mother gave such an earnest speech, and the friar testified so solidly in my favor, that my father was won over and resolved to place me elsewhere, as will be seen in the following chapter.

CHAPTER 3

The long-postponed day arrived when my father and the good friar decided to send me to a third school. I was disheartened, weeping, and fearful, expecting to find myself faced with the sequel to the cruel old man from whose clutches I had just been rescued, despite the constant attempts by my father and the reverend to bolster my spirits.

At last we entered the new school; but what was my surprise when I saw what I never expected, nor was ever used to seeing! It was a tidy, spacious classroom, full of light and ventilation, which were not blocked by its handsome exhibit cases; models and samples here and there about the room were held by amusing figures that grasped bouquets of roses, pleasantly and exquisitely painted, in their left hands. It seemed that my teacher had read no less than wise Blanchard's *School of Manners*, and that he proposed to carry out the projects put forth by the author, for his classroom overflowed with light, cleanliness, curiosity, and happiness.[1]

My first glance at the school's agreeable exterior greatly lessened the terror with which I had approached it; and I grew altogether peaceful when I saw the happiness painted on the faces of the other children who would be my classmates.

My new teacher was no stern, saturnine old man, as I had imagined he would be; quite the contrary: he was a semi-young man, thirty-two or thirty-three years old, slender in body and average in height; decently dressed in fashionable clothing, and very clean; his face displayed the sweetness of his heart; his mouth was set in a prudent smile; his lively and penetrating eyes inspired confidence and respect; in a word, this kindly man seems to have been born to guide children in their early years.

After my father and the friar left, my teacher led me to the corridor; he began to show me the flowerpots and ask me which flowers I could name, making me reflect on the varied beauty of their colors, the sweetness of their fragrances, and the artful mechanism through which Nature distributes the earth's sap through the various branches of plant life.

Then he had me listen to the sweet singing of several colored birds that hung in cages like those in the classroom, and he said: "Do you see, child, the exquisite beauty that Nature holds even in the handful of little flowers and animals we have here? For Nature is the minister of the God we believe in and worship. The greatest wonder of Nature that might astonish you was made by the Creator through a simple act of His supreme will. That fiery globe above our heads, which has burned for thousands of years without ever consuming itself, which maintains its flame with who-knows-what fuel, which not only gladdens but gives life to man, to beast, to plant, and to stone; that Sun, my child, that lamp of day, that eye of heaven, that

---

[1] [French Jesuit *abbé* Jean-Baptiste-Xavier Duchesne Blanchard (1731–1797) published his *L'ecole des moeurs, ou, Réflexion morales et historiques sur le maximes de la sagasse* in 1773. A Spanish translation appeared in 1786. –Tr.]

soul of Nature, which has illuminated so many peoples with its beneficent brilliance, gaining worship for itself as a deity, is—so that you understand what I am saying— nothing more than a plaything of His supreme Omnipotence. Consider now how powerful, wise, and loving your great God is, for the Sun that astonishes you, this sky that gladdens you, these little birds that entertain you, these flowers that delight you, this man who teaches you, and everything that surrounds you in Nature, came from His divine hands without the least effort, all perfect and destined for your ser- vice. And you, are you too small a thing to recognize this? And if you do recognize it, could you be so low as not to give thanks to God for all these favors He has done you without your deserving them? I couldn't think such a thing of you.

"Look, then: the best way for a person to show his gratefulness to his benefactor is to serve him however he can, never displease him, and do whatever he asks. That is what you should practice with your God, for He is so good. He asks that you love Him and that you observe His commandments. In the fourth of these, he orders you to obey and respect your parents, and after them, your superiors, among whom your teachers have a very distinguished place. Now it is my turn to be your teacher, and your turn to obey me as a good pupil. I should love you as a son and teach you with sweetness, and you should love me, respect me, and obey me just as you do your father. Do not fear me, for I am not your executioner; treat me courteously, but at the same time cordially, considering me a father and a friend.

"We do have whips here, and ones made of wire that cut the flesh; we have canes, dunce caps, stocks, shackles, and a thousand ugly things; but you won't see them so easily, for they are locked up in a storage room. Those horrible instruments that fore- bode pain and disgrace were not made for you or the other children you have seen here, for you were all raised in no ordinary cradles; you all have good parents who have given you beautiful educations and have inspired in you the finest sentiments of virtue, honor, and shame; and I do not think—nor do I expect—that you would ever put me in the difficult situation of having to use such repugnant punishments.

"The lash, my child, was invented to punish the rational man by shaming him, and to drive laziness from the unreasoning beast; but not for the decent child with a sense of shame, who knows what he should do and what he should never perform, not out of fear for the harshness of his punishments, but persuaded of his duty by teaching and convinced of his own interest.

"Even irrational animals are tamed and can learn solely through continuous teaching, without need for punishment. How many times do you think I have had to whip these innocent little birds to make them trill the way they do? As you can imagine, not once; for neither am I capable of such tyranny, nor would the little creatures withstand it. My efforts to teach them, and their industry in learning, have accustomed them to twittering in the ordered way you hear.

"So if mere birds need no lash to make them learn, how could a boy such as you? Dear Jesus, what an idea! What do you say, am I fooling myself? Will you love me? Will you do as I say?"

"Yes, sir," I said, and kissed his hand, moved to love by his sweet nature. Then he hugged me, brought me to his room, gave me some crackers, sat me on his bed, and told me to stay there.

It is incredible how a sweet, affable character—especially that of a superior—can command the human heart. My teacher's character so tamed me in his first lesson that I always loved and revered him with all my heart, and for the same reason, I obeyed him happily.

The bell rang for noon prayers, and my teacher called me to school to pray with the other children; we finished, and then he allowed us to jump and scamper about, all in good company, but within his sight, so that our playing was innocent. Meanwhile the serving men and maids began arriving for the children in their care, until the maid from my house arrived and took me home; but I noticed that my teacher handed her the book that I was to read, and gave her a note for my father, in which he told him that I should first study the general histories by Fleury or Pintón, and once I had a sound basis in their instruction, that it would be worthwhile to put in my hands *The Happy Man, The Famous Children, Recreations for the Sensitive Man,* or other such short works;[2] but that it would never do for me to read *Solitudes of Life,* the *Novels* of Zayas, *The Civil Wars of Granada, The History of Charlemagne and the Twelve Peers,* nor any such foolishness, which, far from shaping children's spirits, collaborate in corrupting them, whether by disposing their hearts to lewdness or by filling their heads with fables, boastful deeds, and ridiculous tales.[3]

My father followed my teacher's suggestions, and he was happy to do so, once he saw that the recommended works had nothing vulgar about them.

I stayed in the company of this dear man for two years, and came out with a middling understanding of the rudiments of reading, writing, and counting. My father had a respectable little suit made for me the day I had my public examination. He stretched his means in order to give my teacher a fine gift, which was indeed well earned. My father thanked him appropriately, as did I with many embraces, and we said farewell.

---

[2] [The teacher's recommended works—staples of Spanish and Spanish-American education in the late 18th century—are all didactic histories and Catholic moral works: Claude Fleury, *Catéchisme historique, contenant en abrégé l'histoire sainte et la doctrine cretienne* (Paris, 1683; *An Historical Catechism, Containing a Summary of the Sacred History and Christian Doctrine,* London, 1726), translated into Spanish in 1717 and reprinted many times; José Pintón, *Compendio histórico de la religión, desde la creación de mundo hasta la presente* (Madrid, 1754), reprinted twenty times by 1804; a didactic work by Portuguese scientist Theodoro de Almeida, *El hombre feliz independiente del mundo y de la fortuna* (Spanish translation, Madrid, 1783; Portuguese original, Lisbon, 1779); a French children's reader by A. F. J. Fréville, translated into Spanish as *Historia de los niños célebres* (Madrid, 1800); and French author François-Thomas-Marie de Baculard d'Arnaud's compendium of moral exempla, translated into Spanish as *Recreaciones y desahogos del hombre sensible* (Madrid, 1798). –Tr.]

[3] [The works he counsels against are all popular novels: Cristóbal Lozano, *Soledades de la vida y desengaños del mundo* (Madrid, 1658); María de Zayas y Sotomayor, *Honesto y entretenido sarao* (Zaragoza, 1637; *The Disenchantments of Love,* Albany, NY, 1997) and *Saraos* (Barcelona, 1647; reprinted under the title *Novelas ejemplares y amorosas,* Madrid, 1795); Ginés Pérez de Hita's novelized history, *Guerras civiles de Granada* (1595, 1604; *The Civil Wars of Granada,* London, 1801); and Nicolás de Piamonte, *Historia de Carlo Magno y los Doce Pares* (Seville, 1528), a reworking of the medieval romance of *Fierabras.* See Spell, pp. 153 and 159. –Tr.]

Perhaps you will find it striking, my children, that having been given such a bad nature by my physical and moral education, through no one's ill will but rather my mother's excessive love, and having been further corrupted by the perverse example of the children at my first school, I could have been transformed in an instant from bad to average (for I have never been good) under the direction of my true teacher; but don't be so surprised, for a good education, guided by a superior talent and vigilant wisdom, and above all by a good example, is so powerful that it forms a standard by which children will almost always direct their actions.

Therefore, when you have children of your own, be sure not only to instruct them with good advice, but to encourage them with good examples. Children mimic their elders, and they are very lively mimics: they immediately imitate whatever they see the grown-ups do, and unfortunately they are better and quicker at imitating the bad than the good. If your children see you praying, they'll pray too, though most likely they'll get bored and fall asleep. Not so if they hear you saying crude or insulting words; if they find you angry, vengeful, lustful, drunken, or gambling; they will eagerly learn those things, find a certain gratification in them, and their desire to completely satisfy their passions will make them imitate your disorderliness as meticulously as possible; and then you won't dare rebuke them, for they will answer: that's what you taught us, you've been our teachers, and we are doing nothing that we did not learn from you yourselves.

Crabs are animals that walk sideways; when some civilized crabs became aware of this deformity, they tried to correct the defect; but an elderly crab said, "Gentlemen, it is a mistake to suppose that we might correct a bad habit that has grown worse with age. The surest thing is to instruct our young people in how to walk straight, so that when they correct this slovenliness, they can then teach their children, and our posterity will be able to rid themselves forever of this cursed way of walking." All the crabs without exception celebrated this ruling. The mother and father crabs were put in charge of carrying it out, and with good arguments they convinced their children to walk straight; but the little crabs said, "Show us how, mother, father!" That was the thing. The crabs set out to walk, and they walked sideways, against every rule they had just laid down in words. The little crabs, naturally, did what they saw and not what they heard, and so they kept on walking as they ever had. This is a fable as far as crabs go, but as for men, it is an obvious truth; for, as Seneca says, "the road that leads to virtue by the way of rules is long and difficult; but the one that goes by the way of examples is brief and efficient."

Thus, my children, you should behave with the utmost circumspection in front of your own children, so that they may never see any bad deeds you commit now and then in your poverty. To tell the truth, if you are to be bad (may God forbid), I would rather you act hypocritically than flagrantly before my grandchildren, for they will be less harmed by watching your pretended virtue than by learning shameless vices. I am not saying that hypocrisy is good or excusable, but being bad is worse.

Not only do we Christians recognize our obligation to set a good example for our children; even the pagans understood this truth. Among others, Juvenal is worth noting when he says in his Satire XIV what I will translate as follows:

Let not the child observe, by ear or sight,
Any unworthy thing in your own house.
From your tender maiden, keep away
Seductions that might lead her astray,
And never hearken to the honeyed voice
Of he who lies awake to ruin her.
The child is due the greatest reverence,
And if you plan to carry out some sin,
Do not disdain his years, few though they be,
For in most people, malice early grows;
But rather, if you would commit a crime,
Your child should stop you, though he cannot speak:
For you are his censor, and tomorrow
Your example may make him provoke your wrath.
(And you should note, your child will look as much
Like you in habits as he does in face.)
When he commits some horrifying crime,
Not losing sight of where you've gone before,
You'll want to rectify and punish him;
Your street will echo with the fuss you'll make.
You may do even more then, if you have the will:
You'll disinherit him, filled as you'll be with rage;
But in that case, with what kind of justice
Could you invoke a father's liberty,
If you, old as you are, in his presence
Do not keep your own worse sins concealed?

They gave me a few days off in my house as a kind of graduation gift, and then tried to find me an occupation.

My father, who, as I have told you, was a prudent man and always looked beyond the surfaces of things, took into consideration the fact that he was already old and poor, and determined to find me a trade, for he said that, no matter what, it was better for me to be a bad workman than a good vagabond. But scarcely had he communicated his intention to my mother when—Lord of my soul! What a fuss and hullabaloo the sweet lady raised! She loved me dearly, true enough, but her love was disorderly. She was good and sensible, but full of common notions. She told my father, "My son, a trade? God forbid! What would the people say if they were to see the son of Don Manuel Sarmiento apprenticed to be a tailor, a painter, a silversmith, or whatever?"

"What could they say?" my father replied. "That Don Manuel Sarmiento is a decent but poor man, and a true upright man; and that, since he can't leave his son a great inheritance, he wants to provide him with a useful and honest means of support, rather than overburden the commonwealth with one more idler, and that means of support is nothing other than a trade. That's what they can say, nothing else."

"No, sir!" my mother replied, electrified. "You may wish to find Pedro some manual trade in spite of his high birth, but I do not. For, poor though I be, I remember that my veins and the veins of my son flow with the blood of the Ponces, Tagles, Pintos, Velascos, Zumalacárreguis and Bundiburis."

"But my dear," said my father, "what does the illustrious blood of the Ponces, Tagles, Pintos, or any other lineage on earth have to do with your son learning a trade so that he can provide for himself honorably, since he has no relatives who will guarantee his sustenance?"

"So," my mother pressed him, "so, you think it's fine for a noble child to become a tailor, a painter, a silversmith, a weaver, or some such thing?"

"Yes, my darling," my father replied quite phlegmatically, "I do think it's fine, very fine indeed, for a noble child, if he is poor and unprotected, to learn any trade whatsoever, no matter how manual it be, so that he will not have to go around begging for his meals. What I think is bad is for a noble child to go about penniless, dressed in rags or dying of hunger, because he has no trade or means of profit. I think it is bad if he has to earn his bread by wandering among the gaming tables, looking for a chance to swipe some gambler's ante,[4] place a bet, or cage a croupier's gratuity. I think it is even worse for a noble boy to go around spying out people's midday meals so he can join in as a guest—or as I would say, as a shameless sponger, because guests are those who are invited to eat at others' houses, while these scamps go where no one has asked them to come; rather, in exchange for filling their bellies, they make themselves everyone's laughingstocks, suffer a thousand snubs, and in the end, they cling tighter than a bunch of leeches, so that sometimes they can only be sent away with curses. I do think that all these things are bad for a noble; and what I think is worse, the absolute worst imaginable, is for an idle, depraved, and poor young man to go about cheating one man, swindling another, and pulling every trick he knows, until he is finally unmasked, is revealed as a thief, and ends up humiliated by public punishment or in prison. You've heard of some of these scoundrels, and you've even seen the corpses of some of these nobles, dead by the hangman's noose right here in the Mexico city plaza. You knew one of these nobles, a very noble young gentleman indeed, scion of an ancient lineage, nephew of no less than a prime minister and secretary of state; but he was depraved, profligate, and (being a cad) jobless; he topped off his wicked deeds by murdering a poor itinerant juggler on Platanillo Hill on the road to Acapulco, while robbing him of some trifle that he had acquired with his own work and sweat. The nobleman fell in the hands of the Acordada, was sentenced to death, sat on death row, was reprieved by the viceroy out of respect for the uncle, and languished in prison for many years, until the Count of Revilla banished him for life to the Mariana Islands.[5] That's the sorry portrait of the depraved and jobless nobleman. His ancestral house lost no luster because of the

---

[4] [The author here includes a note explaining Mexican gaming slang: *arrastrar un muerto* (literally, to drag a dead man), "to steal a gambler's bet when he is not looking." –Tr.]

[5] [This anecdote is based on the true story of Pedro Antonio Fernández Bazán, who robbed and murdered his partner in 1784, was sentenced to death by the Acordada (a special tribunal established in 18th-century Mexico to deal with the endemic problem of highway robbery), had his sentence commuted in 1789 by the second Count of Revilla Gigedo (viceroy of New Spain, 1789–1794), and was exiled to the Spanish penal colony on the Marianas, east of the Philippines. For the full source, see Spell, p. 176. –Tr.]

base behavior of one knavish kinsman. Had they hanged him, his uncle would have still been where he was, on top of the world; for just as no one is wise because his father knew a few things, nor brave because of his father's deeds, likewise no one is dishonored or discredited by his sons' behavior, however bad. I have brought up this horrendous case—and God forbid anything of the sort happen again!—so you'll see what is liable to happen to a nobleman who, relying on his nobility, does not wish to work, poor though he be."

"But must he fall so low?" my mother said. "Must my little Pedro end up as cruel and wicked as Don N. R.?"

"Yes, my dearest," my father replied, "being in the same predicament, it makes no difference whether it's Juan or Pedro; it is a natural thing, and the miracle would be if it didn't happen in just the same way, circumstances being equal. Does Pedro enjoy some special privilege that would keep him, supposing he were poor and unemployable, from becoming one more criminal and thief, just like Juan and all the other Juans in the world? Has the Father Eternal signed some document that guarantees us our son won't be steeped in vice, nor suffer the hapless fate of all his equals, especially when he sees himself pressed by need, which almost always blinds men and makes them stoop to the most shameful crimes?"

"All that is fine," my mother said, "but what will his relatives say when they see him working a trade?"

"Nothing. What should they say?" my father replied. "The most they could say is: my cousin the tailor, my nephew the silversmith, or whatever; or perhaps they will say: we don't have any relatives who are tailors, and so on; and maybe they will never speak to him again; but now, you tell me: what will his relatives give him, the day they see him jobless, tattered, and dying of hunger? Come on, I told you what they would say in one case, now you tell me what they would say in the other."

"Could be," my good mother said, "could be they'd help him out, if only so that he won't tarnish their golden reputations."

"You can laugh at that, dear," my father replied. "So long as they can keep his hands off their gold, they won't care much about what he does to their golden reputations. Most rich relatives have a well-rehearsed routine for avoiding the hint of shame their poor relations' rags might cause them: they roundly deny the relationship. Stop fooling yourself; if Pedro has any good luck or gains any standing in the world, not only will his true relatives recognize him, he will discover a thousand new ones, though they're no more closely related to him than the Grand Turk, and he will have such a swarm of friends continually at his side that he won't be able to move; but if he is poor, as will be likely, he will have nothing but the peso he earns. This is a truth, and an ancient and well-established one in this world; that is why our elders wisely said, 'there is no better friend than God, and no closer kinsman than a peso.' Have you seen how your uncle the captain still visits us? How my nephew the priest sends us his regards? And the Delgado cousins, Aunt Rivera, Grandma Manuela, and all the rest? That is because they can see that, poor though we be, thanks to God, we still have food on our table, and I do my best to be of service to them. That's why they visit us, that and nothing else, believe me. Some come to ask me for a loan, others to help them out with one obligation or another, some to pass the time, some to snoop around the inside of my house, some to have lunch or a cup of chocolate; but the day I die, if you end up poor, you will see—yes, you will see—how quickly friends and kin will evaporate, like mosquitoes fleeing from smoke. Knowing all this, I would like for my son Pedro to learn a trade, since he is poor, so that he won't depend on family nor strangers after my days are done. I warn you, men often find more comfort among strangers than kin; but be that as it may, it is best for each to rely on his own work and his own business and not be a burden to anyone else."

"You've almost stunned me with all these things," my mother said; "but what I see is that an hidalgo without a trade is better accepted, and treated as more distinguished in any decent place, than any hidalgo who is a tailor, tinker, painter, or so on."

"There's your coarse and unfounded fear," my father replied. "He doesn't have to have a trade; but he must have some honest business. An office employee, a military officer, or some such, will be treated better than a tailor or any manual tradesman, and rightly so; it is right and just for people to make distinctions; but the tailor, even the shoemaker, will be held in higher esteem anywhere than any hidalgo who is a lazy, ragged, swindling rogue, which is what I do not want my son to become. All this aside, whoever told you that having a trade is debasing? What's debasing is bad actions, bad behavior, and bad education. Is there any baser job than herding pigs? Well, that did not stop a Sixtus V from becoming the pontiff of the Catholic Church. . . . "

But you will discover the outcome of this argument in the fourth chapter.

CHAPTER 4

IN WHICH PERIQUILLO TELLS US OF THE OUTCOME OF THE
CONVERSATION BETWEEN HIS PARENTS, AND ITS RESULT, WHICH WAS
THAT THEY SET HIM TO STUDY, AND OF THE PROGRESS HE MADE

My mother, despite all that had been said, was obstinately opposed to teaching me a trade, insisting that my father send me on to higher education. His Worship told her, "Don't be foolish; what if Pedro is disinclined towards his studies, or has no aptitude for them—wouldn't it be outrageous to send him in a direction he does not want to follow? The silliest thing some parents do is to make their son become a lawyer or a priest by brute force, even when he has no vocation for such a career, nor any talent for letters: a baneful process, whose pernicious effects are daily bemoaned when we see all these paper-pushing lawyers,[1] murderous doctors, and ignorant, dissolute priests.

"Even to teach children a trade, we must first consult their characters and physical constitutions, because one who would make a good tailor or painter would not be good as a smith or carpenter, trades that call not only for inclination, but for bodily aptitude and robust strength.

"Not every man is born fit for everything. Some are good at letters—and not in general, for one who would make a good theologian might not be so good a medical doctor; and one who would be an excellent physician might be a mere run-of-the-mill lawyer, if his character isn't taken into account; and so on with all the men of letters. Others are good at arms, but inept at commerce. Others excel at commerce and blunder at letters. Others, finally, are quite talented at the liberal arts and unfit for manual arts, and so on for every type of man.

"Indeed, men who are fit for all the arts and sciences[2] in general can be considered either phenomena of Nature or testimony to the divine Almighty, who can do whatever He will.

"Nevertheless, I firmly believe that these 'omniscient' men, whom the world has celebrated time and again, are but freaks (so to speak) of understanding, of hard work, and of memory, and they have astonished people through the generations insofar as they have acquired knowledge of many more sciences than is common among their most knowledgeable contemporaries, and perhaps have held this knowledge to a higher degree; but in my opinion, they have not gone beyond being phenomena of talent, rare in truth as that is; yet they are infinitely limited, and will never deserve their sacred renown as omniscient, for if 'omniscient' means that one knows everything, I say there is only one omniscient being in or outside of Nature, which is God. This Supreme Being is certainly the one and only true omniscient, for

---

[1] [*Abogados firmones,* "signature-signing lawyers":] So we call the lawyers who, having few clients, go to the offices of notaries, and in older times to the benches of solicitors, to sign their names for four reales or a peso on written documents that, by law, must carry a lawyer's signature. –E.

[2] [Science (*ciencia*): Lizardi uses this word in its older meaning (still common in Spanish) of "any field of knowledge," not strictly limited to the physical or natural sciences. –Tr.]

He is the one and only one who truly knows everything that can be known; and in this sense, admitting another man to be omniscient would be to admit another God, an absurdity far from the minds of even those who honor the profound Leibniz with this pompous title.[3]

"Perhaps this great man would be incapable of resoling a shoe, embroidering an epaulette, or doing a thousand other things that we see as mere trifles and results of purely manual art; and if this celebrated genius were alive today, he would no doubt have to renounce many of his precepts and axioms, in the light of newer discoveries that have been made.

"I tell you all this, my dear, so that you may reflect that all men are finite and limited; that we can barely succeed in one thing; that the most celebrated geniuses have not been more than great; but they have not even remotely been universal, for that is the prerogative of the Creator; and that, it follows, we should examine our children's inclinations and talents in order to guide them.

"I do not remember where I read that the Spartans used the following stratagem to start their children on the right career. In a great hall, they would prepare a variety of instruments belonging to the arts and sciences that they knew; suppose that in that hall, they put instruments for music, painting, sculpture, architecture, astronomy, geography, and so on, without neglecting arms and books as well; this done, they cleverly arranged for several children to enter the hall alone, where they played with whichever instruments they wished, while their parents hid, observed their children's actions, and took note of the things toward which each child was inclined on his own; and when they noticed that one child was constantly attracted to arms, or to books, or to any science or art, from all the instruments that he had at hand, they did not hesitate to devote him to that thing; and their prudent examination was almost always crowned with success.

"I have always liked this lovely skill of tracking down a child's aptitude, just as I have always reproached the common corrupt practice of many parents, who foolishly and madly push their boys into college, without taking the least effort to investigate whether they have any aptitude for letters.

"My dear, this error is as deeply rooted as it is crude. A child who is a slow and shallow learner will never make progress in any science, no matter how much time he spends sitting in the classroom or handling his books. Neither books nor colleges can give talent to one born without it. Donkeys enter the colleges and universities every day to deliver loads of coal or stone, and when they leave, they are still the same dumb brutes they were when they entered; for just as the sciences are not isolated within the precincts of the universities or high schools, neither are these schools able to communicate an iota of science to one who lacks the talent to understand it.

"Apart from this, there is another powerful reason that would keep me from resolving to send my son to college, even if I knew that he had a wonderful aptitude for study, and that is my poverty. I barely have enough to pay for food with my salary; where am I to get the ten pesos for the monthly room and board, and all the

---

[3] [Gottfried Wilhelm Leibniz (1646–1716), the German philosopher and mathematician. –Tr.]

decent clothing that a college student needs? And this, you can see, is an insuperable obstacle."

"No," said my mother, who up until then had only listened without even parting her lips, "no, that is no reason, much less an obstacle, because we can solve everything by sending him as a day student."

"Very well," said my father, "you've beaten me there; but let's see how you get out of this next difficulty. I am already old, I am poor, I have nothing to leave you; tomorrow I may die and leave you widowed, alone, without shelter or food, with a grown boy at your side who at most will know how to speak some poor Latin and confuse everyone with a handful of *ergos* and pedantries that he won't even understand as they leave his mouth; but in reality all this means nothing, because unless the boy has someone who will continue fostering him, he will remain stuck in midstudies, unable to become priest nor lawyer nor doctor, nor anything else that will support his way of life nor help you with his letters; and the worst of all this is that he will no longer be any good for the arts, for he will not set himself to learn a trade for three strong reasons. First, because of a certain vain humor that boys tend to contract at college, which means that any boy who has so much as entered college (especially if he wears the scholar's sash) and has learned to spout a bit of Cicero or the Breviary, will think it beneath him to stand behind a counter or to learn a trade in a workshop. That is true even if he is nothing but a sorry grammar-school graduate; and what if he has attained the high-sounding and colorful title of Bachelor of Arts? Oh, then he will be persuaded that the earth doesn't deserve him. Poor boys! That is the first thing that ruins them for the arts. The second reason is that, since they are already grown, material labor becomes tedious for them, whereas they find it shameful to apprentice themselves at an age when others are already tradesmen, and it would even be fairly difficult to find a master tradesman who would take on the education and sustenance of such hulking brutes. The third reason is that these boys have already been around the block—that is, they've tasted freedom, so that they will never submit themselves to what they would so easily have accepted when they were young children. So just think what a state your Pedro will be in, if we send him to college and I die, leaving him (as is likely) halfway through his studies; for he will be up in the air, unable to go forward nor back. And when you see that rather than having a staff you can count on to support you in your old age, you will have by your side a lazy good-for-nothing who won't do a thing to help you (for stores don't give credit for syllogisms or Latin phrases), then you will curse all your son's studies and degrees. Therefore, my dear, let's do now what you will wish you had done after I am gone. Let's have Pedro learn a trade. What do you say?"

"What can I say?" my mother replied, "except that you are doing everything in your power to mortify me and turn my poor baby into an unhappy wretch, trying to make him common by making him a craftsman, and that is why you have spent so much time talking and pontificating. So, what, do you already know that he is stupid? Do you already know that you are going to die when he is halfway through his studies? And do you already know, finally, that when you die, every other resource is going to be cut off? God does not die; the boy has relatives and godparents who can help him; there are plenty of devout rich men in Mexico who can protect him; and I who am his mother will beg for alms to sustain him until he makes it. No, but you don't love the poor boy; nor me, either, and that is why you are trying to saddle me with this affliction. What am I to do? I'm as wretched as my son. . . . "

Here, my dear mother, bless her soul, began to cry, and with a couple of tears she brought all my good father's firmness and solid reasoning crashing down; for as soon as he saw her crying, he hugged her, for he loved her tenderly, and told her, "Don't cry, my dearest, it isn't so bad as all that. What I have told you is what reason and experience have taught me; but if what you want is for Pedro to study, then let him study and good luck to him; I won't stop it; perhaps God will let me live to see him through it, and if not, His Majesty will open a path for you, since He knows your good intentions."

My mother consoled herself with this prescription, and from that moment, she tried to get me to study; and I was fitted out with black clothes, a Latin grammar book, and all the other odds and ends I needed.

It seems that my father had spoken prophetically, for everything turned out just as he had said. Indeed, he was knowledgeable about the ways of the world and shrewd in his judgment; but most of the time, he lost these virtues, for he yielded so willingly to my mother's whims.

It is all very good and just for men to love their wives and to please them in everything that does not run counter to reason; but not that they indulge them so far as to ride roughshod over justice in order not to upset them, running the risk that they themselves and their children will harvest the fruits of their imprudent love, as happened to me. This is why I am alerting you to live with this warning: you should love your wives as God commands you and as Nature sensibly inspires you to do; but do not make yourselves effeminate, as brave Hercules did, who, having defeated lions, wild boars, hydras, and everything else that opposed him, let himself be so conquered by his love of Omphale that she stripped him of the Nemean Lion's skin, dressed him as a woman, set him to spinning yarn, and even scolded and punished him when he broke a spindle or failed to finish some chore she gave him. How shameful it is to be so feminized, even in a fable!

Women know very well how to take advantage of this mad passion, and they try to dominate such butter-soft men.

It is infuriating to see so many men who, not recognizing or understanding how to uphold their character and superiority, let themselves droop until they become their wives' servants. There is no secret, no matter how important, that they do not reveal to their wives; they do nothing without asking their opinion; they don't take so much as a step without asking for permission. It does not take much coaxing for women to want to leave their sphere, and when they realize that they have gained a man's submissiveness with their beauty, then they go ahead and develop their full dominant spirit, and there you have it: an Omphale in every woman, and in every downtrodden man a sissified, shameless Hercules. In such cases, when women do whatever they fancy at their own discretion, when they think nothing of men, when they cuckold them, when they give them orders, insult them, even lay hands on them, as I have seen many times, all they are doing is carrying out their natural inclinations and punishing the baseness of their husbands or lovers for not preventing them.

God save us from a man who fears his wife, who needs to ask her opinion before he can do this or that, who knows he has to tell her where he's been and where he's going, and who, if his wife screams and yells, can only resort to caresses and endearments to calm her down. Such a man, unworthy of that superior name, is ever ready to be a cuckold and an incompetent family head—for he does not guide his children, she does. His own boys soon note their mother's superiority and pay their father not the slightest attention, especially when they see that, should they commit some rascally act for which their father wants to punish them, they have only to seek refuge with their mother, for she will defend them, and if need be, will raise a ruckus with their father, and so thus sin can be committed and the penalty avoided.

Right was Terence to say that mothers abet their children's wickedness and obstruct the fathers who would correct them. I will set this in a little verse so that you may remember it:

> Often mothers will assist
> The evils of their sons,
> Keeping fathers' punishments
> From being justly done.[4]

It is true that my father was not the effeminate sort of man, nor my mother the arrogant type of woman I have mentioned. My father sometimes held his own, and my mother never lost her temper nor stuck her hand, as they say, in the collection box;[5] what happened was that, when her hints and pleas were not enough to dissuade my father from his intentions, she resorted to tears, and then it would be a miracle if she didn't get her way, because the tears of a beautiful and beloved woman are the most effective weapons for defeating even the most circumspect man.

Nevertheless, sometimes he held his own with the utmost vigor. It would have been better had he always maintained an even character; but we men cannot control our hearts all the time, much as we should do so.

At last, the day arrived when they sent me to study; the school was that of Don Manuel Enríquez,[6] a figure well known in Mexico, as much for his good manners as for his pleasant disposition and established ability to teach Latin grammar, for in his time, none of the many private tutors in this city could challenge his primacy; yet due to the common and tenacious prejudice that still reigns here, he taught us much grammar and little Latin. Teachers are ordinarily happy if they can teach their pupils a multitude of rules that they call *palitos*, "handles"; if their students can recite a few short phrases; and if they can translate the Breviary, the Council of Trent, the Catechism of St. Pius V, and, with luck, a few bits from the *Aeneid* and Cicero. "Such a

---

[4] *Matres omnes in peccato adjutrices, et auxilio in paterna injuria esse solent.* [Terence (186–159 B.C.), *Heauton Timorumenos*, Act V, scene II, lines 991–93. –Tr.]

[5] ["Stick her hand in the collection box": *alzarse con el santo y la limosna*, literally "to steal the saint and the alms." Images of saints were sometimes sent around a neighborhood from house to house, together with a collection box for alms. To keep the saint and the alms, rather than send it on to the next house, implied a betrayal of trust. –Tr.]

[6] [Lizardi went to the school of Manuel Enríquez de Agredo in the 1790s. See Spell, p. 173. –Tr.]

method teaches boys to be big talkers, but does not teach them Latin," as Father Calasanz says in *Discerning Genius.*[7] That is how I turned out, and it was the best I could have done. I got my head filled with little Latin rules, riddles, phrases, and plays on words; but as for a pure and faithful understanding of the language, not a word. I was not bad at making a fair translation of the homilies of Breviary and the paragraphs of the priests' catechism; but Virgil, Horace, Juvenal, Persius, Lucan, Tacitus, and so one would have escaped my understanding untouched if I had had the fortune to meet them, with the exception of the first poet I mentioned, for I know a few short bits of his that I had heard my wise teacher translate. I also knew how to count the meter of verses, and the difference between hexameter, pentameter, and so on; but I never learned to write a distich.

Despite this, in three years I finished my elementary education satisfactorily; they assured me that I was a fine grammarian, and I believed it better than if I had seen it for myself. God bless you, self-love! How easy it is for you to fool us, even when we have our eyes wide open! The fact is, I took my public examination in all the parts of grammar and came out on top; my teacher and friends were all happy, and my beloved parents more puffed with pride than if I had passed the Mexico bar examination.

This performance was followed by gifts, embraces, thank-yous to my teacher, and the end of my primary studies; though I shouldn't end before telling you some of the other things I learned in those three years. Here, there were many more than the few children at my good school: an endless number of boys, between boarders and day students, all of them sons of their own mothers, all so different in character and education; and since I was a first-class troublemaker, I had the cursed luck of being able to pick all my friends from among the worst boys, and they quickly and faithfully returned my attention; as you can see, and as everyone knows, birds of a feather flock together; the donkey does not lie down with the wolf, nor does the dove nest with the crow; like loves like. Thus I did not associate with sensible, honorable, reasonable boys, but with naughty and mischievous ones, in whose friendship and company I did myself in a little more each day—as will happen to you and to your children, if you ignore my lessons and fail to insure that they make only good friends, or no friends at all; for it never fails that, as the divine axiom tells us, "with a saint, you will become a saint, and the corrupt will corrupt you." That is precisely what happened to me; to be sure, I was already corrupt, but in the company of these bad students, I became utterly lost.

I imagine that when you read these sentences, you will exclaim: how did our father change so quickly? For in the school he had just left, hadn't he forgotten all the bad attributes he had acquired in his first school? How could he go through such a sudden metamorphosis? My children: the habits, good or bad, that are imprinted on us in childhood send down very deep roots; that is why it is so important to guide boys and girls well when they are very young. The vices I picked up when I was young—through my mother's spoiling me, my old aunts' flattery, my teacher's indolent methods, the abominable example set by all my unruly companions, and above

---

[7] [Ignacio Rodríguez de Calasanz,] *Discernimiento [filosófico] de ingenios [para artes y ciencias* (Madrid, 1795)], p. 162.

all through my depraved and ill-inclined nature—deeply penetrated my spirit; I had a terrible time ridding myself of them, at the expense of many reprimands and hugs from my good teacher, and of the constant good example set for me by other children. I think that, had I never lacked such precepts and schoolmates, I would not have strayed again, but rather would have established a refined, religious conduct; but alas! we cannot place our trust in forced or fleeting reforms, for as soon as respect or fervor fails, the Devil carries off that sort of reform, and there we are, back in our former guise, or worse.

That was my experience, to my great detriment. My passions were stifled, not dead; my depraved inclinations had merely withdrawn, but still remained in my heart as much as ever; my bad temper had not been extinguished, but was merely hiding, like hot embers under a dusting of ash; in a word, I did not act as naughty or brazen as before, out of the love and respect I felt for my prudent teacher, and out of the bit of shame that the other children instilled in me with their good actions, but not because I lacked the desire or disposition to continue.

Indeed, once I was separated from these witnesses whom I respected, and joined up again with other companions who were as dissipated as I, again I gave free reign to my passions, which ran unbridled with the wildness of youth and left the circle of reason, much as a river leaves its banks when the dikes that contain it are removed.

Without a doubt, I was the wickedest boy among the most boisterous students, for I was the *ne plus ultra* of the clowns and jokesters. This quality alone proves that mine was not the best of characters, for in the wise opinion of Pascal: "Joking man, poor character."[8] In the colleges, as you know, phrases like *pull a trick, play a prank, do a practical joke,* and so on, really mean *mock, insult, provoke, mortify, offend, bother,* and *injure* some other poor boy by every possible means; and what is most unjust and opposed to all the laws of virtue, good breeding, and hospitality, is that the comedians who play these jokes show off their odious talents on the poor new boys just entering college. It would be altogether appropriate if these dimwitted buffoons were tied to a column in the college yard and given a hundred lashes for each of their "pranks"; but how regrettable it is that the professors, tutors, administrators, and other persons of authority in their communities should wash their hands of all responsibility for these crimes—which is what they are, and serious ones too, though they are passed off as "boys' play" even when their victims complain—ignoring the fact that their acquiescence legitimizes these abuses and allows for the solid formation of cruel spirits in the abusers, such as I was, who could watch one of these hapless boys crying after I had utterly afflicted him with insults and taunts; and his tears, which, springing from the wounded feelings of an innocent child, should have moved me to pity and stayed me, served me instead as an appetizer and a motive for laughing and for redoubling my taunts with greater determination.

Just consider, then, how lovely a character I had, for I was held to be the best prankster in college, and my companions said I could play practical jokes with the

---

[8] [*Diseur de bons mots, mauvais caractère,* Blaise Pascal, *Pensées,* 46. Lizardi may have read this in the Spanish translation by Andrés Boggiero, *Pensamientos de Pascal sobre la religión* (Zaragoza, 1795), p. 245. Spell, p. 169. –Tr.]

best, which was as much as to say that I was the most contemptible of the lot, and that no one, good or bad, could help feeling put out if they heard my wicked tongue speak against them. Do you find anything favorable about this situation, my children? Doesn't this alone tell you how depraved my spirit and condition were? For a man who takes pleasure in afflicting his neighbor can but have a mean soul and perverse heart. Nor does it help to say that lots of boys play pranks; for all that shows is that, if they are bad as boys, they will be worse when they grow up, if God and reason don't moderate them, which is not what commonly happens. I had a crowd of classmates, and by observation I have seen that scarcely a one of these jeering geniuses has turned out good; and the worst of it is how many of them there are in our colleges.

From the way I began, you will see that I was completely depraved. And so I went on to study philosophy.

CHAPTER 5

PERIQUILLO WRITES OF HIS MATRICULATION INTO THE SCHOOL OF ARTS;
WHAT HE LEARNED; HIS GENERAL EXAMS, HIS DEGREE, AND OTHER
CURIOUS EVENTS THAT WILL BE LEARNED BY THOSE WHO WISH TO KNOW

I finished grammar school, as I have said, and entered the grand old College of San Ildefonso to study philosophy under the direction of Doctor Don Manuel Sánchez y Gómez, who lives today, an example to his pupils.[1] It was not yet common, in that illustrious college, that seminary of the learned, that ornament of knowledge for the metropolis—it was not yet common, I was saying, to teach modern philosophy there in all its aspects; its lecture halls still resonated with the *ergos* of Aristotle. There you could still hear debates over the Rational Being, the Hidden Properties, and the Prime Matter, which was defined in relation to Nothingness, *nec est quid*, and so on. Experimental physics had never been mentioned on that campus, and the great names of Descartes, Newton, Musschembroek, and others are scarcely known within the walls that had nurtured Portillo and other celebrated geniuses.[2] In short, the Aristotelian system that dominated the loftiest intellects of Europe for so many centuries had not yet been entirely abandoned when my wise teacher first dared to show us the path of truth, while trying not to stick out too much, for he selected the best in Aristotle's logic and what he felt was most probable in the modern authors, through whom he taught us the rudiments of physics; and in this way, we became true eclectics, who would not stick capriciously to any one opinion nor defer to any system simply because we were well disposed toward its author.

In spite of this prudent method, we still learned plenty of the sort of nonsense that has been taught out of habit and that should have been gotten rid of, as is shown both by reason and by the proofs of the illustrious Feijóo, in Discourses X, XI, and XII of the seventh volume of his *Teatro crítico*.[3]

Just as I had learned, as I have told you, many impertinent plays on words in my grammar studies—such as *Cara coles comes; pastor cito come ad oves; non est peccatum mortale occidere patrem suum,* and other such foolishness—so also in my scholastic studies did I straightaway learn a thousand ridiculous sophisms, which I used to show off in front of my most naïve classmates; for example: "Kissing the dust of the

---

[1] [Lizardi enrolled in 1797 in the College of San Ildefonso, founded in 1585 and run by the Jesuits until their expulsion from the Spanish realms in 1767. It was situated in a fine building built in 1749, two blocks north of the Cathedral, and served as an auxiliary to the University of Mexico (founded in 1553, about five blocks south). After 1910, the building housed the National Preparatory School and was painted with murals by José Clemente Orozco; today it is a museum. Don Manuel Sánchez y Gómez may be modeled on Lizardi's teacher, Manuel Antonio de Sanchristóbal. Spell, p. 173. –Tr.]

[2] [Antonio Lorenzo López Portillo (1730–1780), Mexican writer, philosopher, and mathematician. –Tr.]

[3] [Benito Jerónimo Feijóo y Montenegro (1676–1764) was a key Spanish Enlightenment thinker; he published his collected works in *Teatro crítico universal, o discursos varios en todo género de materias para desengaño de errores comunes* (13 volumes, 1727–1760). –Tr.]

earth is a humble act; woman is the dust of the earth; therefore," and so on. "The apostles are twelve in number; St. Peter is an apostle; ergo," and so on. And you'd better believe I could toss out an *ergo* with more poise than the best professor in the Paris Academy, and use it to negate the most obvious truth; that is to say, I argued and debated ceaselessly, even about things that are beyond all understanding; but I knew how to base my reasoning on my lung capacity, in the words of Padre Isla. Thus, no matter how many times my companions beat my arguments, I never gave in. I might as well have told them: you can outreason me, but you'll never outshout me; so that I constantly illustrated the common saying, "He who has the worst case puts it forth the loudest."

Just imagine how stubborn and stupid I became after I had learned the cheap tricks of reduction, reduplication, and equivalence, and especially certain foolish verses that I should write down for you, just so you can see what men come to through letters! Read and marvel:

> Barbara, Celerant, Darii, Ferio, Baralipton.
> Celantes, Davitis, Fapesom, Frisemorum.
> Cesare, Camestres, Festino, Baroco, Darapti.
> Felapton, Disamis, Datisi, Bocardo, Ferison.[4]

What do you think! Aren't these great verses? Don't they seem more suited for decorating drugstore phials than for teaching solid and useful rules? Well, my children, I immediately realized the fruits of their invention; for I could fool my friends as easily with *Barbara* as with *Ferison*, since I produced nothing but barbarities with each word. I learned to create sophisms rather than to recognize and dispel them; to obscure the truth rather than investigate it; a natural outcome, given the obsessions of schools and the pomposity of boys.

In the midst of this hubbub of shouting and exoticized wordplay, I learned to distinguish between a syllogism, an enthymeme, a sorites, and a dilemma. The latter terrifies many married men, because it catches them on its horns.

Not to exhaust you, I passed my course in logic with the speed at which lightning flashes through the atmosphere without leaving us any sign of its passage; and thus, after long and continuous debates on the operations of the intellect; on natural, artificial, and utile logic; on its formal and material objects; on the means of understanding; on whether or not Adam lost knowledge through sin (something not even the devil would debate); on whether logic is a science or an art; and on 30,000 other such posers, I had become about as logical as a tailor, but very happy, and quite satisfied that I could get in the last *ergo* with the Stagirite himself. What I did not know is that you can tell a tree by its fruit; and if that is true, then my setting off to debate any subject whatsoever was as much as to let everyone around know how incompetent I was. Be that as it may, I was more puffed up than a pumpkin, and told everybody who would hear that I was a Logician, the same as almost all my classmates.

---

[4] [This mnemonic verse was composed by the medieval logician Peter of Spain (*Tractatus* IV, c. 1230) to represent the 19 forms of valid syllogisms in the Aristotelian system. –Tr.]

I had no better luck with physics. I spent little time trying to distinguish the particular from the universal, or learning whether a given factor applied to the properties of all bodies, or whether another factor was limited to certain specific types. Nor did I find out what experimental or theoretical physics were; nor try to distinguish between a repeatable experiment and a rare phenomenon of unknown cause; nor did I stop to learn what mechanics means; what the laws of movement and inertia are; what the terms *force* and *power* mean, and what they are composed of; even less did I discover the meanings of *centripetal force, centrifugal force, tangent, attraction, gravity, weight, potential, resistance,* and other trifles of the same sort; and you can imagine that if I was unaware of these things, I was even more ignorant of the meanings of *static, hydrostatic, hydraulic, barometric, optical,* and 300 such tongue twisters; but on the other hand, I fervently debated whether the essence of matter was knowable or not; whether a given ternary dimension was the essence of matter or of water; whether or not Nature abhors a vacuum; whether infinite division was possible; and other similar hullabaloos that it made blasted little difference whether we knew or not, for all the good they could do us. True, my good professor taught us a few principles of geometry, calculation, and modern physics; but whether out of the short time we spent, the superficiality of the few rules that we could cover in that time, or my lack of studiousness (which was the most likely cause), I didn't understand a single word of all this; yet when the course was over, I nevertheless said that I was a Physicist, though I was merely an ignorant nitwit; for after I had passed a physics exam by rote, and after I had spoken of this great science with such self-satisfaction in every gathering I found, I couldn't have explained, if my life depended on it, why hot chocolate foams when it is beaten, why a flame has a conical figure and not some other shape, why a cup of soup or any other liquid cools off when you blow on it, nor any of the other puzzles that we find at hand every day.

In the same way and no better, I said that I understood metaphysics and ethics, and all but claimed to be a second Solomon after I finished the course in Arts, or rather it finished with me.

Meanwhile, two and a half years went by, a length of time that might have been better employed with fewer scholastic rules, an exercise or two in useful problems of logic, teaching the most basic principles of metaphysics, and as much theoretical and experimental physics as possible.

My teacher, I think, would have done exactly that if he hadn't feared being singled out and perhaps becoming the target of a few carping critics by departing entirely from the ancient routine.

It is true—and I will always concede this in honor of my teacher—as I was saying, it is true that we no longer debated the nature of the Rational Being, Hidden Properties, Formalities, Quiddities, Intentions, and the whole swarm of meaningless terms with which the Aristotelians endeavored to explain everything that escaped their understanding. It is true (we say with Johan Burkhard Mencke) that "these questions are not heard as often now in our schools as in past years; but have they been entirely abolished? Are our universities entirely free of the dregs of barbarity? I am afraid that in some of them, the old ways still hold sway; if not throughout, then perhaps rooted in enough subjects to hold back the progress of true wisdom."[5] This critic's declarations are certainly quite appropriate in our Mexico.

At last, the day arrived for me to receive the degree of Bachelor of Arts. I passed my exams with satisfaction and came out grandly, just as I had in my grammar school examination; for as the respondents were not trying to show off themselves, but rather to show off their boys, they did not get wrapped up in their questioning, but at once pronounced themselves satisfied with the least-vigorous answer, and we were left feeling as smug as could be, thinking that they had no questions on which they could press us. How blind is self-love!

So the upshot of it all was that I came off perfectly well, or at least so I persuaded myself, and they gave me the great, the resonant, the resounding degree of Bachelor, and I was approved *ad omnia.*[6] Dear God, what a laudable day that was for me, and how happy the hour of the graduation ceremony! When I took the college oath; when, standing at the front of the hall between two college officials shouldering maces, I heard myself called a Bachelor in the midst of that general pomp, and by no less than a Doctor who wore a shiny tasseled cap of pure silk on his head, I thought I would die, or at least go mad, with joy. By then I had formed such a high opinion of the bachelor's degree that, I assure you all, at that moment I wouldn't have traded my title for that of a brigadier or field marshal. And don't think I am being hyperbolical, for when they bestowed my title upon me, in Latin and formally authorized, my enthusiasm grew so much that, if I hadn't felt restrained by my respect for my father and my guests, I would have run through the streets, as Ariosto did when Maximilian I crowned him poet.[7] That is what can happen to us when we are suddenly and excessively excited by our passions, whatever those may be, for they can deceive us and make us act fevered, demented, or out of our minds!

We arrived at my house, which was filled with old ladies and young women—relatives and servants of the guests—who, as soon as I entered, bowed and curtsied a thousand times for me. I reciprocated, more puffed up than a turkey-cock; you can tell how vain I was. My poor, foolish mother was exceedingly hospitable; her elation gleamed in her eyes.

I shed my graduation gown and we entered the wide drawing room where we were to be served lunch, the center toward which the bows and curtsies of all these gallant gluttons were aimed. Believe me, my children, whenever you see great crowds drawn to a fiesta, whether a wedding, a baptism, or any other ceremony, what attracts most people is the *chow.* Yes, *free grub, free grub* is the bell that calls the crowds to visit, and the flag that recruits so many friends of the moment. If these were mere ungarnished fiestas, you wouldn't find them quite so frequented.

---

[5] [*Declamaciones contra la charlatanería de los eruditos* (Madrid, 1787 [1715]), p. 131. See Spell, p. 150. –Tr.]

[6] For everything; this phrase was used to designate the titles of those approved to continue studying any of the major fields, as opposed to those who are not generally approved but who can only continue in the fields designated in their titles. –E.

[7] [Spell (p. 150) notes that this is a confused citation from Mencke's book; Ariosto was crowned poet laureate by Charles V, not Maximilian I. –Tr.]

And do not think such public freeloading goes on only in Mexico. You can hear the same story the whole world over, and as proof, it is so common in Spain that they have a little rhyme on the topic. It goes like this:

> We're coming to scrounge,
> Virgin of Illescas,
> We're coming to scrounge
> And not for the fiesta.

And that's how it is, children, everyone comes to scrounge where the scrounging's good, not to wish you well or to congratulate you. What more? As I've seen, there's no lack of scrounging even at funeral wakes; rather, wakes usually begin with sighs and tears and conclude with cookies, cheese, liquor, chocolate, or lunch, depending on the hour; you see, bread is a cure for sorrow, as you must have heard it said, and a full belly makes for a happy heart.

Don't be offended by my digressions, for, apart from the fact that they may prove useful to you if you know how to take advantage of their teachings, I warned you from the outset that they will come frequently in the course of my work, which is the product of my inactivity as I lie in this bed, and not of serious study and planning; thus I am writing down my life as it comes back to me, and decorating it with the bits of advice, criticism, and erudition that I can muster in my sad state; assuring you all sincerely that I am far from pretending to be wise, but that I do wish to be useful to you as a father, and that I would like it if reading my life were profitable and entertaining for you, and that you might drink the salutary bitterness of truth from the gilded cup of jokes and erudition. Then I will indeed be content, and will have fulfilled the duties of a solid writer, according to Horace, who says, in my free translation:

> The writer has accomplished what he ought
> When the reader is amused and also taught.[8]

But in the end, I do as well as I can, though not so well as I would wish.

We sat down at the table and began to eat gaily, and as I was the reason for the fiesta, everyone directed their conversation toward me. All they talked about was the boy with the bachelor's degree; and knowing how happy my parents were, and how conceited I was about my title, they all poked us not where it hurt, but where it felt good. Thus all I heard was: "Have some more, Bachelor"; "Do drink up, Bachelor"; "Please see here, Bachelor"; and *Bachelor* this and *Bachelor* that, at every turn.

Lunch ended; dinner then followed, and at night came the dance; and the whole time was a continuous bachelorization. God help me, how they bachelored me that day! Even the old wives and the housemaids gave me my bachelorizings from time to time. Finally, God Almighty willed the bash to come to an end, and with it ended all

---

[8] *Omne tulit punctum qui miscuit utile dulci, / Lectorem delectando pariterque monendo.* [Horace, *Ars Poetica* (*The Art of Poetry*), vv. 343–44. –Tr.]

the bachelory. Everyone went home. My father was left sixty or seventy pesos the poorer, for that is what the celebration had cost him; I was left with one more cause for pretentiousness; and we went to sleep, which was what we most needed.

The next day, we woke up at a fine hour; and I, who shortly before had been so vain of my title, and so satisfied to hear how everyone feasted my ears by repeating it, had already lost all taste for it. How true it is that man's heart is endless in its desires, and that only solid virtue can fill it!

Don't imagine that I am just pretending now to be all holy and that I am writing down these things to make you think I have been a good person. No; I am far from a vile hypocrite. I have always been depraved, as I have told you, and even now, as I lie prostrate in this bed, I am not what I ought to be; but this confession should assure you of my truth, for it does not come from any virtue that can be found in me, but from the knowledge that I have of virtue, a knowledge that vice itself cannot obscure, so that, should I rise again from this illness and return to my erring ways of old (may God forbid), I will not retract what I am writing to you now; rather, I will confess that I act badly though I know what is good, as Ovid put it.

Coming back to myself, I was saying, two or three days after my graduation, my parents decided to send me to amuse myself at a cow branding that was to take place on a friend's hacienda near this city. And, indeed, I went. . . .

CHAPTER 6

IN WHICH OUR BACHELOR REPORTS WHAT HAPPENED ON THE HACIENDA, WHICH IS CURIOUS AND ENTERTAINING TO HEAR

I reached the hacienda accompanied by my father's friend, who was no less than the owner of the estate. We dismounted and everyone there greeted me favorably.

On the occasion of the amusement provided by the branding, the house was filled with brilliant people, both from Mexico and from the other towns all about.

We entered the house, I picked out a good seat by the sitting room,[1] for I never liked leaving the company of skirts for long; and after they had spoken of various country matters that I did not understand, the great lady, who was the wife of the hacienda owner, entered into conversation with me, saying, "So tell me, young sir, what did you think of the countryside you have passed through? It must have caused you to take notice, for they say it is the first time you have left Mexico."

"So it is, ma'am," I told her, "and I truly love the countryside."

"But not as much as the city, isn't it true?" she said.

Out of politeness, I replied, "Yes, ma'am, I like it here, although, to be sure, I do not dislike the city. It all seems fine to me in its own fashion; and so, in the country-side I am happy in a country way, and in the city I am entertained in a city way."

They celebrated my answer as if it were a pronouncement worthy of Cato, and the lady continued the praise, saying, "Yes, indeed, the college boy is talented, though it would be more seemly if he weren't so mischievous, from what Januario has told us."

Januario was a young man of eighteen or nineteen years—the lady's nephew, my own classmate, and a great friend. I turned out as I did because he was such a joker and a tremendous rogue, and I never fell out of step with him, nor did I neglect to learn from his every lesson. He had been my closest friend since my first school, and he was my constant *ahuizote*[2] and my inseparable shadow everywhere I went, for he

---

[1] [Sitting room: *estrado,* a term that was already passing out of date in Lizardi's time. According to Spell (p. 175), "this was a dais or slightly elevated and railing-enclosed platform in the drawing-room, on which the ladies, seated on cushions scattered about, entertained their gentlemen friends, who sat nearby on chairs or stools—a custom reminiscent of Spain." –Tr.]

[2] [*Ahuizote* (from Nahuatl *ahuitzotl,* a kind of salamander): curse, nemesis. The explanation by the editor of the 4th edition follows: –Tr.]

It seems that this phrase had its origins in pagan times among the indigenous Mexicans, who were governed from the year 1482 to 1502 by the emperor Ahuitzotl, which, in the Mexican language [Nahuatl], means *omen.* This cruel and bloodthirsty man caused more than 64,000 human victims to die in the dedication of the main temple of Mexico, according to various authors; but Father Torquemada attests that during the four days of celebrations, 72,344 prisoners were sacrificed. This massacre caused such a horrified impression on his subjects, the Mexicans, that ever since, they have given the name *ahuitzotl* to all persecutors, or anyone who causes any kind of harm.

For the comfort of humanity, there are plenty of reasons for sound critics to argue that, if this event (unequaled in the annals of barbarism) is not a fable, it is at least quite exaggerated; we must suspect that some mistake has been made, either in the numbers that the authors found in

attended the second and third schools where my parents sent me; he left these schools with me, and with me he entered grammar study in the house of my teacher Enríquez; when I left there, he left; I entered San Ildefonso, he entered as well; I graduated, and he graduated on the same day.

He was graceful, tall, and elegant of body; but as it was a law in my above-mentioned school that no one could escape without a nickname, we would stick one on anybody, even a Narcissus or an Adonis; and following this rule, we gave Don Januario the nickname *Juan Largo*, Long John, in this way combining the sound of his name with the most distinctive perfection of his body. But after all, he was my teacher and my most constant friend; and in carrying out these sacred duties, he did not neglect two things that concerned me deeply and that stood me in good stead throughout my life, and these were: to inspire me with his bad habits; and to divulge my gifts and my sobriquet, *Periquillo Sarniento*, the Mangy Parrot, everywhere; so that, thanks to his loving and active diligence, I have kept it through grammar school, through my study of philosophy, and into public life whenever possible. Tell me, my children, if it would not be ungrateful for me, in my life story, to neglect to name and profusely thank such a useful friend, such an effective teacher, the public crier of my glorious deeds; for all these titles were faithfully fulfilled by the great and meritorious *Juan Largo*.

I did not know, however, whether these ladies had been fully informed about me, nor whether they knew my resonant byname. I was smugly horsing around in the sitting room, as they say, with the lady and a group of girls, not the least lively and talkative of whom was the daughter of the lady who had flattered me, and she struck me as no bale of hay herself, for on top of the fact that there is no such thing as an ugly fifteen-year-old (and she was fifteen), she was altogether beautiful and her figure quite attractive: a powerful motive for me to try to behave as affably and circumspectly as I could, in order to please her; and I had noticed that whenever I made some tasteless collegiate joke, she was the first to laugh, and she readily applauded my wit.

So I was coming off well and feeling at home, when I heard the sound of horses arriving in the patio of the hacienda, and before there was time to ask who it was, there appeared in the middle of the room, wearing a fine rain cloak, sun scarf, field boots, and the full get-up of a respectable country squire. . . . Who do you think it could be? Who else but Juan Largo, that devil, repaying me for my dark sins, my dear friend and flatterer! He saw me the second he entered, and, greeting everyone else all at once and in a rush, he ran up to me with his arms held wide and gladdened my ears as follows: "Hey there, my dear Mangy Parrot! Great to see you round here! How's it going, brother? What're you up to? Have a seat. . . ."

You cannot imagine how angry I was to see how the villain had, in one instant, exposed my mangy parrotry in front of all those respectable gentlemen—and what

---

their manuscript sources, or in their interpretation of the Mexicans' numerals and hieroglyphs, or in the meaning of phrases in their language. But this subject is not to the point here; the fact is that the shocking number of victims sacrificed by Ahuitzotl on this occasion must have scandalized his vassals, giving rise to the phrase. –E.

hurt me more, in front of so many mocking girls and women, for as soon as they heard my honorable titles, they set to guffawing as impudently as they could, without the least consideration for my little self. I don't know if I turned yellow, green, blue, or red; what I do remember is that, in my anger, the room grew dark around me and my cheeks and ears burned hotter than if I had rubbed them with chili. I looked at the accursed Juan Largo and tossed him some reply filled with scorn and solemnity, thinking I could correct the girls' mocking and my friend's insolence by acting haughty; but I achieved just the opposite, for the more serious I grew, the more fervently the girls laughed, so much so that it seemed somebody must be tickling the little piggies, and that rascal Juan Largo added yet more tasteless jokes to the mix until they redoubled their cackling. Seeing the fix I was in, all I could do was to give in to my embarrassing bad luck and conceal the pique I felt, laughing along with everyone; though if I were to tell the truth, my laughter was not very natural, but somewhat more than forced.

In the end, after they were done parroting my nickname and had dissected the rotting carcass of its mangy etymology, since they had no more spleen for laughing, and that rogue had run out of repartee for insulting me, the scene came to a close and, thanks be to God, the storm passed.

That was the first time I realized how odious it could be to have a nickname, and how vile is the character of the jesters and comics who cannot keep faithful even to their own shirts; for they are capable of losing their best friends, just not to forgo the joke that pops into their mouths on the best of occasions; and they have the skill to insult and embarrass anyone with their vulgar gags, and at such a bad time for their victims that it seems they are being paid to do it, which is what my dear schoolmate did to me, making me look so bad precisely when I was hoping to come off well with his cousin. My children, you should loathe the friendship of such fellows as this.

Dinnertime came, they set the table, and we all sat according to our class and character. I was seated across from a young curate from Tlalnepantla, who sat next to the parish priest of Cuautitlán (a town seven leagues from Mexico), a fat and grave old man.[3]

Everyone ate gaily, and I along with them; being a lad, after all, I was not resentful, especially when they endeavored to please me with the abundance of exquisite dishes and tasty sweets; for Don Martín (that was the hacienda owner's name) was fairly liberal and rich.

During the meal, they spoke of many things that I did not understand; but after they had removed the tablecloths, a lady asked if we had seen the *commit*.

"The *comet*, you mean, ma'am," said the curate.

"That's it," replied the matron.

"Yes, we've been seeing it for the past few nights from the terrace of the rectory, and have been greatly entertained by the sight."

---

[3] [A curate (*vicario*) and a parish priest (*cura*) are both ordained priests, but the former has a lower rank, being a mere hired assistant of the tenured *cura* of his parish. Tlalnepantla and Cuautitlán lie north of Mexico City (and today form rather industrial suburbs of the capital), near the town of Tepotzotlán, where Lizardi lived as a child. –Tr.]

"Ay, what an ugly sort of entertainment!" said the matron.

"Why, ma'am?"

"Why? Because that comet is an omen of some great harm that wants to befall us."

"You can laugh at that," said the young cleric. "Comets are heavenly bodies like any other; what happens is, they only appear from time to time, because they have a long way to go, and therefore they are long in coming, but not malicious. Otherwise, here's our friend Januario, who is well informed of what comets are, and why they delight our eyes, and he will do us the favor of explaining it all clearly to everyone's satisfaction."

"Yes, Januario, come on, tell us all about it," said his young cousin.

But Juan Largo, that devil, knew no more about comets than he did about pyrotechnics; he was not stupid, though, so without missing a beat, he replied, "Cousin, I'll leave that job to my friend the Parrot, for two reasons: firstly, because he is a very capable boy; and secondly, as yours is a request that will display the brilliance of the explicator of cometly causes, the rules of etiquette require us to hand such shining opportunities to our guests. So please, ask our Mangy little friend to explain it all; you'll see what a sharp beak the boy has. If he can't keep up with us, then I'll explain, not what comets are or where they wander—for our friend the priest has set us straight on that—but rather what all the heavenly bodies are, what each one is called, where they go, what they do, how they pass the time, in as much detail as you could want to know, and I will be happy knowing that I will have to sate your curiosity no matter how long-winded your questions, never fearing that you might not believe me, for as my uncle Quevedo said:

> "A lie about the stars of night
> Is the safest lie of all to make,
> For no one's ever going to take
> A trip to find if you were right.[4]

"So there you have it, Poncianita. My good friend Perucho will explain the comets up and down, backwards and forwards, while I, with the permission of all the gentlefolk here, go saddle my horse."

Talking and walking, he shot out of the salon, paying no attention to what I was saying, which was that the reverend fathers who were there could satisfy the lady's curiosity better than I could.

"Not I, sirs," I was saying. "It would be terribly rude to show off in front of my superiors."

The parish priest, who was as sly as he was serious, hearing my urbane pretense, smiled like a rabbit and said, "You should all know that, ages ago, my parish had a

---

[4] [Though attributed to the celebrated Spanish poet Francisco Quevedo, this ditty was actually written by Agustín de Salazar y Torres, in *La segunda Celestina*. See the note by Carmen Ruiz Barrionuevo in her annotated edition of *El Periquillo Sarniento* (Madrid: Cátedra, 1997), p. 175. –Tr.]

priest who was very foolish and vain, one of the greatest fools ever; well, one day he was happily preaching whatever rubbish came into his head to a group of poor Indians, who were the only ones that could bear listening to him. He had reached the most fervent part of the sermon when into the church walks my lord the archbishop, making his holy rounds. The moment he entered, the audience grew restless and the preacher became alarmed; he was knocked further off his guard than if he had seen the Devil. He shut his mouth, took off his cap, and when His Grace asked him to continue, exclaimed: 'How could I, Your Grace, my lord, in the presence of my prelate, be so rude as to dare continue my sermon! I cannot. Please, Your Grace, come up and finish it, while I finish the mass *pro populo.*' The archbishop could not help laughing at the urbanity of this ignorant priest, and not only did he take him down from the pulpit, he sent him away from the parish. See if that isn't relevant."

This said, the fat priest fell silent. The curate and the women laughed, and I couldn't help blushing, though I was not entirely sure whether he had told the story because of my behavior or that of Juan Largo; but I was not kept in suspense for long, for that busybody of a curate quickly showed how shrewd he was by telling Poncianita, "You choose, dear child, who should explain what comets are, the college boy or me; and if you were to choose me, I would obey at once, because I don't like making people beg, nor am I capable of snubbing the ladies."

No doubt he winked, because Largo's cousin immediately turned to me, "I want you, sir, to do me this favor."

There was no escape; I was determined to satisfy them; but I had no idea where to begin, for blast if I knew the first word about comets or *commits*; nevertheless, with a certain pride (the most essential garb of any ignoramus), I said, "Well, ladies and gentlemen, comets, or *commits* as some call them, are larger than any other stars, and being so huge, they have the most longest tails. . . . "

"The most longest?" asked the curate.

And I, not realizing he was amazed to discover that I didn't even know how to speak proper Spanish, replied in all my vanity, "Yes, father, the most longest of all; haven't you seen them?"

"Dear me, God bless us," he answered.

I continued, "These tails come in two colors, white and crimson; if they are white, they portend peace or some happy news for the people; and if they are red, as if tinged with blood, they portend wars or disasters; that is why the *commit* that the Three Kings saw had a white tail, because it foretold the birth of the Lord and the worldwide peace that King Octavian made for the occasion; and this much cannot be denied, since there is never a birth on Christmas Eve that doesn't have a little comet with a white tail. The reason we don't always see them is that God keeps them far away, and only lets them into our sights when they need to portend the death of some king or other, the birth of some saint, or peace or war in some city, and that's why we don't see them every day; because God doesn't make miracles unnecessarily. The comet of these past days has a white tail, and surely it portends peace. That," I said, quite satisfied, "that is all there is to say about comets. At your service, ma'am."

"Thank you very much," she said.

"No, not very much," said the curate; "for the young gentleman, if you don't mind my saying so, has not told us a word of sense, but rather a devilish concoction of absurdities. You can tell that he hasn't studied a single word of astronomy, and therefore he has no idea what fixed stars are, or planets, comets, constellations, ephemeredes, eclipses, and so on, and so forth. I am not an astronomer either, my little friend, but I have acquired some small inkling of the subject; and superficial as it is, it suffices for me to recognize that you know less, which is why you come out with these barbarities; and the worst thing is, you pronounce them so proudly, thinking you know what you are saying and that what you are saying is true; but next time, don't be so naïve. You should know that comets are not stars, nor are they produced by miracles, nor do they foretell wars nor peace, nor was the star seen by the kings of the Orient when our Savior was born a comet; nor was Octavian a king, but rather Caesar or emperor of Rome; nor did he create worldwide peace at that divine birth, but rather the Prince of Peace, Jesus Christ, wished to be born when peace reigned throughout the universe, as it did in the time of Octavian Caesar Augustus; nor, finally, should you believe any of the other inanities that people say about comets; and so that you won't think I am just saying this to hear the tinkling of my voice, I will briefly explain to you what a comet really is. Listen up.

"Comets are planets, like all the others; that is: the same as the Moon, Mercury, Venus, Earth, Mars, Jupiter, Saturn, and Herschel,[5] which are all spherical bodies (in other words, perfectly round; in lay terms: they are balls); they are opaque and give off no light of their own, just as Earth does not give off light, for what they reflect or send our way is communicated to them by the Sun. The reason why we see comets at such long intervals is that their path is irregular with respect to the other planets; meaning, the latter have spherical orbits around the Sun, and the former orbit elliptically; some travel in a circular and others (the comets) in a elongated path; and that is why, as they have a longer way to travel, it takes us longer to see them; just as you will see someone who makes a trip to Mexico and back sooner than one who might go from here to Guatemala and back; for the first has a shorter trip to make than the second. The tails that we see on them are, according to those who understand them, nothing other than a sort of vapor that the sun draws out from them and illuminates, in the same way that it illuminates a beam of atoms when it shines through a window; and it is the same Sun, depending on the direction from which it communicates its light to the vapor, that makes these comet tails look white or red to us, a conclusion at which we may arrive without torturing our understanding, for every day we see clouds illuminated with white or red coloring, depending on their position relative to the Sun.[6] By virtue of this, we have nothing favorable to expect from the white color of a comet's tail, nor anything adverse to fear from its red color.

"That is what has been established as most probable by physicists in this matter; all the rest is nonsense, to which no one pays attention anymore. If you would like to study these things more deeply, you should read Father Almeida, Brisson, and other

---

[5] [*Herschel:* Uranus, discovered by William Herschel in 1781. –Tr.]

[6] These explanations by the deputy priest show that he was not very knowledgeable about the subject, either. –E.

authors who have been translated into Spanish, who treat the matter *pro famatiori*—that is, extensively. As for being extensive, I have gone on longer than I should in explaining this subject, and indeed have verged on pedantry, for this matter is foreign and perhaps unintelligible to all our listeners, excepting the priest; but your vanity and ignorance have obliged me to treat this singular matter among all these folk, and by the same token, I recognize that I have broken the rules of good breeding; but these gentlefolk in their wisdom will forgive me, and you will either thank me or not, for my good intentions, which amount to making you realize that you should not open your mouth to talk about things you don't understand."

Just imagine how I felt after such a liturgy. I instantly recognized that the father was right, hurt as I was by his sharp reproach, for though I was ignorant, I was never stupid, nor was my head made of *tepeguaje*,[7] I was easily tamed by reason, for in reality the truth is sometimes so penetrating and well demonstrated that it gets into our heads despite our self-love. What poor wretches are those whose minds are so obtuse that they cannot grasp the most obvious truths! And even more wretched, those who are so obstinate that they close their eyes to keep from seeing the light! How little hope either type has of ever being tamed by reason! I felt embarrassed, as I was saying, and I think my shame was written all over me, for I dared not utter a single word, nor did any words come to me. The ladies, the priests, and the other fellows at the table only stared at each other and at me, making me blush more and more.

But the curate himself, a very prudent man, got me out of the spot I was in quite cunningly, saying, "Ladies and gentlemen, we have talked long enough; I am going now to say vespers, and the young ladies will want to rest a bit before our evening entertainment at the bull ring."

He got right up from the table, and everyone else did the same. The ladies retired to the inner rooms, and as for the men, some lay down on sofas, others picked up books, other sat down to cards, and yet others picked up their shotguns and went out to pass the time in the orchard.

I was left the odd man out, though many gentlemen offered me their company; but I thanked them and excused myself with the pretext that I was exhausted from the trip and was accustomed to taking a short nap.

When I saw that everyone was either sleeping or enjoying themselves, I went into the hallway and lay down on a bench, and began to reflect on myself and the letdown I had just suffered.

Surely, I said, surely the priest shamed me; but after all, it was my own fault for chattering about things I did not understand. No doubt about it: I'm a thickheaded, stuck-up boor. What have I ever read about planets, stars, comets, eclipses, or anything else the father told me? When have I seen so much as the covers of the books he mentioned, or even heard of them before now? Why the devil did I get it into my head to try explaining something I don't understand, and to be so dimwitted, yet proud, about my explanations? What was I thinking of? Here's the thing: I got a bachelor's degree in philosophy, so I'm a physicist. I detest my physics and all the physicists in the world, if they're as pinheaded as I am. Damn my sins! What will

---

[7] [*Tepeguaje:* the hard, dense wood of a tree native to tropical Mexico. –Tr.]

that curate say? What will the priest say? And what will they all say? Well, what could they say, except that I'm an ass? That knave Juan Largo didn't dare display his ignorance. No two ways about it: knowing when to keep quiet is a lesson to be learned, and silence is the best cover for a lack of education. Juan Largo, by not talking, left everyone in doubt about whether he knows about comets or not; while I, by talking too much, only managed to display my blockheadedness and expose myself to public shame. But it's done, and there's no two ways about it. So now, to keep it from being a total loss, I'll have to give satisfaction to the father himself, who understands my foolishness better than any of the rest, and beg him to give me a list of the authors I should study; for physics is surely a science that is not only very useful, but entertaining, and I would like to know something about it.

With this resolved, I got up from the bench and went in search of the curate, who had just finished vespers, and I recanted fully before him.

"Father," I said, "what must you have thought of the novel explanation of comets that you heard me give? Come now, you could not have been expecting that kind of after-dinner entertainment; but I truly am a dunce, and I admit it. After I learned a couple of basics of physics in college, and a few properties of bodies in general, I got used to calling myself a physicist, and I firmly believed it and thought there was nothing left to learn about the field. On top of that preconception, I did well in all my exams; the guests at my graduation party praised me and gave me presents; and besides, not a week has gone by since I graduated with a bachelor's degree in philosophy, and they told me that I had passed *in every subject*; I thought I was truly a philosopher, that my title proved my wisdom, and that the passport they had given me *in every subject* authorized me to debate about anything, even with Solomon himself; but now you have given me a lesson that I want to take advantage of; because I like physics, and I'd like to know in which books I can learn a little about it; but only if they teach it as clearly as you do."

"This is a good sign that you have an uncommon talent," the father told me; "because, when a man recognizes his errors, confesses them, and tries to rid himself of them, he gives us hope; for that is not the way of miserable minds, who err and recognize their errors, but whose pride does not allow them to repent; and thus they deprive themselves of the light of education, like the imprudent patient who will not show his wound to the doctor and therefore deprives himself of medicine and gets worse. But where did you learn the heap of superstitions that you told us about comets? Surely they did not teach you that at college."

"Not in the least, as you can see," I replied. "The cornucopia of erudition that I spouted forth can be attributed to the old ladies and cooks at home."

"Nor are you the first," the father said, "to suck up such absurdities with your first milk. The truth is that these are all lies and old wives' tales. As for you, what you should do is study hard, for you are still young and can improve yourself. I'll give you the list you asked for, of authors in whose works you can easily read about these matters, and I will also give you a few lessons while we are here."

I thanked him, captivated by his fine character; I was about to ask him a boyish favor, when we were called to the entertainment in the horse-shoeing corral.

CHAPTER 7

Although we had been called, the curate continued to speak: "In regard to your asking me to inform you about the best authors on physics, it really won't be necessary to write a list, because there are just a few that I would advise you to read, and you can easily memorize their names. First you should read *Experimental Physics* by Abbés Para and Nollet, father Don Teodoro de Almeida's *Philosophical Recreations*, and Brisson's *Dictionary of Physics* and *Treatise on Physics*. If you read them carefully, you will learn enough to be able to speak knowledgeably about physics wherever you go; and if you'd like to add to this the study of natural history, which is so closely related, you might profitably read Pluche's *Spectacle of Nature*, or even better, *Natural History* by the famous Comte de Buffon, commonly known as the Pliny of France.

"These studies are useful, pleasant, and entertaining, young friend, because the mind does not encounter in them the abstractions of theology, the uncertainties of medicine, the intricacies of law, nor the ruggedness of mathematics. It is all satisfying, all delightful, all enchanting, and all educational, both physics as well as natural history. It doesn't exhaust you to study it, and you don't tire of it as an occupation. Its teachings are sweet, and it is served in a golden cup.

"Those who look at the universe from the outside are surprised by the lovely perspectives it offers; but they merely surprise themselves as little children do when they first see some pretty toy. The philosopher, looking at the universe with different eyes, goes beyond simple surprise: he knows, observes, scrutinizes, and admires everything about Nature. If he lifts his mind toward the heavens, he loses himself among those spaces filled with the most sovereign majesty: if he turns his attention to the Sun, he sees an enormous mass of intense fire, which is penetrating and inextinguishable, but at the same time beneficial and advantageous to all of Nature; if he observes the moon, he knows that it is a globe with mountains, seas, valleys, and rivers, no different from the globe he walks on, and that it is a mirror reflecting the brilliant light of the Sun and communicating its influences to us; if he observes the planets, such as Venus, Mercury, Mars, and the rest of the multitude of heavenly bodies, both fixed and wandering, he contemplates no less than an infinity of worlds, some lit from within and others reflecting light from without, some suns and others moons that constantly observe the movements and orbits prescribed for them by the Almighty since the beginning. If he lowers his reflections to this planet we inhabit, he wonders at the economy with which it was crafted; he sees water suspended on earth, held back only by a frail dusting of sand; sees towering mountains, thundering cascades, cheerful springs, tame creeks, swift-flowing rivers; sees trees, plants, flowers, fruits, jungles, valleys, hills, birds, wild beasts, fish, man, and even the contemptible little crawling insects; and all of it, all of it offers him a theater for his curiosity and investigation.

"The atmosphere, clouds, rain, morning dew, hail, ignis fatuus, aurora borealis, thunder, lightning flashes and blasts, and all the meteors of Nature present a vast field for his detailed and meticulous examination; and after he has admired, contemplated, examined, meditated on, pondered, and sharpened his mind upon this prodigious chaos of heterogeneous beings, as admirable as they are incomprehensible, he pauses to reflect that his knowledge or ignorance of these same things leads him, as if by the hand, to the very foot of the Creator's throne. Then the true philosopher cannot but be overwhelmed and fall prostrate before the Supreme Deity, confess His power, praise His providence, silently recognize the sublimity of His wisdom, and give infinite thanks to Him for the deluge of benefits that He has rained down upon His creatures—the most noble, the most exalted, the most privileged, and the most ungrateful of His earthly creatures being Man, under whose feet (as the voice of truth tells us) He has put all creation: *Omnia subjecisti sub pedibus ejus.*[1] No sooner does the philosopher reach these lofty and necessary heights of knowledge than he becomes a contemplative theologian, for just as all the spokes of a cartwheel rest on the axle that forms their center, so all creatures recognize their central point in the Creator; thus, any impious atheist who denies the existence of a God who has created and preserved the universe, is working against the common testimony of all nations, for the most barbarous and savage nations have recognized this sovereign principle; because the heavens themselves proclaim the glory of God, the firmament announces His wondrous works, and all the creatures that reveal themselves to our sight are guides leading us to adore the wonders that we see. But as you can see, atheists are all brutes who only seem like men, or men who voluntarily wish to be less than brutes. This much is obvious. . . . "

And at that, seeing how late we were in coming, the girls and the gentlemen of the hacienda came to call us again to go see the cowboys' and foremen's tricks, and we had to suspend, or rather cut off entirely, a conversation that I had found very sweet; because I was truly more entertained by it than by the rowdiest bull ring.

They were amazed to see the father and me so united, thinking that I would have held some resentment for the bit of blushing he had caused me after dinner; even in their joking banter, they revealed what they were thinking; but no matter how debased I have been, God has given me two gifts that I do not deserve. The first is a mind that bends to reason; the second, a noble and sensitive heart, which has never let me give in to my passions. I put it this way, because when I have at times committed excesses, it has been difficult for me to subordinate my spirit to my flesh. That is, I have committed evil knowing what I was doing and riding roughshod over the protests of my conscience, and in the full awareness of justice, as befalls every man who slips into crime. Because of these good qualities, which, as I say, I have noted in my soul, I have never been vengeful, not even against my enemies, much less against someone who I knew had counseled me well, if perhaps somewhat harshly; which is not a common thing, because our self-love ordinarily suffers from the gentlest corrections; and because of this, the people at the hacienda were amazed by the friendly harmony they observed between me and the father.

At last we arrived at the place where the circus had been set up for our entertainment, a great corral where comfortable benches had been arranged. The curate and I sat together, and we passed the afternoon watching them brand the yearling bulls

---

[1] [Psalms 8:8 (8:6): "Thou hast subjected all things under his feet." –Tr.]

and the horses and mules that they had. But I noticed that the spectators showed less pleasure when they were marking the animals with hot irons than when they were fighting the yearlings or breaking the colts, especially whenever a young bull threw one of the boys, or a young mule shook off a rider; because then their laughter was boundless, no matter how much compassion the affliction displayed on the face of the injured rider might inspire.

Since I had never before observed such a scene, I couldn't help feeling moved when I saw a poor fellow limp away from under a mule's hooves or a steer's horns. At such a moment, I could only consider the pain that the wretch felt, and this personal compassion would not let me laugh, though everyone else guffawed to bursting. The judicious curate—if only he could have been my mentor always!—noticed how serious and silent I was and, reading my heart, said to me, "Have you ever seen the bullfights in Mexico?"

"No, sir," I answered, "this is the first time I have ever seen this kind of entertainment, which consists in hurting poor animals and exposing men to the blows they give in revenge—something they deserve, in my judgment, on account of their wicked inclination and barbarity."

"So it is, my young friend," the curate told me; "and I can tell that you've never seen even worse things. What would you say if you saw the bullfights that they have in the big cities, especially during what they call the Royal festivals? Everything you see here is mere child's play; the worst that happens is that the young bulls toss the boys around a little, and the colts and mules throw them, which normally leaves the riders beaten and bruised, but not wounded or dead, as occurs in the public festivals in the cities that I mentioned; for there, since they fight bulls chosen for their fierceness and their naturally sharp horns, one all too frequently sees horse intestines wrapped around bullhorns, men severely wounded, and a few deaths."

"Father," I said to him, "is that how rational beings act, exposing their lives to be sacrificed by an enraged beast? And do so many people troop in to enjoy the blood of the brutes spilled, and perhaps even that of their fellow men?"

"That is precisely what happens," the curate answered me, "and it will keep happening in the realms of Spain until at last we forget this custom, as repugnant to Nature as it is to the enlightenment of the century in which we live."

We had a long conversation about this, since it is a very fertile topic, and when my friend the curate finished, I said to him, "Father, I am thinking: as soon as my devilish schoolmate Januario, or Juan Largo, finds out about the nonsense I said about comets and your proper reproach, he is bound to start mocking me loudly at table in front of everyone, because he is a great prankster and loves to play practical jokes on anyone whatsoever, no matter how fine the company; and to be sure, I wouldn't like to be embarrassed again as I was at midday, but if he is such a bad friend and so indiscreet, he could suffer some unlucky break just as I did, if you were to make him look bad with a little problem in physics, which he understands no better than he does shoemaking; so I ask this of you: do me a favor; put a little red in his cheeks for being so cocksure of himself."

"Look here," the father said to me; "I will gladly help you improve yourself, but that would be revenge, a vile passion that you should curb your whole life long;

taking revenge denotes a low soul, one incapable of overlooking the slightest affront. Pardoning insults is not only the characteristic sign of a good Christian, but also of a noble and great soul. Anyone, no matter how poor, feeble, or cowardly, is capable of avenging an offense; that doesn't take religion, talent, wisdom, nor nobility, high birth, education, nor anything that is good; all you need is to have a debased soul and to let your anger run wild, and then subscribe to the bloody emotions it inspires. To forgive an affront, to pardon those who offend us, and to repay evil with beneficent acts, you not only need to know the Gospel (though that should be sufficient), but to have a heroic soul and a sensitive heart, and those are none too common; nor is it a common occurrence to find heroes like Trajan, of whom it is said that, when he was receiving his subjects in public audience, a shoemaker went up to the throne pretending to beg for justice; he drew close to the emperor, and taking advantage of his lowered guard, slapped him. The people surged forward, and the sentinels wanted to kill him on the spot; but Trajan would not allow it, wishing to punish the man himself. With the traitor held tight before him, Trajan asked: 'How have I offended you? What motive did you have to injure me?' The shoemaker, being as thickheaded as he was vain, replied: 'Sir, the people say their blessings for your amiable character; I have no complaint to make of you; rather, I committed this sacrilegious crime, knowing that I would die, so that future generations would say that a shoemaker had the courage to slap the emperor Trajan.' 'Very well, then,' Trajan said; 'if that was your motive, I won't let you surpass me in courage. I also want posterity to say that, if a shoemaker dared to slap the emperor Trajan, then Trajan had the courage to pardon the shoemaker. You are free.' No need to praise this act; it recommends itself, and you can deduce from it and from thousands of similar acts along the same lines that, to seek revenge, you have to be low and cowardly; but not seeking revenge takes nobility and courage; for knowing how to conquer oneself and tame one's passions is the most difficult conquest of all, and therefore is the most praiseworthy victory and the most reliable proof of a magnanimous and generous heart. For all these reasons, I think that it would be good for you to forget and overlook Mr. Januario's insults."

"Well, father," I said, "if it takes more courage to pardon an insult than to inflict one, then from now on I declare that I won't take revenge on Juan Largo or on anyone else who ever affronts me in this life."

"Oh, Don Pedrito!" the curate answered me. "How valuable such resolutions would be in this world if only they were carried out! But there is no reason to declare a resolution arrogantly, because we are all weak and frail, and we cannot trust our own virtue, nor feel secure in our word alone. In the hour of the storm, sailors make a thousand promises, but when they pull in to port, they forget them as if they had never been uttered. When the earth trembles, all you can hear are prayers, acts of contrition, and pledges to reform; but when the quake ends, the drunks head back to their cups, the lewd back to the ladies, the gamblers back to the card tables, usurers back to their profits, and everyone back to their old vices. One of the most unbecoming things about man is his confidence in himself. That confidence is what makes young people liable to prostitute themselves, prudish souls to stray, administrators of justice to yield to temptation, and the wisest and saintliest of men to become delinquents. Solomon lied; and St. Peter, who thought himself the bravest of the apostles, was the first and only to deny his divine Teacher. So we shouldn't put too much trust in our own strength, nor chatter too long about our word of honor, for until the moment comes, we're all as firm as a rock; but, when it arrives, we're a miserable bunch of reeds, bending to the first breeze that hits us."

Our conversation continued a bit, until the evening ended and, with it, the entertainment, entailing our return to the salon of the hacienda.

Since the only point of being there was to pass the time, everyone entertained themselves doing whatever they enjoyed best, and thus they took up their cards and their mandolins and began to have fun amongst themselves. I did not yet know how to play cards (or more to the point, I had no funds to gamble), nor how to strum the mandolin; so I went to the far end of the sitting room to listen to the singing of the girls, who calmly raked my patience over the coals; for two or three of them would draw close to me, and one would say to another, "Tell me a story, girl—just not the one about the Mangy Parrot."

Another would ask me, "Sir, since you have studied, tell us: how can parrots talk like people?"

Another would say, "Oh, girl, my arm's so itchy! You think I've caught the mange?"

And so the ladies went on making fun of me all night, until it was suppertime.

The table was placed, we all sat down, and among us there was my very good friend Juan Largo, who, up until then, had been playing ombre[2] or some such card game.

Many topics were discussed throughout supper. I horned in on a topic or two, but only after being provoked, and always with the addition of: 'It seems to me . . . ,' 'I don't have the wits . . . ,' 'I have heard it said . . . ,' and so on; but I no longer spoke as arrogantly as I had at midday, so intimidated was I by the sermon that the curate had preached to my face. How useful a lesson can be when it comes at the right time!

The meal ended, and my good friend Juan Largo, directing himself toward me, began to pour out his clownish genius, just as I had expected he would.

"So, Periquillo," he said to me, "you're saying that comets are sort of like trumpets? You were brilliant in your midday act! Yes, I've heard all about your witticisms; what I didn't know was that I had so great a physicist as one of my classmates—not just a physicist, either, but an astronomer as well. No doubt but that in time you'll become the best almanacker in the kingdom. What celestial object would even try to hide from a man who knows so much about comets?"

The women, who almost always act on the first thing they notice, and who heard only a cheerful ribbing in his derision, began to laugh and to stare harder at me than I would have liked; but the father curate, who liked me and recognized the shame I felt, managed to extract me from that trap, saying to Don Martín (who, as I said, was the owner of the hacienda), "So, do you know that the day after tomorrow you'll be having a solar eclipse?"

---

[2] [*Ombre:* an old Spanish three-player card game (called *hombre* or, as here, *manilla* in Spanish). —Tr.]

"Yes, sir," said Don Martín, "and I'm all in a dither about it."

"Why?" asked the curate.

"What do you mean, why?" said the landowner. "Because *eclimpses* are the devil, is why. Two years ago now, I'm remembering, my wheat was growing along just fine, and then because of a darn eclimpse, it got all sucked dry and turned out short as can be, and not just that, all the calves and baby animals that was born those days got sick and most of 'em died. So just you see if I don't have good reason to be afraid of them eclimpses."[3]

"Don Martín, my friend," said the curate, "I think the lion is not as fierce as it's made out to be; what I mean is, the poor eclipses aren't as devious as you imagine them to be."

"How could that be, father?" said Don Martín. "You know a lot of things, but I've got lots of 'sperience, and like everybody knows, 'sperience is the mother of know-how. No doubt about it, eclimpses do a lot of damage to the fields, to the cows, to people's heaf, and to pregnant women, too. Five years ago now, I'm remembering, my wife was expecting, and you might not believe it but my son Polinario was born harelipped."[4]

"And what caused that misfortune?"

"What else could it be, sir?" said Don Martín. "It was because the eclimpse took a bite of him."

"Don't fool yourself," said the curate. "The eclipse is a very upright fellow, and neither bites nor bothers anyone; otherwise, let's hear from Don Januario. What does our bachelor have to say?"

"There's nothing for it," he replied, full of satisfaction that his opinion had been sought. "No, there's nothing for it," he said; "the eclipse cannot eat the flesh of children still in their mothers' wombs; but it can hurt them through its malign influence, and make them be born harelipped or hunchbacked, and through the same malignancy, it is even more likely to kill young animals and suck the wheat dry, as my uncle has said, testifying to his experience; for as you see, Father, *quod ab experientia patet non indiget probatione.* That is to say: what has been shown by experience needs no other proof."

"I am not surprised," said the father, "that your uncle thinks in this manner, because he has no reason to think otherwise; but I am very shocked to hear a college man produce the same sort of thing. Along these lines, tell me, what are eclipses?"

"I think," said Januario, "that they are run-ins between the Sun and the moon, in which one or the other has to come out the loser, depending on the strength of the victor; if the Sun wins, it is an eclipse of the moon, and if the latter wins, the Sun is eclipsed. Up to this point, there can be no doubt; because if you watch the eclipse in a bowl of water, you can materially see how the Sun and the moon are

---

[3] [*Eclimpses:* Lizardi represents the landowner's rustic speech with phonetic spellings throughout, emphasizing his deviations from standard Spanish. I have substituted equivalent English mispronunciations (as here, *eclimpses* for the typical Spanish mispronunciation *eclises*). –Tr.]

[4] [The belief that solar eclipses cause ruined fields, miscarriages among people and cattle, harelips, and other calamities remains common in rural Mexico. –Tr.]

fighting; and you can observe what one or the other eats in the struggle; and if these two bodies have the ability to do so much damage to each other, rock-solid as they are, how could they help but damage the tender seedlings or delicate infants of this world?"

"That's what I say," responded good old Don Martín. "Look here, Father, tell me if I'm right or wrong. No two ways about it, my nephew's real edgicated; right now, he up and explained eclipses just the way my late brother, who was a man of many letters, used to tell it; and up there in our homeland, the Huasteca, everybody said he was a fountain of know-how.[5] Ah, my brother! If he was alive, how happy would he be to see how far his boy Januario's come along!"

"Not very happy, if you'll pardon my saying so," said the vicar; "for this gentle-man doesn't understand a word of anything he's said; rather, he's a philosophical blasphemer. What are all these brawls and run-ins, these blasted, fatal influences that you think eclipses produce? I'll have you know, Don Martín, sir, that the greatest eclipse ever could do no greater harm to you or your plants or animals than to take away your light for a short while. There's never been any such brawl between the Sun and the moon, nor any of this other claptrap. Tell me, could you get into a fistfight from here with someone standing in Mexico?"

"No, of course not," said Don Martín.

"Well, the same is true of the Sun in relation to the moon," the curate went on; "for a great many leagues separate those bodies."

"Can you see all that?" asked the bumpkin. "Well, I don't understand it."

"Then I will make you see it all clearly," said the father. "You should know that whenever an opaque body is placed between our eyes and a luminous body, the opaque one impedes our view of that portion of light which it covers with its disk."

"Now I don't understand it, nohow," said Don Martín.

"Well, you are going to understand me," the father replied. "If you put your hand between your eyes and the candlelight, clearly you won't be able to see the flame."

"That much I can understand."

"Well, then you just understood the eclipse."

"Is it possible, father," said Don Martín, "is it possible that it's that easy to under-stand eclimpses?"

"Yes, my friend," said the curate. "What happens is, since your hand is larger than the candle flame, whenever you put it in front of the flame, it will cover it com-pletely, making a total eclipse; but if you put it in front of a bonfire, surely it will only cover up a part of that flame, for a bonfire is larger than your hand; and thus you can say that you've made a partial eclipse—that is, that you have covered up one part of the bonfire's flame. Now do you understand?"

"Yep, real good," said the bumpkin. "But can you understand eclipses of the Sun and the moon just as easy?"

"Yes, sir, you can," said the father. "I already told you that the Sun lies many leagues distant from the moon; it is much larger than the moon, just as the bonfire is much larger than your hand; therefore, when the moon passes between the Sun and

---

[5] [The Huasteca is the semi-tropical coastal region northeast of Mexico City. –Tr.]

our eyes, it covers up a part of it, which is the part we cannot see; so what looks to Januario and to you and to others like a bite taken out of the Sun, is nothing other than a hand passing in front of the bonfire. Do you understand?"

"Completely," said Don Martín, "and if I follow you, there can never be a total eclimpse of the Sun, because the moon's a lot tinier and can't cover it all up."

"That would be true," said the curate, "if the moon always passed at the same distance in relation to the Sun and our eyes; but as it sometimes passes very close to us, it screens the Sun totally from us,[6] in the same way that, if you were to put your hand very close to your eyes, you wouldn't see any of the bonfire, even though your hand is much smaller than the bonfire; and now, I do believe that you've understood me."

"And what about the ones of the moon?" asked the bumpkin.

"The same way," said the father; "just as the moon covers or darkens a piece of the Sun when it stands between it and ourselves,[7] so the Earth covers or darkens a piece or all of the moon when it stands between it and the Sun."

"That's got to be it," said Don Martín, "and now I'm thinking, I've seen a few total eclimpses, like you say, of the Sun and the moon, when it's been all covered up, so's we've been left all in the dark. So it don't matter that the bonfire might be bigger than the hand. And it's really possible that that's all eclimpses are?"

"Yes, sir," said the father, "that and nothing else; and since there are 365 days in the year, or 366 in a leap year, we have the same number of eclipses—and all of them total, which is the best part."

"How can that be true, father?" exclaimed Don Martín.

"You know it's true," said the curate. "Can you see the Sun at night?"

"No, sir, not even a pinch," replied Don Martín.

"Well, there you have it: the Sun is eclipsed entirely; and in order for you not to see me, it makes no difference whether I close myself in my bedroom, or you close your eyes."

"That's true," said Don Martín; "and following what you tole me before, and what you just now tole me, I think the world's got to be a lot bigger than the Sun, and it can't be smaller, from what we're seeing."

"Well, yes, it can be smaller, friend," said the curate, "and indeed it is as small in relation to the Sun as an almond in relation to a coconut."

"Well, then," replied Don Martín, "we're back to what you said before, that even though my hand's smaller than a bonfire, I can cover it all up if I put it real close to my eyes."

"So it is," said the curate, "you can cover it all, or not, depending on the distance at which you place it in relation to your eyes. If you place it far from them, it will not cover the whole bonfire, and you will see some part of it; but if you place it in front of your nose, you won't see a thing."

---

[6] The distance of the moon from us is not what produces total eclipses, but rather its complete interposition. –E.

[7] The curate knew quite well that what is darkened is not the Sun, but the Earth, which falls into shadow; but he explained it in this way so that Don Martín would understand.

"Course I won't, now," said Don Martín; "and not just the bonfire, I won't even see the gate to the hacienda, which is that much bigger, or anything else, and that's because I'll almost cover up my eyes when I put my hand so close."

"So there you have the reason," said the father, "why we sometimes see total eclipses of the Sun caused by the moon; because even though the moon is much smaller than the Sun, if it passes close to us, as it actually does sometimes, it has the same effect as holding your hand in front of a bonfire; and the Earth does the same thing, in spite of its small size, eclipsing the Sun for us every night because it is right next to us."[8]

"I understood the whole deal about eclimpses, father curate," said Don Martín, "and I think anybody would understand it, no matter how dull their brains. Did you understand it, my daughter? Did you all understand it, girls?"

All the girls replied unanimously that they did understand it, very well indeed, and that they now knew they could make an eclipse of the Sun, the moon, or a bonfire whenever they wished; but good Don Martín went on to ask, "Tell me, then, father, if that's all eclimpses are, then why are they so harmful that they make us lose our plants or our animals, and even make our children fall sick and come out with defects?"

"That is a common error," replied the curate. "Eclipses have nothing to do with such misfortunes. Plants are lost because they are not weeded at the right time, or because they lack water, or the seed was damaged or frail, or the earth lacks nutrients or is tired, and so on. Cattle miscarry or calves are born ill because the females have been injured, or they suffer from some particular illness that we do not understand, or because they have eaten some harmful plant, and so on; finally, we ourselves fall ill because of overwork, or some disorder in our food or drink, or because we heedlessly expose ourselves to the open air when our bodies are overheated, or a thousand other assaults of which there no end; and children are born harelipped, stunted, defective, or dead because of their mothers' imprudence in eating noxious foods, playing, running, lifting heavy objects, working too hard, falling into vehement rages, or being hit in the belly. So you can see that the poor eclipses are not at fault in any of this."

"Fine," said Don Martín, "but why do these misfortunes happen exactly when there's an eclimpse?"

"The unfortunate thing about eclipses," said the curate, "is that such misfortunes ever coincide with them; because the poor folk who understand nothing blame the eclipses straight away for every failure in the world. Likewise, when someone falls ill, the first thing he does is to look for what's to blame for his illness, and perhaps he thinks it was caused by something completely innocent. So, my friend, let's not be common, nor detract from the honor of the poor eclipses, which is a sin of restitution."

Everyone applauded the curate and gave my friend Juan Largo a good case of sunburn, so that his ears were ringing when he got up. A short while later, we went to bed.

---

[8] This coincides with the inaccurate explanation noted above. –E.

CHAPTER 8

IN WHICH PERIQUILLO WRITES OF SOME ADVENTURES THAT
HAPPENED TO HIM ON THE HACIENDA, AND HIS RETURN HOME

The following day, we arose quite contented; the priest called for his carriage, the curate ordered his horse saddled, and they left for their respective homes. The curate gave me a very fond farewell, and I replied in the same tenor, for he was a likeable and benevolent man, neither proud nor thick-headed.

They went away in the end, and I was left without their useful company. My brother Juan Largo, stupid and shameless as ever (for it is the property of a fool not to care a whit about anything in this life), at lunchtime began to mock me about the comet; but I parried him, defending myself with the nonsense he had said regarding the eclipse, and with that jab I left him blushing; and he must have noted how silly it is to throw stones at the roof of your neighbor when your own is made of glass.

Whether it was because I was new in the house, or because I had a more prudent and jovial character, the ladies, girls, and everyone else loved me more than they did Juan Largo, who was crude and vain by nature. This being so, whenever I made some tasteless joke, they applauded it endlessly, which my rival Januario resented; so he tried to take his revenge every time he had a chance, and I could not escape his pranks, for he laid his traps under a cloak of friendship. How abominable are the base souls who weave treachery in the shadow of virtue itself!

As I did like him, for my part, and he, for his part, had a scheming character, he dissimulated his evil intentions, and I walked right into his plots without suspecting a thing.

Every afternoon, we went out on a horse ride. You can just imagine how fine a rider I was, never having ridden anything but the cheap horses one hires in Mexico: thin, overworked animals possessed of an imponderable tameness and insipidity. The horses on the hacienda were nothing of the sort, for almost all of them were sprightly and full of verve—motive enough for me to be afraid of them; which is why they saddled up the horse of the lady of the hacienda for me, or that of her young daughter; and every afternoon, as I said, Januario and I went out on a horse ride with the administrator's two sons, a couple of fine young good-for-nothings.

Of the four, I was the worst horseman, or as they say, the best college boy; they therefore played a thousand tricks on me in the countryside, like pulling my horse's tail, hobbling it, spooking it, and doing all they could to provoke it, tame as it was, into throwing me, which they constantly managed to do without much difficulty; so that, although the bruises I got were light and hardly dangerous, since I always fell on grass or sand, I nevertheless received so many of them that I don't know how they failed to frighten me off. Yet after my good friends had laughed their fill at my expense, they always consoled me by telling me about the spills they had taken when they were learning to ride, and then they added: "Don't worry, man, this is nothing; even if you broke a leg every time you fell, or bashed a rib, you would take it as a stroke of luck when you saw how useful these horse lessons are for learning how to handle them; because, friend, there's no two ways about it, it takes a few blows to make a rider of you; and you yourself must notice that you aren't as clumsy as you used to be; no, you're holding on longer and sitting better, and if you stick around the hacienda a few more days, you'll have to give us all a lead start when we race."

Who would believe that such frivolous flattery was the medicinal balm that those rascals applied to my weals and bruises? And who would believe that I felt quite pleased with them, and that I forgot all about their merrymaking when I fell, and the groans that it sometimes cost me to get back up? Well, who else would believe it, but someone who knows that adulation holds so much space in our hearts that it pleases us even when it comes from our own enemies?

That rogue Januario never tired of hurting me in every way he could, while always feigning the sincerest friendship with me. One Sunday afternoon when they were holding a bullfight with some yearling bullocks, he put it into my head to enter the bullring with him to fight, arguing that the yearlings were small; that their horns weren't sharp; that he would teach me how; that it was great fun; that men should know how to do everything, especially on a farm; that being afraid was for women; and who knows how much other nonsense, until he had demolished all the outrage I had expressed to the curate the first time I saw such a fracas between man and beast. The horror that the sport had first inspired in me dissipated, I lost my earlier circumspection toward it, and, disregarding everything, I entered the corral on foot, for I felt safer that way.

At the beginning, I called the bullock from a distance of ten or twelve yards, a head start from which I could easily escape its anger by climbing the fence of the corral; but since there is nothing in this life toward which we do not lose our fear through repetition, bit by bit I lost my fear of the yearlings, seeing how easily I could escape from them; and, egged on by the encouragement of my good friends and comrades, who constantly shouted: "Get in there, college boy; go in closer, man, don't be a chicken; go on, you pansy," and other provocations of the same sort, I kept getting closer and closer to their respectable crowns, until on one of these passes Juan Largo tiptoed up behind me, and when I tried to flee, I couldn't, because he hampered my way by pretending to collide with me; with this timely aid, the bullock caught up to me and, lifting me in the air with its head, threw me to the ground four or five yards away, like a ripe sapodilla, to my displeasure. The fall and the shock left me shattered; but even so, since fear is swift-footed and I was afraid of a repeat event, for the bullock was preparing to conclude its triumph, I jumped straight up without noticing that I had lost the buttons and belt of my pants; and so, as they fell down around my ankles, I stood there as if in shackles, unable to step forward or back and cutting the most shameful figure; but the damnable yearling took advantage of my ineptitude at running and hit me with a second blow, but with such fury that I thought it had smashed all my ribs with one of the towers of the Cathedral, and that it had tossed me higher than the orbit of the moon; but when I hit the ground like a sack of bricks, I lost all awareness of everything in this world.

I was knocked out; they covered me with blankets and picked me up, and the day's entertainment ended with that scare; the ladies all thought that I had received a mortal blow to the head.

God willed that it be nothing but a fleeting loss of my senses; for, with the help of some black wool,[1] alkali, bandages, and so on, I revived in half an hour, with no complaints other than a bit of pain in my coccyx, which did bother me more than I would have wished.

But when I had returned to full consciousness, I saw myself lying stretched out in bed, tightly wrapped, surrounded by all the gentlemen who were on the hacienda, all of them full of apprehension, some asking me: "How do you feel?" Others: "What do you have?" And everyone: "Where does it hurt?" And in the midst of this throng, I noticed that my pants were loose, for my belt had broken, and I remembered standing there in shirttails and the rest of what I had just gone through, and I was filled with shame (a passion that did not entirely elude me) and wished that I had fallen honestly, as Caesar had under Brutus' knife.

I thanked them for their care, replying that no great damage had been done; but even so, the lady of the hacienda made me drink a glass of vinegar water, and a bit later a potion of *calahuala*,[2] with which I was completely restored by the following day.

My good friend Januario, during the first hours of my injury, when everyone else feared it might be something serious, displayed his deep distress with all the hypocrisy he could muster; but the next day, when he saw I was out of danger, he took charge and began to rain down all his buffoonery upon me, turning me red over and over again in front of the girls by shamefully recalling my recent adventure, emphasizing my nakedness, the position of my shirt, and the indecency of my fall.

Since he was able to provoke the girls' laughter with his foolery, and I could not deny it, I felt terribly ashamed, and could only resort to begging him not to make me blush in those terms; but my begging only served to spur on his blasted verbosity, which added to my shame and to my anger.

To calm me down, he said, "Don't be a fool, brother, I'm only kidding. This afternoon we're going on a ride to Cuamatla—just wait till you see what a nice hacienda it is. Which horse do you want them to saddle up for you, Little Almond or my aunt's Smokey?"

I answered him the first time he mentioned the idea, "Friend, I'm thankful for your kindness; but don't bother having them saddle up anything for me, because I never plan to mount another horse nor mare again in my life, nor stand in front of so much as a cow, much less a bull or even a bullock."

"Come on, man," he said, "don't be such a coward; you can't be a horseman without taking a few spills, and a good bullfighter dies on the horns of the bull."

"Well, then, why don't you go die, and good luck doing it," I replied to him, "and you can take as many spills as you'd like, because I'm not tired of living yet. Why do I need to go home with one rib fewer, or with a broken leg? No, Juan Largo, I wasn't born to break horses or herd cows."

In two words: I never again mounted a horse in his company, and never so much as watched another bullfight with him, and from that day forward, I began

---

[1] The common people believe that black wool, not white, has the virtue of reviving a person who has lost consciousness, a superstition to which the author alludes here. –E.

[2] [*Calahuala*: a fern native to Peru, used in the Americas as a medicinal herb. –Tr.]

to mistrust my friend a little bit. Happy is he who learns his lesson when he first falls into danger! Even better: "happy is he who learns his lesson when others fall into danger," as the ancient saying went: *Felix quem faciunt aliena pericula cautum.* You can call that: turning adversity itself to your advantage.

Three days after this conversation, the entertainments ended and each guest went home. The wicked Januario had noticed that I looked fondly at his cousin, and that she was not put off by this, and he endeavored to play another prank on me worse than the one with the bullock.

One day when Don Martín was not at home, because he had gone to visit a nearby hacienda, Januario told me, "I've noticed that you like Ponciana, and that she loves you. Come on, tell me the truth; you know that I'm your friend and that you've never kept a secret from me. She's pretty; you've got good taste, and I'm only asking you because I know that I can help you gain what you desire. The girl is my cousin and I can't marry her; so I'd be happy if her love went to such a good friend as you are to me."

Who would have thought that this was the net that this devil was spreading to catch me, so he could have a laugh at the expense of my honor? Well, that's what happened, because I, simple as ever, believed him, and said, "It is obvious that your cousin is worthy; I cannot deny that I love her; but I also cannot know whether she loves me or not, for I have no way to find out."

"Why not?" said Januario. "What, haven't you ever told her how you feel?"

"I've never spoken to her about that," I replied.

"And why not?" he insisted.

"What do you mean, why not?" I said. "Because I'm ashamed; she'll say that I'm being forward, or she'll go tell her mother, or she'll send me packing. Besides, your aunt is very suspicious; she never gives us a chance to talk or even leaves her alone for a second; so, how do expect me to have time to hold such a conversation with the girl?"

Januario laughed heartily, made fun of my fear and caution, and said, "You're such a prude; I never took you to be so dull and useless; just look at the enormous difficulties you'd have to surmount! Not a bit of it, you chicken. All women want to think that someone is in love with them, and even if they don't repay it, they are thankful to be told so. Now, haven't you heard it said that nobody can hear you unless you speak up? So go ahead and speak, you savage, and you'll see how you get what you want. If you're afraid of my old aunt, I'll team up with you and arrange things so you can speak with my cousin alone, for as long as you want. What do you say? You want to do it? Speak; you'll see that I'm simply your true friend."

With this sort of advice, and seeing how opportunity was handing me what I most desired, it was not long before I accepted his obliging proposal, and I thanked him more than if he had done me a true favor.

The rogue went away for a short time, at the end of which he returned quite content and told me, "It's all done. I gave Poncianita an emetic and made her spill her guts to me; she sang like a canary, confessed how much she loves you. I told her that you're dying for her and that you want to talk to her alone. That's what she wants, too, but she's got the problem of her mother, who's on top of her all day like a jail guard. It looks like a huge difficulty, but I've devised the best method for you two to get what you want, never fear, and this is it: my uncle shouldn't be back until tomorrow; you know where the bedroom is where she sleeps with her mother, and you know that her bed is the one on the right as soon as you go in; so this very night, between eleven and twelve, you can go talk to her as much as you'd like, knowing that at that hour the old lady will be in the deepest part of her sleep. Poncianita is in on it; she just told me that you should go in carefully, without making any noise, and that if she isn't awake, you should touch her pillow, because she sleeps very lightly. Just look at that, Mr. Periquillo: how quickly we've conquered all the difficulties that had you cowering; so you have no excuse to be so dull, take the chance before it gets away, I've done everything for you that I can."

Again I thanked my great friend for his hard work, and I stayed there weighing the pros and cons, thinking of what I would say to that girl (for in truth my naughtiness went no further than wanting to talk), and wishing that the hours would speed by so that I could make my visit at the witching hour.

Meanwhile, that traitor Juan Largo, who hadn't mentioned a word to his cousin about my flirtations, went to see his aunt and told her to keep an eye out for her daughter, because I was an utter cad; that he had already noticed that I was sending her thousands of signals at the dinner table, and that she was responding; that sometimes he had looked for me in my bed at night, and that I was missing; so she should move Poncianita to a different bedroom with a serving girl, and that she herself should take her daughter's bed that night, and should lie there quietly, to see if he wasn't wrong. All this struck the lady as a good idea; she believed it as if she had witnessed it, thanked Januario for the zeal he showed for the honor of his house, promised to take his advice, and, without any further investigations, she closed herself in a room with the innocent girl and gave her the tanning of her life, according to what one of her serving girls told me when she came to work at my house two months later, for she had heard the gossip that the rogue had spread, and had witnessed the unjust punishment of Ponciana.

There are two lessons you should learn from this event, my dear children, which you should apply throughout your lives. The first is: do not be quick to reveal your secrets to everyone who tries to sell himself as your friend; for one thing, he might not be a friend at all, but a traitor, like Januario, trying to take advantage of your simplicity to ruin you; for another, even if he is a friend, the time might come when you fall out with each other, and then if he as base as so many are, he will take his revenge by revealing any defects you made known to him in secret. In any case, it is better not to express your secrets than to risk doing so: "If you want your secret to remain hidden," said Seneca, "do not tell anyone, for if you cannot remain quiet yourself, how do you expect others to keep it in silence?"

The other lesson that this story offers is that you should not get carried away by the first idea that anybody offers you. Believing the first thing we are told, without investigating how likely it is, or how truthful the messenger is who gives us the news, implies an unforgivable frivolity, which should be classified as foolishness; and such foolishness can be and often has been the cause of irreparable harm. Because of wicked Haman's gossiping, all the Jews almost perished at the hands of the deceived

Ahasuerus;[3] and because of the gossiping and calumnies of that damnable Juan Largo, his young cousin suffered an unjust punishment and loss of repute.

Throughout that day, the lady frowned and acted rudely toward me; but being a boy, I never imagined that I was the cause of her displeasure, attributing it to some illness or some disagreement with the serving family. I was surprised that the girl was not at dinner, but all I did was miss her.

Night came, we had supper, and I went to bed and fell asleep without recalling the date we had made; but Januario, the dog, lay awake waiting for my ruin, and when the hour came and he saw me happily snoring away, he got up to waken me, saying, "What do think you're doing, you blasted lazybones? Come on, it's eleven already, you're keeping Poncianita waiting."

I was feeling more sleepy than naughty, so it was more by force than by free will that I climbed from bed in my underclothes; barefoot and trembling from cold and fear, I went to my beloved's bedroom, unaware of the scheme that my great and generous friend had contrived for me. I tiptoed in quietly, approached the bed where I thought the innocent girl was sleeping, and touched the pillow; then, when I least expected it, her old mother walloped me full in the face, so soundly that I saw the sun at midnight. The shock of not knowing who had hit me counseled me to hold my tongue; but the pain of the blow forced a shout from me that was louder than the wallop itself. Then the fine old lady grabbed me by the shirt and, sitting me down next to her, said, "Shut your mouth, you impudent brat. Who were you looking for here? I know all about your games. Is that how you honor your parents? Is that how you repay the favors we've shown you? Is that how a well-born and well-raised child behaves? How are you any different from the plain, uneducated country bumpkins? Rogue! Rapscallion! Cad! How dare you hurl yourself onto the bed of a young maiden, the daughter of a lady and a gentleman who have treated you so well? You should be thankful that, out of respect for your good parents, I don't order my servants to beat you to a pulp; but tomorrow my husband returns, and I'll have him take you back to Mexico the same day, because I don't want rogues like you around my house."

Full of fear and confusion, I kneeled down to her, and cried and pleaded that she not tell Don Martín, until at last she gave me her promise. I went back to bed and noticed how hard the contemptible Januario was laughing under his covers; but I pretended not to see.

The next day, Don Martín came back, and the lady had the coach made ready under the pretext of some urgent business or other in the capital; and without seeing the poor girl again, I was taken to my parents' house; but as she had promised, the lady did not let her husband in on what had happened.

---

[3] [In the book of Esther. –Tr.]

CHAPTER 9

We arrived at my house, where I was very well received by my parents, especially by my mother, who could not get her fill of hugging me, as if I had just returned from some dangerous expedition to faraway lands. Don Martín stayed at our house for two or three days while he wrapped up his business, and then he retired to his hacienda, leaving me quite content because my misdeeds had been passed over in silence.

One day my good father called me in alone and said, "Pedro, you have become a youth without knowing when you left childhood, and any day now you will enter the fullness of manhood without knowing where your youth has gone. What I mean is: today you are a lad, tomorrow you will be a man; you have a father who can give you direction, give you advice, and support you; but tomorrow, when I die, you will have to find your own direction and earn your own way at the cost of your sweat or your endeavors, or else perish if you cannot; for as you see, I am a poor man, and have no inheritance to leave you other than the good education I've given you, although you have not taken as much advantage of it as I had hoped.

"In virtue of this, let's think today about what tomorrow will bring. You have already studied grammar and philosophy; you are in a good position to continue in the field of letters, whether by studying theology or canon law, civil law or medicine. The first two of these fields bestow honor and assure a good living to those who devote themselves to them with talent and hard work; but in order to enjoy the fruits of working in these careers, you practically have to be a cleric, for if you remain a layman, no matter how good a theologian or canon lawyer you might be, you will never be able to preach from a pulpit, nor resolve a matter of conscience in a confessional; thus, these two fields are sterile for the layman, who can only study them for enlightenment, if he doesn't need to use his books in order to eat.

"Medicine and civil law are useful fields for the layman. Both are good in themselves and profitable for the practitioner, as long as he is good at them—that is, as long as he has taken advantage of his studies; thus, it would be foolish and stupid for a dime-a-dozen theologian, an ignorant doctor, a shyster, or a pettifogger to accuse these sciences of the discredit that he himself has earned, or to blame these fields for his own lack of employment; for no one thinks highly of trembling and incompetent hands, nor wants to entrust soul nor health nor worldly goods to them.

"This is to say, dear son, that you have four paths through which you can enter the most opportune sciences for earning a living in our country; for although there are others, I do not recommend them to you, because they are sterile in this kingdom; they would serve to enlighten you, yet as occupations, they would perhaps not prove very useful. These are physics, astronomy, chemistry, botany, and so on, which form part of the first science I mentioned.

"Nor would I persuade you to devote yourself to what they call belles lettres, which is better suited to delighting the mind than filling the purse. Let's imagine you are a great rhetorician, more eloquent than Demosthenes: what good will that do you, unless you can show off your oratory from a pulpit or a lawyer's bench? That is, unless you are a priest or a lawyer. Now, imagine that you've devoted yourself to the study of languages, both living and dead, and that you've gained an exquisite command of Greek, Hebrew, French, English, Italian, and others; you cannot make a living on that knowledge alone.

"But I would advise you even more energetically to stay away from poetry, if you are tempted to make that your occupation; for dealing with the muses is as enchanting as it is fruitless. When someone is very poor, it is commonly said that 'he is writing verses.' It seems that the terms *poet* and *pauper* are synonymous, or that having the skill to poetize is to be cursed to perish. Some friends of Pindar have managed to turn their inspiration into fortune, but they are few and far between. Virgil was among them; he was a protégé of Augustus; but it is not easy to find an Augustus or a Maecenas to sponsor another Virgil; rather, many others who have had the two requirements set by Horace for making poetry, which are *inspiration* and *art*, have had to go begging when they tried to rely on that skill, and others, more prudent than they, have stayed away from it, seeing poetry as a trade that is injurious to their chances of finding a better position; such a one was Don Esteban Manuel Villegas, who has given us his *Erotics*. Therefore, on this matter I advise you, in the words of Bocángel himself:

> If you are to write verses, write few,
> However much genius you have;
> For even though taste may applaud,
> Talent is bound to begrudge it.[1]

"Which is to say: even if you have a taste for writing verses, and even if they are good and you become famous for them, write few; don't become so entranced or wrapped up in that practice that you neglect to do anything else; because unless you are rich, in the end your talent will begrudge what you've done; for your purse will feel the pinch, and money will hold a grudge against you, as it does against almost every poet. The great Ovid's father told him not to devote his life to the muses, on the grounds of the poverty that he could expect from them; for as he reminded him, the famed poet Homer himself died a poor man: *nullas reliquit opes.*[2]

"This is not to tell you that poetry and the other sciences I have mentioned are useless; rather, many of them are not only useful, but necessary in certain professions. For example: dialectics, rhetoric, and ecclesiastical history are quite necessary to the theologian; chemistry, botany, and the entire field of physics are equally essential to the medical doctor; logic, oratory, and erudition in secular history are not mere ornaments, but indispensable supports for anyone who would be a good lawyer. Finally, the study of languages furnishes literate men with an exquisite and copious erudition in their respective fields, one which can only be obtained by imbibing from the original founts; and sweet poetry serves them as a spicy delicacy or a

---

[1] [From Gabriel Bocángel's poem *El Cortesano* (1655). –Tr.]

[2] [Ovid, *Tristia*, book 4, 10, line 22: *Maeonides nullas ipse reliquit opes*, "Even Homer stayed poor." –Tr.]

refreshing drink, sweetening and cheering their spirits when they flag from the detailed attention they must lend to serious and irksome affairs; but such studies, when considered separately from the main fields (if they can be separated), will be no more than ornaments; they might put food on the table now and again, but not always—at least not in America, where there are no opportunities, rewards, or incentives for dedicating one's life to the sciences.

"Therefore, the conclusion that we can draw from all of this is that a poor man such as you, who follows a career in letters in order to make a living, finds that he must needs become a priest specializing in theology or canon law; or if he is a layman, a medical doctor or a lawyer; so now you can pick which kind of study you like best, in the awareness that finding the good fortune that will make you happy throughout your life will depend upon your making the right choice.

"I am not demanding a sudden or unpremeditated decision from you. No, dear son, this is no sneak attack. I am giving you eight full days to think it over. If you have friends who are wise and virtuous, convey to them any doubts that occur to you, get their advice, take advantage of the lessons they can give you, and above all, consult yourself; examine your talents and interests; and after you do all this, you will settle prudently on the career in letters that you want to embrace. Understand that, if you deduce from your consultations and from examining yourself that you will not make a good man of letters, neither cleric nor layman, you should not feel embarrassed or ashamed to tell me so; for thanks be to God, I am not a ridiculous father who will get annoyed if you inform me of some disillusionment you might come to as the fruit of your reflections. No, dear Pedro; tell me, tell me in complete frankness, how you are thinking now; I put Nebrija's *Grammar* in your hand as a compromise with your mother; but now that you are grown, I'd like to compromise with you, because you are the hero of this scene, you are the one who has the greatest interest in your own success, so you have to consult your own inclinations and aptitude for one thing or the other, and not your mother's or mine.

"I am not one of those parents who want their sons to be priests, friars, doctors, or lawyers, even if they are unsuited for or repulsed by those professions. No; I am well aware that the most important thing is that our children not turn out lazy and idle, but devote themselves to being useful to themselves and to the State, rather than a burden to society by becoming vagrants, and that it is not only the sciences that make this possible; one can also earn one's bread honorably through the liberal arts or manual trades.

"And so, dear son, if you do not like letters, if you find the road toward them too rugged, or if you surmise that you are not likely to advance very far no matter how hard you apply yourself, making the work that you put into your education fruitless, I repeat, do not worry. In such a case, turn your gaze to painting, or music, or whatever trade suits you. There are plenty of tailors, silversmiths, weavers, blacksmiths, carpenters, tinkers, carriage builders, potters, and even tanners and shoemakers in this world who make a living through the work of their hands. So tell me what you want to be, which trade you have an inclination for, and in which line you think you will earn an honorable sustenance; and believe me, I will happily see to it that you learn it, and I will support you for as long as God gives me life; understanding that no trade is base in the hands of an upright man, and there is no craft more contemptible, no trade or skill more abominable, than having no craft, trade, or skill in the world. Yes, Pedro, being lazy and good-for-nothing is the worst fate that can befall a man; because his need to make a living, together with his ignorance of how to do so or in what, will all but lead him by the hand to the most shameful vices: which is why we see so many swindlers, so many men who would pimp their own wives and daughters, and so many thieves; and this is also why we have seen so many people filling our jails, prisons, galleys, and gallows.

"So, dear son, take your time while you consult your character and inclinations; judge prudently; embrace one way or another in which you will be able to earn a living for all the days that heaven gives you; and so, avoid becoming an odious burden on your fellow men, whom you should rather benefit to the extent you can, for that is what the just society in which we live demands.

"But even though you will judge this examination for yourself, you should also be aware that, for that very reason, you will have to be scrupulously honest and not let yourself be governed by flattery, for then you would be wasting your time; your speculations will be in vain, and you will only be fooling yourself, if you do not test your capabilities and analyze your character as if you were examining a stranger, and that would not be doing yourself the slightest favor. In his *Poetic Arts*, the great Horace counsels poets: 'that to write they should select the material that best suits their strengths, and should see how much weight their shoulders will bear, and how much they can withstand.'

"For it is true that, if a man's strengths are greater than the burden, he will easily carry it; but if the burden is greater than his strengths, it will crush him, and he will fall shamefully beneath its weight.

"The truth of the saying that *we cannot all do everything* enters easily into our hearts; but the pity is that, although we recognize this truth as evident, we only see it regarding everyone else, but not with regard to ourselves. When someone tries to take on this or that and it turns out badly, we say, 'Oh! Well, if he gets into something that he doesn't understand, how can he help but fail?' But when we take on something ourselves, we think we'll be able to get ours. And if we fail? Oh! Then we have thousands of excuses close at hand to keep ourselves from admitting that we are clumsy and scatterbrained.

"That is why I will never tire of repeating to you, dear son, that before you embrace one field of letters or another, one manual trade or another, and so on, you should think it through, and see whether or not you are suited to it; for even if you have more than enough inclination for it, if you do not have the talent you will go wrong—for you need both talent and inclination to take on such an enterprise—and you will expose yourself to intense criticism.

"Cicero was a storehouse of Roman eloquence; he had an inclination for poetry; but he did not have the talent specific to poetry, which is called *poetic inspiration*; because of which he composed a ridiculous cacophony, or grating sound of words, in the verse that Quintillian among others criticized:

O fortunatam natam me consule Roman.

"Juvenal said that if Cicero had written his *Philippics*, which so inflamed Mark Anthony's spirit, in such bad verse, he never would have had his throat slit.

"The famous Cervantes was a great genius but a miserable poet; his prose writings gained him immortal fame (though as for pesetas, he died a beggar; after all, he was one of our writers); but his verses, especially his comedies, no one remembers. His masterpiece, *Don Quixote*, did not give him a free pass to keep people from pestering him over his poor poetry; at least Villegas, in his seventh elegy, says in a conversation with a friend:

> From Helicon you'll go to the conquest
> Better than Cervantes the poetaster,
> For writing *Quixote* was no excuse.[3]

"This brief pair of examples will show you the truth of what I have told you. So go ahead, son; think it all over and decide what you will be in the world; because our aim is that you not end up vagrant and jobless."

My father left, and I stood there like a fool on the eve of the storm, for I still did not perceive how sound his teachings were. Nevertheless, I realized that His Grace meant for me to select a trade or profession that would put food on my table for the rest of my life; but I made no use of this realization.

For seven of the eight days he had given me to make my decision, I thought only of going to visit my friends and of loafing around, as was my habit, backed by the acquiescence of my ingenuous mother; but on the eighth day, my father nudged my memory, saying: "Pedrillo, you know what you have to tell me tonight, regarding what I asked you eight days ago." I instantly remembered the deadline, and went to find a friend with whom I could discuss the matter.

I found one, indeed; but what a friend! Just like all the other friends I had then: the sort of friend that disorderly boys, such as I was, normally have. His name was Martín Pelayo, and he was scarcely less annoying a pest than Juan Largo. He was about nineteen or twenty years old; a bigger card sharp than Birján;[4] more amorous than Cupid; a more fervent dancer than Bathylo; stupider than me; and lazier than the biggest drone in the best beehive. Despite these nullities, he was studying to be a father, so he claimed, though he had as much of a vocation for the priesthood at the time as I did to become a hangman. Nonetheless, he had already tonsured his hair and he wore clerical habits, because his parents had forced him into the clergy, in the same way you might force a nail into a wall: by hammering at it; and they had done this so as not to lose the income from a couple of juicy chaplaincies that they had inherited.[5] How sick I am and will always be of entailed estates and inherited chaplaincies!

---

[3] [This is the same Villegas mentioned above: *Eroticas,* part 2, Elegía VIII, vv. 79–81; cf. Espasa-Calpe 1956 edition, p. 232. See Ruiz Barrionuevo, p. 218. –Tr.]

[4] [Birján (or Vilhán) was the legendary inventor of the Spanish card deck. –Tr.]

[5] [A chaplaincy (*capellanía*) was an endowed position for a priest, who typically would say a specified number of masses per year in honor of the founders of the endowment. Much of the fabled wealth of the colonial Mexican church was locked into such chaplaincies, which were endowed

But be that as it may, this was the distinguished professor, the dignified elder, the virtuous sage whom I selected to ask for advice, and you can all imagine how well he might have fulfilled my father's good intentions. And so it was.

As soon as I informed him of my doubts and told him a little of what my father had preached to me, he laughed out loud and said, "Why even ask? Study to be a cleric, like I did—it's the best career, trust me. Look here: everybody will look up to a cleric; everyone will admire and respect him, even if he's a dolt, and will cover up his defects; nobody will dare stick a nickname on him or contradict him; there's always room for him at the best dance, at the best gaming table, and he isn't ignored even in the ladies' sitting rooms; and on top of it all, he will never be short a peso, even if he gets it from a Mass that he says poorly and on the run. So don't be a fool, study for the priesthood. Look here: the other day I was at this gaming house and I didn't feel like losing the hand, even though the fellow across the table had played an ace against my first card; so I grabbed the whole pot—that is, my own money and the other fellow's, too. The owner complained and swore, rightly, that it was his; but I shouted, raged, cursed, took the money and left the house, and nobody dared make so much as a peep, because they all figured me to be a deacon at the least; and you know that if I had been a doctor or a lawyer and had done the same thing, either I would have left without a penny, or they would have mounted such a battle that I might not have even gotten my ribs out of there intact. Therefore, once again I tell you, study to be a cleric and forget about anything else."

I replied, "I like everything you've said, and you've got me convinced; but my father told me that I have to study either theology, canon law, civil law, or medicine; and to tell the truth, I don't think I have enough talent for any of them."

"Don't be an idiot," Pelayo replied. "You don't need to study so much or work so hard to be a cleric. Do you have a chaplaincy?"

"No, I don't," I replied.

"Well, don't worry about it," he continued; "get yourself ordained as a language specialist;[6] that is bad, because the poor curates are like servants to the parish priests, and some will even force you to make their beds for them; but that isn't much compared to the advantages you gain; and as for what your father says about having to study theology or canon law to become a cleric, don't you believe it. Just study a few definitions in Ferrer or Lárraga, and that'll be more than enough; and if you dip into Cliquet or the Salamanca course, well![7] Then you'll be the consummate moral theo-

---

by wealthy families and used to support a priest who usually came from those same families, thus keeping the wealth in the family. Together with *mayorazgos* or entailed estates (mentioned in the same line), endowed chaplaincies were one of the main methods used by wealthy families to circumvent Spain's strict inheritance laws and keep their estates intact. –Tr.]

[6] ["As a language specialist" (*a título de idioma*): that is, an assistant priest licensed to carry out his sacramental and liturgical duties in an Indian language; Periquillo's father soon explains to him what this meant in practice. –Tr.]

[7] [The sources mentioned are authors of the common Spanish textbooks of theology of the era; respectively: Vicente Ferrer (1675–1738), a Spanish Dominican friar; Francisco Lárraga, another Spanish Dominican of the same era; José Faustino Cliquet, a Spanish Augustinian; and the 14-volume course in theology taught at the University of Salamanca, Spain's oldest university. In the

logian, a Seneca in the confessional, a Cicero in the pulpit; you'll be able to decide the toughest case of conscience that ever was, and your preaching will win you more devotees than all the Massillons and Bourdaloues—who were a couple of great orators, from what my professor tells me, because I've never cracked open their books."[8]

"But, man, the truth is," I said, "I don't think I'd make a good priest, because I like women too much, so I think I'd be better off married."

"Perico, you're such a fool!" Pelayo answered. "Can't you see, that's just the devil tempting you to keep you away from the holiest of professions? Do you think that being a priest is the only way you can sin along those lines? No, friend; laymen and even married men commit the same kind of sins. And that's aside from the fact that—who cares? . . . But I don't want to open your eyes to such things. Just get yourself ordained, man; do it and stop making so much noise about it, and later you'll thank me for my good advice."

I said goodbye to my friend and went home, resolving to become a cleric come what may, because I so enjoyed the flattering picture of the profession that Martín had painted for me.

Night fell, and my good father, never negligent about my welfare, called me into his study and said, "Today is the deadline I gave you, dear son, for seeking advice and deciding on the career that best suits you in the sciences or arts, because I don't want you to be wasting so much time. Tell me, then, what have you thought, and what have you decided?"

"I have decided, sir," I replied, "to be a cleric."

"I think that is very good," my father said, "but you don't have a chaplaincy, and in that case you will have to study some Indian language, such as Mexicano,[9] Otomí, Tarascan, Mazahua, and so on, so that you can find an appointment as a curate administering the sacraments to those poor people in their villages. You do understand that?"

"Yes, sir," I replied, because it did not cost me anything to say yes, not because I understood any of the obligations of a curate.

"Well, then, you must also know now," my father went on, "that you will have to go without grumbling wherever your prelate sends you, even if it is to the poorest village in the Hot Country,[10] even if you dislike it or find it damaging to your health, for the harder you work in your career as a curate, the more merits you will acquire toward being made a parish priest some day. These villages that I've mentioned are very hot and you will find little or no company there, except that of coarse

---

next chapter, Periquillo's father (expressing Lizardi's opinion) mocks these works as insufficient training for the seminarian. –Tr.]

[8] [Jean-Baptiste Massillon (1663–1742) and Louis Bourdaloue (1632–1704) were the most famous French preachers of their time. –Tr.]

[9] [Mexicano: that is, Nahuatl or "Aztec," the main Indian language of Mexico City. The four languages mentioned are the principal indigenous languages (in decreasing order) of central Mexico. –Tr.]

[10] [Hot Country (*Tierra Caliente*): the tropical lowlands of Mexico, which, in the colonial era, were the breeding grounds of many tropical diseases and considered virtual death traps. –Tr.]

Indians. There you will suffer from riding on horseback at all hours to take confessions, being burnt by the sun, lashed by fierce thunderstorms, and being kept up many late nights working. You will constantly battle the scorpions, ticks, chiggers, mites, nits, midges, mosquitoes, and other poisonous insects of the same sort that will quickly drink up your blood. It will be a miracle if you don't have to suffer through the tertian fever that they call 'the chills,' which is normally followed by consumptive jaundice; and in the midst of these travails, if you come up against a parish priest who is sullen, surly, and thick-headed, that will give you a tremendous opportunity for practicing patience; and if you fall in with one who is lazy and pampered, he'll pile all the work on your shoulders while keeping the most lucrative rewards for himself. That is what it means to go into the priesthood and be ordained as a language specialist or manager. Do you like that?"

"Yes, sir," I replied out of a sense of obligation, for in truth, my spirits had been chilled by the details he gave me on the difficulties and travails that curates tend to suffer; but I said to myself: Does he have to have guessed it right? Will I have to go to the Hot Country, to some miserable village? Will there have to be scorpions, flies, or any of the other bugs my father mentioned to me? Will I have to get the chills, and will the priests I work for have to be so pampered or so surly? Maybe it won't be like that, and I'll find a good village and a good parish priest, and then I'll have a fine old time, I'll have money, and in a couple of years I'll get myself a rich little parish, and then I can rely on my own curates, flop down on my back, and live high on the hog.

I was spinning all these stories to myself while my father went to the door to send a servant out for tobacco. His Grace returned, sat down, and continued his conversation as follows: "So, Pedrillo, granted that you have resolved to be ordained, what do you want to study? Canon law or theology?"

I was surprised, because as much as I liked the idea of making money while lying around lazily scratching my belly, I loathed studying and any kind of work just as much.

I remained silent for a short while, and my father, noticing my hesitation, said, "When you decided to devote yourself to the Church, you anticipated what kind of studies you would have to undertake, so you have no reason to delay your answer. What, then, will you study? Canon law or theology?"

Frowning deeply, I replied, "Sir, the truth is, I don't like either of these fields, because I don't think I will be able to learn them, because they are so difficult. What I want to study is ethics, since they tell me that's all I'll need to become a curate, or at most a sorry parish priest."

My father rose rather vexed from his seat on hearing this and, pacing up and down the room, said, "Will you look at that! That's just the sort of erroneous opinion that corrupts boys. That's how they lose their love for learning, that's how they stray and let themselves go, that's how they soak up the most ignoble ideas; and then they embrace a career as priests because they think it's the easiest to take up, that it gives the best returns and requires the least amount of learning. De facto, they study a couple of definitions, and a couple of the commonest ethical cases; they latch onto a synod; and if they happen to strike it lucky there, they become instant priests, and increase the number of idiots who bring dishonor to the whole profession." Turning to face me, he said, "The fact is, son, I know several curates who are steeped in the detestable maxim that has been instilled in you: that you don't need to know very much in order to become a priest; and I have seen a few, unfortunately, who have put down their *acocotes* in order to pick up the chalice, or who have taken off their mule skinner's smock to put on the chasuble,[11] and have slackened off and gone into something for which they had no calling; but don't you believe, Pedro, that all it takes is a bit of half-swallowed grammar and half-digested ethics, as you seem to think, to become a good priest and to exercise honorably the terrible burden of the cure of souls.

"I know too well that there was an era (as Abbé Andrés tells us in his *History of Literature*)[12] when learning had fallen into such decline in Europe that anyone who could read and write had all he needed to become a priest, and if he knew, perchance, a bit of plainsong, that qualified him as a doctor; yet who could doubt but that the holy Church was grieved by this general ignorance, and that it acquiesced in the ineptitude of such ministers because of the darkness of the age and the dearth of suitable candidates, and so that the people would not lack spiritual nourishment? And thus, to keep her children from perishing from hunger when, by the grace of Jesus Christ, there was bread in such abundance, she sadly had to trust crude hands to distribute it, and to confide the administration of the wine of the Lord to unskilled workers, for there was no other way.

"But just as it would have been a gross error to say back then that you only needed to know how to read in order to be worthy of holy orders, though such a thing may have occurred, it is just as gross today to suggest that for obtaining such a high honor, it is *more than enough* to know a little bit of grammar and another bit of ethics, even though there are too many who lack any learning when they are ordained; for we have plenty of evidence that the Church only tolerates this practice, not that she likes it.

"Quite the contrary; she has always desired that the ministers of the altar be fully endowed with learning and virtue. The holy Council of Trent declares: 'that ordained priests should know Latin and be educated in letters; desires that as they age, they should grow in merit and greater education; declares that they be suitable for administering the sacraments and teaching the people; and finally, declares that seminaries be established in which a number of youth always be educated in ecclesiastic discipline, who should learn grammar, plainsong, ecclesiastic reckoning, and other useful and honorable fields; that they memorize the Holy Scriptures, the

---

[11] [*Acocote:* a large, hollow gourd with a long neck, used to suck the sap from the *maguey* or century plant in order to make *pulque*, the lightly fermented drink of the Indians of central Mexico; the chalice is the communion cup, held only by priests. Muleteers provided the main means of trade between cities and the countryside, and were often of mixed ethnic background; the chasuble is the outer vestment worn by a priest during Mass. The implication of both phrases is that uncultured men of questionable (that is, non-Spanish) ethnicity and rural backgrounds have become priests. –Tr.]

[12] [Giovanni (Juan) Andrés (Spanish Jesuit, 1740–1817), *Origen, progeso y estado actual de toda literatura*, written in Italian and translated into Spanish by Carlos Andrés, published in 10 volumes in Madrid, 1794. –Tr.]

ecclesiastic books, the homilies of the saints, and the formulas for administering the sacraments, especially those conducive to hearing confession, and other rites and ceremonies. Thus will these colleges be perennial nurseries for ministers of God.' (Session 23, chapters 11, 13, 14, and 18.)[13]

"So you see, dear son, that the Holy Church has always wanted her ministers to be well endowed with the greatest wisdom, and rightly so; because, do you know what a priest is, and what he should be? Surely not. Listen, then: a priest is a sage of the law, a doctor of the faith, the salt of the earth, and the light of the world. Now, tell me if someone could hold such a position, or even deserve it, if he is satisfied with knowing grammar and a dash of ethics; and tell me if he can reputably obtain an honor that requires so much learning, by getting away with learning so little, even if he learns that little bit very well. How, then, can he be ordained with half-digested grammar and poorly learned ethics?

"On the other hand, when we see so many wise and virtuous priests who, even when they are old, ill, and tired, and when their trembling heads have turned white from age and long study, still do not let books stray from their hands; still do not understand the mysteries of theology well enough; still struggle to penetrate many obscure passages of the Holy Bible; still confess that they are ever the disciples of the holy fathers and doctors of the Church, and recognize that they are unworthy of the sacred character that adorns them; what judgment, then, should we make of the high honor of the priesthood? And how will we convince ourselves of the great reserves of holiness and wisdom that such a profession requires in its members?

"And if, after these serious considerations, we gaze in the other direction and see how calmly and smugly so many young lads saunter into the Sanctum Sanctorum, after a couple of swipes at Nebrija and a couple more at Father Lárraga; if we see that some of them are scarcely ordained when they put aside not only those two poor books, but perhaps, or not even perhaps, the Breviary itself; and if, finally, we take a step outside the capital and the cities where the bishops and canons reside, and we see incidents of scandalous, unbelievable ignorance,[14] and from those pulpits we hear stupidities and absurdities that were never written—what sort of judgment can

---

[13] [Spell (p. 155) notes that this is not a quotation but a paraphrase of many passages in the acts of the Council of Trent. –Tr.]

[14] Such is the case that follows. In some village in Spain, the distinguished Dr. Suárez made confession before celebrating Mass, and the miserable curate who took his confession was so ignorant that he did not know the form of absolution. The penitent himself had to keep prompting him, the way one does with a student who tries to recite something he has not learned; but at last, with this help, our curate absolved the priest, who, as soon as he had finished saying Mass, went to see the parish priest, full of outrage, and rightly so, and informed him of what had happened; but what was this theologian's surprise when he heard the parish priest tell him, in measured tones, "Father, that curate is such a fool; I have told him more than once that he shouldn't interfere in absolutions, he should just hear the confessions and send the penitents to me so that I can absolve them"?

I know that this case will seem incredible; but only to those who have never left Mexico or other cities, for those of us who have been around the little villages far from the cathedrals will believe it as if we had seen it ourselves, for we have witnessed even more pathetic things of the same sort, and I would cite a few if they were not so generally well known.

we make about such ministers? Or of their virtue? Or of their rightiousness in the spiritual administration of the wretched villages entrusted to their care? Oh! To recount all the damage they have caused, you would have to say what Aeneas said to Dido when he told her of the fall of Troy: 'Who could hold back tears when recounting such a tale?'"

At this, my father took out his watch and said, "Tonight's discussion has been long, but I still have not told you everything you need to know about this important matter; nevertheless, we will leave it pending until tomorrow, because it is ten in the evening, and your mother is waiting for us at supper. Let us go."

CHAPTER 10

PERIQUILLO'S FATHER CONCLUDES HIS LESSON; PERIQUILLO
DECIDES TO STUDY THEOLOGY; HE ABANDONS IT; HIS FATHER
WANTS HIM TO LEARN A TRADE; HE RESISTS; AND OTHER MATTERS

We had supper, contented as always, and went to bed as we did every night. I could not help brooding over what my father had just said, and had to admit that what he said was gospel, because there are some truths that you can just plain see, whether you like it or not; but no matter how convinced I was by the arguments I had heard, I could not make up my mind to study canon law or theology, as my good father intended, for just as I loved my free and lazy life, I abhorred hard work. Finally I fell asleep plotting how I could become a cleric and make money without working, and how I might escape my good father's intentions. Many children spend sleepless nights weaving such plots without realizing that they plot their own ruin.

The next day, after my father returned from Mass, he called me into his room and said, "I do not want us to forget last night's discussion. I was telling you, Pedro, how much towns suffer when their priests and curates are ignorant or immoral, for sheep can never be safe nor well cared for if they are in the power of thick-headed or slothful shepherds; and the reason I told you that was to prove to you that a priest can never have enough wisdom, especially if he is in charge of caring for a town; and for further confirmation of my point, listen:

"In every town there might be—and in many there actually are—a few mystical souls who aspire to perfection through the ordinary path, which is that of mental prayer. And what kind of direction could a half-ignorant curate give such a soul if, out of sloth or ineptitude, he has not studied the appropriate theology, indeed has not so much as cracked open the books of St. Teresa, *The Mystical Lantern* by Father Ezquerra, *The Mystical Disillusions* by Father Arbiol, and perhaps not even Kempis or Villacastín?[1] How can he direct a virtuous and abstract soul, if he himself is ignorant of the path? How could he plumb the spirit and tell if the soul is deluded or truly favored, if he has no idea what the purgative, illuminative, contemplative, and unitive ways are?[2] If he does not know what revelation, ecstasy, swooning, or rapture are? If the difference between consolation and curtness is news to him? If he is surprised

---

[1] [These are important and popular works and authors in the vein of Spanish Catholic mysticism. St. Teresa of Avila (1515–1582), Spanish mystic, nun, and poet, and the first woman declared a Doctor of the Church. José López Ezquerra, *La lucerna mystica pro directoribus animarum* (Zaragoza, 1713, published in Latin). Antonio Arbiol (1651–1726), Franciscan from Aragón; his widely disseminated work *Desengaños místicos* was Lizardi's main source for the discussion that follows, according to Spell (p. 155). Thomas à Kempis (1379–1471), Dutch canon and attributed author of the popular spiritual tract *Imitatio Christi* (1415). Tomás Villacastín (1570–1649), Spanish Jesuit and author of *Manual de consideraciones y exercicios espirituales para saber tener oración mental* (*A Manuall of Devout Meditations and Exercises, Instructing How to Pray Mentally,* 1618). –Tr.]

[2] [Purgative, illuminative, contemplative, and unitive ways: these constitute the mystical path to union with God, according to the teaching of St. Teresa of Avila. –Tr.]

to hear the terms holy kiss, divine embrace, and spiritual marriage? And if (not to bore you with matters you do not understand) he is completely ignorant of the beautiful works that divine grace brings about in devout, spiritual souls? Isn't that true? Don't you realize that if you set out to sail a ship to Cádiz, Cavite, or any other port, with all the knowledge you have of navigation (that is, none whatsoever), you would certainly ground any unhappy vessel they might entrust you with on some shoal or reef, or lose it in some gulf, without ever reaching your destination? You should be able to understand this, because the comparison is very simple. Well, the same thing happens with these unhappy "Lárraga's-enough-for-me" curates,[3] who can barely absolve a common sinner (like the Indians who only know how to steer a canoe to Ixtacalco). The poor fellows are blind, and the souls who aspire to enter through the way of perfection are also blind and need a good guide to direct them. They won't find that in these dull-witted directors, so what happens (saving a special favor of grace) is that they either become lukewarm, or become lost; and their guides either become confused, or fall rashly into the delusional errors that such mystical souls convey to them.

"This is a terrible truth, but it is a truth that no wise priest would deny. What I see (and what particularly confirms my opinion) is this: that the most virtuous, saintly, and wise priests are very hesitant to confess and direct nuns and other spiritual souls, and when they do direct them, they are very effective in never letting go of the sounding plumbs of doctrine and prudence. Apart from this, they consult with the Theologian in Chief—with God, I mean—during their moments of prayer; and, as they know that they must do whatever they humanly can in order to hit the mark, they discuss their doubts with other wise and spiritual men. That is what I see, and that is what makes me think that, when the spiritual direction of mystical souls is entrusted to a bunch of poor, half-ignorant clerics who barely know enough to say Mass and absolve a penitent in virtue of the promise of Jesus Christ, they can only succeed by accident. Therefore, dear son, I am firmly convinced that if the holy Church could arrange it so that all of her ministers were theologians and holy men, she would omit no sacrifice to attain that goal; but the lack of the necessary talents and men makes her furnish the faithful with ministers who are useful only for the simple administration of the Sacraments.

"There is yet more. I have told you that priests are the teachers of the law. They exclusively can explain the dogma and the interpretation of the Holy Scriptures. They must be very well educated in the revelation and tradition on which our faith is founded, and they, in the end, must demonstrate to the face of the world that our holy religion and beliefs are solid and unshakable.

"Well, now, let's imagine an unlikely but not impossible case. Let's imagine that one of the poor little curates we are talking about, or a once-a-week friar—a 'Mass-and-stewpot' priest, as they say—has an argument with a heretic about the verity of our religion, the justice of its dogma, the divine nature of its mysteries, the reality of the fulfillment of the prophecies, the evidence of the coming of the Messiah, the calculation of the weeks in Daniel, or some such thing (and mind you, the heretics who

---

[3] [Lárraga: see Chapter 9, footnote 7. –Tr.]

promote or enter into such arguments, blind as they are to faith, are not blind to learning: I have lived in a port city, and have met and dealt with a few of them). How would he recognize their sophisms? How would he evade their arguments? How would he distinguish between their malice and the intrinsic power of reason? And how could the truth emerge triumphant from his lips in all its natural splendor? It is a fact that if Ferrer, Cliquet, Lárraga, or some other summarizer were all we had to counteract the heretics, I don't know how St. Augustine would have come out against the Manicheans, or St. Jerome against the Donatists, or the other holy fathers against all the heresiarchs and heretical scum they combated and confounded with the brilliance and soundness of their arguments.

"From everything I've said, you should conclude, dear Pedro, that to be a worthy priest it isn't enough to know just what is sufficient for the job; you must imbue yourself, steep yourself in sound theology, and in the ecclesiastic rules or laws that are the canons of the Church.

"To this you should add the fact that letters are so proper to being a priest that, since the mid-13th century, only men of letters have been promoted to the clergy, according to the Law of Justinian, 6, ch. 4, and 123, ch. 12. Hence, Julian Antecessor wrote: 'He who is not a man of letters cannot be a cleric.' Thus the title of *cleric* began to be used to signify an educated man of letters, and that of *layman* to denote an ignorant man, or one who didn't know letters, which is why they also gave the title of *cleric* to educated laymen; while, on the other hand, illiterate churchmen were also called *laymen*. 'He is called a *cleric*' (in the words of Orderic Vital, book 3), 'because he is imbued with the knowledge of letters and other arts.' In the *Crónica andrense*, we also read the following words: 'With the consent of certain Romans, he appointed as his subordinate a very *cleric* Spaniard named Burdino.' And in the history of the bishops of Eistet: 'This Bishop Juan was very *cleric* in canon law'—that is, very learned. The same meaning can be found in the early French language, in which *clerc* meant scholar, and *clergie* meant knowledge and learning.

"All this erudition and more was collected by Mr. Muratori in his brief treatise entitled *Reflections on Good Taste* (chapter 7, pages 70, 71, and 72), where you can read it, confirming that you must be a man of letters to merit the title of cleric; while on the other hand, he who does not have letters cannot be a *clerical* father, but merely a *lay* father.[4]

"I have told you more than enough; so, if you want to be a clergyman, tell me, what have you decided to study?"

Seeing the assault I was under, I had no choice; I answered my father that I would study theology; and two days later, there I was, a student theologian, sporting the clerical habit.

Soon enough I met my friend Pelayo at the University and told him about what had happened with my father and how, unable to escape his insinuations, I had chosen to study theology.

"That'll be a great waste of time, since you don't like studying," my friend told me; "but if you don't have any choice, what else can you do? Sometimes we've got to

---

[4] [Muratori: see the author's Prologue, footnote 7. –Tr.]

compromise with these old eccentrics, even if we'd rather not, even if we just do it to fool them while we go ahead with our own plans. My father also goes on about it, as follows: he's stuck on my studying canon law *a fortiori*—that is, like it or not; and he even talks about master's degrees and tasseled caps; but I'm not vain and don't think about such things; all I want to do is finish my canon law course, well or badly, get my little certificate, get myself ordained, and get rid of all these books and headaches. You can do the same: put up with your university courses with the patience of a penitent, and when you least expect it, you'll find that you've been made a Bachelor of Theology, because as long as they say that's what you are, that's good enough.

"No point in giving yourself a hard time or burning up your brains studying books. Study the courses that your professor tells you, learn to handle the *ergo* by imitation, and spend a lot of time at the university, because the classes are important, my boy; the classes are more important than learning itself, because you have to get that grade. They know and we know that most of us students don't go to the university to learn anything, but to pass the time jawing with each other; the truth is, though, you've got to get a certificate saying you took classes for the amount of time fixed by statute, or you won't graduate even if you know more theology than St. Thomas; and if you do get it, you'll be a bachelor even if you couldn't say who God is according to Father Ripalda;[5] but that's how it is, that's how we're going to do it, and that's how you and I will get through the easiest. I'm hardly ever absent at the university, just once in a while; but I do skip the classroom a lot. On Sundays, Thursdays, and holidays we don't have classes; and I jump ship one or two days a week; you won't believe how little that embarrasses me. That's what you should do, if you don't want to let studying theology get to be too much for you. Hang out with me, snatch every penny you can from your father, and trust me, you won't just live the good life, you'll become civilized; because, let me tell you, you're a Mexican bumpkin, and I want to get you out into the open. Yes, I'll take you to the houses of a few fine young ladies where we have social gatherings; you'll learn how to dance, to waltz, to have a conversation with decent folk. Aside from that, I'll sit you down in the sitting rooms and make you communicate with the ladies; because talking with women is the most enlightening thing around. Finally, I'll show you how to play billiards, manille, three-card monte, and ombre, because all those skills are the qualities of a refined and enlightened lad, and that way we'll have a great time. A year from now you won't recognize yourself, and you'll thank me for the good offices of my friendship."

At last I saw a ray of hope when I heard Pelayo's proposal for our new life plan, because I aspired to nothing beyond amusing myself and having a good time; so I thanked him for the interest he had taken in my progress, and from that day forth, placed myself under his protection and direction.

He immediately set about performing his duties, taking me to the social gatherings he frequented at several more-or-less decent houses, where young, titled ladies lived, such as *La Cucaracha, the Ballmaster, the Bonebreaker,* and others of

---

5 [Jerónimo Martínez de Ripalda, the author of the most commonly used Spanish Catechism. –Tr.]

the same ilk. It goes without saying that the men and women who attended these gatherings were, under their cloaks, frock coats, and skirts, girls and young men of finely sharpened tongues: that is, spoiled, profligate lads and lasses, and rogues by profession.

With such fine companionship and the direction of my sage mentor, within a few months I had become a good mandolin player, a tireless dancer, an everlasting party-hopper, wit, windbag, smart-aleck, and a first-class *lépero*.[6]

Since my teacher had proposed to civilize me and enlighten me in all the ways of chivalry then in fashion, he taught me to play billiards, ombre, whist, and other card games; he did not omit to instruct me in the stratagems of roulette, nor in the wiles of playing monte through skill: not just any old way, hoping for a favor from God or for whatever luck has in store—for as he liked to tell me, 'he who plays clean, goes home cleaned out'—but always with a touch of diligence.

I spent a whole year learning all these gimmicks; but in the end I became a master of the craft and qualified as an expert in cardsharping and respectable *leperage*; for there are two classes of roguery: one is the lowdown, dirty sort, as practiced by the drunks and derelicts who play knucklebones or pitch-and-toss on the street corner; who slug it out on the street; who swear scandalous obscenities; who go around with barefoot, ragged, *leperish* women; and who get drunk publicly in the taverns and *pulque* stands;[7] and these are called everyday rascals and *léperos*. The other class of respectable roguery is that practiced by respectable lads who, straying from the path, with their cloaks, frock coats, and even their perfumery, are lifelong idlers, perennial members of every social gathering, ready to woo any coquette who comes along or seduce any married women they find handy; gamblers, swindlers, and cardsharps whenever they get the chance; hecklers at dances, the nightmares of other guests, gate-crashing freeloaders, impertinent, shameless, thick-headed *a nativitate;* feather-brained chatterboxes, well-dressed automatons, to the scandal and detriment of the unlucky society in which they live: these are the respectable rascals and *léperos*, and it was in this kind of rascalry, as I said, that I could have set myself up as a public expert, so much did I get out of the lessons of my teacher and the examples of my classmates in the short space of one year.

My poor father was quite unsuspecting of my contemptible progress, and quite pleased with Martín Pelayo, who frequently visited my house; for as I told you before, your grandfather was as good of heart as he was sound of mind. In effect, he was a virtuous and upright man, and since such people are easily fooled by the cunning of the wicked, my friend and I kept my good father well deceived; for I was a

---

[6] [*Lépero:* rotter, swine, rogue; this usage is peculiar to central Mexico. Francisco J. Santamaría notes: "The *lépero* should not be confused with the *pelado,* two types of the Mexican people, especially the capital. The former is characterized by his low moral condition; the latter only by his humble social condition. The *lépero* may or may not be poor; the *pelado* may or may not be morally questionable" (*Diccionario de mejicanismos,* Mexico, 1978, p. 661, my translation). –Tr.]

[7] [*Pulque:* a slightly alcoholic drink made from fermented maguey (century plant) juice; this was the main alcoholic drink of Mexico before the Spanish conquest and, under colonial rule, became associated with Indian and lower-class drinking habits. –Tr.]

great scoundrel, and Pelayo an even greater one, so between the two of us, we handled my gullible father like putty. He believed Martín, that rogue, to be a refined, well-behaved, and studious lad; and Martín, in my defense, earnestly praised my talent and hard work, bamboozling them even more—or rather, bamboozling my father, for my mother had no need to be convinced; since she loved me without prudence, she pardoned my worst transgressions because of my age, and passed over my lesser ones as amusing childish pranks.

But just as false coin cannot circulate for long without revealing the poor die or the alloy with which it was cast, so wickedness cannot continue too many days under the cover of hypocrisy without manifesting its filth. That is precisely what happened to me, for my father, one day when I least expected it, asked me when my final examination would be, or if I was in a position to take it. If he had instead asked whether I was ready to dance a jig, corrupt a young lady, or lay up a hand of monte, of course I would quickly have responded in the affirmative; but he had asked me a difficult question, because with all my homework I had no time for any other studying, so my copy of Billuart was still clean and almost untouched.[8]

Nevertheless, I had to give some sort of answer, and it was: that my professor hadn't said anything, but that I would ask him.

"No," my father told me, "don't ask him anything; I'll do it."

It was an unlucky time for my father to take on such a commission, because he went on the second day of school and asked my teacher about the state of my studies, and he said that if I was up to the challenge of an examination, then he would make arrangements to cover the expenses.

My teacher, as truthful as he was serious, replied, "Friend, I was hoping that you would see me, so that I could tell you that your boy shows no promise of improving: not because he lacks the talent, but for want of hard work. He is very neglectful; it is a rare week that he doesn't miss one or two days of class, and when he does come, it is to cause trouble and make the other students waste their time. In view of this, you can just imagine how ready he is, and how far along he has come. In addition, I have noticed certain friendships and bad inclinations that he has, which make me fear for the boy's ruin in the near future; so, as a good father, you should keep watch over his behavior, and see in what you might engage him rigorously, for otherwise the boy will be lost, and you will have to account for him to God."

My father took leave of my teacher feeling quite embarrassed (as he later told me), and filled with righteous anger against me. Poor fathers! What hard times their bad sons give them! He went home at midday; greeted me dyspeptically; went into his bedroom with my mother; who, some two hours later, came out bleary-eyed from crying and ordered the table set.

My father scarcely ate, nor my mother; I, shameless as ever and not knowing the crux of their displeasure, did all I could to lick the dishes clean; for in the end, shamelessness goes hand-in-hand with gluttony. During dinner, my father did not

---

8 [Charles-René Billuart (1685–1787), Belgian Dominican, editor of a compendium of the theological works of St. Thomas Aquinas that went through several editions in the 18th century. See Spell, p. 154. –Tr.]

utter a word, and as soon as it was over, they cleared the table and gave thanks to God;[9] my father retired for his nap, telling me in great earnestness, "This afternoon, don't go to school; I need you here."

Since guiltiness always shows, I felt a good deal of dread, fearing my father might have learned of some of my extracurricular games, and might wish to use a cudgel to give me the award I deserved for them.

Later I conceived that I had been the cause of his anger, of the sparseness at dinner, and of my mother's tears; but as I was satisfied that she did not just love me, but adored me, I had no trouble asking her, "Ma'am, what news is it that my father has?"

To which the poor woman answered with her tears, and she recounted to me everything that had happened to my father with my teacher, and told me he had resolved to set me to work at a trade. . . .

"At a trade?" I asked. "A trade? May God forbid it, ma'am. What will it look like to have a Bachelor of Arts and a student of theology transformed from one day to the next into a tailor or a carpenter? What kind of jokes would my classmates make about me? What would my relatives think? What will people say?"

"Well, son," my mother replied, "what do you want me to say? I have pleaded long enough with your father; I've cried to him; but he's unmoved, there's no way to convince him. He says he doesn't want the devil to take him, and you with him, just to please me. I don't know what to do. . . . "

"Don't cry, ma'am," I told her; "I know what has to be done. I'm sure my father isn't really hoping to see me as a tinker or a tailor. So, have all the barracks closed? Have they run out of uniforms and army rations?"

"What do you mean by that, Pedrito?" my mother asked.

"Nothing, ma'am," I replied, "except that before I learn a trade, I'll join the army, because I've got a good body for being a soldier, and they'll take me in with open arms."

At this my mother redoubled her wailing, and said, "Ay, my sweet little boy! What are you saying? A soldier? A soldier? God forbid! Don't be rash, and don't lose hope; I'll beg your father again this afternoon, and if he says you're not up to studying and that he has to find you an occupation, let's see if he can get you a place in a store."

"Quiet, now, mother," I said. "That would be worse. How would it look to see a bachelor all dirty and covered with lard, and a theologian serving twelve pennies–worth of chilies in vinegar? No, no; I'll be a soldier, and that's that; because if my father is tired of supporting me, the king is everyone's father, and he has thousands of pesos to clothe me and keep me fed. This afternoon I'll sell myself to the China regiment,[10] and tomorrow I'll come see you dressed in my conscript's uniform."

Every time I remember this and other hard times I gave my poor mother, and the

---

[9] [The first edition adds, in parentheses: "A Christian custom which I always observed in my parents' house, and which I have later missed in most gentlemen's houses." –Tr.]

[10] [That is, the Spanish regiment stationed in the Philippines. The Philippines, a Spanish colony since 1565, was administered from Mexico, where it was commonly known as "China." See Spell, p. 174. –Tr.]

tears she shed for me, I feel my heart break to bits from sadness; but it is too late now to repent, and these lessons only serve to teach you, my children, to look always upon your mother with true love and respect, and not to imitate bad sons, such as I was; rather, pray to God that he not punish the erring ways of my youth as harshly as they deserve, and remember that He tells you, in the words of the Sage: "Honor thy father, forget not the groanings of thy mother. Remember that thou hadst not been born but through them: and make a return to them as they have done for thee."[11]

Finally this scene ended with my mother begging, pleading, wailing for me not to join the army, swearing to me that she would intercede again with my father that he desist from his intention and not force me into a trade; and with this promise I calmed down, since it was precisely what I had desired and the reason why I had so grieved Her Grace, not because I had any idea of going into a military career, since I looked upon every type of work with a certain horror.

It would have been so much better if my mother had broken every chair in the room on my head, and had bandaged me up and packed me off to the nearest barracks, and if there I had been fitted out right away with a conscript's clothes! That would have been the end of my bachelor days and all the worries they brought; but that's not what she did, and she had to go on suffering, as God alone knows.

A while later, my father emerged, with his hat and walking stick, and said, "Get your cloak and let's go."

I got it and left fearfully with His Grace, and my mother stayed behind to worry. After a short walk, my father stopped in a vestibule and told me, "Friend, I am now disabused about you and know that you are all but a lost case, and I do not wish for you to be lost entirely. Your teacher has informed me that you are lazy, idle, and dissolute, and that studying is not your destiny. Bearing this in mind, it is not my wish that your destiny be picking locks, nor swinging from the gallows. Right now, choose which trade you will learn, or I will take you from here and give you to the king in the China regiment."

All the groaning I had used on my mother turned to submissive pleas with my father, since I knew that he never lied and was resolute; so all I could do was humble myself and beg him to please give me a little time to investigate which trade might be best for me. My father granted me three days' clemency, as if I had been sentenced to hang, and we returned home to find my poor mother ill from a hemorrhage she had suffered from the grief I caused her and the scare that it gave her.

As said before, my father loved her extremely, and so, filled with regret, he could only hope that medicine would help her. Indeed, the next day she was better; but she continued to cry now and again, because I had told her of my father's resolution, and she, in the midst of her pain, had not forgotten to beg him not to find me a trade, to which my father answered that first she should recover from her attack, and then they would see what had to be done in the end.

This answer greatly distressed my mother and made me feel uneasy, because I had never seen my father so firmly resolved, nor so seemingly aloof from my mother; so I came to understand that, this time, I would not escape from some apprenticeship.

---

[11] [Ecclesiasticus 7:29–30 (7:27–8). [Tr.]

Not knowing what else I could do to escape the iron rule of some master crafts-man, I dreamed up the most devilish plot I could in such difficult straits, which was to go see my charitable tutor and wise friend, the illustrious Martín Pelayo. With the mutual trust we had, I walked straight into his room uninvited, and there I found him swinging back and forth, holding onto a rope that dangled from the ceiling, humming boleros, and leaping across the floor. He was so entranced in his dancing lesson that he didn't notice when I entered and kept jumping around like a billy goat, until I asked him, "What's all this, Martín? Have you gone crazy, or are you studying acrobatics?"

Then he saw me and answered, "I'm not crazy, and I don't plan to be a trapeze artist, I'm just working on learning how to do the octave that these boleros call for."

Seeing how slow he was being, I said, "Set your lessons aside for a bit, because I've got an important piece of business to ask you about, and it is something that only your friendship can save me from."

He then politely undid the rope, sat down on his bed with me, and said, "I didn't know you were here on business; but tell me whatever it is, because you know how highly I think of you."

I told him all my troubles point by point, rounding it off by telling him that, to escape the dishonor that awaited me as an apprentice, I had thought of becoming a friar. He listened to me seriously and then said, "Perico, I'm sorry about the misfor-tune that your father's ridiculous and scrupulous character is causing you, but given that he's left you no middle ground between becoming a manual craftsman or a sol-dier, and that your only means of escape from those choices is to become a friar, I'd have to agree with you; because, better one-eyed than blind; it would be worse to be Perico the Tailor, or Private Perico, than Father Pedro. It's quite true that a friar's life has its unbearable inconveniences, like studying, helping the community, observing the rules, being subordinated to your prelates, and suppressing or being deprived of the liberty that you and I so enjoy; but it's all a matter of getting used to. Besides, in exchange for those nuisances, the office has its considerable advantages, such as the honor that living the religious life extends over all its individuals, even laymen; the respect that a holy habit instills; and above all, my boy, having your lunch money paid up forever. You know that craftsmen and soldiers don't enjoy all those conve-niences; so I think you should carry out your plan."

"Well, I've come," I said, "to discuss my plans with you, and to beg you to ask your father to give me a letter of recommendation for your uncle, the provincial of San Diego,[12] so that he'll admit me; because this is urgent, and waiting is dangerous, since as soon as I get a certificate of admission, my father will stop being angry and will look at me differently."

"Well, that's the least I can do," Pelayo told me. "Come by early tomorrow, because I will have my father write the letter tonight."

---

[12] [Provincial of San Diego: the provincial is the superior in a province (jurisdictional division) of a Roman Catholic religious order. San Diego was the province of the *Dieguinos,* a strictly obser-vant order formed within the Franciscan movement. The monastery of San Diego (today con-verted into a museum, the Pinacoteca Virreinal) sits on the western edge of the Alameda park in central Mexico City. –Tr.]

With this consolation, I left Martín, feeling happy, and went home.

When I went inside, I saw we had visitors: Don Martín from the hacienda; his wife, the lady who had given me that wallop; their daughter; and the famous Januario or Juan Largo. The whole family had come on a trip to Mexico, for everything grows irksome in this world, so that those who live in cities look for entertainment in the countryside, and those who live in the country yearn to entertain themselves in the city; yet neither group manages to satisfy their desires for long; for sadness does not reside in the city nor in the country, but in the heart, and so our boredom and worries follow us wherever our hearts may go.

After I had greeted the visitors and we had finished paying the courtesies then in fashion, I stepped aside into the corridor with Januario, and we spoke at length about various matters, with the greater part of the conversation dealing with my life; I told him about my adventures and my latest resolution to become a friar, to which Juan Largo quickly replied, "Yes, yes, Periquillo, become a friar, my boy, become a friar; you couldn't do better than that. Not everybody does what he should; most do what suits them best for their personal ends: one guy gets ordained because he's useless for anything else, or to keep from losing a chaplaincy; another marries the first woman he sees just to avoid conscription, though he has no love for her and no money to support her with; another joins the army so that the civil authorities won't pursue him for thieving or some misdeed he's committed; and finally, people do a thousand things that they find disagreeable, just to avoid some turn or other that they think will be worse for them; so, what'd be so new or so strange if you joined the friars to avoid learning a trade or becoming a soldier? Yes, Perico, you're doing it right; I love your determination; but step lively, brother, step lively and get it over with, the quicker the better."

Thus the great man concluded his sermon. He clearly told me many truths; but they were half-truths. If, after telling me all this, he had gone on to say that such people are not doing anything just nor worthy of an upright man, and that usually the tricks and contrivances they use to evade punishment, to get out of working, to fool their superiors, or to avoid some misfortune that they see (or think they see) approaching, are nothing but palliatives and placebos, which, after taken, turn to horrible poisons whose dire consequences they will regret for the rest of their lives—if he had told me this, I repeat, then perhaps, perhaps he might have made me open my eyes and back down from my attempt to become a friar, for which I had neither temperament nor vocation; but unfortunately for me, the first friends I had were bad ones, and consequently, their advice was even worse.

The next day I went to Pelayo's house, where he handed me his father's recommendation; his father, not content with giving it to me, thinking me a very virtuous young man, promised to go speak in my favor with his brother the provincial, so that he would dispense with all the exams and delays suffered by those who aspire to wear the habit in such austere religious orders.

It seems that I was being helped along by what they call rogue's luck, because everything advanced smoothly in accordance with my desires.

I received the letter gratefully, thanked my friend for his efforts, and went home again.

CHAPTER 11

PERIQUILLO DONS THE FRIAR'S HABIT AND REGRETS IT ON THE SAME DAY; WITH OTHER RELEVANT AND ENTERTAINING STORIES

I spent that whole day waiting quite contentedly for the next morning to come, when I would go see the provincial. I did not want to go that very afternoon, because I wanted to give Pelayo's father time to put in a word for me as he had promised.

Nothing particular happened that day, and bright and early the next morning, I left for the San Diego monastery. Passing through the empty Alameda,[1] I stopped in front of a tree and made it stand for the provincial in my imagination; and there I began to practice how I would speak to him in a submissive tone, with my head bowed, eyes lowered, and both my hands hidden in the crown of my hat.

With these and all the other outward shows of humility that hypocrisy could suggest, I went on to the monastery.

I arrived and wandered around the cloisters asking for the prelate's cell; they pointed it out to me; I knocked, entered, and found the father provincial seated at his desk, on which sat an open book that, no doubt, he had been reading before my arrival.

After greeting him I kissed his hands with all the formalities I had just been practicing, and delivered to him the letter of recommendation from his brother. He read it and, looking me over from head to toe, asked me if I wanted to be a friar in that monastery.

"Yes, father," I replied.

"And do you know," he continued, "what it means to be a friar, and how strictly we observe the Rule of Our Father St. Francis? Have you thought that over?"

"Yes, father," I replied.

"And what moves you to come here and shut yourself up in these cloisters, secluding yourself from the world, now that you are in the flower of your youth?"

"Father," I said, "the desire to serve God."

"And a very good desire that is, I think," the provincial said; "but why can't you serve God in the world? Not all the righteous nor all the saints have served Him in monasteries. The mansions of our Heavenly Father are many, and many the paths by which He calls His chosen. Concerning the gift of grace, all social stations and all places on Earth are appropriate for serving God. There have been married saints, celibate saints, widowed saints, anchorite saints, courtier saints, idiot saints, learned saints; doctors, lawyers, craftsmen, beggars, soldiers, and rich men have been saints; in a word, there have been saints from every walk of life. It therefore follows that to serve God, you do not need to be a friar, but rather to observe His holy law; and that law can be followed in palaces, in offices, on streets, in workshops, in stores, in the countryside, in cities, in barracks, on ships, and even in the midst of the synagogues of the Jews and the mosques of the Moors. Taking religious vows is the most perfect

---

[1] [The Alameda: the oldest public park in Mexico City, eight blocks west of the central plaza. –Tr.]

life; but unless it is embraced with true vocation, it is not the surest life. Many men have been damned in the cloisters who might have been saved in the secular world. The thing is not simply to start off well; constancy is required. No one achieves the crown of triumph except by struggling vigorously to the end. At your age, you must mistrust these religious impulses or passions, which rarely turn out to be more than a grass fire, going out as easily as it is lit. Thus it happens that many men do not take vows, or if they do profess, they do it because of the old *what-will-people-say;* and since they profess unwillingly, they become bad friars and disobedient libertines who, with their vices and apostasies, give more work to their superiors, scandalize the laymen, and, along the way, discredit the holy orders. For as St. Teresa says, and it is clearly true: the world wants those who follow virtue to be quite perfect; it forgives them nothing; it observes, notices, and criticizes everything about them most scrupulously; and so it is that the men of the world easily excuse the grossest vices of their fellow laymen; but they are terribly scandalized if they notice any vice in some friar or another, or some soul dedicated to virtue. They scream to high heaven, and speak out not only against the friar who scandalized them, but against the honor of the entire order, without weighing in the scales of justice the many righteous and orderly men they see in the same order, or even in the same monastery. So that young people without the vocation for it will not be lost by embracing a way of life that can certainly not be one of leisure, but of constant work, and so that we prelates may fulfill our obligations and not allow our orders to be discredited through their bad sons, we must examine the spirits of our candidate prudently and exactingly, even before they enter as novices; for the novitiate is a time for them to experience life in the order; but the prelate should examine their spirits even before they become novices. By virtue of all this, if you want to serve God in our order, do you know that the first thing you have to renounce is your will, since you are to have no will other than that of your superiors, whom you must obey blindly?"

"Yes, father," I said.

"Do you know that you have to renounce the world and all its pomp and vanities forever, just as you promised in baptism?"

"Yes, father."

"Do you know that you are not coming here to be idle nor to have fun, but to work and keep busy all day long?"

"Yes, father."

And "yes, father," and "yes, father," I replied to about seventy "do-you-knows" that he asked me, so that I thought my time had come and I was already receiving the sacrament; the upshot of this whole examination was that he gave me my certificate on the spot, telling me to ask my father to come see his reverence.

My studied words and my hypocrisies were so well done that the good prelate swallowed them whole and formed a favorable opinion of me. Well, of course: he was a good man, I was a rogue, and I've mentioned before how easily rogues fool upright men, especially when they catch them unawares.

The blessed provincial hugged me as I took my leave and said, "Go with God, dear child, and pray to Him to keep you for His good purposes, if that be best for His greater glory and the good of your soul. Tell Him every day, with all your fervor,

Confirma hoc Deus!, quod operatus es in nobis,[2] and dispose your heart a little more each day to receive the fertilizing grace of the Holy Spirit, that it may produce the finest fruits of virtue."

With this, I kissed his hand and returned home.

Who would believe that when I left the monastery, I felt a certain goodness in myself—that I thought I really had a vocation for the religious life? I could not forget the old prelate's venerable visage, his words, so penetrating and full of devotion, which echoed so strongly in my heart, his prudence, his likeable character, and the bewitching totality of his true virtue, which could have won over vice itself.

"Indeed," I said to myself, "what a stroke of luck: that I was born to be a friar but didn't know it, and that God should have made use of this accident to subdue me and set me on the path that's best for me! No doubt about it, that must be it. I remember hearing it said that God can draw straight lines with twisted rulers, and this must be one of them, no two ways about it."

These and other such arguments filled my imagination as I walked home from the monastery.

When I arrived, I went in to see my mother and told her everything that had happened to me, showing her my certificate admitting me to the monastery of San Diego. As soon as my mother saw it, I don't know how she did not go crazy with pleasure, believing that I was a very good lad and would become another St. Philip of Jesus at the least.[3] There is no reason to doubt my mother's surprise or be amazed by it; since she found my transgressions so charming, and my virtues so bright, what else could she have thought?

My father came in from the street, and my mother, full of jubilation, thrust all my plans upon him, showing him, at the proper time, the provincial's certificate.

"You see, dear?" she told him. "See how the lion is not as fierce as it's made out to be? See how Pedrito wasn't as bad as you said? As a boy, he's been very mischievous, but what boy isn't? You wanted him to be a saint from the day he was born; and it was a good wish, dear, but not a very wise one. How can children start from where we've finished? You have to give these things time. Now you see how suddenly he's changed. Did you ever expect it? Just yesterday you were saying that Pedro was a rogue, and today you see how he's become a saint; yesterday you thought he'd be the black sheep of his lineage, and today you can see he'll be the most illustrious in the family, because a family that counts a friar among its members cannot be of obscure origins; at least, that's how I understand it, and I will hold on to that faith and belief,

---

[2] "Oh God! Confirm what Thou hast wrought within us." –E. [This line is chanted by a newly ordained ecclesiastic as part of the ordination service. –Tr.]

[3] [St. Philip of Jesus (San Felipe de Jesús): the first Mexican martyr and patron of the Archdiocese of Mexico. He is described as an impetuous youth who traveled to Manila to join the Franciscan missionary effort there; tiring of the constraints of the order, he returned to Mexico after his novitiate, only to change his mind and become ordained in the monastery of Santo Domingo. On his return trip to Manila, a storm blew the ship to Japan, where he and his companions were executed in 1597. He was beatified soon after his martyrdom and was popularly considered a saint in Mexico, though he was not officially recognized as a saint of the Church until 1862. –Tr.]

even if they tell me (as they already have) that this is a preconception of those who have deeper roots in America than in other parts of the world; but I don't believe it: I think that, if a family has a friar for a relative, you can reckon it every bit as noble as Prester John of the Indies, without having to look at pedigrees or genealogies or any of the other trifles that we nobles like to boast, because those are things that only the members and friends of the house know; but everybody else, who doesn't see them, cannot know whether they are noble or not. But it's different if you have a friar for a relative, because that's something everyone can see, and no one can doubt that he is noble, and then so are his parents, his grandparents, great-grandparents, and great-great-grandparents; and, if the friar could get married, his children, grand-children, great-grandchildren, and great-great-great-grandchildren would be noble—very, very noble. So tell me if I'm not right to be happy, and if you shouldn't be happy, too, about Pedrito's new resolution."

Through a little hole in the door, I had been listening in and spying on this whole scene, and I saw that my father was reading and re-reading and looking over the cer-tificate, once, twice, three times; and I even noticed how he made to rub his eyes more than once, even though he had no sleep to rub from them. So dubious was he of my telling the truth that he could hardly believe what he was reading!

Despite his surprise, he heard my mother's speech quite well; and when she fin-ished, he said, "God help you, dear, but you are naïve! How much nonsense can you say all at one time? If anybody had been listening to us, I would be ashamed; because truly noble families, such as yours, have no need to appear noble by scheming to place a child in a religious order, nor do they show it off when they do have one; rather, that kind of scheming and showing off are clear signs that they are not recog-nized as noble, or at least that they have no other way of proving it; and it's a very risky way of doing it, open to a thousand ruses; but that's not important for now, for in any case, true nobility consists of virtue. That is its touchstone and its legitimate proof, not fancy positions, whether religious or lay, because we often see those filled by people who, because of their poor morals and so on, are unworthy of holding them. The important thing for now is this certificate. I'm astonished, and I cannot figure out how this has come about. Yesterday Pedro was so profligate and errant that he continually skipped his classes to go scalawagging with his friends; today, could he be so obedient and virtuous that he wants to be a friar and join the strictest and most observant order? Yesterday he was so lazy that, even though he was supposed to be studying theology, he put up thousands of stumbling blocks; today, could he be so resolved to work for a community? Yesterday so dissolute, and today so retiring? Yesterday one way, today completely the other? I can't understand it. I haven't forgot-ten that God is mighty and can do whatever He wants; I am quite aware that He made a saint out of Mary Magdalene and a confessor out of Dismas,[4] turned Saul into Paul and Aurelius into Augustine, and other sinners into as many humble ser-vants who have constructed His church; but such cases are hardly common, because it is rare for a sinner to heed the calls of grace; the normal thing is to scorn them

---

[4] [St. Dismas (San Dimas) is the traditional name given to the "Good Thief," one of the two thieves crucified at the same time as Jesus, as told in Luke 23:39–43. –Tr.]

continually, which is why the world is so lost. I don't know why this strikes me as one of Pedro's tricks. . . . "

"Hush," my mother said; "since you don't love the poor boy, even if he performs miracles you'll think they're bad. You believe his faults too easily, even when you don't see them for yourself; but you doubt his virtue, even when you see it in front of you. That's just what they say: 'pretend the dog has rabies, and most likely they'll kill it.' "

"What are you talking about, dear?" my father said. "What virtue should I see here? What have I ever seen in Pedro?"

"What better proof of virtue can you have than this certificate?" my mother said.

"No, this certificate is no proof of virtue," my father replied. "What it proves is that he had the skill to fool the provincial enough to get this from him, for his own purposes."

"You must be saying and doing all this to get out of spending money on his habit and his profession of vows; but you won't have to squeeze anything from your stones to spend on my son. He still has his uncles; and otherwise, I will go beg for the money he needs."

So asserted my mother, to whom my father prudently replied, "Don't be a fool, woman. It's not the expense, it's my experience that tells me not to trust Pedro. I know his disposition, and I've examined his character, and that is why I doubt that his vocation is true. He is my son and I do love him, love him very much; but my love can't cover up what I know about him. I know that he doesn't like to work, that he enjoys freedom, friends, and luxury all too much, and that he is very flighty in his way of thinking. Besides, he's very young and has a long way to go before he really understands things. All this tells me that he'll barely last two or three months in the monastery before he sees how much work the order demands and he leaves. That is what I want to avoid, not the expense, because I've always been happy to pay every expense when it has been for his good. Nonetheless, I will gladly and willingly as ever spend whatever is necessary on this occasion, and will congratulate myself that I've done it to benefit him."

With this, the session ended, and the old couple went to their dinner.

That night my father called me in alone and asked me a thousand questions, to which I answered *Amen, amen*, as hypocritically as I had with the provincial; His Grace preached me a fine sermon, explaining what the life of a friar is like; how perfect his station is; what his duties are; how fearsome the results that await one who takes vows for such a station without having the vocation for it; and who knows what else: all of it right, true, well put, and all for my own good; but that is precisely what boys pay the least attention to, so it's no wonder that they forget it straight away. The fact is, I sat through the sermon with my eyes lowered and with such modesty that it seemed I was already a novice. I played the role so well that my father thought it was the absolute truth, and he offered to go see the father provincial for me the next day; he blessed me, I kissed his hand, and we each went to bed.

I went to sleep content and satisfied, because I had fooled them all and had escaped becoming an apprentice or a soldier.

When I woke up the next morning, my father had already left the house, and when he returned at midday, he told me in front of my mother, "Pedrito, I just saw the provincial; everything is in order, and one week from today, if God gives me license, you will join the order."

My mother rejoiced, and I pretended to rejoice more when I heard the news.

We ate, and that afternoon I went to see Pelayo and told him how well my business had gone. He congratulated me as follows: "I am happy, brother, that everything has gone so well for you. The thing for you is to put up with the friars' peculiarities, especially during your novitiate year, because I can assure you that they have first-class oddities; and the matter of getting up in the middle of the night, praying all day long, speaking little, fasting a lot, whipping yourself raw, sweeping the cloisters, studying, and tolerating all those serious friars your whole life long, is an endless job, an everlasting worry, a continual servitude, and an uninterrupted series of chores from which only death can free you; but, in the end, you've gone and done it, and now you've got to bite your tongue; because otherwise, what will your father say? What will your mother say? What will your relatives say? What will the provincial say? What will the acquaintances of your house say? What will my father say? What will everybody say? If you were to repent now, it would be a scandal for the public, a dishonor for you, and a horrible shame for your parents; so there's no two ways, brother; what's done is done, as the saying goes, so make the best of it; now you've got to become a friar, like it or not."

There are some men whose characters are so venomous that they do evil even when they think they are doing good. They are like the cat that scratches when it shows affection. Such was Pelayo's character; after telling me how highly he regarded me, it seems he always went out of his way to cause me trouble or pain; for he first painted monastic life to me as a paradise on earth, and then after I had committed myself to it, he represented it to me as a dungeon, discrediting it from either side.

I took leave of him feeling quite saddened, and was just about to withdraw from my plot; but a touch of shame, and that *what-will-they-say* of the world, which is the reason we almost always disregard the laws of God, made me compel my inclinations, set aside my fears, and go forward with my false and foolhardy effort.

During that week, we prepared everything I would need for joining the order; all my friends, relatives, acquaintances, well-wishers, and ill-wishers were informed, and my father received a thousand congratulations from them, and my mother a thousand felicitations, which together add up to 2,000 empty pieces of blather—or as we say, politeness, etiquette, and formality—which altogether contain not an ounce of anything useful, for all that their numbers multiply.

My parents were busy that week receiving visits and preparing everything I would need to take my vows, and I was busy going around with Pelayo, taking leave of the ladies in our social gatherings, with no little pain in my heart, for I deeply regretted this abrupt separation from my sinful distractions.

My wonderful Pelayo took it upon himself to announce my new intentions wherever we went, and to tell them how soon I would become a novice. I begged him to keep it quiet, but he felt it would be a burden on his conscience to keep it to himself, and since all the houses we visited were those of frivolous folk, they gave me a terrible going-over, especially the women. One lady said to me, "Ay, what a pity! You're too young a boy to be locking yourself up!"

Another, "How funny! And so young."

Another, "Won't you remember me?"

Another, "You aren't really going to take those vows?"

This one, "I don't think you're made for being a friar: too young, not ugly enough, and too funny."

The other, "A dancer and a friar? Come on, I don't believe you."

And so on, with all the women; and whenever someone uttered a few wicked tales or obscene words (which they did constantly), one of the women would mock me tastelessly, "Ay, girl! How can you say such a thing? Hush up, don't bother the servant of God here."

Despite all the jokes, I had as much fun as possible, as my way of saying goodbye. I turned a deaf ear to them, and danced, played the mandolin, chatted, seduced, and did things that are best left in silence. Such were the preparatory exercises in which I spent the week prior to my friarization. So it happened.

Not content with my allotted freedom to be out in the street until eight at night (the appointed bedtime for a future friar), nor satisfied with the merrymaking set up for me by my teacher Pelayo, my own festive nature, and the flightiness of the ladies we visited, I still aspired to seduce Poncianita, the daughter of Don Martín the hacienda owner, who visited my house daily; but the girl was virtuous, discreet, and playful. She knew my character well, and took me to be what I was—that is, a rakish and wicked lad, but in reality a fool; so she always responded to my shows of affection and endearment, but in a great variety of ways, and she always made me think she loved me. Therefore, being both more wicked and more foolish than she, I thought I might manage to conquer her some day; but she, being more honorable and more quick-witted than I, knew that day would never come, and indeed it did not.

One day I passed a note to her that contained a string of foolish, flirtatious remarks, and ended by assuring her of my good intentions and saying that, if I were not about to enter the monastery, there was no one I would rather marry than her. Here you can tell quite well what sort of person I was, and how compatible utter ignorance is with utter wickedness; but what deserved the most applause was the droll response she wrote to my message, which went:

> Sir: I appreciate your good intentions, and if I could, I would reciprocate; but I am in love with another young gentleman; yet if I were not, there is no one I would rather marry than you, even if it meant getting a dispensation. May God make you a good friar, and give you good luck in your struggles.
>
> –You-know-who.

I can scarcely exaggerate how agitated I felt on receiving this message. She had made me jealous, made me fall in love, and made me furious, in such a way that I could hardly sleep that night, the last night before I was to enter the monastery. How inflamed could my passions be? But dawn came at last, and as I began to see other objects, the uproar within me subsided.

Afternoon arrived; I took leave of my mother, aunts, and family friends, all of whom I embraced contritely, not forgetting to show the same courtesy to Mistress Poncianita, who reciprocated my embrace with some disdain, since her mother was present, and she did not really love me as she had expressed.

After we finished with the string of embraces, tears, and fooleries, we set out for the monastery: my father, myself, my uncles, and several guests who were to serve as witnesses to my hypocrisy.

Luck—my bad luck—soon presaged my misfortune, as I saw it; for the silence in which we traveled, and the long series of coaches that followed our own, seemed like nothing so much as a funeral procession, and all those who saw us on the streets thought the same. Indeed, they would have been perfectly right to give their condolences to me and my parents.

We arrived at San Diego; the father provincial was notified; he received us with his accustomed good character and joined us in the coach in which I rode with my father; we turned then towardTacubaya, where San Diego has its novitiate house.[5]

After we stepped down at the door of the monastery, all our things were arranged, and we went to the choir of the church, where the ceremony took place. I put on the habit, but I did not take off my bad qualities; I found myself dressed as a friar and mixing with them, but I did not feel the slightest inward change: I remained as bad as ever, and then I experienced for myself the saying that "the habit doesn't make the monk."

My father took leave of me and of that venerable community; the other guests did the same; and Juan Largo gave me a huge embrace, at which time I told him: "Don't forget to come and see me." He promised he would; everyone left; and there I was, alone and bashful among the friars, or as the saying goes, like a dog in the wrong neighborhood, tail between my legs.

The coarseness of the woolen tunic immediately felt odd to me. Refectory time came, and the frugality of the supper offended me. I went to bed, and could find no way to make myself comfortable; the plank bed hurt me all over, and since I had never tried out these kinds of mortifications, not even on a lark, I felt them all too sharply.

I turned over and over and could not sleep, thinking about Poncianita, *La Zorra*, *La Cucaracha*, and other vermin just like them, and I sincerely repented my decision, cursed the help I had gotten from Pelayo, and wished myself to the devil together with the recommendation that had so quickly gotten me into this prison, for that was what I called my new station; though it was not the station's fault but my own, as I was not equal to it.

"Aren't I a fine savage, and an idiot to boot," I said to myself, "for sentencing myself, of my own free will, to this frightful jail cell and this miserable life? What funds have I stolen? What money have I counterfeited? What heresies have I

---

[5] [Now a neighborhood in central Mexico City, Tacubaya was then a town just outside the city limits, about three miles southwest of the Alameda. –Tr.]

preached? What house have I burned down? What dreadful crimes have I committed to suffer what I'm suffering? Who the devil put it into my head to become a friar, just to get out of being an apprentice or a soldier? Surely I would have had a better time of it in either of those jobs, because I'd be able to eat my fill whenever I wanted, and whatever I felt like eating; I could wear a shirt, even if it was just one of coarse cotton; I could sleep on a mattress (if I had one) as late as I wanted on my free days; and finally, I could enjoy my freedom, going around to dances and parties with my friends and lady acquaintances; and I wouldn't be here, with this sackcloth stuck to my hide, barefoot, underfed, lying sleepless on these hard planks, locked up, forced to work, and never seeing a girl or anything that resembles one, to top it all off. Blast me, and blast the hour when it occurred to me to be a friar!"

That was how I talked with myself, and so do all young people of both sexes, especially the miserable girls, who embrace the religious life without inspiration from God or a perfect vocation: a holy life, a peaceful, sweet and heavenly life for those called to it by grace; but a hard, difficult, hellish life for those who get themselves into it without a vocation. How many young people experience this in themselves, when the hour is too late! Be careful, my children, be very careful about mistaking your vocation, whatever it may be; be careful about entering a way of life without consulting anything beyond your immediate self-interest; and finally, be careful about taking on a burdens that you cannot bear, lest you perish under their weight.

Swearing and cursing, as I said, I fell asleep around eleven thirty at night, and had scarcely closed my eyes when the novice in charge of wake-up came into my cell and said, "Brother, brother, it is time for us to rise; let us go to Matins."

I opened my eyes, realized I had no choice but to obey, and got up, muttering a blue streak under my breath.

I went to the choir and, half asleep, grumbled through whatever I could understand of the service, and when the task was done, returned to my cell, wishing I could at least have a spot of hot chocolate at that hour, because I was certainly hungry; but there was no one I could ask to bring me some.

Deep silence reigned in that dormitory, and amid the dread that it caused me, to allay my hunger, my sleeplessness, and my desperation, I indulged myself once more in my libertine and melancholy ideas, and I became so absorbed in them that I spilled plenty of tears of rage and remorse; but sleep at last overcame me at four in the morning; but such is the luck of the lazy! I had barely begun to snore when along comes the brother novice to wake me to go to Prime.

Again I awoke filled with anger, cursing myself like a convict; but deep in my heart, without speaking a single word, saying only to myself: "Isn't this the most tedious life ever? Can you imagine anyone going to the trouble that this little friar has taken to keep me from sleeping? No doubt but he's my *ahuizote*; he's another Dr. Pedro Recio, because if the one in *Don Quixote* took each dish away from Sancho Panza as soon as he started to eat, this one comes to wake me up as soon as I fall asleep."

Thinking all this nonsense, I went to the choir, prayed louder than a blind beggar, and when I sang, I did it with my mouth open wide—but from hunger, because

I hadn't liked the supper of the night before and so had barely tasted it, and therefore my stomach was thin as a thread. I was hoping the Prime service would end so I could go get my fill of chocolate, and I promised myself it would be good and plenty, for in the lay world I had heard that the friars drink the best Caracas cocoa, and when someone had a large cup at home, they'd say: "That's a friar's mug!" So I told myself: "At least, if supper was bad, breakfast will be splendid. Yes, no doubt about it; I'll soon be blowing on a great big cup of the best chocolate, and have the biscuits to go with it, or if not, then three pennies' worth of bread spread thick with butter, at the least."

This was my holy contemplation as we finished praying and left the choir; but imagine how sad and angry I felt when the clock rang six, six thirty, seven, and no chocolate appeared; nor did it appear all morning long, for they told me it was a fast day! That was when I commended myself to Barabbas, cursing with redoubled fervor my blasted desire to become a friar; more so, when two other novices came and, showing me two leather buckets, said, "Brother, come now with us; please take these buckets and let us sweep down the monastery before it is time to go to choir."

"This gets worse and worse," I said to myself. "No sleep, nothing to eat, and they work you like a mule on a waterwheel! Is this what it means to be a novice? Is this what it means to be a friar? Me and my blasted shallowness, and the horrid advice that Pelayo and Juan Largo gave me! There's no two ways about it, I'm no friar; I've got to get out of here, because if I try to stick it out another week, the devil will carry me off from lack of sleep, hunger, and exhaustion. Yes, I've got to get out; got to get out . . . but so soon? I've barely warmed my spot, and I already want to leave? That can't be. What will everyone say? I've got to put up with it for two or three months, like someone who has to drink tobacco water, and then I'll cover it up when I leave by feigning illness—though I'll hardly have to pretend, because with a life like this, I'm likely to be sick enough, and God save me I'm not pushing daisies after spending so much time inside these holy walls. What else can we do!"

So I spoke with myself as I carried water and dumped it by the pailful over the halls, feeling all sad and crestfallen; but I was amazed to see how joyfully my companions, the other two friars who were even younger than I, swept up; as you can see, they were a virtuous pair and had entered the monastery with true vocation, not to loaf and get out of work, as I had.

One of them, the younger boy, was very joyful; his color was white, his hair was red, his little eyes very bright blue, his mouth filled with a modest smile, and since he was weary from work, he had taken on a pretty blush that made him look like a St. Anthony. He noticed how sad and dismal I looked, and, thinking it the result of my excessive austerity and the doubts that worried me, the innocent boy went up to me and said most pleasantly, "What's the problem, brother? Why are you so sad? Cheer up; you can be joyful and still serve God. Our Lord is all goodness. We are His sons, not His slaves; He wants us to love Him like a father and to adore Him as the Supreme Lord, not to cower in servile fear of Him; no, He is not our tyrant! He is a God full of sweetness, not a parricidal God like the Saturn of the pagans. His sight alone rejoices the saints and creates all the happiness in heaven. Serving Him should inspire His servants with the utmost mutual trust and good joy. Holy King

David expressly tells us: 'Serve ye the Lord with gladness,'[6] and Ecclesiasticus says: 'Drive away sadness far from thee, for sadness hath killed many, and there is no profit in it.'[7] But what else? Jesus Christ himself commanded us to 'be not as the hypocrites, sad.'[8] So cheer up, brother, rejoice and get rid of your doubts and baneful ideas, which neither honor God nor profit our souls."

I thanked the good young friar for his advice, and I envied him his virtue, his serenity, and his joy; for there is something about sound virtue that endears itself to even the wicked.

Time came for Mass at the monastery, and we went to the choir. Then I noticed that some of the fathers I had seen around the monastery were not present. I asked why, and was told that they were dignified fathers who had retired or were exempt from attendance at community events. That consoled me somewhat, for I thought: "In case I do take vows, which I doubt, when I become a dignified father, I'll finally be free of all this." We went to the choir.

---

6 [Psalms 99:2 (100:2). –Tr.]
7 [Ecclesiasticus 30:24–25. –Tr.]
8 [Matthew 6:16. –Tr.]

CHAPTER 12

ON ADVICE, GOOD AND BAD; THE DEATH OF PERIQUILLO'S FATHER; AND HIS LEAVING THE MONASTERY

I stayed in the choir for Terce and Mass, but paid them as much attention as the lectern did. It all passed me by while I nodded my head, blinked my heavy lids, and yawned as if I had neither eaten nor slept. The officiating friar noticed, and when we left he said to me, "Brother, one might think that you are more than a bit slack; you had best mend your ways, since this is no place for sleeping."

I couldn't help feeling annoyed, being unaccustomed to such scoldings; but I dared not say a word in reply. I passed through the chapel and went back to cleaning my holy barracks.

The blessed hour for refectory arrived, and though it was a communal meal, it tasted to me like manna from heaven, since hunger is the best cook.

In the end, bit by bit, I got used to suffering a friar's labors and a novice's imprisonment, and to having a perpetually empty stomach, comforting my sleepy eyes, stimulating my work-weary limbs, and tolerating the other hardships of the religious life, in the hopes that after putting up with it for six months, I might feign illness and get back to the garlics and cabbages I had left in the street.

These hopes were encouraged by my father's visits from time to time; but even more by the ever-Christian, prudent, and charitable advice of my two mentors, Januario and Pelayo, who used to come see me by permission of the father in charge of us novices, to whom my father had recommended them. One of them would say, "Quite right, Perico, getting out of here is the best thing you could do. Just two days, and look how skinny, sad, and sickly you've gotten: all you need is a sheet pulled over you, and no doubt somebody'd come along to bury you—these blessed friars would be glad to do it, too; for all their sanctimoniousness, they're rather unbearable and short on judgment. They seem to think a novice should turn into a candidate for sainthood just like that; they notice everything, they punish everything; they don't forgive or forget anything; you can tell that none of the teachers here can remember ever being a novice himself."

That was what the less wicked of my friends, Pelayo, used to tell me; while that devil Juan Largo was worse; he blasphemed every monk and friar in the world; and you can only imagine the terms he used, if he managed to shock me, being a bit worse than Barabbas myself.

It will certainly not do to set down on paper everything he said about all the religious orders, especially about mine, though my order was scarcely to blame for the fact that a rogue such as myself should have joined it without vocation or virtue, simply to avoid my father's just designs; but through his advice, you may infer the depths of wickedness that his heart concealed.

"Don't be a fool," he'd say, "just make a run for it, head for the street; don't stick around till you start liking it here, because then you might up and take vows, which is as good as burying yourself alive. You're a boy, savage! Get out and enjoy the world. The girls you went with are always asking me about you; my cousin has been crying constantly—she misses you, and says she wishes you weren't a friar, because she'd like to marry you. So come on, run for it, Periquillo, my boy, get out and marry Poncianita; she's Don Martín's only daughter and she's loaded with pesos. Now, while she loves you; you've got to take your chance, because if she loses hope that you might leave, and then falls in love with someone else, you'll lose it all. If only I weren't her cousin! You'd better believe I wouldn't be giving you this advice then, because I'd be taking it for myself; but I can't get married to her, and in the end she's going to marry somebody or other, and that somebody should be none other than you, my good friend, because if the Moors are about to steal something, better that the Christians steal it first. What do you say to that? What can I tell you? When are you going to take off?"

I was clumsy enough as it was, but after all this scoundrel's visits and persuasions, I grew more and more corrupted, until I became so slovenly that I didn't do a single thing right, as the rule of obedience ordered me. If I were to serve as acolyte, I would stand restlessly by the altar, my head spinning like a windmill, as I turned my eyes to gaze at every woman who entered the church; if I were to sweep the monastery, I would do it very badly; if I served food in the refectory, I would break the plates and bowls; if I had to go to some service in the choir, I would fall asleep; in a word, I did everything badly, because I did everything against my will. So it was a rare day I wouldn't enter the refectory wearing a pillow, a broom, or a pottery shard, together with a blindfold or some other sign of my wicked ways—or of the friars' ridiculous punishments, as I liked to say.

The first few days, the saddle chafed me a little;[1] that is, I was annoyed by such farces and mockeries, as I called them, though the proper term is *penitences;* but after a while I began to grow accustomed to them, until it no more bothered me to walk into the choir wearing a string of cobblestones around my neck than it would have to wear a rosary in Jerusalem.

So, between falling down and getting back up again, and driving the blessed friars to distraction, I managed to finish six months of my novitiate, which was what I had fixed on from the beginning as the time I would head for the street and return to my wanderings in the secular world. I was busy thinking what disease would be good to contract (or to pretend I had contracted) in order to whitewash my fickleness, and had finally settled on epilepsy and was just about to give my father's sensitive heart the fatal blow by writing him of my decision to leave, when Januario arrived with the sad news that my father was seriously ill, and that the doctors had declared his case hopeless.

This news grieved me, and I endeavored to hasten my departure; but Januario stopped me, saying that there was still plenty of time and that I should hold off on my resolution for the moment, because it would make nothing better, and it might happen that this new affliction would make my father take a turn for the worse, and that my haste might shorten his days; so I should calm down, and later, whether my father lived or died, I could go through with it more successfully and with fewer obstacles.

---

[1] Periquillo could scarcely get away with this comparison with horses, if it were not that he is speaking of himself. –E.

That is what I did, and I confess that he convinced me; for, bad as he was, on this occasion he counseled me like an upright man.

My children, men are like books. You know that no book is so bad that there is no good in it; likewise with men: no man is so perverse that he does not, on rare occasions, have some good sentiments; and in this sense, the greatest sinner, the most dissolute libertine, can give us sound and edifying advice.

Five days after my conversation with Januario, Don Martín came to see me. Preparing my spirit with consoling words that his sense of charity suggested to him, he gave me a sealed letter from my father, together with the news of his passing.

Nature squeezed my heart, and my tears displayed my feelings in abundance. Don Martín repeated his consolations, and went to give the father provincial alms to say Mass for the departed. The curate, the choristers, and my fellow novices entered my cell and consoled me with the help of religion; and after my sorrow had abated somewhat, they retreated to their tasks. Two days went by before I dared open the letter, for every time I thought of opening it, I would read its little envelope, which said: "To my dear son Pedro Sarmiento. May God keep you in His Grace for many years to come." Then my heart would shudder terribly and I could do nothing but kiss it and dampen it with my tears, for those few letters reminded me of the love that he had always felt for me, and of his constant virtue, which always inspired me.

Oh, children! How true it is that we only recognize a good father, a good wife, a good friend, when death has closed their eyes! I knew my father was good, but I didn't really recognize it until I received news of his passing. Then, in a single glance I saw his prudence, his love, his wisdom, his congeniality, and all his virtues, and at the same time I came to see the teacher, the brother, the friend, and the father I had lost.

On the third day, I opened the letter, the contents of which I read so many times that it remained in my memory; and as the document is a worthy inheritance from your grandfather, I wish to leave it written down here for you.

> Dear son: From the edge of the tomb I am writing you this letter, which, according to my wishes, will be delivered to you after this body of mine is buried.
>
> I have no goods to leave your poor mother other than a handful of coins and the sparse furniture in the house, that she may spend the few days of her sad widowhood unburdened by worries; as for you, dear son, what can I leave you but these maxims, written in my trembling and moribund hand, by which I have tried to inspire you all my life? Make room for them in your heart and be sure to bring them to mind often. Observe them, and you will never regret it.
>
> Love God, fear Him, and recognize Him as your Father, your Lord, and your Benefactor.
>
> Be loyal to your country, and respect the established authorities.
>
> Behave toward everyone as you would have them behave toward you.
>
> Harm no one, and never neglect to do whatever good you can.

Do not upset your mother nor provoke her weeping, for the tears spilled by a mother over her bad son cry out to God for vengeance against him.

Never scorn the outcries of the poor, and may they find a shelter from their poverty in your heart.

Do not judge men's merit by their outward appearance, for most often that is deceptive.

Never make it your goal to distinguish yourself in anything.

If you profess in your holy order, never forget the vows by which you will have dedicated yourself to God.

Do not strive to achieve the honorary positions in the order, and do not be saddened if you fail to achieve them, for that is inappropriate to a true religious who has abandoned the world and its pomp.

If you become a father, teacher, or prelate, do not forget the observance of your Rule;[2] rather, you should then be even more modest in your habit, more punctual at choir, and more edifying in all matters, for it would be unreasonable of you to demand that those under you comply strictly with their duties, if your example teaches them otherwise.

Do not get mixed up in the affairs and assemblies of laymen, that your laxity might scandalize them; for a friar who looks right in choir, in cloisters, at the altar, pulpit, or confessional, looks out of place on a stroll or at a gathering, in a gaming room, dance, bullring, or sitting room.

Do not let the tufts of hair around your tonsure grow out until you look like a pheasant or peacock, for that style alone shows how little religious spirit a friar has, and declares out loud how attached he is to the world and its ways.

Finally, if you do not profess, keep the precepts of the Ten Commandments in whatever walk of life you find yourself. These are few, easy, useful, necessary, and profitable. They are based in both natural and divine law. What they demand of us is just; what they prohibit is in our own benefit and that of our fellows; nothing about them is awkward, except to profligates and libertines; and finally, except by observing them, it is impossible to achieve inner peace in this life, nor eternal happiness in the next.

Remember this, then, please; and remember that within a short time you will be on the path that your father is now entering. His blessings and God's be with you forever. At the gate to eternity, your loving father.

–Manuel.

---

2 [Father (i.e., priest), teacher, prelate: these are public roles that friars could play in "the world"— that is, outside of the confines of the monastery—while still being bound by "the Rule": that is, the laws governing their order. –Tr.]

This letter had no effect on me other than to sadden me for a time, without its truths going deeply into my heart, which yet lacked the disposition to receive such healthy seed.

Two weeks passed, and in that short time, I all but forgot my feelings at the death of my father and the warnings in his letter (that is, the remorseful spirit in which I first read it), and could remember only the freedom that I craved.

At the end of this time, Januario came to bring me a message from my mother, saying she had been left sad and bereft in her solitude; and he told me it was time to move ahead with my plans, for with the death of my father there was nothing to stop me from leaving; in fact, it might be a consolation for my mother; and other such advice, with which I soon made up my mind.

I showed Januario my father's letter; as soon as he read it, he burst out laughing, and said, "It's a great sermon, no doubt about it; brother, your father sure picked the wrong vocation. He would have made a better missionary than a married man; but they say that advice and mustaches have gone out of style. It's a wonderful inheritance, though I wouldn't give a penny for it. If your father had left you a coin for every piece of advice, you would have had something to thank him for; because one good peso, my friend, is worth more than ten gross of warnings. Keep the letter, and get yourself out of here so you can see what you can do with what your father left behind; because otherwise, what is your mother going to do? In a couple of days, she'll go through it, and it will be gone, and neither you nor she will be able to enjoy it."

I thanked him for what I took to be his good advice, and told him to suggest to my mother that I might be leaving, giving her the pretext of my illness and of how useful I might be by her side. Januario offered to carry out the deed and to return the next day with her answer.

I could hardly keep still, awaiting my mother's resolution—not because I wanted to get her consent, for I did not think it necessary, but so that I could bind her affections and get her to hand over to me unreservedly the scant means that my father had left behind, and so that she would trust me as if I were a good son.

Everything went according to plan, and the next day Januario returned to tell me it was all on course; he had gone on about my ersatz illness to my mother, telling her that I cried constantly for her; that I wanted to leave, not so much for my health as to serve her and keep her company; but that I was waiting to hear her opinion, because I was such a good son that I would never make a move without her approval. My mother replied that she would welcome my leaving, for my health was more important than anything else, and one can serve God anywhere.

"No sooner said than done," I said when I heard the message. "Tomorrow we'll eat together, Januario. . . ."

"And go visit Poncianita first thing," he told me, "because that devil of a girl's looking prettier day by day."

We spent the allotted time until the next bell in these and other such edifying conversations; the bell tolled and Januario left, while I stayed waiting for night to fall so that I could notify the father who headed the novitiate about my decision.

Night came at last, later than usual, it seemed to me. As soon as I had a chance, I entered the father superior's cell; I told him that I was ill, and that, in addition, my mother had been left widowed and impoverished, and that I was her only son, so I planned to return to the lay world; so I asked him to please have my clothes returned to me.

The good friar listened to me with the patience of a saint, and said that he would see what he could do; that these were temptations from the devil; that if I were ill, the monastery had doctors and medicines, and that they could treat my illness as well there as at home; that if my mother was left widowed and impoverished, she had not lost God, who is the Father of us all and never forsakes His creatures; and finally, that I should think it over.

"I have already thought it over, father," I said, "and there's no other way; I've got to leave, because the religious life isn't fit for me, and I'm not fit for religion."

These words angered the reverend father, and he said, "Religious life is fine for everyone who is fine with it; but you are quite right to say that you are not fit for religion, as I have suspected several times in the past. God go with you. Early tomorrow I will inform our father provincial, and you may go home or wherever you will."

I retired from his sight, and that night I did not feel like going to choir and refectory (nor did they insist on my going, either), and between nine and ten the following morning, the father superior called me in, solemnly stripped me of my habit, and gave me my clothes. I left for the streets, heading immediately toward Mexico.

After I had rested for a bit on a bench in the Alameda, and had shaken off the dust of the road I had walked from Tacubaya, I headed home with my cloak wrapped around me and my scarf tied around my head, filled with confusion, thinking it was almost as if I were excommunicated and separated from those servants of God. I cannot describe the dread that overcame my heart every time I turned my head and saw the sacred walls of San Diego, storehouse of the virtue and quietude from which I was withdrawing.

"No doubt about it," I said to myself, "I've just left a refuge of innocence; I've abandoned the only plank I might have held on to in the shipwreck of this mortal life. God will see me as ungrateful, and men will scorn me as fickle. . . . Oh, if only I could go back!"

I was lost in these serious meditations, when one of my old companions recognized me and tugged on my cloak; with him was one of the most forward coquettes I had ever flirted with before I entered the monastery.

After the three of us had greeted each other, he asked me when I had left, and why. I replied that I had left that very day, because of the death of my father and my own illness. They thought I had done the right thing, and took me to have breakfast at a cheap tavern, where I ate like crazy and drank every bit as much, and with the help of this meal, drove away my sorrows.

They took leave of me, and I went home. As soon as my mother saw me, she began to hug me and to weep bitterly; but she declared herself happy to have me back in her company. Who could have told her that her troubles would begin from that day forth, and that far from lending her the promised consolation and relief, I would become a fatal burden upon her? But so it happened, as you will see in the next chapter.

You are about to learn, gentle reader—and learn so that you can tell the story—that when I was at home the other night, pen in hand, scribbling the notes for this little book, one of my friends, one of the few who are worthy of being called friends, walked in: a fellow of advanced age and profound experience, named *Understanding;* on seeing him, I jumped to my feet to show him the customary courtesies that politeness demands.

He replied in kind and, sitting down on my right, said: "Please continue with your work, if it is anything urgent, because I simply came to visit out of friendship."

"No, sir, it is nothing urgent," I said, "and even if it were, I would gladly interrupt it for the sake of your welcome conversation, for I rarely have the honor of a visit from you; and I appreciate this occasion even more today, since I can take advantage of it to ask what they are saying out there about *The Mangy Parrot,* for you visit many wise men, and you even honor coarser fellows such as myself from time to time."

"Are you asking me about that little book, whose first volume you recently published?"

"Yes, sir," I replied, "and I would like to know what opinion the public has formed of it, so that I may continue my labors, if they have formed a good one, or abandon it if the opposite is true."

"Well, listen, please, my friend," *Understanding* told me; "you have to realize that the public is everyone and no one; that it is composed of the wise and the ignorant; that each person holds fast to his own opinion; that it is morally impossible to please the public—that is, to please all of them at once; and that if the fool acclaims a work, the wise man will only approve of it by coincidence, and by the same token, if the wise man applauds something, it will be a miracle if the fool acclaims it. Since these platitudes are as true as they are old, let me tell you that your book is going through the same trials in the tribunal of public opinion that all its companions have undergone—all the works in its class, I mean. Some people give it more acclaim than it deserves; others wouldn't read it for anything; and others, finally, compare it to the *Annals* of Volusius,[2] or to the thorny thistle that could only please a donkey's harsh palate. You should accept these facts as true, for as you well know, it would be easier for a honeycomb to escape a lad's sweet tooth than for the most sublime work to escape the caviler's bared fangs."

"It is true, sir, that I know all this, and I know that my poor works contain nothing that deserves the slightest applause, and I am saying this without a trace of hypocrisy, but rather with all the sincerity I feel; and I am amazed at the public's generosity when they gladly read my clumsy scribblings at their own expense, graciously forgiving the

---

[1] [This prologue was written for the second volume of the 1816 edition, which began with Chapter 13; it has appeared in various places in later editions, according to the whim of the editors. –Tr.]

[2] [An allusion to a line in Catullus, *Poems,* 36: 1 (*Annales Volusi, cacata carta*—roughly, "Annals of Volusius, soiled toilet paper"), which Lizardi found quoted in Mencke's book (Spell, p. 150). –Tr.]

ordinary thoughts, the unpolished style, and perhaps a few gross errors; so the least I can do is consider them all more judicious than Horace, who said in his *Ars Poetica* that he would pardon a few defects in a good work: *Non ego paucis offendar maculis;* and he also said that there are some defects that deserve to be pardoned: *Sunt delicta tamen quibus ignovisse velimus;*[3] but my readers, in exchange for whatever they enjoy here and there in my little books, have the patience to pardon the innumerable defects that abound in them. May God repay them and preserve the mildness of their characters. Nor am I one to aspire to having endless numbers of readers; nor do the cheers of the ignorant, novel-loving mob appeal to me. I am happy with few readers: if they are wise, their approval will do me no harm; and, not to bore you, sir, when I say all this I recall the views of Horace, John Owen, and Iriarte, and I agree with what the latter said in his fable of the dancing bear:

> If the wise man disapproves, bad;
> If the fool applauds, worse (Fable III).[4]

"True, it would be very nice to have, not more readers, but many more buyers; or at least, all the buyers it takes to pay for the printing costs and compensate me for the time I put into writing. As long as there were enough, I would be more than satisfied, even if I didn't have a single person singing my praises, recalling what the celebrated poet Owen[5] says about authors and admirers in one of his epigrams:

> Few[6] suffice, one suffices
> From whom one might crave applause;
> And if no one were to read me,
> No one would suffice as well.

"Yet despite all this sound advice, I would love to know what people think of my little book, so that I can settle accounts with my purse—don't think it is for any other reason."

"Well, friend," said *Understanding*, "it may console you to know that so far I have heard more people speaking well of it than badly."

"So there are also people speaking badly of it?" I asked.

"How could there not be?" he told me. "There have always been people who speak badly of the best works—did you think *Periquillo* could somehow laugh at all the gossips?"

---

[3] [Horace, *Ars Poetica,* verses 351–52 and 347. –Tr.]

[4] [Tomás de Iriarte, *Fábulas literarias.* Ruiz Barrionuevo (p. 293) points out that this is a loose paraphrase; Fable III ("The Bear, the Monkey, and the Pig") actually concludes: "When the monkey disapproved, / I began to doubt myself; / But since the pig has praised me, / I must dance very badly." –Tr.]

[5] [Welsh poet John Owen (1564?–1622) was famed for his witty and mordant Latin epigrams (*Epigrammatum*, 1606), which were widely translated and frequently reprinted in Europe; a Spanish translation appeared in 1682. The quotation is from the Spanish translation of Liber 2, epigram 1: *Sat mihi sunt pauci lectores, est satis unus. / Si me nemo legat, sat mihi, nullus erit.* –Tr.]

[6] Admirers.

"But what are they saying about Perico?" I asked; and he answered me:

"They say that this Perico fellow talks more than he needs to; that he looks liable to leave no stone unturned when he dresses down everybody; that he pretends to be a critic so that he can get away with slandering every class and corporation in the State, which is a wicked, dirty trick; and they ask who made him the public's pedagogue so that he could claim to rail against abuses when what he really does is satisfy his own scathing, carping character; if his goal were to teach his children, why didn't he do it like Cato the Censor,

> Who educated his son
> With a good heart,

and not with satire, criticism, and vulgarity; that, if he is publishing these scribblings to gain a reputation as an editor, they actually bring him into disrepute, because they spell out his stupidity in block letters; and if he is doing it in the hopes of making money off his readers, it is an odious and illegal business, for no one should try to make a living at the expense of his brothers' reputations; and finally, that if the author is so zealous, so well behaved, and so opposed to abuses, then why doesn't he start by reforming his own, since he clearly has plenty of them?"

"Oh, *Understanding*, sir!" I exclaimed, clenched by fear. "Is it possible that they are saying all these things?"

"Yes, my friend, they are indeed."

"But who is saying it, brother of my soul?"

"Who else do you expect," answered *Understanding*, "but those who have been embittered by the truths you have forced them to drink in the cup of fable? Who would you expect to speak well of *Periquillo*—a bad father, a mother who spoils her children, an inept tutor, a dissolute cleric, a coquette, an idler, a thief, a grifter, a hypocrite, or any of the other sinners you describe? No, my friend, there is no way those people would speak well of this work or of its author, as long as they live; but you should bear in mind that there is one tremendous advantage that you gain from having that sort of rivals, for without wishing to, they themselves will give your work a good reputation and make it clear that you are not lying in anything you write; and so, please keep on writing, and pay no attention to this sort of backbiting (because it cannot and should not be called criticism). Just repeat from time to time what you have so often proclaimed and printed—that is, that you never portray any particular person in your writing; that you only ridicule the vice, with the same laudable goal that so many valiant geniuses have had when they have done the same, both in and beyond our Spain; and to prove it to them, recite along with the divine Canary Islander (Iriarte):

> My admonishments are all meant
> For everyone, and for none:
> Blush and you just blame yourself;
> And if you don't, please hear them.
>   And since they do not censure

Anyone in particular,
If you think they apply to you,
Well—that is your own problem" (Fable I).

Saying this, *Understanding* left (for his full name is *Universal Understanding*), first adding that he was badly needed elsewhere; and I took up my pen and wrote down our conversation, so that you, my friend, my reader, might work up an appetite and then get back to reading the brief history of the famous *Mangy Parrot*.

CHAPTER 13

We are now entering the most disorderly period of my life. All my misbehavior up to now had been merest child's play compared with the offences that were to follow. I myself am aghast, and the pen falls from my hand, when I write about my scandalous conduct and recall the terrible risks I took and the turns of events that continually threatened my honor, my life, and my soul; for obviously, the more depraved a man is, the more exposed he is to greater dangers. Everyone knows that life is a constant tissue of squalor, scares, risks, and worries that menace us from every angle; but the orderly conduct of an upright man frees him from most of these, making him as happy as one can be in this miserable life; while on the other hand, a depraved and profligate man not only cannot free himself from the evils that naturally assail us: he gets himself into even more trouble through his very laxity, and calls down upon himself a shocking amount of danger and distress that he would not remotely experience if he would only live as he ought; and from this simple premise, you can see why the most depraved men are those who suffer the most adventures, and perhaps have the worst time of it even in this life. I was one of them.

For six months I stayed at home, living the most hypocritical life I could; for I recited the rosary every night, as had been my late father's custom, I rarely went outside, I went to no parties, I frequently spoke of virtues and godly things, and in a word, I played the role of an upright man so well that my mother believed it and was beside herself with happiness; but that's not half! Even Januario swallowed it whole, veteran though he was in rogueries, and he believed it so thoroughly that one day he told me: "Periquillo, I'm amazed at you: you must have been born to be a friar after all. Here I was expecting you to run out and grab the first fruits of your absolute freedom, and thinking the two of us would have our very reasonable bit of fun, but I see you shut inside and playing the anchorite in your own home." Poor Januario! My poor mother! And poor everyone, for I persuaded them all of my virtue, when what they really saw in me was the most refined wickedness!

I was trying to gain my mother's good regards, so that she would trust me entirely and not withhold the meager inheritance my father had left her, a goal that I achieved without difficulty through my wicked stratagems.

In effect, my mother revealed the bit of wealth that had been left, and even made me the administrator of the estate, which amounted to 1,600 pesos in silver coin, about 500 in recoverable debts, and around 1,000 more in jewelry and furniture. Few assets for a rich man, yet a very reasonable bit of principal for any poor but hardworking and upright man; but that was exactly where I was lacking, so I squandered it all in no time, as you will see.

Any reasonable amount of capital will flourish in the hands of a man who behaves well and applies himself to his work; but no amount is ever enough to thrive in the hands of a lad such as I was: not only dissipated, but dissipating.

Money in the pocket of an immoral, dissolute youth is like a sword in the hands of a wild man. Since he doesn't know how to use it properly, all he can do with it is injure himself and injure others, opening wide the door to all his passions, making it easier to indulge all his vices, and thereby occasioning all sorts of illness, squalor, danger, and misfortune.

To keep entailed estates from being thus depleted, and to forestall the utter ruin of such prodigal sons, governments step in, take over the administration and management of the capital, and appoint guardians to watch over the heirs and hold them to a diet, as if they were young children or lunatics; for otherwise, they'd go through all the money in the banks of London in the blink of an eye, if only they could get their hands on it.

What a shame that men who, for the most part, are well born and unaffected by insanity should need to have the law subordinate them to a guardian and reduce them to the status of wards, as if they were madmen or children! But so it is, and I have known a few of these headless heirs.

If I had inherited an entailed estate, I would have had no trouble going through the entire fortune in two weeks, for I was lazy, depraved, and wasteful: three qualifications that, by themselves, are more than enough to consume any fortune, no matter how splendid and opulent.

Tying this back to the thread of my story, let me say: I was getting tired of simulating virtues I did not possess, and in a desire to break that reputation and take off that mask once and for all, one day I said to my mother, "Ma'am, before we know it, St. Peter's day will be here."

"And what do you mean by that?" Her Grace asked me.

"What I mean," I replied, "is that it will be my saint's day, and a very good day for us to come out of mourning."

"Ay, God forbid!" my mother said. "Me, come out of mourning so soon? Don't even think it. I loved your father dearly, and it would be an offense to his memory if I were to come out of mourning so quickly."

"Quickly, ma'am?" I said. "Hasn't it been six months already?"

"So?" she said, utterly scandalized. "Do you think six months too long a time to keep in mourning for a father and a husband? No, son, one should keep strict mourning for a full year for such a person."

As you can see, my mother was one of those old-fashioned ladies who are convinced that wearing mourning clothes proves your feelings for the departed, and who rate your feelings by how long you dress in black; but this is one of the endless inanities that we imbibe with the first milk from our mothers.

It is true that we should regret the passing of those we love, and more so the more closely we are bound to them by relations of friendship or kinship. This feeling is natural, and so ancient that, as we know, the most civilized republics ever to exist in the world, Greece and Rome, not only used mourning clothes, but made even more tender demonstrations for their dead than we do. Perhaps it will not annoy you to learn about them.[1]

---

[1] [According to Spell (p. 151), Lizardi probably took the long explanation of ancient burial customs that follows from Luis Moreri's *Dictionary* (see author's Prologue, footnote 3), and from J.

In Greece, when a sick man expired, his relatives and friends who were by his side would cover their heads as a token of the grief they felt, so as not to see him. They would cut the tips of his hair, and they would press his hand as a token of the pain that his separation caused them.

After his death, they would encircle his body with candles; they would place him at the entrance to the house, and near him they would place a glass filled with holy water, which they would sprinkle on those who attended the funeral. All those who went to the burial and all the kin wore mourning clothes.

The funerals lasted nine days. The body was kept in the house for seven days, on the eighth it was burned, and on the ninth its ashes were buried.

The Romans did things in almost the same way. After the sick man had expired, they would cry out three or four times to show their feelings. They would place the body on the floor, wash it with hot water, and anoint it with oil. Then they would dress it and adorn it with the insignia of the highest position he had held.

Since these pagans believed that every soul had to cross a river in hell called Acheron in order to reach the Elysian Fields, and that there was only one boat on this river, owned by a boatman named Charon who was interested in making sure that no one crossed the river without paying him their toll, to this end the Romans would put a coin in the mouths of their dead. Next, they would display the body to the public, surrounded by lit candles, on a bed in the doorway of the house.

When it was time for the burial, the body was brought to the tomb either on men's shoulders or on litters (just as we used to bring them in carriages). The body was accompanied by mournful music and by hired weeping women, called *praeficae* or paid mourners, whose forced lamentations set the key for the music and the pitch that the funeral procession had to follow.

The slaves freed by the departed in his will would go, wearing hats and carrying lit candles; his sons and male relatives, with their faces covered and hair hanging limply; his daughters, with their heads uncovered; and all his other friends with untied hair and mourning clothes.

If the departed was famous, his body was first brought to the plaza, and from the column known as the Speech Column, one of his sons or relatives would deliver a funeral oration in praise of his virtues. That is how long ago our funeral sermons began.

Afterward, the body was taken to be buried; the place of burial changed. For some time, the dead were buried in the homes of their children. Then, seeing how harmful this practice was, it was established as good policy for the dead to be buried in unpopulated land; from that time forward, each man had a tomb constructed to hold himself and his family.[2] The Greeks kept the same custom, except for the

---

J. Barthélemy, *Viaje del joven Anacharsis en Grecia* (Madrid, 1813; translated from French, orig. 1788). –Tr.]

[2] A wonderful provision, which we have seen imitated in Mexico since the epidemic of 1813, abolishing the outmoded abuse of burying the dead inside the churches and moving burial grounds to suburban cemeteries in keeping with the decisions made by our city councils. Let us hope this is not forgotten, and that lapses will not be tolerated or go unpunished!

Lacedaemonians. Poor people who could not afford this luxury were buried, as they are everywhere, in the bare ground.

Later it became the custom to burn the bodies of dead heroes. For this purpose, they would put the body on a pyre,[3] which was a tall pile of dry firewood, which they sprinkled with fragrant liquids and perfumes, and the relatives would set fire to it with the lit candles they carried, averting their faces as they did so.

While the body was burning, the relatives would toss on the flames the decorations and arms of the departed, and some of their own hair, in demonstration of their grief.

After the body had been consumed, the fire was put out with water and wine, and the relatives collected the ashes and deposited them in an urn with flowers and fragrances. Then the priest would sprinkle everyone with water to purify them, and as they left, they would recite out loud: "*Aeternum vale*"—that is, "Farewell forever": a good wish, which better explains our own *Requiescat in pace* (Rest in peace). This done, the urn was deposited in a tomb, on which they would engrave the epitaph and these four letters: S.T.T.L., which stands for *Sit tibi terra levis* (May the earth be light upon you), so that passersby might wish him rest. Among ourselves, we might see a cross along a road, or a little *retablo*[4] painted of some person killed on the street, placed there so that we might pray for their soul.

At the end of the service, the house of the departed was closed and was not to be opened again for nine days, at the end of which they held a commemoration.

The Greeks would place flowers, honey, bread, arms, and food around the funeral pyre. . . . Offerings! Just like the offerings of the Indians! How ancient and superstitious our origins are![5] The whole ceremony would end with a meal served at the house of some relative. We even imitate this, remembering that "mourning is lighter on a full stomach."

And could the Greeks and Romans have been the only ones who expressed their feelings so effusively at the deaths of their kin and friends? No, my children. Every nation, in every age, has voiced its sorrow for this cause. The Hebrews, the Syrians,

---

[As Lizardi indicates in this note, the custom throughout the Catholic world was once to bury the dead inside the church building itself. In response to growing population, continuing epidemics (such as the devastating one that swept across central Mexico in 1813–1815), and new ideas about the communicability of disease, municipal governments in Spain and Spanish America prohibited such burials between about 1780 and 1830, creating cemeteries removed from the church grounds for the first time. –Tr.]

[3] This custom is imitated by our "pyres" [platforms for displaying the caskets at funerals]. This is why they are elevated, crowned with lamps, decorated with jars that disperse pleasant smells, and adorned with busts of the dead and the insignia of their positions.

[4] [Retablo: known outside of Mexico as *exvotos,* these are small, often crude paintings commissioned by individuals or families, either in honor of a miraculous cure or escape or, as here, in memory of a death. –Tr.]

[5] Even today, there are villages where the Indians set out an *itacate* for their dead: that is, a bundle filled with things to eat and a few small coins. In other villages, they hide a piece of paper covered with foolish statements written for the Eternal Father, in addition to equally superstitious offerings. Elsewhere we will say who continues to follow such abuses.

the Chaldeans, and the men of the most remote antiquity manifested their sensitivity for their deceased, one way or another. The barbarous nations feel and express their emotions just as the civilized ones do.

It is right to regret the dead, and in the sacred Scriptures we read these words: "Weep for the dead, for his light has failed"—that is, his life *(Supra mortum plora, defecit enim lux ejus)* (Ecclesiasticus 22:10). Jesus Christ wept for the death of his dear Lazarus; and so it would be dreadfully absurd to take as evil the feelings inspired by nature itself, and to blaspheme against the outward displays that express them.

So I am far from wanting to criticize either such feelings or our tokens of them; but I am just as far from thinking proper such abuses as we have noted in these tokens, and I believe that all sensible men will agree on this; for who could judge reasonable the Romans' hired weeping women, or the coins they put in the mouths of their dead? Who would not laugh at the foolishness of the Copts, who in their funerals run through the streets crying out loud alongside their hired mourners, rubbing mud over their faces, beating and scratching themselves, waving their wild hair, and performing all the excesses of raging lunatics? Who would not be horrified by the cruelty with which, in other barbarous lands, the principal widows of the kings or mandarins are buried alive, and so on?

In truth, we all criticize, revile, and ridicule the abuses of foreign nations, while at the same time we fail to recognize our own; or, if we do recognize them, we do not dare to part with them, venerating and conserving them out of respect for our elders who established them.

Such is the case with the abuses we note today in our condolences, funerals, and mourning. After a sick man dies among us, we normally cry out loud to express our feelings. If it is a rich house, the normal thing is to send the body to the mortuary; but if it is a poor house, there is no escaping the *wake*. The latter amounts to laying the shrouded body down on the floor, in the middle of four candles; reciting a few devotions and rosaries; drinking a couple of chocolates; and (to keep from dozing) telling stories and allaying sleep with foolishness and perhaps with criminalities. I myself have seen people whittling away at reputations and courting their loves in the presence of the dead. Surely such doings make fine prayers for the souls of the dead.

The cries, sighs, and weeping calm down a bit in the interval between the death of the kinsman and the act of removing him for burial. Then, as if a dead body could be of any profit to us, as if they weren't doing us a huge favor by removing that filth from our house, and as if the dead man himself were about to be quartered live, the grief of his kin redoubles, their cries grow louder, their laments reach up to high heaven, tears flow with abandon, and sometimes fainting spells and convulsions become indispensable, especially among pretty, young, bereaved ladies,[6] whether caused by sensitivity or by playfulness. And watch out: some girls are so skilled in feigning an epileptic attack that it seems like the real thing. Some find that these are generally effective means of attracting the consolations and indulgence of the fellows they like.

---

[6] I have observed that such attacks almost never afflict old or ugly women. Perhaps some doctor may know the cause of this phenomenon, and will know why one such girl whom I knew never had such an attack when her stockings were dirty.

We will leave the bereaved embroiled in their weeping and fainting, while we go on to observe the funeral.

If the dead man is rich, you know, pomp and vanity will follow him to the grave. The inmates of the poorhouse will be invited—how many times!—to such funerals, so that they may bear candles for the dead who, in life, had so loathed their company.

I don't think it a bad thing that the poor should accompany the rich when the latter die; but it would doubtless be better if the rich would accompany the poor while they are alive: that is, by visiting them in the prisons, the hospitals, and in their miserable huts; and if their business keeps them from accompanying and consoling them in person, at the least their money could keep them company and alleviate their poverty. I refer to the money that is wasted a thousand times on luxury and immoderation. If that were the case, not just the poor who were being paid would attend the funeral, but all the poor who had received aid. They would go without being called, weeping as they marched behind the body of their benefactor. In the midst of their grief, they would say: "Our father has died, our brother, our friend, our guardian, our everything. Who will console us now? Who will take the place of this benevolent spirit?"

That would indeed be an honor, and higher praise than the flattering heart of a kinsman could ever give; for the tears of the poor at the death of the rich honor their ashes, perpetuate the memory of their names, vouch for their charity and benevolence, and attest to the happiness of their fortunes after death more soundly, truthfully, and forcefully than all the pomp, vanity, and flash of a funeral. Wretched are the rich whose deaths are neither preceded nor followed by the tears of the poor!

Back to the funeral. Next come several old men, called Trinitarians, outfitted in red suits; then a few priests, together with lots of lay brothers dressed as clergymen; this cortege is followed by the body and, behind it, a number of coaches.

The church where the last rites are held is filled with blazing tapers and a magnificent, elegant bier. The music is likewise solemn, though funereal.

During the vigil and the Mass, which for some heirs is not a requiem Mass but a Mass of thanksgiving, the bells never cease to deafen us with their tiresome clamoring, which repeats to us:

> This bell that tolls in sorrow
> Is not for he who died,
> But to let me know that I
> Am bound to die tomorrow.

It would be well for the rich to take this sort of reminder to heart, since church bells toll only for them, and should remind them that they are as mortal as the poor for whom the bells never toll, or if they do, only for a short time and with little enthusiasm; so that it is the poor who really are "the dead who make no noise."[7]

---

[7] [The Mexican proverb, *Hay muertos que no hacen ruido, y son mayores sus penas* ("There are dead who make no noise, and their suffering is all the greater"—that is, some ghosts do not ostentatiously groan and clank their chains, despite their grievous sins), is used to allude to rich people who hide their wealth. –Tr.]

The funeral concludes with all the pomp that can be managed or that is desired, making sure that the dead man's casket is well lined, studded, and even gilded (I have seen this myself), and perhaps kept in a private tomb, since mausoleums are exclusively for the use of princes—as if death did not make us all equal, a truth to which Seneca testified when he said (Epistle 102) that *aequat omnes cinis*, "ashes equalize everyone." Who could distinguish the ashes of Caesar or Pompey from those of the poor peasants of their time?

The whole shindig costs an arm and a leg, and sometimes these expenses (as vain as they are useless) entail such reprehensible abuses that the authorities are obliged to contain them through laws, which declare that if funeral expenses are out of proportion to the means and rank of the departed, they should be modified by the relevant local judge.[8]

The most serious difficulty here is that of knowing when these expenses are excessive. I admit that only in very rare cases could a judge make such a decision, for he would almost never have enough inside understanding of the affairs of the deceased; thus he could determine it was excessive only by looking at rank. Let us suppose: when a known plebeian wants to be buried with as much pomp as a count, even then, if he has enough money to pay for it, I couldn't say for certain that he is making a mockery of the law; but Horace did know for certain, saying that: "everything—virtue (meaning the praise that is virtue's due), fame, and splendor—obeys the beauty of riches, and whosoever is able to accumulate riches will be illustrious, brave, just, wise, and whatever else he wants."[9]

Speaking as a Christian, however, I will not refrain from setting the rule for where we should decide that a funeral is excessive.

I know that this rule will seem too nitpickingly scrupulous, but I assure you that it is infallible and very easy. It is simply that what is spent on luxuries at a funeral should not come out of what is owed to creditors nor to the poor.

So, if the creditors have been paid and the poor have been given a few alms, can't the deceased freely dispose of his fifth of his estate?[10] Yes, he can, I reply; but I immediately ask: would it not be better to take what you would spend on luxuries and employ it rather among the poor, of whom there are always plenty? Indisputably. In that case, what luxuries can legitimately be used among Christians? None, in truth. That is what I would say if I were speaking with Christians. If I were speaking with pagans who were considering professing Christianity, I would be less scrupulous in my opinions. Let us go on to another matter.

In accordance with the abuses we have noted among the funerals of the rich, we

---

[8] Law 12, title 13, paragraph 1; and 30, title 13, paragraph 5.

[9] [*Omnis enim res, / Virtus, fama, decus, divina, humanaque pulchris / Divitiis parent; quas qui construxerit, ille / clarus erit, fortis, iustus.* Horace, *Satires* II, 3, 94–96. –Tr.]

[10] [In Spanish inheritance law, each son and daughter was entitled to an equal share of four-fifths of each parent's estate (after leaving one-half to the surviving spouse, if any). A parent only had discretion over the remaining fifth of the estate in his or her will, and could, for example, leave it all to a favored son, to charity, or to pay for masses in his or her own memory. Lizardi clearly finds this system very just, and in the novel he frequently criticizes the attempts of wealthy families to circumvent it. –Tr.]

observe almost the same ones among the poor, for as they too are vain, they wish to mimic the rich insofar as they can. They do not invite the inmates of the poorhouse, nor the Trinitarians, nor the crowd of lay brothers; nor are they buried in monasteries, nor in elegant caskets, nor do they do everything that the rich do—not because they lack the will, but the pennies. Nevertheless, they do as much as they can. They call upon another group of raggedy, hunched old men called the Brothers of the Holy Name; they pay for their seven assistant priests, their High Mass, their plain coffin, and so on, and all this by spending money that will doubtless be found wanting, before the nine days of the funeral are up, to buy bread for the bereaved.

The custom is to shroud the dead in the humble woolen tunic of St. Francis; but if, in its day, this was a pious custom, it has become corrupt.

Far be it from me to carp at true piety and devotion; the object of my current criticism bears solely on the simoniac commerce in shrouds, and the preconceptions under which the common people labor, to dress their dead in blue, and at such expense.

Shrouds are sold at the excessively high price of twelve and a half pesos for a man, or six pesos and two reales for a woman. The poor try to order a shroud almost the moment a sick man dies. And if they don't have enough money? They take out a loan, go into debt, even beg for alms so that they can get it; their children go without bread for the money they waste on a useless and loathsome rag, which is all the best shroud is when it goes on a dead man, who no longer is in a position to earn any indulgences; and since one can only receive the spiritual grace of indulgence if he is in a state of merit, it follows that, if they don't dress the sick man in a shroud while he lives, after he has died it will do him no more good to wear it than it would to wear the robes of the Emperor of China.

Children, if you, in the course of your lives, have any relative whose passing occurs during a period of your own destitution, do not fret over the funeral nor over the shroud. A funeral can be paid for with three pesos and four reales, which you should distribute in this form: twelve reales for a coffin; one peso for the coffin-bearers; and one for the gravedigger who will fashion the tomb for you in the cemetery.

The shroud will be cheaper if you accept your poverty. The Jews used to tie up their dead in cloths that they called cerements, and then they would wind them in a clean sheet. You can do the same, and yours will be as well shrouded as the best of them. Indeed, the shroud of Jesus Christ was no different.

After the funeral there follow the condolences. To receive them, the doors are closed, the ladies of the house sit in the sitting room, and the gentlemen on the chairs, all dressed in black and keeping utterly silent during this ceremony, or whispering at most, not to give the bereaved an epileptic fit—a degree of moderation and respect that perhaps was not observed quite so scrupulously when the deceased was sick.

I have noticed another abuse in these happenings, which is that the conversations that they have with the bereaved are aimed at celebrating and expounding upon the virtues of the departed; remembering the causes of his illness, what he suffered, the cures he was administered, how long he was on his death bed, and other such impertinences; by retelling which, they further torment the grieving spirits of his family.

This custom of giving condolences comes down to two things. First, to demonstrate that we share in the feelings of those to whom we give our condolences, either because we are related to them or because of our friendship with the deceased. Second, to console the bereaved insofar as we can, offering them our temporal assistance and assuring them that we will add our intercessory prayers to their own in remembrance of their soul in need.

As you can see, this entire ceremony is almost always a solemn farce, a routine performance, and one of our best-received customs.

This proposition will not seem too audacious if you note that not only the distant relatives and friends of the deceased, but even his closest and most favored, will after a very short time cease to bring him to mind, because in the course of time the heart grows calm, the tears dry, the sense of loss is filled, the benefits are forgotten, and all is erased, despite how many cries, tears, fusses, fits, and humbug were lavished upon the scene of his death.

And if their sons, their wives, and their brothers can forget like this, what hopes can the poor dead have for all the prayers of intercession that are promised by those who only attend the wake so they can drink chocolate, and who give their condolences because the banquet attracts them, no matter how much they claim, on taking leave, that "though sinners, we will never forget you in our prayers"?

This is a very serious matter. Let us leave it pending, while we finish refuting the abuse of talking about the dead while giving condolences; because, if one of the objects of these "condolatators" is, as we have said, to ease the grief of the bereaved, it seems a tactless error to renew their motives for sorrow, even while we seek to console them.

It could do nothing but torment the heart of the wife or son of the deceased to hear someone say: "Don Fulano was such a good man! So considerate! So nice!"— "Oh, my dear!" says another woman, "you have a thousand reasons to cry for him; you'll never find another husband like the one you just lost!" And other such idiocies, which are so many screws squeezing the heart of those you should be consoling. Thus, these polite flatteries are indiscrete tortures for the grieving spirits.

Wouldn't it be so much better to substitute this imprudent formula of giving condolences by another, opposite form, in which either we discuss festive or indifferent matters, or, better, we reduce this piece of etiquette simply to putting our goods and resources at the disposal of the bereaved, should they need them? By doing so truthfully, without humbug, when the bereaved were satisfied of our truthfulness they would surely be more consoled than by all the panegyrics that the "condolatators" now dedicate to their dead.

And going back to them, I say: I pity the fellow who dies if he hasn't managed during his life to pave the road to his salvation, relying instead on his children, friends, and executors.

All too frequently we see many people, perhaps with plenty of resources, who have neither given alms while they lived, nor paid for a Mass, nor repaid their debts, nor made restitution for past sins, nor practiced any of those obligations imposed on us by religion and our own interests; but a time comes when our ears cannot help hearing the truth. The doctor informs them of their death sentence; they recognize that the prognosis is no mistake, for their constitutions are growing steadily weaker; their hearts are gripped by the fear of what eternity has in store for them; they call the confessor and the notary; the two arrive at almost the same time; they confess quickly,

God knows how; the will is written next; everything is arranged; they declare their debts, order them paid, and name executors to carry out their will; they ask for alms to be given in what are called compulsory bequests, some to the poor and others to say a few Masses for their souls; and with all this done, they receive the sacred Viaticum and holy oils, and the sick die comforted; but oh! how little trust they should place in such measures when they are made on the edge of the tomb itself.

At that hour, they give alms and ask (sometimes) to have restitution made, because they cannot take their fortune with them to the grave. They die confident that their executors will carry out their wills, but how often are those who draw up wills fooled? How many times have executors turned into heirs, and guardians into estate holders? Too many to count. No, there is nothing rare about the complaints one hears every day from poor minors who have been left on the street by the bad faith or bad administration of such gentlemen.

All this should teach you not to wait until the hour of gestures, as they say, to put your affairs in order, for then your haste and panic will greatly diminish your likelihood of success.

We now get to the mourning period, when, as you saw with my mother, there is also room for abuse. The custom of keeping mourning is simply that of wearing black in order to display our feelings upon the deaths of our friends or kin; but this color, required by custom, is merely a token, not a proof of our feelings. How many wretches do not wear mourning on the death of those they most love, because they do not own black clothes? Yet their sorrow is undeniable. On the other hand, how many young widows, how many bad and self-interested sons and nephews, who were waiting for the death of the deceased so that they could come into possession of his goods, will keep the strictest mourning dress, not just to follow the custom, but to convince us that they are stricken by feelings they have never had?

Color, physicists tell us, is an accident that does not alter the substance of a thing; thus, a good son will feel the loss of his father, the good wife of her husband, and good friends, of their friends, whether they dress in black, blue, green, scarlet, or any other color. On the other hand, a kinsman who did not love his relative, who may have wished him to expire so that he might inherit something, will not feel it any more sharply no matter if he wears every scrap of black baize from every mourning-clothes store in the world.

In some provinces of Asia, the color white has been adopted for mourning clothes; and among ourselves, when we dress in black for Good Friday and the Day of the Dead,[11] we can see that we do not do it out of grief but luxury.

In the end, I do not regard it as an abuse to wear black in such cases, but I do take it as such to prescribe a certain number of days for wearing mourning clothes, in order to denote our greater or lesser grief, depending on the degree of kinship we have with the deceased.

As you have seen, in my mother's time the established period to wear mourning clothes was one year for one's parents, children, and close companions; six months

---

[11] [Day of the Dead (here, *el día de Finados*): November 2, All Soul's Day in the Catholic calendar, is a traditional day for remembering the dead and visiting cemeteries. –Tr.]

for brothers; three for nieces and nephews; and so on.[12] This can be nothing but foolishness; for if one truly loved the deceased, and if mourning dress were proof of one's feeling, one would never take it off, because the motive for wearing it would never end; and if one did not love them, it would make no difference whether one wore mourning for a few months or for many, because the black clothes would prove nothing about one's feelings.

I shared some of these reflections with my mother, until I took away her enthusiasm for her whim, and she offered me to have us come out of mourning on St. Peter's day, which was all I wanted, so that I could also take off the mask of virtue that I had been feigning and indulge myself freely in every vice around, fully enjoying my freedom and squandering with my friends the few means my father had scrimped and saved to leave for my poor mother's sustenance.

In keeping with this decision, I ordered myself a suit fit for a dandy, which I would wear that day, and we arranged a lunch and dinner, and a dance for that night.

My long-desired saint's day came, the 29th of June; I took off the black rags that once had served me as a schoolboy's outfit, and dressed to the nines in my secular clothes. It seemed that a bell had rung to call all my relatives and acquaintances; many who had not been back at our house since my father's funeral, and some who had not even come to give my mother their condolences, crashed the party that day, feeling quite at home and not a bit ashamed.

As you might have guessed, the first in were my closest friends, Januario, Pelayo, and others like them, who brought with them to the dance their titled ladies, who were also mine. In a word, the smells of turkey and of pineapple-flavored *pulque*[13] attracted a number of my friends, family, and acquaintances to my house that day, all of whom came to wish me well on my saint's day. God bless them.

They licked up the lunch, consumed the dinner, and when the time came, enlivened the dance tremendously, for they sang, danced, frolicked, got drunk, trashed the house, and in the end left, some of them muttering about the lunch, others about the dinner, others about the dance, and all of them about something that they had come to enjoy.

What stupidity it is to hold a public party! You waste your money, suffer a thousand inconveniences, lose a few things, and always come off badly with the very people you meant to honor; and you get back in muttering and grumbling what you expected to get in thanks.

Despite all this, since I didn't think like this back then, nothing bothered me, nor did I think about anything but having fun and a good time by spending money; though the truth is that at the time, they flattered me quite a bit, especially the coquettes, for whose praises I decided that the money we had wasted and the inconveniences my mother had put up with were all worth it.

---

[12] In the city of Mexico, one rarely sees this now; but in the villages, towns, and other cities of the kingdom, these abuses are still strictly observed.

[13] [*Pulque*: as noted above, this slightly alcoholic Mexican drink was associated with the lower classes; it was sometimes "cured" or flavored by mixing in various fruit juices. –Tr.]

CHAPTER 14

PERIQUILLO CRITICIZES DANCES, AND MAKES A LONG AND USEFUL
DIGRESSION, SPEAKING OF THE BAD EDUCATIONS THAT MANY PARENTS
GIVE THEIR SONS, AND THE BAD SONS WHO GRIEVE THEIR PARENTS

When everyone had tired of dancing and drinking, the dance ended, as all dances do. A little past twelve midnight, the most prudent (or least foolish) guests began leaving—those who had not made it their goal to stay up late. The ones who stayed behind, whether because they missed the bustle and din of those who had gone, or because they themselves were tired, barely roused themselves to dance. The candles burned low and begged for a changing of the guard; the musicians (who never overlook a chance to tip the bottle on such occasions) rarely hit the right notes when they played a request; one of them was even trying to strum his mandolin on the wrong side of the bridge.

Januario, handy as ever in such affairs, said to me, "Man, how sorry the dance has gotten, and so early!"

"But what can we do about it?" I said.

"What can we do? Cheer things up!" he replied.

"Cheer it up, how?" I asked.

"With a little something. Don't you have some liquor?"

"Yes," I said.

"And sugar, and lemons?"

"Those, too."

"Well, have them bring it all to your room."

I did as Januario asked, and in an instant he whipped together a mixture of liquor, sugar, and lemon, which they call punch; he made them put fresh lamps under the shades, and he started serving his infernal beverage by the barrelful to the musicians and the guests, at which the party went straight to the devil.

At first there was a little order in the way they danced; some musicians knew what they were playing, and some dancers knew what moves they were making; but as the sweetened liquor began to kick in, their heads became completely unhinged; the little bit of respect and moderation that had once reigned was set aside; the women forgot their shame, and the men their consideration.

A second and a third round of punch were served, and the uproar was complete; it was no longer a dance, but a bash and a criminal scandal.

The people who put on dances, especially this sort of dance (and few are any different), are procurers and front-men for a thousand scandalous indecencies. Perhaps they don't plan them, don't want them, and are even disgusted by them; yet for all that, it is their permissiveness that gives rise to such brazen lewdness, for any good philosopher knows that "the cause of a cause is the cause of its result"; therefore, anyone who puts on a dance should keep many things in consideration to avoid such scandalous licentiousness, for otherwise he will be nothing but a procurer in the eyes of the public, and in the eyes of God he will be held to account for every sin committed in his house.

The main considerations that someone planning a dance should keep in mind can be reduced, I think, to the following:

First, that the women who attend should be honest, honorable, and never single or free women, but daughters or wives; and that they should go with their fathers or husbands, so that both they and the libertine lads will be restrained by their respect for these men.

Second, that none of the latter should ever be knowingly invited, no matter how exquisitely skilled in dancing they might be: better someone who dances badly, than someone who seduces well. Normally these dancers, or "useful" lads, as they are called, are a bunch of outrageous rogues; they go to a dance with only two objects in mind: to have fun and to "tease," in their words. This teasing amounts to seductions and crudeness. If they can, they pervert the maiden and corrupt the married woman, and all without love, but out of depravity or simply to pass the time.

On some occasions (if only it were not so often!), they achieve their goals, and scarcely do they satisfy their lust when they abandon, in favor of some other object, the wretched madwomen who prostitute their honor and virtue because of the artful verbosity of an immoral, lascivious, and stupid youth who is good only for dancing.

But even when they run into a wall of stone—I mean, when by good fortune all the girls at a dance are judicious, honest, and demure, knowing how to mock the lads' flirtations and conserve their honor untouched in the midst of the flames, like the thornbush that Moses saw burning without being consumed, which is surely a miracle—even in such rare cases as this, the "useful" boys do business.

When they can do nothing else, when the young women close their ears to them, they don't give up or get discouraged. Since all the effort and adulation they put into seducing arise from depravity, not love, they don't mind being snubbed, nor does a lack of response cool their ardor. Quite the opposite. They keep right on skipping and hopping, satisfying themselves with what they call "the broth."

This broth—watch out, you fathers and husbands who know what honor is and who want to maintain your own honor as you should!—this broth consists of the pawings they give to your daughters and wives,[1] their license passing thousands of times from hand to mouth, so that open pawing turns into furtive kissing, which the less scrupulous women do not take badly, and which women known for their prudence and honor put up with and pretend to ignore, in order to avoid trouble.

So it is that self-respecting, honorable husbands or fathers, who would be shocked to see their wives or daughters give their hands to any man in their house, at one of these dances will tolerate watching them being embraced, touched, ruffled, and pawed more roughly than a fat horse's haunches.

---

[1] This is especially the case in the contra dance and the "waltz," which is nothing other than what we used to call the *alemanda*. The difference is that the latter was danced slowly, while the waltz is a rapid frolic, and the dust it raises serves well to hide or dissimulate an exchange of words or assignations, a pinch, an embrace, a kiss, or even worse, which I do not name out of respect for modesty.

The worst thing is that all this pawing and groping, accompanied by the customary giggling and chatter, are to many women as venial sins are to the soul, with the difference that venial sins *warm* the soul and dispose it to commit mortal sins, while this pawing, this broth of which we have been speaking, *inflames* some young women and disposes them to toss aside their honor, and that of their fathers and husbands. One cannot take too many precautions to avoid such excesses.

The third consideration that those who put on dances might keep in mind would be not to have any spirituous liquors on hand. If it is necessary to offer something to the guests, out of courtesy or affection, it would be better to give them wafers and ice milk, lemon ices, tamarind ices, or the like, rather than "snacks" and wine, brandy, punch, or other such liquors, which confuse the mind, confound the reason, and upset the physical constitution of both sexes, the necessary results of which are desires, permissive thoughts, and amorous delights—and in one or another person, other even more sinful things.

Much of this could be avoided by the simple rule I have just set down for you, for as the ancient saying correctly put it, *sine Cerere et Baccho friget Venus,*[2] which is the same sentiment put forward by this couplet:

> Little to eat and no spirits to drink:
> If that does not quench lust, at least it allays it.

The fourth and final consideration that should be kept in mind is that dances should end no later than twelve midnight. That allows more than enough time for each guest to go home well entertained, if he is a rational person; because everything that happens past that hour should no longer be called entertainment, but vice, inconvenience, and foolishness.

I wish that all those who throw dances would hold to these four simple rules, and I think (though I cannot guarantee it) that they would not be sorry to have followed them.

Finally, I am not denouncing dances, but rather the scandals that take place at dances. Take away everything that makes them sinful and dangerous, leaving them as a kind of indifferent amusement, and they will be bad for those who go there to be bad, and honorable for the honorable; but until that happens, no dance, whether for its abuses or for the sins it occasions, can be free from the definition given by one father of the Church, who said that "a dance is a circle whose center is the Devil."[3]

Dancing is not bad; what may be bad is the way you dance and the object you have for dancing. David danced before the Ark of the Lord, and the Israelites danced before the golden calf of Belial. Both danced, but so differently, and for such different objects! Therefore they also received such different rewards.

---

[2] ["Without Ceres (goddess of grain) and Bacchus (god of drink), Venus (goddess of love) languishes." From Terence, *The Eunuch* (IV: V, 732). –Tr.]

[3] [Spell (p. 156) identifies the source of this quote as Ignacio de las Erbada's moralistic tract *Fantasmas de Madrid, y Estafermos de la Corte, obra donde se dan al público los errores y falacias de trato humano* (Madrid, 1761–1763), I:307. –Tr.]

Some moralists are so austere, they argue that all dances are voluntary proximate occasions of sin,[4] and therefore they find that all are illicit. I respect their opinion, but I cannot agree. I am more lenient, and say there might actually be some dances (unlike the usual ones, however) that present no occasion for scandals, lascivious songs, pawing of flesh, drunkenness, and the other abuses that occur in most of them. And what sort would they be? The sort that should be thrown by people of good conscience.

If all the guests are honorable, so will the dance be. The difficulty consists in throwing a dance with a sense of order.

Letting everyone else do whatever they wish in their own houses, and returning to my own, I was saying: when all the guests were exhausted from leaping, drinking, and chatting, things gradually became as quiet as could be, for most of them could no longer stand on their own feet.

The musicians let their instruments fall next to their chairs, on which they stretched out as best they could; the women went up into the sitting room, and the men sat down to tell stories and talk nonsense to keep from falling asleep, for it would soon be daybreak, which was what they were waiting for, so that they could go out for coffee.

It wasn't a bad plan, but neither the men nor the women were in control of themselves; rather, the liquor was in charge, and it was drugging them a little bit more with each passing minute. So it happened that, with some talking and others listening to nonsense, they all fell asleep, some to one side and some to the other, and one of the first to sleep was Januario.

My dear mother had gone to bed quite early, leaving me in charge of caring for the house, which I did; for although I was as sleepy as the best of them, I dared not fall asleep, fearful that one of them might try carrying off with something. Personal interest is the dickens. As far as one's health goes, there are few things that rob one of as much sleep.

I was on the lookout, watching them all, listening to the snores and stomach noises they were all making, some more, some less. I was not altogether pleased by the music, nor by the smell; besides, I could scarcely stay awake.

True, the courtyard was locked and I held the key, so I could well have gone to bed; but what stopped me was the thought that no one was at home but my mother, myself, and a good but old and slumberous serving woman who could happily sleep through an earthquake. It wasn't right to ask my mother to get up and open the door each time one of those sluggards woke up from his hangover and asked to leave for the street, so the only one who could do sentry duty was me; therefore, to keep from falling asleep, I set about having my bit of fun with the sleeping guests, knowing that most of them were sleeping a double sleep—one natural, the other liquor-induced.

One of the risks that drunkenness carries for all who fall prey to it is that of being exposed to the derision of any and all, which is what happened to my guests. Some,

---

[4] [A voluntary proximate occasion of sin is one that is easily avoidable (voluntary) and will likely lead to sin (proximate); Catholic doctrine demands that such situations be avoided. –Tr.]

I painted dirt on their faces; others, I hid their things; still others, I sewed their clothes to their neighbor's; and thus I pulled a thousand pranks.

A new day dawned, a fresh breeze blew, I threw the balcony window open, and with the light and the sound of church bells and the noise of people walking in the street, they started waking up; and when they saw each other's faces covered with speckling and frillwork, they couldn't help laughing, especially the women; but no sooner did they jump up than, to their great dismay, they heard their dresses rip, or even saw them torn to shreds.

Some of the women pretended not to mind, but others cursed the idle rogue who had caused them so much harm, for harm it was; but villains, such as I was, pay no attention to such matters; the thing is to have fun at others' expense, and if you can manage to do that, you don't care whether your pranks do damage to their interests or even to their health.

When the first flush of anger had passed, and when some had cleaned themselves, others had mended their dresses, and all had settled down, they left for the cafés or their own houses—all but Januario and three or four friends of his and mine, who, as the greatest freeloaders and scoundrels of the lot, stayed to finish off at breakfast the relics of the evening's feast; but at last they had their breakfast and, seeing that there was nothing left to graze on from the party, they went out and I went to bed.

I slept like a hound until twelve noon, when I got up and found the poor old cook railing against the dancers.

"Ma'am," she was telling my mother, "haven't these rakes committed a fine disgrace, leaving the house the way they did after drinking and enjoying themselves all day long? Look here, ma'am, I've spent the entire day cleaning up their mess, because—dear Jesus! How they left it! It was filthy. Vomit in the hallway, nastiness on the stairs, this here, that there; even the drawing room, ma'am, even the drawing room was a pigsty. Ugh! Have you ever seen such dirty, gross people? But what saddens me most, ma'am, is the flowerpots. Look, will you please, how they've left them, all broken. Ay! The folks who go to dances must be evil by nature—they're not satisfied with drinking, having fun, getting soused, and leaving the house a mess, but they have to do wickedness like this, too!"

My mother consoled the old woman, telling her, "Right you are, Nana Felipa, they're a bunch of indecent, gross, badly bred rogues to do so much damage at the very house where they are having fun; but there's nothing you can do about it for now. As you know, my husband was never in favor of these bashes, so I have no experience with this sort of ill manners; but I give you my word that this will be the first and the last time it happens."

I was none too happy with this sentence, because, since I had neither spent my own money, nor done any work for the party, I would have been happy to have kept having dances at my house, three times a week at least.

Nevertheless, I went no further for the moment than to laugh heartily at the old woman, and at a fine hour in the evening, I took my hat and went out into the street.

I first returned at nine at night and found my mother in a serious mood, for she asked me where I had been, saying that she was amazed by the license I was taking, that I was her son, that I shouldn't think that the death of my father had made me the absolute master of my freedom, and other things along these lines, to which I replied that those times were over, that I was not a boy any more, that I shaved now, and that if I wanted to go out into the street and hang around, it was to see how I might make out living.

Such rude replies saddened my mother, and she immediately knew what would come next, which was that I would take off the mask and completely cease to respect her, and so it happened.

I wish that I could pass over this short and nasty time in silence, and that you could remain ignorant, my children, of how impudent an insolent and ill-bred son can be; but, since I have set out to give you a faithful mirror in which you will see virtue and vice as they are, I should keep nothing from you.

Today you are my young ones, mere playful children, but tomorrow you will be adults, parents, and heads of families, and reading my life story will then teach you how you should handle your own children, so that you will not have to put up with what my mother had to put up with from me.

My mother lived for two years after the death of my beloved father, and it was a long time, given the headaches I gave her during those years, which I regret every time I recall them.

Constantly dissipated, idle, and badly employed, I thought only of dances, games, women, and everything that might tend to pervert my behavior more and more.

The bit of money that had remained in the house was not enough to satisfy my desires. It soon vanished. We found ourselves reduced to moving into a small apartment in a tenement, but since we could not even afford that, a few days later I put my mother in a wretched, low room, which pained her terribly, as she was not accustomed to such treatment.

Her poor ladyship reproached my evil ways; she made me see that they were the cause of the sad state to which we had been reduced; she gave me hours of advice, pleading with me to dedicate myself to something worthwhile, to confess, to abandon the friends who had done so much harm to me and who might even have led me to the threshold of my final perdition. In a word, the miserable lady did all in her power to make me reflect on myself; but it was too late.

Vice had hardened my heart; its roots were deep, and neither sound advice nor soft nor harsh reproach made any imprint on it. I listened in a fury to everything she said and obstinately rejected it. If she exhorted me to virtue, I laughed; if she painted the ugliness of my vices, I grew exasperated; not only that, but on such occasions I would show my disrespect for her by making replies unworthy of a well-born, Christian son, making my poor mother weep inconsolably.

Oh, my mother's tears, shed through her own fault as well as mine! If from the beginning, if during my childhood, if, before I had become the absolute master of my vicious passions, she had corrected my first impulses of passion rather than flattering me with her endearments, indulgence, and affection, I would surely have grown accustomed to obeying and respecting her; but quite the opposite was the case: she welcomed my first indiscretions and even forgave them because of my age, forgetting that vice also has its infancy, its solidity, and its old age in the moral life, just as man does in physical life. Beginning as a child, or a trivial vice, it grows through habit and causes the man to perish, or else reaches decrepitude at the same time that, with the passing of the years, the man's passions wither.

How it would have profited my mother and me if she had not opposed my father's plans so often, if she had not prevented him from punishing me, and if she had not indulged me so with her imprudent love! I would have grown used to respecting her, I would have grown up pious and orderly, and under that system I would not have suffered so much toil in this world, nor would my mother have been the victim of my disobedience and abuse.

The most lamentable aspect of this deplorable case is that there are any number of parallels. The sons of permissive widows are almost always lost and ill bred; and what can the mothers of such sons be, but hapless women?

What normally happens is that the father is an ordinary man who manages to inspire a few Christian, moral, polite sentiments in the child, and thereby lead him away from all the baseness to which man naturally inclines. This makes the child cry; the mother grieves and hampers the father. The child is mischievous, and she applauds; he shows bad manners, she forgives him; he produces a few indecent words, because he heard them either from the servants or in the street, and she celebrates them. The father is driven up the wall by all these things, but does not dare try to reproach them or punish the child, because he knows that when he does so, the mother will pounce like a lioness; whether because he loves her too dearly, or because he does not want their marriage to become a living hell, he consents to her will and leaves the boy's transgressions unpunished; the boy laughs with satisfaction at the impunity that his mamá insures, gives free rein to his vices, which, as we have said, are still boy-vices, childishness, trivialities; but at an adult age, they become scandalous crimes and misdemeanors.

Nonetheless, the father's presence almost always serves as a kind of brake, yet when he dies, all is lost. With the only dike breached, frail though it may have been, the full pent-up river of passions comes rushing forth, crushing everything that stands in its path.

Then the widow recognizes how fierce a heart devoted to its own liberty can be; she tries to oppose it for the first time, but it is too late; the torrent comes rushing down with uncontainable force. She tries advice, employs endearments, compiles lists of reproaches, ventures a few threats, uses up her store of tears, seeks punishment, and perhaps, in desperation, bursts out in curses against her son;[5] but nothing suffices. The hardened, obstinate young man, accustomed to never obeying nor respecting his mother, spurns her advice, derides her endearments, mocks her reproaches, laughs at her threats, enjoys watching her tears, evades her punishments, and replies to her imprecations with more of the same, if he does not contemptuously lay his vile hands, as has happened, on his mother's person.[6]

This entire lamentable catastrophe could be avoided if children were educated

---

[5] Such curses have often been seen to come true. Sons should take care not to deserve them, and parents not to utter them. Both are wrong. [The theme of the "mother's curse" is a frequent one in Mexican *corridos* or ballads. –Tr.]

[6] An outrageous crime, yet one that has indeed occurred more than once.

well and scrupulously. And how many main obligations might parents have toward the education of their children? Just three, in the judgment of a great man of the Church who flourished in Mexico.[7] To wit: to teach them what they need to know; to correct them when they do wrong; and to set them a good example. Three things that are quite easy to say, but very difficult to put into practice, to go by the multitudes of ill-bred and vice-ridden children we see; yet not because they are difficult to observe (for the Lord's yoke is light), but because such fathers and mothers make not the remotest effort to practice the three precepts we have suggested; rather, they seem to avoid them as much as they can.

As for instruction, they are happy to give their children the most superficial sort, relying on tutors, or mercenary teachers,[8] who perhaps, seeing how the parents spoil the child, do nothing but flatter him, thus harming both their pupil and their own consciences.

As for correction, we have already commented on these parents' neglect, especially the mothers'.

Finally, as for setting an example, what is it that children normally see at home? Luxury among the people, excess at table, pride before the servants, haughtiness and disdain for the poor.

That's it, more or less; we all know what children see and hear in many houses. And since the examples we set are the greatest inducements that children of this age can have, to do good or to do bad, what kind of hearts could they have, given these examples? The results tell us: spoiled child, haughty adult; pampered child, stubborn adult; neglected child, incorrigible adult; and so on.

All this could be corrected by proper education, which should begin early. This advice comes from the Holy Spirit, which says: "If you have children, instruct them

---

[7] Father Juan Martínez de la Parra, of the Society of Jesus. [Spell (p. 157) identifies the work by the Mexican Jesuit (1655–1701) as *Luz de verdades católicas y explicación de la doctrina cristiana* (Mexico, 1691; 26 editions); he points out that it was Lizardi's source for his comments on the Lacedaemonians and Solon later in this chapter, and other examples in the next chapter. –Tr.]

[8] Here we are speaking of decent, well-born parents who work in this way, not of the common people, who harbor no normal feelings, for the latter cannot be corrected by criticism nor by persuasion. Those barbarians who take their son with them so that he can watch them when they are carried away by drinking cheap brandy in the street; those who take their children to the gaming table, and even gamble with them; those in whose pigsties nothing is ever heard but curses, swearing, quarrels and obscenity, and so on: not only can these sorts never give their children a good education nor set them a good example, because they are mere rational beasts, but for the same reason, they always get the children mixed up in their errors and prejudices, and with the examples they set, their children form devilishly bad hearts. This is a sad truth, but if you tried to disprove it, you would find evidence in its favor at every *pulque* stand, tavern, billiard room, jail, and street in this city, all of which are filled with no other vermin than these depraved idlers. What a wonderful thing it would be to make them useful to the State and to themselves! What better steps toward this could be taken than to take charge of their children, offering them a good education, by love and by force? And what better means than the project of free schools, which I proposed in my *Mexican Thinker*, numbers 7, 8, and 9? I guarantee that, if this plan is put into practice everywhere, within ten years our commoners will not be as stupid, depraved, and useless as they are now. It would be like turning stones into sons of Abraham.

from their youth" (Ecclesiasticus 7:23).[9] A tree should be straightened when it is a slender rod, not when it has grown strong and become a trunk. Doctors say that cures should be given at the outset of an illness, before it takes shape, before the blood is depraved and the humors are corrupted. Skillful surgeons set bones right after they are dislocated, and splint them right when they are broken; for otherwise, they grow together disjointed, and a cure becomes impossible.

That is precisely how children should be educated: when they are small, before they grow into solid trunks. Their faults should be corrected the moment they are noticed, for otherwise, they will grow up disjointed.

These truths are clearer than water, more common than days; no one can say they have never heard them; yet for all that, all we see are ill-bred, stupid boys, on their way to becoming idle, depraved, ruined men.

This is only because we act against everything that we know to be true. We pamper our children because they are children, and because we love them too much; when they become young men, they fill us with grief and disgust, and then come the if-onlys and the damn-it-alls, but to no avail.

Isn't it so much better and so much easier to tame the horse when it is a colt than when it is old? Parents have a very useful set of reins and spurs for this purpose, and if they know how to manage them prudently, they can hardly help producing good results. The rein is the law of the Gospel, well inspired; the spur is their good example, constantly practiced.

The cattlemen in our country say that the best horse needs spurs; and so we can say that the most obedient and good-natured child has to observe good examples in order to form sound morals in his heart and not be corrupted. This is the most effective spur to keep children from straying.

A good example is a better prod than all the advice, insinuations, sermons, and books. All of these are fine, but in the end they are just words, which are almost always carried away by the wind. Teaching that enters through the eyes makes a better impression than that which comes in through the ears. Brute animals cannot speak, yet they teach their children, and even rational beings, through example. Such is its strength.

It is no surprise that the drunkard's son should be a drunkard; or the gambler's son, a cardsharp; or the haughty man's son, haughty, and so on; for if that is what he learned from his parents, no wonder he should do what he saw being done. "The cat's kitten hunts mice," the saying goes.

What is to wonder at, or better, to laugh about, is that, as I just pointed out, when the son or daughter is grown, and has become a full-grown rogue, and commits terrible crimes and causes great disgust, then the parents pretend to be shocked, and they cry out: "Who would have thought it of my son! Who would have believed it of Fulana!"

Fools! Who would think it? Who would believe it? Everyone in the world, because everyone has seen how you raised them. The only miracle would be if you

---

[9] [In the King James version: "Hast thou children? Instruct them, and bow down their neck from their youth." –Tr.]

had educated them well and given them good examples, and they had turned out disobedient and depraved; but if they turn out bad when they were raised on no teachings at all, and have seen only the worst examples, it is the most natural thing in the world; because every effect corresponds to its cause. Who has ever been surprised to see cotton burn when a flame is put to it, or a piece of paper stained when it is dipped in an inkwell? No one, because everyone knows that it is natural for flame to burn a combustible, and for ink to stain whatever is susceptible to its color. Well, it is equally natural for children to be set aflame by bad education and to be contaminated by bad examples. The important thing is to give them neither.

That is why the Lacedaemonians had the custom of punishing parents for their children's crimes, pardoning the latter for their lack of awareness and accusing the former for their malice or indolence.

Wenceslaus and Boleslav, princes of Bohemia, were brothers, sons of the same mother; the former was a saint, whom we venerate in our altars, while the latter was a cruel tyrant who took his own brother's life. Different natures, different fates; but to what can these be attributed other than to their differing educations? The first was educated by his grandmother Ludmilla, a pious, saintly woman; the second, by his mother Drahomira, a monstrous, vile madwoman. That is how powerful good or bad education in early youth can be!

When we consider the wrongs that parents commit by neglecting their obligations to their children, we are not exonerating the latter for their misdeeds and disobedience. Both sides do wrong, and both upset the natural order, infringe the law, and do harm to the societies in which they live; and if they do not mend their ways, both will damn themselves, for as we read in the holy book: "The children gather the wood, and the fathers kindle the fire" (Jeremiah 7:18).

It is true that God says "the spoiled son shall be his parents' shame and their confusion"; but the divine Scriptures are also filled with condemnations of such children. Listen to these from the books of Proverbs and Ecclesiasticus: "He who curses his father shall lose his life, and shall soon reside in the shade of the tomb. He who disdains his mother shall have bad fame, or shall be dishonored. He who afflicts his father or flees his mother shall be ignominious and wretched. The curse of the mother ruins even the foundations of the houses of bad sons," and finally: "May ravens devour the body and pick out the eyes of he who dares mock at his father."[10]

These curses horrify us, but then, could any sons be so iniquitous, ungrateful, and heartless as to deserve them? Solon himself doubted it, and therefore, when he gave the Athenians their laws and set down punishments for every crime, he set none for the ungrateful or parricidal son,[11] saying that he was not convinced such sons could exist. Oh! We cannot pretend to have such doubts, for we can see thousands of sons unworthy of that name, as perverse and ungrateful as they are toward their parents.

On the other side, God lavishes blessings on good sons who are loving and obedi-

---

[10] [These biblical citations and those that appear two paragraphs below are rough paraphrases of Proverbs 20:20, 19:26, 30:17, and Ecclesiasticus 3:2–15. –Tr.]

[11] It amounts to the same thing to kill one's parents by grief as by poison or knife. Either way, one takes their lives.

ent toward their progenitors. He says that they "shall have a long life, for the blessing of the father establishes the houses of children": that is, their temporal happiness. "The honor that they give in tribute to the father, will result in glory for the son or his good name. The Lord will remember the good son on the day of his tribulation. He will hear his prayers and pardon his sins." And finally, "the blessings of God will accompany them for all time."

The love, respect, and gratitude that sons owe their parents are so just, deserved, and natural that the pagans themselves, though ignorant of the true God and unschooled in His blessings and curses, have recommended them to us not only in their writings, but through their works.

How strong was the love of that young Roman woman who, seeing her father imprisoned and sentenced to die of hunger, found a way to feed him through a crack in the prison door! And how? With her own breast milk. An action so tender that, when the judges learned of it, they granted a pardon to the poor old man.

How high was the respect of those two noble sons, Cleovis and Viton, who for lack of horses, pulled the carriage themselves to drive their mother, the priestess, to the doors of the temple! An action that Cicero praised and that the Romans so applauded that they venerated those two reverent sons as if they were gods.

How pious was Aeneas, for when the city of Troy was in flames on the fatal night of its destruction, when all was horror, terror, and confusion, when no one thought of anything but saving themselves from death, he ran to where his old father Anchises stood, lofted him on his shoulders, ran with him through the flames, and assured his life, saying:

> Come now! Hold my neck, for on my shoulders
> I will save you, my beloved father!
> So sweet a burden never could
> Weigh me down nor seem like work to me.
> Whatever may come after, for now the risk
> Or the good fortune of us both shall be as one.[12]

Don't heroic examples like these enchant, enrapture, entrance good sons? And don't they shame and confound bad sons? These shining actions were not undertaken by saintly Christians, nor by anchorites in the desert, but by heathens, pagans who knew not the light of the Gospel, nor did they know of its unfailing promises; yet nonetheless they loved, venerated, and succored their parents to the extremes that you have seen here, with no other guide than Nature, and no more self-interest than the inner satisfaction that is one of the fruits of virtue.

But bad sons not only fail to venerate their parents, they insult them; far from succoring them, they wastefully spend all they own, abandon them, and leave them to perish in poverty. Woe betide such sons! And woe betide me, for I was one of them! And the troubles and unpleasantness I caused my poor mother sent her to the grave, as you will see in the next chapter.

---

[12] [*Aeneid*, II, vv. 707–11. –Tr.]

CHAPTER 15

PERIQUILLO WRITES OF HIS MOTHER'S DEATH, AND OTHER
MATTERS THAT ARE NOT ALTOGETHER DISAGREEABLE

With what constancy does the hen afflict her breast a dozen times a day over her eggs! When she feels life stirring in them, how quick she is to break the shells and help her little chicks emerge! And when they do, how closely she watches over them! How tenderly she feeds them! How fiercely she defends them! How calmly she tolerates them, and how carefully she shelters them!

Likewise do the cat, the dog, the mare, the cow, the lioness, and all other animal mothers care for their children. But when their children are grown up, when they have passed beyond childhood (so to speak) and can find their own food, all their mother's love and tenderness stop then and there, and with beak, teeth, or horns, she tosses them aside forever.

Not so with rational mothers. What infirmities they suffer in pregnancy! What pains and risks they expose themselves to in childbirth! What illnesses, cares, and sleepless nights they tolerate in raising their children! And when the raising is done—that is, when the child is no longer a child, when he is a young man and can fend for himself—his mother's worries never cease, nor does her love diminish, nor her cares vanish. She remains always a mother, and she always loves her children with the same constancy and enthusiasm.

If our mothers acted toward us like the hens, and their love only lasted as long as our infancy, still we could never repay them the good they had done us, nor thank them enough for the toil we had given them; for giving us physical existence and watching over us to preserve it are no little things.

Surely for no other reasons does Ecclesiasticus exhort our respect and gratitude for our parents. "Honor thy father," he says in chapter VII, "honor thy father and forget not the groanings of thy mother. Remember that were it not for them thou wouldst not exist, and behave towards them with the same love that they showed for thee."[1] And St. Tobias the Elder told his son: "Thou shalt honour thy mother all the days of her life, for thou must be mindful what and how great perils she suffered for thee in her womb" (Tobias, ch. IV).[2]

In view of this, who could doubt that we are obliged by both Nature and religion not only to honor our parents at all times, but to support them in their need, under threat of grave sin?

I say "at all times," for there is an abuse among some people who believe that after they get married they become exempt from their obligations as sons or daughters, and who neither feel forced to obey and respect their parents as they once did, nor do they accept the slightest burden of caring for them.

---

[1] [Ecclesiasticus 7:29–30 (7:27–28); here, Periquillo paraphrases the second verse, which his father quoted to him five chapters earlier. –Tr.]

[2] [Tobias 4:3–4. –Tr.]

I have seen many of these sons and daughters, who, having contracted matrimony, begin to treat their parents with a maddening indifference and detachment. "No," they say, "now I'm emancipated, I've left your parental authority, times have changed," and their first act on taking possession of their new liberty is to smoke tobacco in front of their parents.[3] Next, they begin to speak to them with a kind of spitefulness, and finally, they do not lift a finger for them, even in their need.

Regarding the first obligation, that is, respect and veneration, children are never exempted from these, no matter what state they find themselves in, or what post they have been given. Parents are always parents, and children always children, and children are always praised, never vituperated, for respecting their parents. Solomon was married and was king, and he descended from his throne to receive his mother Bathsheba with the utmost submissiveness;[4] Pope Boniface VIII did the same with his mother; and so do all good sons, yet by humbling themselves so they gain only glory, blessings, and praise.

In regard to the support that children owe their parents in their hour of need, our obligation is all the greater. A woman cannot excuse herself from it by saying: "My husband doesn't give me enough"—she should ask him for it, for if he is a good son, he will give it; and if he won't, she should skimp on her spending and give up luxuries; however, that there should be money for dresses and dances and other extravagances, but not to help her mother, is a matter for scandal; so much that one can scarcely conceive that such daughters might exist.

We see this more frequently among men, who quickly say: "Oh, I'd help my parents; but I'm a poor man, I've got a wife and kids to care for, and I can't make ends meet." Hullo! This is no just excuse, either. Just let them ask the theologians, and they'll see that they're obliged to part their bread with their parents; and some would even say[5] that if the need is equal, it is a grave sin not to help their parents even before helping their own children.

Not supporting your parents in extreme cases is like killing them; a crime so cruel that the ancients, astonished by its enormity, deemed that one who committed it would be justly punished by being sewn into a bull's hide, to die there of suffocation, and then thrown thus into the sea, so that his body would never find the rest of the tomb.

Well, how many hides would we need to bundle up all the ungrateful children we see scandalizing the world with their base and villainous acts? Back then I would have earned one myself; for not only did I not support my mother, but I spent the little bit that my father had saved up so that she could support herself.

---

[3] Smoking is not bad; it is one of the tolerable vices, and even though it is often pernicious to the health and burdensome to the purse, custom now favors it; but taking a drag in front of your parents? That is not bad, either; it is just as legal as doing it in front of anyone else. No father will be scandalized to see his son taking snuff in his presence; but for all that, the same custom that tolerates taking snuff even in church, by the nose, does not tolerate taking it through the mouth, nor in front of one's parents or superiors. This is a prejudice, but a permissible one, by which we can prove our respect for certain people and places.

[4] [I Kings 2:19. –Tr.]

[5] St. Thomas. [The citation is perhaps to the chapter on the Fourth Commandment in the Catechism of St. Thomas Aquinas. –Tr.]

What a case! Of the handful of rules I was taught in school, I forgot some entirely after my father died, and I practiced others completely. After the inheritance was gone and my mother's jewels were sold, I forgot *addition*, for I no longer had anything to add; I never learned to *multiply*; but I learned *short division* and *long division* perfectly well, and soon divided everything that came my way among my friends and all our girlfriends; and so the bit of money we had was so quickly spent; nor was that enough, for there was always *subtracting* from my creditors, and I could do this lesson from memory, for if you owe one person four, and another one six, and another one three, and so on, and you don't pay any of them, you owe them all. This is what I knew how to do the best: owing, destroying, wasting, falling into debt, and never paying anyone in this life; and these are the lessons that all libertines know from A to Z. They can't add, because they have nothing to do it with; they can't multiply, either, because they waste everything; but subtracting from whoever lets their guard down, and dividing the little that they acquire with the other lazy swindlers they call their friends, that they can do with the best of them, and they don't have to turn to the rules of arithmetic to get it done. And that is what I did.

Between one thing and another, not a peso was left in the house, nor anything worth so much as a peso. Today we'd sell a knife, tomorrow a fork, the next day a niche, the following day a wardrobe, until all the furniture and furnishings were finished. Next went my mother's clothes, which the pawnshop[6] and the stores made quick account of, because, as we had nothing with which to redeem them, all her garments were lost for a trifling sum.

The truth is that I didn't spend it all myself; some of it was consumed by my mother and Nana Felipa. We were like the madman of whom Father Almeida speaks,[7] who had taken to the mad notion that he was the Holy Trinity; one day, someone asked him how that could be, seeing how ragged and tattered he was? To which the madman replied, "Well, what do you want, seeing as I have three mouths to feed?" So it was in our house, where there were three of us eating and no one looking for food. Of course, when there was any to be had, I would waste enough for thirty, and so I alone should take the blame for the complete destruction of my house.

My poor mother wore herself out convincing me to find some profession that might help us; but that was the last thing on my mind. First, because I liked freedom more than work, like any good libertine, if there is such a thing as a good libertine; second, because, what kind of profession could I have found that would be compatible with my uselessness and vanity, based on my nobility and my resounding, empty title of Bachelor of Arts, which, as far as I was concerned, was as good as a title of count or marquis?

My father's prediction came true to the letter; and then my mother, despite her affection for me, which never faltered, recognized how wrong she had been to oppose my learning a trade.

---

6 [The *Montepío* or Pawnshop was a government-run agency founded in 1775, in order to provide loans for the poor. It was located to one side of the Mexico City cathedral. –Tr.]

7 *Recreaciones filosóficas*, t. IV, Tarde 19.

Knowing how to do something useful with your hands—by which I mean knowing some manual craft or liberal art—is never reprehensible, nor is it contrary to a
noble background, nor to the studies and illustrious schooling that such a background might give; rather, there are many occasions when the most illustrious nobility does not avail a man, nor having had much wealth in the past; and at such times,
having a skill and knowing how to do something by himself are infinitely valuable.

"Dishonor," says an author who wrote almost at the end of the last century,[8] "dishonor should arise from idleness or from crime, not from an occupation. Every individual in the social body should consider himself a child of one large family."

What would have happened to Dionysius, king of Sicily, when he lost his throne
and wandered incognito and fugitive because of his tyranny, if he had no skill by
which to live? He would surely have perished in the clutches of beggarliness, or else at
the hands of his enemies; but he knew how to read and write, no doubt very well, for
he undertook to become a schoolteacher, and he lived from that office for some time.

What fate would have befallen Aristipus if, when he arrived at the Isle of Rhodes,
having lost all his wealth in a shipwreck, he had no other means of support? He
would have perished; but he was an excellent geometer, and when his skill became
known, the islanders gave him such a fine welcome that he never missed his homeland nor his wealth, and in proof of this he wrote these memorable words to his
countrymen: "Give your children the kind of riches that they will not lose even
when they emerge naked from a shipwreck."[9] How fitting this advice would be for
many mothers and many little noble boys!

If one of our lawyers, theologists, or canon lawyers were shipwrecked in Peking or
Constantinople, would he be able to earn his bread with his profession? No, because
in those great cities our religion does not reign and our laws do not rule; and if he
didn't know how to sew a shirt, weave a jacket, make a pair of shoes, or do any such
thing with his hands, he would find all his conclusions, arguments, systems, and erudition as useful for supporting himself as a physician would find his bromides on an
uninhabitable desert isle.

This is the truth, but unfortunately the ignorant prejudice against it is held
almost universally among the rich and those who deem themselves blue-blooded.

I said "almost," which is nonsense: leave out the "almost." This ignorant notion is
utterly widespread, so much so that it is backed up by the hoary and vulgar prejudice
that "the trades debase those who exercise them," and this error is followed up by an
even more damnable one, which is the disdain with which the poor manual crafts
are viewed and treated. Fulano is an upright man, but he is a tailor; Zutano is a
noble born, but he is a barber; Mengano is a virtuous man, but a shoemaker. Oh!
Who will make way for him? Who will seat him at their table? Who might treat him
with distinction and esteem? His personal qualities recommend him, but his trade
brings him low.

---

[8] Licenciado Don Francisco Xavier Peñaranda in his *[Resolución universal sobre el] sistema
económico y político más conveniente a España* [Madrid, 1789].

[9] [The quote is from Pedro Murillo Velarde, *Catecismo o instruccion christiana en que se explican los
mysterios de nuestra Santa Fe,* Madrid, 1752, p. 291 (Ruiz Barrionuevo, p. 320). –Tr.]

So would many people argue, but I would say to them: sirs, if you had no riches nor any means of support other than making shoes, sewing jackets, preparing hats, and so on, is it not true that you would then denounce the rich men who would treat you with the same stupid vanity that you now display toward craftsmen and artisans? There can be no doubt.

And if, to consider an impossible case, if one day all these artisans were to conspire against you and refuse to serve you, despite your money, would you not then go about barefoot? Yes, because you don't know how to make a pair of shoes. Would you not go about naked and dying of hunger? Yes, because you know how to do nothing to clothe yourselves, nor how to cultivate the land so that you might feed yourselves with its fruits.

Therefore, if in reality you are a useless bunch—even though you play the same role in this world that the actors play in that comedy titled *Fortune's Children*—why so haughty? Why so finicky? Why so scornful of the very ones you need the most, those on whom your brilliant good fortune depends?[10] If you act this way because those who exercise such trades to support themselves are poor, then you are tyrants, for it is only because of their poverty that you look down on those who serve you, and who perhaps keep you fed;[11] if you only treat them in this haughty fashion because they live from their own labor, then in addition to being tyrants, you are stupid; and if not, then I ask you: what do you live from? You, mine owner; you, hacienda owner; you, merchant: you would die of hunger and perish in destitution if Juan didn't labor in your mine, if Pedro didn't cultivate your fields, and if Antonio didn't consume your products, all by the sweat of their brows, while you, loafing lazily, perhaps, perhaps serve only as a scandal and a burden upon the republic.

Thus would I speak to the proud and foolish[12] among the rich; while I would encourage you, oh honorable poor![13] to endure their insults and affronts, to resign yourselves to Divine Providence and to continue honorably with your toil, satisfied that there is no base trade if the man is not base; nor are there any riches or distinctions that might acquit a man of a reputation for stupidity or depravity if he deserves it.

How often do ignorant or crime-ridden men ride past in gilded coaches that shake the foundations of your humble workshops? How many of the sauces that season the quail and pheasant at their tables are concocted of intrigue, crimes, and usury, while you and your children eat, in sweet tranquility, a simple tortilla, dampened perhaps with the sweat of your brow?

My dear children, it is not the trade that debases the man (I will never tire of repeating this truth); it is the man who debases himself with his wicked conduct; nor does a poor birth or a manual trade hinder a man from being given, by those who

---

[10] It is a given that the poor are the vassals of the rich, and the ones who increase their riches.

[11] The wretched day laborers who cultivate the haciendas, the workers who labor in the mines, and the artisans who work the looms, and so on, feed and support the luxury of the rich.

[12] It is to these that I speak.

[13] It is to these that the following apostrophe is dedicated, not to the wicked poor, for if the latter are insulted because of their misconduct, they well deserve it. To be a rogue, on top of being poor, is a terrible disgrace.

appreciate merit, the place he has earned with his virtue, skill, and knowledge. Good witnesses to this truth are all the clever poets, accomplished painters, excellent musicians, distinguished sculptors, and other skillful practitioners of the liberal and mixed arts, whom the world has seen visited, enriched, and honored by the popes, emperors, and kings of Europe. This is clear proof that distinguished merit and extraordinary skill not only are no barriers to honor, but are often the magnets that attract honor to their practitioners. In this very book, it has already been mentioned that Sixtus V, before he came to govern the Catholic Church as pope, was a pig herder[14]—an example that can stand in for all the others that are recalled in ecclesiastic and profane history; although vanity has made such examples rare in our time.

But we have to say it all. I don't know whether it is more amazing to see a man raise himself up from the trash heap to a high position, or to see others who, having attained such a post, do not forget their humble origins. I believe that, just as the latter is the right thing to do, it is also the more difficult of the two, bearing human pride in mind; and being more difficult, it is of course more amazing.

For a man to pass from a poor to a rich state, from plebeian to noble, from herdsman to king, as has happened, might be a chance effect in which the man himself has played no part; but if, seeing himself raised up far above the rest, he does not become arrogant or conceited, but shows himself to be human, affable, and courteous toward his inferiors, remembering what he had once been: that is, indeed, amazing, for it is proof of a great soul, one capable of holding his passions in check at any stage of life, something that does not come easily to man.

Most commonly, we see endless numbers who were born rich and great, and who are proud and haughty by nature; in other words, that is how they saw their houses being run as far back as they can remember; flattery rocked them in the cradle, and

---

[14] This pope was born in a village in the Ancona district on December 13, 1521. His father was a poor farmer (according to Moreri), or a wine grower (according to the author of the *Diccionario de hombre ilustres* [Spell, p. 151, identifies this book as Ladvocat's *Dictionnaire historique portatif,* Paris, 1752; *An Historical and Biographical Dictionary,* Cambridge, 1799]), named Peretti, and his mother was Mariana. He was herding piglets when a Franciscan friar who was not familiar with the road passed by and took him to be his guide; enchanted with the keenness of his replies, the friar brought him to his monastery. Soon thereafter, the young man took the habit of the Seraphic order, and, rising in accord with his application and talent, he came to sit in St. Peter's chair. He reestablished the edition of the Vulgate Bible to its original purity; canonized St. Diego, a Spanish Franciscan; added St. Bonaventure to the list of Doctors of the Church; ordered the celebration of the feast of the Presentation of the Blessed Virgin; and did many other excellent things. During a terrible famine that beset Rome and caused an uprising there, he constructed several buildings, cleared a number of roads, and promoted the famous temple or dome of St. Peter, in whose construction (which it was thought would never end) 600 laborers worked daily. Finally, he erected an obelisk in St. Peter's Square that rose 72 feet high. Nor was this the only Pope to come from a poor and humble background. St. Peter aside, St. Dionysius, John XVIII, Damasus II, Nicholas I, and others came from obscure lineages. Adrian IV and Alexander V depended on alms to eat when they were children; Urban IV was the son of another pig herder; Benedict XI was the son of a laundry maid; Benedict XII was the son of a miller; and so on. (See the history of the popes.) All of which proves that neither an obscure birth nor the deepest poverty is an obstacle to attaining the most honored positions, when a man's knowledge and virtue make him worthy of them.

they have inhaled vanity since their first breath. They inherited (to put it simply) nobility, money, titles, and with all that, the haughtiness and domination that they exercise over those below them.

That is bad, terrible, because no rich man should forget that he is first a man, nor that the poor and the plebeians are his fellow men; nevertheless, if any vices can be forgiven, it seems that the rich man's pride deserves some indulgence, considering that he has never seen the face of poverty, nor has he ever been free from the flatterers who constantly sweet-talk and kneel before him. You would have to be an Alexander not to fall into the temptation of letting yourself be decked out like a Nebuchadnezzar.

But the poor who were born among clods of dirt in some hamlet or miserable little village, whose fathers were some poor wretches, and who were swaddled as infants in the coarsest cloth; who were raised so and grew up so, battling misfortune and indigence, never hearing as much as an echo of adulation, indeed, becoming inured to scorn; of these men, I ask, if Providence has seen fit to elevate them to some brilliant position, why should they immediately banish such memories and forget such origins, to the degree that they not only despise the poor, not only fail to support their relatives, but—more detestable yet!—they deny their lineage altogether? Such pride is unforgivable.

These are not mere fictions of my pen; the world is witness to these truths. How many people, reading these lines, will say: "My brother the doctor doesn't speak to me"; others: "My sister, the married woman, doesn't greet me"; others: "My uncle the prebendary looks right past me," and so on, and so on, and so on?

I hate to say it, but perhaps this vice and ingratitude were why they invented the hackneyed saying, "If you want to see a contemptible character, give him an office." It shows a baseness of spirit[15] to let your blood degenerate and allow your kin to perish in poverty simply because they are poor, when you might easily favor them due to the lofty position you occupy.[16]

But whether it is pride, villainy, or whatever we want to call it, that is what we see in practice. And if such people are so haughty toward their own blood, what won't they do toward their dependents, subordinates, and other poor people whom they consider unworthy of their affability and courtesy?

What we see, none too rarely, is that many men who were thoughtful, affectionate, and well-bred with everyone in the sphere of the poor, as soon as their fortunes shift and they are raised from the ashes, become proud, puffed up, irksome, and detestable.

The famous Father Murillo, in his Catechism, citing Pliny and Strabo, says that Alexander's horse Bucephalus allowed anyone to pet it and lead it when it was unsaddled, but as soon as it was richly saddled and harnessed, it became untamable, and would only obey the young Macedonian. The good Father's meditation on this story

---

[15] Just as a plebeian may have a noble soul, so may there be a contemptible soul in a noble, and this is what we call a base soul or baseness of spirit.

[16] Without acting contrary to justice, let it be understood, for such help would not be a virtue, but an offense.

is so much to the point that I will quote it here word for word. "There are those," he says, "who are friendly to all when they are unsaddled, but as soon as they see themselves decked out with a robe, a tassel, a high post, I was even going to say with a friar's shroud, there is no getting along with them."[17]

No, children, I beg you not to add to the numbers of these proud ingrates. If, tomorrow, luck hands you a good position, placing you (as they say) on the top of the heap, or if you have wealth and influence, then distribute your favors to as many as you can without harming justice, for to do that is to be truly great. The higher you are elevated, the greater your benevolence should be. Cicero said, in his defense of Q. Ligario, that "nothing makes men seem more like God than this virtue." The world will always respect the august names of Titus and Marcus Aurelius. The latter filled Rome with glories and happiness, while the first was so inclined toward doing good deeds that, the day he did not do one, he said that he had wasted the day, *diem perdidimus*.

On the other hand, you should never let riches or distinguished positions go to your head, for that would be the surest proof that you do not deserve them and that you have never enjoyed them. When we see someone get dizzy when he rides in a coach or boards a boat, we can easily tell that it is the first time he has set foot in such a vehicle and that it has gone to his head. There is a reason why our popular adage goes, "A horseshoe that clatters is missing a nail," and this is why.

How differently the world judges those who have come from poor or obscure origins, and who, suddenly finding themselves with extraordinary wealth or offices, do not let the heights of their offices go to their heads, and are not dazzled by the brilliance of their wealth, but remain steadfast in their former simplicity and sweet nature, and thereby conquer the hearts of everyone they meet! Must we not admit that such men's hearts are magnanimous, that gold neither stuns nor excites them, and that, though they were born without high posts and honors, they always deserved them?

And if these same men, instead of abusing their power or money by oppressing the helpless and trampling the poor, were to recognize a fellow man in each of these wretches, and so were to treat him sweetly, inspire him with hope, and favor him as much as they could, isn't it true that instead of backbiters, malcontents, and grumblers, they would have an endless number of friends and admirers who would smother them with blessings, wish for their continued rise, and praise their memory even after the end of their days? Who could doubt it?

A no less laudable quality for one of the rich men of whom I have been speaking is a sincere and unaffected candidness. Knowing how to admit our own defects is a virtue that brings the immediate benefit of saving us from the embarrassment of having someone else rub them in our faces; and if being born poor or without a pedigree is a defect,[18] by admitting it ourselves we put a good muzzle on our enemies and malcontents.

---

[17] [Pedro Murillo Velarde, *Catecismo*, p. 323–24. –Tr.]

[18] These are not defects. The world scorns the poor and those who do not shine with nobility; but this is just one of the inanities of which the world is full. Defects that do not depend on a man's free will are not reprehensible, nor should they be thrown in a man's face. To do so is foolishness.

This truth was well understood by a certain Willigis, the son of a poor wheel-wright who rose by his virtue and learning to become archbishop of Mainz in Germany, and who, in order not to become conceited because of his high position—or, as we have suggested, not to give his rivals any work to do—put a cartwheel on his coat of arms, with this motto: *Memineris quid sis et quid fueris. (Remember what you are, and what you were.)* Far from diminishing his good name, his humility raised it so high that after his death, Emperor Henry II commanded that the cartwheel remain always on the coat of arms of the archbishops of Mainz.[19]

Agothocles, who became a king, and a rich king at that, could have dined on gold and silver, yet he ate on simple pottery plates, to remember that he was a potter's son.

And finally, Pope Boniface VIII was the son of very poor parents; when he became the pontiff of Rome, his mother went to see him; she entered finely dressed, and the Holy Father did not even speak to her; rather, he asked: "Who is this lady?" "This is Your Holiness' mother." "That cannot be," he said, "for my mother is very poor." Then the lady had to take off her beautiful gowns and return to see him wearing a humble dress, on which occasion the Pope received her and gave her every honor that the mother of such a good son deserves.[20]

So you see, my dears, that neither working at a trade nor poverty debases a man, nor are they obstacles to obtaining the most brilliant posts and offices if he comes to deserve them through his virtue or learning. You should soak up these truths, and follow these examples constantly—not those of your bad father, who, having become accustomed to laziness and license, did not want to devote himself to learning a trade, nor seeking a master to serve, for he was noble; as if nobility might support idleness and licentiousness.

My poor mother wore herself out giving me advice, but in vain. I got worse day by day, and moment by moment gave her new sorrows and vexations, until, hounded by poverty and oppressed by the burden of my wickedness, the wretched lady became bedridden with the illness from which she died.

During that time, how hard it was to find a doctor! What worries to pay the apothecary! What distress to buy the food! But not for me, no—for good Aunt Felipa! Because I, as great a rogue as ever, scarcely stopped by the house at noon and night to gorge myself on everything I could find, and to ask, for politeness' sake, how my mother was feeling.

---

[19] [Lizardi collected this and the following two examples from Juan Martínez de la Parra, *Luz de verdades católicas*. The third example refers to an incident in the life of Boniface IX, not Boniface VIII as Martínez de la Parra erroneously wrote (see Spell, p. 157). –Tr.]

[20] It is also known that Benedict XI, who was the poor son of a laundry maid and who rose to the papacy, pretended not to recognize his mother when she came dressed in silk, and that when she returned to visit him in her humble dress, he recognized her and lavished honors on her. History tells us that Benedict XII, born the son of a miller, never wanted to recognize his father except when he dressed in his miller's clothes. These heroic examples of humility have been written down so that the merit and virtue of these personalities might be further enhanced. See Guillermo Burio's *Onomástico*, secc. X, fol. 358. [The note refers to Guillaume Bury, *Romanorum pontificum: Brevis notitia*, 1675. –Tr.]

Many years have passed, I have wept many tears and paid for many masses for her soul, and still I cannot quiet the terrible cries of my conscience, which incessantly tell me: "You killed your mother with worries; you did not support her when she lived, after plunging her into poverty; and in the end, you did not close her eyes when she died." Oh, dear children! God forbid you should suffer such remorse! Love, respect, and support your mother always, for that is what the Creator and nature demand.

Fortunately, the fever she suffered was so furious that the doctor had her prepare for her demise on the same day, and the following day she lost all consciousness.

I said that this was fortunate, because if it weren't for this malady, she would have suffered doubly with the pain and with the grief that her ungrateful and worthless son's base behavior must have caused her.

For the six days she lived, her entire delirium consisted of giving me advice and calling out for me, from what the neighbor women told me; and when I was at home, I heard only: "Has Pedro come home? Is he here? Give him some supper, Aunt Felipa; son, don't go out, it's late, something bad might happen to you in the street," and other things along the same lines, proving the love she had for me. Oh, my mother! How much you loved me, and how poorly I repaid your endearments!

In the end, Her Grace expired when I was not at home. I learned of it in the street, and did not return home or set foot in the neighborhood until the third day, so that I would not become involved in all the expenses associated with her burial, for I was penniless as always, and my parish priest was not very fond of performing his services on credit.

On the third day, I began showing my face and pretending I had just heard the news, telling everyone I had been in jail on account of some lawsuit, with a prayer on my lips, trying to learn my mother's fate, and who knows how many other lies; and with these and a couple of tears I managed to win back the scandalized neighbor women and the furious Nana Felipa, from whom I learned that, seeing that I wasn't going to show up and that the corpse could wait no longer, she had swept up everything she could find, even the mattress and my few rags, and had sold them for the first price she was offered at the flea market,[21] and so resolved the problem.

This news grieved me, or that part of it that concerned me directly, since her maneuver had left me with the clothes I had on my back and no change of shirt, for all the shirts I had owned amounted to two.

Next she told me that I owed the doctor for who knows how many house calls, and the apothecary for who knows how many prescriptions; since I had no intention of paying them, I didn't bother finding out the amounts.

When all is said and done, I cannot remember Aunt Felipa, that good old woman, without feelings of tenderness. She was nursemaid, sister, friend, daughter, and mother to my own mother all that time. Whether by begging or borrowing, she fed her, treated her, served her, held the wake for her, and buried her,

---

[21] [The Mexico City *baratillo,* or flea market, was built in 1793 at the corner of Allende and Donceles, a site occupied today by the Chamber of Deputies. –Tr.]

with utmost love, charity, and zeal; she played the role that should have been mine, to my humiliation, and that you might learn that there are faithful, loving servants who are grateful to their masters, often more so than the children themselves; and note that after my mother reached her final state of poverty, she told Nana Felipa to look for another job, because she was no longer able to pay her salary; at which the dear old woman wept and replied that she would not leave her until death parted them, and that until then she would serve her without pay, which is what she did, for everywhere there are heroic servants like the coppersmith of St. Germaine.[22]

But I had not won Nana Felipa's love quite so well, despite the fact that she had reared me, as they say. Like all good women, she endured the nine days of mourning at home, although enduring them was not the worst of it, but rather having to feed me each of those nine days, at the expense of a thousand loans and a thousand embarrassments, for not a stick remained in the house.

But, seeing my shamelessness, she told me, "Pedrito, you know I don't have a penny to my name; I'm stripped bare and out of a job because I gave it all up to serve and accompany my dear lady's soul, may she enjoy God's grace; but now, my little boy, she's died, and I've got to go out and make a living; because you don't have any money and no way to get it, and I don't neither, so what else can we do?"

As she said this, she was crying like a baby and leaving the house all at the same time, and none of my arguments could persuade her to stay. She did the right thing. She knew what kind of bread I kneaded, and what kind of life I had given my poor mother; what hopes could she still have for such a vagabond?

Just look at me here in my house of mourning, which cost twenty reales a month in rent that hadn't been paid in seven months; with no bed, sheets, or clothes but what I was wearing; with nothing to eat and no one to feed me; and in the midst of these afflictions, here comes the damnable landlord pestering me to pay him; calculating for me that 20 times 7 is 140, which comes to sixteen pesos and four reales, and letting me know that if I don't come up with the cash, a token to pawn, or a guarantor for a loan, he'll go see a judge and have me thrown in jail.

Fearful of this new misfortune, I offered to pay him the next day, begging him to wait while I collected a debt to my mother.

The poor fellow believed it and let me go. Losing no time, I wrote a document for him in which I said that a good payer does not worry about pawning some tokens, and that I therefore signed over to him all the goods I had left in my house, a list of which I left on the table.

Having written the letter, sealed it with wax, and left it and the key with the landlord's wife, I set out to try new adventures and to make my rounds, as you will discover in the next chapter.

---

[22] ["The Coppersmith of St. Germaine" was a story by Stéphanie-Félicité comtesse de Genlis, in her moralistic children's book *Les Veillées du Château* (Paris, 1784; *Tales of the Castle,* London, 1785); the book appeared in Spanish translation in 1788, and in Mexico City, this story was also adapted as a play, which Lizardi could have seen. –Tr.]

But before closing out this one, you should learn that the next day the landlord came to collect, asked for me, was given the letter, read it, asked for the key, opened the room to see what goods I had left, and came across the promised list, which said:

List of the valuable goods and furnishings that I surrender to Don Pánfilo Pantoja for seven months' rent that I owe him for this room. To wit:

Two couches and four stools, made of straw, tattered and infested with bedbugs.

One old bed that once was green, also infested.

One small corner table, broken.

One large, ordinary table, missing a leg.

One small bookcase, missing the key and two shelves.

One sleeping mat, five yards long, with 5 million bedbugs a yard.

One niche altar of ordinary wood with a piece of glass, and inside it a wax saint, which you can no longer tell who it is because of the ravages of time.

Two large canvases, whose paintings can no longer be discerned for the same reason; but the burlap bag in which they are stowed can be discerned.

Two old wooden fire screens, golden, one with the window broken, the other missing the window altogether.

One worm-eaten desk.

One large box, missing the bottom and the key.

One scruffy, very ancient cloth trunk.

One easy chair, missing a foot.

One dull-sounding guitar, made of shingles.

One pair of candle-snuffers, twisted out of shape.

One basin for holy water, of Puebla pottery, chipped.

One Jerusalem rosary with its cross inlaid with mother-of-pearl, without any defects other than missing three or four beads out of every ten.

One incomplete volume of *Don Quixote,* minus engravings.

One copy of Lavalle, somewhat old, covers missing.

One mountain of old novenas.

One copper candlestick.

One large candle holder, missing the barrel.

Two pewter spoons and one fork with one tine.

Two Puebla mugs, handles missing.

Two Puebla bowls and four broken plates.

One deck of mismatched cards.

About twenty stories and novels, and other assorted pamphlets.[23]

One dozen pots and pans, between the whole and broken ones.

One saucepan with a hole.

A piece of a grindstone.

One mortar, no pestle.

The brush for the chamber pot.

The water jug.

The well bucket.

The poker for the fire.

The lock on the door.

One small, cracked chamber pot.

Two usable chamber pots, not empty.

All the above is for the landlord. If there is any money left over after his debt is paid, please invest it in masses in honor of my late mother.

—Mexico, November 15, 1789. Pedro Sarmiento.

The sorry landlord cursed himself on reading this list, while as I have told you, I was occupied with more pressing affairs.

---

[23] [The third edition reads: "About twenty *Diarios, Gacetas,* and other papers," referring to the two Mexico City newspapers of the time—anachronistically, since the *Diario de México* began publishing in 1805. –Tr.]

CHAPTER 16

Alone, poor, and abandoned by his relatives, Periquillo meets
Juan Largo, who persuades him to embark on a scoundrel's
career, specializing in being a pest of the gaming tables

Finding myself alone, orphaned, poor, and without house nor home nor a place to sleep, like the accursed Jews, since there was no parish or neighborhood that I could call my own, I could only hope to find a mother who would swaddle me, as they say; and so I headed into the street, ragged, downcast, and brooding, as soon as I had given the list of my exquisite possessions to the landlord's wife.

The first step I took was to try my relatives' patience on both my mother's and my father's side of the family, thinking I might find some consolation for my sorrows among them; but I was only fooling myself. I told them the story of how my mother had died and I had been left orphaned and helpless, topping off the tale with a plea for their protection; some of them told me that they hadn't known that their sister had died; others pretended it was news to them; all of them feigned sympathy for my loss; but none of them offered me the slightest help.

I left each of their houses in indignation, feeling that I had never had any relative who cared about my situation other than my departed mother, for whom I began to grieve more vividly at the same time that I conceived a mortal hatred toward my entire horde of heartless aunts and uncles.

Is it possible, I wondered, that this is what relatives are like in this world? That they can care so little to see their own kin perishing, being so closely related? Are these the laws that nature sets? Is this how man respects the claims of blood? And even so, are there madmen who have any trust in their family? When my father was alive, when he had a bit of wealth and they came to our house to be fed, these same relatives made a great fuss over me, and even gave me a bit of change for treats; if we had any kind of entertainment, or if it were a day for long tablecloths, as they say, they'd all come piling in, many of them without waiting to be invited; but when all that ended, when poverty took hold of my house and there was nothing left to skim, they withdrew, and never again returned to see me or my mother. It is not surprising, then, that I'm being dismissed so curtly from their houses now. I should even thank them for not denying that they know me and for not throwing me down the stairs. If I ever have children, I'll have to counsel them never to trust in their relatives, only in the pesos they earn on their own. That peso is, indeed, their closest relative—the most generous, the readiest to serve, the most useful in every situation. In the end, these other relatives are just flesh and bone, like all animals: ungrateful, vain, self-interested, and useless. When their kinsman can help them, they visit him and fawn on him ceaselessly; but if he's poor, like me, they not only fail to help him: they even are ashamed of being related.

I was walking along, absorbed in these thoughts and trembling with rage against my contemptible kin, when I turned a corner and, in the distance, saw my friend Juan Largo approaching me. My heart leapt in delight, feeling that this encounter would necessarily be a happy one for me.

As soon as we were close, he said, "Ah, Periquillo, my friend! What're you up to? How are you doing? How's things?"

I told him my troubles in an instant, concluding by heaping slander on my uncles.

"And what have those gentlemen done to you," he asked me, "to put you in such a bad mood with them?"

"What do you think they've done?" I replied. "Nothing but despise me and refuse to give me any help, forgetting that I have the same blood as them and that they owe my father a thousand favors!"

"You're right," said Juan Largo; "relatives today are a bunch of wretched tight-wads. I just had an even worse time with that old dog, my uncle Don Martín. You should know that ever since I left this city, going on a year now, I've been living with him on the hacienda; but a damnable cowboy gave false witness against me about two weeks ago, claiming I had sold ten of their calves, even though I swear to you, brother, that it wasn't more than seven; but there are people who would leave Mass early just to tell a lie and ruin your reputation. My uncle believed him from the first word, and he pinned the blame on me for all of his losses at the hacienda since I moved there; he swore at me and threatened me to make me confess; but I've never been more prudent, and never held my tongue more carefully. I kept quiet, and I will continue to keep quiet for all eternity if they continue demanding that I confess; which is why Don Martín got angry and threw me in a room where he took one of those vines that the army corporals use and gave me such a heap of lashes with it that I still haven't come to; and that's not all: he stripped me of all my plain old rags and took away both my little horses, and threw me into the street—that is, into the road, which is the closest street to his house—swearing before the entire court of heaven that if he ever set eyes on me again out there, he'd send a bullet flying my way; and he added that I was a rogue, a bum, a thief, and an ingrate who was robbing him blind after eating him half out of house and home. 'And so, curse you, rogue,' he told me, 'curse you, you aren't my nephew the way you thought; you're just a wretched, wicked hanger-on, and that's why you're so contemptible, because I don't have any thieves for nephews.'

"That's how angry my uncle got with me; and when I found myself abandoned, poor, beaten to a pulp, and left in the middle of the road, I resolved to come to this great city, and that's just what I did. It'd be about a week or ten days since I got here; I went looking for you right away at your house; I didn't find you there, or anyone who could tell me where you lived. I've found Pelayo, Sebastián, Casiodoro, the Mayorazgo,[1] and other friends, and they've all told me how long it's been since they've seen you. I've asked Chepa la Guaja, and La Pisaflores, and Pancha La Larga, and La Escobilla, and the other girls about you, and they all answered that they don't know where you live. In short, during this brief time, I have not stopped try-ing to find out about you for a moment, but all in vain. So tell me: why did you leave your house?"

---

[1] [The Mayorazgo: this nickname literally means "the entailed estate," implying that the friend is wealthy (see Lizardi's critique of *mayorazgos* in Chapter 29). –Tr.]

I replied, first, to keep from having to pay a few bills I owed; and second, because my house was a wretched little room and so indecent that I was ashamed to have visitors there.

Januario approved of my actions, and I asked him, "So what are your plans now? How are you making a living?"

"As a *pest of the gaming tables*," he replied, "and if you don't have a job and want to do the same, you can join me, and I hope to God[2] we won't die of hunger, since four eyes see better than two. It's an easy business, not much work; it's fun and it pays. So, you want to?"

"You bet," I said. "But tell me: what do you mean by being a *pest* of the gambling tables? What's that?"

"That's what they call the ones who go gambling," Januario told me, "without having a penny on them, but who just play *by their wits*; and they're the ones that the gamblers fear, because they don't have anything to lose, and with a clever move, they often sneak a win."

"I'm liking your plan more and more," I said; "but tell me, what do you mean, *play by their wits*?"[3]

"Playing by your wits," Januario answered, "means making money without risking a dime of your own on a bet."

"That's got to be hard," I said, "because I've heard it said that you can do anything without money except gamble."

"Don't you believe it, Perico. We *pests* have the advantage of gambling without a penny, because getting money by winning the pot doesn't take skill: it just takes luck and being able to guess what's coming next.[4] The trick is to win it without putting down a bet."

"Well, if that's it, I'll call myself a *pest* starting this second; but tell me, Juan, how do you go about playing by your wits?"

"Look," he replied; "you make sure to find a good spot (because a front-row seat is more valuable at a gambling table than at a bull fight); and when you're sitting there, you *eyeball* the dealer so you can catch him if he's *grifting* or *copping a peek*,

---

[2] A crude and foolish thing to say, though it is no stranger to certain tongues. We should never hope that God will help us take vengeance or satisfy some sinful passion, for that would be to abuse His generosity and justice, thinking Him capable of consenting to our vices. God permits sin, but does not like it.

[3] Although, as noted, Perico was a lost soul, he had not yet learned many acts and terms from the school of the depraved. Januario was the one who finished his training.

[4] [Much of the following chapter deals with the game of *monte,* which was the gambling fad of Mexico City in the 1790s (see Spell, p. 180). In monte, the dealer plays against all the other gamblers. He begins by turning a set of two cards face up (this set is called the *albur*), and then a second set of two cards (the *gallo*). The gamblers place bets on these cards, and then the dealer turns over the rest of the deck one card at a time. The first card of each set that is matched by a card of equal value from the deck wins the amount that was bet on the opposite card in the set.

[Lizardi is highly critical of the gamblers' dissolute life, but at the same time he seems to revel in their slang (the editor of the fourth edition has eight explanatory footnotes in the next paragraph alone), much of which I have translated into rough equivalents drawn from U.S. gambling slang. –Tr.]

and then you *blow the whistle* on him, because they always give a little something to the snitch in these run-ins. Or you can *hedge* your bets, *nail* a card, *cop the kitty*, or if nothing else works, walk off with a bet when it's payoff time, and then you say: 'I'm an upright man, and I didn't come here to swindle anyone, and I vow to St. So-and-so and swear to St. Thus-and-such, and may all the devils take me if this bet isn't mine.' And when things get hotter, you add: 'Isn't that right, Don Fulano? You tell 'em, Don Zutano,' until in the end nobody is sure who the money belongs to, and whoever's holding the bet wins it. That's the riskiest way to play by your wits, because you might run up against some hothead who'll beat it out of you, but that's not what usually happens, and when you're in a tight spot you've got to take risks. The thing is, I'm not going to go without dinner or skip my supper, because if nothing else has paid off and the game is coming to an end, I'll walk off with six or eight reales in my purse by grabbing somebody's bet, even if it's my own mother's. But you always have to keep in mind, starting right now, that you're never to swipe somebody's ante or walk off with someone else's bet if it comes to a peso or more; just swipe small bets and tiny antes, like three or four reales, which they always double when they pay off, and since the amounts are small, they let it pass, and no one notices which of the two of you is pulling off the fraud, and so you end up making money from it; but that doesn't happen with bigger bets, because those attract attention and nobody lets them pass unnoticed; instead, the owners keep their eyes peeled and fixed on their money, and that leaves you too exposed."

"I truly thank you, Januario my friend, for wanting to help me find a way to keep myself fed, which is something I certainly need to do; and I also thank you," I said, "for your advice and counsel; but I'm just a bit scared that I might end up getting a thrashing or worse in one of these deals, because the truth of the matter is that I'm clumsy and not the old hand that you are, and I'm afraid that I'm likely to bungle it all badly from the word go, and just when I think I'm going to rake in the hay, instead I'll find the field mowed down to the bare ground."

My show of fear made Januario angry, and he said, "Get out of here, brute! What a good-for-nothing you are. You, get a thrashing? What a joke! What do you think, they're going to spot your dodge right away? I'd expect your hand to tremble the first time you grab a half-real; but it's all a matter of practice, and later on you'll be nicking fifteen or even twenty pesos, cool as can be, and I'll tell you how.[5] I'm sure you know that getting started is always the most difficult part; once you overcome that, everything becomes more bearable. March bravely into your new job as a *pest*, which is really incredibly cushy, and don't be afraid that anybody will give you a thrashing

---

[5] These were Perico's friends and the advice they gave him. Surely the devil himself could not have given worse advice. Father Jerónimo Dutari was quite correct to say that bad friends are devils that don't frighten. The way that his friend is inciting him here to rob and cheat is how it is usually done in practice, and that is how it actually happens: one begins with fear, but later the vice becomes familiar. Therefore it is best never to begin.

[Spell (p. 157) identified Dutari as the Jesuit author of *Vida christiana, o práctica fácil de entablarla con medios y verdades fundamentales contra ignorancia o descuidos comunes* (Mexico, 1724). The quote (cited again in Chapter 30 below) appears on pp. 29–30 of the 18th edition (Madrid, 1794). –Tr.]

or a drubbing, since you must have heard it said that Fortune smiles on the daring and repels the cowardly; she's already abandoned you—in fact, she's repelled you but good: do you want to end up even worse off? And besides: suppose they finally start up a campaign against you or me, after we've spent three or four months eating, drinking, and spending the gamblers' money: who's to say they'll beat us? We can give as good as we get, can't we? And finally, say we come out of it with a broken head or a disjointed rib: it takes a little risk to rent a house; life isn't all sweetness and light; and if that's what happens, we can always resort to doctors and hospitals. So come on, Perico, let's get cracking and leave poverty and hunger behind, because if you don't take any risks, you'll never cross the sea. And besides, there are even more profitable ways to play by your wits, and some of them might be less dangerous."

"So tell me what they are, then," I said, "because I'm bursting to find out."

"One of them," Januario told me, "is to volunteer to help deal the cards to the other gamblers, and this job usually gets you a good tip—a croupier's gratuity—if the owner is free with his money and wins; and even if he isn't and he loses, as a croupier you never lose so long as you're not a fool, because if you just keep *raking off the pot* now and then, your accounts will balance out just fine; but you have to do it with style, because otherwise, you'll be too exposed."

"What does that mean," I asked, "that bit about *raking off the pot?* I don't understand the professional terms of this business very well."

"*Raking off the pot*," my teacher said, "means rat-holing as much of it as you can, a little bit at a time, while your partner shuffles the cards, by pretending that you're scratching yourself, dusting the table, picking up a cigarette, folding your handkerchief, or doing whatever business you think will serve you to get the job done; but as I said, you have to do it very craftily, and if you can do that, your croupier's tip will be worth a good eight or ten pesos to you at least.

"Another job you can pull is to have a friend that you trust, like me, sitting next to you at the gaming table, and then every time the owner of the money lets his guard down, you pass your friend four pesetas, pretending that you are changing a peso for him.[6] That money, your partner takes and bets it fearlessly; if he gets beaten, you just advance him a few more pesetas; when his bet pays off, you always give him a little extra money to sweeten the pot, all without fear, because as long as the owner thinks you're honest, he'll be putty in your hands. If he's winning, the money will dazzle him, and if he's losing, his losses will blind him; so he'll never reflect on what kind of job you're doing—and lots of times it's an excellent job that gets pulled, because there have been times I've seen the croupier and his *front* (that's what they call the partner) knock over the entire pot between them. In a case like that, the two of them never leave together; they go out one at a time, not to raise suspicion, and meet at a prearranged place to split the loot, and hallelujah.

"The third, best-paying, and quickest job is to take the whole pot with a single hand, if your partner has the dough to cover it; and if not, in a few different hands, since it comes to the same thing, which is to knock over the pot. But to pull this one off, the croupier and his front both have to be very shrewd; the whole trick consists

---

6 [Peseta: in colonial Mexico, two *reales* or one fourth of a peso. –Tr.]

of stacking the cards and holding the deck so you know where the packet is, so the stacked hands will come off on top when you cut; and you also have to arrange whether your front is going to bet on the top card or the bottom card, the inner or the outer, or on the one-and-one, so that you don't make a stupid mistake and lose your money, which is what they call *going down the chute on a cinch hand.*

"To get a good start in this career, and to be able to progress in it, it is essential that you learn about *stacking, pulling through, crimping, burying, pegging, palming, taking a free ride, flashing a hold-out,* and other such refined and exquisite skills, and it doesn't make any difference whether you understand them now or not;[7] I'll teach them all to you in the next two or three weeks, because if you put your mind to it and if you're not dull-witted, that will give you plenty of time to master the subject, with the help of my lessons.

"But it is a fact that, if you want to come out on top in most situations, you have to work with your own tools; and so, it is essential that you know how to make card decks."

"That's another thing," I said, quite surprised, "because, can't you see that it would be impossible for me to do that, given that I lack the main thing, which is money?"

"And why would you need to have money to make decks?" Januario asked me.

"What do you mean, why?" I said. "For plates, paper, ink, paste, presses, printers, and everything else you'd need to print the cards; and besides, even if I had the money, I wouldn't dare make them; don't you know that if they caught us, they'd ship us off to prison as smugglers?"[8]

Juan Largo roared with laughter at my simplicity, and said, "I can tell you're still a poor, naïve boy, and you still have milk on your lips. Pumpkin head! To make decks like I'm telling you, you don't need all the stuff or money that you seem to think. Look, I've got all the tools of the trade here in my bag."

And saying this, he showed me a few rectangles of tin, a sharp pair of scissors, a bit of gum, and a small brick of India ink.

It flustered me to see so little equipment, and I found it hard to believe that you could make a deck of cards with just that; but my teacher broke my astonishment by saying, "Don't be so amazed, stupid. Making decks the way I'm telling you doesn't involve gluing paper, engraving plates, printing them, and all the other things card manufacturers do; that's a different trade. Making them the way gamblers do means dolling them up: for that, all you need is the handful of tools you see here, and with just these you can trim them down along the top or the sides, or give them the kind of corners they call *ears*; or you can color them, or scrape their edges (what they call *sanding*), or gum them, or any other skill that you can hope to learn; all toward the honest end of taking the shirts off the backs of the careless."

---

7 Periquillo could easily have explained how these hoaxes worked, but no doubt he was careful to keep quiet, preferring to warn the more gullible readers about the dangers of gambling, without teaching them to the more malicious. It is good to know that tricks exist, but not to know how to pull them off.

8 [Under Spanish rule, manufacturing playing cards was a government monopoly. –Tr.]

"The truth, brother," I said, "is that all the jobs you're talking about are very good, but they amount to robbery and theft, and I doubt there's a confessor who would absolve them."

"Well, well, now," said Januario, shaking his head, "aren't you fresh! So, now that you're running around like a lost sheep, homeless and naked, not a bite to eat and not a battlement to hang yourself from, you start getting scrupulous? Idiot! If you're so virtuous, why did you leave the monastery? Wouldn't it have been better for you to stay there, eating for free and all meals guaranteed, not wandering here and there dying of hunger? Come on! I feel sorry I wasted so much saliva enlightening you, for your own good and to keep you from dying of hunger. Animal! If everybody thought like you, if they all considered that the money they won were stolen and should be returned, and that otherwise the devil would carry them off, do you think there could be as many idlers making a living from gambling as there are now? Do you think they all trust to luck and honesty and that's how they survive? No, Perico, they play with the long cue,[9] and they always add their bit of skill; if not, what would they live from? They'd win one day a month, and lose the other twenty-nine, because you must have heard that gambling takes away more than it gives, and that's especially true if you try to be very scrupulous; because he who plays clean, goes home cleaned out; and for that reason, the first thing that the young gentlemen who are my comrades and companions do, before they embark on a cardsharping career, is hide their consciences under their pillows, lay back from work, and get up-to-date. That said, every single one of the ones I've known has his own devotion. Some pray to the blessed souls, some to the Holy Virgin; this one to St. Christopher, that one to St. Gertrude; and finally, we all place our hopes in the Lord, that He will give us a good death.[10] So don't be a fool, Periquillo, pick your own devotion, and go ahead, man, go ahead, don't be afraid; it'll be worse if you keep your lips sealed and bear it,[11] because wherever you go, expect it or not, you're likely to meet people who won't give you so much as a rope to hang yourself. You just saw how your own uncles treated you. So, if you can find a crust of bread among your own people, what hopes do you have left for your future? I'm back in Mexico now, I'm your friend, and I can teach you and train you; if you let this opportunity slip, tomorrow I might be gone and you'll be left here begging for handouts; because it isn't every shark who likes to teach his skills, since they're afraid of raising crows that might scratch out their eyes tomorrow or the next day. In sum, Perico, I've said plenty. Only you can say what you'll do, since I'm only doing this out of charity."[12]

Since, on the one hand, I felt that need was pressing, and that I had no useful skills, and on the other hand, since Januario's projects were all too flattering, for they

---

[9] An allusion to the game of billiards, or rather pool, for billiards was not played widely at the time. −E.

[10] A terrible hope. We should never place our hopes in God in order to offend Him; nor make use of the devotions to the saints for that purpose; rather, it is an outrage to invoke them in the belief that they will intercede with God for those who offend Him with such hopes.

[11] It is not worse to be poor than to be a thief; but in practice, we say that many people become thieves to avoid poverty, and how many bad people there are.

[12] Wonderful charity! And many examples of charity that we see in the world are similar.

offered me nothing less than the possibility of making money without working, which had always been my aspiration, I had no trouble making up my mind; and so I thanked my teacher, whom I acknowledged from that moment on as my protector, and promised that I wouldn't stray a whit from the observance of his precepts, regretting my scruples and warnings, as if man should ever regret not following in the footsteps of iniquity; but the fact is that we often do just that.

During our conversation, Januario noticed that my lips were white, and he said, "It looks to me like you haven't eaten lunch."

"Nor breakfast, either," I replied, "and I'm sure it's already half past two in the afternoon."

"It's not even one yet," Januario said, "but the clock of a hungry stomach always runs fast, just as it always runs slow for a full stomach. For now, stop your worrying; let's go eat."

"Praise be!" I said to myself, and we left.

That was the first day I had ever experienced the terrible power of hunger, and perhaps that was why, as soon as I set foot in the tavern doorway and the smell of the dishes hit my nose, I thought that, at the very least, I was entering into earthly paradise.

We sat at the table, and Januario very jauntily ordered two dinners at four reales each, and a pint of wine. I was surprised at my friend's generosity, and fearing that he was going to come up with one of his tricks after we had finished eating, I asked him if he had the means to pay, because everything he had ordered came to at least a couple of pesos. He smiled and said he did, and so that I would eat at ease, he showed me about six pesos in coins large and small.

At that point, they began bringing the food: a pair of bread rolls and table settings, two bowls of soup, one dish of noodles and one of rice, the stewpot, two main dishes, wine, dessert, and water; a frugal dinner for a rich man, surely, but to me it seemed fit for a king, or an ambassador at least; because if there's no such thing as bad bread to a good hunger (even if the bread really is bad), then by the same reasoning, when the bread is good in itself, it must seem unsurpassable. The fact is that I didn't eat the food, I bolted it down, so fast that Januario told me, "Slow down, man, slow down, they're not going to snatch the plates away from us."

Between bites we frequented our wine glasses, which put us in a fairly cheerful mood; but the meal ended, and to settle it down we took out our tobacco and continued our conversation.

I asked my mentor, more out of curiosity than friendship, where he lived. He replied that he had no house, nor did he need one, because the whole world was his home.

"Where do you sleep, then?" I asked.

"Wherever night finds me," he replied; "so you and I are equals in that respect, as well as in furnishings and clothes, because all I own is what I'm wearing on my back."

Amazed, I said, "How could you spend your money so freely, then?"

"That," he replied, "is nothing to be surprised at; all of us *pests* and gamblers do the same whenever we are *on a hot streak*—that is, where we're winning like I was last night, because I used a stake that I had put together to *bull the game*, and I won twelve pesos; because I'm a *driller* whenever I have the chance, that is, I bet fearlessly, since I have nothing to lose even if I *tap out*, and I have the door open for making another play by my wits."

"Maybe that's why," I said, "I've heard monte players say that they're more afraid of one coin in the hands of a *pest* like you than they are of a hundred pesos in a gambler's hands."[13]

"That's exactly why," said Juan Largo; "because, since we are always playing by *mouth bets*, that is, without risking anything, it hardly bothers us if we take four reales and double them for eight straight hands, and then get taken for 120 pesos on the ninth hand; because if we win, we've made 256; and if we lose, we haven't lost anything that was ours, and in that case, we already know the way to make more business. That's not the case with people who *bull the game* with money that cost their own sweat and labor, because they know what it cost them to earn it, and so they're fond of it and they gamble cautiously, and they're too cowardly to bet a hundred pesos, even if they're winning; and that's why we call them *tight players*. That's also the reason why we are such free spenders when we're on a hot streak, spending and showing off freely, because it doesn't cost us anything, nor is the money we throw away the last that we expect to come across while we're on this road. Make no mistake, the most free-spending people around are the gentlemen who own mines, the employees who openly manage their masters' money, the children of well-off parents, cardsharps such as myself, and everybody[14] who gets money without working for it, or who manages someone else's, in cases when it's hard to make them give exact accounts."

"But, man," I said, "I don't doubt everything you're saying; but haven't you even bought yourself a sheet or a blanket to sleep on?"

"I wouldn't even think of getting into that right now," Januario answered me; "don't be a fool—if I don't have a house, why should I want a sheet? Where would I keep it? Am I supposed to carry it around with me? You get scared too easily. Look: gamblers like myself play the role of comedians; sometimes we go around dressed quite decently, other times in rags; sometimes we're married, other times we're widowers; sometime we eat like marquises and other times like beggars, or maybe we have nothing to eat; sometimes we walk the streets, other times we're in prison; in a word, sometimes we do well and other times badly; but we're used to this life; we care no more about what's past than about what's to come. In this profession, the important thing is to set aside your soul and your sense of shame, and believe me, if you do the same, you'll live the life of the angels."

I began to worry a bit on hearing such a naïve confession about the wretched life I was going to embrace, especially considering that it must be true in every detail, as Januario was speaking under the inspiration of wine, an oracle that rarely lies; rather, among its thousands of bad qualities, it almost always has the good one of being neither flattering nor false; and even though my inspired friend declared it was time to

---

[13] [Apparently Lizardi has forgotten that Periquillo did not understand the gambler's term *pest* (*cócora de los juegos*) when Januario first used it a few pages back. –Tr.]

[14] Not everybody; rather, all those who act badly.

change topics, which I did, I pretended not to understand, whether not to offend my benefactor or because I wanted to find out for myself whether that kind of life was for me; and so, I contented myself merely with asking him once more where he lived. To which, unperturbed, he replied roundly, "Look: sometimes I stick around a dance like a weed, and I spend the rest of the night on the sofa; other nights I go to a tavern, and make like a rock; and other nights, which is most of them, I spend the night in the *arrastraderitos*.[15] That's how I've managed the last few days I've been back in Mexico, and that's how I expect to manage it until I've raised 500 or 1,000 pesos from gambling, because at that point I'll have to start thinking differently."

"And what are those *arrastraderitos*," I asked, "and what do cover yourself with when you sleep there?"

To which he answered, "*Arrastraderitos* are the filthy, unusable pool rooms that you must have seen in some low storefronts. These aren't places for shooting pool, because they are so plain awful that you couldn't shoot a dime's worth in them; they are just pretexts or fronts for setting up a few miserable games of monte. All the dodgers, sticky-fingers, and such lowlife and deadwood gamble in these wretched dives. As a rule, all the games they play there are crooked; and as soon as some innocent chump happens in, they'll strip the rags off his back, and they'll take his shorts, too, if he's wearing any. These greenhorn gamblers don't understand how crooked the game is, so they're called *pigeons;* and like the pigeons they are, they'll get plucked clean at the drop of a hat. So, since the only folks who go to these *arrastraderos* are lost souls, without a drop of education or good upbringing, and God only knows if they even have religion, all that goes on inside them is robbing, and borrowing, and gambling, and swearing, and cursing, and so on, all without the slightest respect, because there's no one there to restrain them as there would be in the more decent gambling halls. That's where I spend most nights, for one small coin that I give to the operator, or two coins if I have them; he loans me the table cloth or somebody's pawned cape or blanket, full of lice, and that's how I manage. So there's your answer, and why don't you see if there's anything else you need to know, because you ask more questions than the catechism."

If I had been anxious before about the picture he was painting to me of the pestish lifestyle, after he filled in the highlights and shadows with these details on the *arrastraderos* I was stunned; but for all that, I did not act rudely, and I determined to accompany him until I saw the end of the comedy in which I would so soon be acting.

We left the tavern and began roving the streets for the rest of the afternoon. At a fine hour of the night, we went to the gaming hall. Januario began betting the bit of cash he still had, and was cleaned out in the blink of an eye; but he thought nothing of it. Every time I looked, he had money on him, and he was always handling coins, whether they were his or someone else's; the whole business was constantly getting him wrapped up in arguments, remonstrations, and complaints, but he was able to shake them all off and end up on top.

---

[15] [*Arrastraderito:* this term, explained below, was passing slang from the Mexico City of the late 1700s, and was already long out of date when *Periquillo* was written. No doubt Lizardi enjoyed the way it incorporated the more common Mexican slang term *arrastrado*, "down-and-out." –Tr.]

The gaming ended around eleven at night, and we went back to the streets. I was starting to think we'd have to go on the Diet of Worms,[16] but my fears were proved wrong when Juan Largo knocked on a storefront, and after giving them I don't know what password, the door opened; we entered and ate supper—not as decent as our dinner had been, but enough to stave off hunger.

After we finished supper, Januario paid and we left. Then I said, "Man, I'm amazed, because I saw you get cleaned out as soon as we entered the gaming hall, and even though you always had money, I could have sworn that you left the place without a penny, and here I see you paying for supper; no two ways about it, you're a wizard."

"The only wizardry here is what I've already told you. The first thing I do is squirrel away six or eight reales to see me through the night from the first racket I pull off; once that's safe, I can play by my wits all night long without worrying about whether my rackets will pay off or not. If one of them pays, great; and if not, I got through another day, which is the most important thing."

As we talked, we reached another low storefront, even filthier than the one where we had supper. My mentor knocked, gave the password, the door opened, and by the light of a guttering candle-end from a corner of the room, I saw that this was the *arrastraderito* about which I had heard so much.

Januario spoke in a low tone with the owner of that hellish den, a mulatto wrapped in a coarse blue blanket who had already stripped for bed, and who brought us two filthy, ragged blankets, saying, "I only got up to answer the door because you're my friend, since I've got a headache that's making the world swim." And that must have been true, to judge from how drunk he was.

We weren't the only ones that the naked rogue was putting up for the night. Four or five other wretches, all in the buff and, as far as I could see, half drunk, sprawled liked pigs over the bench, table, and floor of the pool room.

Since the room was small, and our companions the sort of people who eat cold, dirty food for supper and who drink *pulque* and *chinguirito*,[17] they were producing an ear-shattering salvo whose pestilent echoes, finding no other outlet, came to rest in my poor nostrils, thus giving me in one instant such a migraine that I could not bear it, and my stomach, unable to withstand the fragrant scents, heaved up everything I had eaten just a few hours earlier.

Januario noticed my sickness and, understanding the cause, said, "Well, you're in a sad state, friend; you're too delicate to be poor."

"That's out of my hands," I replied, and he told me, "I can see that; but don't let it get to you, it's just a matter of time, and you're just getting started, as I told you this morning; but let's go to bed and see if you don't feel better."

The noise that my evacuating stomach made woke up one of the *léperos* there, and as soon as he saw us, he started to spew a blue streak of abuse out of his devilish mouth.

---

[16] [Lizardi's pun is just as bad: "we would have to read the Nicene Council," where the Spanish *Niceno*, or *ni ceno*, means "I don't even eat supper." –Tr.]

[17] [*Chinguirito*: cheap, illegally brewed rum. –Tr.]

"You raggedy sons of b . . . !" he said. "Why don't you go home and vomit on your mamas, if you're already so drunk, and not come here to rob people of their sleep at this time of night?"

Januario signaled to me to keep my mouth shut, and we lay down on the billiard table; and between its hard planks, my migraine, the fear instilled in me by these naked men whom I charitably judged to be merely thieves, the countless lice in the blankets, the rats that ambled over me, a rooster that spread its wings from time to time, the snores of the sleepers, the sneezes that their backsides produced, and the aromatic stench that resulted, I spent the most miserable night.

CHAPTER 17

Counting the hours and the cock crows, I spent the night unable to sleep a wink and anxious for dawn to break so that I could escape from that dungeon, until at last God allowed the sun to rise, and those naked vagabonds began to wake up.

The first words out of their mouths were shameless; their first request was to *make their morning*. As soon as I heard their demands, I decided they were crazy, and I told Januario, "These men must not have a drop of sense, because they all think they can make the morning. What a funny bit of madness! What, do they think it hasn't been created already? Do they think they can do something that is reserved for God alone?"

Januario burst out laughing and said, "I can tell that so far you've only been a part-time rogue, a decent scoundrel, and a sheepish rascal. Indeed, you're still ignorant of many of the most common clichés in the leperish dialect; but luckily you have me at your side, because I won't let any chance slip by me if I judge that I can use it to teach you whatever you'll need to know to become a skilled old hand, whether you want to be a decent scoundrel or a 'bare *chichi*'[1] like these fellows here. For the moment, let me tell you that among these folks, *making their morning* means breakfasting on booze, because they're on bad terms with chocolate and coffee, and at this time of day they'd rather spend a real or two on a glass of bad rum than on a mug of the most delicious chocolate."

I had scarcely settled this doubt when several others were raised by one of those rowdies, who I later learned was a journeyman shoemaker, for he said to one of his companions: "Chepe,[2] let's *make our morning* and then get to work, because last Saturday we agreed with the master that we'd go, and he's bound to be waiting."

To which Chepe replied, "The master can go to . . . , 'cause I don't feel like working at all today, for two reasons: first, because it's *Saint Monday's*, and second, because yesterday I got drunk and today I've got to *heal up*."

I was baffled by hearing these things, which were all enigmas to me, until my teacher said, "Listen: it is an ancient and almost irreparable custom of most journeymen that they never work on Monday, on account of how wiped out they are from their Sunday drunks, and that's why they call it *Saint Monday's*—not because every Monday is an official feast day, which you know it's not, but because these profligate journeymen take the day off to *heal up* from their hangovers, as this one said."

"And how do they heal from their drunken sprees?" I asked.

---

[1] These folks typically wear their blankets or shawls thrown over their left shoulders and tucked under their right arms, which leaves their right teats exposed if they are shirtless; and since *chichi* means teat or breast in Mexicano [i.e., Nahuatl, the native language of central Mexico], this phrase is applied to men who leave their chests exposed or habitually go shirtless.

[2] A nickname for José, the same as Pepe. –E.

"By going on another," Januario replied.

"But then," I said, "the excess of rum must have the same effect on Monday as it did on Sunday, so if a drunken spree on Sunday calls for another spree on Monday to heal it, the Monday spree must call for another one on Tuesday, the Tuesday spree will call for a Wednesday spree, and we are consequently forced to conclude that the sprees will catch up with each other, and the first will never be healed by such a preposterous cure. The truth is, I think this is an even crazier idea that these fellows have than the one of *making their morning,* because believing that you can cure one bender with another is like thinking that you can heal a burn by burning yourself again, or a wound with another wound, and so on, which is obviously nonsense."

"You're quite right," Januario answered, "but these people don't understand arguments. They're depraved and lazy, they work to keep from dying of hunger and perhaps to scrape enough money together to keep their main vices going, and for them that is almost always drunkenness; so as long they have something to drink, they hardly care if they don't have anything to eat, or if they eat any old rubbish; and that's why, no matter how good they are at their crafts, no matter how much they work, they never thrive, they never look decent, because they squander everything; and so you see them naked as these two, who might be the finest journeymen that the master has in his shop."

"What pitiful men!" I exclaimed; "and if they're married, what a miserable life they must give their poor wives, and what a poor example they set for their children!"

"Just imagine," said Januario. "They keep their wives unclothed, hungry, and beaten, and their children naked, dinnerless, and ill-mannered."

As we spoke, we left that pigsty and went for coffee. For the rest of the morning, which we spent visiting friends and wandering the streets until noon, I was nipping and scratching myself, such was the crowd of lice that gotten onto me from the damnable rag of a blanket. And that was hardly the worst of it: my friends made me the butt of their obnoxious jokes because of all the insects that were crawling all over me, which were so white and bloated you could see them a league off; every time one of them came into view, one friend would say, "Don't do that, not to my friend Periquillo, because I'm here now!"

Others would say, "Man, that's what you get from looking for girlfriends on the cheap."

Others, "How strong you are! Look at the huge beast you're carrying!"

And so they all ribbed me to their hearts' content, and they did not they spare my companion, who was also drowning in lice.

At last the clock struck noon, and Januario said, "Let's go to the gaming hall, because I don't have a penny for dinner; and don't act dumb, get to work. Wherever you can, grab hold of a bet and say that it's yours, and I'll swear by every saint in Heaven that I saw you lay it down. But remember my warning: it should be a small bet, two or three reales at most, because if you go and do something foolish, we're likely to tap out."

Indeed, we went to the gaming hall and found good seats, things heated up, as they say, and I eyed first one bet and then another and another; but I couldn't make up my mind to take any of them, out of pure fear. I would try to extend my hand,

and it seemed that someone was holding it back and whispering to me: "What are you doing? Leave it where it is, that isn't yours. . . . " Our conscience certainly warns us and reproaches us, secretly but effectively, when we attempt to do bad; the thing is, we never want to listen to its cries.

Januario just looked at me, and I could tell that he was ready to eat me alive with his eyes, from rage. If he had had venom in his gaze, as liars claim the basilisk does, I would never have risen alive from the table: so fierce was his glance. Some people seem bent on making others turn out as depraved as they are, and this villain was one of them.

At last, fearing his anger more than I did God, and to appease his desires rather than my own (which is something that goes on in the world every day), I resolved to confiscate a peseta at pay-out time. When the poor man to whom the money belonged was about to grab his four reales, I was already holding them. Then came the whole business of "That's my money," "No, it's mine," "I'm telling the truth," "Me too"; and more than a bit of "All right, now," "We'll see about that," "I'm ready when you are," and all the bluster typical of such quarrels; until Januario, in an upright tone of voice, told the loser, "Friend, don't get hot-headed. I saw you place your peseta bet, but the coin that this gentleman picked up is his, have no doubt about it, for I just lent it to him."

With this the fight cooled off, that poor wretch was left without his coins, and I was left holding them tight.

They all but melted in my hand, but I couldn't bring myself to bet them on a single hand—not because I didn't have the courage to bet four reales, for as you know, I knew how to gamble, though without much skill, and had gambled away everything my mother owned—but because I was afraid to lose them and be left without anything to eat. Such was the fear that hunger had instilled in me the day before!

Januario recognized what I was doing, and he signaled to me that I should bet it without a worry, since he had already squirreled away enough for grub.

With this assurance, I bet double-or-nothing on five hands in a row, and when I found myself holding sixteen pesos, I felt as if I had inherited an estate; for you know it had been many days since I had a real to my name.

My companion signaled me to deep-pocket them, which I did, thinking that we were about to go eat; but that was the last thing on Januario's mind; instead, he sat there like a lump until the big game was finished, at which point he asked me for the money, took out four pesos of his own and one of his decks, and started shuffling, saying, "Come on, try your luck with this little pot."

As soon as the big gamblers saw how small the bank was, they started leaving; but the poor ones lined up to bet right away, which is what they call *coming in on the thin edge.*

The bank slowly began to fatten, so that by two in the afternoon, that drone had something like seventy pesos.

Just then, two well-dressed bumpkins walked in, brimming with pesos. They began to bet heavy—twenty and twenty-five pesos at a time—and began to lose at the same rate. On every hand, when I saw them lay down their sausage rolls of pesos, I felt my blood sink to my toenails, thinking that if they just won two hands we'd be out all our labor and have to leave penniless, dreaming about what we once had, which was intolerable to me, in keeping with the cardsharp's maxim: *you feel more strongly about the child you raise than the child you give birth to.*

But those men, I came to realize, were quite mistaken, because whenever they bet ten or twelve pesos on a hand, they won; but whenever they bet forty or fifty pesos between the two of them, they lost, no matter how cautiously they played.

In this way, they were each bled dry almost at the same time, and when one of them lost the last hand that he had a bet riding on—a jack against an ace, and the ace came up—he grabbed all four jacks and ate them, as if he were eating four ladyfingers, while he ripped the other cards to shreds; and once he concluded this important business, he left with his companion, both of them glowing scarlet red and sweating like pigs. That's how steamed they were!

Januario, with a wide smirk, counted 300 pesos and change; he gave a tip to the owner of the house, and tied up the rest in his handkerchief.

The other cardsharps were drooling over the winnings and begging for their share; but he didn't give a penny to any of them, saying, "When I tap out, nobody gives me anything; so when I win, there's no reason why I should give anybody a penny, either."

This hardness did not seem right to me, because, as bad as I was, I still had a sensitive heart.

We went outside and walked to the tavern, which was nearby. We ate in high style, and when dinner was over, my patron told me, "So tell me, Señor Perico, how do you like the profession? If you hadn't made up your mind to go for it with that bet, would you have more than a hundred pesos to call your own? Come on, take your dough and spend it on whatever you wish, because it's all yours and you can enjoy it to your heart's content, with God's blessing;[3] though I think it would be best to set aside fifty pesos for us both to serve as our stash; and let's go to the Parián[4] right now, or better yet, to the flea market, and buy ourselves some decent clothes, and then we'll have a better time of it: people will treat us better everywhere and give us more opportunities to get more; because I assure you, brother, that even if they say *the habit doesn't make the monk*, I don't know what it is about this world that if you go around dressed decently—in the street, on strolls, making the rounds, at the gambling halls, in dances, even in church—you'll get a little attention and respect. In the end, it's better to be a well-dressed rogue than an upright man in rags;[5] and so, let's go."

His words did not fall on deaf ears; I jumped up and grabbed my money, which amounted to less than what Januario kept; but I pretended not to notice, satisfied that when it comes to self-interest, the best of friends will want to come out ahead.

---

[3] This is the last straw: nothing that is wrongly acquired could be blessed by God.

[4] [The Parián: a large building on Mexico City's central plaza that formed the fashionable commercial hub of the city, from its construction in 1703 until it was sacked in a riot in 1828. –Tr.]

[5] Not in the least. It is true that the world is full of stupid people who judge a person by his external appearance, and so perhaps they honor a decently dressed rogue; but the first time they are let down, they see things as they really are.

We went to the flea market and bought shirts, shorts, vests, cloaks, capes, hats, handkerchiefs, shoes, and even some watch cases or hollowed-out junk watches, but they looked good.

All fitted out, we went to take a room in an inn until we could find an adequate place to live. As for beds, we had nothing, but although I pointed this out to Januario, he told me, "Be patient, because later we'll have enough for everything. For now, the main thing is for us to put on a good appearance in the street, and even if we eat badly and sleep on the bare floor, nobody will see that. What, do you think that every fop and dandy you see in public has a bed to sleep on and plenty to eat? No, my boy; most of them are like us; everything is appearance, and on the inside they are suffering cruelly. We call those fellows *rotos*."

I accepted everything, and was very happy with the bit of clothes I got and with the fact that I would not be spending another night in that damnable *arrastraderito*.

We arrived at the inn, took our room, and closed the door behind us, wildly happy. That night, Januario did not want us to go gambling, because, as he put it, we should let our winnings rest. We went to see a comedy, and when we returned we had a fine supper and then slept on the hard floor, which we were able to cushion a little with our capes, both new and old.

I slept like a child, which is the best comparison, and the next morning, we had the barber come visit us, and once we were all embellished we got dressed and went out, starched and ironed, into the street.

Since our main objective was to be seen by our friends, the first visit we made was to the house of Dr. Martín Pelayo; but what was our surprise when, thinking we would find the old Martín, we found a new Martín who was different in every way from the one we had known; for the old one was as dissolute a young man as the two of us, while this was a serious, virtuous, and established little cleric.

As soon as we entered his room, he stood up and politely offered us seats; he told us that he was a deacon, and was set to be ordained a priest in the upcoming ember days. We congratulated him; but Januario tried to mix in his usual coarse jokes and impudence, to which Pelayo, in a very serious tone, replied: "Lord help me, Señor Januario, are we always going to be children? Will this puerile humor never cease? One must draw distinctions between one age and the next: at one age, the mischievousness of little children is delightful; at another age, the good cheer of youth; and at our age, the seriousness and solidity of men is what counts, because we are grown enough to need barbers. I'm not old, and even if I were, I would have nothing against being festive. Indeed, I like cheerful, jovial men, the sort of whom it is said: *When he's around, sadness leaves*. Yes, friends, there's nothing that puts me out more than irritable, gloomy, melancholy types; I avoid them as abominable misanthropes, and I judge them to be arrogant malcontents, unsociable grumblers, and fit company for bears and tigers. On the contrary, as I said, I feel most at home with men who are thoughtful, affable, educated, and cheery. Their company delights me, entices me, enraptures me; and I could spend days and weeks with any one of them; but it would have to be someone of that caliber, because, as for someone who is stupid, loudmouthed, arrogant, and impudent, who could put up with them? Those types aren't festive; they're fools; their character is despicable, and their habits gross.

When they talk, they shout; when they want to entertain, their jokes irritate; because men who have no talent or education can't put forth good, cheerful, or reasonable ideas; rather, their gags offend the honor and reputations of others, and their witticisms puncture their neighbor's good name, if not his heart. I tell you all this, friends, in the hopes that you will avoid such coarse jokes at all times. There is a proper time for everything. A noisemaker from Holy Week would sound out of place to children on Christmas, and nobody would decorate a Holy Week shrine with tinsel from Christmas Eve.[6] That is what I have been led to believe by experience, and by the snubs that I have seen many jokers suffer."

Soon after he said this, Father Pelayo deftly changed the subject; but my companion, who had understood him and who was as steamed as water for chocolate, could not take much more. We soon said good-bye and left.

In the street he told me, "Could you believe that show-off? Who wouldn't have seen through him! Now that he's ordained in the Gospel, he pretends to be all polite and proper; but give that bone to some other dog, because we know that it's pure hypocrisy."

I cut short his conversation, because sometimes it disgusted me to talk behind people's backs, and we went on to visit other friends who received us better, and even gave us a bit of breakfast.

In this way, we passed the morning until the noon hour tolled, at which time we went to the inn; we took twenty-five pesos from our stash and went to the gambling tables.

On the way there, I said to Januario, "Man, if the bumpkins come back, as soon as they win a hand, that'll be the end of us."

"No it won't," he told me; "I hope they do come! What, do you think it's up to them whether they win or lose? No, my boy, it's in my own hands. I know them well, and I've seen that they always bet on the face cards; so I set up the cards so that if they don't bet very much, I'll let the face card match; but if they bet a lot, I'll take it all with one card. That's the problem with gambling like an amateur, or with using a set system."

"What—do gamblers use systems?" I asked.

And he told me, "What cardsharps call a system[7] is nothing but a string of coincidences (so long as you shuffle the deck well), because, if a four comes up against a

---

[6] [In Catholic services, wooden noisemakers or rattles are used instead of the usual handbells during Holy Week, on Good Friday. Tinsel: *lama,* a plant similar to Spanish moss, is used in Mexico as a Christmas decoration, much as tinsel is used in the U.S. –Tr.]

[7] [The following footnote on gambling systems, all aimed at deciding which card to bet on in the game of monte, has been moved here from Chapter 18, since these systems are first mentioned here. –Tr.]

A "system" (*regla*) is what gamblers call any order of cards or combinations that they use to pick their bets. Thus, *big and little* is one system, and there is nothing here to explain: for any two cards dealt on the table, one will have a higher value, and that is the *big,* while the other is the *little.* For example, if one is a 4 and the other is a 3, the first is the *big* and the other is the *little. Judía* refers to the biggest face card and the smallest spot card; *contrajudía,* vice-versa.

Evens and odds are the even and odd numbers, but the trick is to distinguish them when both cards have the same value; for example, if a 2 and a 4 come up, both are even: which is the

jack, that's a coincidence; and if a seven then comes up against a king, that's another coincidence; if a five comes up against a queen, there's another one; and so on: even if you make ten or twenty *contrajudías*, they just add up to ten or twenty coincidences, a single string of coincidences. There's no better or surer system than *pulling through, stacking, burying*, and the other tricks I use, and there's even an exception to those, which is when someone else notices what you're doing and uses it to beat you; that is why one of our sayings is: *there's no system that beats eyeballing*. All the other systems—*judía, contrajudía*, evens and odds, places, and all the other so-called systems—are fads, obsessions, and vulgar superstitions that we constantly see men falling into who aren't vulgar at all in any other respect, but it seems that when it comes to gambling, nobody is the master of his own judgment. So bear in mind, there are just two systems: luck and dodges. Luck is more lawful; but dodging is more certain."

Just then we reached the gaming hall, and Januario sat in his usual place, but he didn't risk more than a peso, because he had come with the intention of dealing monte; for, as he liked to say, that way our money would be safer, since *there is one thing that's always so: the guy who deals will keep the dough*.

As soon as the game ended, we set up our little game, and we won ten or twelve pesos, since the fat pigeons we were expecting never came; still, we were satisfied enough, and we left.

And so we spent some six months this time around, winning almost every day, even if not by much. During those months, I learned every kind of trickery Januario wanted to teach me; we bought beds and some more clothes, and lived like marquises.

There was nothing about gambling that I didn't observe in that time. I learned that it truly is *the melting pot of men*, for in it they reveal their unvarnished passions, or they have to be very much in charge of themselves not to reveal them, which is a rare thing, for self-interest blinds men, and in a gambling den the only thing they think of is winning.

There you can see who is ill-mannered, because he will sit on the table, wear his hat indoors, not give up his chair even to those who most deserve it, blow cigarette smoke in the face of whoever sits next to him regardless of whether he is a person of respect and character, and commit whatever discourtesies he wishes without the slightest consideration. What is worse is that there is an axiom, as vulgar as it is false, that goes: *in the gambling den all men are equal*; and, under the cover of this

---

even and which the *odd?* If a 7 and a 5 come up, which of the pair is *even?* The explanations are confusing, but if you keep in mind that *the bigger card keeps its value,* it all becomes clear. Thus, in the first case, the 4 is *even* and the 2 is *odd*. In the second case, 7 is *odd* and 5 is *even*. For the face cards, today [using the modern, 40-card Spanish deck] the jack represents 8, the queen is 9, and the king is 10; but in the era when the book is set [using an earlier, 48-card deck], decks had eights and nines, so the jack represented 10, the queen 11, and the king 12. Thus *evens and odds* is always subject to the general rule that *the bigger card keeps its value*.

   Inner place and outer place: the first is where the first card is dealt, or where the table is marked with the number 1; the second, with the number 2.

   There are a great many other systems that have been invented by the whims of each gambler; but this note is limited to those that are mentioned here in the book. –E.

parsimonious phrase, the ill-mannered never refrain from their discourtesies, and few decent and honorable persons dare insist on the respect that they deserve.

In the same way that the discourteous man reveals his lack of education in the gambling den through his foolishness and vulgarity, the immoral man reveals his bad conduct with his curses and crassness; the fraud reveals his character through his vows; the swindler shows his bad faith through his trickery; the ambitious man discloses his greed through his voraciousness at gambling; the miser displays his stinginess through his timid and penny-pinching bets; the spendthrift, his profligacy through his imprudent magnanimity; the scoundrel, his cheekiness through his boldly begging for a handout from his own shadow; the idler . . . but why am I wearing myself out? For you can get to know every vice there, since they are on naked display. The immodest, the swindler, the haughty, the sycophant, the ungodly, the indulgent father, the over-soft husband, the profligate, the harlot, the bad wife: all of them, all of them freely admit which leg they limp on; and no matter how hypocritical they might be out in the street, in the gambling den they lose their heads and suspend any semblance of virtue, letting themselves be seen as they really are.

Curse the vacuities of the gambling den. One of these is the obscene way things are always decided there. If someone carries cash, he'll be offered a seat, and when he wins a bet, he'll be praised as a good bettor and a skilled gambler; but if someone comes without cash, or loses it on a bet, he'll get no seat, or will have it taken away, and before long they'll be calling him a *rockhead*, a term that some of them use to designate a fool.

In sum, I learned and observed everything that there was to learn and observe in this career. At the time, it served to my detriment; today, it serves me to warn you against its fatal consequences, in order that you may avoid them.

I would not have you be gamblers, my children, but in case you do place a bet sometime, let it be little, let it be your own, let it be free of trickery; for I would rather have you taken for fools than for thieves, which is all that cardsharps are.

Many say that they gamble *to help with their necessities*. This is an error. Of every 1,000 who go to the tables with the same objective, 999 return home as needy as before; or perhaps worse, since they leave behind the little that they had, and perhaps they contract new debts, and their families will perish all the more rapidly.

You must have heard it said, or you will when you are bigger, that many people make their living from gambling. I could scarcely believe that these people might be any others than those who *play with the long cue*, as they say—that is, the cheats and thieves, who deserve prison and the gallows even more than the rogues Maderas and Paredes,[8] because people can take precautions against a known thief, but not against a cheat.

People such as these, I can believe, sometimes do support themselves by gambling; but for upright men—those who work and those who, as they say, *depend on God's good will* when they gamble—I maintain that this would be a physical

---

[8] Two famous thieves who lived in Mexico City. [According to Spell (p. 181), Paredes was imprisoned in 1789, and "el Pillo Madera" was publicly executed before a huge crowd in 1791. –Tr.]

impossibility, because gambling might yield them ten pesos today, but tomorrow it will take away twenty. I know all this, and I am speaking to you from experience.

Another class of persons who support themselves by gambling. . . . Is anyone listening in on us? . . . Well, let me tell you: there are certain gentlemen who have plenty of money, which they could use to make a more honest living, but not wishing to work, they make a business and find their profits in gambling, putting their money into various houses where they hold monte games.

Since this manner of gambling is very advantageous to those who run the banks, they normally win, and sometimes they win so much that I know a few who ride in carriages and amass great wealth. How is that? Well, people make greater efforts to be placed as *dealers* or *croupiers* with these fine gentlemen than they would to become a master of the best craft; and rightly so, since these gentlemen display their wealth so ostentatiously and throw their pesos around so openly that no office employee or colonel could imitate them. So you see, as long as there are little lords like these who have a daily wage of six, eight, or ten pesos, on top of what they get on the side, people are going to want to get their hands on the latter.

There are also constant entreaties for the lords of monte to send money to the gambling houses, to cover the tips that they give to the owners of those houses, which certainly add up to enough to support a poor and honest family.

These are the persons who, I cannot deny, make a living from gambling; but how few of them there are! And if we scrutinize how they do it, we are forced to consider even these few men as criminals, even if we can believe in good faith that their games are entirely clean. If not, let me ask you: should gambling be deemed a branch of commerce, and an honest way to make a living? The answer is either yes or no. If yes, then why is it so rigorously prohibited by law? If no, then why does it have so many patrons who defend it with all their might? Let me answer.

If men would not pervert the order of things, gambling would hardly be prohibited as an evil; rather, it would be so legal that it would be classed with the moral virtues of other innocent pastimes; but inasmuch as the greed of gambling goes beyond the limits of entertainment—and in the games about which we have been speaking, many people ruin others without the slightest consideration or fraternity—enlightened governments have found it necessary to take up the question, trying to contain this pernicious abuse through the severe penalties imposed under the laws against such offenders.

The fact that gambling has patrons who defend it, and proselytes who follow it, is beside the point. Every vice has as much, but no vice can be classified as a virtue on account of patrons or proselytes, whose justifications are worthless insofar as they are not determined by reason, but by sordid self-interest and open egotism.

Who are the people who support gambling and defend it so earnestly? Examine closely and you will see that they are the cheats, the good-for-nothings, and the idlers, sometimes considered poor, other times considered rich; and any defense from such a class of advocates must be considered suspect, if only because they are the interested party.

To say that gambling is licit because it is profitable to some individuals is nonsense. For a thing to be licit, it is not enough that it be profitable; it must also be honest and not prohibited. Otherwise, someone could argue that robbery, usury, and prostitution are licit, because they yield profit to the thief, the usurer, and the whore. That would be an error; to defend gambling as licit with the same argument, then, would be to commit the same error.

But, without going into the matter very deeply, it is plain to see that this much-lauded profitability for the few in no way balances the damage done to the many. What do I mean, it doesn't balance? It is, indeed, tremendously damaging to society.

Let us count up all the rogues, swindlers, and thieves who make a living from gambling; add to them the few who are not thieves, but make their fortunes with gambling; add their dependents; tally up the families who support themselves on the tips they get as owners of the gaming houses; let us not forget what is spent on servants and *armadores;*[9] let us make note of how much some of them hoard and how much others spend wantonly, without passing over the lavishness with which they spend, dress, eat, and show off, each of them in proportion to their abilities; and after we finish with this accounting, let us calculate the daily amount that these leeches suck from the State in order to support themselves at the State's expense, as they do with such liberality; and then we shall see how many families must be ruined in order to support these idlers.

You don't have to be a mathematician to comprehend this truth; going from one gaming hall to another in a single day would suffice, for there you would see that those who gain the most are the monte dealers.[10] Ask each of the cardsharps and gamblers how he did, and for every four or six who say they won, forty will reply that they lost the last penny they had.

Therefore, this proposition is self-evident: *all those who support themselves by gambling are so many sponges on the population, sucking the substance of the poor.*

All these reflections, dear children, should serve to keep you from getting mixed up in the labyrinth of gambling, for once you fall into it, you will have to repent, perhaps for the rest of your life; because in the long run, it rarely fails to cause outsized afflictions; and even the pleasures that it gives are repaid at excessive interest, with such worries and troubles as: sleepless nights, empty stomachs, arguments, enmities, predicaments, fear of the law, fines, jail, shame, and others along the same lines.

I learned about all these things in Januario's company, and something else as well, because at last we did go broke. We began to sell our clothes and everything else we owned; we *hit a bad streak*, as the sons of Birján say; we began to eat badly; to lose sleep, with nothing to show for it; to pay fines, and so on, until we were back where we were before, and worse, because now everyone knew us as swindlers and looked more closely at our hands than our faces.

---

[9] This is the name we give to those who recruit gamblers to come play; they also get paid for doing this job.

[10] Together with the *Imperial* bankers. This is another game that is worse than monte, as it incites people's greed even more because of its excessively large payoffs. I have seen men walking around as if out of their minds, using paper and pencil to make their imaginary computations and calculations. Good grief, as if it weren't enough for the game to leave them stone broke, it also has to pack them off *imperially* to beg for a number from [the Mexico City insane asylum] San Hipólito!

In the midst of this sad situation, and to top it all off, that rogue Januario gulled a bumpkin into backing a game of monte, telling him that he had a very skillful friend, an upright man, who would deal the game using his money. The poor bumpkin fell for it and agreed to give the money the following day. Januario let me know what had happened, and told me I was to be the dealer.

We agreed that I would stack the cards so that Januario would raise the bet, and another friend of his, who had sold a horse to get in on the scheme, would meet it and win the whole pot, and then we would later split the money like brothers.

It was no trouble for me to agree, since by then I was as great a thief as he.

The next day arrived; Juan Largo went to get the bumpkin, who gave me a hundred pesos and told me, "Take good care of 'em, sir, and I'll give you a big tip if we win."

"It's a deal," I replied.

And I set about dealing the cards in my own way, following the advice of my diabolical teacher.

In half a flash, the money was gone, because selling the horse had brought us ten pesos, and thus, in four hands that I stacked and Januario raised, our third partner took it all in discord.

The latter left first to disguise his involvement, and a while later Januario left too, making signs that I should stay. The poor bumpkin was stunned, thinking about how his money had disappeared without a trace; all he said, from time to time, was: "Look here, sir, what a pity! I didn't even have any fun!" But one of the onlookers knew Januario and me all too well: he noticed how I had *pulled through* when I shuffled, and, very cautiously and with a thousand excuses, he let the bumpkin know that I had handed over his money.

Then the rustic, more crafty at seeking vengeance than at gambling, took me to an inn under the pretext of paying for my dinner. I resisted, not out of fear of what would happen to me, but out of a desire to collect my prize for the tricks I had pulled; but I couldn't escape; the bumpkin took me to the inn, closed the door to the room, and gave me such a magnificent thrashing that he dislocated my shoulder, broke my skull in three places, smashed in a few of my ribs, and if the noise hadn't forced the other guests to come to the door and deliver me from his hands, I would surely not be here to write my life story; because I would have met my end then and there. Even so, I was left senseless at his feet, and only woke up in the place that you will see in the next chapter.

CHAPTER 18

I am sure that if the bumpkin had killed me, he would have found himself in dark straits, for the law would have accused him of treachery, since he had planned and premeditated his act, and had beaten me black and blue without giving me a chance to defend myself, and that kind of vengeance, given its cruelty and the circumstances, was an abominable crime; yet my own act of handing his money over to others in four hands of monte was hardly any better.

His crime was contemptible treachery and assault; mine was diabolical meanness and treachery; but with this difference: when he committed his crime, he had been infuriated and provoked by my own, yet I committed mine not only without having been offended, but after he had offered to give me a good tip.

Thus, judged without passion, the crime that I committed was worse and more shameful than his; and so, had he killed me that day, I would have died, and for good reason, because if it is true that we should not harm or deceive anyone, much less should we do it to those who give us their trust.

I spent two hours meditating in almost these very terms after I revived and found myself in a bed in the Hospital of San Jácome,[1] where I had been brought by order of the authorities.

After a while a notary arrived, surrounded by his satellites, to take down my declaration of what had happened.[2] You will understand that I was in screaming pain, both from the intense agony caused by the dislocations and fractures, and from the agony that I had suffered in the treatment, which was on the rough and besotted side, being a hospital treatment, after all.

Being in this state and having the notary come in to swear at me and threaten me so that I would confess all my sins to him in front of everybody in the room were fresh ordeals that tormented my spirit—the last thing I needed to have in pain.

Finally I swore to everything he wanted to hear; but I said what was best for me, or at least what did me the least harm. I related the deed, omitting the matter of the swindle, and said truthfully that I didn't know my enemy and had never seen him

---

[1] There is no hospital by this name in Mexico. The purpose of this disguise is that the criticisms will not fall on any particular hospital. The abuses criticized here occur everywhere. May they be corrected!

   [Hospitals in colonial Mexico were charities (usually associated with a church or Catholic brotherhood), whose patients were those who could not afford to bring doctors to their own homes. –Tr.]

[2] [Notary publics or scriveners (*escribanos*) were important figures and crucial functionaries in the justice system of Spain and its empire, as we will see in great detail a few chapters later. Their position in the legal system was somewhat lower than that of a lawyer, but much greater than that of a notary in the U.S. system. –Tr.]

before in my life. In this way the interrogation ended, I signed the declaration with great difficulty, and the notary left, together with his retinue.

Since the blows to my head were many and well planted, it was not easy to stanch the flow of blood; the wounds were constantly bleeding, and with this loss of blood I became so weak that I frequently fainted, so often that it was thought the fainting spells were symptoms of a mortal injury, or that under one of the contusions I had broken some essential organ.

With these fears in mind, they made efforts to have the chaplain come, which at last he indeed did. I confessed, full of fear; because, seeing all these preparations, I too swallowed the idea that I was dying; but my fear did not improve my confession. Just imagine: it took place in a rush, without any disposition, and in the midst of pain; how well could it come out? Badly, of course. A *come on, hurry it up* type of confession. The second it was over, they brought the viaticum and committed a second sacrilege, and I came to understand how contingent last rites are when they are carried out in circumstances as rushed as mine.

By this point, it must have been eleven at night. I had not wanted to eat anything, because I had lost my appetite; nor could I get to sleep, because of the acute pains I was suffering, since I didn't have a whole bone in my body, as they say; but my wounds stopped bleeding, and an intern took my pulse, made me bite down on a spoon, performed who knows what other balderdash, and decreed that I would not die during the night.

Hearing this news, the orderlies[3] went to sleep, leaving me a bowl of *atole*[4] and a jug of drink by my bed so that I could have a sip whenever I desired.

The quack's favorable diagnosis did not fail to console me somewhat, and I myself felt my own pulse every now and again to see if I was still as weak as before, and since I found that it was weak—weaker indeed than I had hoped—at one in the morning I resolved to drink my atole and eat my crust of bread, though it nauseated me, to fortify myself a little.

With tremendous difficulty I picked up the cup and, using the spoon to force down the sips, I tucked the atole away in my stomach.

I reflected often on the reasons for my malady, and each time I had to admit that the bumpkin had been in the right. No doubt about it, I told myself: he all but killed me, but it was my own fault for being a rogue, a traitor. How many people deserve the same kind of punishment for the same kind of crimes!

Exhausted by this philosophizing (calamitous and unwelcome as it was, since there was nothing that could be done about it), I was just starting to fall asleep when the groans of a moribund patient lying next to me interrupted my sleep, and I could perceive the poor wretch comforting himself in a languid voice, which could barely be heard, saying: "Jesus, Jesus, have mercy on me!"

The fear and sorrow that this sad spectacle evoked in me made me raise my voice

---

[3] [Orderlies: *enfermeros,* which could also mean "(male) nurses," but it is clear that these men had no specialized training in nursing. –Tr.]

[4] [Atole: a Mexican drink (Nahuatl *atolli*) made of hot water and finely ground cornmeal, like a thin gruel, often sweetened with sugar. –Tr.]

as loud as I could, and I yelled to the orderlies: "Hullo, friends, get up, a poor man is dying in here!" I shouted four or five times, and either the rogues did not hear me, or they pretended to be asleep, which is what I suspected was more likely the truth; and so, offended by their laziness, I threw the jug of drink in their direction with such good aim that I gave them all an involuntary bath.

They could no longer pretend, so they got up, snarling at me like tigers and pelting me with their shameless curses; but I took advantage of my blessed infirmity and stopped them short, telling them with a grace that they had not anticipated: "Rogues, shiftless bums, uncharitable fools, you sleep and snore when you should be keeping watch, so that you can notify the father chaplain on duty in case one of your patients is dying, like this poor fellow who is about to expire. Tomorrow I will tell the supervisor, and if he does not punish you, the notary will come and I will ask him to notify his excellency the viceroy about these abuses, and to tell him from me that you were all drunk."

My threats and faultfinding frightened those laggards, and they begged me not to tell their overseer; I offered to keep quiet so long as they kept an eye on their patients.

While we were engaged in this conversation, the poor wretch on whose account I had troubled myself died, so that when they finally went to see about him, he was already but a soul.

As soon as those disorderly orderlies saw that he was no longer breathing, they tossed him off the bed like a hot tamale, carried him almost naked to the morgue, and presently returned to collect the poor dead man's gear, which amounted to a short poncho and an old pair of white pants made of rough fabric, a piece of steel for striking flint, a rosary, and a box of cigarettes that I think the poor wretch never had a chance to open.

Quick as a breeze, they settled his final testament and divvied up his goods, with one of the two orderlies who were there getting the pants and the rosary, and the other the poncho and the bit of steel; but over the question of who would get the box of cigarettes, they engaged in such a stormy argument that they almost came to blows, until another orderly counseled them to split the cigarettes between them and throw away the box.

They took the advice and went back to bed; I was left to grumble about their meanness and greed for an estate like that; but around three in the morning I fell asleep, and the fact that I slept well was a sign that my pain had subsided.

The next morning, the orderlies woke me for my atole, which I drank with considerably more appetite than I had the day before. In a short time the doctor entered to make his rounds in the company of his apprentices. We had some seventy patients in the ward, but even so, the visit lasted less than fifteen minutes. The whole gang passed by each bed; the doctor barely touched the patient's pulse, dropped it instantly as if it were on fire, and went on to do the same with the next one, ordering the medicine according to the bed number—for example, he would say: "Number 1, bloodletting; number 2, same; number 3, normal diet; number 4, emollient enema; number 5, diaphoretic drinks; number 6, anodyne poultice"—so it was little wonder that he finished his rounds so quickly.

Because of a clerical error, they had put me in the medical ward, when they should have tucked me away in the surgery ward, and this fluke allowed me to observe the abuses that I have been relating. No doubt, the day before, some poor fellow had died of fever in my bed, number 60, so the doctor, without glancing at me or examining me, looked only at the prescription sheet and the number on the bed, and believing that I was the feverish patient, said, "Number 60: caustics and liquids."

"Caustics and liquids!" I exclaimed. "Holy Mother Mary, don't torment me or hurt me any more than I already am! The bumpkin didn't manage to beat me to death yesterday, so please, sirs, don't you kill me today with hunger or burns."

My lamentations made the doctor realize that I was there not for fever but for wounds. Boldly taking charge of the situation in order to cover up his bewilderment, he asked, "What are you doing here, then? Go on, get to your own ward."

Thus the doctor ended his rounds, and we patients were turned over to the secular arm[5] of interns and faith-healers. When I saw two orderlies come in carrying a pitcher full of drink at eleven in the morning, and go around giving a cup of it to each patient, I was chilled. How is it possible, I wondered, that a single drink could be appropriate for all their illnesses? God save us.

Then the surgeon entered with his assistants, and they fixed me up in no time; but with so much brusqueness and so little charity that, in truth, I did not even thank them, because they hurt me far more than necessary.

Dinnertime arrived and I ate what they gave me, which was . . . just imagine. That evening, the atole supper followed; and for another poor fellow, the one in number 36, the orderlies set up a crucifix in front of his bed with a candle at its feet,[6] and then went to sleep, leaving it up to him to die whenever he felt like it.

For two months I lay observing such things that one could scarcely believe, and which one could only hope might be corrected.

I was on the way to recovery when one day Januario came to see me, wrapped in a torn serape, wearing a broken-down hat, in shirtsleeves,[7] with torn and filthy pants and leather button-up shoes that were older than the hat.

Since I hadn't left him in such a sorry state, nor had I ever seen him looking so ragged, I was shocked to think that there had been some terrible event on account of which my friend was coming in disguise; but he relieved me of my fear by telling me that these were his own clothes, indeed, they were all he owned, because he had been attracting troubles the way a street dog attracts beatings; that since the day of my accident, he hadn't been able to get back on his feet; that all the gamblers knew the whole story, so they wouldn't let him back into any gaming den, since they all

---

[5] [Lizardi makes sardonic use here of the vocabulary of the Inquisition, in which suspects were first examined by Church authorities and then "turned over to the secular arm" (i.e., the civil authorities) for punishment. –Tr.]

[6] In most hospitals, they call this lazy and uncharitable ceremony *putting up the tecolote*. [*Tecolote*, from the Nahuatl *tecolotl*, is the common Mexican word for owl; since pre-Hispanic times, the owl has been considered a portent of death in Mexico. –Tr.]

[7] [In shirtsleeves (*En pechos de camisa*):] A vulgar phrase, meaning that he had no jacket or waistcoat.

treated him as a traitor; that on the day of the incident, as soon as he noticed I was missing and heard that I had gone off with the bumpkin, he was afraid of what might happen, so he went to the inn that night to find out about it, and was told that as soon as my attacker recovered from his anger and realized what an outrage he had committed, in fear of the authorities he had saddled his horse and had beaten a hasty retreat, riding off so swiftly that when the constables had gone to look for him, he was already far from Mexico; that our partner, the rogue who had bet on the four hands of monte, had also taken off to who-knows-where with all the money, so that Januario hadn't made a penny from all his efforts;[8] that Januario had chased him on foot all the way to Chilapa, where he was told he had gone; that his journey was in vain; that he got together with other artful sorts and went on a mission[9] to Tixtla, hoping to make some money, since there was a fiesta there; but the Subdelegado there was very opposed to gambling, so he couldn't do anything; that he lived from begging, and returned to Mexico; that he had arrived two days before, and as soon as he found out I was still in the hospital, he had come to see me; that he was perishing; and finally, that he hoped I would leave the hospital soon so that the two of us could see what we might do.

Januario gave me this whole long report, and he did not do it in brief. I told him the details of my misfortunes, and he answered, "Brother, what can you do! If you want to grab the ripe fruit, you have to be ready to get the green fruit, too. You were happy and contented with the pesos that you won, so you should be just as happy with the pummeling you were given. That's the thing about our profession: we can have wonderful adventures, but we're just as likely to suffer bad ones. I would have said the same if it had happened to me, but don't despair; just get better, because the sea won't always be becalmed. If you leave and I don't hear about it, look for me in the *arrastraderito* where we stayed that night, because I don't have any other house right now—but neither do you. You know that we're old friends."

With that, Januario said good-bye, leaving me in the hospital, where three days later they gave me a clean bill of health, just as they do soldiers in the army.

I left fit and healthy, according to the doctor; but according to my limp, I still needed more *calahuala* water and more plasters; but what could I do? The medical practitioner said that I was well, and he had to be believed, despite the fact that my body contradicted him.

---

[8] It often so happens, that those who make the plans and take the risks of a robbery are not the ones who reap the rewards.

[9] *Going on a mission (ir a misión or ir de misión)* is what criminals call the trips they make out of the cities to rob, with a deck of cards, the poor wretches who lower their guard and fall into their hands. It is a rare fiesta for the patron saint of a town or for the installation of a new priest or civil authority that is not full of these malevolent missionaries. They are the parasites of the pueblos. A thousand times to one, they will go there broke, naked, and on foot, and then return on horseback, well dressed, and carrying the many pesos that they have stolen. It would be good if every judge acted like the one in Tixtla: that is, not allow them to enter their territory.

[Tixtla and Chilapa are towns about 120 miles south of Mexico City in the modern state of Guerrero; Tixtla is on the road to Acapulco, and Chilapa lies in the mountains about 25 miles east. –Tr.]

In the end I left, all sickly and shabby; but when I left, where was I to go? To the street, because I had no home to speak of; and I left worse off than I had entered, because my clothes were in bad shape when I arrived, but when I left they were beyond hope. I don't know why.

Impoverished and in tatters, alone, infirm, and very hungry, I wandered in the glare of the sun all day long, looking for my protector Januario, putting my hopes on his leavings, even though I considered him scarcely any less wretched than myself.

My efforts were in vain; it was one in the afternoon, and I had nothing in my stomach but the bit of atole I had drunk that morning in the hospital; moreover, when I drank it I had recalled the ditty that goes:

> Here's the last cup of atole
> I'll ever drink in your house.

The fact is, I was so hungry I couldn't see straight, and because of the blood I had lost and the bad time I had of it in the hospital, I was completely debilitated.

There were no two ways about it: at three in the afternoon, I ducked into a passageway to take off my waistcoat, which I then pawned. I had to work so hard to get them to loan me four reales for it! They refused to go any higher, because they said that it was no longer worth anything at all; but at last they loaned me that much, and I furnished myself with cigarettes and went to a cheap restaurant to eat.

My heart was somewhat more content after I satisfied my stomach. I spent the whole afternoon continuing my efforts of the morning, but I had nothing to show for all the walking I did, since I did not find my companion; after night fell and the clocks struck eight, I was filled with fear, thinking that if I stayed out in the street, I was liable to be found by some night watch or patrol and spend the night in jail.

These terrors made me resolve to go to the *arrastraderito*, which had become as hard for me to do as to go to the hospital itself; but need overrides everything else.

I reached the damnable hovel with one and a half reales (because I had stopped on the way to eat half a real's worth of beans). I entered and no one questioned me; I saw the gaming table arranged like a painting of the souls—souls of the damned, that is.[10]

Some fourteen or sixteen people were there, and among them all I didn't see a single white face or half-dressed body. All of them were *lobos* and mulattos,[11] all in the buff, betting their half-reales on cards that were so filthy only they could read them.

They were stripping each other of their clothes, sometimes to pawn them, sometimes to bet them, until some of them were left as they were when their mothers gave them birth, wearing nothing but a *maxtle*, as they call it, which is a cloth they use to cover their shameful parts, and there was at least one rogue who wrapped himself up in a blanket together with another, whom he called his pal.

---

[10] [The blessed souls in purgatory are popular subjects for religious icons in Mexico and, in some paintings, are contrasted with the tormented souls of the damned. –Tr.]

[11] [*Lobo:* a person of mixed Indian, African, and European descent. –Tr.]

That miniature hell abounded in curses, obscenities, and blasphemy. Between the gambling, the crowd, the close space, and the cheap rum, it was blazing hot, it stank of sweat, and it seemed like . . . well, I have already made the best comparison: hell.

When they saw me draw near the table to watch them play, thinking I had some money they offered me a seat on the corner of a bench that had a slat jutting out, catching me in the wrong place and leaving me in an embarrassing position.

Despite my discomfort, I did not stand up, thinking that it would be too much courtesy to show that crowd. I took out a small coin and started gambling like the rest of them.

It did not take me long to lose it, and I continued with another, which suffered the same fate in fewer minutes; and I did not dare gamble the third, reserving it to be able to pay for staying the night.

I was about to get up when the dealer recognized me and asked, "Who did you come looking for?"

I told him I was looking for Don Januario Carpeña (for that was my companion's last name). They all laughed boisterously at my reply, and seeing that I had taken offence at their laughter, the dealer asked me, "Maybe you're looking for Juan Largo the traitor, the guy who came here the other night?"

I couldn't deny it; I said that was him, and he answered, "Friend, that guy isn't a Don any more than he's a Doña—at the very tops he's Don Sleeping Mat or Don Stark Naked, like the rest of us. . . . "

Just then, the man in question came walking in, and as soon as they saw him, everyone started kidding him, saying: "Oh, Don Januario! Oh, Señor Don Juan Largo! Come in, please, sir. Where have you been, sir?" and other nonsense, which all boiled down to mocking him for the way I had spoken about him.

He had not seen me, and since he had no idea what was going on, he stood there like a bumbling idiot until one of the naked fellows cleared it all up for him by saying, "Here is someone who has been inquiring about the great gentleman Don Januario Garrapiña."[12]

And saying this, he pointed to me.

No sooner did Januario see me than, in his excitement, he expressed his friendship in the finest way he knew how: he greeted me by wrapping his arms around me and saying, "Is it possible, Periquillo Sarniento, that we have met again?"

When our brothers heard my nickname they redoubled their cackling and began to demand the etymology of the name, an explanation that Januario did not deny them.

And here they all started up again, mocking me and *parroting* me as much as they could, since in the end they were crude and obscene folk; but as much as their jokes offended me, I had no choice but to bear it and face the music, as they say; because if I had tried to get that riffraff to treat me as my background demanded, I would only have given them a better motive to make fun of me. These are the let-downs to which a man exposes himself by being lazy, dissolute, and shameless.

---

[12] [*Garrapiña:* slang for "thief" (a pun on the name Carpeña). –Tr.]

When they saw how jolly I was and how, far from getting angry, I went along with their jokes, they all became my friends and comrades, branding me as one of their own, for as they said, I was a regular guy, and with this intimate trust we cheerfully began to speak with each other on informal terms—a normal custom among ill-mannered people, who start off affectionately and more often than not end up insulting each other, even if they are decent fellows.[13]

Just look at me now, a brother of such a community, a member of an academy of scoundrels, and a partner in a conspiracy of drunks, swindlers, and petty thieves. Come on, that night I was in top form, and how well I honored my good father!

What would my mother have said if she had seen the descendant of the Ponces, Tagles, Pintos, Velascos, Zumalacárreguis, and Bundiburis involved with that indecent rabble? She would have died a thousand deaths, and a thousand times more would have resolved to apprentice me to the lowest trade sooner than let me become such a tramp; but mothers never believe in what will happen, and they even think that such examples are nothing but fairy tales, or that even if they are true, they say nothing about their own children. In the end, those of us who stayed there went to bed as best we could, and I spent the night as God willed.

For the next six or eight days, I stayed with that family, and in that time, Januario left me uncloaked, for one day he borrowed my cloak to do some business or other, and he took it away and left me without a serape. He came back without it at four in the afternoon, shocking me almost to death with the thousand lies he told, and he topped it off by telling me he had pawned the cloak for five pesos.

"Five pesos, God Almighty!" I said. "How is that possible, if it is so torn and patched that it isn't worth half that much?"

"Oh, what a fool you are!" he replied. "If you had only seen all the things I did with those five pesos, you would have been amazed; you know what a go-getter I am. I got it up to about . . . let me see. Fifteen plus seven makes twenty-two, plus . . . nine?, thirty-one . . . plus twelve? Well, about fifty pesos, something like that."

"And where are they?" I asked.

"Where should they be?" said Januario. "I was betting them on a *contrajudía* that I had all wrapped up; I put all the money on a three against the jack, and. . . . "

"You went bust," I said; "the jack came up and the devil took the money, isn't that it?"

"Yes, brother, that's it; but if you had only seen what a pretty three it was! The little card, the *contrajudía*, the odd, on the outside place . . . [14] Damned if the three didn't have them all."

"Damn *you*, and the three, and the four, and the five, and the six, and the whole deck of cards, now that you've left me without a cloak. I swear to the devil! That was

---

[13] The use of the word *tú* [the informal Spanish way of saying "you," which contrasts with the polite and formal form *usted*], far from enhancing friendship, as some people vulgarly assume, diminishes it, because excessive intimacy is normally followed by scorn; and scorn, by anger; and then, good-bye friendship! Using polite and affectionate terms of address conserves good friendships.

[14] [Footnote 7 to chapter 17, on gambling systems, was placed here in the fourth edition to explain the terms *chiquito, contrajudía, nones,* and *lugar de afuera.* –Tr.]

the only possession I had. It was my mattress, my blanket, my everything, and now you've gone and made a *pilhuanejo* of me?"[15]

"Don't get so worked up about it," Januario told me. "I've got a project all thought out that'll get us both lots of money, maybe even tonight—but you've got to keep it secret. For now, here's my serape, and it will serve well enough for both of us."

I asked him what the deal was. Bringing me to a corner of the room, he told me, "Look, when someone's in the position that we're in now, they've got to be determined and ready to do anything, because dying of hunger is worse. So listen up: there's a rich widow who lives near here, and she doesn't have anyone to keep her company aside from her maid, a good-looking girl whom I've tried to sweet talk, though I haven't gotten anywhere. This widow is the one who'll have to help us out tonight, whether she likes it or not."

"How is that?" I asked.

To which Januario replied, "In the gang here, there's a companion they call *Culás el Pípilo*, Nicky the Gobbler, a crafty little mulatto with lots of spirit, and a great friend of mine. He's proposed to me that tonight between ten and eleven, we could go to that house, surprise the two women, and fill our bags with coins and jewels, because the old woman's got lots of both. Everything's ready: we've agreed on the plan, and we have a picklock that fits perfectly. All we need is a companion who'll stay in the courtyard while we move forward. Nobody better than you for that job. So buck up: maybe I lost your rag of a cloak, but now in exchange I'll be putting a considerable sum of money in your hands."

I was astonished at Januario's determination, unable to convince myself that he would be capable of stooping so low as to declare himself a burglar; and so, far from agreeing to accompany him, I endeavored to talk him out of his plan, expostulating on the injustice of the deed, the dangers to which he would be exposing himself, and the shame that would await him if he were caught.

Januario listened to me attentively, and when I came to a pause he told me: "I never thought you would be so hypocritical or so stupid that you would dare to pretend you were virtuous or to give your own teacher advice. Look here, you mule: I know perfectly well that robbery is unjust, and that the profession carries its risks; but tell me: what doesn't? If a man goes into long-distance trade, he can get lost; if he goes into farming, one bad rain can ruin the ripest harvest; if he studies, he could be a fool, or fail to make a reputation; if he learns a manual craft, he might spoil his jobs, or fall into debt, or turn out to be clumsy; if he goes for working in an office, he might not find a mentor and never get a promotion in his life; if he enters a military career, he might get killed on his first campaign; and so on, with all of them.

"So if everyone were so afraid of what might happen, nobody would have a peso, because nobody would risk trying to get it. If you are trying to tell me that all the ways I have just mentioned are just, but what I proposed to you is wicked, let me tell you that robbery is nothing but taking away what belongs to someone else against their will, and according to this truth, the world is full of thieves. The thing is that

---

[15] [*Pilhuanejo* or *pilguanejo*: originally meaning a priest's servant, this Mexican Spanish word had come to mean an insignificant or despicable person. –Tr.]

some people can steal while keeping the appearances of being just, and others can't. Some do it in public, others in private. Some under the cover of the law, and other by declaring themselves outlaws. Some expose themselves to bullets and the hangman's noose, and others promenade and sit safely in their houses. Finally, my brother, some steal in the divine way and others in the human way; but everybody steals.[16] So that's no argument for keeping me from carrying out what I've determined to do; because, as they say, *everybody's evil,* and so forth.[17]

"What is so much better about robbing with fountain pens, with yardsticks, with measuring scales, with prescriptions, with oils, with papers, and so on, and so forth, than robbing with picklocks, ropes, and master keys? Stealing is stealing; it all comes out the same, and a thief is a thief; it's the same to rob from a carriage as to rob on foot; and a city thief is at least as harmful to society as a highway robber.

"Don't furrow your brows at me or start acting shocked in your sanctimonious way. I'm not telling you all this just because I want to be a thief; others have said the same thing before me, and they haven't just said it, they've published it, including virtuous and wise men like the Jesuit father Pedro Murillo Velardo, in his Catechism. Listen to what he writes in book II, chapter XII, page 177:

> There are countless forms, ways, and manners to steal (says the father). The child steals, the grown man steals, the craftsman steals; the soldier, the merchant, the tailor, the notary, the judge, the lawyer; and although not everyone steals, all types of people steal. And the verb rapio can be conjugated in all persons and tenses.[18] People steal actively and passively, by circumlocutions and with the future participle, rus.

"End quote.

"So what do you think now? With so many thieves out there, what difference will I make? None at all, because one more chickpea won't burst the pot. Do you know who acts shocked at thieves and their robberies? Those who are in the business themselves, fool. They are their worst enemies; that's why the saying goes, *the cat hates it when someone else can scratch.*

---

[16] Only Januario could speak so generally, because he was a hopeless case. The words in our mouths rise from what fills our hearts. Not everyone steals; but there are so many thieves, and self-interest is so powerful, that there is scarcely anyone who can be trusted. Upright men are lost among the dishonest, and when it comes to self-interest, there are few men who have many scruples against committing fraud or holding onto other people's things. This is a bitter truth, yet it is a truth. We should examine it dispassionately.

[17] [The saying that Januario begins to quote is *mal de muchos, consuelo de tontos;* literally, "harm for many people is a consolation for fools," or roughly, "misery loves company." By quoting only the first three words (relying on the double meaning of *mal* as "evil," as well as "harm, damage"), Januario twists the saying to mean "everyone does it," but his ellipsis pointedly implies that his argument is a "consolation for fools." –Tr.]

[18] In other words, in the present tense: I steal, you steal, he steals, we steal, you steal, they steal. The past tense: I stole, you stole, he stole, and so on. The future: I will steal, you will steal; and so on, with all the other tenses and persons. What a shame! Many people do not know how to read, yet they can conjugate this verb without blinking an eye.

"I don't remember if it was in an old book titled *The Delights of Discretion* or in another called *Spanish Medley,* but I'm sure it was in one of them, that I read that amusing story about the sharp-witted madman who lived in Seville, named Juan García, who, seeing a thief being escorted to the gallows one day, began to laugh loud and long, and when he was asked what there was to laugh about in such a gloomy spectacle, he replied: 'I'm laughing to see the big thieves bringing the small fry to be hanged.' Draw your own conclusions, my dear Perico."[19]

"The only conclusion I can come to," I replied, "is that when a man is resolved, as you are, to do anything no matter how evil, he interprets every argument in his own favor, even if it goes counter to him. Everything you've said is true enough. Who could deny that there are lots of thieves, if we see them all around? Do people gloss over robbery by giving it different names? Obviously. Do people usually steal under the appearance of legality? That's clearer than water. But does the fact that men kill thousands of people in wars, both just and unjust, ever prove that murder is legitimate? The repetition of an act will make it habitual, but not just, if the act is not good in itself.

"What Father Murillo says does not prove anything, either, because he said it to satirize stealing, not to praise it. But, so that I won't owe you anything, let me repay your little story with another that I also read in a Jesuit's book, and it has the advantage of proving what you're saying and also what I'm saying: that is, that many people steal, but that does not make stealing legitimate. Follow me.

"In the middle of a canvas, someone painted a prince, and by his side a minister, who said: 'I serve only this man, and so I serve myself.' Then, a soldier who said: 'So long as I rob, these two rob me.' Following him came a farmer, saying: 'I feed and feed off these three.' By his side, a craftsman who confessed: 'I cheat these four and they cheat me.' Then a merchant who said: 'I strip these five when I dress them.' Then a lawyer: 'I destroy when I defend these six.' A bit farther on, a doctor: 'I kill when I heal these seven.' Then a confessor: 'I damn when I absolve these eight.' And finally a devil, stretching out his claws and saying: 'Well, I'll take all nine for myself.' And so, each linked to the next, men go about studying how to commit frauds in violation of the Seventh Commandment, and linked together in these chains, they go down to hell. End citation: from the Christian, zealous, and erudite father Juan Martínez de la Parra, moral sermon 45, page 239 of the 24th edition, printed in Madrid in 1788.

"So you see that, even if everybody steals, as you say, everybody does wrong, and the devil will take them all, and I don't feel like getting mixed up in this business."

"You're so sanctimonious," Januario told me, "and to tell the truth, that isn't virtue, it's just fear. Why don't you have the same scruples about pulling a trick, cashing someone else's bet, or swiping the ante, since you do it so much better than I do

---

[19] [According to Ruiz Barrionuevo (p. 387), the books mentioned are Bernardino Fernández de Velasco y Pimentel, *Deleite de la discreción y fácil escuela de la agudeza* (Madrid, 1764), and Melchor de Santa Cruz Dueñas, *Floresta española de apotegmas* (Toledo, 1574). The first contains anecdotes about Juan García, and the second has others about another *loco,* Garci Sánchez, but neither recounts the story in question. –Tr.]

now? And how come you didn't have any scruples about handing over the bumpkin's hundred pesos? You know perfectly well that all this is just stealing under another name."

"That is true," I replied, "but if I did it, you instigated it, because on my own I would never have the nerve. I realize that it is robbery, and that I did wrong; and I also realize that from these swindles, cheats, and tricks, things lead in that direction: that is, to becoming a flat-out thief. Friend, I don't hope that you should think of me as virtuous. You can suppose that fear alone is what makes me pull back; but you can be absolutely sure that I have not the slightest appetite for dying on the gallows."

We conversed like this for a long time, until at last we resolved what you will discover if you read the chapter that follows.

CHAPTER 19

IN WHICH OUR AUTHOR RECOUNTS HIS TIME IN PRISON, HIS LUCK
IN FINDING A FRIEND THERE, AND THE LATTER'S LIFE STORY

After many debates that we had on the preceding topic, I told Januario, "For the last time, brother, I'll accompany you wherever you want to go, as long as it's not to go stealing; because the truth is that the profession doesn't attract me; and I only wish I could get this foolishness out of your head."

Januario thanked me for caring about him; but he told me that if I didn't want to accompany him, I should stay behind; but that I should keep the secret, because he had made up his mind to escape poverty that night, come what may; that if they could carry it off without raising a ruckus, as he and the Gobbler had it planned, the next day he would bring me a better cloak than the one he had gambled away, and we would get away from such hardships.

I promised to keep absolutely quiet, thanking him for his offer and repeating my advice and my pleas, but nothing could stop him. Before leaving, he hugged me and put a rosary around my neck, saying, "Just in case we never see each other again by some accident, wear this rosary so you'll remember me."

With that, he left, and I stayed behind crying, because I liked him despite knowing what a rogue he was. I don't know what it is about being in contact with someone since childhood that engenders such brotherly affection.

My friend left, and I spent a very sad evening, mourning his decision to go and worrying about some ill-fated mishap. By nine at night, I could no longer contain myself, missing my companion, and in the fashion of lovers I went off to hang around the street where he told me the widow lived.

Tucked into a doorway and hidden thanks to the lack of street lights, I observed how, around half past ten, two hulking shapes arrived at the house that was destined for burglary; I instantly recognized the shapes as Januario and the Gobbler: they broke in silently; they pulled the door almost closed behind them; and I walked casually over to light a cigarette on the candle in the lamp of the night watchman who was sitting on the street corner.

When I got there, I greeted him with great courtesy; he responded in the same tone; I gave him a cigarette, lit my own, and had barely begun to strike up a conversation with him while waiting for my friend's results, when we heard a balcony window open and a girl, no doubt the widow's maid, let out a terrible scream: "Watchman, sir! Guard! Thieves! Come quick, please God, they're going to kill us!"

So the girl screamed, but over and over again, and very loud. The guard jumped up right away, whistled as best he could, and waved his lamp around a few times in the crossroads to call his companions, and he told me, "Friend, help me out here— take my lamp and let's go."

I took the lamp, and he slung his short cape across his shoulders and hoisted his pike; but while he was doing all this, the thieves escaped. The Gobbler, whom I recognized by his white hat, passed by almost next to me, and no matter how the watchman and I ran (because I was also pretending to run), we weren't able to catch up, because he sprouted wings on his feet. The watchman shouted in vain: "Stop him, stop him!", because the streets around there are hardly crowded at night, and there were few stoppers in sight.

So the Gobbler escaped, and so did Januario with less excitement, since he took the other crossroads, where there was no night watchman, nor anyone to bother him about anything.

Meanwhile two other guards arrived, and directly behind them a night patrol. The girl was still screaming from the balcony, calling for "a father" and saying that they had killed her mistress. We all turned toward her voice and entered the house.

The first thing we found was the girl, crying in the corridor and telling us, "Ay, sirs! Bring a father and a doctor, because those tramps have killed my mistress!"

The patrol sergeant, two soldiers, the watchmen, and I, still holding the lamp in my hand, all entered the bedroom where the lady was lying stretched out on her bed, which was covered with blood, and she gave no signs of life.

The horrendous sight of that spectacle surprised us all, and filled me with fright and pity: fright, for the risk that Januario was running if they caught him, and pity, considering the injustice with which they had sacrificed this innocent victim to their greed.

Soon after, the doctor and the confessor arrived at almost the same time, having been called by one of the soldiers on the sergeant's orders as soon as he had heard the girl screaming in the street.

As soon as they got there, the priest approached the bed, and seeing that, regardless of whether he jostled or spoke to her, she did not move, he gave her a conditional absolution and stepped aside.

Then the doctor approached and, being more skilled, he noted that she had just fainted and that the blood was from her womanly period. We went into the drawing room, comforted to know that it wasn't the misfortune we had thought, while the doctor and the servant administered household remedies to the patient.

With this business done, and the lady revived from her fainting spell, the sergeant called the maid to see what was missing in the house. She looked it over and said that nothing was missing except for the silverware that her mistress had been eating with, and the little string of pearls that she had worn around her neck, because as soon as one of the thieves had carried her to the bed, the other pocketed the fork and spoon; and since there weren't enough of them, or since they didn't think to stop her, she had run out to the balcony and started to shout for the watchman, and hearing her screams, the thieves merely ran away from the house.

I was standing there with the lamp in my hand, with my serape open and with the kind of serenity that innocence lends; but all the time that the wicked servant was giving this testimony, she never took her eyes off me, staring at me from head to foot. I noticed it, but didn't think anything of it, attributing it to the fact that she thought I wasn't bad looking.

The sergeant asked her if she recognized either of the thieves, and she replied, "Yes, sir; I know one of them, called Señor Januario, but they've nicknamed him Juan Largo, and he never leaves that little gambling dive around the corner, and this gentleman's got to know him better than me."

She then pointed at me, and I stood there thunderstruck, as they say. The sergeant noticed my distress and said to me, "Yes, friend, the girl is right, no doubt. Your face has fallen too much, and your guilt is accusing you. Are you the watchman for this block, by chance?"

"No, sir," I said; "rather, when this lady stepped out to the balcony to scream, I was puffing on a cigarette with the watchman, and we were the first two who came here to help them. This gentleman can tell you."

Then the watchman confirmed the truth of what I had said; but instead of being convinced, the sergeant continued, "Yes, yes; no doubt you're as good a trickster as the watchman. Watchmen? *Hanged* men, that's how I hope to see you both, for being the robbers' lookouts! If they didn't have you covering their backs, if you hadn't been drunk, or sleeping, or away from your posts, there is no way there could be so many robberies."

The watchman fretted and swore, testifying with me that he hadn't been away or asleep; but the sergeant paid him no mind, instead asking the girl, "And you, my girl: what grounds do you have for saying that this man knows the thief?"

"Oh, sir!" the girl said, "lots and lots! Just look at this here serape he's got on: it's the same one as belongs to Señor Juan Largo, because I know him well, since every time I went to the store or the plaza, he'd be hanging around me; and to prove it, that rosary on the gentleman's neck is mine, 'cause that rogue caught me yesterday by the front of my blouse and by my rosary, and he tried to pull me into an empty entranceway, and I yanked and got away, and I even tore my blouse, just look here, and my rosary was still in his hand and it busted; to prove it, it's bound to be rigged up and it's bound to be missing some beads; and the cord's pretty new, it has four strands and it's pink and green silk, and in that little satchel there should be two little images, one of my patron St. Andrew Avellino and another of St. Rosalia."

All these proofs from the wicked girl chilled me, considering that none of it could be a lie, since the rosary had come from Januario's own hand, and he had told me about his infatuation with her.

The sergeant made me take it off; he undid the satchel, and there you had it, everything the girl had declared, to the letter. No further proof was needed. In an instant they tied my arms together, elbow to elbow, with a rifle sling, without paying any more attention to my oaths and allegations, for the sergeant answered them all with, "Fine, tomorrow we'll see how this all turns out."

With that they took me down the staircase, and the maid also came down to shut the door, and seeing that she couldn't get the key in, she noticed that the problem was the picklock, which they had left in the lock. She took it out and handed it to the sergeant. She locked her door, and I was taken away to headquarters.

When I was turned over to that guardhouse, the soldiers there asked my escorts why they were bringing me, and they replied: for being a *filch*, that is, a thief. The busybodies thoroughly cussed me out, as if they were happy that I had fallen and that somehow made them into upright men. They wrote down something or other and then left, but before they went, the sergeant told his partner, "Take care with this one, because he's a prisoner of some consequence."

As soon as the sergeant of the guard heard this recommendation, he ordered his men to put my legs in stocks. The patrol left; the soldiers curled up again on their cots; the sentinel went back to shouting *who goes there* to every passer-by; and I was left to struggle with the pain of being in stocks, the drubbing of lying on a rough log floor, the multitude of bedbugs and fleas that had me surrounded, and worst of all, a bewildering jumble of sad thoughts that suddenly attacked me.

You can just imagine what kind of night I spent. I couldn't close my eyes all night long, thinking about the terrible and shameful state to which I found myself reduced through no fault of my own, just for maintaining my friendship with a rogue.[1]

Day broke at last; reveille sounded; the soldiers got out of bed with their customary cursing, and when time came to send in the night report, they dispatched it to the major on duty, and they sent me, bundled up like a bottle-rocket, along with it to the city jail.[2]

As soon as I passed through the narrow entry into the central patio, they rang a bell, which as they later told me was something they did with all the prisoners, so that the warden and the upstairs watchmen would be advised that a new prisoner was coming.

Indeed, a short time later I heard one of them start shouting: "New man! New man coming up!" My companions informed me that I was the one they were calling, and the trusty—a huge, fat man with a bullwhip tied around his waist—brought me upstairs and pushed me into a long hall where, behind a small desk, sat the warden, who asked me my name, where I was from, and who had brought me to the jail. Not wanting to stain my family name, I told him my name was "Sancho Pérez," that I was born in Ixtlahuaca,[3] and that some soldiers from the main headquarters had brought me.

They noted all this down in a book and sent me off. After I came downstairs, the trusty charged me some two and a half pesos for my *entry fee*. I didn't know the jargon there, so I told him I didn't want to join any religious brotherhoods in the jail, and therefore I didn't need to pay any such fees. The damnable slave driver, thinking I was making fun of him, gave me a punch that left me spitting blood. "Listen up, mug," he spat, "nobody makes fun of me—not real men, and for sure not some snot-nosed brat. I asked for the entry fee, and if you don't want to pay up, you'll clean floors, you lousy filcher."

Saying this, he left, but he left me there in a sea of affliction.

There must have been a million prisoners there in the patio. Some white, others black; some half-dressed, others decent; some stripped naked, others wrapped in threadbare blankets; but all of them pale, and with their sadness and desperation painted in the haggard color of their cheeks.

It seems, however, that none of them cared a hoot about that life, because some of them were playing monte, others were dancing in their shackles, others were singing,

---

[1] This happens to many people, yet the young never learn from these examples. One should hold on to a good friend at all costs, and flee from a bad one as soon as he lets himself be known, because "better alone than in bad company."

[2] [The Mexico City jail (*cárcel de la corte*) was located, until 1835, inside the Ayuntamiento, or city council building on the Plaza Mayor opposite the Cathedral. –Tr.]

[3] [A town fifty miles west of Mexico City. –Tr.]

others were knitting socks and lace, others were chatting, and each of them was finding some distraction, except for a handful of snoops who surrounded me to dig into the reason for my incarceration.

I answered ingenuously, and as soon as they heard they went away laughing, and in an instant everybody knew me as *the filch*.

No one consoled me, and the interest they showed in learning the cause for my arrest was mere curiosity. But so that you will learn that in the worst place in the world, there are good men, pay attention.

Among those who listened to the snooping prisoners' examination of me, there was a man about forty years old, white, fairly good in appearance, dressed in his shirtsleeves, blue corduroy pants, purple poncho, leather country leggings, button-up shoes, and a white cocked hat. After the rest of them had left me alone, this man came up to me and, with an affability that was new to me in that place, said, "Young friend, would you like a cigarette?"

And he gave me one, sitting down next to me. I took it, thanking him for being so obliging, and he urged me to come to his cell and to breakfast on the food he had.[4] Again I displayed my gratitude, and went with him.

After we got to his room, he took down a *tompiate*[5] that he had hanging on the wall, took out a crust of cheese and a bread roll, and put them in my hand, saying, "The lodgings couldn't be worse, nor is there anything better to offer you; but what can we do? Let us eat this little bit that God has given us, and please judge me by my affection, not by the hospitality I can show you, which is all too little and too crude."

I was surprised to hear such gracious words from such a seemingly ordinary man, and, as amazed as I was moved, told him, "I give you my endless thanks, sir, not so much for the hospitality you have shown me as for the interest you have displayed in my unfortunate luck. The truth is that I am astonished, and can hardly believe it possible to find an upright man such as you must be in this horrific place, this storehouse of wickedness and iniquity."

The good friend answered me, "It is true that jails are built to hold rogues and delinquents, but sometimes there are even bigger and more powerful rogues who make use of them to oppress the innocent, accusing them of crimes they have not committed, and they normally attain these goals through their intrigues and cunning, deceiving the integrity of the most vigilant judges; but, according to your opinion, I am doubtless deceived in my own."

"What is your opinion, sir?" I asked.

"Mine," he answered, "is what I have just stated: that is, that although jails were instituted to hold delinquents, men's wickedness has been able to twist that aim, and in many cases has made jails serve to deprive upright men of their liberty; so many examples of this abound that we need look for no further proof. This notion of mine, and some strange sympathy that I felt, made me pity you as soon as I saw how

---

[4] [Prisoners (or their families) were responsible for providing their own food in colonial jails and prisons. –Tr.]

[5] [A basket or pouch woven from palm leaves. –Tr.]

badly the trusty treated you, and I formed the idea that you were an upright man who had perhaps been buried alive in this dungeon by some powerful enemy, as I have been; but you have made me change my way of thinking, for you believe that jails hold only criminals, so I am now convinced that you, being an inexperienced youth, must have committed some crime, more out of human squalor than wickedness; but even if that is the case, my son, do not think that I am scandalized, much less that I have ceased to love and pity you; because in man we should abhor the crime, but never the person. Therefore, please ask the trusty's permission to move to this cell, and if you are afraid of him, I will ask for you, and when they bring your bed, put it next to mine, both so that you can avail yourself of my help insofar as I can offer any, and can free yourself from the taunts of the other prisoners, who, being coarse folk that lack any principals or education, always entertain themselves by mocking the poor newcomers who come to reside in these walls."

I repeated my thanks to him, adding, "I can do no less than deem you a sensitive and upright man, or more properly, a beneficent genie who has deigned to dedicate himself as my guardian angel in the midst of my helplessness, and I am ashamed to have explained myself so clumsily as to convince you that I thought everyone in jail might be a rogue, for surely, if you were not one of the exceptions to this rule, I myself disprove the poor opinion I had formed of jails. . . . "

"So then," the friend interrupted, "you are not here for committing some crime?"

"As you see, I am not."

And at once I told him the story of my life, point by point, up to the unhappy moment of my arrest.

The companion listened to me with great courtesy, and when I concluded, told me, "Friend, the candor with which you have related your adventures has confirmed the first impression that I immediately had of you; that is, that you were a well-born lad, and that some unforeseen misfortune had brought you here; but though you are suffering, it is clear that you are not entirely innocent. You did not steal, nor did you take part in the robbery; but, oh, my friend!, you have on your conscience the tears that you caused your mother, and perhaps her death, which you probably hastened with your erring ways; and crimes committed against one's parents cry out to heaven for revenge. For now, all you can do is recognize this truth, repent, and trust to Divine Providence, which, even when it punishes, always aims its decrees at our own good. As for me, as I have already told you, you can count on my friendship and on my poor means, which I will most happily use to help you."

For the third time I thanked him, mindful that his offer was not mere words, as such things usually are; and with my curiosity goading me to know who this kind man was, I could not contain myself, and without skirting the topic I begged him to do me the favor of informing me of his misadventures. He gladly answered my request in these words:

"Don Pedro, even if I were not obliged to reciprocate the trust you have shown me by recounting your tragedies, I would be happy to do what you have asked me, because it is well known that, though communicating one's sorrows may not heal them, it certainly does alleviate them. Keeping this in mind, you should know that my name is Antonio Sánchez; my parents were well born and orderly in behavior, and both had handsome inheritances that I would have enjoyed in my turn, had not Providence destined me to suffer from the moment I was born; not that I complain of my fate when I remember my misfortunes, for I would be a blasphemer if I were to speak resentfully about a God who loves me infinitely more than I do myself, and who infallibly disposes all for my benefit; but only in the way of telling my life history, let me say that since I was born, I have been assailed by misfortunes, because my mother died the moment I left her womb, and as everyone knows, being an orphan from birth brings with it a long series of calamities to those of us who have suffered such a misfortune.

"My good father spared no expense, worry, or fatigue to make up for this lack; and so I spent my childhood between wet nurses, governesses, and maids, with the cheerfulness proper to that age, without failing to learn the principles of religion, etiquette, and elementary education, which my loving father did not forget to teach me with the great care and affection that all good fathers show to their first and only children.

"I had reached the age of fifteen when my father sent me to secondary school, where I remained three years, contented and filled with innocent satisfactions, which ended for me with my noble father's death, which left me under the guardianship of the executor of his will, whose name I will leave in silence so as not to reveal the author of my misfortunes. You will recognize from this turn of phrase that my guardian quickly did away with my estate, leaving me in the clutches of destitution, and when he had nothing else to do, he fled from Orizaba,[6] my native town, without leaving me so much as a recommendation for his business partner in Mexico.

"When this partner discovered my guardian's absence and the sinister reasons for it, he went to my school, wiped clean my tuition debts, brought me to his house, informed me of my sad situation, and concluded by telling me that he was a poor man with a large family, that he felt sorry for my misfortune, but that he could not take me on, and that I should therefore solicit the protection of my relatives and see how things went for me.

"Imagine how this news made me feel. I was eighteen years old then, and entirely inexperienced; but by God's special grace, I had not taken up any shameful vices, nor did I think as most young lads do; and so I said that within a week, I would make up my mind about what to do, and would let him know.

"Immediately I went to see a poor student, an upright fellow whom, after recounting to him my misfortunes, I entrusted with selling my bed, books, mantle, divan, clock, and everything that I thought might be worth something.

"Indeed, my friend carried out the matter efficiently and promptly, and the next day brought me a hundred and some odd pesos. I gave him his tip, and changed most of the pesos into gold, using the rest to buy a cloak and a used pair of boots.

---

[6] [Orizaba is a town 150 miles east of Mexico City, on the road to Veracruz, the principal Atlantic port of Mexico. Situated at the foot of the Pico de Orizaba, the highest mountain in Mexico, it has a semi-tropical climate, and in the colonial era it was known for its tobacco production. As the son of a wealthy man, Antonio was sent away to school in Mexico City. The towns of Jalapa and Veracruz, mentioned below, are relatively nearby. –Tr.]

"With this matter concluded, I went to the inns to look for a traveler who might be on his way to my homeland. Fortunately, my search was not in vain; I found a mule driver who was going to carry cigarettes there and bring tobacco back, and for ten pesos I arranged to make the trip with him. Then I notified my guardian's business partner of my decision; he approved of it, I bid farewell to him and his family and went to the inn, and two days later we left for Orizaba.

"This journey seemed very different to me from those, along the same road, that I had made before when I went on vacations, especially when my father was alive; but these were different times, and I had no choice but to adjust myself to circumstances.

"At last I arrived without incidence in the town and, suspecting that one or another of my well-to-do relatives might treat me with a certain detachment, I decided to stay at the house of some old aunts who I knew loved me, and who would not disdain to shelter me.

"I was not wrong in my way of thinking, because as soon as they saw me, the poor dears began to weep as if they had known about my ill fate before I did myself; they embraced me and let me into their little house, assuring me that I should look at it as my own.

"I showed them my gratitude as best I could, telling them I was thinking of moving to a store, an hacienda, or something of the sort, so that I could begin to learn how to earn my bread by the sweat of my brow, which was as much as I could now aspire to.

"The sweet old ladies were touched by these things, and I redoubled my thanks for their expressive sentiments.

"I had spent six days lodged in their house when, one afternoon, there walked in a very decent gentleman, whom I did not know; my aunts treated him familiarly, because they washed and mended his clothes when he passed through there, and availing themselves of this rapport, they said to him, 'Señor Don Francisco, do you know this child?'—pointing to me.

"The gentleman said he did not, and they went on, 'He is our nephew Antoñito, the son of your friend, our late lamented Don Lorenzo Sánchez, may he rest in peace.'

" 'Is it possible,' said the gentleman, 'that this unfortunate lad is my friend's son? What is he doing here, so indecently dressed? Was he not in school?'

" 'Yes, sir,' my aunts replied; 'but since his father's executor wasted his entire inheritance, the poor child has been reduced to searching for a way to earn a living through labor, and in the meantime he has come to stay with us.'

" 'I had heard news of that rascal's villainy,' said the gentleman, 'but I couldn't believe it. And what, then, my young friend—did he leave nothing for you?'

" 'Nothing, sir,' I answered; 'merely to be able to move to this town, I had to sell my mantle, bed, books, and other trifles.'

" 'Lord help me! Poor boy!' continued Don Francisco. 'Those wicked, wicked executors, how badly they carry out testators' wishes, enriching themselves at the expense of others and leaving their miserable wards out of doors! My young friend, don't lose heart; be an upright man, because not all those who put food on their tables have inherited their wealth, nor do the gallows hang every thief there is, for if they did, all these thieving executors would not be strolling around laughing, like your father's. Can you write reasonably well?'

" 'Sir,' I said, 'you shall see my handwriting.'

"Then and there, I wrote something or other on a piece of paper.

"He liked my handwriting very much, and he examined my ability to keep accounts, and seeing that I knew a little something, he proposed that if I wished to go with him inland,[7] where he had an hacienda and a store, he would pay me fifteen pesos a month for the first year while I was in training, in addition to clean clothes and board.

"I saw a new chance opening up with this position, which seemed unsurpassable, since I had no other position, nor any hopes of finding one; and so I instantly agreed, and my aunts and I thanked him many times.

"The gentleman was to depart the next day for his destination; and so he told me that from that hour on, I was on his account, and I should bid farewell to my aunts and leave with him for his place.

"I resolved to do this, and I took out of my pouch four ounces of gold that remained from liquidating my possessions, giving three ounces to my aunts, who refused to take the gold no matter how much I swore that they should, assuring them that I had only saved it with the aim of giving it to them once I had found employment, which was now the case, so that I should consequently show my gratitude.

"Even so, my aunts refused to accept the gold, and we said good-bye to each other amid tears, embraces, and promises to write. The next day, we left Orizaba, and a month and few days later reached Zacatecas, where my master had his hacienda.

"Before setting me up in his store, he had the tailor and the seamstress come, and he promptly made me linens and suits, everyday wear and fancy clothes, and bought me a bed, a trunk, and all the necessities.

"I was happy but embarrassed to see his munificence, reckoning that between the amount he had spent on me and my puny salary of fifteen pesos, I had sold myself to him for four or five years at the least.

"Once I was outfitted, he brought me to the store, recommending me as his protégé, and put me at the disposal of the head cashier.

"I could never finish if I were to try telling you all the favors I owe this man, my new father, for I adored him as a father, and he loved me as his son; for he was a widower and had no heirs. Suffice it to say that during the twelve years I lived with him, I applied myself so much, worked so tenaciously and loyally, and so won his affections, that not only did I become the head cashier and his chief confidant, but he always called me son, and I in turn treated him as my father.

"But the goods of this life do not endure, and so a time came when I lost the bit of repose that I had achieved.

---

[7] [In colonial Mexico, "inland" (*tierra adentro*) implied the expansive and sparsely populated mining region in the north. As we will soon see, the gentleman's hacienda is in Zacatecas, 350 miles north of Mexico City. –Tr.]

"A fellow for whom he had vouched in the administration of the Royal Treasury went bankrupt, and my master covered what he owed with the greater part of his estate; soon afterward he contracted a terrible fever, from which he died at the end of two weeks, leaving me wracked with sorrow, which my tears tried in vain to relieve; I did not dry my tears for many days, in spite of being named heir to everything he had left, which, after being sold, amounted to 8,000 pesos.

"I endeavored to distance myself from those lands, both because I wanted to remove from my view objects that renewed my sense of his absence every day, and because I wanted to shelter and look after one of my poor aunts who was still alive.

"With this in mind, I made out a bill of exchange for Veracruz, and left with two serving lads and my luggage for my homeland. I arrived after a few days, took a house, furnished it, and on my first visit to my beneficent aunt, brought her back with me.

"Afterward I went to Veracruz, put my few resources to use, and dedicated myself to inter-city trade, in which I did not do badly, for after six years my assets amounted to 20,000 pesos.

"But it seems that the one they call Fortune soon ceased to smile upon me. I struck up a close friendship with two rich merchants of Veracruz, and they proposed to me that, if I wished, I could enter into a partnership with them on a certain deal involving some valuable contraband onboard the frigate *Anfitrite*.[8] Toward this, they showed me the original invoices from Cádiz, on top of which prices the owner had added a very small profit for himself; since all the goods were English, and had been selected and paid for on the side, the owner was content with fifteen percent, but under the condition that we would give him the money in cash before we unloaded them, and that the unloading would be at the expense and the risk of the buyers.

"This condition bothered me a little, but my partners urged me on, assuring me that it was a mere detail, since the guards had already been paid off, and that one night the merchandise would be unloaded along the coast using two small boats or launches from the port itself.

"Since the greed that profit stirs up will ride roughshod over anything, I easily agreed with my comrades, thinking to make myself a respectable sum of money in two months.

"With this resolution, I went about liquidating everything I owned, and I put all my cash in the hands of my friends, who concluded the deal with the mariner, putting the full amount that they agreed on at his disposal.

"Everything was prepared for safely unloading the contraband, and that is what would have happened, if one of the guards we had paid off hadn't made a deal of his own, giving the viceroyalty the most exact and circumstantial description of the clandestine unloading, after which they took measures and precautions against us as

---

[8] [Spain had a 40-cannon frigate by this name, which plied the Veracruz-Cádiz route in the late 1700s; it was captured by the British in the early 1800s, and lost at sea in 1806. Spain's restrictive trade policies meant high prices for poorly manufactured imported goods, and thus led to widespread smuggling of contraband merchandise throughout the colonial era. –Tr.]

the case demanded, so that we only found out what was going on when the cargo was already on land and confiscated.

"There was nothing we could do to recover it, and we took to escaping in person. I was the poorest of the three, and doubtless the greediest, because I invested everything I owned in the deal, and for that reason I lost everything.

"Just imagine me: left penniless from one day to the next, and losing in one hour everything I had acquired in eighteen years of work.

"I was at the brink of despair, and more so when my poor aunt died, for she could not withstand this hard blow; but in the end I managed to grin and bear it, as they say; by selling what little I still had, and collecting on a few small debts I was owed, I put together around 2,000 pesos, and with that money began to work again; but my trade was so underfunded that the most I could do was simply get by.

"During this time (the lunacy of men!), during this time I took it into my head to get married; and indeed I did marry a girl, from the town of Jalapa, who had an extraordinary face, a beautiful disposition, and a simple heart; altogether, she was one of those girls that you Mexicans call bumpkins.

"The many good qualities that she had and I came to know made me love her more and more each day, and so I endeavored to please her in everything she desired.

"One of her desires was to come to Mexico to see everything she had been told about this city, where she had never been. She only needed to drop me a hint about it, and I arranged to bring her. . . . If only I had never thought of doing so!

"I must have had about 2,300 pesos when I began my journey to this grand capital, where I arrived very happily with my wife, planning to spend the 300 on showing her around, and to use the 2,000 to buy some cheap merchandise, returning to my homeland within the month, satisfied that I had pleased my love, and with my assets intact; but how mistaken are the judgments of men! Providence had other plans devised to punish my excesses and test my spouse's honor.

"We stayed at the Mesón del Ángel,[9] and straight away I called a tailor to come make my wife dresses in the fashion of the day, which he quickly did, being well paid: for craftsmen's hands move with the same alacrity as that with which they are paid.

"Two days later, the tailor brought the clothes, which fit my wife to a tee, for she was as graceful of body as she was handsome of face. And besides, though she was a country lass, she was not one of those wild bumpkins who grow up among the cows and pigs in the ranches; she was a refined and educated girl from Jalapa, the daughter of a gentleman who was captain of one of the companies in the Tres Villas regiment;[10] so you will understand how easy it was for her to pick up the graceful style that the ladies of the court here call *aire de taco*, a foppish air.

"To be sure, no sooner had I begun to present her on promenades, at dances, in the theater, and at social gatherings, than I noticed with a foolish satisfaction that everyone praised her merits, many of them too expressively. Who would believe that

---

[9] [An inn that was located near the Plaza Mayor, according to Spell, p. 182. –Tr.]

[10] [Tres Villas regiment: a militia regiment raised by the "Three Towns" of Orizaba, Jalapa, and Córdoba, and used primarily to patrol the Veracruz-Mexico road. –Tr.]

I was so dim-witted as to think there was no risk in the adulation and flattery that was heaped on her? So it was; and I responded with gratitude; and harmed myself even further, by showing her off in as many public places as I could, congratulating myself that they were celebrating her merits and envying my happiness. Fool! I did not know that a lovely woman is a jewel that acutely excites the covetousness of man, and that in such cases, one risks one's honor by exposing her too often to the curiosity of all; but. . . . "

This was as far as my friend's conversation had reached when it was interrupted by a series of shouts, "New man! Out here, Sancho Pérez! Out, filch! Out, son of a b . . . !"

My friend pointed out that they were, doubtless, calling me. So it was, and I had to leave our conversation pending.

CHAPTER 20

I suspended my friend's conversation, as I said, to go see what they wanted from me. I went upstairs, filled with anger at seeing the crude way I was being treated by that loudmouthed savage, mulatto, or demon (who was a prisoner who had been given the job of calling the others), who led me to the same hallway or room where the warden had registered me; he did not bring me to the warden's desk, though, but to another, where a darkish and enormously fat fellow was sitting, in whose eyes glimmered the fire that encased his heart.

When we reached the desk, the old rogue told me, "This gentleman is the secretary who called for you."

The secretary then turned to face me and, gazing with his hellish eyes, said, "Wait here."

The loudmouth left, and I stood back a bit from the desk, frowning darkly and waiting for him to finish chewing out the poor Indian who was in front of him.

After he finished with the Indian, he called me and, making me cross myself, asked me if I knew what it meant to swear an oath: that I should not lie nor break my oath under any circumstances, but rather tell the whole truth about whatever I knew that I might be asked, though they hang me for it. Would I swear to do that? I replied in the affirmative, and he added, as seriously as a saint, "If you do as you say, may God aid you; if not, may He bring you to account."

With this formality out of the way, he began to ask me who I was, what my name was, my status, my age, my profession and marital status, and where I was from. All these questions were beginning to make me feel desperate; I was thinking that at the rate he was going, he would be asking me the color of the first baby clothes I wore.

All this questioning and requestioning led me to tell him everything about how I had acquired the maid's rosary, my friendship with Januario, my acquaintances in the gambling dive, and other such things that seemed like trifles to me at the time.

Thus he filled up something like two sheets of paper with writing, made me sign them, and then sent me back to my fate.

I went downstairs feeling content, wishing to hear the rest of my friend's tragedy; I found him lying on his bed, entertaining himself by reading a book.

When he saw me, he closed his book, sat up in bed, and asked me how it had gone. Neither well nor badly, I replied, for it had only amounted to the notary's asking me a thousand questions and writing two sheets of paper, which I had signed; and now I was free to go back to enjoying his amiable conversation.

He answered me politely, and said, "The series of questions they asked you is called taking the preparatory declaration. It is important for you now to bear carefully in mind the answers you gave, so that you do not get mixed up or contradict yourself when they take your confession after charging you, which is the most serious step in the trial, and the one on which the defendant's success or failure usually depends."

"Holy Virgin Mary! That is terrible!" I said. "Because they asked me an infinite number of questions and things, and most of them seemed trifling to me. Who could ever remember what I answered to them all? And how long will it be before they take my confession?"

"That won't be for quite a while," said Don Antonio, "because for a small-time robbery like this, normally nobody pushes for a settlement, and in that case the trial goes through routine channels; and since such trials normally yield no profit to the notaries, because the delinquents have no means to fall back on, they let them sleep as long as they can; so you can expect to see your confession coming around in about three months, more or less, more or less."

"This news distresses me greatly," I told him, "for two reasons: first, because of how long I will be detained in this vile house; and second, because in that long time, I will easily forget how I answered the questions just now."

"As far as your detention goes," my friend answered, "it is not a very long time. The three months that I mentioned are how long I conservatively estimate you will have to wait before the second phase of your trial begins, but. . . . "

"Forgive me," I interrupted, "but what is this about a second phase? What, won't it be the final one, and once my innocence is established, won't they throw me out of here?"

My friend laughed at my simple-mindedness, saying, "How easy it is to see that this is the toughest spot in which you've ever found yourself in your life! Yes, it's too obvious, not only that you have never been in jail before, but that you've never met anyone who has."

"True," I said, "and I have been friends with some regular scoundrels; but not with anyone who has been in jail, that I know of, and that is why all this strikes me as new. But what, will my business still be moving so slowly three months from now?"

"Yes, my dear," replied my friend. "Trials (unless they are scandalous, urgent, or pushed along by one of the parties) move on leaden feet. Haven't you ever heard the old bromide about how long they keep prisoners in jail? If the case doesn't amount to much, for a month; if the case is more clear, for a year; if its gravity shows, then only God knows. Well, that should be enough to tell you that men can spend an eternity in here."

"What if they are innocent, though?" I asked.

"That makes no difference," the friend replied. "Even though you are innocent, since you have no money to push your case along or to prove your innocence, until it becomes apparent in the course of things—and a slow course that will be—a long time will pass."

"That is outrageously unjust," I exclaimed, "and the judges who consent to it are all tyrants, hiding their true natures from humanity; for if jails were not built to oppress but to hold delinquents, much less were they meant to torment the innocent by depriving them of liberty."

"Well said," my friend agreed. "Depriving a person of liberty is a great evil, and if we add to that deprivation the disgrace of being in jail, it is not merely a great, but a terrible evil; so much so that we have laws meant to provide some people, in certain cases, the means of paying bail and thus escaping from being entombed in these horrific places; but you should know that the judges are not at fault for the sluggishness of these trials, nor for the losses that the wretched prisoners suffer on that account. The notaries are to blame for these and other harms that are inflicted in jail, because they are responsible for moving a prisoner's business along or letting it fall dormant; and as I have already told you, run-of-the-mill trials move slowly, because they would not leave them much time for card parties."

"That is to say," I rejoined, "that most notaries are venal, and that they only work, toil, and deal with any business if it is in their own interest; but if there is nothing in it for them, you cannot count on them, for lack of a damned profit."

"At least," my friend replied, "I wouldn't generalize the proposition so broadly, except that I have heard so many poor wretches in our company here mourning their sluggishness; but, Don Pedro, the notaries have a huge influence on the prisoners' fates. If they want to, they can sweeten a case; if not, they can sour it; this truth is as sad as it is well known. Even children say that *it's all up to the notary,* and those who are not children take comfort when they have the notary on their side, especially in a criminal case."

"If that is true," I said, "can notaries fool the judges whenever they wish?"

"Clearly they can," my friend replied, "and all the responsibility that should fall on the magistrates or judges falls instead on them, because of their abuse of the trust that such judges place in them. Don't think this is too bold a proposition. If I were at liberty to do so, I could tell you about recent and original cases that I witnessed personally, and to some of which I myself was a party; but you will be talking with other prisoners less scrupulous than I, and they will be able to give you all the details of everything I tell you. The pity is that the worst notaries—the most corrupt and venal ones—are the most hypocritical, and they are the ones who are best at winning the judges' trust and good will; they commit their intrigues and crafty tricks by dint of that trust, and they gain more satisfaction the surer they are that their bad faith will be believed. Again I say that these truths are hard for the wicked; but for the wicked, what truths are soft? If a judge, even the most upstanding and righteous judge, is taken in by a notary, how can he know whether a defendant is innocent or guilty, when the notary alone has taken his declaration? And if, when he presents his account of the declaration, he adds guilt or suppresses favorable testimony, depending on his own interests? In such a case, if the judge lets his conscience rest on that of the notary, clearly his sentence will reflect the way the notary has depicted the defendant's crime. This is seen very frequently in the towns, and also in the cities, especially with common crimes that do not amount to something horrible. That is, in crimes such as gambling, housebreaking, pickpocketing, drunkenness, lewdness, and so on; for in important crimes such as murder, substantial robberies, sacrilege, and so on, we know that judges do not rely on notaries, but personally attend the declarations, confessions, identity parades, and other inquiries that such trials require."

"I must confess to you, sir," I said, "that this news leaves me very distressed, both because the crime I am supposed to have committed is precisely the kind whose investigation is subject to the notaries' iron rule, and because I have no cash to push the case forward; and, finally, because I do not dare doubt a word of what you have said."

"Nor should you," he answered, "for even if this place were not filled with witnesses to its truth, I myself am proof of what I say. Yes, friend; I have spent two years in prison because of an unjust libel, and my enemy would not have found it so easy to get rid of me if he hadn't counted on the help of a venal and deceitful notary."

"Well, as you have mentioned this point," I said, "please continue the conversation of your misfortunes, which, if I am not mistaken, we left off when you were telling about your pleasure in showing off your madam in the best circles of Mexico."

"That is true," said Don Antonio, "and I have paid for that foolish pleasure with an uninterrupted series of troubles. My wife was skilled at dancing and even at ballet, though not as an artist, but rather, as they say, as an amateur. I wanted her merits to shine through in everything, and so that she would not be seen as a mere amateur dancer, I hired a good teacher, whose lessons she put to good use, and within a short time she became so advanced that she could compete with the best ballerinas in the theater, and since her gracefulness and natural beauty favored her, she attracted attention everywhere, and harvested the fruits of her talent in cheers, adulation, and applause.

"I was enchanted with my darling companion, believing that, though all envied me, none would dare seduce her from me; and even if they did, her constant honor and virtue would make a mockery of my rivals' wicked pursuits.

"With this confidence, I freely went with her everywhere I was invited, which was to almost all the best dance parties in Mexico. At those gatherings, what compliments and honors we were given! What plum positions and lucrative jobs I was offered! What patronage was extended to me, and how many gifts and visits I received! And could I have really been so unwise in the ways of the world and so idiotic as to think that all these adulations were for me? Oh, it should have been me carrying the packsaddle, rather than the donkey with the icon![1]

"One night a respectable lady invited my wife to a dance at her house on the occasion of her saint's day. I happily took her there, as was my custom. My wife was among the first women to dance, being asked by a distinguished man of wealth and nobility (if there can be true nobility where virtue is missing), whom we will call the Marquis of T. This gentleman was mad about my wife from that moment on; but he knew how to disguise his mad passion.

"He finished the dance, and since my wife and I were known in that house, he found it easy to gather information about who we were, where we were from, the state of our fortunes, and everything else he wanted to know; and with this information he sat down next to me and began, with the greatest courtesy, to involve me in conversation, and between one thing and another we began to chat about trade and the great advantages that it offered.

"With this motive, I told him about the setback I had suffered because of the contraband that had been confiscated from me. He put on a show of grief and sympathy

---

[1] [The donkey with the icon: Ruiz Barrionuevo (p. 413) has identified the source of this image as a story in Murillo Velarde's catechism, in which a donkey carrying an icon of the goddess Iside thinks that the homage that people pay to the goddess is directed at him, until they tell him: "Why are you acting so proud? You are the same ass as ever." –Tr.]

for my misfortune, and more so when he learned how little capital I had been left with. But at last he asked, 'What business do you plan to go into, with so little money?'

"I replied, 'I plan to return to Jalapa in two weeks, use the few resources I have left to buy some cheap merchandise, and leave my wife at her mother's house while I continue peddling.'

" 'Friend, that is foolishness,' said the marquis; 'I think that no matter how much you work, you will never prosper; because such a pitifully small stash can only yield pitifully small profits, which you will no doubt have to spend on traveling expenses and food, and you will never have 10,000 pesos to your name, nor be able to expect any rest.'

" 'That is how I see it,' I told him; 'but one has to work to be able to eat, and if that is all I can manage, that is no small thing.'

" 'Fine,' said the marquis; 'but when an upright man is offered an advantageous opportunity, he should not neglect or disdain it.'

" 'That is what no one has offered me,' I answered.

" 'So, if you were offered an opportunity,' the marquis said, 'would you accept it?'

" 'Precisely, sir,' I replied; 'I am not that stupid.'

" 'Well, friend,' he continued, 'cheer up, because your situations and the ill luck you have suffered have moved me greatly. You were born to be wealthy; but luck is always cruel to the good. Nevertheless, I will not express my compassion with mere words: a mysterious sympathy draws me to you; I am rich . . . and finally, I want to make a man of you. Where do you live?'

"I replied that I was staying at the Mesón.

" 'Fine,' he continued, 'tomorrow wait for me between eleven and twelve, and you may be sure that you will not regret the visit. Do you know who I am?'

" 'No, sir,' I said, 'only that I am at your service.'

" 'Well,' he went on, 'I am your friend, the Marquis of T., and I have wealth and the desire to use it to help you'

"I thanked him appropriately, adding if his lordship did not wish to go to the trouble of passing by my house, I would pass by his at whatever time he preferred.

" 'No, no,' he answered; 'I truly like to visit the poor, and besides, I go on these walks for the sake of my health, because it is good for me to do some exercise on foot.'

"This said, a few people began to join a contra dance, and when they came to invite the marquis, he stood up and went to ask my wife to dance at the same time that another captain was asking her the same. As you may imagine, they got into a heated argument over which of the two would dance with her, each of them citing the factors that he thought favored himself; but since neither could answer the other's counterarguments, and since each of them declared that he could not go away dissatisfied, nor allow his honor to be sullied in public,[2] they went on, each

---

[2] Strictly speaking, *honor* is nothing other than the endeavor to conserve virtue; that is, any man can rightly say that his honor is offended if he is slandered by being called a thief, if his wife is seduced, or if some vice is imputed to him, and in such cases (if he is innocent, that is), it would be quite licit for him to defend himself and vindicate his honor according to the dictates of justice; but unfortunately the word *honor* has been corrupted, and has been made a synonym of *revenge, vanity,* and other whims of men. Many think that their honor consists of showing off

word surpassing the last, until they were saying such offensive things that if the women had not become upset and if various fellows had not intervened, they would have come to blows; but the ladies had made sure to hide their dress swords.

"In the end they calmed down, like it or not, and the upshot of the matter was that my wife did not dance with either of them, and rightly so, which left them both somewhat satisfied; though everyone else was upset, and I most of all, to see the absurdity of the two rivals, who were acting as if they were fighting over something that belonged to them.

"The marquis told me, with some haughtiness in his voice, 'Come, let us go, Don Antonio.' Not daring to oppose my supposed protector, I obeyed and left with him and my wife, no doubt leaving behind plenty of material to exercise the malicious carping of those who stayed.

"We went outside; the marquis made room for us in his carriage, and ordered it to stop at a tavern.

"My wife and I resisted; but he insisted that my wife should have a little something for supper, and that if she wanted to be entertained that night, he would find some other dance, and if there were none, he would hold one at his own house. We thanked him for the favor, but begged him not to put himself out, because it was already late.

"Meanwhile we reached the tavern, where the marquis had a splendid table set, in the tavern style—I mean, abundant rather than clean or tidy; but even so, and with just the three of us having supper, he had to pay two ounces of gold, for the scullion charged him that much.

"After we left the tavern, I tried to say good-bye; but the marquis would not allow it, instead taking us to the Mesón in his carriage before returning home.

"I had a faithful servant named Domingo who has a role to play in this story; it was his job to open the door for us no matter when we came back, which is what he did that night.

"We had already eaten supper, so we had nothing left to do but go to bed, though I could scarcely contain myself with delight, thinking about the good fortune that awaited me with that gentleman's protection. My wife noticed my disquiet and asked me the reason for it; I related to her everything that had happened to me with the marquis, which brought the poor dear tremendous joy, for she did not suspect, nor did I, that his protection was aimed against her honesty and my honor.

"There are many such protectors in the world, people who cannot give half a real in charity and who sacrifice their respect and their money chasing their passions. We settled down to sleep peacefully for the rest of the night.

"The following day, at the hour set by the marquis, he arrived at our house. It fell precisely on the king's birthday or some such holiday; the upshot was that my protector came in a splendid carriage decked out for the festivities.

---

their wealth, even if they have to stoop to unseemly and forbidden means to sustain it; others think it means taking revenge for the slightest offense, and that duels are always justified by honor; others believe their honor consists in getting whatever they want, like the marquis; others demand that their underlings show them the most meticulous veneration; and others have other such ideas; but the truth is that none of these is honor.

"He greeted us affectionately and courteously, and after making a mild criticism of the events of the previous night, he told me, 'Friend, I have come to fulfill my word, or rather to guarantee my word to you, because once the Marquis of T. says something, he fulfills it, just as if it were a written contract. I have 10,000 pesos set aside to outfit you, along with an itemized memorandum for you to take to the fair of San Juan de los Lagos,[3] with the understanding that all profits will be yours. So, let's roll up our sleeves and get to work! What do you think?'

"I thanked him for his generosity, promising that within ten or twelve days, I would receive the memorandum and leave for San Juan.

" 'But why wait until then?' asked the marquis.

"I told him that it was because I wanted to take my wife to her mother's house, because I had no house in Mexico that I could rely on to leave her, nor did it seem proper to me that she should stay alone, entrusted solely to the cares of a maid.

" 'Your second point is well thought out,' said the marquis, 'but not your first, because I intend to do you yet another favor so as not to lose my money, which is certainly what would happen if I were to defer sending my merchandise as long as you propose; because, please see here, it will take at least six days to find the mules and drivers, to get the items on the memorandum together, and to prepare everything. Apart from that, it would take you at least twelve days to reach your destination; the fair will be starting very soon, and I do not want the person who goes (if you decide against it) to lose time, but rather to hurry up and get the advantage of being among the first vendors there. That is my decision; but I don't mean it as a cowardly attack that catches you unawares. I am going to the ceremony, and in an hour I will be back here. Meanwhile, take your time deciding what you would like to do, and then you can let me know, for my information.'

"That said, he left.

"Who would have thought that when the marquis showed the least interest in whether I left Mexico quickly or not, that was precisely when he was using all his tricks to speed my departure? Oh, despotic poverty, how you force upright men to risk their honor so they can shake you off!

"My wife and I were left in a sea of doubt, thinking about which decision we should take. On the one hand, I realized that if I passed up that opportunity, I was not likely to find another one like it, especially at my age; on the other, I did not know what to do with my wife, nor where to leave her, because I had no satisfactory house in Mexico for that purpose.

"We were going through a thousand calculations, unable to make up our minds, and in this state of anxiety and hesitation we found the marquis returning from doing his courtesy call. He entered, sat down, and said to me:

" 'So, what have you both decided?'

---

[3] [San Juan de los Lagos: an important market town 275 miles north of Mexico City on the road to Zacatecas. The image of the Virgin of the Conception (popularly known as the Virgin of San Juan de los Lagos) is perhaps the second most popular religious figure in Mexico, after the Virgin of Guadalupe in Mexico City; her feast days (December 8 for the Conception and February 2 for the Purification) long ago gave rise to month-long fairs that draw huge crowds from the entire "inland" region north of the capital. –Tr.]

"I replied in a way that recognized the desire I had to take advantage of his favor, and the obstacle that I was weighing before accepting it, which consisted in having nowhere to leave my wife. To this he replied, quite craftily, 'Very true. That is a powerful and a just motive for a man of such honor as yourself to eschew the most advantageous offers; indeed, before departing from a lady so meritorious as is yours, you must think the matter over very carefully, and should you decide to go, you would necessarily have to leave her in a house that is both honorable and secure; not because the lady would be unable to safeguard herself under any circumstance, but because of the indiscretion with which the malicious common herd think about a beautiful woman alone, and also because of the seductions to which she would be exposed; not to go on for too long, and with your forgiveness, madam: a woman's heart is not invincible; no woman can guarantee that she will not fall in a world so filled with snares; the finest garden needs a fence and a watchman; and on top of that, here we are in this city of Mexico . . . this Mexico, overflowing with rogues and opportunities. So I praise you for your rightful hesitation, and of course I would be the first to talk you out of thinking any differently. This was the only way that I could find to help you, but God keep me from being even a distant cause of your disquiet, or perhaps of. . . . No, friend, no; better to lose everything else, because honor comes first.'

"Here the marquis paused his conversation, and my wife and I were unable to disguise the feelings that came to us when, in one moment, we saw all the hopes we had built up for rapidly changing our fortunes frustrated. Oh, damned self-interest, how lightly you imperil us miserable mortals!

"My pious protector was very astute, and so he easily recognized in our fallen faces the effectiveness of his depraved machinations, which he was able to carry out thanks to my wife's innocence.

"So it happened that, pained to see that she, though guiltless, was the obstacle to my good fortune, she told me, 'But look, Antonio, if all that is keeping you from accepting the gentleman's favor is not having a place to leave me, that is easy to fix. I'll go with you, though it's true that I don't know how to ride a horse. . . .'

" 'No, no,' said the marquis, 'absolutely not. What an idea! How could I allow you to be exposed to illness on such a long trek? Nor would it be honorable of Don Antonio to permit it. Do you not see that if upright men work, it is so that their wives might enjoy certain comforts? How could I hand you over to the burning sun, the sleepless nights, the lack of food, and the other hardships of a long journey? No, my lady, do not even think it. Instead, let me propose a better solution, and if you both agree to it, I think you will have no reason to repent.'

"As hopeful as we were foolish, we begged him to reveal his solution, and the marquis, who did not have to be begged very long, said, 'Well, sir, madam: I have an aunt who is not merely honorable but saintly, if I may say so. She is a poor old woman, a lay sister in the order of St. Francis, a maiden who remained unmarried so that she could dress saints' images and scold children; she is very punctilious, and she is always praying—one of those women who go to confession every day. Her house is like a convent; what am I saying? It is even worse. Hardly anyone ever goes to visit, and the only visits she allows are from *old ladies*, as she says; because she would never let any *pants*, as she calls men, set foot in her drawing room for all the money in the world. By evening prayers, she is already locked up in her house with the key under her pillow. The only walks she takes are to the church, and to the hospitals on Sundays to console the sick women. In a word, her life is as settled as could be, and her house could serve as a model for the strictest convent. But do not think, madam, that for all this she is a gloomy and ridiculous old woman. Not at all: she is very gentle and affectionate, and is so sweet and amusing in her conversation that by herself she can entertain every woman who visits. Finally, if you are capable of subjecting yourself to such a recondite life for the two or three months at most that your husband might be away from you, it seems to me that there is nothing more fitting.'

"My wife—whom I had actually taken out of her routine, as they say, because she was raised in a house as devout as the one that the marquis just painted for us—did not doubt for a second before replying that she only went to dances and on outings because I took her, but if I should ever want to leave her at home, she would gladly stay, and would miss nothing except for my company. I was very happy with her docility, and accepted the marquis' new favor, thanking him again and feeling quite content to see my hopes revive and my wife so well taken care of.

"The marquis declared that he was equally content to have been of service to me, and he said good-bye, promising to return the next day, both to introduce me in the warehouse where I was to order and pick up the merchandise, and to take us to his good aunt's house.

"My wife and I spent the rest of that day joyously counting and recounting the profits we saw coming, strolling in our fool's garden.

"The following morning, the marquis showed up very early at the Mesón. He had me ride in his carriage with him to the warehouse, where he told them to order me the merchandise from the memorandum that he had mentioned the day before, and said that they should give it to me with whatever adjustments I wanted to make to the list, and that he was merely there to vouch for me and give to give me his recommendation.

"When the merchant heard this, thinking that the marquis was telling the truth, he bowed and scraped before me, and was much more courteous and affectionate toward me when I left than he had been when I entered his house. As you know, he did not do this for me, but for the pesos that he planned to get from my pockets.

"With this step taken, we returned to the Mesón, the marquis had my wife dress up, and we went to Chapultepec,[4] where he had a splendid breakfast and dinner waiting for us.

"We spent a very cheery morning in the countryside there in that woods, which is lovely by its very nature. In the afternoon, around four, we returned to the city and went to see his aunt's house.

"We got out of the carriage; the marquis entered and rang the entranceway bell; an old maidservant came down, asking who was there. The marquis replied that it was he.

---

[4] A lovely woods outside of Mexico, though it has nothing of note other than the palace built by Don Bernardo de Gálvez, former viceroy of New Spain; however, it is a popular place for outings. [Chapultepec Park is almost in the center of modern Mexico City. –Tr.]

" 'I will let the lady know, then,' said the maid, 'because we don't open the doors to any man here, unless my mistress sees him through the hatchway in the drawing room. Please wait.'

"Indeed she kept us there cooling our heels for about a quarter of an hour, until we heard a little window slide open in the ceiling of the entranceway itself. We raised our eyes and saw the venerable old lady, her head wrapped in a wimple, looking at us very slowly through her eyeglasses and turning around to ask who it was.

"The marquis, sounding annoyed, said, 'It's me, Aunt, it's me, Miguel. Are you going to open up or not?'

"To which the old lady replied, 'Oh, yes, Miguelito! Now I recognize you, sweetheart, they'll open up for you now; but what about this other fellow, is he with you, son?'

" 'Oh, fiddlesticks!' said the marquis. 'Who else is he going to be with?'

" 'Well, don't get angry, now,' said the old lady, 'they're coming.'

"With that, she closed the hatchway, and the marquis said to us, 'What do you think about that? Have you ever seen such a tightly kept cloister? But don't be stunned, dear girl, because the lion is not as fierce as it's made out to be.'

"Just then the old maidservant arrived and opened the front door. We entered and climbed the stairs, and the aunt was already waiting for us in the front hall, dressed in her blue habit and her reverend wimple, wearing eyeglasses, with a fine cotton rebozo, and holding her rosary. Since I owe many favors to this good lady, I keep her image very much alive in my memory.

"She received us with a great deal of affection, especially my wife, whom she embraced with tremendous expressiveness, showering her with *my dears* and *sweethearts* as if she had known her for years. We went inside, and soon they brought us some very good cups of chocolate.

"The marquis told her the reason for our visit, which was to see whether she would mind if that girl stayed at her house for a few days. She declared that it would give her the greatest pleasure, but that her only shortcoming was that she disliked outings and visits, because they put the soul in peril, and she then went on for about half an hour, talking about virtue, scandals, obligations of atonement, death, eternity, and so on, enlivening her conversation with a thousand examples, all of which had my innocent wife enthralled and entertained, for she had a good heart.

"After we had set the date for my wife's entrance into that miniature monastery, the lady said, 'Nephew, sir, please come see my little house, and let my novice come see if she likes the convent.'

"We consented to the reverend lady's request, and my wife was very pleased with the clean and tidy little house, especially the windows, birds, and flowerpots.

"We spent the afternoon in this, and then took our leave, my wife being completely captivated by the lady.

"We stayed at the Mesón and the marquis went to his house. Over the next six days, I received the memorandum, hired mules, and prepared everything for my trip; but during all that time, my protector never neglected to lavish attention on my wife and take her on outings, because he said it was necessary to entertain the new nun.

"It is true that I could not help feeling a bit bothered to see the extremes to which the marquis went with her, but since I was confident about my wife's love and orderly conduct, I had no trouble communicating my fears to her, to which she replied that I should set them aside: on the one hand, because she loved me dearly and would never be capable of offending me for all the gold in the world; on the other, because the marquis was the most gentlemanly man she had ever known, for even when she went out, with my permission, with him and a maid in his carriage, he had never taken the slightest license, but had always treated her with respect. Secure in this knowledge, I relaxed and planned to leave this city for my destination.

"One day I told the marquis that everything was ready, and he, who wanted nothing more than to be free of me, told me that he would come by that afternoon to take me to his kinswoman's house, and that I could leave the following morning.

"My wife asked me to leave her our servant Domingo, so that she would have someone she could trust if she needed to have anything done. I agreed to her wish without delay, and the marquis did not object; on the contrary, he said, 'Better, let's give Domingo a downstairs room, and he can serve you and my aunt as doorman and as company.'

"While the marquis went out to eat, I packed my wife's trunk, leaving her a thousand pesos in gold and silver, in case she should need anything.

"When the marquis returned, there was nothing left to do but take my wife to her new house; her separation was, naturally enough, a tearful one; but in the end she stayed and I left on the same evening, sleeping outside the city limits."

This was as far as Don Antonio got when one of the jailhouse rules again interrupted his conversation.

CHAPTER 21

The reason behind this new interruption of my conversation with Don Antonio was the fact that, around five in the afternoon, the warden came downstairs to lock all the prisoners into their respective cells, accompanied by two others who each carried a bunch of keys.

After he finished locking up the prisoners in the first courtyard, he moved on to the second; and the fierce trusty, who was still upset with me, separated me from Don Antonio's company for no reason and took me to the smallest, dirtiest, and most crowded cell. I was the last to enter, and when they closed and locked the door, we were left there, thick as flies in the old boys' jail.

Unfortunately for me, among all the sons-of-guns who were locked up in that cellar, I was the only white, for they were all Indians, blacks, *lobos*, mulattos, and mixed, which gave them all the reason they needed to make me the target of their obnoxious jokes.

About six in the evening, they lit a small candle, and those gentlemen all gathered around its sad light; one of them took out a disgustingly filthy deck of cards, and all of them started gambling whatever they had.

They called me to join them, but since I didn't even have an eighth of a real, I excused myself, openly confessing the feebleness of my purse; but they refused to believe it, thinking instead that I was either stingy or vain.

They played until nine or so, by which time the candle was barely more than a stub; no one had another candle, so they decided to have supper and go to bed.

The circle disbanded and they began to warm their little potfuls of porridge on a small brazier that burned coal dust.

I was hoping that some kind soul would invite me to have supper, just as Don Antonio had invited me to eat dinner; but my hopes were in vain, because all those poor men seemed to have goodly appetites and to be badly hungry, judging from the way they gulfed down their porridge when it was practically still cold.

During the card game, I had stayed in a corner, wrapped up in my serape and praying the rosary with more devotion than I had shown at my prayers in some time; for you see, what sailor doesn't cry out to God during a storm?

The swears, curses, and indecent words that this family mixed in with their fights over the cards were innumerable and horrifying, so much so that, even though they were not new to my ears, they scandalized me terribly nonetheless. I was corrupt, but these things typically filled me with disgust and loathing. There is something about a good education in early childhood that can serve as a powerful brake, slowing us down on the most headlong rush into vice; unhappy is the man who makes it a habit to go against his principles!

After they finished their suppers, each of them made his bed as best he could, and I, who had no sleeping mat or anything that could serve as one, seeing no other way out, doubled my serape to make it into both mattress and blanket, and used my hat as a pillow.

With all my cellmates in bed, they slowly began to make fun of me, saying, "So tell me, friend, did you also fall into this rat-hole for being a *filcher*? That's great! So Spanish gents are thieves now, too? And they always say robbery's just for us puny folks!"

"Don't wear yourself out, Chepe," another one said; "as for that, they're all the same, white or black; everybody sticks a good finger into the pie whenever he gets a chance. The thing is, you and me might steal a rebozo, or a cloak, or sumpthin' like that; but these guys—when they steal, they steal big."

"And being as that's how it is," said another, "I bet my buddy here, when he got to stealing, he musta stoled like 200 or 500 pesos; and I bet he makes out, too, eh? I bet he does!"

And so they all went along, each saying worse things about me than the last; at first I tried to make excuses for myself, but when I saw that they just made even more fun of my excuses, I had to keep my mouth shut, and by wrapping my serape around me after the candle went out, I pretended to sleep, and with that stratagem their gabbing quieted down for quite a while, so that I thought they had fallen asleep.

But just when I was most convinced of this fantasy, they started hurling pitchers of urine at me; but so many, so full, and so well aimed, that in less time than it takes to tell the tale, they had turned me into piss soup, all washed up and shot to hell.

That was when I really lost patience, and started cussing them out shamelessly; but instead of drawing back or getting angry, they started up their fun again, whipping me all over with I don't know what, because I could feel the blows, but the next morning I didn't see any switches.

Finally, tired of laughing and harassing me, they went to bed, and I stayed crouching by the door, naked and unable to lie down, because my serape was soaking wet, and my shirt, too.

Lord help me! Just imagine how distressed my spirit was that night, finding myself in jail, on trial for robbery, impoverished, with nowhere to turn, surrounded by that rabble, and without a hope of even getting some rest from sleep, for the reasons I have given! But in the end, since sleep is a brave fighter, I had to give in, and slowly I fell asleep, though in fits and starts, leaning against the door; but scarcely had I begun to sleep when a rat jumped on me—and such an enormous rat that, by its weight, it seemed as big as a grocer's cat; the thing is, it was big enough to wake me up, fill me with terror, and take away my sleepiness, for I still believed that devils and ghosts had nothing else to do at night but wander around frightening sleepers. The truth of the matter is that I couldn't sleep anymore that whole night long, assaulted by fear, by heat, by the armies of bedbugs that had me under siege, by the ear-splitting snores of those rogues, and the damnable effluvia that their gross bodies exhaled; together with other things not fit to speak of, for that cellar was drawing room, bedroom, guest room, kitchen, toilet, and dining room all in one. How many times I recalled the thankless nights I had spend in Januario's *arrastraderito*!

At last God deigned to give His light to the world, and I, being the first one up, began to recover my things, which were still half-wet for all that I had wrung them out: so you can imagine the flood of urine they had endured; but in the end I put on my shirt and shorts, and I had a hard time putting on my pants, because my beloved companions had made sure to steal all the buttons, thinking they were silver.

At six in the morning, they came to open the door, and I was the first to leave, dying of hunger and lack of sleep, both to go complain to my friend Don Antonio and to wait for the sun to dry out my rags.

Good Don Antonio indeed sympathized with my bad luck, and consoled me as best he could, promising me that I would never spend another night like that among those rogues, for he would ask the trusty to let me stay in his cell.

"No, friend!" I told him; "I'm afraid you will embarrass yourself in vain; because all the begging in the world wouldn't soften that slave driver."

"Don't you worry," he answered; "I know the language these people understand, which is money; so, with the four or five reales that we'll give him, you'll see how you will get everything you need."

I had not yet finished thanking my friend when again they shouted for me, and I, thinking that I was being called for another declaration, ran out and saw that they were just calling me to help clean out the cell where they had done so much harm to me the night before. Cleaning the cell amounted to taking out the barrel of waste, emptying it out in the common toilets, and washing it.

I don't know how I kept from spilling my guts out in that operation. My pleas and promises did me no good there, for the damnable dodderer in charge of the operation, seeing my resistance, began to untie the bullwhip that he wore for a belt; and so to save myself from worse afflictions, like it or not, I carried out that revolting job, and when I was finished I returned to my good friend's cell, my only consolation in that vale of tears.

As soon as I saw him, tears did come to my eyes, and again I recounted my latest punishment. He did not tire of consoling me and relieving me in every way he could.

He first had me lie down on his humble bed; he gave me a cup of hot chocolate and some cigarettes, and then ran out to look for the fierce trusty, from whom he got what he wanted by paying the unjust *entry fee*[1] and giving him I don't know how much more as a tip; and with that, thanks be to God, they left me in peace.

I did not have the words to express my gratitude to Don Antonio after I found out (for another prisoner told me) all he had done for me; he merely assured me that they would no longer be tormenting me. This is the true characteristic of a good friend and a kind soul: don't brag about your good deeds, but do them without mentioning them, and even try to keep your beneficiary from finding out so that he won't have to go to the trouble of thanking you. But such friends are so rare, and it is so rare for charity to be done with such perfection! Ordinarily, people do most charitable deeds, or favors that go by that name, so that they can pass themselves off

---

[1] It appears that this tax, imposed by greed, might be a reasonable fee in this kingdom for exempting oneself, with a small payment of money, from the onerous job of cleaning the cells; but it should only be used in case there are no prisoners sentenced to labor in the jail; when there are such prisoners, however, they should clearly do this job, and thus poor wretches should never be forced to do the work just because they do not have enough money to pay this unjust toll, which always ends up in the pockets of criminals, since it is normally collected by the trusties. This abuse takes on an even worse aspect when we consider that it is prohibited by law.

as good and generous Christians (which actually is just hypocrisy), rather than to benefit anyone; and this goes strictly against the very rules of charity, for Jesus Christ said that we should not let our left hand know what our right hand does. That is, all the good that a man does should be done for God without expecting any reward from men, because if men pay the reward, God owes nothing; let's be clear about this: publicizing the good we have done by bestowing our favors, or tacitly coercing our beneficiary into showing us his gratitude, is reward enough in itself.

Don Antonio was very prudent, and since he knew that I hadn't slept at all the night before, he had me lie down and did not wake me until one in the afternoon, to join him for dinner.

When I awoke, I had gotten my fill of sleep, but my stomach was calling out for food, and I satisfied this need at the kindly prisoner's expense. After our frugal meal was finished, he said, "Friend, I do believe that despite the troubles you have just suffered, you must still have some curiosity about learning the rest of the origins of my own hardships."

I told him that was the case, because to tell the truth, his conversation was a soothing balm that healed my afflicted spirit; and Don Antonio picked up the thread of his story in this way:

"I recall," he said, "that we had gotten to the point where I had left this city with my mules and drivers, while my wife stayed here in the old aunt's house, with no other company on her part than our serving lad Domingo.

"I would prefer not to recall what came next, because in spite of the time that has passed, the wounds from my injuries still hurt when I touch them, though they are beginning to form scars; but I cannot leave you wondering about the end of my story, both so that you might be consoled to see that I have gone through greater troubles than you, though blameless, and so that you might learn about the world and its wiles.

"There is nothing in particular that I can tell you about myself, because there is nothing particularly interesting about the life of a traveling merchant, nor about his residence in his destination at the end of his journey; at any rate, I traveled and reached my own destination without mishap, while my wife was awaiting the most terrible storm.

"After the marquis, that rogue . . . pardon me for that unseemly epithet, as I have pardoned him for the injuries he caused me. So, after he found out that I had left Mexico, he set about revealing his perfidious intentions.

"He began frequenting the hypocritical old woman's house at all hours, for she was not as virtuous as she appeared, nor was she the kinswoman she claimed to be; she was nothing but a refined procuress, and with that kind of help, you can imagine how easy he thought it would be to conquer my wife's heart; but he was utterly mistaken, because when women are honest, when they truly love their husbands and are imbued with solid virtue, they are more unyielding than a rock.

"Such was this heroine of conjugal fidelity. The marquis' cunning tricks, his gifts, his cajolery, his respects, his seductions, his promises, even his threats, along with the repeated and fervent efforts of the damnable old woman, were futile. With all these, the marquis could squeeze no more juice out of my wife than he could have gotten from a flint; when he became desperate, when these repeated experiences made him recognize that hers was not a heart that he was meant to conquer, but that he would have to turn to more powerful weapons, he resolved to do so, and to satisfy his appetite by sheer force.

"Having made this decision, one night he resolved to stay in the house in order to put his wicked plan into practice; but as soon as my faithful wife realized this, she took advantage of a moment's distraction to slip downstairs to Domingo's room and to tell him, 'The marquis has been trying to woo me for days; tonight it appears that he wants to stay here, no doubt with evil intentions; the entryway door is closed; I couldn't leave even if I tried; my honor and your master's honor are at risk; I have no one else to turn to for help, and no one who might free me from the danger that threatens me, but you. I put all my trust in you, Domingo. If you are an upright man and you respect your masters, tonight is the time to prove it.'

"Poor Domingo, all upset and embarrassed, said, 'Fine, my lady, Your Grace, please tell me what you want me to do, and I promise to do whatever you ask me.'

" 'Well, son,' my wife told him, 'what I want you to do is to hide in my bedroom, and if the marquis goes out of control, as I fear he will, I want you to defend me, come what may.'

" 'Well, Your Grace has nothing to worry about. You can go on back, you don't want them to miss you and start suspecting; and I swear to you that unless the marquis kills me, he will never get what's in his wicked thoughts.'

"On that simple promise, my wife went back upstairs content, and she was lucky not to have been missed.

"Suppertime came and Domingo entered to wait at table as always. The marquis endeavored to fill my wife's stomach with wine; but she politely refused as much as she could without appearing rude.

"After supper, over dessert, my rival called on all the eloquence of love so that my wife would consent to his lurid desires; but she was accustomed to resisting his assaults, and merely reproduced the admonitions she had given him a thousand times before; but in vain, because the marquis was blind, and each admonition only egged him on.

"This struggle must have lasted about an hour, time enough for the maid to fall asleep and for Domingo to hide under my wife's very bed without being noticed; my wife, seeing that her admirer was keeping her long, rose from the table and said, 'My lord Marquis, I am feeling somewhat indisposed; please allow me to retire, for it is quite late.'

"With this she left for her bedroom, anxious that Domingo might have forgotten his responsibility; but when she entered, our faithful servant let her know where he was, telling her not to fear.

"Despite this company, my wife did not want to undress nor to put out the candle, as was her custom, apprehensive about what might happen—what, in fact, did happen.

"It would have been about midnight when the marquis opened the door and came tiptoeing in, believing that my wife was asleep; but as soon as she heard him, she jumped to her feet.

"The gentleman was a bit startled by her unexpected preparedness; but when he had recovered from his first embarrassment, he asked her, 'Madam, what is it that has you up and fully dressed at all hours of the night?'

"To which my wife replied with great sarcasm, 'My lord Marquis, when I noticed that you were staying in this saintly lady's house, I assumed that you would not leave without paying your respects to this bedroom at some unearthly hour of the night, despite the fact that I have done nothing to deserve such favors; and therefore I decided not to undress or fall asleep, because it would not be a decent way to wait for such a visit.'

"It would seem normal that the marquis should desist from his intentions, seeing how he had been anticipated and reproached in such a timely fashion; but he was blind, he was a marquis, he was at home, and as far as he knew, there were no witnesses nor anyone who could stop his wickedness; and so, after trying his pleas, his promises, and his endearments one last time, seeing that they were all futile, he embraced my wife as she walked around the room and threw her onto the bed on her back; but she had not yet hit the mattress before the marquis himself was spread out on the floor; for Domingo, as soon as he recognized the critical point when he was needed, jumped out from under the bed and grabbed the marquis by the legs, to test his ribs against the bed platform.

"My wife has written to me that, if the reason had not been so serious, she would have had a hard time restraining her laughter, for the scene called for nothing less. She immediately sat down on the edge of her bed, and saw the enemy of my honor stretched out at her feet, not daring to stand nor to speak a word; because there was big, strong Domingo kneeling on his legs, pinning him to the floor and threatening his life with a dagger, and asking my wife, seething with wrath, 'Do I kill him, my lady? Do I kill him? What do you say? If my master were here, I would have done it already, so's no point in waiting, why not save him the trouble? I bet when he finds out he'll be real glad I did it.'

"My wife did not give Domingo a chance to finish talking; rather, fearing that some misfortune might occur, she held back his knife-wielding arm and, with pleas and orders as his master, between a thousand scares and challenges, she managed to wrest the dagger from his hand and make him free the marquis.

"That poor man stood up, filled with anger, shame, and fear, all inspired by the lad's savage determination. The only satisfaction my wife gave him was to order Domingo to retire to the side room, and stay there; after he obeyed, she told the marquis: 'Do you see, sir, the risk to which you have been exposed by your inconsiderateness? I assumed, as I implied a short while ago, that you had decided to stain my honor and that of my husband by force, and to prevent it I had this servant hide in my bedroom. What I had feared came to pass, and this poor country boy, who has little understanding of etiquette, thought that the only way to halt your designs was to throw you on the floor and murder you, which he would have done if I had not taken the proper steps I did to stop him. I recognize that he was terribly out of bounds, and I beg you to forgive him; but you must also recognize and admit that the fault was your own. I have told you a thousand times how very grateful I am to you, and that I will always remember you for the favors you have done both for me and for my husband, and much more when I see that neither he nor I deserves them;

but, sir, I cannot repay them in the coin that you demand. I am married, I love my husband more than myself, and above all, I have my honor; and once honor is lost, it can never be restored. You are intelligent; you should recognize that I am in the right; try to rid yourself of the thoughts that torment you and disturb me; and if that is not good enough, I offer to serve you as the lowest maid in your household.'

"The marquis kept profoundly quiet while my wife was speaking; but after she finished, he stood up, saying, 'Madam, I am now informed of the reasons that motivated you to make this treacherous attempt on my life, and I am half convinced that if you had no husband, you would love me, for I am not that contemptible. I will try to remove this obstacle, and if you do not return my affection, you will remember me—I swear it.'

"Saying this, he left the bedroom without waiting for an answer, and looking at Domingo in the doorway, he told him, 'You have acted like a base villain against whom I would not find it decent to exact satisfaction man to man; but you will learn who the Marquis of T. is.'

"My wife, who wrote these things to me in as much detail as I am telling them to you, did not understand that those threats were directed against me and the life of my servant.

"She waited for dawn to attempt freeing herself from the risks to which her honor was exposed in that corrupt house, and much more so when the servant told her what the marquis had said to him, adding that he was thinking of leaving the city the next day, because he was afraid the man would have him murdered.

"My wife approved his decision; but she pleaded with him to leave her in some safe place, away from that house, and my serving lad solemnly promised to do so; which goes to show that among people who are wrongly called *ordinary*, there are also noble and generous souls.[2]

"The sun tore through the veil of dawn and showed its resplendent face to mortals, and my wife instantly attempted to leave that house; but where to go, if she had absolutely no understanding of Mexico? But, oh, Domingo's loyalty! He arranged everything, and told her, 'The important thing is that Your Grace shouldn't be here, even if that means staying in the middle of the plaza. I'm going to call the porters.'

"Saying this, he went outside and soon returned with a pair of Indians, whom he urgently ordered to carry my wife's bed and trunk; and although the hypocritical old woman attempted to stop him, saying that they should wait for the marquis, the lad, filled with wrath, said: 'Wait for the marquis, that empty sack? He's a rogue, and you're a procuress; and now I'm off to report you to the local judge.'

"That was all it took to get the old woman to give up her attempts, and fifteen minutes later my wife was in the street with Domingo and the two porters; but as soon as they overcame one difficulty, they found more new ones to solve.

---

[2] It is true that servants are called domestic enemies, that they normally lack good backgrounds and education, and that they almost always serve for the money rather than for love; but it is no less true that this is not a universal rule. There is a bit of everything; in the same way, there are haughty and arrogant masters whose harsh treatment is unworthy of their domestics' love. Treat servants affectionately and humanely, and they will rarely fail to repay their masters with love, gratitude, and respect.

"My wife was standing exhausted in the middle of the street, with hired porters and nowhere to go, when faithful Domingo recalled a certain Nana Casilda who had washed our laundry when we were staying at the Mesón; and without another thought, he had the porters go there.

"And so they arrived, and while the porters unloaded the things, he informed the laundress of what had been happening, adding that he would leave my wife under her care, because his life was at risk in this great city; that his lady had money and that she needed nothing except for someone who could keep her safe from the marquis; and that his master was a very honorable and very upright man who would not neglect to pay for the favor she was doing for his wife. The good old woman offered to do all she could for her part, in our honor; my faithful companion gave Domingo one hundred pesos so that he could return to his homeland and wait for us there; and with that, he left tearfully for Jalapa, being warned that he should not let on about anything to my wife's mother.

"After the lad departed, the little old woman went right away to discuss the matter with a wise and virtuous cleric whose laundry she washed; and he, after speaking with my wife, arranged things so that my wife spent the night in a convent, from which she wrote to me about the whole tragedy.

"Let us leave this noble woman safe and sound in her cloister, and let us look at the snares that the marquis set for me, being all the more vengeful when he found my wife had fled the old woman's house, and could not even guess where she was hiding from his sight.

"The first thing he did was to send me a private messenger notifying me that he was ill, and that as soon as I had read his letter, I should bundle up the remaining stocks and return as quickly as I could to Mexico, because that was in his best interest.

"I immediately obeyed my master's orders and set out on my return, but I did not know what trap he had set for me.

"This was it: in one of the country inns where I had to stay on the way, my master had posted two or three rascals with evil intentions (for gold can buy anything), who pretended to be my friends, without my being able to see through them, and told me that they had come to accompany me by the marquis' wishes.

"I sincerely believed them, because the less malicious a man is, the more easily he can be deceived; and so I chatted with them without restraint. That night we had supper together and toasted each other amiably; and they, losing no time to set their intrigues in motion, got my servants drunk and, when the time was ripe, hid a considerable amount of tobacco[3] among the bundles of clothing, and then went to bed.

"The next morning, we all got up at the crack of dawn to return here to the capital, which we reached that very day, marching at top speed. They took my cargo through the city checkpoint[4] without a problem and without looking through it;

---

[3] [Selling and transporting tobacco was a strict government monopoly in the Spanish empire. –Tr.]

[4] [The checkpoint (*garita*) was "a small structure at the entrance to a city where merchandise being brought in was examined and taxed"; Mexico City had eight such checkpoints (Spell, p. 183). –Tr.]

truth to tell, though, I could not tell what they were up to with the checkpoint guards, for not all guards are honest, and so many of them can be bought cheap.

"I did not pause to consider this, thinking that my partners were simply chatting with the guards, who perhaps were acquaintances of theirs; and so, trusting in this presumption, we came to Mexico and to the very house of the marquis.

"After I dismounted, the marquis ordered the mules unharnessed and the cargo stored away, while at the same time giving me a thousand greetings.

"Although I already had on me my wife's bad news, which I had received on the road, I could not refuse to accept his courtesies, and although I wanted only to go see her in the convent, I was obliged to hide my feelings and submit to the marquis' requests.

"Despite my being exhausted and worn out from the trip, I could not sleep that night, thinking about my beloved Matilde, for that is my wife's name; but at last dawn broke and I got dressed, waiting for the marquis to awaken so that I could leave his house.

"He woke up soon after; but he told me that he wanted us to close our accounts that very morning, because he had a loan hanging over him and he wished to know how much he had to cover it.

"Although I found him tiresome, I did not imagine that he was planning to use those moments to ruin me, and for my part I also yearned to turn his profits over to him and to make a break, once and for all, with the connections that had given rise to his friendship with me; so it was easy for me to agree to do what he wanted.

"I therefore began showing him the accounts, but then two or three of his friends entered the office, and we suspended our operations during their visits, quite to my displeasure, for I was in a rush to rid my sight of that betrayer; but that was not feasible, since the rogue took his friends to the dining room under the pretext of politeness and affection; and he did not let me separate from them, but rather treated me with excessive familiarity and warmth; and in this way we all sat down together for breakfast.

"We had scarcely finished when a footman entered carrying a message from a corporal of the guard, who was waiting in the courtyard with four soldiers.

" 'Soldiers, in my house?' the marquis asked with feigned surprise.

" 'Yes, sir,' the footman replied, 'soldiers, and customs guards.'

" 'God save us! What is going on? Let's solve this now.'

"Saying this, we all went down to the courtyard where the guards and soldiers stood. They saluted my master courteously, and the corporal or head of the troupe asked which of us was the employee who had just returned from inland.

"The marquis replied that I was the one, and they immediately informed me that I was being placed under arrest, and at the same time, the soldiers surrounded me.

"You can imagine the shock that overcame me when I saw myself taken prisoner, without having any idea why; but I was even more overwhelmed when the marquis asked the reason and was told that I was being held for smuggling contraband, and that I had used his own merchandise to slip a good quantity of tobacco into the city, hidden among the bundles, which should still be in his warehouse; that the accusation had been very direct, for it had come from none other than the mule driver who had personally bundled up the tobacco; as proof, the bundles that carried the most tobacco would be those marked with a T; and finally, that by the director's order, they were warning his lordship the marquis to answer their charges and hand over the goods to be confiscated.

"The marquis said, in deceitful pretense, 'But that cannot be; this fellow is an utterly upright man, and I was so confident of him that I entrusted him with my interests, with no other guarantee than his word; how, then, could he possibly have acted so villainously as to attempt to shame me and ruin himself? Come on, that's more than I can understand!'

" 'Well, sir,' said the guards, 'here's the notary, who will record everything we find in the bundles; let's inspect them, and we'll clear up our doubts.'

" 'So we will,' said the marquis, and as if he were filled with anger he called for the keys. The keys were brought; the men opened the warehouse, untied the bundles, and found them almost entirely filled with tobacco.

"Then the marquis, donning an expression of indignation and throwing in my direction the gaze of an angered rich man, told me, 'This cheat, swindler, rascal, and ingrate: is this the way he repays me for my favors? Is this how he remunerates the blind and foolhardy trust I placed in him? Is this how he recompenses my services, which he did nothing to deserve? Finally, is this how he returns the generosity with which I gave him my money, so that he alone would profit from its use without sharing a penny with me, an almost unparalleled deed? Was the rogue not satisfied with robbing and defrauding me, but he tried to compromise a man of my honor and my class? It is all well and good for him to pay for the fraud he has committed against the Royal Treasury by rowing in a slave galley or dragging his chains around a prison keep for ten years; but as for me, who will make clean the reputation he has made me incur, at least among those who do not know the truth of the case? And who will restore my capital, for it is clear that whatever tobacco you find in the bundles, that much textile and other merchandise is missing? I will vindicate and purify my honor to the end; but how can I retrieve my capital? Come now, this isn't the time to keep quiet or to feign meekness. Tell the truth, in front of the notary: did I tell you to traffic in tobacco? Do I have any interest tied up in this contraband?'

"I had remained silent throughout this nefarious reprimand, stunned not by my guilt, since I had none,[5] but by my surprise at what they found, and by the insults I was hearing from the marquis' mouth; yet I could do nothing less than break the silence that followed his questions, and admit that he did not have the slightest role in the affair, but that neither did I; for God knew that it had never crossed my mind to invest a single real in tobacco. They all laughed at that, and after giving the marquis a summons to answer their charges, they carted the bundles off to the customs house, and carted me off to this prison, without having the fleeting pleasure of seeing my dear wife, the innocent cause of all my misfortunes.

---

[5] Perturbation is not always proof of guilt. It is a very ambiguous proof: an upright man will be more readily stunned than a brazen criminal when he finds himself accused of a crime that he has not committed. If one turns pale, one's face falls, and one begins to babble, that is proof of dread or shame, but not always of the truth of an accusation.

"For two years now, I have been living here in the mansions of crime, considered simply one more delinquent; for two years, I have struggled without resources against the marquis' treacheries, while he has endeavored to bury me in some prison—for throwing me in jail was not enough to satisfy his vengeful passion, because after I proved with infinite trouble that, according to the muleteers' testimony, I had no knowledge of the tobacco, he has continued trying to ruin me by demanding I repay the rest of his money that he says is missing; for two years, my wife has been suffering in her own honorable imprisonment; and for two years, I have been resigned to bearing her absence, along with many other troubles that I will not mention; but God, who never fails the innocent who truly trust in His supreme Providence, has declared Himself satisfied and has sent me consolation in the nick of time; for just when the judges who had been deceived by my powerful enemy's duplicity, and by the intrigues of the venal trial notary that he had bought with doubloons, were preparing to confine me to prison, the marquis fell deadly ill, and in that hour he became convinced of his iniquity, and in fear of the terrible leap he was soon to make into the other world, he handed his confessor a letter written and signed in his own hand, in which, after begging my sincere pardon, he admits to my good conduct and confesses that everything he had imputed to me was mere libel and the effects of an unruly and vindictive passion.

"I have a copy of this letter, and it has been given to the judges in private, so that it might not cause harm to the marquis' honor; and therefore, from one day to the next, I expect to gain my freedom and compensation for the money I have lost.

"This, my friend, has been my tragic adventure. I have told it to you so that you might not lose hope, but rather might learn to resign yourself to your troubles in the sure faith that if you are innocent, God will return for your sake."

This was the point that Don Antonio had reached when the time came for us to separate, so that we could pray the rosary and retire to our beds. Nevertheless, after supper, when we were more alone, I told him the following:

CHAPTER 22

Don Antonio is released from jail; Periquillo gives himself over to the friendship of his roguish companions; and what happened between him and El Aguilucho

After we had gone to bed, I told Don Antonio, "Dear friend, this moment has truly brought me both pleasure and sorrow. It has been my pleasure to learn that Your Honor emerged unharmed in regard to your faithful spouse and the marquis, given his public and solemn retraction, which will shortly return you to freedom so that you may enjoy the loving company of your wife, who has proved so faithful and so worthy of your love. It is my sorrow to realize how short a time I will have for enjoying the amiable company of a man who is generous, charitable, and unselfish."

"Please save your praise," Don Antonio told me, "for someone who deserves it. I've done nothing for you but what I would hope others would do for me if I were to find myself in your situation, and in so doing, I've merely fulfilled the obligations that religion and Nature have imposed on me. And, as you can plainly see, someone who does merely that deserves neither praise nor recognition."

"Oh, dear sir!" I said, "if everyone would do no more than what they ought, the world would be a happy place, but so few carry out their duties that the shortage of righteous men makes those few all the more estimable, so I will hold you in high regard for as long as I live. If only my luck were different! Then my gratitude wouldn't be mere words; for if, as you say, someone who merely does what he ought doesn't deserve praise, then someone who shows gratitude for a favor is doing neither more nor less than what he ought: for who could be so contemptible as to receive as great a favor as I have, and not acknowledge it, announce it, and give thanks for it, despite his benefactor's modesty? My father, sir, was very honest and given to reading, and I remember hearing him say that the man who invented prisons was the man who did the first favors; this is easy enough to understand when it comes to grateful men, but who could be so odious as to receive a benefit and not give thanks for it? Indeed, an ingrate is worst than a wild beast. You have seen how grateful dogs can be, and you must remember the lion who had a thorn removed from his paw by a traveler, and when the traveler later fell prisoner and was sentenced to be a victim of the wild beast in the circus of Rome, by chance, or in order to teach the ingrates a lesson, the lion that was to devour him turned out to be the same one whose paw he had healed, and to the spectators' amazement, after he recognized his benefactor by his scent, instead of attacking him and tearing him to pieces as would have been natural, he came up to him and licked him, and gave him a warm welcome with his tail, mouth, and body, out of respect for the man who had done him a favor.[1] Who, then, could fail to acknowledge a favor? There is a reason why the ancient laws set no punishment for ingrates: the legislator thought such a crime impossible; and for the same reason, Ausonius said that 'Nature produces nothing worse than an ingrate.'

---

[1] Note that when the Romans threw criminals to the lions, they would reduce the beasts' feed in order to make them more fierce through hunger.

"So Don Antonio, my friend, please tell me if I can decline to thank you for the favors you have done me."

"I never speak out against what reason tells me," he replied. "I recognize that it is right and proper to thank a benefactor; that is what I do, and publicly, too, for if I can do nothing more, announcing the good done for me is half payment, since I have no other way of repaying it; but even so, I wish they wouldn't do the same for me, because I have no desire for the person who receives any little favors I can do to repay me for them, but rather to be repaid by God and the testimony of my conscience; because I too have read in the author whom you cite that 'whoever does a favor should not recall what he has done.'

"And so, to finish with this subject, the important thing is that you should not be overwhelmed by your troubles, nor get discouraged when I am no longer around, for Providence is still with you, and will be there to support you when I am gone, just as it is doing now through me, since I am nothing more than an instrument being put to use at present."

In such amiable conversation, we fell asleep, and the following day I was unexpectedly called upstairs. I was frightened as I went up, not knowing why they needed me; but my doubts were soon dispelled when the notary announced that they were going to have me make my "confession with charges."

They made me swear on the cross and they beseeched me in every way they could to confess the truth, under the oath that I had sworn.

The last thing that would have occurred to me was to confess a single word that might harm myself, for I had heard the *léperos* say that in these cases, "better to be a martyr than a confessor." I did swear to tell the truth, however, since saying "yes" couldn't harm me.

They started asking me many of the same things they had already asked in the preliminary declaration, and I repeated the same lies to many of the same questions that I suspected were not in my favor; and so I denied my name, my homeland, my marital status, and so forth, and added, in regard to my trade, that I was a farmer where I was from; I confessed, because I couldn't deny it, that Januario was my friend, and that the serape and the rosary belonged to him; but I didn't tell them how they had come into my power, but claimed instead that he had pawned them to me.

They next brought several charges against me, but nothing induced me to make the statement they wanted, so in view of my resistance they ended the inquest, had me sign the declaration, and sent me out into the courtyard.

I quickly obeyed, since I wished to be out of their presence. I went back down to my cell, and when I did not find Don Antonio there, I went out in the courtyard to take some sun.

While I was busy doing that, a few members of the brotherhood of gamblers gathered near me and, spreading a small blanket on the ground, sat down to play a round of cards in peace and good company—which the trusty would have disrupted in no time if they hadn't paid him a couple of reales for a license, because he grubbed that much money or more, depending on the size of the bets, for so-called licenses before every gaming party.

I was amazed to see that they gambled more freely and at less cost in jail than out on the street, and while I was at it, I envied the trusties' perks, because apart from the general ones, this trusty whom I have mentioned had a few others that left him a tidy profit, since he smuggled in liquor through a third party and sold it whenever he felt like it; gave out loans against pledges, taking in two reales profit for every peso lent; and had other business ventures, each of them every bit as legitimate and honorable as those I have described.

I had a desire to mix in with the gamblers to see if I could *play by my wits*, using one of the tricks Juan Largo had taught me; but I didn't get my nerve up at the time, since I was new and I could see what class of people was playing, any one of whom could have given me lessons in the art of cardsharping; and so I contented myself with passing the time by watching them.

After a long time of idleness, which is the only kind of time that is spent in our jails, I repeated my trip to the cell, and there was Don Antonio waiting for me. I told him the whole story of what had happened between me and the notary, and he seemed amazed, telling me, "I find it hard to believe that you have gone through the confession with charges so fast, for I told you just yesterday that you could expect that step to come three months from now, and indeed I could cite many examples of such delays to you. True, when the judges are active and there is no obstacle impeding them, or when there is an urgent need to conclude the case, this business can be finished quickly. But let's look into this: did you make many citations? Because if that is the case, the trial will become more complicated or be delayed."

"I don't know what citations are," I replied.

To which Don Antonio answered, "Citations are the references that the prisoner makes to other fellows, calling on them as witnesses or citing them for any sort of meddling in the case; then it is necessary to take their testimony and examine it to see the truth or falsity of everything that has been said; and this is called *deposing cited witnesses*. As you can see, such proceedings naturally take time."

"Well, friend," I said, "we're badly off; because, to prove that I didn't go out with Januario on the night of the robbery, I testified that I had been in the pool room with all the folks who were living there, and there are a lot of them."

"You really did do badly," Don Antonio told me, "but if you did not have a more favorable proof, you couldn't have left it out. After all, if your business keeps going at the same speed with which it has begun, you can hope to leave here soon."

We spent the rest of that day in this and other conversations, while my charitable friend gave me food to eat; and during the fifteen or twenty days that we were together, he not only gave me all the help he could, he also taught me through his good advice. Oh, if only I had taken it!

Whenever he saw me joining up with some prisoners whose friendship he did not think good, he would tell me, "Look here, Don Pedrito: as the saying goes, every sheep with its mate. [2] You might try not being on such familiar terms with that class of people, such as N. and Z.; not because they are poor and dark-skinned—those are accidents, on account of which you should never disdain a man nor part with his

---

2 [That is, birds of a feather flock together. —Tr.]

company, especially if his dark color and his torn clothes cover, as they often do, his underlying virtue—but because that is frequently not the case. Instead, common birth and personal shabbiness are usually the best witnesses to a lack of any education or manners; and you have seen how the friendship of a few folks of that class can bring no honor or profit; and you must remember how, as you have told me, the missteps you have suffered and tight straits you have found yourself in have been due to none other than your bad friends, even those from the class of the well born, such as Señor Januario."

That was the tenor of all the advice this good man gave me, and so, between the favors he showed me and the sweetness of his character, he captivated my good will to the extent that I loved and respected him as I did my father.

This reminds me that, owing to God, I had a noble heart that was pious and malleable to reason. Virtue enchanted me, when I saw it in others; atrocious crimes horrified me, and I could not make up my mind to commit them; and sensitivity stirred in my gut in the presence of any pitiful scene. But what do such good qualities do for us if we do not cultivate them? What do we gain if the ground is fertile but the seeds that are planted there are tares? That is precisely what happened to me. My malleability helped me follow the impetus of my passions and the example of my bad friends; but when I saw a friend who was good, I rarely failed to fall in love with virtue, and if I could not make up my mind to follow it with any constancy, at least I felt inclined toward good and I restrained myself so long as I kept that stimulus in view.

That's what happened with me as long as I had Don Antonio's company: far from debasing myself or becoming more contaminated by the depraved examples of the ordinary prisoners that we call the riffraff, which is what I had experienced in the pool room; far from that, I say, I was somehow acquiring the habit of thinking honorably, and I did not dare associate with that rubbish, because of the shame it would cause my friend and because of the force that his soft and effective persuasion had on me. How true it is that an honorable friend's example can sometimes serve as a better restraint than a superior's orders—especially if the latter only gives orders, not examples!

But since I was barely beginning my apprenticeship as an upright man through my good companion's examples, as soon as I no longer had those before me, all my good behavior and self-mastery came crashing down, just as a cripple will hit the ground as soon as he loses his crutch. What happened was that one morning, as I sat alone in my cell reading one of Don Antonio's books, he came back down from upstairs and, giving me a hug, told me jubilantly, "Dear Don Pedro, God has finally made innocence triumph over slander, and allowed me to attain the fruits of my innocence by giving me full enjoyment of my freedom. The warden has just given me my release. I don't plan to waste one more moment in this prison, so that my good wife might have the pleasure of seeing me free and by her side as soon as possible; and for that reason, I've decided to leave straight away. I am leaving you my bed, and that chest with everything it contains, so that you might make use of it until I can have it taken out from here; but I am trusting you to take good care of it for me."

I promised to do everything he asked me, congratulating him on his freedom and giving him all the thanks he deserved for the favors he had done me, begging him to remember his poor friend Perico when he was back in Mexico and not to forget to visit him from time to time. He offered to do that for me, placing two pesos in my hand, and, embracing me in his arms again, he told me: "Yes, my friend . . . my friend . . . poor boy! Well born, but such bad luck. . . . Good-bye. . . . "

This sensitive and generous man could not restrain his tenderness: his tears interrupted his words, and without giving me time to speak a word myself, he left, leaving me sunk in a sea of affliction and sorrow, not so much because of how much I needed Don Antonio, but rather because I missed his company; for indeed, as I have said already and will never tire of repeating, he was very friendly and generous.

That day I did not eat dinner, and that night I had a very meager supper; but since time is the best cloth for wiping away the tears we shed over the dead and the absent, by the next day I was settling down, bit by bit; though the truth is, the only thing that quieted down was the excess of my grief, not my love or my gratitude.

No sooner did my companions, those scoundrels, see me without Don Antonio's respect, and realize that I had been left to guard his few things, than they endeavored to win my friendship, and to that end they frequently came up to me, gave me cigarettes at every opportunity, invited me to a shot of liquor, asked me about the progress of my case, consoled me, and did everything their skills suggested to them so that they could gain my trust.

It didn't cost them much work, because, being the fine fool I was, I'd think: No, these poor fellows aren't as bad as I thought at first. A base color and tattered clothes don't always prove that men are wicked; indeed, they may sometimes conceal souls as honorable and sensitive as Don Antonio's; and what do I know but that I might find, among these wretches, one who will take my friend's place?

Tricked by these hypocritical feelings, I resolved to become a comrade of that rabble, forgetting the advice of my absent friend, and what's more, the testimony of my conscience, which was telling me that, if not absolutely then most of the time, it is rare to find an unprincipled and uneducated man who isn't also dissolute and depraved. By the third day after Don Antonio's departure, I was already a close companion of those rogues, getting along with them as tightly as if we had known each other for years; because we not only ate, drank, and gambled together, we spoke on familiar terms and tussled with each other like a bunch of kids.

But the person with whom I became friendliest was a fat little mulatto. Squat, stout, big-headed, naked, and all too shrewd and daring, he was called El Aguilucho, the Eagle, and I never knew him by any other name; the truth was, this one fit him to a tee, on account of both his quick wit and his sharp grasp. He was an astute and light-fingered thief, one of those small-time burglars who can never pull off a worthwhile robbery, yet would risk twenty-five lashes in the stocks for a two-bit piece of glass or a one-and-a-half-bit cut of cloth. In other words, he was one of those pickpockets or purse-snatchers, but he was subtle in the profession. Nothing escaped his claws, not the best-hidden handkerchief, not the most tightly tied rag on the clothesline. Just imagine what a thief he was, if all the other prisoners, who were likewise professors of the same art, threw in the towel to him, admitted his primacy, and guarded against him as if they were the slowest learners in the business!

He himself boastfully vaunted his crimes, detailing them to me quite frankly, and I held up my end by recounting my adventures point by point, without hiding the fact that, just as they had nicknamed him the Eagle, I was likewise known as the Mangy Parrot.

Revealing that secret was all I had to do for everyone there to discover it, and from that day forward, they didn't know me by any other name in the jail. This was, as I have said, the wonderful fellow with whom I struck up the closest friendship. You can imagine what kind of examples, what kind of advice, and what kind of favors I received from my new friend and from all his pals.

During this time, I used up the two pesos that Don Antonio had left me, and I no longer had anything to eat or anything to gamble. It is true that my friend El Aguilucho shared food from his plate with me; but it was such food that I swallowed it with the greatest repugnance, for it amounted to a bit of watered-down *atole* in the morning, a chunk of undercooked steer in chili broth at midday, and a few peas or lima beans at night, all of which the others gulped down happily, both because they weren't used to better provisions and because this was the sort of stuff they were given as charity; but I scarcely touched it, so if it hadn't been for a benefactor who deigned to help me, I would have perished in jail from illness or hunger, since it is a sure thing that if I had eaten their peapodish rations or their semi-living steer steaks, I would have fallen gravely ill, and if I hadn't eaten it, there being no other food to be had, debility would have sent me to my grave.

But neither happened, because on the fourth day of Don Antonio's absence, I received from the street a basket with plenty of fairly good food, though I was unable to find out who had sent it, for every time I asked the runner, all I could get out of him was that "a friend" had sent it, and had ordered him to say that I didn't need to know who it was.

Having learned that much, I took the basket, gave thanks to my unknown bene-factor, and ate with a very good appetite, almost always together with El Aguilucho or some of his brother prisoners. But since their friendship was neither real nor aimed at my welfare, but rather at getting whatever benefits they could out of me, they never ceased insisting that I gamble, and they did this through the Eagle, who would tell me every fifteen minutes, "Friend Periquillo, come on, let's play, man. What are you doing here, all sad and curled up in a corner with a book in your hand, looking like a saint on a side altar? Look, the only way you can have a good time in jail is to spend it drinking or gambling, because there's nothing else to do here. In here, a blacksmith, a tailor, a weaver, a painter, a gunsmith, a tinker, a tinsmith, a wheelwright, or any kind of artisan, as soon as he finds himself deprived of his free-dom, is also deprived of his trade, and is therefore forced into the deepest poverty, along with all his family, on account of the idleness to which he is reduced; and those who don't have a trade perish by the same means; and so, pal, since there's nothing else to do, we spend our time gambling and drinking while we're waiting for them to hang us or send us to eat fresh fish in San Juan de Ulúa;[3] because the only

---

[3] [San Juan de Ulúa, on an island at the entrance to the Veracruz harbor, was a fortress that dou-bled as a prison. —Tr.]

other thing we could do would be to take our own lives, before the hangman or our hardships have a chance to do it for us."

My friend concluded his persuasive argument, and I said to him, "I never imagined that a man of your appearance could speak so reasonably; because, to tell the truth—and not to make you angry—the people of your class never express themselves in this way."

"Even though that rule isn't as universal as you presume," he answered, "I nevertheless must admit that you are for the most part correct; yet the roughness and ignorance that you have noticed among Indians, mulattos, and the other castes are not because of any defect in their minds, but because of their complete lack of culture and education. You must have seen that many of those same folks who can't speak well are able to make a thousand clever objects with their hands, such as little boxes, writing cases, dolls, noisemakers, and all sorts of knickknacks that attract the attention of boys, and even of those who are no longer boys. What is most noteworthy about this is the price for which they sell these things, and the kinds of tools they use to make them. The price is at most a half- or a quarter-real, and the tools amount to a piece of a knife-blade, a strip of tin, and usually nothing else. This proves quite well that they have more talents than you would concede to them, because, even without being sculptors, carpenters, wheelwrights, and so on, and without knowing anything about the rules of those crafts, they can make a figure of a man or an animal, a table, a wardrobe, a toy carriage, or anything they want, all pretty and agreeable to the sight; if they had learned those trades, they would clearly be able to make perfect works in their line. In the same way, then, you should consider that if they could dedicate themselves to studies, and if their everyday commerce were with civilized people, many of them would be as knowledgeable as the best scholar, and they would be capable of standing out among the ranks of the learned, regardless of the darkness of their color.[4] I, for example, speak regular Spanish because I was brought up at the side of a wise friar who taught me to read, write, and talk. If I had been raised in the house of my aunt the offal-vendor, surely at this time you would find nothing amazing about me. But let's leave this philosophizing to the students. Here it doesn't matter if you speak well or badly, if you're white or black, ragged or decent; the important thing is to see how you'll pass the time, and how we can fleece our companions for their coins; so let's go play, Periquillo, let's go play, don't be afraid; I'm not bad at all at cards; I know more about cards than I do

---

[4] People in this city still remember the black lay brother who was a keen-witted poet of improvised verse, of whose many impromptu witticisms the most celebrated is what he said to the wise Jesuit father Samudio on the occasion when the latter asked a companion whether the black man he saw nearby was the one about whom he had heard so much; our man heard him and replied:

> I am the little black poet,
> Though I've never been able to study—oh,
> If I weren't as black as jet,
> I'd be another Padre Samudio.

[For more on *el negrito poeta*, see Chapter 26. –Tr.]

about gelding fighting cocks; I can win a hand of monte against twenty cards. So let's get going, man."

I told him that I'd be happy to go if I had any money, but at the moment I didn't have a dime.

"Not a dime!" the falcon exclaimed. "That can't be. Then why do you want those sheets or that mattress that you have on your bed, or the other gear you're storing in the chest? Here the trusty, or other fellows whose consciences are as clean as his, would lend you eight-for-two with those things as collateral, either against winnings or on the whistle."

"Getting a kickback of two reales for lending eight is something I understand," I said, "and I know that that's called *lending eight-for-two*; but as for the business with the *winnings* and the *whistlings*, I don't know what all that's about. Please explain that part to me."

"To lend against winnings," he replied, "means to loan someone money with the obligation that the person in question must pay the lender half a real or one real for every hand of monte he wins; and to lend on the whistle means to make a loan for a specified amount of time, without interest, but under the condition that if the collateral isn't redeemed when the time is up, the person loses it irrevocably in exchange for the money that was lent, and the owner has no right to demand payment for the excess value."

"Fine," I said, "now I know how the business works, and just as I figured it, one way or another the borrower is very likely to lose what he pawns, while the money-lenders are on the verge of being carried off by the devil."

"Don't let it worry you," said El Aguilucho, "whether they get carried off or not; what do you care? Are you their mother? The thing is to get them to provide us with the coins we need for gambling, and as for the rest, that's their problem."

"That's all fine, brother, but these things aren't mine, so how could I pawn them?"

"With your hands," said my wonderful friend, "and if you don't want to do it, I'll do it for you, because I know very well who makes loans and who doesn't in our house. Maybe what's stopping you is what you will tell Don Antonio when he comes back for them, isn't that it? Well, look, the answer is simple, natural, and one that he'll have to accept whether he likes it or not, and it's that you got robbed. Don't imagine that Don Antonio could doubt it, because we've robbed him before— myself and others who aren't as feeble-minded as you; so he'll have to remember and say, 'If they robbed me, and I'm the owner of my things, then how could they have helped robbing this fool, who's new here, and who couldn't have kept as close watch over my things as I did myself?' Besides, even if he didn't think along these lines, even if he thought it was all a trick that you pulled on him, what could he do to you? You're in jail already, my boy, not further in, not further out. But don't worry about him finding out, because in here we all cover up with the same blanket,[5] and we won't squeal on you even if the devil takes us.

---

[5] A common phrase, meaning that two or more people give excuses for each other, thus covering up their joint tricks and deals. –E.

"I believe everything you're telling me," I answered, "but look: this fellow is a good man; he's put his trust in me; he considers himself my friend, and he's proven his friendship by doing me lots of favors. So how could I possibly treat him this way?"

"You're such a brute!" said the Sparrowhawk. "First, Don Antonio became friends with you for his own purposes, because he wanted someone to talk to, but he couldn't get any support from the rest of us since he was so stuck up, ridiculous, and mysterious. Second, once he's swept away by his freedom, he'll never give a second thought to these odds and ends, just as he hasn't remembered in the four days since he left. Third, in case he does remember, he'll just have to believe your excuse and not charge you with the robbery; and fourth and finally, this isn't what you could call injuring a friend, since you're not taking away his wife or his reputation or his property, or sticking him with a knife, or doing him any harm that you know of. You're just selling one of his knickknacks or another, out of necessity and without letting him find out, which is the sign of a great friendship. If you were to do him any harm in the certain knowledge that he would find out, well, that would be a sign that you wanted to injure him; but selling four rags of his, when you're certain he'll never learn about it, is indisputable proof that you love him well, which should calm you down inside."

In the end, the little mulatto rogue did and said so much that I, who had little need for convincing, was persuaded, and for five pesos I pawned a very good pair of blue cloth trousers with silver buttons that I found in the chest, and we lost no time heading off to set up a game of monte. Like flies to honey, all the blanket-robed scoundrels gathered to play. They sat in a circle, and my friend began to deal while I happily paid.

El Aguilucho was indeed a cardsharp, but he wasn't as skilled at cheating as he had said, because he did such a clumsy and obvious false cut in one hand on which he had twelve pesos riding that everybody saw it, and beginning with the fellow who had placed the bet, supported by his friends, and then the dealer supported by his, things got so hot that in a second we were at each other's throats, rumbling all in a knot, people on top of people, rolling across the gaming table, throwing horrific punches at each other and sometimes at our own friends, since we were so tightly packed and so blind with rage that we jabbed left and right without bothering to aim, and we tended to land our best blows on our best friends. In my case, certainly, I got such a fierce punch from El Aguilucho that I was covered in blood, and it hurt so bad that I thought I had spat my brains out through my nose.

The uproar in the courtyard was so great that the trusty couldn't even stop it with his whip, until the warden came, and since he wasn't the worst warden there could be, we quieted down out of respect. After we had calmed down and I had gone back to my cell, my companion El Aguilucho came looking for me. Since he was used to brawls like this, both in jail and on the outside, he was cooler about it than I was, and so he asked me scornfully how things had gone for me in battle.

"Like hell," I replied. "All my teeth are loose, and my nose is broken, and what hurts most about it all is that you were the one who did me the big favor."

"I don't know about that," said the little mulatto, "but I don't deny it either, because when I get angry I don't pay any attention to how I shower my affections or on whom. You saw how those devils almost had me with my face squashed against the ground, so I couldn't tell where my fist was going. Still, forgive me, brother, because I didn't do it on purpose. And did you really lose so much blood?"

"It couldn't have been that much," I answered, "but I'm feeling pretty faint."

"Don't worry about it," he went on. "You know, every cloud has a silver lining, and a good swift punch in the face like that, every now and then, is usually very good for your health, because it's a great way to get a cheap bloodletting that clears out your head and prevents a fever."

"Damn you and damn your cures," I said, "and you'd better not ever give me another one of your bloodlettings like this one. But tell me, how'd we do with our coins? Because it would be the devil of it if, on top of being bled and bruised, we came out broke, too."

"Not at all," my pal told me; "I'd sooner have left my guts in the hands of my enemies than a single real. As soon as I noticed that we were all getting angry, I made sure to tuck away the dough, so when things blew up, the coins were already safe and sound."

"But where?" I asked. "Because you don't have a jacket, or a shirt, or trousers, or anything you could use. So where did you hide it so quickly?"

"In the waistband of my underpants," he answered, "and inside the sash; and it was when I was putting it there that they grabbed me, like you saw, because if they had caught me with two free hands at the beginning of the fight, those so-and-so's would've had a second fighting cock to deal with; but we're still young, and there's lots of days in the year."

"Come on, drop your grudges," I said. "Let's see how much of it I get, because I'm dying of hunger and I'd like to send for some lunch."

"That business had been taken care of," El Aguilucho answered me, "and to prove it, here comes Tío Chepito the runner with your food."

And indeed, there came the little old man with a basket bulging with pig's feet marinated in chili, beef jerky in *tlemole*, bread, tortillas, beans, and other such provisions. The Eagle called in his other pals and we all sat down in a circle and ate in peace and good company; but in the middle of our joy we remembered the pulque, and its absence saddened us all; yet, in the end, some cane liquor made up for the lack, and the toasts came so thick and fast that, being hardly accustomed to so much drinking, I was so knocked out that I had no idea what happened next nor how I had gotten out of there. The fact of the matter is that, when I revived later that night, I found myself in my bed, not very clean and with a powerful headache; and in this state, I took off my clothes and tried to go back to sleep, which I did not find hard to do.

CHAPTER 23

IN WHICH PERIQUILLO RECOUNTS HOW HE WAS ROBBED IN JAIL; HOW
DON ANTONIO BID HIM FAREWELL; THE TROUBLES HE SUFFERED; AND
OTHER THINGS THAT PERHAPS WILL NOT DISPLEASE THE READERS

After day broke, the prisoners all woke up in my cell; I was the last to wake, feeling very hungry since I hadn't had supper the night before. The first thing I did was go to get a piece of chocolate for breakfast; but imagine my surprise when I looked in my pocket for the key to the chest and didn't find it there, or under my pillow, or anywhere, and, plagued by my hunger, I broke open the chest and found it swept clean of all Don Antonio's things, which I had been watching with such loving care! I admit I very nearly cracked my head against the wall in anger and despair, just thinking about the reality of what had happened—that is, that my very own companions, as soon as they saw me drunk, had taken the key from my pocket and had pinched everything the wretched chest held.

I was correct in my judgment, but I wasn't able to catch the thief or collect the stolen goods, and that made me more furious, so that I didn't stop to think about the baneful effects that drunkenness entails; for, with his faculties asleep and his senses paralyzed, a drunk is left in a state of insensibility that makes him no better than a log, and in that miserable condition, he is liable not only to be robbed but to be injured and even murdered, as we have seen in numerable examples.

That was the last thing I was thinking of, though it would have been very helpful to me in keeping me from contracting that horrific vice, which I did contract, though not very frequently.

Baffled, sad, chapfallen, and melancholy, I sat on the bed biting my nails, staring at the poor chest that had been emptied of everything including dust and straw, cursing the thieves, blaming this fellow and that, and forgetting all about my chocolate; though even if I had remembered it at that moment, what good would it have done me, since there wasn't even a trace left of there ever having been any squares of chocolate in the chest?

While I was making these reflections, my pal El Aguilucho arrived, and with a very pleasant face, he greeted me and asked how I had slept last night. To this I replied, "It wasn't the worst night ever, but this morning has been a dog."

"But why, Periquillo?"

"What do you mean, why?" I said. "Because I've been robbed. Look what they've done to Don Antonio's chest."

El Aguilucho leaned over to look at it, and he cried out as if wounded by my misfortune, "You're right, man, that chest is emptier than the basin that Don Quixote called 'Mambrino's helmet.'[1] What wickedness! What knavery! What infamy! I'm not astonished by robbery; come on, that's my business, too, so how could it shock me? What irritates me is when they rob my friends; because there's no doubt about it, Periquillo, you don't get burned unless you're close to the fire. Yes, I'm sure of it,

---

[1] [In *Don Quixote*, part I, chapter XXI. –Tr.]

the thieves were inside the house, and I'll bet you they were some of the same rogues who were here having lunch with us yesterday. If I had caught scent of their intentions, none of this would have happened, because I wouldn't have left your side, but instead I was trying to make up for what I had spent, so I went and gambled all the money we have left, and we went bust; but don't you worry, because tomorrow is another day."

"So you mean," I said, "you don't even have enough money left to buy breakfast?"

"Breakfast? Cash?" he replied. "Last night I had to go to bed without a cigarette! But tell me, what did they take from the chest?"

"A trifle," I told him: "two shirts, underpants, boots, good shoes, corduroy trousers, two handkerchiefs, a few books, my chocolate . . . and finally, everything."

"What a dirty trick!" said the mulatto. "I'm sorry about it, brother, and I'll be on the lookout in all the cells and mezzanines to see if I can track down any of the things you mentioned, because if we can just find one thread, don't you worry, it'll all appear; but for now, don't let it get you down, straighten your back, hold your head up, stand tall, come on, get yourself out here and calm down, because we aren't made of rags; more stuff got lost in the Flood, and it all belonged to other people, just like what you've lost. So let's get going, Periquillo, come on, don't be a fool, you'll get your breakfast."

Like it or not I got out of bed, hungry for the promised breakfast. We went to the trusty's cell, where El Aguilucho had a talk with him in private. The slave-driver opened a chest, from which I imagined he would take out a square or two of chocolate and maybe a bread roll, but instead I saw him take out a bottle and a glass, into which he poured about half a pint of liquor, which my pal picked up and passed from his hand to mine, saying, "Drink up, Periquillo, make your morning."

"Man," I said, "I'm not used to having anything for breakfast except chocolate."

"Well, this is chocolate," he answered. "The thing is, the chocolate you've drunk in the past was ground on a grinding stone, and this is made by machine; but, my boy, you've got to believe this is better, because it fortifies your stomach and puts new life in your head . . . so come on, drink up, because our good trusty is waiting to get his glass back."

With these and other arguments, he convinced me, and between the two of us we took turns swigging the half-pint, with my share going to my head faster than was good for me; but at last, with this slight aid, two hours later I was feeling happy and had forgotten all about the robbery.

In this way, we spent about the next two weeks, with me giving El Aguilucho food to eat, and him giving me liquor to drink, in mutual and reciprocal harmony; though the truth is, he was constantly telling me we should sell or pawn the sheets and the mattress from my bed; but he couldn't get me to do that at the time, because I swore up and down to him that I wouldn't sell them for anything in the world, and to make sure of it I brought them to the trusty and begged him to keep them safe for me until their owner came to take them back home with him.

The trusty did me the favor of watching them, and I was left without anything to cover me but my worn serape, at which my crafty friend lost his hopes of getting his hands on them; but even so, he didn't act like he had been hurt by me, whether because he was one of those people who have no shame, or because it wasn't in his interest to be too fastidious and lose out on the free grub he scrounged from me every day at noon, when he never failed to show up at my side; for the food that my anonymous benefactor sent me was worth a little flattery, being both flavorful and abundant, and I don't mean just for El Aguilucho's crude palate, but for other more exquisite tastes.

I gathered that this rogue had been the foremost agent of my robbery, which was indeed the case, but I pretended not to know this because, I reasoned, that would make me too hated among those folks, and in any case it would be easier to free a Jew from the Inquisition than a single real from what they had most likely already consumed.

We carried on with this pretense, as I got back in swigs of liquor what I would give the Sparrowhawk in mouthfuls of food.

One day, as I sat picking the lice out of my dirty and tattered shirt, I was called upstairs. I ran up, thinking it must be some other judicial proceeding; however, it wasn't the notary who had called me, but my good friend Don Antonio and his wife, who were generous enough to visit me.

As soon as he saw me, he embraced me with great affection, and his wife greeted me affably. For my part, despite the pleasure I felt at seeing my true and generous friend, I couldn't help feeling rather alarmed, thinking that he had come back for his things and that I would have to give him the shocking bill; but Don Antonio quickly put me at ease, for after a few words, he asked me why I was so dirty and shabby.

"Because, as you know," I answered, "I have nothing else to wear."

"What do you mean?" my friend said. "What happened, then, to the bit of clothes that I left in the chest?"

I blushed at hearing this question, and couldn't help but concoct a crafty lie, for without answering his question directly I indicated that I hadn't used it because it wasn't mine, and I said all this with fear, which he took to be the effect of shame. "Since the clothes are yours, not mine. . . . "

"No, sir," Don Antonio broke in, "they are yours, and that is why I left them with you. Use them in good health. I asked you to guard them for me in order to test you; but since you've been able to keep them safe, please use them."

Hearing about this donation, I regained my composure, though I silently cursed myself to think that, while he had freed me from my responsibility for his clothes, those damnable thieves had prevented me from wearing them. I asked him if he were going to be taking away his bed, so that I could go get it ready. He told me, no, he was giving me everything. I thanked him, as was proper, for his affection and charity, and I admitted to the lady all the favors that I owed her husband, speaking freely in praise of him; but he cut my panegyric short by relating to me that, as soon as he had left jail, he had gone to see his wife, who had a sealed letter for him that had been delivered by a gentleman, asking him to come to the gentleman's house as soon as he had read it, on urgent business; having done so, he had learned from the same gentleman's own mouth that he was the prime executor of the marquis, who had asked him insistently to spare no pains in getting Don Antonio released from prison, and to beg his pardon once more in the marquis' name, and to give him 8,000 pesos in cash, both to repay him for his work and to indemnify him to some extent for the harms he had inflicted, and that he give his wife a diamond surrounded by rubies, which he had set aside as the price for his lewdness had she acceded to his illicit seduction; but having tested her conjugal fidelity, he now gave it to her as a small tribute to her virtue, beseeching them both to forgive him and to commend his soul to God. Don Antonio and his wife showed me the ring, a jewel worthy of a rich marquis; but they both were moved to pity when they finished telling me what I have just written, and the young lady added, "When I realized what that poor gentleman's evil intentions were, and saw how much Antonio had to suffer on his account, I abhorred him and thought that my hatred would be everlasting; but when I saw his repentance and his determination, in dying, to satisfy us, I recognized that he had a great soul, I pardoned him, and I feel sorry for his early death."

"You are quite right, my darling, to think this way," said Don Antonio, "and we should have pardoned him even if he had not given us satisfaction. The marquis was a good man, but what man, no matter how good he is, is not moved by passions? If we would remember our own squalor, we would be more indulgent with our enemies and would absolve the injuries we receive from them more easily; but unfortunately, we are very stern judges of others; we forgive them nothing, not even an oversight, not even a mistake, not even a slip; while we wish that they would forgive us everything all the time."

We spent much of the morning in these conversations. He asked me about the progress of my case and whether I had anything to eat. I said, yes, every day I was brought a basket of food for dinner and supper, two bread rolls, and a box of cigarettes, which I always received with thanks, but that I felt sorry not to know whom I was thanking, for the runner did not want to tell me who my benefactor was.

"That makes little difference," said Don Antonio; "the important thing is that he keeps up with the charity he has begun, and I trust to God that he will continue."

Saying this, they rose and took leave of me, Don Antonio adding that they would leave this capital city the next day for Jalapa, where I could write to them about what happened to me, for hearing from me would delight them both, and that if I were to leave prison and wish to go there, given that I was single, I would not have trouble finding a way to make an honorable living.

Don Antonio was not, as you have seen, one of those friends whose friendship is all talk; he always confirmed through his acts what he said with words; and so, after he concluded what I have just said to you, he gave me ten pesos, and the lady his wife another ten, and with more embraces and courteous expressions, they bid me an emotional farewell, leaving me feeling sadder than the first time, because I now figured that I was absolutely beyond his help.

El Aguilucho did not neglect to keep everything that happened during our visit under observation, and he didn't so much as blink when my benefactors were taking their leave of me, so he saw quite well what kind of gift they gave me, and he must have been celebrating the good news, since he considered himself to be the joint heir, along with me, of Don Antonio.

After Don Antonio had gone, I went back down to my cell in bewilderment; but my very dear friend El Aguilucho was waiting for me there with a tall glass of liquor and a couple of sausages, though I don't know to where he could have sent for them so quickly; and without letting on that he had been on the lookout for my movements, he told me, "Let's go, Periquillo, my boy! You've had me sitting here all this time, waiting for you to start my breakfast! My goodness, what a long visit! I bet it was Don Antonio, come to collect his stuff. How'd it go? Did you come off all right? Did he believe the robbery story?"

"I came off well and badly," I answered. "Well, because my good friend not only didn't charge me anything for what he had left in my care, he even gave it all to me, and a few more coins to help me out; and I came out badly because I think this will be the last aid I get, since he's leaving tomorrow for his homeland and his family, and aside from feeling sorry for his absence as a friend, I'll miss him as a benefactor."

"You're right to say that, and you're right to feel sorry," said the Sparrowhawk to the foolish little bird, "because you sure don't find friends like that every day; but what can you do! God is great and He didn't raise people so that they'd die of hunger. By hook or by crook, you'll see that you'll never lack for anything if you stick with me. I'm a poor black man, but, brother, even if I say so myself, my color doesn't do me justice; yet I'm a good friend and I'll scrape the ground before I let you go without. I don't know if you noticed me up there, when you were having your visit. I didn't want to tell you, and that's why I pretended when you came back down, but I went up as soon as I heard that Don Antonio was the one who had called you, to get the witnesses ready in case he tried charging you and you faltered; but when I saw him say good-bye and embrace you, I got over the worry you had been causing me, and I came down to get this bite to eat ready for you, and if you don't like it, I'll have something else brought for you, because I still have four reales here that I just won playing *rentoy*.[2] Do you need them? Here, take them."

"No, brother," I said, "God bless you, but for now I'm set."

"I wasn't asking how old you were," said the little black man, "I was just telling you: if you need 'em, spend 'em, and if not, throw 'em away; but let me tell you, it hurts me more to get snubbed by a friend than to be stabbed with a knife. If you weren't my friend and I didn't hold you in as high esteem as I do, you can be sure I wouldn't be offering you anything."

"Thank you, Eagle," I said, "but I don't mean it as a snub; it's just that today I am in very good shape."

"Well, I'm as endlessly happy for your good fortune, as if it were my own," he replied; "but look how tasty these little sausages are. Eat up. . . . "

Flattery is cunning, and since it can worm its way into someone's heart through the most cautious and circumspect of ears, how could it not get in through mine, which were unwary and unaccustomed to its wickedness? As it happened, I was completely enchanted by the black man, and all the more so when, after a long series of toasts, he told me with great seriousness, "Friend Periquillo, I am a friend of friends and not of money. Maybe you aren't sure about this part of me, because you see me here shirtless and wrapped in an old blanket, but I'm going to give you some proof that will convince you of what I'm saying. We've drunk more than normal,

---

[2] [*Rentoy:* an old card game, played with partners. –Tr.]

especially you, as you're not used to liquor. I wouldn't say you're drunk, but you are starting to get ripe. I'm afraid you might go overboard and have the same thing happen as the other day: that is, that you'll pass out and get robbed of the money you've got in your pocket; because in here, my boy, when it comes to swooping down on loot, even the slowest one of us can fly like the wind, and if there's one Eagle, there's more sparrowhawks, gyrfalcons, falcons, and other birds of prey than you can count; so I think the most reasonable thing we could do would be to go and have the trusty guard those coins you've got, because if you just give him a little tip—since he 'can't walk without a lantern'—he'll keep them safe for you in his trunk, and then you'll have a peso or two when you need them, instead of letting other rogues enjoy your money. Not only won't they thank you for it, they'll think you're a brute for not having learned your lesson from the skimming they gave you not long ago."

I thanked him for his advice, not anticipating the shrewdness of his self-interest, and went to find the trusty, to whom I handed, one by one, the twenty pesos that I had just received. With this business done, my great friend told me to go wait for him in my cell, and he would be there soon.

I obeyed him to the letter and, sitting down on my bed, told myself, "No two ways about it; he's a fine black man; his color doesn't do him justice, as he says; until today, I hadn't realized how much he loves me; he really is my friend, and worthy of the name. Yes, I'll love him, and after Don Antonio I'll prefer him to anyone else, because he has the best quality you could hope for in a friend, which is unselfishness."

I was in the middle of this mistaken soliloquy when my pal walked in bearing cigarettes, sausages, and liquor, and told me, "Alright, brother Perico, now we can smoke, eat, and drink at ease, confident that your pennies are all safe."

And so I did, without having to be asked twice, until the freely flowing liquor left me sound asleep. Then my tender friend put me into bed and carefully wolfed down all the food that I had been brought.

That afternoon I woke up feeling fresher, for the liquor fumes had dissipated, and El Aguilucho, who was beginning to carry out his plans, had me redeem the trousers I had pawned, telling me it would be a pity to lose them for so little money. His aim was to take advantage of my funds little by little, and to this end he peddled an endless string of flattery, assuring me that all his advice was only for my own good; and thus, for my own good, he advised me to redeem the trousers and to ask for the bed clothes that I had put in safekeeping and the money that I had deposited; and for my own good, and desirous of my advancement, of course, he invited me to gamble; he plotted with another fellow; and within the space of two days, they left me without a penny, and within a week, without bedspread or mattress, sheets, chest, or serape.

Once he saw me reduced to absolute penury, he drummed up some pretext or other to quarrel with me, and abandoned my friendship entirely. This business done, he only tried to make fun of me whenever he could. A natural result of his wicked condition, and a just punishment for my reckless trust.

It is true that the cold that penetrated me through the holes in my rags, the lice that crawled over my tattered clothes, the bit of shame that I felt from my indecency, the ingratitude of my friends and especially of El Aguilucho, and the hardness with which the ground received me at night, were motive enough to fill me with confusion and sadness; however, this passion would cool somewhat around midday, when I would be delivered the basket and satisfy my hunger with a little well-seasoned food; but later, when even this disappeared because my guardian angel stopped coming at midday, without my knowing why, I wished myself to Barabbas and the whole inferno, cursing my recklessness and misconduct, though it was already too late.

Naked and starving, I suffered a few more months of prison, which left me on tenterhooks, as they say, because my health was wracked until I was left pallid and skinny as a bone, and for good reason, because I ate little and badly, while the lice ate well and plenty, there being an infinite number of them.

After all the hardship and squalor I had to tolerate by day, there followed, as I have just mentioned, the horrible torments that awaited me at night in my rough bed, which amounted to an old straw mat covered with bedbugs and nothing else, because I had nothing to use for pillows, sheets, or mattress but my indecent patch-work clothes, which promptly and perceptibly began to diminish before my eyes, since they were constantly being put to work. Consider, my children, what bitter nights and bitter days your father lived through, in this wretched situation; but consider, too, that men expose themselves to this low state and worse for being mindless rogues. I have already told you that the more disorderly a young man is, the more likely he is to become a victim of poverty and all the misfortunes of life, while an upright man—that is, a man of moral and religious behavior[3]—has a powerful shield to keep himself safe from many of these misfortunes. That is what I repeat to you now. But let's leave everyone else to do what they want with their behavior, while we go back and pick up the thread of my story of toil and hardship.

By day I suffered unbearable hunger and nakedness, and by night, the bed and the lack of covers, and I would have remained uncloaked the whole time I was in jail if it hadn't been for an entertaining incident, which went as follows:

A poor country bumpkin, who was also a prisoner there, came up to me one morning when I was in the courtyard, waiting for the sun to come up and avenge me for the insults of the cold night, and he told me, "Look, sir, I sure'd like to tell you about sumpthin' so as you could get me out of this fix I'm in, and I'll pay you whatever it takes. Thing is, though, look here that I don't want any of my companions to find out about it, 'cause they do like to make their jokes."

---

[3] An opportune reflection on Periquillo's part! Some people confuse the idea of *hombría de bien*—of being an upright man—with that of luxury and money, and in their opinion the term *hombre de bien* (upright man) equals rich or semi-rich, while they judge that *poor* is the equivalent of rogue; so, reasoning from these false premises, they are likely to deduce such nonsense as this: Pedro is rich, he has money, he dresses decently; therefore, he is an upright man. Juan is poor, he has no job, he dresses in rags; therefore, he is a rogue. Such absurd conclusions and stupid ideas should have no place in the minds of men! If behaving in accordance with healthy morals is the surest witness for determining true *hombría de bien*, who could doubt that it is often observed among the poor, just as it is often lacking among those who are not poor? Clear proof that the luster or obscurity of the person is not the best thermometer for grading the characters of men. It is true that flashiness and squalor are often the award or punishment for our good or bad conduct; but there are so many exceptions to this observation that it could hardly be adopted as an infallible rule.

"That's fine," I replied; "please tell me whatever you wish, because I will help you willingly and in complete secrecy."

"Well, you should know that my name is Cemeterio Coscojales."

"You must mean Eleuterio," I said, "or Emeterio, because *Cemeterio* isn't a Christian name."

"Sure enough," said the bumpkin, "it's sumpthin' like that, just that with all my worries, half the time I don't even get my own name straight; but anyway, sir, now you know it, so on to the story. I'm from San Pedro Ezcapozaltongo,[4] about eighteen leagues away from this here city. Well, sir, there's this girl lives there, name of Lorenza, the daughter of old man Diego Terrones, who shoes and trains horses, not that there's too many of 'em thereabouts. Well, me, day in and day out, being as her house is fence to fence with mine, the devil made me go and fall hopeless in love with la Lorenza, seeing as how, oh, sir! she's such a devilish pretty girl, just see here: tall and plump and strong as an elephant-ear tree, or at least a live oak; round and ruddy face, with dark eyes and good, big nostrils; she don't have no defecks, 'cept being a little cross-eyed and missing her two front teeth, and that's just because this mule give her a good back-leg kick, because she slipped up and let go his hoof one day when she was helping her father shoe him; but for all that, the girl's right pretty in everything else. Well, sir, it's true, I wooed her, I give her things, and I begged her, and I kep' at it so long that after awhile, like it or not, she came around and tole me she'd marry me; but thing was, when? 'Cause wouldn't it be the devil of it if I was to fool her and leave her in the lurch. So I tells her, how'm I gonna go and fool her, since I'm dying for her, just that we couldn't up and have us a wedding too soon because I was poorer than Adam and the priest was stubborn as they come, he won't do no wedding on credit even if the devil himself brings him the bride and groom, or no funeral even if the dead man's stinking up his house for a whole week, so then, if she love me, she should wait three or four months for me, just till I got in my corn harvest, and it was lookin' good, I had a dozen bushels sowed in my fields. She came around to everything just like I wanted it, and from that day on, we seen ourselves like man and wife, we was that much in love. Well one night, sir, I was comin' home from my field and thinkin' about talkin' to her over the fence like we always done, and I spy somebody scrunched up there talkin' with her, and I right away got angry as a bassinet, I was so angry."

"You mean, angry as a basilisk," I interrupted, "because bassinets don't get angry."

"If you say so, sir, except I can conceive of things, but I don't give birth," the bumpkin continued. "But the thing is, is that I went over to that scrunched-up somebody, angry as Santiago, and soon as I got there I saw it was Culás the guitar-man, because he could play a jarabe and he knew how to strum a guitar like he was makin' it talk. As soon as I get there I says to him, so what do you think you're doin' here. And him, all stuck up–like, he tells me, whatever he feels like it, that I'm not his father to go around checkin' on him. Then me, being as I was in charge of things there, I couldn't take much more from him, so I picked up a digging-stick that I got

---

[4] [San Pedro Azcapotzaltongo, known today as Nicolás Romero, is a town on the northwestern edge of Mexico City. The man's pronunciation of his town's name is typical of country speech. –Tr.]

from a field hand and I landed him such a whomp on the back of the head that he fell down in a heap, ready for confession. Well, right then the deputy comes walkin' by, doin' his rounds with his *topiles*,[5] he hears Culás screamin', and run as I might, they caught up with me and drug me back, tied up tighter'n a bottle rocket, to his office. So right away I gives my declaration, and the surgeon says he ain't too sure about the patient, 'cause he was all wounded and oozin' lots of blood. So after that, they took poor ole Lorenza and put her in shelter in the priest's house, and me in the jail, where they stuck me in the stocks. Next day, la Lorenza sends me a missage by the priest's old cook, tellin' me it weren't her fault, that Culás had called her over to the fence and he had been standin' there pretendin' he was givin' her a missage from me, tellin' her I tole her to go out to the store with him, and other stuff that I forget; but the old lady tole me the poor girl was cryin' all inconsolable. Next day the deputy sends me to this here jail on a mule with a couple of shackles on me and big pile of papers that he give to the Indians who brought me here, so they'd give 'em to the judge here. I been in prison for three months now and I don't know what they're gonna do with me, though Lorenza wrote me that Culás is all up and healed and goin' around playin' his guitar again. So, sir, I'm beggin' you to do me a favor, and I'll pay you whatever you want, by your patron saint and your mother's bones, to write me two letters, one for my godfather, who's the barber there where I'm from, to see if he'll come fix up all this stuff for me, and another one for my darlin' Lorenza, tellin' her, since I know she left the shelter and Culás is still runnin' around after her, to watch it and not do sumpthin' foolish, and not to act like that, and everything you can think up, sir, that ought to be put there; but in your hand, because I'll pay you."

My client finished his long-winded report and request, and I asked him when he needed the letters.

"Right now, sir," he told me, "right away, because the mail goes out tomorrow."

"Well, friend," I said, "give me two reales to buy the paper, please."

He immediately gave them to me, and I had the paper brought and sat down to write the pair of muddles, which came out any old how; but the fact was that the bumpkin liked them so much that he not only paid me the twelve reales that I asked for them, but what I was even more thankful for, he gave me a bit of rag that once had been a cloak: it was falling to pieces, missing half the collar, and so short it only reached down to my knees. What could you expect of it, since its owner had lost it on a four-real bet? The rag was bad, terrible, but I saw it as the solution to all my problems. With the twelve reales, I ate, had a smoke, drank my chocolate, had supper, and still had a bit left over; and with my cape, I slept like a Dutchman.

I thought my luck might be changing; but that rogue El Aguilucho relieved me of my error by pulling an especially obnoxious joke on me, which was as follows.

---

[5] [Deputy: the deputy district governor (*teniente de alcalde mayor*, or as the storyteller calls him, the *tiñente*) was the government-appointed head of a small subprovince in colonial Mexico. *Topil* (or *topile*; from Nahuatl *topileh*, staff-bearer, referring to the person who carries the *vara de justicia*, the staff or wand representing public office): this was an Indian constable who performed police and other low-level government functions in a small town. –Tr.]

The day after my good fortune with the cape, he entered my cell bright and early and, sitting down next to me, said in a very sad and serious tone, "This is a little too much negligence, Señor Perico, and the truth is, the moments are precious and can't be allowed to pass by so coldly, all the more so when the danger threatening you is so terrible and so near. I have been your friend, and I hope you recognize that I still am, even when you have nothing to offer me; but someone has to rouse you, after all, if only out of charity, and shake you from your idleness."

Frightened and disturbed, I asked him what had happened.

"What do you mean?" he said. "Haven't you heard about the sentence that came down from the bench yesterday, that as soon as the upcoming feast days are over, you are to be given 200 lashes as punishment while being marched through the usual streets with the picklock hanging around your neck?"

"Holy St. Barbara!" I exclaimed, pierced to the quick. "What has happened to me? They're going to give 200 lashes to Don Pedro Sarmiento? To a man who's a hidalgo on all four sides? To a descendant of the Tagles, the Ponces, the Pintos, the Velascos, the Zumalacárreguis, and the Bundiburis? And on top of that, to a Bachelor of Arts, a graduate of the Royal and Pontifical University of this city, whose graduates enjoy the same privileges as those of Salamanca?"

"Come on," said the black man, "this isn't the time for that sort of exclamation. Don't you have any relative of means?"

"Yes, I do," I answered.

"Well, get moving," said El Aguilucho; "write to him to work from the outside to get your case going forward with the judges, and to send you two or three ounces of gold to keep the notary happy. You could also buy a sheet of stamped paper[6] and present a petition to the criminal court, invoking your privileges and appealing the sentence until your nobility can be proved. But do it quickly, friend, because delay means danger."

Having said this, he got up to leave, and I thanked him effusively.

Endeavoring to put his advice into action, I checked my pocket to see how much money I had left for paper, filing the petition, and writing a letter to my uncle, Licenciado Maceta; but, dear me, what a jam I found myself in when I saw that I barely had three and a half reales, and was in dire need of another five! In this tight a spot, I went to see my friendly bumpkin; I described my troubles to him and begged him by all the saints in heaven for a little help. The poor fellow sympathized with me and, with tremendous generosity, gave me four reales, telling me, "I'm sorry, sir, about your worries; I don't have any more than this, so take it, because anybody here could loan you the other real, or give it to you out of charity."

I took my four reales and thanked him, on the verge of crying; but I couldn't find another heart as sensitive as his among the nearly 300 prisoners who inhabited that place.

---

6 [Stamped paper (*papel de parte*, also known as *papel sellado*): legal papers such as lawsuits, petitions, witness testimony, and so on, had to be written on paper that carried an official stamp, which the government sold for four reales a sheet. –Tr.]

So I bought the stamped paper, and half a real of regular paper for the letter, keeping three reales in reserve and coming up one and a half reales short of what I would need for filing the petition and paying the runner.

That very day, I did my report as best I could and wrote the letter to my uncle, in which I informed him of my misfortunes; of my innocence, which I had in my favor, at least in everything that was substantial; of the state I was in; and of the insult that threatened the whole family; and I concluded by telling him that, even though I had concealed my name, giving it as Sancho Pérez, the pretense would not do any good once they took me out onto the street, since everyone would recognize me, and then our disgrace would be revealed; and so, for the honor of his relative, my father, and that of his own sons and grandchildren, if not for me, he should help redeem me from this insult by sending me quickly a little something to win the notary's good will.

I closed the letter and gave it on credit to Tío Chepito the runner, for him to take to my relative. This was around vespers; but I still needed one more real to have the four it would take to pay the doorman for presenting my petition.

All night long I couldn't sleep, between worrying about the fearful lashings, and doing the calculations to see where I could come up with the other real I needed so badly. I was still sunk in these sorrowful thoughts the next day. I set about scrutinizing everything I had and examining my clothes piece by piece, to see if I owned anything that might be worth a real and a half; but how much could it be worth! To put my shirt on my body, I had to call the pieces by number; my trousers were barely hanging onto the waistband; you couldn't even use my socks to plug a drain; my shoes looked like two turtle shells and only stayed on my feet out of respect for the laces I had made from a couple of bottle-rocket strings; I had no rosary; and I needed my fragment of a cape more than all my other treasures put together.

I was losing all hope of being able to file my petition that morning, since I had nothing worth a single real, when by luck I raised my eyes and saw, hanging from a nail, my hat, and considering it a worthless article in that dungeon, yet the finest thing I owned, I exclaimed in my glee, "Thanks be to God, at least I have a hat that can do me some good right now!" Saying this, I took it down and sold it for a peseta to the first person I saw, which solved my worries and gave me enough for breakfast to boot.

It must have about ten in the morning when Tío Chepito came wandering in with my uncle's reply, which I will set down for you word for word, so that you will learn, my children, never to place your trust in friends or relatives, but only in your own good behavior and in whatever you are able to acquire, be it a little or a lot, through your honest labor and industry. The reply went like this:

SEÑOR SANCHO PÉREZ:

If you are who you say you are, and if you are publicly insulted as a thief, you may believe that I will not be the least bit worried, for the rogue is the one who will be suffering punishment for his own crime. The warning that you have given me to the effect that my family will be dishonored is very frivolous, for you should know that the insult only falls upon the criminal, while his other kin remain untouched. Therefore, if you are guilty, bear with it on that account; and if you are innocent, as you swear to be, bear with it for the sake of God, because Christ suffered worse for our sakes.

May His Majesty aid and comfort you.

Sincerely, Licenciado Maceta.

There is no need to expound, to anyone who can imagine himself in my place, on the lamentable impression that this bitter reply made upon me. Suffice it to say that it was enough to leave me prostrate on the floor with a sudden fever.

As soon as they noticed me there, they carried me up to the infirmary, where charity swiftly came to my aid.

When they found me with a clear head again, the doctor, who fortunately was skillful and had noticed my delirium and informed himself about my case, had the notary himself set me straight, along with the warden, because I had never been given any sentence, nor did I need to fear the threatened lashing.

Then, as if they were bringing me back from the grave, I regained perfect consciousness, I calmed down, and my health began to recover day by day.

When I was nearly well again, the notary came down to ask me, on the judges' behalf, to turn in the person who had put that fiction in my head; for they knew my whole tragedy, both because I had told them in the petition, and because they had read the letter from my uncle that I have retold to you, and they had formed the idea that I was undoubtedly well born, and they must therefore have been annoyed by the obnoxious joke and they wished to punish its author.

The notary and the warden tried everything they could to get me to reveal the name; but after I reflected on their plans, the results that my denunciation might cause El Aguilucho, and the fact that no good could come my way by denouncing that foolish wretch, who was already serving a long enough sentence for his crimes, I didn't want to give him away, but would only say that there were so many prisoners there, I couldn't be absolutely certain who it was. The magistrates' agents couldn't get anything else out of me no matter how they tried, and so, forming the opinion of me that I was an idiot, they left.

I was happier in the infirmary than in my own cell, both because I was better taken care of, and because there were, after all, some people there with reasonably good backgrounds, whose conversation I enjoyed more than that of the scoundrels in the courtyard.

When the notary saw my handwriting in the petition, he was captivated by it, and that was precisely the same time that his copyist had quit; so, taking advantage of his friendship with the warden, he proposed to me that if I wanted to write copy in longhand for him, he would pay me four reales a day. I agreed instantly, but I warned him that I was not decently dressed for going upstairs. The notary told me not to worry about it, and indeed the next day he outfitted me with a shirt, vest, jacket, trousers, socks, and shoes; all second-hand, but clean and not very old.

I was dressed up to the nines, so that all the prisoners were amazed to see my transformed appearance; but what else, since I didn't recognize myself when I saw how different I looked from night to morning?

I began to serve this man, my first master, so reliably, staunchly, and effectively that within a few days I had completely won his affection, and he grew so fond of me that he not only helped me in jail, but got me out of there and took me home to give me a job, as you will see in the next chapter.

CHAPTER 24

IN WHICH PERIQUILLO DESCRIBES HOW HE GOT OUT OF JAIL, CRITICIZES
BAD NOTARIES, AND FINALLY, RELATES THE REASON WHY AND THE
SHAMEFUL WAY IN WHICH HE LEFT THE HOUSE OF CHANFAINA

There are times when men find themselves so beaten down and in such tight straits
that the most roguish rogues have no other way out but to pretend to have the virtue
that they lack in order to win the friendship of the people they need. That is precisely
what I did with the notary, for even though I was an irreconcilable enemy of work, I
saw myself confined to a jail cell, poor, naked, starving, without any way to make a
penny, and fearing for hours on end the baneful results of the suspicions against me;
given this, I pleased him in every way I could, and he showed more and more affection toward me: so much so that within fifteen or twenty days, he concluded my case
by making them see that there were no witnesses or plaintiffs against me, that the suspicion was trivial, and who knows what all. The important thing is, I was set free
without having to pay court costs, and I went to work for him at his house.

This, my first master, was named Don Cosme Casalla. The prisoners called him
Chanfaina—Chili Stew—either because of the assonance of that word with his
name, or because he tended to make a stew of everything.

That man was so audacious that on one occasion I saw him do something that
shocked me, and that still scandalizes me today as I write about it.

The case was this. One night, a well-known and rather criminal thief fell into the
hands of justice. The business of drawing up his case went to another notary, not to
my master. The prisoner was persuaded, and he frankly confessed all his crimes
because they could not be denied. During this time, a sister of the thief, not bad-
looking, came to see my master and intercede on her brother's behalf, bringing him
some little gift or other; my master excused himself, saying that he wasn't the notary
working on the case, and that she should go see the one who was. The girl told him
she had already seen that notary, but to no effect, because the notary was very punctilious and had told her that he could never do anything that went against justice,
nor was it up to him to move the judges' hearts in his favor; he would only report on
what came up in the case, and the judges would pass sentence based on what they
found appropriate, and thus he had no say in the matter. Despairing at this bad
news, she had therefore gone to see my master—knowing how compassionate he
was and how much influence he wielded in the court—to beg him to look on her
with charity; for, although she was poor, she would thank him for this favor her
whole life long, and would repay it in any way she could.

When my master, who knew more shortcuts than the devil, heard this proposition,
he took a better look at his supplicant's tearful eyes, and, thinking they weren't unworthy of his protection, offered it, saying, "Come on, beautiful, don't cry, you have me
here. Don't worry, no blood will flow because of your brother's case; but. . . . "

After that "but," he stood up and I couldn't hear what he added in an undertone.
However, the girl said "Yes, sir" two or three times and left quite content.

A few days later, one afternoon when I was writing for my master, the same young woman came in, utterly terrified, and told him, half crying and half scolding, "Don Cosme, I never expected this from your politeness, nor did I think that anyone could take such advantage of an unfortunate woman. If I did what I did, it was to free my brother, as you promised me, not because I needed somebody else to tell me, 'Go rot.' I may be as poor as you see me here, but I've never gone walking the streets, because if that were the case, I'd have more than enough people who could raise me from this poverty, since you can always find a torn stocking to go with a broken leg; but curse me and curse the day I came to see you, thinking you were an upright man who could keep his word. . . . "

"Hush, woman," my master said, "you've strung together more nonsense than words. What's happened? What's wrong? What have they told you?"

"Oh, just a trifle," she said. "That my brother has been sentenced to eight years in the Morro fortress in Havana."

"What are you saying, woman?" my master asked in sudden alarm. "That can't be. It's a lie."

"The devil, it's a lie!" said the grief-stricken woman. "I've just said good-bye to him, and tomorrow he leaves. Oh, my dear brother! Who could have thought this would happen, after I've done all I could for you . . . !"

"What do you mean, tomorrow, woman? What are you talking about?"

"Yes, tomorrow, tomorrow. They cuffed him this afternoon, and he's in the list to be taken away."

"Well, don't you worry," said my master, "because all the devils will take me before I let them take your brother to prison. Get along, go home and stop worrying, because tonight your brother will be free."

This said, the girl went outside and my master went to the jail, where he found the prisoner handcuffed to another one, ready to leave on the chain gang the next day, just as his sister had said.

The notary was shaken to see this, but he didn't faint; instead, pulling one of his tricks, he unchained the condemned prisoner from his companion and, in his place, chained up a poor Indian who had landed there for drunkenness and wife-beating. That poor wretch went to serve eight years in the Morro fortress of Havana in the place of the pretty girl's thieving brother, who walked out at vespers that evening, free and unfettered, warned not to walk in Mexico during the day—though he never went outside at night, either, because, fearing that the notary's ruse would be discovered, he left the city as soon as he could, the better to keep this injustice under wraps.

If my friend Chanfaina was capable of committing an offense like this, what would stop him from drawing up a document without the proper proofs; knowingly accepting false witnesses; certifying something that he had not seen; serving as both notary and lawyer for the same party; commissioning me to take a deposition; neglecting to put his seal whenever he felt like it, or other such illegalities? He did all this with the greatest nonchalance, and he rode roughshod over every law, order, and royal decree that got in his way, whenever any thieving, selfish interest got in the way between the law and his rackets: and I say thieving, because he was such a venal man that he would commit the dirtiest tricks for just an ounce or two of gold, and sometimes for less.

Apart from this, he was extremely bloodthirsty and cruel-hearted. Any wretch who fell into his hands for a criminal trial was on his own, if he was poor, and was sure to land a prison term at least; and he was extremely boastful about this, considering himself a man of justice and integrity, bragging that because of him, a rotten member of the body politic had been amputated. In a word, he was a wicked man in every sense.

It must seem that I am being reprehensibly ungrateful for revealing the bad conduct of the man to whom I owed my freedom and, for some time, my living. However, since it is not my intention to attack his memory or grumble about his behavior, merely to use it to show how some of his fellow notaries act, and to do so at a time when the original man is no longer among the living and, moreover, did not leave any relatives who would be offended, thinking men will naturally forgive me on this account, especially when they learn that he didn't do me these favors for my sake, but rather so that he could use me for little pay; for in nearly one year that I worked for him, apart from four old pieces of clothing and one or two reales that he gave me for cigarettes, I can safely state that, like the prisoners in the fortresses, I was working for my rations and not for a wage, because even though he had offered me four reales a day, those remained nothing but an offer.

Nevertheless, I shouldn't pass over in silence the fact that I proved worthy of learning all his bad habits at his side *pro famatiori*, as the scholars say; what I mean is, I learned them well and became very diligent in the art of plotting intrigues by pen.

During the short period that I have spoken of, I learned to draw up a power of attorney, issue a document, cancel it, incriminate a prisoner or defend him, produce a brief, conclude a trial, and do everything a notary can do, though I would only do a so-so job of it all—the same way everybody else does it: that is, by routine, by formulas, and by habit or imitation; but hardly ever because I truly understood what I was doing, except when I worked for my own wicked purposes, since in that case I did know the wrong I was doing and the good that I was neglecting to do; but as for the rest, I was no more than an interloping paper-pusher, an ignorant semi-lawyer, and a depraved scribbler.

Given these laudable circumstances, my *maestro*[1] trusted me without the slightest reservation. Clearly, who better to trust than a disciple who has imbibed your spirit?

One day when he was not at home, I was passing the time by issuing a bill of sale for a certain piece of land that a lady was going to dispose of. I was just about to finish it when the licenciado Don Severo, a wise and honest hypochondriac, entered in

---

[1] [*Maestro*: the word means either teacher or, in this case, a master craftsman who serves as a teacher or instructor for an apprentice or journeyman in his trade. The usual translation of the word in this sense is *master*, but Lizardi makes a point of contrasting the ideally educational relationship between teacher and apprentice (*maestro, aprendiz*) with the hierarchical and merely functional master-servant relationship (*amo, criado*). Chanfaina was Periquillo's *amo*, since he treated the young man as his hired servant, and also his *maestro*, since he taught him a little bit of his profession. –Tr.]

search of my master Chanfaina. As soon as he sat down, he asked for the notary, and then he said to me, "What is it that you are doing?"

Not knowing his character, nor his profession, nor his intelligence, I answered that I was making a document.

"How's that?" he went on. "Are you copying it into testimony, or issuing an original?"

"Yes, sir," I said, "the latter: I'm issuing an original."

"Well, well," he said. "And what kind of document is it?"

"Sir," I replied, "it is a bill of sale for a field."

"And who is making the sale?"

"Doña Damiana Acevedo."

"Ah, yes," said the lawyer, "I know her very well! She is my in-law—she has long been betrothed to marry my cousin Don Baltasar Orihuela; to be sure, the young lady is a bit too fashionable and spendthrift. Is she really in a position to sell pieces of land that could be part of her dowry? Though in that case, I don't know how she could draw up a bill of sale. Let's see, please read it to me."

Playing the brute and not realizing with whom I was speaking, I read the document, which went exactly as follows:

In the city of Mexico, on the 20th of July, 1780,[2] before myself the notary and witnesses, Doña Damiana Acevedo, citizen of this city, states: that for herself and in the name of her heirs, successors, and children, if she someday has any, she sells forever to Don Hilario Rocha, born in the town of Carbón and a citizen of this capital, and to his family, a house situated in the Calle del Arco of the same, which she owns and possesses; which belongs to her by inheritance from her deceased father Don José María Acevedo; which is composed of four tall rooms, which are: drawing room, bedroom, guest room, and kitchen; one closet, a hayloft, and a stable; it has a frontage of fifteen feet and a depth of thirty-eight, all of which agrees with the respective clause in the testament of her above-mentioned deceased father, by which title it belongs to the seller, who declares and assures that she has not previously sold, disposed of, or pawned it, and that it is free of any tribute, lien, chaplaincy, entail, trust, bond, lease-hold, mortgage, or any other kind of encumbrance; which she bestows with all its structures, entrances, exits, uses, customs, and rights of way in form of law, in return for 4,000 pesos in valid coin, minted with the Mexican die-stamp, which she has received to her satisfaction. And from this day forth, for all time, for herself and for her heirs and successors, she abdicates, gives up, disowns, waives rights to, removes herself from, and parts with the ownership of, dominion over, title to, say in, recourse to, and any other rights that she might have over the mentioned house, which she cedes, surrenders, and conveys entirely, with all the royal, personal, useful, mixed, direct, executive, and other pertinent actions, to the above-mentioned Don Hilario Rocha, to whom she

---

[2] [The third edition has the date as 20 July, 1776; in either case, the point is that Periquillo has falsified the date, since (according to the chronology of the novel) this scene is set in the 1790s. –Tr.]

confers irrevocable ownership with free, forthright, and general administrations, and who acts as proxy in his own interest, that he may enjoy its use and without dependence on nor interference from the seller; may change, sell, use, and dispose of the house as his own possession acquired with just and legitimate title; and may take and seize, on his own authority or judicially, actual ownership and possession that belong to him by virtue of this instrument; and so that he need not take it, but rather that it be known for all time that it is his, she formalizes this bill of sale in his favor, an authorized copy of which she shall give him. She likewise declares that the just price and value of the property is the above-cited 4,000 pesos, and that it is not worth more, nor has she found anyone who would give her more for it; and if it is or should be worth more, she freely makes a pure, mere, perfect, and irrevocable donation of the excess, of the type known in law as *inter vivos*, to said Rocha and his heirs, waiving for this purpose Law I, Title XI, Book 5 of the *Recopilación*, which deals with this matter, as signed in Alcalá de Henares, as well as the law of *non numerata pecunia*, and that of the *Senatus Consultum Velleianum*, and she submits to the jurisdiction of the judges and magistrates of His Majesty, foreswearing the law of *si qua mulier*, that of *si convenerit de jurisdictione omnium judicum*, and all others whatsoever that may be found in her favor, for herself and for her heirs, taking on, in addition, the obligation that no one shall disturb him nor file suit against him in regard to the ownership, possession, or use of said house, and if he should be so disturbed or sued, or should any encumbrance appear, after the seller and her heirs and successors are summoned in accordance with law, they shall go to his defense and shall take up the suit at their expense in all venues and tribunals until judgment shall be executed and the buyer left in free usage and tranquil possession; and should such outcome not be possible, they shall give him another house equal in value, structure, place, rent, and amenities, or, in its absence, shall restitute him for the amount of money he has expended; the improvements he shall have made at the time, including practical, necessary, and voluntary ones; the greater value it may have acquired over time; and all the costs, expenses, and damages, with interest, consequent to all that has been executed solely in virtue of this document and sworn statement by the possessor or representative in whom its value shall be relegated, exonerating him of other proofs. Therefore, and in observation of all the above described, she obliges her person and goods present and future, all of which she submits to the judges and magistrates of His Majesty so that she be compelled to such observation as if by sentences passed, confirmed, and not appealed in any venue, renouncing her own jurisdiction, domicile, and residence as prescribed by law, and so she declares. And, Don Hilario Rocha, hereto present and known to me upon my sworn word, having been instructed in the contents of this instrument, its localities, and its conditions, declared: that he accepts and has accepted the purchase of said house as described above, and he obliges himself. . . .

"Enough of that," said Licenciado Severo; "it would take a tall glass to keep listening to such a tiresome instrument—not only tiresome, but ridiculous and poorly done. Do you, my little friend, have any understanding of what you have put down there? Do you know this lady? Do you understand what rights she is renouncing? And. . . . "

My master Chanfaina entered just then, and when he was informed of the questions that the licenciado was asking me, he said, "There is little reason why this boy should answer any questions you might ask him, because he is no more than a diligent little scribe. The document that you have just heard is one he made by following the blank form that I left him and the others that he has seen me draw up, and since he has a good memory, everything turns out easily for him."

We should note that, at the time, neither I nor my patron knew that this Don Severo was a licenciado; we just thought he was some poor fellow who was planning to hire us. Given this error, my master, being very ignorant and therefore very proud of himself, thought he would dumbfound his visitor by talking his usual arrogant nonsense, and so he went on: "If you have any doubts, my dear sir, you should ask me about them, and only me, and I will completely satisfy your curiosity. You must have heard who I am, for you have sought me out; but if you haven't, then let me tell you that I am Don Cosme Apolinario Casalla y Torrejalva, royal notary and receiver of this Royal Audiencia,[3] at your service."

"Yes, I know all about your skills and talents, sir," said the lawyer, "and I celebrate the good fortune that has brought me to the house of a man of your accomplishments, especially since I am always eager to learn new things, and I always endeavor to ask those who know more than I do, so that I can overcome my ignorance. In view of this, and before getting to the business that I have come for, I would like to ask you about a few minor things that I just have been hearing and that I do not understand."

"As I have said, friend," Chanfaina replied with his customary arrogance, "ask whatever you wish, and I will happily resolve your doubts."

"Well, sir," the lawyer continued, "please tell me: what do the waivers in the document mean? What is the meaning of the law *si qua mulier*? What is the law of *sive a me*? What is the significance of *si convenerit de jurisdictione omnium judicum*? What benefit from the *Senatus Consultum Velleianum* can women waive? What is the meaning of *non numerata pecunia*? What do they mean by *I renounce my own jurisdiction, domicile, and residence*? What is Law I, Title XI, Book 5 of the *Recopilación*? And finally, who can and who cannot issue bills of sale? Which laws can they waive, and which can they not? And what are the people they call instrumental witnesses, and what purpose do they serve?"

"You have asked so many questions," said my master, "that it isn't easy to give you a detailed reply, but to allay your doubts, let me tell you that the laws that are being waived are all a bunch of ancient relics that don't mean anything, and so we notaries don't worry our heads with trying to learn them, because knowing the laws is a matter for the lawyers, not for us. What happens is that, since it is the established fashion

---

[3] [The Royal Audiencia was the judicial and legislative body that governed the colonial province of Mexico. It was composed of several *oidores* (judges) and presided over by the viceroy of New Spain. –Tr.]

to put those things in bills of sale and other public documents, we notaries who are alive today put them there, and the notaries who will be living a century from now will put them there, with as much knowledge about the matter as the first notaries who ever were; but as I'm saying, it doesn't make any difference whether or not you know what this hairsplitting means. Are you with me? As for what you've asked regarding the kind of people who can issue a bill of sale, I have to say that anybody who isn't insane can do it. At any rate, I would draw up a document for anyone who paid me money for it, no matter who it might be; and if he had any sort of impediment, I'd see how I could remove it and qualify him. Are you with me? Finally: instrumental witnesses are just figureheads, or better said, assumed names; for if Juan wants to sell, and Pedro wants to buy, why should it matter if there are any witnesses to their contract or not? So you see, I and many of my companions, as well as almost all the mayors, deputy mayors, and magistrates out in the towns, draw up these instruments alone in our homes and courthouses, and when we get to the witnesses, we put down that it was Don Pascasio, Don Nicasio, and Don Epitacio, even if there aren't any such men within twenty leagues of us, and the fact remains that the bills of sale have been issued, the properties have been sold, our fees have landed in our purses, and nobody bothers to reprimand us about it even if they know all about this trifling matter. That, friend, is all there is to say about this particular point. If you have anything else to ask, please go ahead, because you will get your answer *in terminis*, pal, *in terminis*: definitively."

The licenciado rose from his chair and, half stuttering with rage and looking like a rabid dog, said to my most illustrious patron, "Well, sir, Don Cosme Casalla, or Chanfaina, or Cucumber, or whatever your name is: for your information, the person who is speaking to you is Licenciado Don Severo Justiniano, a lawyer before this same Royal Audiencia, on which you will soon find me serving; and then you will know, if you do not want to learn it now, that I am a doctor in both civil and criminal law, and that I have not been speaking with you out of mere bluster, as you have; and in this regard, I repeat that you are a man of accomplishments, though your accomplishments are not in learning, but rather in wickedness and ignorance. Savage! Who made you a notary? Who examined you? How were you able to fool the judges—perhaps by answering common questions, or ones you had studied or been warned about, or by hypocritically satisfying the tough cases they posed?

"You, and other notaries as driven by passion and malice as yourself, are to blame for the fact that the common people, who are rarely correct in their judgments, view this noble profession with dislike and even, I would say, with hatred, lumping educated and God-fearing notaries together with you swindling students of crime, safe in the knowledge that there are more of the latter than the former.

"Yes, sir: the notarial profession is honorable, noble, and decent. The law terms it *public and honest*; it prescribes that 'the man who would exercise this profession should be a free, Christian man of good repute'; it assures that 'promoting notaries is a matter reserved for the king. For in them is placed the watch and fealty of letters made in the court of the king, and in the cities, and in the towns. And they are, as it were, public witnesses in suits before the law and in the pacts made by men betwixt themselves'; and it declares that in order to be admitted to the exercise of this office, 'they should verify to the magistrates, with confirmation from the solicitor general, their domiciles, purity of blood, legitimacy, loyalty, skill, and good life and customs.'[4]

"Isn't it a pity, then, that through their fraud, stupidity, and petty thefts, a handful of rascals should besmirch a profession that is so laudable for society? At least, they have besmirched it in the opinions of the many; for the few are well aware, in the phrase of a modern author, that 'the abuse of such a modest ministry should not lower it, or any other profession in the Republic, in the estimation and appreciation that are its due.'

"The document that you have put together, or have had put together for you, is a hodgepodge of simple-minded phrases that are not worthy of criticism, and in itself it proclaims your ignorance, even if you refuse to admit it. So you are convinced that a notary has no need of knowing the laws, which is exclusively the business of lawyers? No, no, sir; notaries should also study the law, in order to carry out their profession in good conscience.[5]

"This assertion should be obvious, and if not, take a look at all the sloppiness and incompetence of the botched mess that you have concocted here. You cite and waive laws that have nothing to do with the case at hand, thereby demonstrating your ignorance, while at the same time you neglect to state the lady's age, a crucial piece of information for making this a valid legal document, for she is older than twenty-five, unmarried, and not a dependent child, and thus can freely administer her possessions and may sell them on her own account, just as any free man can; and it is consequently absurd for her to waive any law from the *Senatus Consultum Velleianum*, as that has no place here, nor does it benefit her. I will have you know that the law in question was enacted in Rome when Velleius was consul, on behalf of women, stating that they cannot take on obligations nor go bail for anyone, and in order for them to do so in certain cases, they must waive this Roman law, or rather the paternal dependencies that benefit them, in which case the contract will be valid and they will be obligated to fulfill it; but when they are qualified by law and they undertake an obligation on their own accord and in their own interest, this clause is to be excluded, because in that case, no law exempts them from the obligation they have undertaken.

"The same can be said of the other nonsensical waivers you've put here, such as *si qua mulier, sive a me*, and so on, for those are drawn up to ensure the possessions of married women, or their dowries, and thus they only benefit married women, who alone can waive these benefits, not unmarried women such as Doña Damiana Acevedo.

---

[4] The laws cited can be found in the prologue to *Febrero ilustrado*. [This work, Lizardi's source for many of his critiques of notaries, is an edition of José Febrero's six-volume work on the notarial art, *Librería de escribanos e instrucción jurídica teórico-práctica de principiantes* (Madrid, 1769–1786), as revised and reprinted by José Marcos Gutiérrez; see Spell, p. 163. –Tr.]

[5] "It is impossible for notaries to exercise their office," writes Don Marcos Gutiérrez in the cited work, "unless they have a good grasp of jurisprudence; for otherwise they are bound to commit an endless number of absurdities that will give rise to costly and interminable litigation, because of which innumerable citizens are victimized in their goods and in their rights."

"But for you to truly understand the extent of your ignorance, and that of all your fellow notaries who draw up instruments full of these Latin tags, laws, and waivers, not understanding what you are talking about but only putting them there because that is how you have seen it done in the protocols from which you took your blank forms, listen here: you say that you sold the house for 4,000 pesos, which the seller received to her satisfaction, and a bit further on, you say that she waives the law of *non numerata pecunia*. If you knew that this law speaks of uncounted money, not of money that has been counted and received, you could have avoided this mistake. Finally, when you put down any old names as the instrumental witnesses, while making the document by yourself, as you have said, if you do not explain this clause to both parties along with the laws that they are waiving, this clumsy error could annul the entire transaction; because notaries are absolutely required to inform both parties of the laws that you call *ancient relics*; but since 'notaries[6] for the most part know next to nothing about the contents of the laws that the parties in question waive, how could we imagine that they could inform anyone about something we do not believe they know? Shall we, perhaps, bring the notary to trial and examine him on the contents of these laws, so that, if he responds correctly, we should believe that he informed the parties well, and if he cannot reply in person, we should form the opposite opinion? That would be best.'

"Therefore, Señor Casalla, be diligent: be diligent, and act like an upright man, because it is sad that on account of your faults and those of others like you, the good notaries must suffer the vexations of this business. The business that I have come on calls for a notary with more abilities and better conduct than you have shown, and so I have decided not to entrust it to you. Study more, behave better, and you will never lack for food to eat with greater tranquility of spirit.

"And you, my little friend," he said to me, "study, too, if you want to follow in this career, and don't learn how to rob with the pen, for then you are no better than another bird of prey. Good-bye, gentlemen."

We never again saw or heard from the licenciado after he finished reprimanding my master, who was so shaken that he didn't know if he was in Heaven or on Earth, as he later told me.

I was reminded of my first schoolteacher after he had been similarly humiliated by the priest; but my master wasn't the sort of person to let himself be drowned in a little bit of water; rather, he was very brazen or shameless, and so he hid his discomfort behind a jaunty air, and after he had recovered somewhat, he told me, "Do you know, Periquillo, why that lawyer spewed all his claptrap? Well let me tell you, it's for no other reason than that one cat hates to be clawed by another. These little scholars are all so envious: they can't stand to see eyes in somebody else's face, and they'd like to do it all themselves—be they lawyers, judges, agents, court reporters, attorneys, notaries, or even constables and executioners—so they could swindle the litigants out of body and soul. Just look at this rascal Severillo and the lecture he hurled at us, that big hypocrite, like he's so educated, as if it were the same thing to concoct a

---

[6] Aliaga [Manuel Aliaga Bayod y Salas Guasqui], *El escribano perfecto, Espejo de escribanos* [Tarragona, 1788–1799], volume 2, chapter 1, clause 13, folio 62.

brief by coining forty texts as to draw up a public document. Right there, you can tell the difference between a lawyer's work and a notary's: you can toss away a lawyer's brief, if it comes to that, as a useless piece of paper, while an instrument that we notaries authorize is kept and made part of the permanent record. That little scholar is scandalized by things that he doesn't understand, but it would never shock him to leave a litigant shirtless. Yes, I know him too well: and he must think I'm a pretty baby, trying to feed me atole with his finger! And not just him, or the judges in their robes. You know why I took the tack of keeping quiet? It's because he's so nosy; and besides, I have my suspicions that he's an adviser to His Excellency. He's up for a judgeship on the Audiencia, and I don't want to expose myself to any trouble, because rogues like him don't leave a book unopened or a shelf untouched when it's a matter of taking revenge. If it hadn't been for that, I would have shown him how I deal with spoiled brats. No matter, let him come back to my house some other day and try busting my head; maybe I won't be able to restrain myself, and then he'll abandon it like a rat does a sinking ship."

After my master finished letting off steam with me, he opened his little bookcase, refreshed himself with a tall glass of Castile's finest, and went out to play a few hands of cards while waiting for dinnertime.

Although the licenciado's arguments had made a great impression on me, Chanfaina's lies and sarcasm rather went to my head. The upshot was that I decided not to part company with him until I had become a middling notary; but we can't always do everything we plan.

At two in the afternoon, my maestro came home, happy because he hadn't lost at gambling; I set the table; he ate and went to sleep the siesta. I went to do the same in the kitchen, where I was well served by Nana Clara, who was the cook. Afterward I went out to the street corner to pass the time with the shopkeeper while I was waiting for my patron to wake up. Once he awoke, he left my writing tasks for me, as always, and left for the street, returning home at seven at night with a new guest, a woman who was going to stay with us.

I recognized her as soon as I saw her. Her name was Luisa, and she was the sister of the thief that my master had freed from the chain gang more easily than Don Quixote had freed Ginés de Pasamonte.[7] As I have mentioned, the girl was far from ugly, and my master found her very good-looking. If only I hadn't thought the same!

As they were walking in, my master told her, "Go ahead, child, change out of your street clothes[8] and go with Nana Clara so she can inform you what you have to do."

She went away humbly, and when we were alone, Chanfaina told me, "Periquillo, you're going to have to give me your thanks for this new servant I've brought home; she's going to be the chambermaid, so you'll be spared some of your chores, since

---

[7] [In *Don Quixote*, part I, chapter XXII. –Tr.]

[8] [The verb used here, *desnúdate*, literally means "take off your clothes" or "get naked," to which the editor of the fourth edition added this note: "In that era only the poorest people lacked cleaner or more decent clothes for going outside, and so *take off one's clothes* meant to take off the street clothes while keeping on the house clothes." –Tr.]

you won't have to sweep the floors anymore, or make the bed, or wait at table, or clean the candlesticks, or do any of your other obligations except for running errands. The only thing I'm asking you to do is to keep a close eye on her and let me know if she sticks her head out the balcony window too often, or if she leaves the house, or if anyone comes to see here when I'm not home. In short, keep an eye on her and tell me everything you notice. After all, since she's my servant and she's under my care, I'll have to answer to God for her, and I'm rather conscientious and would rather not damn myself through someone else's sins. Understand?"

"Yes, sir," I answered, laughing to myself at his stupidity in thinking me capable of swallowing his hypocrisy.

For you see, the big numbskull took me to be a good boy, or an idiot. Since I had played the role of the upright man so vividly during the nearly two months I had lived with him, neither going out for strolls even when he gave me permission, nor making the slightest slip with the old cook, my friend Chanfaina thought I was very ingenuous, or who knows what, and he entrusted his Luisa to me, which was like entrusting a spongecake to a hungry dog. And so it happened.

That night we had supper and I went to bed without getting myself mixed up in any further designs. The next day, the little chambermaid gave us our chocolate; made the beds, swept, polished the copperware (for there was no silverware), and got the house sparkling clean, as women like to say.

For six or eight days, la Luisa played the servant's role, waiting at table and treating Chanfaina as her master in front of me and the old woman; but he couldn't put up with the dissimulation for long. After that stretch of time had passed, he started letting her eat out of his plate, though she was still standing; then he had her sit down a few times; and finally, he threw off all pretense and sat her at his side like an aristocratic lord.

The three of us ate dinner and supper together in peace and good company. The girl was pretty, cheerful, vivacious, and witty; I was young, not too bad-looking, and I could play the mandolin and sing fairly on key; my master, for his part, was nearly an old man, and had none of my talents. Leaving aside his rackets with the pen, he was very foolish in everything else; he spoke with a nasal twang, and splattered spittle all over whoever was listening to him, because the French disease and the mercury treatment had left him without teeth or uvula; he was hardly generous; and on top of all these fine qualities, he had the laudable one of being extremely jealous.

You can imagine that it wouldn't take me much trouble to conquer Luisa, having such a contemptible rival. And that is what indeed happened. Before long we plotted together and came to an agreement, amicably exchanging our mutual affection. My poor master was delighted with his chambermaid and completely satisfied with his scribe, who didn't dare raise his eyes to look at her in font of his master.

But she was a rogue and a joker, and she took advantage of my master's simplicity, putting me in some terrible spots in his presence; sometimes she made me laugh and at other times she made me feel uncomfortable with her vulgar jokes.

On a few occasions, she would say to me, "Señor Pedrito, you are so gloomy! You seem like a novice or a friar who just got ordained; you don't even lift your eyes to look at me. Am I so ugly that I scare you? What a bore! God save me from you. You must be the biggest crook around. That's right, Don Cosme, God save our beehives from these fellows who don't eat any honey."

Other times she would ask me if I was in love with some girl, or if I was planning to get married, and 30,000 other such stupidities, each one of which threatened to expose our wicked relations; but since my good maestro was dull-witted, that was the last thing he was thinking about; instead he would ask me, in regard to her, whether I had noticed any signs of restlessness, and I would answer, "No, sir, nor would I allow it, since I see your interests as my own, especially when it comes to this."

This completely satisfied the poor man that we were both faithful. But since there is nothing hidden that does not become revealed, in the end he discovered our wicked carryings-on in a way that could have cost me plenty.

One morning Luisa was on the balcony, and I was writing in the drawing room. I got a craving for a cigarette and went to light up in the kitchen. Unfortunately, the hearth was being stoked by a pretty-looking girl named Lorenza, Nana Clara's niece, who came to visit her every now and then with an eye to the perks that the good old woman gave her; the cook, however, wasn't home at the time, having gone to the plaza to buy onions and other necessities for cooking. I thus found myself alone with the girl, and since she had a merry heart, we began to have some fun together. At the same time, Luisa began to miss me; she went looking for me and, finding me with someone else, became furiously jealous and reprimanded me in the harshest terms, saying, "Very well, then, Señor Perico. So this is how you spend your time, romping around with this tremendous street girl. . . . "

"Street girl? No," Lorenza said, bursting with rage, "the street girl is her, and her mother, and her whole race."

And without any further ceremony, they had at it, each of them grabbing the other's braids, getting in some good scratches, and saying some lovely things; and making such a clamor and commotion about it that everybody within two leagues of the house could have heard the fight and what it was about. I was doing everything in my power to separate them, but it was impossible, given how determined they were not to let go.

At this time, Nana Clara came in, and seeing her niece covered in blood, she did not stop to find out what had happened, but threw down the basket of vegetables and attacked poor Luisa, who was not exactly in one piece, telling her, "You're not getting away with this, you pig, you scrounger, you upstart! Not with my niece, you don't. Now you'll see who's who." And as she made these fervent prayers she was raining down blows with the ladle.

Given those odds, I couldn't allow the pair to maim my poor Luisa, so, seeing that my pleas to leave her alone were getting nowhere, I resorted to force and started beating the old woman on the back of the neck.

That kitchen was in such an uproar that I can't imagine Caesar's battle in Pharsalia was any more terrible. Since we weren't standing still in one place, but falling down and picking up and moving on all over, and the kitchen was narrow, in a second all the pots were broken, the food was spilled, the fire was out, and the ashes whitened our hair and dirtied our faces.

It was all shamelessness, shouting, beatings, and disorder. Not one of the women in the fight had escaped a bloodletting according to El Aguilucho's method, and they were disheveled and beaten to a pulp besides, nor had I kept clean in this performance. The battlefield, or kitchen, was scattered with plunder. In one corner there was a clay pot smashed to bits, in another the water tank, here a frying pan, there a bunch of onions, over there the grinding stone, and everywhere the vestiges of our clothing. The dog added his barking to our shouts, and the cat, its hair all on end, didn't dare come down from the chimney.

In the middle of this performance arrived Chanfaina, dressed in his proper suit, and seeing his Luisa bled, beaten, bathed in blood, and surrounded by the cook and her niece, he didn't wait for explanations, but grabbed a cudgel and had at the pair of them, and with such passion and rage that a few blows were enough to end the fight, leaving the unhappy chambermaid, who had certainly received the worst of it.

When we had all come to our senses, not so much out of respect for our master as for fear of his cudgel, the notary began to take down our testimony on the cause or reason for such an outrageous brawl. Old Nana Clara said nothing, because she really didn't know anything about it; Luisa also said nothing, because it wasn't in her interest; I said even less, because I was the main actor in that scene; but the damnable Lorenza, being the best informed and most innocent, immediately explained the contents of our proceedings to my master, telling him that it had been nothing other than an assault and a provocation by that jealous street girl who was there in his house, who might be my girlfriend, since it was because of her jealousy of me and her that she had started this scandal. . . .

That's as far as I listened to Lorenza, because as soon as I realized that she was revealing more than was necessary about our ignoble relationship, and that my master was staring at me with wildly furious eyes, I felt afraid like a man and ran down the stairs like a jackrabbit, and in so doing, I instantly confirmed everything Lorenza had said, thoroughly inflaming my patron, who didn't want to let me leave his house without a proper farewell, and so ran downstairs after me like a thunderbolt, so precipitously that he didn't notice he was running out without hat or cape and with his ruffled collar hanging to one side.

Chanfaina chased me for some two blocks, incessantly shouting, "Stop, villain! Stop, rogue!" But I played deaf and didn't stop until I had lost sight of him and found myself far away and safe from the cudgel.

This was the honorable and splendid way in which I left the house of the notary: worse than I had entered, and without learning the slightest lesson, for in each of these stories, I started my series of adventures anew, as you will see in the next chapter.

CHAPTER 25

In which Periquillo recounts the reception that a barber gave him; the reason why he left his house; about finding a job in an apothecary shop and leaving it; and other curious adventures

It's incredible how much ground can be covered by a coward on the run. When the scene I have just described took place, it was noon on the dot; my master lived on Calle de las Ratas, but I ran with such a will that by a quarter past twelve I was resting in the Alameda.[1] True, I arrived shaken with fright and covered with sweat; but I thought little of that, or of having lost my hat and broken my head, or of being beat to a pulp and starving to death, considering that I was safe from Chanfaina, whose cudgel I feared less than his backbiting pen, for if he had me in his grasp he would no doubt beat me, plot some slander against me, and have me sent to break coral stones in San Juan de Ulúa.

And so I took this evil turn to be a good thing, or rather, I sanely decided to choose the lesser of two evils; but that's fine for the moment of decision, because once it is past, we recognize any evil for what it is, and then it bitterly vexes us.

Which is what happened to me when, sitting on the bank of a ditch, resting my left elbow on my knee, holding my head with the same, and using my right hand to scratch in the earth with a small stick, I contemplated my sad situation. "What will I do now?" I asked myself. "The state I'm in now is just too wretched. Alone, practically naked, my head broken, starving, no shelter, no idea what to do, and on top of it all, with an enemy as powerful as Chanfaina, who'll never rest until he finds me so he can take revenge for my infidelity and Luisa's. Where will I go? Where can I spend the night? Who would pity me, much less give me shelter, when my appearance is so suspicious? Staying here would never do, because the guards would kick me out of the Alameda; walking the streets all night is too daring, because I'd be exposing myself to being caught by a night patrol and being delivered quicker than ever into Chanfaina's hands; finding a place to sleep in some secluded cemetery, like the one of San Cosme,[2] would be the safest thing . . . but aren't dead people and ghosts a matter for respect and fear? It's out of the question. So what will I do, and where will I eat tonight?"

I was absorbed in these melancholy thoughts, unable to find the thread that would lead me forth from this bewildering labyrinth, when God, who never abandons even those who offend Him, made a venerable old man pass by close to me, who, together with a boy, was busy catching leeches in the ditch with a *chiquihuite*;[3] and as they went about their business, they greeted me and I replied politely.

---

[1] [Calle de las Ratas, "Street of the Rats," an actual street in colonial Mexico City, is today the block of Bolívar between Mesones and República de El Salvador, a mile southeast of the Alameda; for this and the next note, see Spell, p. 184. –Tr.]

[2] [San Cosme: this Dieguino monastery, church, and cemetery was a mile west of the Alameda and, at the time, lay on the western outskirts of the city. –Tr.]

[3] [*Chiquihuite* (from Nahuatl, *chiquihuitl*): a basket or box made from woven sticks, made by Indian artisans in central Mexico. –Tr.]

When the old man heard my voice, he stared at me attentively, and after pausing for a moment, he jumped out of the ditch, threw his arms around my neck with great expressiveness, and said, "My precious Pedrito! Can I really be seeing you again? What is all this? What are these clothes, what's all this blood? How is your mother? Where are you living?"

To all these questions I said not a word, surprised to find a man I didn't know calling to me by name and speaking with unexpected familiarity; but when he realized the cause of my embarrassment, he said, "What, don't you know me?"

"No, sir, to tell the truth," I answered, "though I am at your service."

"Well, I certainly do know you, and I knew your parents and owed them a thousand favors. My name is Agustín Rapamentas;[4] I shaved the late gentleman Don Manuel Sarmiento, your dear father, for many years, yes, many years, on top of which I knew you when you were just this high, son, just this high; I could almost say I saw when you were born; and don't try to deny it; I loved you very much, and I used to play with you when your father would go to get a trim."

"Well, sir, Don Agustín," I said, "now I'm starting to remember bits and pieces, and you are right, it's just as you said."

"Well, so, what are you doing here, son, and in this state?" he asked me.

"Ay, sir!" I replied, wailing like a widow. "I have the worst kind of luck: my mother died two years ago; my father's creditors threw me out into the street and seized everything in the house; I've kept going by serving one master after another; and today, because the cook didn't heat the soup enough and I served it cold to my master at table, he threw me and the soup out at the same time, and the bowl broke my head; but that wasn't enough to stop his rage, so he grabbed the knife and chased after me, and if I hadn't taken a shortcut, I wouldn't be here to tell you about my misfortunes."

"Imagine the villainy!" said the ingenuous barber. "And who was your cruel and vengeful master?"

"Who else, sir?" I said. "He was Marshall de Birón."[5]

"How's that? What are you talking about?" said the hair trimmer. "That can't be; there's no such person in the world. It must be somebody else."

"Oh, yes, sir, that's true!" I said. "I was confused; his name was Count . . . Count. . . . What a memory, dear God! It was Count . . . Saldaña."[6]

"That's even worse," said Don Agustín. "What, have you lost your mind? What are you talking about, son? Can't you see that the titles you're mentioning are those of comedies?"

"That's true, sir. I've forgotten my master's title, because it's been two days since I left his house; but for the case at hand, it hardly matters if I don't remember his title,

---

[4] [Rapamentas: roughly, "Shavement," a Dickensian name that hints that this character is a barber. Barbers at the time also performed bloodletting (thus the leeches), surgery, and dentistry. –Tr.]

[5] [*El mariscal de Birón* (or *Virón*): Charles, Duke of Byron, Marshall of France, was the subject of several works, including a "famous comedy" by Juan Pérez de Montalbán and a burlesque by Juan Maldonado. –Tr.]

[6] [*El conde de Saldaña*: a heroic comedy by Álvaro Cubillo de Aragón. –Tr.]

or give him the title of a comedy, because if we look at it in all seriousness, what title in the world isn't a comedy? Marshall de Birón, the Count of Saldaña, the Baron of Trenk, and a thousand others were real titles of nobles; they played their role, they died, and their names stayed behind to serve as titles of comedies. The same thing will happen with the Count of Campo Azul, the Marquis of Casa Nueva, the Duke of Ricabella, and every other titled noble who lives among us today: tomorrow they'll die, and *Laus Deo* to them; their names and their titles will remain here to remind us, on rare occasions, that they ever walked among the living, just as Marshall de Birón and the great Count of Saldaña once did. Therefore it makes no difference, by these lights, whether I remember or forget the title of the master who beat me. What I'll never forget is his damnable action, for actions are what stick in men's memories—either to inveigh against them and regret them, or to laud them and praise them; but not titles and honorifics, which die with time and mingle with the dust of the grave."

The guileless barber listened to me in astonishment, taking me for a wise and virtuous man. Such was my wickedness at times, and at times, my ignorance. Today I myself could not define my character in those times, nor do I think anyone could have comprehended it; because on some occasions I said what I truly felt, and on others I did the opposite of what I said; sometimes I played the hypocrite, and other times I spoke out of the convictions of my conscience; but the worst was that when I feigned virtue, I did it knowingly, and when I spoke out of love for virtue I made a thousand inner resolutions to mend my ways, but I never had the determination to see them through.

On this occasion, I was speaking from what I felt in my heart, but I didn't take advantage of these truths; my speech produced a good temporary effect, however: namely, that the barber pitied me and took me to his home and family, which consisted of a good old woman named Tía Casilda and the young apprentice, and there he received me with the sweetest extreme of hospitality.

I had a better supper that night than I could ever have expected, and the next day the maestro told me, "Son, though you're pretty old to be an apprentice"—he was right; I was nineteen or twenty years old—"you can learn my trade if you'd like; it may not be one of the most preferred trades, but at least it feeds you; so work hard, and I'll give you a house and bite to eat, which is all I can do."

I said I would, because that seemed like the best thing for me at the time; and as a result, he obligingly put me to work cleaning the towels, holding the shaving bowl, and doing some of the things I saw the apprentice do.

On one occasion when the barber wasn't at home, to see if I was making any progress, I caught a dog, the apprentice helping me in this task; we tied its front and back paws and its muzzle, sat it down and tied it to the chair, laid out a rag for cleaning the razors, and I started the shaving operation. The miserable dog whimpered to high heaven.[7] What nicks and scratches it got from time to time!

At last the operation ended, and the poor animal was left fit to have its portrait painted; as soon as it found itself free, it ran outside like a soul being carried off by

---

[7] It could not bark, so it only whimpered.

the demons, while I, pleased with this first attempt, decided to try again on a poor Indian who came in to get a trim for half a real. I jauntily placed the towels on him, made the apprentice bring in the shaving bowl with hot water, sharpened the razors, and walloped him with so many scrapes and slashes that the wretched fellow, unable to take my heavy hand, got up, saying, "*Amocuale, quistiano, amocuale*," which in Spanish means, "I don't like the way you do it, sir, I don't like it."[8]

The upshot of it was, he gave me half a real, and also went away half-shaved.

Not yet content with these poor efforts, I dared to pull a molar from an old woman with a raging toothache, who entered the shop in search of my maestro; but since I was determined to do it, I forced her to sit down and allow the apprentice to hold her head.

He did his job very well; the worried old woman opened her nearly toothless mouth after showing me which molar hurt; I picked up the dental scraper and cheerfully began cutting away pieces of gum.

The miserable woman, seeing herself being sliced up like dried beef, and the porcelain bowl full of blood in front of her, said to me, "Young maestro, for the sake of God, when are you going to finish scraping?"

"Don't you worry, ma'am," I told her; "have a little patience, there's just a little left on your jaw."

So it went until I had cut enough flesh off of her to feed the house cat; I grasped the bone tightly with the proper tool, and with a strong and badly aimed jerk, I broke her molar and did terrible damage to her jaw.

"Ay, Jesus!" the old woman sorrowfully exclaimed. "You pulled out my whole jawbone, maestro-demon!"

"Please don't talk, ma'am," I said, "because you'll let in air and ruin your mandible."

"The devil take you and your *mallibles*!" said the poor woman. "Ay, Jesus! Ay, ay, ay!"

"That's enough, ma'am," I said; "please open your mouth so that we can finish taking out the root. Can't you see that your molar is impacted?"[9]

"I'd like to see you impacted into Inferno, you clumsy, worthless, blasted fool," said the poor woman.

Paying no attention to her insults, I said, "Come along, Nana, sit back down and open your mouth; let's finish taking out that darned tooth, and you'll see that one pain will get rid of many others. Come along, please—even if you don't pay me for it."

"Get along yourself, and curse you," the elderly lady said, "and go pull your big drunk mother's tooth, or all her teeth, if she's got any. Those nasty tooth scrapers aren't to blame, it's the fault of whoever put them in your hands."

---

[8] [*Amocualli, quistián*: "Not good, Christian," the latter word being the common term of address for Spaniards in colonial Nahuatl. –Tr.]

[9] [Impacted: Lizardi has *muela matriculada*, "matriculated molar." It is hard to say whether this is a mistake (and if so, whether Periquillo's or Lizardi's own) or an antiquated or regional dental term. In any case, the sense is clear. –Tr.]

Carrying on with this eulogy, she went outside without ever wanting to look back at her place of sacrifice.

I felt a little sorry for her pain, and the boy never stopped reprimanding me for my thoughtless determination, because he said over and over, "Poor lady! She must feel such pain! And the worst thing, if she tells our maestro, what'll he say?"

"Let him say what he will," I replied. "I'm doing it to help him earn his bread; besides, this is how you learn, by trying and practicing."

I told the *maestra*[10] that it had just been the old woman's silliness, that she had a very impacted molar and that I couldn't pull it out with the first yank, something that could happen to the best of us.

That was enough to satisfy everyone, and I continued doing my monkey tricks and getting paid for them, either in money or in curse words.

I stayed in Don Agustín's house for four and a half months, and that was a long time, considering the flightiness of my disposition. It is true that my fear of Chanfaina played a role in this delay, along with my not finding any other shelter—for in that house I ate, drank, and was treated with respect on my maestro's part. Thus, I didn't do any errands, or anything useful except for watching over the barbershop and doing my mischief whenever the opportunity arose; because I was an apprentice of honor, and so pampered and lazy that, though shirtless, I had at least one person who envied my good fortune. That was Andrés, the apprentice, who told me one day when the two of us were talking with each other, while waiting for a customer to come by and try out for martyr, "Sir, if only a body could be like you!"

"Why, Andrés?" I asked.

"Because here you are, a big man already, free to do what you will and nobody to boss you around; not like me, being as I have so many folks to nag me, and I don't know what it is to have half a real in my pocket."

"But as soon as you learn the trade," I said, "you'll have money and be free to do what you will."

"Now, isn't that green of you!" said Andrés. "I've been here two years apprenticing and I don't know a thing."

"What do you mean, not a thing, man?" I asked, amazed.

"Just that, nothing," he answered. "Now that you're here in the house, I've learned a little."

"And what have you learned?" I asked.

"I've learned," the rascal replied, "how to shave dogs, skin Indians, and break old ladies' jaws, which is nothing to sneeze at. May God repay you for teaching me."

"But, what, hasn't your maestro taught you anything in two years?"

"What could he a taught me!" said Andrés. "I spend the whole day doing errands here and in Doña Tulita's house, the maestro's daughter. And there it's worse, because they make me hold the baby, wash the diapers, go to the hairdresser, wash every last dish, and put up with every little nuisance they put in my way, and what with all that, how'm I gonna learn anything about the trade? About all I've learned is how to carry the shaving bowl and the water-heater when my master takes me

---

[10] [That is, the master barber's wife. –Tr.]

with him—I mean my maestro, sorry, my mistake. Lemme tell you: Don Plácido, the tinsmith that lives next door to my grandma, well now, he's a peachy maestro, because, apart from him not being too much of a scold, and him not beating his apprentices, he teaches them real sweet, and he gives them their fair share of coins whenever they do something straight; but as for running errands, never, forget it! On top of, he hardly ever sends them to get a handful of cigarettes, so how much less is he gonna have them go get lard or chilies or pulque or charcoal or anything, like they do here. So that way, the boys learn the trade fast as fast."

"You speak badly," I said, "but what you say is good. Maestros should not be boys' masters, but rather their instructors; nor should the boys be their servants or *pilhuanejos*, but legitimate apprentices; even though, in exchange for the instruction and the food the maestros give the boys, they can send them on errands and put them to service during the hours when they aren't working at their trade, and in things that are proportionate to each boy's strength, education, and origins. That is what I heard my late father, may he rest in peace, say on many occasions. But tell me: what, are you here on a written contract?"

"Yes, sir," Andrés replied, "and I've been an apprentice for two years now, and we're finishing up the third, and the maestro doesn't look to be putting himself out finding a way to teach me anything."

"But then," I said, "if the contract is for four years, how can you learn the trade in the last year, if it goes by like the last three have for you?"

"Just what I say," said Andrés. "With me, it'll be the same thing as what happened to my brother Policarpio with his maestro, Marianito the tailor."

"And what happened to him?"

"What happened? That he spent the first three years of being an apprentice running errands like me here, and in the fourth year, he tells it, the maestro wanted to teach him the whole trade all at once, and my brother couldn't learn it, and the maestro got so angry he cussed out my poor brother, and then he up and buggy-whipped him till the poor kid got tired of it and run off, and from that day to this, we ain't heard from him, and he was such a good person, poor kid, but how could he a turned into a tailor in one year, and all the while running errands, sir, and with all the holidays there are in a year? So I'm thinking the maestro here looks like to do the same with me."[11]

---

[11] We note with great sorrow that the laudable practice of accepting apprentices with a written contract is currently rarely used; but when it was the common usage, apprentices were received under the following conditions and obligations: the teacher obligated himself to teach the apprentice his trade, without concealing anything, within a stated amount of time, normally four years—and to this end, he could punish the apprentice with prudence and moderation and without wounding him or causing serious injury; to give him food, clean clothes, and a bed; if the apprentice did not learn the skill in the stated amount of time, to pay another teacher in the same trade to teach him; and if the apprentice did not wish to do the latter, to keep him in his house as a journeyman, paying him a salary as such every day. The father, relative, or so forth, of the apprentice who signed the contract obligated himself to have the apprentice serve the stated amount of time not only in matters concerning the trade, but in everything he could do to serve his teacher, so long as it was decent and did not take time away from learning the craft. These

"But why didn't you apprentice to be a tailor?" I asked Andrés.

And he answered, "Ay, sir! A tailor? Tailors get sick in the lungs."

"Or a tinsmith?"

"No, sir; don't you know, you can cut yourself on the tin and burn yourself with the tools."

"Well, why not a carpenter?"

"Ay, no! Because they all get hurt in their chests."

"Or a wheelwright, or a blacksmith?"

"God forbid—they look like devils when they're next to the forge, banging on the iron!"

"Well, my precious boy: Pedro Sarmiento, my dearest brother," I said to Andrés, standing up from my chair. "You're my brother, *tatita*,[12] yes, my brother; we're like twins, like *cuates*;[13] give me a hug. From this day on, I'll love you more than ever, because in you I can see the reflection of my own way of thinking; but so much the same, that it's hard to tell which is the prototype, or if you and I are simply identical."

"Why so many hugs, Pedrito, sir?" Andrés asked, quite flustered. "Why are you telling me so many things I don't understand?"

"Brother Andrés," I replied, "because you think the same way I do, and you're as lazy as my own mother's son. You don't find the trades to your liking because of all the hardships they bring, nor do you like to serve, because your masters scold you; but you do like to eat, drink, stroll around, and have money with little or no work. Well, *tatita*, the same thing's true of me; so, as the saying goes, God raises them and they find each other.[14] So tell me if I don't have plenty of reason to like you."

"What you're saying," Andrés rejoined, "is that you're lazy, and so am I."

"You guessed it, boy," I answered, "you guessed it. Don't you see how everything about you makes me like you and recognize you as my brother?"

"Well, if that's all it takes," said Andresillo, "you must have lots of brothers in the world, because there are lots of lazy people who have the same tastes as us; but let me tell you that what gets me isn't the work, it's two things: first, that they don't teach me, and second, the bad temper that the maestro's darned old lady has; 'cause if it wasn't for that, I'd be happy here in this house, because you couldn't ask for a better maestro."

"That's the way it is," I said. "The old lady's a real devil, and her temper is just the opposite of Don Agustín's, because he is prudent, generous, and considerate, and the darned old lady is foolish, grouchy, and mean as Judas. But what can you expect?

---

and other equally just conditions can be seen in *El Febrero ilustrado* by Don Marcos Gutiérrez, part 1, volume 2, chapter 26.

[12] *Tatita*, diminutive of *tata*, which, among the common people, is used instead of *father*, just as *nana* is used for *mother*; among decent folk, it would be said: *Papá, mamá.* –E. [The custom of calling a child "papito" or "tatita" is common in Latin America. –Tr.]

[13] [*Cuate*: from Nahuatl *coatl*, twin; the word is commonly used in Mexico in the extended meaning of "close friend, buddy." –Tr.]

[14] [Another way of saying "birds of a feather flock together." –Tr.]

What good could she be, with her face that looks like a rumpled sheet and her mouth like an old shoe?"

We should note that theirs was a small, one-room house with another tiny room on the second floor—what they call a "cup and saucer" house,[15] and we hadn't noticed that the *maestra* had been listening to us; indeed, had listened to our entire conversation until the point when I began to praise her in the terms just mentioned, when, justly irritated at me, she silently picked up a pot of water that she had boiling on the hearth and threw it straight at my head, saying, "Out, then! Wicked, ungrateful—out of my house, because I don't want uninvited guests hanging around here and speaking badly of me!"

I don't know if she said anything else, because I had gone deaf and blind with pain and rage. Andrés, fearing a worse bath, and learning his lesson from my mistake, fled outside. I, raving and hairless, climbed up the rickety little wooden staircase with the intention of yanking the old woman's braids, come what may, and then leaving the house like Andrés; but the damnable woman was manly and decisive, and so as soon as she saw me upstairs, she picked the knife up from the hearth and boldly attacked me, mumbling at me in her rage, "Oh, you impudent villain! Now I'll teach you. . . . "

I couldn't hear what she expected to teach me, nor did I feel like staying around to learn the lesson; instead, I swiftly turned my haunches, but with such bad luck that I tripped over a puppy and came down the stairs somewhat faster than I had climbed up, and in the strangest fashion, because I went head-first, bruising all my ribs.

The old woman had turned red-hot as a chili against me. She didn't pity me or slow down because of my misfortune, but ran downstairs after me fast as lightning, knife in hand, and so resolute that to this day I am sure that if she had caught me, she would have killed me without a doubt; but God was pleased to give me the strength to run, and in four strides I was four blocks away from her fury. For I certainly had wings on my feet, whenever any danger threatened and there was room for me to escape.

In its bad timing, this was like my departure from Chanfaina's house; but in every other aspect it was worse, because this time I left in a hurry, without a hat, soaking wet, and singed hairless.

Thus I found myself, at eleven in the morning, on the avenue of La Tlaxpana.[16] I stood in the sun, waiting while it dried out my poor clothes, which were going from bad to worse day by day, since I had no change of clothing.

At three in the afternoon they were completely dry, dry as a bone, and I was in bad shape because hunger was assailing me with full force; a few blisters had come

---

[15] *Accesoria de taza y plato*: The origin of this phrase is that, when very poor people who lived in one-story *accesorias* served a little water, they would do so in a common clay pitcher; whereas those who were a bit better off, and who therefore lived in these two-story *accesorias*, served water in a Puebla porcelain cup on a saucer, because the high price of glasses in that distant era put them beyond the reach of everyone but the very wealthy. –E.

[16] [Today the first blocks of the Calzada México–Tacuba, just west of San Cosme; at the time, this was west of the city proper. –Tr.]

up on me because of the old woman's mischief; my shoes, which time had so mis-treated that they stayed on my feet only for the sake of politeness, had abandoned me during my escape; seeing the diabolical figure that I painted without them, since my socks were now uncovered in all their filth and mended tatters, I took them off, and having nowhere to stash them, I threw them away and was left bare of foot and leg; and to top off my misfortune, I was pressed by fear, pondering where I might sleep the night, not daring to decide between remaining in the countryside or returning to the city, as I saw insuperable obstacles on every side. In the countryside I feared hunger, the inclement weather, and the gloom of night; in the city I feared jail and a bad encounter with Chanfaina or the maestro barber; but in the end, at vespers, the fear of where I was won out, and I returned to the city.

By eight at night I was in the Portal de las Flores,[17] starving to death, and all the hungrier because of the exercise I had done with so much walking. I had nothing of any value on me, other than a little silver medallion that I had bought for five reales when I was in the barbershop; it was hard work for me to sell it at that time of night; but at last I found someone who would give me two and a half for it, one real of which I spent on supper, and half a real on cigarettes.

With my stomach bolstered, all that was left was to decide where to spend the night. I walked down street after street, not knowing where to take shelter, until I was passing by the Mesón del Ángel, where I heard billiard balls clacking, and recall-ing Juan Largo's *arrastraderito*, I said to myself: No two ways about it, I've got one thin real left in my pocket for the operator; I'll spend the night here. Said and done: I ducked into the pool hall.

Everybody stared hard at me, not because I looked so ragged, since others there were in worse shape than I was, but because I was so ridiculous, for I was completely barefoot; I was devoid of any underwear; my trousers were black, sewn together from two pairs, full of holes and patches; my shirt was not only torn, but nearly black from filth; my jacket was made from torn calico, with huge, brightly colored flowers; my hat had stayed at the house; and on top of all this elegance, my face was rather extravagant, for it was covered with blisters and my eyes were half-hidden behind the welts that the boiling water had raised on me.

It wasn't surprising that everyone should notice such an odd figure; however, I didn't care a whit about their stares, and would have put up with a taunt or two in exchange for getting off the streets.

The clocks struck nine; they all finished playing and started to leave, except for myself; I immediately began putting out the candles, which did not displease the pool hall operator, who said, "Little friend, God bless you; but it's late and I'm about to close, so you should be going."

"Sir," I said, "I have nowhere to stay. Please do me the favor of letting me spend the night here on a bench; I'll give you the real that I have, and I'd give you more if I had more."

---

[17] [A building where flowers were sold, on the southeast corner of the Zócalo; the building was demolished in 1934 to make room for an expansion of the municipal office building. –Tr.]

As we have said, in every part of the world, in every business and occupation, we can find good and bad men, so it's no news that here in a pool hall, this fellow who worked as a pool-hall operator might be a sensitive and upright man. And so I found him to be, for he told me, "Please keep your real, friend, and you're welcome to stay. Have you had supper?"

"Yes, sir," I replied.

"Well, so have I. Let's get to bed."

He took out a serape and lent it to me, and while we were undressing, he tried to inform himself of who I was and the reason why I had gone there in such a shabby state. In a jiffy I told him a thousand pitiful stories, along with three thousand lies, and so he felt sorry for me and promised that he would speak with an apothecary friend who needed a serving lad, to see if he could find a place for me in his house. I accepted the favor and thanked him for it, and we fell asleep.

The next morning, despite my laziness, I woke up before the operator, swept the floor, dusted, and did everything I could to win him over. He was pleased with this, and he told me, "I'm going to go see the apothecary; but what are we going to do about a hat for you? You look very suspicious in that get-up."

"I don't know what I'm going to do," I said, "because I only have one real, and I'm not likely to find a hat for so little; but while you do me the favor of seeing that gentleman, the apothecary, I'll go out and come back."

This said, I went out, had breakfast, ducked into a covered entrance and took off my jacket, and traded it in the flea market for the first hat they showed me, though it bothered me that I had tricked its owner. The truth was that the hat was little more than a soaked tortilla, so if I thought I had gotten the better of the deal, how bad must the jacket have been? Yet at the moment we made the trade, I recalled that old verse:

> In Segovia, Montalvo got the knot tied
> Though he was limping, one-eyed, and bald:
> Yet Montalvo had been gulled,
> So how ugly was the bride?

Delighted with my hat and to see myself disguised in my own rags, the son of Don Pedro Sarmiento converted into a hired lad, I set off to find my guardian, the pool-hall operator, who told me that everything was set; but that my shirt looked like an old horse blanket; that I should go wash it in the drainage ditch, and that at noon he would take me to my new job; because poverty was one thing, but dirtiness was something else; that one roused pity, but the other led to scorn and loathing; and finally, that I should remember the saying that goes, *as I see you, I'll judge you.*

I didn't think the advice was bad, so I immediately put it into practice. I bought a quarter-real worth of soap, and a quarter-real worth of tortillas and chili, which I ate for lunch in order to have the strength for doing laundry; I went to El Pipis,[18] stripped off my shirt, and washed it.

---

[18] A bend in the city's main drainage ditch, near a bridge in the San Pablo neighborhood, where the very poor go to wash their clothes for free. –E.

It dried in no time, because it was so thin and the sun was shining the way the washing-women like on Saturdays. As soon as I saw it was dry, I picked the lice out of it and put it on, returning with all haste to the Mesón, because I could hardly wait to get that new job; not because I liked to work, but because necessity has an ugly look, as the saying goes, or as I'd say, it looks like a poor man, because that's the ugliest look there is.

When the operator saw me all clean, he cheered up and said, "Now you look like something else. Let's go."

We reached the apothecary shop, which was nearby, and he presented me to the owner, who asked me a pile of questions, which I answered to his satisfaction, and I stayed in his house with a salary set at four pesos a month and board.

I stayed there for two months as a serving lad, grinding sticks, skinning snakes, stoking the fire, running errands, and helping to do everything that I was asked to do and that needed to be done, to the satisfaction of my master and his journeyman.

After I had amassed eight pesos, I bought socks, shoes, a vest, a jacket, and a handkerchief; all from the flea market, but serviceable. I secretly brought the things to the house, and the next day, which was Sunday, I got spiffed up like an alderman.

My master hardly recognized me, and, delighted by my metamorphosis, he told the journeyman, "Just look, you can tell that this poor boy is the son of good parents and that he wasn't raised to be a servant in an apothecary shop. That's how you do it, son: one's good origins always show through, and one of the ways you can tell a man who has good origins is that he doesn't like to go around tattered or dirty. Do you know how to write?"

"Yes, sir," I replied.

"Let's see your handwriting," he said; "write something here."

To show off a little and confirm the good opinion that the master had formed of me, I wrote the following:

> *Qui scribere nesciunt nullum putant esse laborem.*
> *Tres digiti scribunt, coetera membra dolent.*[19]

"Hullo!" my master said in amazement. "The boy writes well, and in Latin. So, do you understand any of what you've written there?"

"Yes, sir," I said; "this says: those who don't know how to write think that it isn't any work; but while three fingers are writing, the whole body is put to trouble."

"Very good," said the master; "and accordingly, you should be able to understand what the label on this phial says. Tell me."

I read *Oleum vitellorum ovorum*, and I said, "Oil of egg yolk."

"So it is," said Don Nicolás. And, placing jars, bottles, phials, and boxes in front of me, he continued asking, "And what does it say here?"

And as he asked, I answered: "*Oleum scorpionum*, scorpion oil . . . *Aqua menthae*, spearmint water . . . *Aqua petrocelini*, parsley water . . . *Sirupus pomorum*, apple syrup . . . *Unguentum cucurbitae*, ointment of squash . . . *Elixir*. . . . "

---

[19] [The lines (translated by Periquillo, below) are a variation on a medieval Latin tag often used to showcase calligraphy. —Tr.]

"Enough," said the master. And, turning to the journeyman, he said, "What do you think, Don José, isn't it a pity that this poor boy should be a servant, when he could be an apprentice, given how much he already knows?"

"Yes, sir," said the journeyman.

And the master went back to talking with me. "Fine, then, boy. From this day on, you are an apprentice; you'll stay here with Don José and enter the laboratory with him, so that you can learn how to work, though from what I've seen, you already know a bit. Here is Palacios' *Pharmacopea*, and Fuller's, and the *Matritense;* we also have Linnaeus' course on botany, and Lavoisier's on chemistry.[20] Study all this and work hard, for you are welcome to use the books."

I thanked him for the promotion that he gave me by raising me from serving lad to apprentice apothecary, and for the new way in which the journeyman treated me, since from that moment on, he no longer called me just plain Pedro, but Don Pedro; however, at the time, I didn't stop to consider how great an effect a decent outward appearance can have in this topsy-turvy world, but now I do. When I was dressed as an ordinary servant, nobody bothered to inquire into my birth, nor my skills; but as soon as I looked halfway neat, I was thoroughly examined and was addressed politely. Oh, vanity, how you lead men astray! Some of my adventures went well and others badly, while I remained the same individual, the only difference being my clothing. How many people experience the same in this world? If they are decently dressed, if they glitter, if they enjoy wealth, then they are judged to be—or at least, flatterers say that they are—wise, noble, and honorable, even if they lack all such qualities; but if they're down on their luck, if they are poor, and besides being poor are ragged, they are reputed to be, and scorned as, plebeians, rogues, and idiots, even if their poverty might be an effect of the very nobility, wisdom, and generosity of those people. What could we do to keep men from basing their opinions on outward appearances or measuring men's merit by their good fortune?

But these serious reflections are only coming to me now; at the time, I basked in my changing luck, and was overjoyed by the lavish title of apprentice apothecary, not knowing that there is a common saying that goes, *A student who is sloppy is fit for sexton or apothecary.*

However, the last thing I was thinking of was working hard to study chemistry and botany. My studying amounted to mixing up a few messes, learning a few technical terms, and figuring out how to dispense prescriptions; but since I was such a good hypocrite, I won the trust and affection of the journeyman (since my master was rarely in the apothecary shop), so much so that after six months I was also helping Don José, who had occasion to go out strolling and even to sleep away from the house.

---

[20] [The books mentioned are, in order and mentioning only the first of multiple editions: Félix Palacios, *Palestra farmacéutica químico-galénica* (Madrid, 1706); Thomas Fuller, *Pharmacopoeia extemporanea* (London, 1701; *A Body of Medicines*, 1710); *Pharmacopea matritense* (Madrid, 1739); Carl von Linne (Linnaeus), *Philosophia botanica* (Berlin, 1740; *The Elements of Botany,* London, 1775); and Antoine Lavoisier, *Traité elementaire de Chimie* (Paris, 1789; *Elements of Chemistry,* Edinburgh, 1790). See Ruiz Barrionuevo, p. 515, and Spell, p. 164, who observes that Lizardi's familiarity with medicine may have derived from his father's profession as a physician. –Tr.]

From that point, or even three months earlier, I was given a salary of eight pesos a month, and I would have become a journeyman apothecary like so many others if an accident hadn't taken me out of that house. But before I retell this adventure, I must first inform you of the circumstances.

In that era, there lived in this capital city an old physician who was known by the nickname Dr. Purgante, because they said that he tried curing every patient he had with purgatives.[21]

This poor old man was a good Christian, but a bad physician and unsystematic; he adhered not to Hippocrates, Avicenna, Galen, or Averröes, but to his whims. He believed that the only possible cause for every illness was an excess of one of the four humors; and thus he thought that draining the excessive humor would remove the cause of the illness. He could have disabused himself of this delusion at the expense of just a few of the victims he sacrificed on the altar of his ignorance; but he never thought he was a mortal; he believed himself incapable of being deluded, and so he acted badly, yet he acted with an erroneous conscience. Let's leave to the moralists the question of whether or not this error could have been overcome, though for my part, I feel that a physician who errs because he will not ask or consult with wiser physicians, out of vanity or on a whim, is committing a mortal sin, for his vanity or his whim could produce a thousand errors, and therefore a million liabilities could be avoided, since each error can cause a thousand mistakes.

Be this how it may in matters of conscience, this physician had a standing arrangement with my maestro. That is, my maestro, Don Nicolás, sent every patient he could to Dr. Purgante, and the physician steered all his patients to our apothecary shop. The former would say that there was no better physician than that old man, and the latter would say that there was no better apothecary shop than ours, and so on each side we both made a good business. The pity is that this is not an invented example, but one that has innumerable originals.

The physician in question knew me very well, since he went to the apothecary shop every night and had fallen in love with my handwriting and my personality (because when I wanted to, I was capable of deceiving the devil), and on at least one occasion he told me, "Son, when you decide to leave here, let me know, because in my house, you won't lack for food or clothes."

The old man wanted to start up an apothecary shop, and he thought that in me he had found a well-educated and inexpensive journeyman.

I thanked him for the favor, promising to accept it if I ever had a falling-out with my master, for at the time I had no reason to leave him.

Indeed, my life was going along famously; a lazybones couldn't have asked for more. My obligations were to order the serving lad to sweep the shop in the morning, to refill the phials with the liquids they required, and to make sure that we kept the latter in stock, either by distilling or infusing them; but I didn't give a hoot about that, since the well water solved all my problems, and thus I would say: So long as

---

[21] [Dr. Purgante: the good doctor's nickname is possibly an allusion to Monsieur Purgon—another doctor who believed that purgatives could cure all ills—in Molière's play *Le malade imaginaire* (1673; *The Hypochondriack*, London, 1709). –Tr.]

the labels are different, it hardly matters if the water is the same—who's going to notice? The physician who prescribes the drugs might only know them by name; and the patient who takes them knows even less, and has almost always lost his sense of taste; so this drug is safe. Besides, who knows if the doctor's ignorance or the bad quality of the herbs might not make the potions more harmful than natural water! It hardly matters, then, if I make all the potions out of water; as the saying goes, *if you're full of life, water is as good as medicine.*

I didn't fail to do the same with the oils, especially those that had a syrupy color. This sort of quid pro quo, of dispensing one thing instead of another if I judged they were equal or equivalent, played a large role in my conscience and in my practice.

These were my many chores, along with concocting ointments, powders, and other drugs, according to the orders of Don José, who loved me dearly for my efficiency.

It didn't take me long to become halfway educated in dispensing medicine, for I understood the prescriptions, I knew where the ingredients were, and I could spout the price list, like all apothecaries. If they say that this prescription costs such-and-such, who is going to check the price, or see whether or not it is just? The only recourse that poor people have is to ask them to give them a little discount; if the apothecary refuses, they go to another shop, and another, and another, and if they all charge the same amount, they have no choice but to bite the bullet and make the sacrifice, because they care about their sick patient and they are convinced that the medicine will cure him. Bad apothecaries know this and they have to be coaxed and implored—that is, if they don't absolutely refuse—to give a discount.

There was one other pernicious abuse in the apothecary shop where I worked that is very common in all the other shops. This was that, as soon as we learned that a certain drug was growing scarce elsewhere, Don José would raise the price, to the point of not selling it by the half-real, but only by the real or more. The consequence of this abuse (which we can unceremoniously term greed) was that a poor beggar who had no more than half a real, and who needed to take a bit of that drug—camphor, for example—couldn't get it from Don José for the sake of God or all His saints, as if you couldn't sell half or a fourth of what you sell for one real, for a half or a quarter-real, no matter how small the amount might be. The worst part is, there are many apothecaries who think just like Don José. All thanks to the Protomedicato,[22] which tolerates them!

In sum, those were my chores by day. By night I was freer, because the master would come for a little while during the morning, pick up the sales receipts from the day before, and not return for anything in the world. The journeyman was confident on this account, and as soon as he saw that I was apt at dispensing medicine, he would put on his cape at seven in the evening and go to pay his respects to his lady-friend, though he always made sure to be back in the shop by early morning.

Given this freedom, I was in heaven, for some friends I had recently made used to come visit me, and we would merrily eat a late supper and sometimes play our games

---

[22] *Protomedicato:* this was the name of a tribunal, composed of medical doctors, that ruled on affairs of medicine. –E.

of monte for two, three, or four reales, all at the expense of the moneybox, to which we had full access.

I spent a few months in this way, and at the end of this time, the master sat down to balance the books, and he found that, though there hadn't been any serious losses, because apothecaries rarely lose, the profits were nonetheless barely perceptible.

Don Nicolás was rather startled when he discovered this devaluation. When he reprimanded Don José about it, the latter justified it by saying that it had been a very healthy year, and that such years are disastrous, or at least not very profitable, for doctors, apothecaries, and priests.

The master was not satisfied with this reply, and with a very serious face he said, "The losses of my house must be due to something else, not simply the temperate climate this year; because even in the best of years, people get sick and die."

From that day on, he began to mistrust us, and to spend few hours away from his house; and within a short time the apothecary shop had returned to profitability, as the drugs were being dispensed more efficiently; the moneybox was suffering fewer raids; and he was not leaving until late at night, when he took home the day's sales. Whenever a friend invited him to go for a stroll, he excused himself, saying that he was grateful for the favor but that he couldn't abandon the responsibilities of his house, and that *a shop owner must keep an eye on his shop*.

This method soon came to bore us, for the journeyman could not go out on the town, nor could the apprentice have his friends over for supper, gambling, and fun at night.

During this time, because of some miscalculation or other, my master got upset with the physician and undid their arrangement and their friendship completely. It is so true that most friendships are tied up with self-interest! That is why so few of them are certain.

I was already thinking about leaving the house, because I was angry with my subjection and with my lack of access to the moneybox, since under my master's gaze I couldn't treat it as familiarly as I had in the past; but what stopped me was not having anywhere to settle or anything to eat if I were to leave.

On one of these days of my indecision, it so happened that I started to dispense a prescription that called for a small dose of magnesium. I poured the water into the bottle, and the syrup, but when I went to grab the jar of magnesium, I grabbed the arsenic jar instead, and mixed in the proper dose. The sorry patient, as I later found out, heartily chugged it down with the greatest confidence, and the women of his house stirred the dregs in the glass with the end of the spoon, telling him to drink it, because the powders were the healthiest part.

Those powders began to take effect, and the wretched patient to scream, assailed by the infernal pains that were tearing at his guts. The house was in an uproar; they called their doctor, who was no slouch, and they told him that when he had taken the potion that had been prescribed for him, his pain and suffering had begun at once. Then the doctor asked for the prescription; he kept it and had them bring the bottle and the glass, which still had the dregs of the powders; he saw them, tested them, and shouted in fright, "They've poisoned the patient—this isn't magnesium, it's arsenic. Bring oil and lukewarm milk, but lots of it, and quickly."

Everything was brought instantly, and with that and more first aid, they say the patient recovered. As soon as the doctor saw that the patient was out of danger, he asked in which apothecary shop they had gotten the potion. They told him, and he informed the Protomedicato, bringing in the prescription, the serving lad who had gone to the apothecary shop, and the bottle and glass, as reliable witnesses to my thoughtlessness.

The judges commissioned another doctor; he and a notary went to the house of my master, who was surprised to receive such visitors.

The commissioner and the notary briefly and summarily concluded the trial, and I confessed and was convicted. They were about to take me to prison, but when they learned that I was not a journeyman, merely a raw apprentice, they left me in peace and placed all the blame on my master, who was given a fine of 200 pesos to be paid on the spot, and threatened with a seizure of property in case of delay; and the commissioner notified him, on behalf of the tribunal and under penalty of closing his shop, that he should never again allow apprentices to dispense medicines, for what had just happened was not the first time that the thoughtlessness of such dispensers had brought patients to grief, nor would it be the last.

There was no way out: my poor master got into the carriage with those two gentlemen, pulling a face like a dissatisfied blacksmith and staring at me in indignation, and told the coachman to go to his house, where he would pay them the fine. The carriage had scarcely left when I entered the back room of the shop, picked up a cape that I had bought and my hat, and told the journeyman, "Don José, I'm leaving, because if the master finds me here, he'll kill me. Please give him my thanks for the good things he has done for me, and ask him to forgive me for this devilry, which was just an accident."

Nothing the journeyman said could convince me to stay. I started to pick up my pace, mourning my misfortune and consoling myself that at least I had come out better than I had from the houses of Chanfaina and Don Agustín.

So, staying in one pool hall one day and another one the next, I spent the next twenty days, until I was left without cape or jacket; and to keep from going barefoot again and even worse, I made up my mind to go serve Dr. Purgante in any capacity; and he received me very well, as will be seen in the chapter that follows.

CHAPTER 26

IN WHICH PERIQUILLO RELATES HOW HE FOUND A JOB WITH DR. PURGANTE,
WHAT HE LEARNED AT HIS SIDE, HOW HE ROBBED HIM AND RAN AWAY, AND
HIS ADVENTURES IN TULA, WHERE HE PRETENDED TO BE A PHYSICIAN

Tell me not who you are, for your works shall tell me.[1] This apothegm is as ancient as it
is true; everyone is convinced of its infallibility; thus, why should I expound upon
my bad actions, when simply relating them is enough? The ideal thing, my children,
would be for you not to read my life story as if you were just reading a novel, but
rather, to carry your considerations beyond the shell of events, by observing the sorrowful aftermath of the laziness, uselessness, fickleness, and other vices that affected
me; analyzing the errant incidents of my life, investigating their causes, fearing their
consequences, and rejecting the vulgar error that you see being adopted by myself
and others; absorbing the solid maxims of the healthy, Christian ethics that my
reflections present to you; and in a word, I hope that you might fathom, in all its
depth, the substance of this work; that you would laugh at the ridiculous parts, that
you would recognize the errors and the abuse and therefore not imitate the first nor
embrace the second; and that wherever you encounter some virtuous act, you would
be enchanted by its sweet power and endeavor to imitate it. This is to say, my children, that I hope you take away three fruits—two primary and one subordinate—
from reading my life: love of virtue, abhorrence of vice, and entertainment. This is
my desire, and for this more than for anything else, I am going to the trouble of
writing to you about my most hidden crimes and defects; if I do not accomplish it,
at least I will die consoled by the thought that my intentions are praiseworthy. But
enough of digressions, for paper is expensive.

When we left off, I had just gone to see Dr. Purgante, and indeed one afternoon
after the siesta I found him in his study, sitting in an easy chair, with a book in front
of him and his snuffbox by his side. He was a tall fellow, thin in face and limbs and
thick in the belly; tanned and beetle-browed, with green eyes, a hawk nose, big
mouth, and few teeth; and bald, on account of which he wore a small wig with curls
when he went out in the street. When I went to see him, he was dressed in one of
those full-length robes that they call kimonos, covered with flowers and foliage, and
a large doctor's cap that had been starched stiff and ironed until it shone.

As soon as I entered, he recognized me and said, "Oh, Periquillo, son! Through
what strange horizons have you traveled to visit this humble abode?"

His style did not take me aback, because I already knew how pedantic he was,
and so I was about to recount my adventure with the intention of lying about everything I thought appropriate; but he interrupted me, saying, "Yes, yes, I know all
about the troublesome catastrophe that befell you with your master in the pharmaceutical. As it were, Perico, you were going to dispatch the pacific patient instanta-
neously and unexpectedly from healing bed to funeral bier through a substitution of
arsenic for magnesium. It is true that your tremulous and reckless hand must take its

---

[1] [The title of a poem that Lizardi published in 1811. –Tr.]

269

share of the blame, but just as much blame should fall upon your pharmacological preceptor; everything came from your following his whims. I had established for him, with documented evidence, that all those toxic and venomous drugs should be guarded under lock and key, with the key empowered to only the most skilled journeyman, and that through this assiduous operation all such fatal missteps could be avoided; yet despite my insinuations, he replied only that to do so would be to single himself out and to go against the pharmaceutical grain, not realizing that *sapientis est mutare consilium* (to be wise is to change opinions) and that *consuetudo est altera natura* (custom is second nature).[2] That is his business. But tell me, what have you been doing in all this time? Because if the news that has reached my auditory apparatus on the wings of fame is not mistaken, several days have passed since you walked away from the offices of Aesculapius."

"That is true, sir," I said, "but shame kept me from coming here, and it had weighed heavily on me, for in these days I have sold my cape, jacket, and handkerchief in order to eat."

"What inanity!" exclaimed the doctor. "Diffidence is *optime bona* (very good) when it arises from a crime of *cogitato*, but not from one committed *involuntarie*, for if the individual knew *hic et nunc* (in the act) that he were doing wrong, he would *absque dubio* (undoubtedly) refrain from committing it. So, then, my dearest boy, would you like to remain in my service and be my associate *in perpetuum?*"

"Yes, sir," I replied.

"Fine. In this *domo* (house) you will receive *in primis* (first off) your *panem nostrum quotidianum* (daily bread); *aliunde* (as well as) the necessary potables; *tertio* (thirdly), your bed *sic vel sic* (depending on your size); *quarto*, the heterogeneous external teguments of your physical matter; *quinto*, the surety of your hygiene, for here we pay great attention to the diet and to the observance of the six natural functions and the six non-natural ones prescribed by the most luminous men of our medical faculty; *sexto*, you will imbibe the wisdom of Apollo *ex ore meo, ex visu tuo et ex bibliotheca nostra* (from my mouth, from your sight, and from our library); *postremo* (lastly), each month you will receive for your *surrupios* (cigarettes) or for *quodcumque vellis* (whatever you wish) a salary of 544 *maravedís*,[3] free of dust and straw, with your only obligations being: to respond to the orders of the lady of the house, my sister; to observe *modo naturalistarum* (by the naturalists' method) when the poultry fowl are prepared to oviparate, and to collect their snow-white eggs, or better said, the chickens *in fieri* (in the making); to serve the victuals at table; and finally, and what I enjoin you to do above all, to attend to the daily refection and immaculateness of my mule, which you must wait upon and serve with greater prolixity than my own person.

---

[2] [The editor of the fourth edition added the translations in parentheses, with this footnote:] For the convenience of some readers, it seemed best to put into Spanish the Latin tags that the doctor strings together, like others that are dispersed throughout the book; and these translations have been inserted into the text, to avoid an annoying accumulation of notes that would interrupt its reading. This note is placed here so that the reader will not find it odd when Periquillo says, on the next page, that *he did not understand many of these terms.* –E.

[3] [*Maravedí*: a Spanish coin last minted in the 1300s, but used as a "money of account" for centuries thereafter, in spite of its miniscule value. –Tr.]

These, oh beloved Perico, are all your obligations and accommodations in synopsis. When I invited you to come to my humble abode and to join me in consortium, I had pondered the notion of establishing a chemical and botanical laboratory; however, a continuous string of disbursements has reduced me *ad inopiam* (to poverty), and has frustrated my primordial designs; nonetheless, I will keep my word to you and admit you to my house, and will compensate you justly for your services, because *dignus est operarius mercede sua* (he who works deserves his pay)."

Though I didn't understand many of his big words, I recognized that he wanted me to be both an upstairs and a downstairs servant; I observed that the work I would be given was not very hard; that the job couldn't be better, and that I was in a state where I would have accepted worse; but I could not comprehend how much my salary would amount to, and so I asked him how much, exactly, I would be making a month. At this, the good doctor seemed to grow angry, and he replied, "Didn't I tell you *claris verbis* (clearly) that you would enjoy 544 maravedís?"

"But, sir," I insisted, "how much cash do 544 maravedís amount to? Because it doesn't seem to me that my work should be worth so much money."

"Yes, it is worth it, *stultisime famule* (most foolish lad), for those hundreds of maravedís amount to no more than two pesos."

"Well, fine, doctor, sir," I said. "No need to get upset; now I know that I have a salary of two pesos, and I consider myself content to be in the company of a gentleman as *sapiente* as yourself, whose lessons will bring me more benefit than did the powders and ointments of Don Nicolás."

"Quite so," said Dr. Purgante, "for if you work hard at your studies, I will open up the palaces of Minerva for you, and this gift will be superabundant in your service, for by my teaching alone, you will conserve your health for a multitude of years, and perhaps, perhaps, you will acquire some interests and estimations."

We came to an agreement on the spot, and I carefully began to fawn on him and his sister—an old *beata rosa* (a lay sister in the Order of St. Rose), who was as ridiculous as my master; and although I would have liked to fawn on Manuelita, their little fourteen-year-old niece, who was pretty as a picture, I couldn't, because the damnable old lady kept a closer eye on her than if she had been made of gold, and well made, too.

For the next seven or eight months, I stayed with my old man, fulfilling my obligations to perfection: that is, serving at table, watching to see when the chickens laid their eggs, caring for the mule, and running errands. The old woman and her brother took me for a saint, because during the hours when I had no chores to do, I would sit in the study, in keeping with the usual concessions, and look at the anatomical prints of Porras, Willis, and others, or amuse myself from time to time by reading the aphorisms of Hippocrates, a bit of Boerhaave and van Swieten, the books by Ettmüller, Tissot, and Buchan, the treatise on fevers by Amar, the anatomical compendium by Juan de Dios López, La Faye's *Surgery,* Lazare Riviere, and other books both ancient and modern, depending on whatever I felt like pulling off the shelves.[4]

---

4 [Spell (p. 165) and Ruiz Barrionuevo (pp. 526–27) have identified these works and authors as: Manuel de Porras, *Anatomía galénica-moderna* (1716); Thomas Willis, *Pharmaceutice rationalis* (London, 1674; *An Exercitation of the Operations of Medicines in Humane Bodies*, London, 1679);

This reading, my observations of the cures that my master prescribed for the poor patients who came to see him at his house—which were always rather so-so, since he made it his rule to follow the old cliché, *you get what you pay for*—and the verbal lessons that he gave me, made me believe that I already knew all about medicine; and one day when he scolded me harshly and was even on the verge of beating me because I had forgotten to feed the mule the night before, I swore to take my revenge on him and improve my fortunes at the same time.

Having made this resolution, that very night I gave milady the mule a double ration of corn and barley, and when the whole house was in the deepest sleep, I saddled her up with all her gear and trappings. I made a package in which I hid fourteen books, some of them incomplete, some in Latin and others in Spanish, because I thought that books tend to lend a lot of authority to doctors and lawyers, even if the books are no good and the doctors don't understand them. In this luggage I stuck my master's cape and ruffled collar, along with an old wig made of pita fiber, a prescription form, and most important, his Bachelor of Medicine title and his examination letter, documents that I remade in my favor with a pocketknife and a bit of lemon, which I used to scrape off and erase just enough to change the names and dates.

I didn't forget to furnish myself with coins, for even though they hadn't paid me any salary the whole time I had been there, I knew where the sister kept a moneybox where she squirreled away everything she saved by not paying me; and, remembering the old saw about *he who robs a thief*, and so forth, I cunningly robbed the moneybox; I opened it and saw with great satisfaction that it held very close to forty pesos in hard cash, though she must have had to soften it to squeeze the coins through the narrow slot.

With this ample traveling fund, I took off from the house at half past four in the morning, closing the courtyard gate behind me and leaving them the key under the door.

At five or six in the morning, I entered an inn, telling them that I had been displeased with the inn I had been staying at the night before and that I wanted a change of lodgings.

Since I paid well, I was promptly attended. I had them bring me coffee and put the mule in the stable, where it was to be well fed.

I didn't leave the room all morning long, wondering which town I should turn to when I left, and with whom I should go—for I didn't know the roads or the towns, nor was it decent for a physician to appear without luggage or a serving lad.

---

multiple editions of aphorisms attributed to Hippocrates; Hermann Boerhaave (Dutch, 1668–1738); Gerard van Swieten (Dutch, 1700–1772); Michael Ernest Ettmüller (Leipzig, 1644–1683); Samuel August David Tissot (French, 1728–1797), especially his *Advice to the People in General with Respect to Their Health* (English translation, 1768), mentioned again below; William Buchan (English, 1729–1805); José Amar, *Instrucción curativa de las calenturas vulgarmente conocidas con el nombre de tabardillos* (Madrid, 1775); Juan de Dios López, *Compendio anatómico* (Madrid, 1750); Georges de La Faye, *Principes de chirurgie* (1739); and Lazare Riviere (French, 1589–1655). –Tr.]

I was still pondering these questions when the clock rang one, the hour when they brought up dinner for me to eat, which is what I was doing when a boy came to the door to beg, by the love of God, for a bite to eat.

The moment that I saw and heard him, I recognized him as Andrés, the apprentice from Don Agustín's house—a boy, I don't know if I mentioned it before, of about fourteen years, but as tall as an eighteen-year-old. I had him enter right away, and after a few words of conversation he recognized me, and I told him all about how I had become a physician and was setting off for some town to find my fortune, because there were too many physicians in Mexico, but that what stopped me was that I had no faithful serving lad who could accompany me and who was familiar with some town where they needed a physician.

The poor boy offered to come, and even begged me to let him accompany me; because he had been to Tepejí del Río, where there wasn't a physician and it was no small town, and if things turned out badly for us there, we could go on to Tula, which was a much larger town.[5]

I was very happy to see how freely Andrés talked, and as I had ordered up some food for him to eat, the poor boy ate it with a ravenous appetite, and told me he had been hiding in an entranceway when he saw me run out of the barbershop, the old lady after me with knife in hand; that I had run right past the same entrance where he was hiding, and that he had run after me soon after the old lady went back inside, but he wasn't able to catch up—and I don't doubt it, as fast as I could run when fear spurred me!

Andrés also told me that he had gone home to his own house and told them all the whole story; that his stepfather had scolded him and beaten him badly, and then had taken him in wooden fetters to the house of Don Agustín; that when the damnable old woman saw that I wasn't coming back, she took her revenge on him by telling on him so often that the maestro lost his temper and decided to give him nine days of lashings, which he proceeded to do, making a sorry sight of Andrés over the course of those nine days, both for the number and the cruelty of the lashes he gave him and because of the fasting that he forced him to endure over that time; that, as soon as the wicked old woman had exacted her revenge, they had freed him, taking off his fetters, preaching a good long sermon to him, and finishing up with that bit about *watch out next time;* but that he had fled from the house the first chance he got, planning to leave Mexico, which was why he was going around all the inns, begging for a bite to eat and waiting for an opportunity to leave with the first traveler he found.

Andrés finished telling me all this while he ate, and I disguised my adventures, making him believe that I had just passed the examination for practicing medicine; I had already hinted that I wanted to leave this city, so I told him that I would gladly take him with me, feeding him and having him pass as a barber in case there was none in the town where we would go to live.

"But, sir," said Andrés, "that's all well and good, but if I hardly know how to shave a dog, how am I going to risk getting into something I don't understand?"

---

5 [Tepejí del Río, a town about 45 miles north of Mexico; Tula, another 11 miles north of Tepejí. –Tr.]

"Hush," I said, "don't be a coward: you should know that *audaces fortuna juvat, timidosque repellit. . . .* "

"What are you saying, sir? I can't understand you."

"That Fortune favors the brave," I replied, "and rejects the cowardly; so, no fainting: after a month with me, you'll become as good a barber as I became a physician in the short time I was with my maestro, to whom I don't even know how much I owe at this point."

Andrés listened to me in amazement, especially when he heard me spouting off my Latin tags, because he didn't know that the most I had learned from Dr. Purgante was his pedantry and his *methodus medendi*, his healing method.

Finally, the clocks rang three and I went out with Andrés to the flea market, where I bought a mattress, a leather cover for storing it, a trunk, a black jacket and green pants with matching black stockings, shoes, a hat, a red vest, a bow tie, and a short cloak for my servant and barber-to-be, for whom I also bought six razors, a shaving basin, a mirror, four cupping glasses, two lancets, an old dress for rags, a pair of scissors, a large syringe, and I don't know what other trinkets; the strangest thing being that for the whole trousseau, I spent no more than twenty-seven or twenty-eight pesos. Obviously, it was all flea-market stuff; but even so, Andrés returned to the inn very contented.

As soon as we arrived, I paid the porter, and we packed our belongings into the trunk. As we did so, Andrés saw that my cash assets amounted to barely eight or ten pesos. Then he said, quite frightened, "Ay, sir! What, are we going to leave with no more money than this?"

"Yes, Andrés," I said. "Why not? Isn't it enough?"

"How could it be enough, sir? Who's going to haul the trunk and the mattress from here to Tepejí or Tula? What are we going to eat on the way? And finally, what are we going to live on once we get there, while we're building up a reputation? That money's going to run out right away, and I don't see that you have clothes or jewels or anything that's worth pawning."

Andrés' reflections did not fail to worry me; but I didn't want to unnerve him any further, and I had also taken it into my head that Dr. Purgante would be on my tail like a compass needle (thus when I went to the flea market, for example, I bought almost all the trinkets mentioned in a single stall), and I was afraid that I'd end up in jail if he found me, and therefore in Chanfaina's hands. That is why I told Andrés, as craftily and pedantically as I could, "Don't worry, son; *Deus providebit*."[6]

"I don't know what you just said," Andrés answered; "but what I do know is that this isn't even enough money to get started."

We were in the middle of this conversation when, around seven at night, I heard the sound of voices and pesos in the room next door. I sent Andrés to see what was going on. He ran off, and returned very happy, telling me, "Sir, sir, what a good game!"

"What, are they gambling?"

"Yes, sir," said Andrés, "there's ten or twelve bumpkins in the room, playing monte, but you should see the sausage rolls of pesos they're betting!"

---

[6] [Genesis 22:8.] God will provide. –E.

The serpent stung me: I opened the trunk, took out six of the ten pesos it held, and gave the key to Andrés, telling him to keep it safe, and not to give it to me even if I began begging and dying to have it, because I was only going to risk these six pesos, and if I were to lose the other four, we wouldn't have anything to pay for our dinner or the mule's feed the next day. Andrés took the key, looking a little sad and distrustful, and I went to crash the gamblers' circle.

They weren't quite the bumpkins I needed them to be; they had a better-than-middling education in the art of the shuffle, and so I had to feel my way cautiously. Nevertheless, I had the fortune to win some twenty-five pesos from them, which made me very happy when I left and found Andrés sitting up, sound asleep.

I woke him and showed him the winnings, which he cheerfully stored away, telling me that he had the trip all set and everything ready; because there were some lads from Tula downstairs who had brought a college boy here and were going home empty; that he had contracted the trip with them, and had even settled on hiring them to do it for four pesos, and that the lads were just waiting for me to confirm the arrangement.

"And why shouldn't I confirm it, son?" I told Andrés. "Go down there and call those lads right now."

Andrés ran down fast as lightning and came right back up with the lads, and I settled with them that they were to give me a mule for my luggage and a saddled horse or mule for Andrés, all of which they agreed to, and also that they were to get up before dawn; and they went off to get some rest.

I then sent my servant to go buy me a bottle of liquor and some cheese, biscuits, and sausage for the next day; and while I waited for him to come back, I had them bring up my supper.

I didn't tire of congratulating myself on my decision to become a physician, seeing how well and how easily everything was coming along, and at the same time I gave thanks to God for providing me as faithful, quick-witted, and helpful a servant as Andresillo, who came back bearing the supplies while I was in the middle of these contemplations.

We both ate supper amicably, had a good shot of liquor, and went to bed early so that we could get up good and early.

At four in the morning, there were the lads, knocking on our door. We woke up and ate breakfast while the muleteers were loading.

As soon as this business was done, I paid the expenses I had incurred for myself and my mule, and we set out on the road.

I wasn't used to traveling, so I soon got tired, and I didn't want to keep going past Cuautitlán,[7] no matter how much the lads insisted that we should sleep that night in Tula.

On the second day, we reached that town, and I found rest or lodging at the house of one of the muleteers—a poor, simple-minded old fellow and an upright man, by the name of Tío Bernabé, with whom I arranged that I would pay for my

---

[7] [A town about 18 miles north of central Mexico City (now almost swallowed by the city's sprawl), just a third of the way to Tula. –Tr.]

food, and Andrés' and the mule's, by serving as the house physician for his whole family, which consisted of two old women, one of them being his wife and the other his sister; two grown sons; and a young daughter of about twelve.

The poor man gladly accepted the deal; and just imagine me now, settled down in Tula, and having to care for the maestro barber—that is what we will call Andrés—myself, and my mule; for, even though she wasn't mine, that is what I termed her; yet every time I looked at her, I seemed to see Dr. Purgante in front of me with his long robe and his tall doctor's cap, flashing flames from his eyes to tell me, "Rogue! Give me back my mule, my trappings, my ruffled collar, my wig, my books, my cape, and my money, for none of it is yours."

There is much truth, my children, in the principle of natural law that tells us that, wherever a thing might be, it calls out for its owner: *Ubicumque res est, pro domino suo clamat.* What does it matter if the executor of a will keeps the inheritance for himself because the children are too young to make a complaint? What does it matter if the usurer keeps his profits? So what if a merchant grows rich on illicit trade? And so what if many others take advantage of their power or everyone else's ignorance, and brazenly enjoy the goods that they have usurped? They will never take pleasure from them without constant anxiety, nor, try as they might, can they quiet their consciences, which will incessantly cry out to them, "This is not yours; this is ill-gotten; restore it to its owner, or you will perish eternally."

That is what happened to me with what I had stolen from my poor master; but, since we rarely look our inner regrets in the face, I managed to establish myself as a good physician in that town, making an inner promise to restore all the doctor's belongings to him as soon as I had earned enough. Though in this, I was doing nothing but flowing with the current.

Since I had not forgotten the principles of courtesy that my parents taught me, two days later, after I had rested, I inquired after the main figures in town, such as the parish priest and his assistant curates, the subdelegado[8] and his director, the tax collector, the postal administrator, a couple of storekeepers, and other decent gentlemen, and through my good patron and Andrés, I sent messages to all of them, offering them my disservices.

They all received the news with the greatest satisfaction, politely thanking me for the courtesy call and making their own fashionable visits to me, which I answered in kind, visiting them at night in my formal wear, by which I mean my cape with its ruffled collar and my wig, because I had no other dress suit either better or worse; the most ridiculous thing about it being that my stockings were white, my pants and shirt were all colored, and my shoes were button-ups, making me look more like a constable than a doctor; and to further enhance the picture of my ridiculousness, I made Andrés come with me wearing the suit I had bought for him, which, as you will remember, was a black jacket and black stockings, green pants, red vest, white hat, and his short-tailed, patched-up blue cloak.

---

[8] [*Subdelegado*: the highest provincial district official under the new *intendencia* administrative system adopted in Mexico in the 1780s; roughly the same as the *corregidor* or *alcalde mayor* (district governor) of the earlier system. –Tr.]

So the main gentlemen of the town had visited me, as I've said, and had formed whatever concept of me they wished; but the common people still hadn't seen me dressed to the nines and accompanied by my squire; so on the Sunday when I made my debut in church dressed in my way, looking like a cross between a doctor and a gendarme, and Andrés looking like something between a crow and a parrot, the people were incredibly distracted, and I think no one heard Mass, they were so busy looking at us—some making fun of our extravagant figures, and others amazed by our clothes. The upshot was that when I returned to my lodgings, I was accompanied by a crowd of boys, women, Indians, and poor farmers, who never stopped asking Andrés who we were. He answered in a very dignified tone, "This gentleman is my master; his name is Dr. Pedro Sarmiento, and the Kingdom of New Spain has never given birth to his medical equal; I am his serving lad, my name is Andrés Cascajo and I am a maestro barber, and so good that I can shave a capon, get blood from a corpse, and dislocate a lion's jaw if it needs a tooth extracted."

These conversations went on behind my back, because, as his master, I didn't walk side by side with Andrés, but ahead of him, all serious and conceited as I listened to him praise me; but I could hardly keep from bursting out in guffaws when I heard the nonsense Andrés spouted and the seriousness with which he said it, and the gullibility of the boys and poor people who followed after us, hanging on my lackey's words.

We reached the house surrounded by our amazed retinue, who were politely dismissed by Tío Bernabé, who told them they now knew where the good doctor lived, should the need arise. At that, they all began to retire to their houses, and they left us in peace.

With the few coins I had left, I had my landlord buy me a few yards of Pontivy linen, and I had a shirt made for myself, and another for Andrés, giving the rest of the cloth to the old woman in return for feeding us for a few days, despite our first payment.

Since people are very gossipy in the towns, just as they are in the cities, the news quickly spread throughout the whole district that there were now a physician and a barber in the head town, and they started coming in from all over to consult me about their illnesses.

Fortunately, the first ones who consulted me were the sort who get better even without being cured, for the assistance of wise Nature is all they need; and others were suffering because they did not want or know how to restrict themselves to the diet that was good for them. One way or another, they got better with whatever I prescribed for them, and I fashioned each of them into a bugle to announce my fame.

After fifteen or twenty days, I knew how to deal with my patients—especially the Indians, who never came with empty hands, but rather would always bring chickens, fruit, eggs, vegetables, cheese, and everything the poor people could get their hands on. Thus Tío Bernabé and his old ladies were very happy with their guest. Andrés and I were hardly sad; but we would rather have had coins; and anyway, Andrés was better off than me, because every Sunday he had a great time skinning the Indians for half a real each, and he became so daring that one time he dared try bleeding one, and merely by accident, it went all right. The fact is that, between the

little he had seen and the practice he was getting, his hand improved so much that
he told me one day, "Well, sir, I'm not afraid anymore now, and I could even shave
the *Sursum corda*."[9]

My fame grew from day to day; but what elevated me to the horns of the moon
was the cure I did (by accident, just like Andrés) for the tax collector, to whom I was
called one night in great haste.

I ran over, praying to God to help me get through this predicament, on which I
thought, with good reason, my happiness depended.

With me I brought Andrés, carrying all his instruments, and in an undertone, so
that the tax collector's servant couldn't hear me, I told him that he shouldn't be
afraid, for I wasn't; that if it came to killing a patient, it made no difference whether
it was an Indian or a Spaniard; and that nobody could have a surer thing than what
we had now: because, if the tax collector got better, he would pay us well and our
fame would be assured; and if he died, as was likely to be the case, given our skills, all
we'd have to do would be to say that he was already with God and that his hour had
come, and we'd be safe, and nobody could accuse us of homicide.

Meanwhile we reached his house, which was a scene of bedlam, because some
were entering, others were leaving, others were crying, and everyone was stunned.

Just then, the parish priest and his curate arrived with the holy oils.

"That's bad," I said to Andrés. "This is a major illness. There's no in-between
here; either we come off well or we come off badly. Let's see how this hand plays."

We all entered the bedroom together and saw the patient, lying face up in bed,
unconscious, his eyes closed, his mouth open, his visage darkened, and with all the
symptoms of apoplexy.

As soon as his wife and her little girls saw me at his bedside, they gathered around
me and, melting with tears, asked me, "Ay, sir! What can you tell us? Will our father
die?"

Affecting a great serenity of spirit and speaking with the confidence of a prophet,
I replied, "Hush, now, girls, no one is going to die! These are mere effervescences of
the sanguinary humor, which, by pressing upon the ventricles of the heart, paralyze
the cerebrum, because they carry the *pondus* of the blood through the spinal chord
and the tracheal artery; but we will get rid of it all in an instant, for *si evaquatio fit,
rececetur pletora*."[10]

The ladies listened to me in astonishment, and the priest kept looking me over
from head to toe, no doubt sneering at my foolishness, which he interrupted by saying, "Ladies, spiritual remedies never hurt or run counter to temporal ones. It would
be best to absolve my friend by dispensation and give him extreme unction, and may
God's will be done."

"Dear Father," I said with all my accustomed pedantry, which was so thick that
it seemed I must have learned it in writing—"dear Father, what you say is correct,
and I would never think of trying to reap someone else's wheat; but *venia tanti*, I
would say that spiritual remedies are not only good but necessary, *necesitate medii*

---

[9] [*Sursum corda:* "Lift up your hearts," a versicle in the Mass. –Tr.]
[10] By performing the evacuation, we will rid him of the plethora. –E.

and *necesitate praecepti in articulo mortis: sed sic est*[11] that such is not our case; ergo, et cetera."

The priest, who was very judicious and well educated, did not want to waste time on my quackery, so he answered me, "Dear doctor, our case is not one for arguments, because time is of the essence; I know what my obligation is, and that is what matters."

He said this and began to absolve the patient, while at the same time the curate applied the holy sacrament of extreme unction. The grieving family, as if those rites were a diagnosis of certain death for the patient, began to stun the household with their wailing; as soon as the clerical gentlemen concluded their business, they retreated to another room, leaving the battlefield and the patient to me.

I immediately approached the bed, took his pulse, looked at the ceiling rafters for a long time, then took his pulse again while making a thousand faces, such as arching my eyebrows, wrinkling my nose, looking at the floor, biting my lips, moving my head this way and that, and pantomiming every figure I thought useful for bewildering those poor people, who stared at me in profound silence, no doubt taking me to be a second Hippocrates; at least, that was my intention, along with pondering the grave danger that the patient was in and the difficulty of curing him, while I repented having told them that it was no cause for worry.

Having finished the pulse-taking, I looked carefully at his face, opened his mouth with a spoon to see his tongue, lifted his eyelids, touched his stomach and feet, and asked the family a thousand questions without getting anything straight, until the lady of the house, who could no longer bear my languid pace, said, "At last, sir, what can you say about my husband? Will he live or die?"

"Ma'am," I said, "that I can't say; only God can tell us what life is and what resurrection is, since He was the one who *Lazarum resucitavit a monumento foetidum,*[12] and if He says so, your husband will live even if he is dead. *Ego sum resurrectio et vita, qui credit in me, etiam si mortuus fuerit, vivet.*"[13]

"Ay, Jesus!" screamed one of the girls, "my daddy's dead!"

Since she was right next to the patient, and her scream was so strange and grief-stricken, and she then fainted in her chair, we all thought that he really had expired, and we surrounded his bed.

The priest and his curate, hearing the commotion, ran in and didn't know who to care for, the apoplectic man or the hysterical girl, since both were unconscious. The lady of the house, whose anger was rising, told me, "Please drop the Latin and see whether or not you can cure my husband. Why did you say it was nothing to worry about when you came in, and assure me that he wouldn't die?"

"I said that, ma'am, not to distress you," I said, "but I hadn't yet examined the patient *methodice vel juxta artis nostrae praecepta.*[14] But please pray to God, and let's see what we can do. First, let's heat up a big pot of water."

---

[11] A necessary means for salvation and for the obligation to fulfill the precepts in the hour of death; however. . . . –E.

[12] Who resurrected Lazarus, who lay rotting in the grave. –E.

[13] [John 11:25.] I am the resurrection, and the life; he that believeth in Me, although he be dead, shall live. –E.

[14] By the method or following the rules of the art of our practice. –E.

"There's plenty of that," said the cook.

"Fine. Then, Maestro Andrés," I went on, "as the good phlebotomist you are, please give this man a couple of bleedings right away in the vena cava."

Although Andrés was afraid, and had no better idea than I did what the vena cava was, he put tourniquets on the patient's arms and gave him two lancet pricks that looked more like knife wounds, and with this relief, after having filled two small bowls with blood, the profusion of which scandalized the spectators, the patient opened his eyes and began to understand what the circumstances were, and to speak.

I immediately had Andrés loosen the bandages and close up the incisions, which was no easy task, considering how long they were!

Then I had them dampen the patient's forehead and wrists with white wine, and comfort his stomach on the inside with atole and eggs, and on the outside with a tortilla and eggs, seasoned with red oil, wine, cilantro, and whatever other garbage came into my head; and I insisted that they not return him to a supinated position.

"What do you mean, supinated position, doctor?" asked the lady; and the priest, smiling, said, "He means, don't let him lie on his back."

"Well, *tatita*, for God's sake," the matron went on, "let's all talk normal so people can understand us."

By this time, the girl had recovered from her fainting spell and was taking part in the conversation, and as soon as she heard her mother, she said, "Yes, sir, my mother is right; I'd like you to know that's why I passed out before, because when you started praying that prayer that the priests recite for dead people when they bury them, I thought my daddy had died and that you were doing the wake for him."

The priest laughed heartily at the girl's simplicity, and everyone joined in with him, because we were all happy to see the tax collector out of danger, drinking his atole and talking calmly like anyone else.

I prescribed a diet for him for the next few days, offering to continue treating him until he was completely better.

They all thanked me, and as I took my leave the lady pressed an ounce of gold into my hand, which I took to be a peso at the time, and I cursed myself to see my success so badly paid, and so I was saying to Andrés when he told me, "No, sir, it can't be a silver peso, because anyway, they gave me four pesos."

"You know, you're right," I replied, and picking up the pace we reached the house, where I saw that it was an ounce of gold, as yellow as the finest saffron.

I was unbelievably happy with my ounce, not so much because of what it was worth as because it had been the first substantial reward I had gotten for medical skill, and this past success would give me a lot of credit in the future, which turned out to be true. Andrés was also quite pleased with his four pesos, even more than with his dexterity; but sounding more empty-headed than a pumpkin, I said to him, "So, what do you think, Andresillo? Could any profession be easier to exercise than medicine? There's a reason why the saying has it that *there's a little bit of doctor, poet, and madman in each of us;* and if we add a smidgen of study and hard work to that, we've got ourselves an accomplished physician. That's what you just saw in my famous cure of the tax collector, who would be pushing up daisies right now if it hadn't been for me. Indeed, I could give a few lessons on medicine to Galen himself, with Hippocrates and Avicenna thrown in for good measure, same as you could teach a few things to the protophlebotomist of the universe."

Andrés listened attentively to me, and as soon as I came to a stop he said, "Sir, if everything about yourself and me wasn't just a lucky break,[15] we're not too bad off."

"What do you mean by *a lucky break*?" I asked; and he replied with sly sarcasm, "Well, a lucky break is what I call it when you're not likely to cure anybody else, or me to do a better bleeding. At least as for me, I'm sure I just had a lucky break, and as for yourself, that must not be the case for you, because I'm sure you know what you're doing."

"And I certainly do know," I said; "what, do you think this is the first time I've skinned a fox? Let 'em bring on the apoplectics by the thousands, and just see if I don't raise them all *ipso facto* from the dead—and not just apoplectics: bring on lepers, psoriatics, syphilitics, gouty men, women in labor, folks with fever, people with rabies, and every ill patient in the world. You did a pretty job of it, yourself, but you have to make sure your fingers don't move so fast, and that you don't stick the lancet in so deep; I wouldn't want to see you cut somebody's artery. But as for the rest, don't worry: by my side, you won't come out of this a mere barber, you'll be a physician, a surgeon, a chemist, a botanist, an alchemist, and if you please me and serve me well, you'll even get to be an astrologer and a necromancer."

"May God make it happen," said Andrés, "so that I'll have enough to eat my whole life long, and so I can support my family, because I'm dying to get married."

We talked on until we fell asleep, and the next day I went to visit my patient, who was already feeling so well that he paid me a peso and told me not to bother myself anymore, and that if he needed my services again, he would send for me; because that is the quaint way people have of getting rid of scrounging doctors, the ones who hang around their houses for the pesetas.

Things happened just as I thought they would. As soon as the poor people heard about the tax collector's happy recovery at my hands, the common folk began to praise me and recommend me openly, for they said, "The principal gentlemen call on him, so he must be a doctor without any equals." The best part of it was that the distinguished sort also got confused and gave me plenty of acclaim.

Only the parish priest couldn't swallow me; instead he told the subdelegado, the postal administrator, and others that maybe I was a good physician, but he didn't believe it, because I was so pedantic and such a big talker, and people with those characteristics were either very stupid or very big rogues, and so no one should ever trust them, whether they were doctors, theologians, lawyers, or anything else. The subdelegado endeavored to defend me, saying that it was natural for everyone to explain things using the terms of his own specialty, and that should not be called pedantry.

"I agree with you about that," the priest said, "but only if one distinguishes among the places and people with whom one is speaking; for if I were preaching a sermon about the seventh commandment, for example, and if I were to use in it such terms as emphyteusis, mortgageable, de facto and de jure possession, extenuated

---

[15] Lucky break (*chiripa*): A term used in pool, and more recently in billiards, to refer to a shot that came out well by accident, and not because of the player's skill. –E.

usury, covenants, reversion sales, and so on, without any explanation, I would surely be acting pedantic, for I must recognize that there would scarcely be two people in this town who would understand me; and so I must explain what I mean, which is what I do, in clear terms that everyone can comprehend; but in the end, Señor Subdelegado, if you want to see how ignorant that physician is, arrange for us to get together here some night, using a social gathering as a pretext, and I promise you that you'll hear him cheerfully blathering nonsense."

"That's just what we'll do," said the subdelegado; "but what can we say about the cure he performed the other night?"

"I would say, without hesitation," replied the priest, "that it was pure coincidence, and smoke and mirrors: a trick that was far easier than it looked."

"Is that possible?"

"Yes, Señor Subdelegado; don't you see that the patient's corpulence and robustness, the strength of his pulse, the darkening of his face, numbing of his senses, his agitated breathing, and every observable symptom he had, indicated that he needed to be bled? The most foolish old woman in my parish could have prescribed that treatment."

"Fine, then," said the Subdelegado; "I want to hear a conversation on medicine between yourself and him. We will schedule it for the 25th of the month."

"Excellent," the priest answered; and they changed the subject.

This conversation, or at least the substance of it, was reported to me by a serving lad in the subdelegado's employ, whom I had cured of a case of indigestion without charging anything, because the poor boy repaid me by telling me everything that was said of me in his master's house.

I thanked him, and devoted myself to studying in my big old books so that the event would not catch me unawares.

In the meantime, I was called one night to the house of Don Ciriaco Redondo, the richest shopkeeper in town, who was suffering from colic.

"Bring the syringe," I told Andrés, "and let's see what happens, because this is another adventure like the one the other night. May God see us through it."

Andrés got the syringe and we went to the house, which we found in an uproar, like the tax collector's; but the advantage here was that the patient was talking.

I asked him a thousand pedantic questions, because I could come up with them by the thousands; and through them I found out that he was a bit of a glutton, and had given himself a devil of a case of overeating.

I ordered them to boil some mallows with soap and honey, and once they had completed that operation, I had the patient drink down a good portion of it, which the miserable fellow resisted, as did his family, saying that it was not an emetic but an enema.

"Please drink it, sir," I said, growing very angry. "Can't you see that if it is an enema, as you say, one can take an enema by mouth as well as elsewhere? So, my dear sir, it's drink your medicine or die."

The sad patient drank down the disgusting potion with such revulsion that he quickly brought up half the contents of his stomach; but it exhausted him, and since the obstruction was in his intestines, it did not relieve his pain.

Then I had Andrés fill up the syringe, and I ordered him to offer his backside.

"Never in my life," said the patient, "never in my life have I let anyone back there."

"Well, friend," I replied, "never in your life have you found yourself in such tight straits; and neither have I, in all my years as a doctor, seen such an obstinate case of colic, because the humor is doubtless very dense and glutinous; but, my dear brother, the enema's the thing, the enema: it's nothing less than the only safe course for the defeated, and if not, we can't expect any other way out—*una salus victis nullam sperare salutem*;[16] and so, if you do not get better with the medicine I have prescribed, we will have to recur to the lancet and open up your intestines, and then cauterize them with a hot iron; and if those operations do not work, the only thing left will be to pay the priest for the cost of burial, because the illness is incurable; for as Hippocrates says, *ubi medicamentum non sanat, ferrum sanat; ubi ferrum non sanat, ignis sanat; ubi ignis non sanat, incurabile morbus.*"[17]

"Well, sir," said the patient, in an undertone that his relatives could not hear, "bring on the enema, if that's the only way to health."

"*Amen dico vobis*," I answered, and immediately ordered everyone out of the bedroom for the sake of decency, except for the patient's wife.

Andrés filled up his syringe and got ready to operate; but how stupid Andrés could be when it came to helping out! It was impossible for him to get anything right. He spilled it all over the bed, hurt the patient, and nothing useful got done until I got upset with his clumsiness and decided to take the remedy into my own hands, even though I had never found myself in such an operation before.

Nevertheless, ignoring my ineptitude, I grabbed the syringe, filled it with the brew, and with the greatest delicacy introduced the narrow end rectally; but whether because I had more talent than Andrés, or because the patient's apprehension was working in my favor, he took more and more of the brew, and I encouraged him, saying, "Grit your teeth, brother, and take it as hot as you can, because this is for your health."

The distressed patient did as much as he could on his part (and most of the time, this is the only reason why the best doctors have any success), and after a quarter of an hour or less he had a copious evacuation, as if he had not moved his bowels in three days.

He was immediately relieved, as he said, but in truth he was completely cured, because when the cause is removed, the effect ceases.

They thanked me to high heaven and gave me twelve pesos, and I went back to my lodgings with Andrés, to whom I said along the way, "Imagine, they gave me twelve pesos in the house of the richest man in town, and in the tax collector's house they gave me an ounce of gold: so is the tax collector richer, or more generous?"

Andrés, always slyly sarcastic, replied, "I don't know about being richer, but there's no doubt he's more generous than Don Ciriaco Redondo."

---

[16] [Virgil, *Aeneid*, II: 354, "The only safe course for the defeated is to expect no safety." –Tr.]

[17] [A saying attributed to Hippocrates (quoted here in Latin translation): "if medicine does not heal, iron (i.e., the scalpel) heals; if iron does not heal, fire heals; if fire does not heal, the case is incurable." –Tr.]

"And why would that be, Andrés?" I asked. "Because the richest man should be the most generous."

"I don't know," said Andrés, unless it's because tax collectors can be richer than anybody else in town when they feel like it, because they manage the king's treasure, and they do their accounts any way they want to. Don't you see that what they call the *tax on the wind* yields a revenue that can't be verified?[18] Figure, they charge one or two reales for each head of cattle that gets slaughtered in the town, whether it's a steer or a cow, a sheep or a pig: who's going to look at their books for that? Figure, all the stuff that gets introduced without an official guide, just with a simple permit, because of how little it's worth; plus, all the little things that get smuggled in and sold, because he comes to an arrangement with the muleteer who carts them in; and finally, there's all the change, which adds up to a lot over the year when you're always rounding up, because, since there's twelve *granos* in one real, if the muleteer owes seven *granos* for what he sold, he'll charge him the whole real, and if a thousand muleteers come to town, he'll charge them a thousand reales. That's what my uncle told me, and he was a tax collector for many years, and he used to say that the *tax on the wind* was worth more than his salary."

As we talked, we reached our lodgings. Andrés and I had supper feeling very contented, tipping the owners of the house, and we went to bed.

Our good fortune continued for about a month, and during this time, the subdelegado arranged the meeting that the parish priest wanted to have with me; but if you want to find out what happened there, you will have to read the following chapter.

---

[18] ["Tax on the wind" (*alcabala del viento*): An excise tax charged to itinerant vendors in a town. The *alcabalero*, or tax collector, was in charge of collecting an excise tax on all items sold in a town, though the typical practice was not to keep accounts of actual quantities bought and sold, but rather to charge merchants a lump sum based on assumptions about how much they might sell during the year. Since itinerant vendors were not resident in the town, there would be no way for a royal inspector to ascertain after the fact how much tax had been collected, and thus the alcabalero could get away with pocketing the tax. –Tr.]

CHAPTER 27

My fame grew from day to day after these stupendous cures, through which I gained
a good opinion even among those who did not count themselves common folk. I ran
out of time to arrange the medicines in my house, and it got to the point where I
had to be cajoled before I would make a visit outside of town, and then only if they
paid me well.

I enhanced my reputation with a medicine kit and a set of barber's tools that I
ordered from Mexico, which, along with a more decent and somewhat luxurious
external aspect (for I had rented a house of my own, and had hired a cook and
another servant), gave me the appearance of a circumspect and studious man.

At the same time, I visited few houses, and made close friends with no one, for I
had heard my maestro, Dr. Purgante, say that it wasn't good for a physician to be very
gossipy, because people would use your friendship to get you to cure them for free.

With these and other simple rules about pennies, I started amassing a pretty pile
of them, for in the short amount of time that I've mentioned, Andrés, the mule, and
I ate very well; we recuperated; and I came to have some 200 pesos, free of dust and
straw.

The solemnity and haughtiness that I displayed in public; the exotic, pedantic
terms I used; the high prices I put on my drugs; the mystery in which I wrapped their
names; the flattery that I lavished on people of means; the high prices I placed on my
answers to the poor; and the good things Andrés said about me in my absence: all
contributed to spreading the fame of my good name in the highest ranks.

As my reputation grew, so did my pile of money; and as both increased together,
my pride, my selfishness, and my arrogance likewise grew. When poor people came
to my house to see me because they had nothing with which to pay me, I treated
them harshly, scolded them, and sent them away unattended. I treated those who
paid me two reales for a visit in almost the same way, because a bottle-rocket would
burn for a longer time than I stayed in their houses. Of course, even if I had stayed
for an hour, they wouldn't have received any better treatment, given that I was nothing but a big talker dressed up as a doctor; but since the miserable patients don't
know how competent a doctor (or one who passes for a doctor) is, it consoles them
when they observe him taking the time to ask them about the causes of their illnesses, and investigating with his own ears and eyes their ages, their states, their business, their constitutions, and other things that seem like trivialities to physicians
such as I was, but that are very important pieces of information to true professionals.

I did not give the same treatment to the rich or to people of distinction, who
would even get angry at the way I wasted time and at the faces I pulled as I tried to
pretend that I was very concerned about their health; but what else could I have
done, if that was all I had learned from my famous maestro, Dr. Purgante?

Despite my ignorance, a few patients accidentally improved, though incomparably more died from my fatal cures. Despite all that, my reputation did not diminish,

for three reasons: first, because most of those who died were poor, and no one pays attention to their lives or their deaths. Second, because I had already attained fame, and so I could sleep soundly even if I killed more Tulans than El Cid killed Saracens. Third, and the point that most favors physicians, because those who got better talked about my skills, while those who died couldn't complain about my ignorance, so I managed to have my successes made public and my errors buried in the earth; though if the same thing happened to me that happened to Andrés, my bonanza would definitely have given out sooner than it did.

What happened was that, even before we had arrived in Tula, the priest, the Subdelegado, and other prominent citizens had been urging their friends to send them a barber from Mexico. After they had experienced Andrés' rough hand, they insisted on their request so strongly that it was not long before Maestro Apolinario arrived, a barber who was indeed educated in the trade and had passed his examination.

As soon as Andrés met him and saw him at work, he felt afraid, and one day, acting more sensible and clever than I, he went to see him and told him his entire story, frankly and plainly, saying that he was merely a barber's apprentice, that he didn't know anything, that what he was doing in the town was out of sheer necessity, that he wanted to learn the trade correctly, and that if the maestro would teach him, he would be grateful and would serve him in any way he could.

Along with this speech, Andrés gave him the barber's toolkit that I had bought for him, which won over Maestro Apolinario, who promptly offered to have Andrés join his house, where he would feed him and teach him the trade as effectively and as quickly as he could.

He then asked Andrés what kind of doctor I was, to which Andrés replied that he thought I was a very good one, and that he had seen me perform some miraculous cures.

He then took his leave of the barber so he could come do the same with me, for he told me about everything that had happened and about his decision to learn the trade properly.

"Because, sir, in the end," he said, "I realize that I'm a brute; this other fellow is a real maestro; so either the people will get rid of me as their barber, or he'll get rid of me by asking to see my examination certificate, and either way I'll lose my reputation, my trade, and my means of making a living; and so I think I'll go with him, seeing as Your Honor already has another servant."

I was going to miss Andrés, but I didn't want to talk him out of his good intention; so I paid him his salary, added a tip of six pesos, and let him go.

During these days, I was called to the house of a rheumatic old man, to whom I gave six or seven purges, in keeping with my system, swindling him out of twenty-five pesos and leaving him worse off than before.

I did the same thing to an old woman with dropsy, whose days I shortened with six ounces of dried rhubarb and ash tree gum, and two pounds of squill.[1]

These were the lovely sorts of favors I was doing all the time, but the blind

---

[1] [Rhubarb, ash tree gum, squill (*ruibarbo, maná, cebolla albarraz*): all three are traditional purgatives and diuretics. –Tr.]

common folk had made up their minds that I was a good doctor, so no matter how loudly the bells tolled, they didn't wake up from their slumber.

At last the day arrived that the subdelegado had set for hearing me debate the priest, which was the 25th of August, for I went to congratulate the subdelegado on his saint's day, and he asked me to stay and eat, insisting on it so much that I could not turn him down.

I noticed that he had his full retinue at his house, not omitting the parish priest; but I pretended that I didn't know what the priest was saying about me, confident that, as much as he knew, he couldn't have as much knowledge about medicine as I did.

With this foolish arrogance, I sat down at table when the time came, and ate and repeatedly toasted to the health of the subdelegado and of all the assembled gentlemen, making them all laugh with my pedantry, except for the priest, who was annoyed by such things.

The subdelegado was well thought of; his table was therefore crowded with the town's principal gentlemen and their wives. The provisions were generous, the dishes numerous and well seasoned. The toasts and cheers came thick and fast, the glasses were in constant danger from all the thumpings they took from forks and knives, and everyone's head was filling up with the spirits of the vine.

At this time, in came the Indian governor with the officials of his government,[2] preceded by drums and pipes, and by two Indians carrying chickens, pigs, and two young sheep.

As soon as they entered, they performed their customary greetings, kissing everyone's hands, and the governor said to the subdelegado, "Great sir, may Your Honor have many more together with all these gentlemen, for the sake of our town."

He then gave him the *xochitl*, which is a bouquet of flowers, in token of his respect, with a piece of paper, full of holes and badly painted, that seemed to hold some verses.

The whole assembly grew curious and demanded to have the verses read publicly. One of the curates offered to do the service, and as everyone fell into a perfect silence, he began to read the following:

Sonnit

Us pore folk of the town
Come here on this joyful day
To wish you a happy birthday
With our sheep and little pigs.

---

[2] [*El gobernador de indios con sus oficiales de república*: the Spanish colonial system combined indirect rule for Indian towns with an overlay of Spanish settlements. In an ancient town such as Tula, the Indian ruler of the province was called a *gobernador* (governor) after the Spanish conquest; together with a town council of Indian officials (*república*), he ruled over the Indian citizens of the town, but was subordinated to the Spanish administrator, represented here by the subdelegado, who directly ruled the non-Indian settlers in the town and its district. –Tr.]

> We hope Your Honor takes them
> And finds them in your intrist
> Being in charge of justice
> And that our luv makes up for
> The prollems with this sonnit
> May you live a thousand years
> And then in heaven until all eternity.

Everyone applauded the "sonnit," redoubling their cheers for the subdelegado and their clinking on plates and glasses, along with more tippling, some doing more of it and others less, depending on each person's inclination.

The priest filled a small glass and gave it to the governor, saying, "Here, son, drink to the Subdelegado's health," while the Subdelegado himself ordered that the governor and all the Indian officials be given dinner in the room next door.

The governor picked up his glass of wine, and the toasting and clamor around the table started up again; the uproar was increased by the disagreeable noise of the drum and pipes, which was already giving us all headaches, until God granted that the whole family of them was called away to eat.

As soon as the Indians had retired from the room, everyone began to admire their "sonnit," which was being passed from hand to hand, but furtively, so that those concerned would not notice.

Parting from this, the conversation circled around from topic to topic until it touched upon the origins of poetry, a subject that a rather quick-witted young woman asked one of the curates, who was known as a poet, to explain; and without waiting to be begged, he replied, "Miss, what I can tell you about this point is that poetry is very ancient in the world. Some say that its origins date to Adam, adding that Jubal, the son of Lamech, was the father of all poets, basing this opinion on the scripture that says, 'Jubal was the father of them that play upon the harp and the organs,'[3] because the ancients knew that music and poetry are closely related; so much so that some people wrote that Osiris, the king of Egypt, was so fond of music that he always had female singers accompany his army, among whom nine were the most distinguished, to whom the Greeks gave the name of *muses*. The truth is that we know from the most ancient history in the world—that is, the books of Moses—that the Hebrews possessed this divine art before any other nation. After the Deluge, it revived among the Egyptians, Chaldeans, and Greeks. Of these, the Greeks cultivated it most diligently, and it was propagated among all the nations according to their genius, climate, or application. Thus we know of no nation anywhere in the world, no matter how barbarous, that has not had knowledge of the poetic art, and even, at times, has had excellent poets. In pagan times here in America, the Indians knew this sublime art and that of music; they had their dances or *mitotes*,[4] in which they sang poems to their gods, and there were even such elegant poets among them that one of

---

[3] [Genesis 4:21. –Tr.]

[4] [*Mitote:* from Nahuatl *mihtohtli*, a kind of dance; applied in the colonial era to Indian gatherings that involved music and dancing. –Tr.]

them, having been sentenced to death, composed such a tender and poignant poem on the eve of his sacrifice that, when he himself sang it, it sufficed to soften the judge who had sentenced him, obliging him to revoke the sentence: which is as much as to say, he was such a good poet that with one of his poems he redeemed his death and prolonged his life. This case is told to us by Boturini in his *Idea of the History of the Indies.*[5] Softening a tyrant's heart is certainly a great deal to ask of anything, yet the effect of poetry on the human heart is well known and long-established, especially when it is accompanied by music. In confirmation of this truth, the fables tell us that Orpheus conquered and tamed lions, tigers, and other wild beasts, and that Amphion rebuilt the walls of Thebes, using only song, harp, and lyre, in order to signify the sovereign power of music and poetry: for by themselves alone, they are sufficient to reduce savages and fierce men scarcely better than beasts to civil life."

"Though I doubt that would be the case," said the subdelegado, "for the author of our 'sonnit,' even if, in singing it, he were to be accompanied by the sweet strains of drum or pipes."

Everyone laughed at the tasteless joke of the subdelegado, who, in hopes of hearing me spout nonsense and anger the priest, then asked me, "What can you tell us about these things, doctor?"

I wanted to look good and to voice my opinion about everything, even things that I didn't understand, having forgotten the lessons that the other good curate had taught me on the hacienda; but I knew nothing at all about a single word that had just been spoken. However, my vanity won out against the limits of my knowledge, and with my accustomed haughtiness and pedantry I said, "There is no doubt that the curate has spoken very well; yet poetry is even more ancient than he says, for he has only brought it back to Adam, while I believe that there were poets even before Adam lived."

This bit of nonsense scandalized everyone, and the priest most of all, for he asked me, "How could there have been poets before there were men?"

"Yet so it is, sir," I calmly replied; "for before there were men, there were angels, and as soon as the angels were created, they intoned their hymns of praise to the Creator, and clearly if they sang, it was in verse; and if they sang verses, they must have composed them; and if they composed them, they knew how to compose them; and if they knew how to compose verses, they were poets. So tell me, everyone, if poetry isn't older than Adam."

When the priest heard this, he merely shook his head and didn't say a single word in reply; as for the others, some smiled and others were amazed by my argument, and more so when the subdelegado went on to say, "No doubt, no doubt about it; our young doctor has convinced us and has taught us an admirable and unheard-of snippet of erudition. Imagine how the antiquarians have strained their heads in search of the origins of poetry, some of them focusing on Jubal, others on Deborah, others on Moses, others on the Chaldeans, others on the Egyptians, others on the Greeks, and all of them sticking tenaciously to their own systems, unable to come to

---

[5] [Lorenzo Boturini (1702–1751), *Idea de una nueva historia general de la América Septentrional* (Madrid, 1746), pp. 96–97. –Tr.]

any accord: and now Dr. Don Pedro has led us out of this bewildering Babel, hurling the bar a hundred yards beyond what the best antiquarians and historians have managed, and raising it up above the clouds, for he makes it ascend up to the angels! Come on, gentlemen, this time let's drink a toast to the health of our young doctor."

Saying this, he picked up his glass, and everyone else joined in, repeating after him, "Long live the erudite doctor!"

As you might imagine, this toast did not lack its round of applause or the usual clinking of glasses, plates, and forks. But who would believe, my dear children, that I could have been so stupid and so uncouth that I didn't realize all this noise was nothing but the flattering echo of the subdelegado's mocking irony? Yet so it was. I tossed back my glass of wine, very satisfied—what am I saying?—very shallow and conceited, thinking it had been not a dry joke about my ignorance, but well-deserved praise for my merit.

But do you think, dear children, that your father, who was still at an age bordering on boyhood, was the only one who ever felt willfully smug about his public reputation? Do you believe that only I, and only at that age, pardoned the mockery of the wise because I imagined it was praise, due to my own ignorance and blind enthusiasm? No, my darlings: in every era, men of every age have been just as stupid and conceited as I was, and have smugly supposed that only they knew, that only they were on target, and that the arcane truths of wisdom were open to them alone. Ay! I don't know if, by the time you read my reflections, this plague of fools might have ended in the world; but if it should unfortunately still continue, I ask you to observe diligently the following lessons: *a willful man is neither wise nor good; a meek man is ready to become good and to become wise; a talkative, vain man is never wise; a quiet, humble man who subordinates his opinion to that of those who know more is positively good: that is, he is a man with a good heart and a perfect disposition for becoming wise some day.* Careful with my digressions, which might be what matter the most for you.

The subdelegado, seeing my serenity, continued, "Young doctor, according to your opinion and that of the curate, poetry is a divine art or science; for whether it was first instilled in angels or men, since neither the former nor the latter had anyone to imitate, it is clear that only the Author of Creation could have instilled it in them; and in this case, tell us: why is it that there are more poets among some nations than others, if all descend from Adam? Because there's no two ways about it: the Italians have, if not the best poets, at least the ones with the greatest facility in rhyming, such as improvisers, those quick-witted people who can versify on the spot and even create a multitude of verses."

I felt myself under assault by this question, for I didn't know how to resolve the difficulty, so I sidestepped it by replying, "Señor Subdelegado, I will not join the discussion, because I don't believe there ever has been or ever could be on-the-spot poets, or improvisers, as you call them. I would therefore have to be convinced of their reality before joining the debate, for *prius est esse quam taliter esse:* first establish that a thing exists, then discuss why it exists."

"Well, there is no doubt that there have been poetic improvisers, especially in Italy," said the parish priest, "and it amazes me that such a well-known fact could have escaped the good doctor's erudition. This kind of ease in versifying on the spot is quite ancient. Ovid admits that it was true of himself, going so far as to say that he would speak about any subject that came up in verse, and this during the time that he was not trying to write poems.[6] I have read what Paolo Giovio said about the poet Camilo Cuerno, a famous improviser who enjoyed many gifts from Pope Leo X because of this skill: the poet was standing by a window, improvising verses while the pontiff ate his dinner, and the pope so enjoyed the quickness of his talent that he passed him the dishes he was eating, and had him drink from his own wine, but under the condition that he had to invent at least two verses on each subject suggested to him.[7] Father Calasanz tells us, in his *Discerning Genius*, about a little boy who scarcely knew how to write, yet was able to come up instantly with verses in any meter that was given to him, and sometimes such witty ones that the wise adults around him were astonished.[8] We could cite several examples of these improvising poets; but why wear ourselves out, when everybody knows that one flourished in this very kingdom, the one known as *el negrito poeta*, the Little Black Poet, about whose swift wit the old folks used to speak?"[9]

"Tell us, Father," said a little girl, "some of the Little Black Poet's verses."

"Many have been attributed to him," said the priest, "and fiction has played a role in each; but to please you, I will recount two or three that I know for certain are his, according to what I was told by an old man from Mexico who said that he heard them from the poet's own mouth. Listen, everyone: one day our black poet entered an apothecary shop, where an apothecary or a physician was speaking with a priest about hair, and at the moment when the black man walked into the shop, he was saying, 'your hairs hang from. . . .' The priest, who knew the poet, incited him to use his skill by saying, 'Negrito, here's a peso for you, if you can rhyme what this gentleman just said, that *your hairs hang from*. . . .' The little black poet said, with his usual quickness,

'I've already won that sum
Unless I lose my wits;
Get out, before there come
A loosened beam that hits
You where your hairs hang from.'

"This was widely known in Mexico. The same phrase was given to Mother Sor Juana Inés de la Cruz, who was a Hieronymite nun, a celebrated genius, and a famous

---

[6] *Scribere conabar verba soluta modis, / sponte sua carmen numeros veniebat ad aptos.* ["When I was trying to write in prose, / of its own accord my song would come in the right rhythms." Ovid, *Tristia*, IV: 10, lines 24–25. –Tr.]

[7] [The anecdote is told in Mencke, *Declamaciones*, pp. 124–25. –Tr.]

[8] [Ignacio Rodríguez de San José de Calasanz, *Discernimiento filosófico de ingenios para artes y ciencias* (Madrid, 1795), p. 203. –Tr.]

[9] [*El negrito poeta*: a semi-legendary figure whose real name was José Vasconcelos (not to be confused with the 20th-century author of the same name), and who was born in Almolonga near Jalapa; see Nicolás León, *El negrito poeta mexicano y sus populares versos* (Mexico, 1912), and Eduardo Montes Moctezuma, *El negrito poeta mexicano y el dominicano: ¿realidad o fantasía?* (Mexico, 1982). –Tr.]

poetess in her time, who earned the epithet of Apollo's 10th Muse, to see if she could rhyme it; but the nun was not able to come up with a verse, and she excused herself very nicely in a set of quatrains, while praising our poet's facility.[10]

"On another occasion, a notary and a constable were walking near him when the notary dropped something; the constable stooped to pick it up, and the other asked what it was. The constable replied that it was a file of papers, and the black man promptly said,

> 'Isn't one of the Devil's capers
> To stoop for a file so contemptible?
> But whenever has any constable
> Not stooped to filing papers?'

"Another time, he entered a house where an image of the Virgin of the Conception was displayed on a table. . . . Just listen to all the discordant things that were there: an image of the Conception, a painting of the Holy Trinity, another of Moses and the burning bush, a pair of shoes, and a couple of silver spoons. Well, gentlemen, the owner of the house doubted the black poet's facility, so he told him that if he could accommodate all those things in a single strophe of four lines, he would give him the spoons. That was all it took for the black poet to say,

> 'Moses didn't dare to look at God
> Till he took off his shoes and his feet were bare;
> So now, by the *Virgen de la Concepción,*
> It's time to give me that silverware.'

"This verse does not display any great ideas or sharp wit, yet the facility with which it accommodates so many disconnected things, and does so with a modicum of sense, is not unworthy of praise.

"Finally, we all know that the hour of death is no time for joking around, yet in the hour of our poet's death, he demonstrated how congenial he found versifying, because when an Augustinian friar came to take his final confession, he said,

> 'Now I know, for sure and of course,
> That death is fast on my heels,
> Because wherever the vulture reels,
> There's bound to be a dying horse.'[11]

---

[10] [The editor of the fourth edition includes Sor Juana's quatrains, with this note:] As the works of Sor Juana are not very common, here we include her answer, which is from volume II of her works. –E. [Her poem (in her *Obras completas*, Mexico: Fondo de Cultura Económica, 1951, v. 1, pp. 276 and 517–18) focuses on the grammatical details of the improviser's rhyme, and thus is essentially untranslatable. –Tr.]

[11] [The Mexican vulture (*zopilote*), a traditional omen of death, is black and bald-headed, inviting a comparison with the black-robed and tonsured Augustinian. –Tr.]

"We should note that this poor black man was an utter commoner, without a drop of education or erudition. I have heard people swear that he did not even know how to write. So if, in the midst of such shadowy ignorance, he was capable of bursting forth with such rapid and witty verses, what might he have done if he had attained the education of such wise fellows as, for example, the good doctor who graces us with his presence?"

"May your life be blessed, Father," I replied.

Meanwhile we finished dinner and the tablecloths were removed, while we remained engaged in after-dinner conversation, without saying grace, which was already falling out of custom in that time; but the subdelegado, who was aching to see the priest and me entangled in an argument about medicine, said to me, "I was certainly hoping to hear you and the father speak about medical practice, because the fact is that our parish priest is quite opposed to physicians."

"He shouldn't be," I said, rather upset, "because our priest should know that God says that 'He hath created medicines out of the earth, and a wise man will not abhor them.' *Dominus creavit de terra medicinam, et vir prudens non aborrebit eam.* He says as well that we should 'honor the physician for his services,' *Honora medicum propter necesitem.* He says. . . . "[12]

"Enough of that," said the priest. "Don't keep piling on texts that I can't understand. Chapter 38 of Ecclesiasticus has fourteen verses in favor of physicians, but the fifteenth verse says, 'He that sins in the sight of his Maker, shall fall into the hands of the physician.' This curse does little honor to physicians, or at least not to bad physicians.

"I know full well that medicine is a very difficult art; I know that it takes a long time to learn; that a man's whole life is not sufficient time; that its opinions are difficult and fallible; that its experiments are practiced on the respectable life of a man; that it isn't enough for a physician to do everything he can on his part, if he is not aided by circumstances, by his assistants, and by the patient himself, insofar as they are able; I know that I am not saying any of this for the first time, but that it was first spoken by the prince of medicine, the sage of the isle of Chios, Hippocrates, the great and sensitive Greek whose memory will not fade so long as men live on earth; the philanthropist who lived to be nearly one hundred and who spent almost all his years attending miserable mortals, investigating the defects of illness, soliciting the causes of diseases and the selection and effectiveness of cures, and applying his speculation and his practice to the object that he set for himself, which was to obtain relief for his fellow men. I know all this, and I know that before Hippocrates, for lack of any other source of help, wretched patients would put themselves on display in front of the doors to Diana's temple in Ephesus, and there everyone would go and see them, pity them, and prescribe for them whatever came into their heads. I know that the cures that were tested for this illness or that were inscribed on what they called *the tablets of medicine;* I know that our Hippocrates, after thirty-five years studying in the schools of Athens from the age of fourteen, and after learning everything that its physicians had to teach him, was not content, but continued

---

[12] [Ecclesiasticus 38:4 and 38:1. –Tr.]

wandering from kingdom to kingdom, from province to province, from city to city, until he found those tablets and used them, together with his repeated observations, to create his celebrated aphorisms; I know that after these discoveries, medicine became a subject of study for selfishness and venality, and not as before, when it was done for friendship toward humankind. I know all this, and many other things that I will not relate, so as not to exhaust my listeners; but I also know that today no one scrutinizes the talent one needs to become a physician, but rather that whoever wants to be one takes it upon himself to become one, even if he lacks the necessary conditions; I know that everyone who has completed the courses required by the University, even if he has learned nothing from the professors' lectures, and who has completed his apprenticeship, perhaps obtaining an unjust certificate from his maestro, is allowed to take the examination, and if he has the examiners in his favor, or if he has the fortune to guess the correct answers to the questions he is asked, even if everything goes according to all the rules that we must suppose are required for such functions, he will be given his certificate of examination, and with it his license to kill anyone with impunity. This I know, and I also know that many physicians are not what they should be—that is, they do not study persistently, they do not practice effectively, they do not observe nature scrupulously, as they ought; they forget that the physician's academy and his best library are the patient's bed, not his gilded bookshelves, his many books, and his excessive luxury, much less the ridiculous pedantry with which he strings together citations, authorities, and Latin tag lines in front of those who cannot understand him.

"I know that a good physician should be a good physicist, a good chemist, a good botanist, and a good anatomist; and yet I see an endless number of physicians in the world who do not know, for example, how sodium sulfate is made and what it is, yet who prescribe it as a specific for certain illnesses in which it is pernicious; who do not know the parts of the human body, the virtues or venomousness of many simples, or the ways in which many things can be broken down or simplified. I also know that you cannot be a good physician if you are not an upright man: that is, if you are not permeated by the most vivid sentiments of humanity, or of love for your fellow men; because a physician who tries to cure someone out of his interest in pesos or pesetas, and not out of love and charity for his poor patient, must surely be very untrustworthy; and the fact is that this is usually the case.

"When physicians take their examinations, they swear to give effective, free care to the poor out of charity, but what do we see? That when the poor come to their houses to consult them about their illnesses without paying anything, they are treated in any old way; but in the case of rich patients who can call physicians to their houses, the latter go promptly to visit them, where they treat them with care, though their care is often mixed with such disregard (if this is not a contradiction in terms) that, with it alone, they kill their patients."

Here the priest took a brief pause, taking out his snuff box, and after he furnished his nostrils with a pinch of snuff, he went on to say what you will see in the next chapter.

CHAPTER 28

IN WHICH OUR PERICO TELLS US ABOUT THE CONCLUSION TO
THE PRIEST'S SERMON, THE UNFORTUNATE HAND HE HAD IN A
PLAGUE, AND THE WICKED WAY HE LEFT TOWN, TOUCHING, IN
THE COURSE OF THE CHAPTER, ON VARIOUS CURIOUS MATTERS

"I wouldn't want you to think, gentlemen, that I am trying to paint physicians in a bad light," the priest went on. "Medicine is a heavenly art, which God has bestowed on man; its worthy practitioners deserve our honors and our praise; but when they are less worthy than they should be, our vituperation is aimed at their ineptitude and selfishness, not the usefulness and necessity of medicine and its wise practitioners. An educated, hard-working, and charitable physician is praiseworthy; but a stupid and venal physician who only went into the profession to make a living because he didn't have the strength to support a *mecapal*[1] is an odious man who deserves a reputation as an assassin of humankind, by the license, albeit involuntary, of the Protomedicato. These were the sort of physicians who were exiled like the plague from many provinces of Rome and other places, and indeed a town can have no worse plague than a bad physician. It would be many times better to leave a patient in the wise hands of Nature than to entrust him to the hands of a foolish and self-interested physician."

"But I'm not one of those," I said rather shamefacedly, because everyone was looking at me and smiling.

"Nor am I talking about you," the priest replied, "nor about Sancho or Pedro or Martín; I am not criticizing any person in particular, and making veiled attacks has never been my habit. I am speaking in general, and only against bad physicians—empiricists[2] and charlatans who abuse this precious and necessary art, which was bestowed upon us by the Author of Nature to ease us of our pains. If anyone who hears me speaking this way believes that I am talking about him, that must be a sign that his conscience accuses him; and in that case, friend, if the shoe fits, then be my guest and wear it. Though the fact is that what you just said, that you are *not one of those*, is exactly what every duffer says in every line of work; yet saying so doesn't make it so."

"But I'm not, sir," I broke in; "I'm not one of those; I know what my obligations are, and I have been examined and approved *nemine discrepante* (unanimously) by the Royal Protomedicato of Mexico; I know what all the branches of medicine are:

---

[1] [*Mecapal*: a strap used by *tamemes* or porters—men (almost always Indians) who carried cargo in colonial Mexico for lack of beasts of burden. The *mecapal* went around the load, which was carried on the porter's back, and passed across the porter's forehead. –Tr.]

[2] [Empiricist (*empírico*): the original sense of the word in Spanish (and indeed in English) was, to quote the 1732 edition of the *Diccionario de la Real Academia Española,* "el Medico que cura por sola la experiencia, sin haber estudiado la facultad de la Medicina, no haciendo caso de saber las complexiones y naturalezas de los hombres, ni poniendo cuidado en investigar las causas de las enfermedades" (the Physician who cures by experience alone, never having studied the science of Medicine, making no point of learning the complexions and natures of men, and paying no attention to investigating the causes of illnesses). Lizardi uses it in this sense. –Tr.]

Physiology, Pathology, Semeiotics, and Therapeutics; I know the structure of the human body; which parts are fluid and which are solid; I know what bones and cartilage are, what the cranium is, and that it is composed of eight parts; I know what the occipital bone, the frontal bone, and the dura mater are; I know the number of ribs, and what the sternum, the scapula, the coccyx, and the tibias are; I know what the intestines, the veins, the nerves, the muscles, the arteries, the cellular tissue, and the epidermis are; I know how many humors man has, and their names, such as blood, bile, phlegm, chyle, and gastric juices; I know about lymph and animal spirits, how they function in the healthy body and in the sick body; I can call illnesses by their proper and legitimate Greek names, such as ascites, anasarca, hydrophobia, cancer, pleurisy, venereal disease, chlorosis, cachexia, podagra, paraphrenitis, priapism, paroxysm, and a thousand other illnesses that the foolish common folk call dropsy, rabies, the French disease, aching sides, gout, and the other usual nonsense; I recognize the virtue of cures without having to know how apothecaries and chemists concoct them, the simples from which they are made, or how they work in the human body; and I likewise know about febrifuges, astringents, antispasmodics, aromatics, diuretics, sternutators, narcotics, expectorants, purgatives, diaphoretics, coagulants, antivenereals, emetics, stimulants, vermifuges, laxatives, caustics, and anticolics; I know. . . . "

"Enough, good doctor," said the priest in great annoyance, "enough, for the love of God, because this is too much learning, and darned if I understand a word you've said. I feel like I've been listening to Hippocrates speaking in his own language; but the fact is, with all this learning, you finished off poor dropsical old Tía Petronila in four days, after she had lived with her *Ay, ay!* for many years before you showed up; and after you came, you helped her pick up the pace, with too many purgatives that were too pungent and in excessive doses, which seemed like a medical heresy to me, because weakness in an old person is precisely a contraindication to purges and bleedings. That was the same reason why another poor gouty or rheumatic old man wouldn't let you kill him off. With all your learning, friend, you're imperceptibly depopulating my parish, for since the day you arrived I've noticed that my parish business is up fifty percent; and although some other priest, more self-interested than I, might thank you for the multitude of funerals you would have sent his way, I don't, friend, because I love my parishioners too much, and I realize that as time goes on you'll take away my job as priest, because once all the people in the parish seat and its dependencies are gone, I'll be the priest of empty houses and uncultivated fields. So imagine how much you know, since even when it redounds in my self-interest, your learning makes me mourn."

Everyone heartily laughed at the priest's irony, and feeling unsettled by this, I said to him while my ears burned, "Father, sir, for one to speak, one must think and be educated about the subject on which one speaks. The cases that you have mentioned to mock me are common ones; it happens every day that a very sick patient dies in the hands of the best of physicians. What do you think, physicians are gods who should be able to give life to the sick? Ovid, in Book One of *Ex Ponto*, says that healing a patient is not always in the physician's hands, and that illness often defeats medicine:

Non est in medico semper relevetur ut aeger,
Interdum docta plus valet arte malum.

"He also says that there are incurable diseases that would not get any better even if Aesculapius himself were to apply the medicine, and that would resist the most clearly indicated thermal waters, such as the waters of El Peñón or Atotonilco here,[3] and one of these illnesses is epilepsy. Listen to his words:

Adferat ipse licet sacras Epidaurius herbas,
Sanabit nulla vulnera cordis ope.

"In view of this, you may be amazed, Father, that some of my patients have died, while patients of the finest physicians die. That would be all we needed, if people thought they could become immortal just by calling the doctor. If one gouty old fellow decides not to continue with me, it proves nothing, except that he has recognized that his disease is incurable; for as Ovid said, gout cannot be cured by medicine: *Tollere nodosam nescit medicina podagram.*—Ovid, *loco citato*."[4]

"I'm the one who must be loco," said the priest, "and an idiot and a fool, for wanting to confer with you about these things."

"You are quite right about that, sir," I said, "if you are speaking sincerely. Indeed there is no greater foolishness than to argue about something one does not understand. *Quod medicorum est promittunt medici, tractant fabrilia fabri,* as Horace said in Epistle 1 of Book 1.[5] Father, each person should argue what he knows; let him speak of his own profession and not get tangled up in what he doesn't understand, remembering that the theologian will speak well about theology, the canon lawyer about canon law, the physician about medicine, artisans about whatever concerns their trades, the pilot about the winds, the farmer about oxen, and so on:

Navita de ventis, de bobus narret arator."[6]

This impolite reprimand was the last straw for the priest, who slapped his hand down on the table and said to me, "Slow down, now, doctor, or rather, charlatan; please pay some attention to where, how, to whom, and in front of whom you are speaking. Do you think I am just a *topile* or some sort of oaf, that you can get upset

---

[3] [There are many thermal baths in Mexico named El Peñón (a Spanish word sometimes applied to a volcano with a small lake in the crater) and Atotonilco (Nahuatl for "place of warm water"). Here Periquillo is probably referring to the ones about 10 miles east of Tula. –Tr.]

[4] [Ovid, *Ex Ponte*, I:3, lines 17–18, 21–22, and 23: "It is not always in the doctor's power to cure the patient; / at times the illness surpasses his skill. / . . . / Even if the Epidaurian (i.e., Aesculapius) himself brings sacred herbs, / he cannot cure a wound to the heart. / Medicine does not know how to lift the effects of gnarled gout. . . . " –Tr.]

[5] [Horace, *Epistles*, II:1, lines 115–16, "Let physicians attend to the work of physicians, and workers handle workers' tools." –Tr.]

[6] ["Let the pilot speak of winds, and the plowman of oxen." Propercius, *Carmina*, II, line 43, as quoted by Jamin, *Le fruit*, p. 58 (see Ruiz Barrionuevo, p. 568). –Tr.]

with me like this and try scolding me like a boy? Or do you believe that because I've put up with you patiently, I can't reason well enough to treat you as what you are, which is a mad, vain, uneducated pedant? Yes, sir, that's all you are, and all you will ever be in the view of anyone with judgment, no matter how much Latin and nonsense you say. . . . "

The subdelegado and all the others tried to calm down the priest when they saw him getting so outraged, while I, feeling none too sure of myself—because all the Indians had run out when they heard the argument, having already finished eating—said to him with a great frown, "Father, please forgive me; if I erred, I did so unintentionally, and not meaning to be impolite, for I should know that you and your fellow priests and curates are always right about everything you say and that no one can argue with you; so the best thing for me to do is keep my mouth shut and not start a kicking match with Samson. *Ne contendas cum potentioribus*,[7] as He said, Who always spoke and always will speak truth."

"See here, everyone," said the priest; "if I were not persuaded that the good doctor says the first thing that comes to his mouth without pausing for reflection, this would have been enough to get me more irritated; for what he is implying is that all priests and curates always want to get their way about everything simply because of what they are, which is undeniably an insult not only to me, but to the entire respectable clergy; yet I repeat that I am convinced about how he came to say these things, and so we must forgive him and set him straight along the way."

And, turning to me, he said, "Friend, I do not deny that there are some clergymen who, because of what they are, always want to get their way about everything, as you have said; but you must consider that this is not true of all the clergy, merely of one or two imprudent priests who, in this or worse things, demonstrate their lack of talent and perhaps vilify their own characters; yet such a case would not be cause for surprise, for in any corporation, no matter how small and how enlightened, there will always be one unruly member; moreover, this should not be taken as the rule, so as to speak unthinkingly of the entire priesthood. I must confess it is true that some individual clergymen might be the way you have said; and I would add that if they do maintain something that is in error, even though they know it is wrong, merely because they are fathers, then they are acting badly; and if they insult any layman, not because of some prior act or because they are enraged by some rudeness against them, but only because they conceitedly think that the layman is a Christian and so has to respect their character to the last, then they are acting very badly, and they should be reproached, for they ought to reflect that their character does not excuse them from observing the laws that social order has prescribed for everyone. You and all the gentlemen listening will realize through this that I am not taking advantage of my office to be disrespectful to anyone, as those who know me and have dealt with me will recognize. If I have gone too far about anything with you, please forgive me, for what I said was provoked by your inadvertent reproach—a reproach that missed the anvil, because when I talk about something, I make sure that I have forces in reserve to back up what I'm saying; and if not, then let's roll up our sleeves. Among

---

[7] [Ecclesiasticus 8:1, "Strive not with a powerful man." –Tr.]

other things, I remember telling you that you were saying things that you did not understand (which is what we call pedantry). I hope that you can make me look bad in front of these gentlemen by doing me the favor of explaining to us what branch of medicine is called *semeiotics*; what the *gastric* or *pancreatic* humor is; what kind of illness *priapism* is; what the *mesentery glands* are; what different types of *cephalalgias* there are; and what kind of remedy an *emetic* is; but let me warn you that I know all this very well, and I have books in my library that explain it all beautifully, and I can show them to these gentlemen in a minute; so don't run the risk of saying one thing for the other, trusting that I won't understand you, for even though I'm not a physician, I have always been curious and have loved reading about everything; in a word, I have been an apprentice of every art, though a journeyman of none. So let's see, then; if you can give me the right answers to what I've asked, I'll give you this ounce of gold for your snuff; and if not, I'll be content to hear you confess that I'm not one of those priests who maintain an argument just because I'm a priest, but that I know what I'm talking about and what I'm arguing."

My blood sank to my toenails when I heard the priest's proposal, because darned if I understood anything he had said, since all I had learned in my maestro's house was those barbaric words, confident that learning them by memory and being able to say them jauntily was the only thing I needed to do in order to be a physician, or at least to seem like one; and so I had no other way out but to say, "Father, please excuse me, but I do not intend to submit to such an examination; the Protomedicato has already examined me and passed me, as my certificates and documents attest."

"Fine," said the priest; "simply by refusing such an easy request, you have satisfied me; but I also declare that I will not submit to unskilled physicians, or those who even appear to me to be such. Yes, sir; I will continue to be my own physician, as I have been up to now; at least I will find it easier to pardon my mistakes; and as for the branch of medicine that deals with maintaining health, which the professionals call *hygiene*, I will be content to follow the rules that the Salernitan School prescribed for a king of Great Britain,[8] namely: drink little wine, eat little supper, exercise, never take afternoon naps or what we call *siestas*, empty the stomach, avoid worries and cares, avoid anger even more so; to which I add, take baths occasionally and the simplest medicines when required: and look at me, healthy and stout as you see me here; because there are no two ways about it, friend, I would be the first to hand myself over to the discretion of any physician if all physicians were what they should be; but unfortunately, it is almost impossible to tell a good physician from a foolish empiricist or a fast-talking healer. Charlatans abound in every science, but in medicine most of all. No layman would dare to preach from a pulpit, to resolve a case of conscience in a confessional, to defend a lawsuit in court; but what am I saying! Who would even dare to cut cloth for a frock coat without being a tailor, or cut

---

[8] [Salernitan School: the teachings of the famed medieval medical school in Salerno, Sicily, were summed up in the 12th-century *Regimen Sanitatis Salernitanum* (over 400 manuscript and printed versions exist), which claimed to be written "for the English king," though scholars believe it originated as a translation of the Arabic medical text *Sirr al-asrar*. Lizardi found the citation in Jamin, *Le fruit*, p. 102. –Tr.]

leather for shoes without being a shoemaker? No one, surely; but who stops before prescribing medicine? No one, either. The theologian, the canon lawyer, the jurist, the astronomer, the tailor, the shoemaker, and all of us are physicians whenever we get a chance. Yes, friend; we all prescribe our cures with a *God help us and save us,* just because we have seen them prescribed before, or because they've worked for us in the past, without bothering to notice how different one person's nature is from another's, without knowing what the contraindications are, and without understanding that what's a cure for Juan is poison for Pedro. Let's take as an example: in some types of apoplexy, a bleeding is necessary and beneficial; but in others the patient cannot be bled without risk, such as a pregnant woman with apoplexy, for whom an abortion is almost necessary. The non-physician does not perceive these complications; he proceeds recklessly and kills with the best of intentions. There is a reason why the Laws of the Indies strictly prohibit the exercise of empiricism. You may read, if you please, laws 4 and 5 of Book V, Title 6, of the *Recopilación,*[9] which speak to this same topic; and even wise physicians (such as M. Tissot in his *Advice to the People*) loudly denounce charlatans.

"I greatly desire that we would observe here the method that is followed in many provinces of Asia with regard to physicians, which is that they have to visit their patients, have to make and pay for their medicines, and have to apply them. If the patient improves, the physician is compensated for his work according to the schedule of payments; but if he dies, the physician has to turn to ridding dogs of fleas. This beautiful measure produces several good results: for instance, that physicians work hard at their studies, and that they are physicians, surgeons, chemists, botanists, and nurses all at the same time.

"And don't you furrow your brows at me," the priest told me, smiling; "our own Spain once had something similar. Among the laws of the *Fuero Juzgo,*[10] in the title on leeches and patients, there is one in Book II that says that the leech (that is, the physician) must come to an agreement with his patients on what they are to pay him for their cure; and if he cures them, he gets paid, but if, instead of curing them, he makes them worse through his bleedings (by which we should understand, through any sort of error), he must pay them for the damage he has caused. And if the patient dies, if he was a free man, the physician is left to the discretion of the dead man's heirs; and if he was a slave, the physician must give his master another slave of equal value.

"I recognize that there is something forced about this law, because who can properly prove that one physician has made an error, except for another physician? And what physician would not support his colleague? And besides, a man has to die sometime, and in such a case it would not be difficult to impute to a physician what is simply the effect of nature, especially if the patient was a slave, for the master would want to recuperate his losses at the expense of the poor physician; but these

---

[9] [*Recopilación de leyes de los Reynos de las Indias,* the standard compilation of laws for Spain's overseas empire. –Tr.]

[10] [*Fuero Juzgo (Forum Judicum)*: a 12th-century legal compilation that long served as the basis of Spanish law. –Tr.]

laws are no longer in use, while I believe that the Asian laws remain in practice, and I like them very much."

By now the subdelegado and all those present were getting uncomfortable with hearing the priest talk so for so long, so they managed to cut him off by setting up a game of monte with a pot of 2,000 pesos, in which (not to tire you) I was cleaned out of everything I had stashed away, and was reduced to beggary.

That night the dancing and the refreshments were brilliant and splendid, insofar as the town's situation allowed. I stayed on there more out of obligation than my own free will after I was cleaned out; and at two in the morning I went home, where I scolded the cook and rapped my servant on the back of the neck, thereby imitating many foolish and imprudent masters who take their anger or some insult they received in the street out on their poor servants, or even on their wives and daughters.

And so I continued on for a few more months, not too bad and not too well. On one occasion they called me to visit a rich old woman, the wife of an hacienda owner, who was sick with fever, and when I arrived I found the priest, whom I feared like the devil; but I didn't forget my charlatanism, and said that it was nothing to worry about and that she wouldn't need to get her affairs in order; the priest, however, had already looked at her, and being more of a physician than I was, he said, "Look here: the patient is an old woman; she has been suffering from this fever for five days; she is very corpulent and at times drowsy; she has been delirious from time to time; she has the purplish blotches on her skin that you would call *petechiae;* it would appear to be a putrid or malignant fever: so let's not wait until she's *catching flies,* or as you would say, until she is *in agone,* to give last rights to her. Besides, friend, how can the physician neglect such an essential point as this, or entrust his patient to such a fleeting hope, and to a sense of security that the physician himself lacks? You should know that in the year 1429, the Council of Paris ordered physicians that they should exhort any patients who are in danger of dying to confess before giving them their bodily cures, and to deny them their assistance if they refuse this advice. In the same year, the Council of Tortosa forbade physicians to make three visits in a row to patients who had not confessed. The Second Lateran Council of 1215 says, in Canon 24, that when physicians are called to their patients' bedsides, they should, *before all else,* advise them to call for the physicians of souls, so that, having taken the necessary precautions for the health of their souls, they might more profitably take the remedies for their bodily health.[11]

"This, friend," the priest told me, "is what the Church has said in Her holy councils: so ask yourself how much our patient has to lose by confessing and taking her last sacrament, especially given the state she's in."

Flustered by all the things the priest had to say, I told him, "Sir, you are quite right; please do whatever you feel is necessary."

Indeed, the priest made good use of the precious instants, confessing her and giving last rites to her, and then I entered and got to work, prescribing caustics, friction

---

[11] [Spell (p. 154) notes that this passage is copied "almost verbatim from Francisco Pérez Pastor's *Diccionario portátil de los Concilios*" (Madrid, 1772). The final reference actually cites Canon 22 of the Fourth Lateran Council, not Canon 24 of the Second. –Tr.]

rubbing, poultices, refrigerants, and exterminants—because within two days she was already resting with Jesus.

Nevertheless, her death, like all the others, was attributed to the fact that she was mortal, that she was in God's hands, that she had reached the end of the line, that her hour had come, and other similar idiocies, for it is not God's will that the physician be reckless, nor is it an absolute decree (as theologians say) that a patient must die, if his nature can still resist an illness with the help of the proper medication; but at the time, I didn't know these theological niceties, nor was I interested in learning them. Afterward I found out that if I had administered several emollient enemas to the patient, and had taken care of her diet and made sure she could perspire freely, she likely would not have died; but at the time, I studied nothing, observed Nature even less, and only aimed at grabbing the peso, the real, or the peseta, depending on how the penitent fell.

I spent a few more months in this way (making it fifteen or sixteen months altogether that I lived in Tula), until that town was hit, as if for my sins, by a devil of a plague, which I never managed to understand; because my patients would come down with a sudden fever accompanied by nausea and delirium, and within four or five days, they'd kick the bucket.

I tried reading Tissot, Madame Fouquet, Gregorio López, Buchan, Vanegas, and every other medical compendium I could get my hands on; but it did me no good: my patients were dying by the thousands.[12]

At last, and to top off all my bad fortune, by following Dr. Purgante's system I took to draining the excessive humor from my patients, and to do this I made use of the fiercest purgatives; and, seeing that they only made my patients die emaciated, I worked to kill them off with the colic called the *ileac passion*, or to poison them once and for all. To do this, I gave them larger-than-regular doses of emetic tartar, in quantities of up to a dozen grains, causing my patients to die in terrible anguish.

For my sins, I ended up doing this to the wife of the Indian governor. I gave her the cream of tartar; she died; and the next day, when I went to see how she was feeling, I found the house swarming with Indian men, women, and children, all of them wailing as one.

I came in there, as foolish as I was shameless. It is worth noting that, by a miracle of God, I was riding my mule—well, not mine, but Dr. Purgante's; but the fact was that the mourners had scarcely seen me when, beginning with a murmuring of voices, such a furious whirlwind of shouts rose up against me, calling me thief and murderer, that I couldn't get over it; and more so when the whole town—for they were all there together, breaking down the dikes of moderation and giving themselves over to tears and vituperation—began picking up stones and hurling them at me in endless numbers, with good aim and loud shouts, while yelling at me in their

---

[12] [Tissot and Buchan, see Chapter 26, footnote 4; Marie de Maupeou Fouquet, *Recuil de receptes* (Lyon, 1667; Spanish translations, 1748 and 1750); Gregorio López (1542–1596), *Tesoro de medicina o de las plantas medicinales de la Nueva España* (several editions); Juan Manuel Venegas (not Vanegas), *Compendio de la medicina, o medicina práctica* (Mexico, 1788). –Tr.]

language: damn you, devil doctor, because you look like you're planning to finish off the whole town.

That was when I put my spurs to the mule and galloped off as fast as I could, armed with my wig and ruffled collar, which I never left behind, so that I would look respectable on all occasions.

The wicked Indians did not forget my house, which found no sanctuary in being next door to the parish priest's, for after they beat the cook and my serving lad, accusing them of covering up my murders, they practically demolished it, breaking my few pieces of furniture to bits and tossing my books and my boots off the balcony.

The uproar of the town was so great and fearsome that the Subdelegado took refuge in the rectory, from which he watched the rumpus with the priest from the balcony, and the clergyman said to him, "You have no need to fear; their rancor is all against the physician. If people would honor all charlatans this way more often, there wouldn't be so many quacks in the world."

This was the glorious way in which my medical adventures ended. I ran off like a hare, and between the speed that I raced her and the bad roads, my mule fell dead two days later in Tlalnepantla. It was to be expected that my ill-gotten gains would meet a disastrous end.

Finally, I sold the saddle and trappings in that town for the first price I was offered; I threw the wig and the ruffled collar into a ditch, not to look so ridiculous; and, walking on foot with my cape over my shoulder and a stick in my hand, I reached Mexico, where I met with the adventures that you will read about in Chapter 29 of this true and incalculable history.

CHAPTER 29

WHICH RECOUNTS THE FRIGHTFUL ADVENTURE OF
THE POTTER AND THE STORY OF THE MAN IN RAGS

There is no ghost or specter that can frighten a man as surely and as constantly as his own criminal conscience. It hounds him and startles him wherever he goes, always in proportion to the seriousness of his misdemeanors, no matter how well he has concealed them. Thus, even if no one pursues the delinquent, and if it has been his fortune that his wickedness has not been revealed, it makes no difference; he is filled with fright and unease everywhere. Any minor incident, a slight noise, the shadow of his own body, is enough to upset his spirit, make his heart tremble, and persuade him that he has fallen or is about to fall into the avenging hands of justice. The hapless fellow cannot live without weariness, cannot eat without bitterness, cannot go for a stroll without apprehension, and even his sleep is interrupted by shocks and sudden starts. This was my inner state when I entered this capital. At every step, I felt I was about to be beaten or thrown in jail. Every time I saw a person dressed in black, I thought it was Chanfaina; every old woman frightened me, for in her I saw the barber's wife; every apothecary, every physician. . . . What am I saying! Even the mules filled me with dread, for they all reminded me of my ill deeds.

A few times I would start to imagine the inward tranquility that a man with a good conscience would enjoy, and I would recall what Horace said to Aristius Fuscus:[1]

> The man who lives a proper life
> And does no wrong to others
> Needs not protect himself with shields
> Nor take up poisoned arrows.
> He passes through all kinds of dread
> Yet him no danger startles,
> For he is sure of his defense,
> Which is a healthy conscience.

But these serious reflections did not go beyond idle imaginings, and never became rooted in my heart; thus I could cast them out of my mind with bad thoughts without making any use of them, and I only tried to run away from the people I had harmed, which was why the first thing I made sure to do was to shed the ruffled cape, both to be rid of that ridiculous article, and to distance myself from an undeniable witness to my faithlessness. To do this, on the same day and the very afternoon that I reached Mexico, I went to sell it in the flea market, or "the louse market" as they call it, because that is where the poorest people trade, and where they sell the dirtiest, most disgusting, repellent, and even stolen goods.

---

[1] This is not a literal translation, but rather an allusion to Horace's [Book 1,] Ode 22, which begins: *Integer vitae scelerisque purus* [The man who is of an upright life and free of sin], and so on.

So, ducking into an entrance way, I folded up the cape and, covered with only my hat and dressed all in black, looking for all the world like a truant schoolboy, went to the most reputable trader in that flea market.

Unfortunately for me, this trader had been warned by Dr. Purgante (whose real name was Don Celidonio Matamoros, though a better name for him would have been Matacristianos);[2] as I was saying, this trader had been asked to recover this cape if anyone tried to sell it, and had been given a very precise description of it.

Two of the signs by which it could be recognized were a row of stitches sewn with green silk thread, and a small hole under the collar that had been mended with blue cloth. I had never in my life bothered to notice such trifling details; so I went to sell it very blatantly, but unfortunately the trader remembered the doctor's request, and the first thing his eyes fell on—before he had even unfolded it—was the row of stitches sewn with green silk.

As soon as I said that it was a cape that went with a ruffled collar, and he saw the contrasting silk in the stitching, he told me, "Friend, this cape might belong to my *compadre*[3] Don Celidonio, or Dr. Purgante, as they've nicknamed him. At least, if turns out to have a little blue patch under the collar, it'll be this one for sure."

He unfolded it, looked it over, and found the patch. Then he asked me if it was my cape, and whether I had bought it or had been given it to sell.

Disconcerted by these questions and not knowing what to say, I replied that I could swear that the cape was not my own and that I hadn't bought it, but that I had been given it to sell.

"Well, who gave it to you to sell? What's his name, and where does he live or work?" the trader asked me.

I said it was a man I barely knew, though he knew me; that I was an upright man, even if the cape was in dispute; but that the fellow was around there somewhere nearby.

Then the trader told a friend of his who was in his stall to go with me, and not to release me until I had turned in the fellow who had given me the cape to sell, because you could tell that I was an honest simpleton, but that this cape had been stolen from Don Celidonio by a servant lad named Periquillo Sarniento that he used to have, along with a mule with saddle and stirrups, trappings, a wig, a ruffled collar, a few books, some money, and who knows what else; so either he should take me to jail, or I should turn in the thief, and when I turned him in, they would let me go free.

With this sentence hanging over me, I set off in the company of my constable, whom I dragged up one street and down another, never managing to find the thief who was always lurking so nearby, until ill luck offered up to me a poor man wrapped up in an old cloak and sitting in an entrance way.

---

[2] [An untranslatable pun: Matamoros literally means "Moor-slayer," a name deriving from the medieval wars between Moors and Christians in Spain; Matacristianos, "Christian-slayer," is a variant on the sardonic Spanish term for a quack doctor. –Tr.]

[3] [*Compadre* is what the godfather of a child and the child's father call each other; it is a close and deeply respectful relationship. –Tr.]

When I saw him there dressed all in rags, I figured him for a thief, as if every man in rags were a thief, and I told my honorary gendarme that this was the fellow who had given me the cape to sell.

The big brute believed me without another word, and he went with me to ask for help from the nearest patrol, which did not turn us down; and so, reinforced with four men and a sergeant, we went back to arrest the man in rags.

The moment the luckless fellow was surprised by a shout of *You're under arrest*, he stood up and said, "Gentlemen, I see that I am under arrest, but what have I done, or what reason do you have for arresting me?"

"For robbery," said the gendarme.

"Robbery?" the pauper repeated. "Surely you have made a mistake."

"No, we haven't made any mistake," said the trader's friend; "we have witnesses to the robbery, and your looks are enough to prove what you are, and everyone else who dresses like you. Tie him up."

"Gentlemen," the poor man said, "don't you see, one devil looks like another; maybe I'm not the one you're looking for; even if there are witnesses who will testify against me, that's not enough proof for this outrage, when we know that there are a thousand villains who would testify against any upright man for two bits; and finally, being poor and badly dressed is not proof that a man's a scoundrel; the habit doesn't make the monk. So, gentlemen, to do this ill deed to me simply on account of my indecent clothes or the depositions of one or two rogues who've been bought for some base price, without any further evidence or investigation, seems to me the sort of trampling that has no place within the prescribed limits of justice. I am a man known to none of you, and one whom you are judging merely by the appearance of my clothes; but a bad cape can cover a good drinker—that is, perhaps under this shabby exterior there is a noble man, wretched but utterly honorable."

"That's all fine," said the self-appointed gendarme, "but you gave this lad (pointing at me) a ruffled cape to sell, which had been stolen along with a mule and its trappings, a ruffled collar, a wig, and other knickknacks; and this same lad has exposed you, so you've got to tell us what happened to all the other things that were lost."

"I don't know anything about any cape or mule or wig, or any ruffle collar or trappings, or anything else you said!"

"Yes, sir," the constable said, "you gave this gentleman the ruffled cape to sell; the gentleman recognizes you, and the person who gave him the cape must know where the other things are."

"Friend," the hard-pressed poor man said to me, "do you know me? Have I ever given you a cape, or have you even seen me before in your life?"

"Yes, sir," I replied, caught between fear and daring, "you gave me that cape to sell, and you were my father's servant."

"You devil!" the poor man said. "What cape did I ever sell you? What do I know about you or your father?"

"Yes, sir," I said, "the gentleman wants to deny it, but this is the gentleman who gave me the cape to sell."

"Well, that's all we need to know," said the gendarme; "tie up the gentleman, and we'll see about it later."

With that, the soldiers tied up the miserable fellow and took him to jail, while they let me go free. That is the kind of outrage that people most often commit when they try to do justice without knowing what justice is.

I walked away without a cape or jacket, but very content to see how easily I had fooled the trader, though on the other hand, I was sorry to have lost the cape and its value.

I was walking along, distracted by these and other such bits of malicious nonsense, when I heard someone behind me shouting, "Stop him! Stop him!"

In that instant, I thought that the poor man I had just slandered had been indemnified, and that the soldiers were coming to catch me and find out the truth, and I scarcely turned my face to see the people running after me when, without waiting for any further disappointments, I took off running down Coliseo Street[4] like a hare.

As I've said before, in situations like this I was fast as a feather to get myself out of harm's way; but on that afternoon, I ran so quickly and in such confusion that when I rounded a corner, I didn't see an Indian potter who was walking along loaded down with his wares, and in a pretty collision I knocked him face down onto the ground, and fell down myself on top of his pots and pans, breaking some of them with my head, while at the same time, the potter and I were both being trampled by a runaway horse, which was the thing they had been shouting for us to stop.

After I saw the horse, I got over my scare, since I realized that I wasn't the object of their hunt; but my sense of consolation was cut short by that devil of an Indian, who quickly crawled like a lizard out from under his *tapextle* of pottery,[5] and held me tight by the kerchief to tell me, full of rage, "Now let's see you pay me my pots, and pay me quick quick, because if not, the divvil take you right now."

"Blast you, Indian savage," I said, "what do mean, I should pay you? Who's going to pay me for getting all cut up and bruised?"

"Did I tell you go get upset, not watch where you running like an excited mule?"

"You're the mule—you, and the big sow who gave birth to you," I said, "you worthless damned four-ears";[6] and I accompanied these quaint compliments with a handsome punch that I landed square on his nose, so hard that I had him spitting blood.

They say that when Indians see themselves stained with their own blood, they lose their nerve; but that wasn't true of him. He turned into a demon when he saw how I had hurt him with my own hand, and in a mix of Mexican and Spanish he told me, "*Tlacatecolo*,[7] bad divvil, thief, son of a demon, now we'll see it, who's who."

No sooner said than done, he started wringing my kerchief with such force that I felt I was going to choke, and with his other hand he picked up little pots and pans

---

4 [Calle del Coliseo: the block of the street now known as Bolívar, about three blocks south of the flea market, in front of the Coliseo theater. –Tr.]

5 [*Tapextle* (Nahuatl *tlapechtli*), a wooden frame for carrying clay pots. –Tr.]

6 In the common way that Indian men cut their hair, they keep a long lock in front of each ear, which they call the *barcarrota* [or *balcarrota*], and in allusion to this, people give them the nickname *cuatro orejas*, four-ears. –E. [On the significance of Indian men's hair, see William B. Taylor, *Magistrates of the Sacred: Priests and Parishioners in Eighteenth-Century Mexico* (Stanford, 1996), pp. 234–35. –Tr.]

7 [*Tlacatecolotl*, Nahuatl ("Mexican") for demon, devil, monster; literally, "man-owl." –Tr.]

very rapidly and broke them on my head; but he was smashing them so quickly and so angrily that, if instead of being delicate little glazed pots, they had been earthen jugs from Cuautitlán, I would have been taking my last breath before long.

I was half suffocated from the way he was twisting my kerchief; my mouth was wide open and I had no means of escape, so I plucked up my courage and, since we were both surrounded by our weapons, the pots, when the Indian bent down to grab one, I picked one up too, and we each smashed them in unison over the other's head.

In a second, a whole crowd of dolts had gathered around, not to defend us, and not to calm us down, but to enjoy watching us.

The multitude of stupid spectators drew the attention of a patrol that happened to be passing by, and making way for themselves with the butts of their rifles, they arrived where we were fighting—two unbeaten and redoubtable combatants.

After a couple of blows with the rifle butts, which we each felt on our backs, we separated and cooled down, and when the Indian informed the sergeant about the harm I had done him, and that I had provoked him by walloping him so furiously and unnecessarily on the snout, he took me prisoner then and there; but when he asked me to pay the four pesos that the potter said his wares were worth, I said that I didn't have a single real, which was true, because on the road I had already spent the little that I got for the trifles I had sold.

"Well, don't worry," the sergeant answered, "you can pay him with your jacket, which has got to be worth at least half the amount; otherwise you can come with us to jail. Or do you mean that, on top of doing so much damage to this poor man, and slapping him, too, you don't want to pay him? We can't have that; so it's give him your jacket, or it's off to jail with you."

I would have given him my pants to stay out of that place, so I took off my jacket, which was a good one, and gave it to him. The Indian wasn't very happy about taking it, because he didn't know what it was worth; he picked up the few *tepalcates*[8] that he thought were still good and left.

I wanted to do the same for my own part, so I looked for my hat, which had fallen off during the brawl; but I didn't find it, nor would I ever find it until Judgment Day, even if I had kept looking for it, because one of the damnable onlookers, seeing it fall to the ground while I was wrapped up in the action, had no doubt picked it up and was planning to give it back to me in three installments.[9]

While I was busy looking for my hat, asking about it, and pretending not to hear the laughter of the crowd, the Indian went far away, the patrol withdrew, the people scattered as they returned to their own ways; and I continued on mine, without jacket or hat, and with a few scratches on my face, lots of bumps, and two or three slight fractures on my head.

This brought an end to the frightening adventure of the potter, and I walked along filled with gloomy ideas, in some pain from the blows I had suffered in our quarrel, thinking about where I would spend the night, though this was not the first time I ever thought about such a problem.

---

8 [*Tepalcate* (Nahuatl *tapalcatl*), a pottery shard or broken pot. –Tr.]

9 Referring to the three installment periods used by swindlers: "late, badly, and never." –E.

Comparing my past position with my present, remembering that two weeks earlier I had been a doctor and a gentleman with servants, a house, clothes, and a reputation in Tula, and now I was wretched, alone, dejected, capeless and hatless, beaten, and without even the worst kind of roof to put over my head for the night in Mexico, my homeland, I remembered the old, old verse that goes,

> Flowers, learn when you look at me
> What happens from night to day:
> Yesterday, a marvel to see;
> Not even a shadow today.[10]

But what most put me out was to consider that both of my latest calamities had come about because of the Indians, and I said to myself, "If it's true that there are birds of ill omen, then the most baneful birds and the worst harbingers for me are the Indians, because they've brought me so many problems."

I was walking along with my chin sunk down against my chest while dusk fell, feeling completely deprived and thinking of nothing other than what I have just mentioned, when a man standing inside a small one-room house woke me from my abstraction, for as I passed by the house he grabbed me by the kerchief and, with a single tug, made me enter against my will; then he closed the door, leaving the room almost entirely dark, since the little light that filtered through its one small window at that late hour was barely enough for us to see each other's face.

The man wrathfully told me, "Don't you recognize me, scoundrel?"

Wrapped in fear, the inevitable garment of a villain, I said, "No, sir, though I am at your service."

"So, then, you don't recognize me?" the angry man repeated. "You've never seen me before? You don't remember me?"

"No, sir," I said, feeling very pressed, "by God, I swear I don't know you."

Through all these questions and answers, he did not let go of my kerchief, and every few moments he gave me a furious squeeze, forcing me to bow down frequently before him.

Just then a little old woman walked in with a candle, and, startled by the scene, she said to the man, "Ay, son! What's all this? Who is this man? What's he doing to you? Is he a thief?"

"I don't know what he is, ma'am," he said, "but he's a rogue, and now that there's some light, I want him to take a good look at my face and tell me if he recognizes me. Come on, rogue, do you? Speak! Why so silent? Just a few hours ago, you saw me and swore that I was your father's servant, and that I had given you a cape to sell. I haven't forgotten you, even though you look a little different now than you did then; so why shouldn't you recognize me, when I haven't changed my clothes?"

---

[10] [This is Luis de Góngora's poem *La brevedad de las cosas humanas* (1621). In Chapter 44, Periquillo will imitate the poem and gloss each line with a *décima* in imitation of Lope de Vega's "beautiful gloss of the same quatrain" in *La moza del cántaro* (Spell, p. 169). –Tr.]

These words, accompanied by the candlelight, made me recognize perfectly the man I had so recently slandered. I couldn't help but confess my wickedness, and feeling cornered by my dread of my victim, who now made my hair stand on end, I kneeled down to beg him to forgive me by all the saints in Heaven, adding to these pleas and prayers a few excuses that were truly frivolous, yet good enough for me: for I told him that the cape had been stolen, but that the person who gave it to me to sell was the doctor's nephew, who was my friend and schoolmate, and so I had availed myself of the lie that I used against him, so as not to lose my friend.

"All that may be true," the slandered man said. "Pick yourself up; I'm not a saint, that you need to adore me. But, since you figure that everybody who wears indecent clothes is a rogue, it wouldn't surprise you if we all had bad hearts; and so, since you judged me a good suspect for being a thief just because I'm dressed in rags, for the same reason, you shouldn't be surprised if I'm vengeful. Besides, the revenge I am planning to take on you is just, because even though I could give you a fierce beating right now (and you certainly deserve it), I only want my satisfaction to come from the side of justice, both to redound to my honor and to serve to correct and reform you, for it is a pity that a lad who is white and seemingly well born should be lost at such an early age on a path that is so hateful and so harmful to society. Sit down here, please; and mother, please go get my children."

Saying this, he went off to speak with the old woman in secret, after which she went into the kitchen, took out a small basket, and went outside, and the man in rags closed the door and locked it.

It chilled me to find myself alone with him, and locked inside; so I knelt down again and told him with the greatest deference, "Sir, please pardon me; I am a fool; I didn't know what I was doing; but, sir, what's done is done; please have pity on me and on my poor mother and my two young sisters, who would die of grief if you were to do me some villainy; and so, by God, by Holiest Mary, by your dear mother's bones, please forgive me for what I've done, and don't kill me without confession, because I swear to you I'm as full of sins as a devil."

"Enough of that, my friend," said the man in rags. "Please stand up. Why so many prayers? I'm not planning to kill you; I'm no assassin, and I'm not going to hire one. Please, have a seat, because I want to give you some idea of the revenge I want to take for the injury you've done me."

I sat down, somewhat calmed by these words, and the man in rags sat down next to me and asked me to tell him my life story and the reason why I was in the condition he found me in. I told him 2,000 lies, which he believed in good faith, demonstrating in this the goodness of his character; and when I observed that he felt sorry for my misfortune, I asked him (after begging his pardon a thousand more times) to tell me who he was and what state his fortunes were in; and the poor man, not waiting to be asked again, told me his life story in this manner:

"Listen closely," he said, "so that you will never again dare to judge men by their appearance alone, without investigating the true depths of their character and conduct. If inherited nobility is a natural good, about which men may justly boast, I was born noble, and there are many witnesses to this fact in Mexico; not just witnesses, but even relatives who are still alive. I owe this favor to Nature, and I would have owed to Fortune the favor of being wealthy if I had been born before my brother Damián; but he, through no merit or choice of his own, was born before me, and became the mayorazgo, the designated first-born heir of the entailed estate, while my other siblings and myself were left to rely on the little that our father left us from his fifth when he died.[11] Therefore. . . . "

"Pardon me, sir," I broke in, "but is it really possible that your own father wanted to leave you and your siblings poor, possibly even destitute, just so he could make his first-born a mayorazgo?"

"Yes, friend," the man in rags replied, "that is just what happened, and that is what happens every day, and the only support and justification for this corrupt practice is our imitation of ancient prejudices. You are astonished, and rightly so, to see this abuse practiced and tolerated in the most civilized nations of Europe, and perhaps you think it is not merely unjust, but tyrannical, for parents to prefer their first-born son over his brothers and sisters, since they are all their children; but you would be even more astonished if you knew that this corrupt practice (for I do not believe it deserves to be called a legitimately introduced custom) has been frowned upon by sensible men, and that monarchs have hedged it around with many tough restrictions, with the laudable aim of getting rid of it.[12] Indeed, it is said that *the*

---

[11] [As noted in Chapter 13, footnote 10, Spanish inheritance law only allowed a parent to freely will one-fifth of his or her estate, while four-fifths were divided equally among all the parent's children without regard to age or gender. To circumvent this restriction and create an estate that would be passed down whole to a single heir from generation to generation, a wealthy family could petition to create a *mayorazgo*, or entailed estate. The *mayorazgo* system left four-fifths of the combined family estate to the first-born son (who was also called the *mayorazgo*); the other heirs could hope, at most, for a share in the remaining fifth. Lizardi has already criticized this institution more than once. –Tr.]

[12] It is worth citing here the words of Don Marcos Gutiérrez, in his notes to *Febrero* [see Chapter 24, footnote 4], part I, volume I, chapter 7: "The same kind of ignorance that has so often accepted humanity's most baneful errors as incontrovertible truths, has permitted and even promoted entailments and mayorazgos in the belief that they are useful to the State, despite their being very injurious to population growth. In every society, population is proportionate to subsistence, which entailed estates diminish excessively by designating a single heir for what should be distributed among many. It amazes me to see so pernicious an institution as mayorazgos propagated throughout almost all of Europe, when at first sight it shocks and offends every humane and sensitive heart to have so many younger children sacrificed for one first-born, and to see them spend their lives in poverty and destitution so that he can show off his wealth, his skills, and perhaps his vices as well. What is important to the State is not that a few families might preserve their glory and splendor at the expense of an endless number who sink into misfortune and obscurity, but that, through a better distribution of wealth, all citizens might live in ease and comfort. These truths, which writers on economics have demonstrated to us with the best of evidence, and which should be better known among the common people, have not escaped the perspicacious eyes of our enlightened government, which at the same time has recognized other ways in which entailed estates have done considerable damage to the State. The clearest proof of all this are the various royal decrees, which by imposing several obstacles to the institution of mayorazgos and entailments, and by conceding certain powers for expropriating their goods, wisely conspire to impede the growth and even to diminish the number of entailed estates that have already been established."

mayorazgo is a right that the nearest first-born son has to inherit the estate, under the condition that he preserve it perpetually whole and within the family; but if I were allowed to define it, I would say: *the mayorazgo is a preference unjustly granted to the first-born son, so that only he may inherit the estate that belongs to all his siblings in equal shares, for they have equal rights to it.* If anyone thinks my definition is harsh, I can convince him of its correctness, unless he himself is a mayorazgo, because in that case, clearly, no matter how convinced he might be in his mind, I would never be able to wrest a confession of this truth from his lips. Friend, if I speak out against mayorazgos, I am speaking with justice and experience on my side. When my father instituted a mayorazgo in favor of his first-born son, perhaps he wasn't thinking of anything other than perpetuating the glory of his house, without foreseeing the damage that would thereby befall his other children; because, before I came to the wretched state in which you see me now, how much I have had to argue with my brother just so that he would give me the food that my father left me in one clause of his testament! And what good has it done me? None at all: since he had all the money and the law on his side, it is easy to imagine that he would have gotten his way every time.[13]

"Speaking as a good son, I would like to exonerate my father from the harm he brought down upon us with this unjust preference; but as an upright man, I cannot help but confess that he did wrong. I only hope that, just as I have forgiven him, God will have forgiven him for the evils he has caused! Although I have been left without anything to eat, I have perhaps had the best of it. We were four siblings: Damián the Mayorazgo, Antonio, Isabel, and myself. Damián, made arrogant by money and flattered by his bad friends, gave in to his vices, of which his favorites were, unfortunately, gambling and drinking; and nowadays, to honor my father's bones, he goes around from game to game and from tavern to tavern, dirty, unkempt, and half insane, relying on a very narrow diet that serves to feed his vices. My brother Antonio entered the Church, not because he had a calling for it, but because my father pushed him into it, and so he has turned into a rather foolish, dissolute, and scandalous clergyman, giving his prelate plenty of headaches. He happens to be free right now; El Carmen, San Fernando, the jail, and Tepotzotlán are his usual residences and places of seclusion.[14] My sister Isabel. . . . Poor girl! I feel so sorry for her whenever I remember her unhappy fate! This poor girl was also a victim of the mayorazgo. My father made her join a convent against her will, the better to secure the entailment for my brother Damián, perhaps without

---

[13] The author cited above says, ironically, that "it is a matter of the greatest importance to the State, and to the founders of mayorazgos themselves, that their memory should be preserved until the most remote posterity for the great feat and heroic deed of having entailed their estates, thereby motivating, as usually is the case, many endless lawsuits, which are so conducive to the welfare and tranquility of families."

[14] [El Carmen and San Fernando were monasteries inside the present-day limits of Mexico City, suitable for locking up an errant priest for a short time; Tepotzotlán was the site of a former Jesuit monastery just north of the city that was used to house a jail for the clergy. In Spanish law of the time, the clergy had a separate justice system from laymen and operated their own courts and jails. –Tr.]

recalling the terrible censures and threats of excommunication that the Holy Council of Trent uttered against parents who force their daughters to enter convents unwillingly;[15] and the worst of it was that he could not allege ignorance, for when my sister saw how he had made up his mind, she plainly confessed to him that she was inclined to marry a young neighbor of ours, who was her equal in birth, in education, and in age, a very honorable boy who was employed in the royal treasury, had an elegant presence, and above all, who was deeply in love with her; and having confessed this, she begged him not to force her to embrace a way of life for which she felt she would not be appropriate, but rather that he permit her to join that kind young man, in whose company she would have been happy all her life long.

"Far from yielding to reason, after my father found out whom my sister wanted to marry, he let his anger carry him away, and scolded her harshly, telling her that her wishes were nonsense and naughtiness; that she was far too young to be thinking about such things; that the lad she loved was a rascal and a rogue; that he'd be likely to waste everything she brought to the marriage; that no matter how good he looked to her, he was no more than a poor man, which was enough to tarnish all the good qualities she imagined he had; and finally, that he was her father and he knew what was for her own good, and all she was supposed to do was obey and keep quiet, and if she dared oppose his will or talk back to him a single word, he'd give her a bullet, or stick her in the Women's Shelter.[16]

"Given his determination and this irrevocable decree, my poor sister was left with no hope of finding a way out, and without any other recourse than wailing, which did her no good.

"After this moment, my father pulled strings so that three days later, Isabel was installed in the convent.

"When her young man found out, he tried to write to her, accusing her of fickleness and inconstancy, but my father, who had every breach covered, must have picked up the letter before it reached the novice, and armed with that letter, his money, and a

---

[15] Session 25, chapter 18: "The holy council anathematizes each and all persons, of whatever character or rank they may be, whether clerics or laics, seculars or regulars, and with whatever dignity invested, who shall [. . .] in any way force any virgin or widow, or any other woman whatsoever, to enter a monastery against her will, or to take the habit of any religious order, or to make profession; those also who give advice, aid, or encouragement, as well as those who, knowing that she does not enter the monastery or receive the habit, or make profession voluntarily, shall in any way take part in that act by their presence, consent, or authority." Thus, as Doctor [José] Boneta [y Laplana] says, echoing the view of the great Suárez, the aggressors of this violence incur three types of excommunication: first, for forcing her to enter the monastery; second, for making her take the habit; and third, for the act of profession. There are cases, this author states, in which robbing or killing can be justified; but as for forcing a daughter to become a nun, there is no case that can ever justify it. In his book, *Gritos del infierno* [*para despertar al mundo*, Zaragoza, 1698], pages 211 and 212.

[16] Women's Shelter (*Las Recogidas*): A building formerly used for the correction of bad women; but due to lack of funds, it has not served that purpose for many years. It was later used as a cigar factory. –E. [According to Spell (p. 188), this women's prison was located eight blocks south of the Viceroyal Palace, near the church of San Lucas. –Tr.]

fast-talking lawyer, he surrounded the poor fellow with such a labyrinth of libels that the best settlement he could get was to leave Mexico and lose his job, in order to avoid even worse results.

"He schemed this whole intrigue not only without my sister's knowledge, but while trying to dispel her passion through the basest means, which was by forging and sending her a letter from her lover, in which he insulted her in a thousand ways, calling her crazy, ugly, and despicable, and concluding by assuring her that he had forgotten her forever, and asserting that he had gotten married to a very lovely young woman.

"This letter was supposedly written outside of this capital; but instead of the effect that my father hoped for, it produced the effect that it could be expected to have on a sensitive heart, which was to fill her with anguish, infuriate her with jealousy, disturb her with desperation, and plunge her into utter dejection.

"A few months after this affliction, my sister completed her novitiate and professed, sacrificing her freedom, not gladly unto God, as the preacher said in the pulpit, but to the whims and sordid self-interest of my father.

"The number of tears shed by this unhappy victim when it came time for her to pronounce her vows were enough to convince all those around her that she was crying from her devout and contrite heart; but my parents and I knew too well the real cause of her tears. My father watched them fall with the greatest coldness and hardness, and I even thought (may his respectable memory forgive me) that it gladdened him to hear the moans of this martyr to obedience and terror, just as it gladdened the tyrant Phalaris to hear the cries and screams of the miserable victims that he enclosed in his brazen bull;[17] but my mother and I cried as much as she did, and although our tears were products of our knowledge of luckless Isabel's sorrow, in the opinions of most people, they passed as the effects of tender religiosity.

"The function concluded with the usual ceremonies and solemnities; we returned home, and my sister returned to her prison (for that is what she called her nun's cell, when she could unburden herself to me in private).

"The turmoil of unsettled passions that had conspired against her, passing from her spirit into her body, caused her such a malignant and sudden fever that in seven days, she was separated from among the living. . . . Ay, dear, sweet Isabel! Beloved sister! Innocent victim, sacrificed on the foul altars of vanity, in the shadow of the founding of a mayorazgo! May your sad shade forgive my father's imprudence, and receive my tender and loving memories in token of the love I always had for you, and the interest that I always took in your unfortunate fate; and you, my friend, please excuse these natural digressions.

"When my father learned of her passing, he received from the hand of her confessor a sealed letter that said the following:

---

[17] The bull of Phalaris is well known among the erudite. It was a large, empty bull made of bronze, inside of which the tyrant would place those he wished to torture, and while they were inside, he would have a fire built around the bull, causing the wretched victims to die in the most terrible agony, their groans crackling in the air but turned into the sound of a bull's bellowing by the infernal machine.

"*Father, sir:*

"*Death will soon close my eyes. Because of you I will die in the fullest bloom of my years. Out of obedience . . . no, out of my fear of your threats, I embraced a way of life to which God had not called me. Forced into sacrilege against my will, I offered my heart to Him at the feet of His altars; but my heart had been offered and consecrated beforehand with all my will to Jacobo. When I promised to be his, I called on God as my witness, and I would have kept that oath forever, and would keep it in the hour of my expiration if it were possible; yet these hopes are fruitless now. I die in torment, not from fever, but from the grief of never having been united with the person I most loved in this world; but at least, amid the excesses of my sorrow, I have the consolation that, by dying, I will escape the painful slavery to which my father . . . what sadness, my own father! . . . condemned me, through no fault of mine. I hope that God will have pity on me, and I hope that He uses His infinite mercy with you.*

"*Your unfortunate daughter, the unhappiest woman,*

"*Isabel.*[18]

"This letter cloaked my father's heart in horror and sorrow, just as night cloaks the Earth's beauty in mourning. From that day forth, he locked himself in his room, where there was a portrait of my sister in her nun's habit; he wept inconsolably, kissed the canvas, and embraced it constantly; he refused all conversation with his closest friends, abandoned his domestic affairs, loathed the tastiest dishes at his meals; sleep fled from his eyes; all entertainment repulsed him; he ran from words of consolation as if they were insults, and even separated from the bed and bedroom of my mother; and to say it plainly, black melancholy filled his heart with darkness, drove the color from his cheeks, and, within the space of three months, led him to his grave, after dragging him through ninety days of a sadly exhausted life. Happy will my father be if this suffering were enough to purge his sacrifice of my sister.

"When he died, my brother Damián, who was already married, entered into absolute possession of the mayorazgo; my mother and I, the youngest son, went to

---

[18] There is nothing unnatural or fabulous about this incident; a thousand just like it have occurred. Dr. Boneta, in his booklet cited above, *Gritos del infierno*, on page 210, states: "One of these women who were forced into convents asked her confessor on her death bed: *Father, if I die, will I cease to be a nun?* And when he replied that she would, she began to close her eyes and make the most furious efforts to speed her death." End of quote. And is this the worst or the only thing that has been seen with these poor women who have become nuns against their will? God wish it were so! But just here in Mexico [City], we have seen the most baneful examples, cut from the same cloth, which we will not relate here because some of them are very recent and considered private by many. How many crimes against heaven weigh on the consciences of those who force their daughters to become nuns, and how many ways do they find to force them! The brevity of a footnote does not allow us to make a complete explication; but God-fearing parents who love their daughters will guard against forcing their preferences, whether by threats or by pleading, by promises, by cajolery, or by arguments, or by anything that smacks of physical or virtual force, if they do not want to appear accused of the severest crime before the most just of judges.

his house, where he treated us well for a few days, after which he changed because of the counsel of his wife, who did not love us, and the disputes began.

"I could not bear to see them harass my mother, so I tried to separate her from a house where we were loathed. Because I was the son of a rich man, my father never taught me any trade or profession by which I could make my living, and so I found myself living in a sad little apartment, with my mother to support, and with no resources other than a few rare handouts from the mayorazgo.

"In this unhappy situation, I fell in love with a girl who had a dowry of 500 pesos; and more for the 500 pesos than for her—or if I may say, more to obtain her money in order to support my poor, beloved mother than for anything else—I married the young woman and received her dowry, which we finished off in four days, leaving me worse off than before, and worse yet day after day, for I suddenly found myself with a mother, a wife, and three young children.

"My misfortunes increased day by day; I was forced to bring my family to live in this sad little one-room house, because my brother proved in court that he was under no obligation to give me anything. My wife, whose noble and sensitive soul was unable to bear my ill luck, lost her life to the rigors of a fatal exhaustion; or to put it plainly, she died of hunger, nakedness, and distress.

"Despite all this, I have never been able to stoop to gambling, drunkenness, swindling, or robbery. My misfortunes pursue me, but my good upbringing keeps me from falling into vice. I am a useless person, not by my own fault, but because of my father's vanity; yet at the same time, I have my honor, and I am not capable of letting myself go like a mayorazgo (I say this because of my brother).

"Here you have, in summary, my whole life: weigh it on the scales of justice and tell me whether I am the rogue you thought I was, or an upright man as I claim; and if, following the demands of reason, you believe I am an upright man, then you should realize that men are not what they outwardly seem to be. You will see men in the world dressed up as sages, who are ignorant fools; men dressed as aristocrats, who, at least by their actions, are common plebeians; men dressed as virtuous, or who pretend to be full of virtue, who are criminals in disguise; men . . . but why wear myself out? In this world you will see men at every turn who are unworthy of the clothing they wear, or who do deserve an honorable name that they lack, though their clothes would not seem to show it; and then you will recognize that no one should be judged by outward appearances, but by his actions."

Just then the ragged man's little old mother knocked on the door; he opened it for her, and she entered, leading three small children in by the hand, who went straight to ask their father for his blessing; he received them with a father's tenderness, and after caressing them, he said to me, "Here you see the fruit of my conjugal love, and my only consolations in the midst of this miserable life."

A few moments after this conversation, the old woman went inside and came out with a small mug of liquor and some rags, and she treated the light wounds on my head. Then came supper, which we all ate together like a family; when it was done, they gave me a poor mattress, which I knew I was taking from the family, and I lay down and slept quite serenely.

The next day they woke me early with chocolate, and after I drank it, the man in rags told me, "Little friend, now you have seen the revenge that I wanted to exact for the way you insulted me yesterday; I have nothing else to give and no other way to show that I forgive you; but I want you to have my friendship, not my trivial hospitality. However, I do ask you never to come down this street, because if the people who know that you slandered me as a thief see you come here, they will not believe that the judge recognized me and trusted me as an upright man, but that the two of us plotted and schemed together, and that would not be good for my honor. This is all I ask of you, and may God help you."

It isn't hard to imagine how such a heroic, generous action moved me. I gave him my most heartfelt thanks, hugged him with all my strength to show him I meant it, and begged him to tell me his name so that I would at least know to whom I was indebted for such charitable deeds; but I couldn't get it out of him, because he told me, "Why do you have to ask so many questions? When I do something good, I am not trying to flatter myself, I am just doing what I ought to do. I do not want to know who my enemies are so that I can take revenge on them, not do I want those who might receive some benefit from me to know who I am, because I do not demand their gratitude in tribute; for benevolence in itself brings the award of the sweet inner satisfaction that it leaves in a man's spirit; and if this were not so, there wouldn't have been so many idolatrous pagans who left us the finest examples of brotherly love. So, please leave your curiosity behind, and good-bye."

Seeing that it was impossible for me to find out from his own mouth who he was, I bid him a very tender farewell, recalling Don Antonio, the man who had done so many favors for me in prison; and I went out into the street.

CHAPTER 30

IN WHICH PERIQUILLO TELLS ABOUT THE JACKPOT HE WON; THE END OF
CHANFAINA THE NOTARY; HOW HE FELL BACK IN WITH LUISA; AND OTHER
DETAILS THAT WILL SATISFY THE CURIOSITY OF THE READERS

I left the ragged man's house then, feeling half bewildered and ashamed of myself, unable to convince myself that such a great soul could fit under such an indecent exterior; but I had seen it with my own eyes, and much as it contradicted my worthless philosophy, I couldn't deny that it was a possibility.

And so, thinking about the man in rags and my friend Don Antonio, I wandered from street to street, without a hat, without a jacket, and without a penny in my pocket, which was the worst of all.

By eleven in the morning, I was so hungry I couldn't see straight, and to make my torment worse, I had to pass by the Alcaicería,[1] which, as you all know, is lined with lunch stands; and since they all keep their dishes out by the door to provoke people's appetites with their aroma, my queasy stomach was crying out for me to swipe a couple of plates of *tlemolillo* with fried *tostaditas* on the side;[2] and so, hungry, voracious, and desperate, I entered an indecent pool hall on the same street, where a circle of scoundrels were gambling. Let me speak clearly: it was an *arrastraderito* just like the one where Januario once put me up.

I entered, as I was saying, and after joining the circle, I took off my vest and tried selling it, which wasn't hard to do since it was in good condition, and I gave it away for the trifling amount of six reales.

I shoved two reales deep in my shoe, saving them for lunch, and I set out to gamble the other four; but I did it with so much care, conduct, and good fortune, that two hours later I had won six pesos, which, under those circumstances and in that poor game, seemed like 600. Not waiting for more, I pretended that I had to go outside to relieve myself, and headed off for a cheap restaurant, and not just to drop in.

Inside the dive, I started sniffing and peeking into the pots more diligently than a hungry dog. I asked for lunch, and bolted down five or six little dishes with the corresponding cups of pulque and bowls of frijoles; and when my appetite was satisfied, I went back to the pool hall, planning to buy a hat, which I obtained easily and at a good price; yet all that I got out of this adventure were lunch and a hat, because everything I had won, I lost again just as easily as I had acquired it. So all I had really done was to keep the money warm, since if I were honest about the accounting, I came out even: the hat cost me two reales, and I had spent four on lunch and cigarettes, which adds up to the six reales I got for selling my vest. This is what normally happens to gamblers: they dream that they are winning, but when all is said and done, they are nothing more than temporary keepers of other people's money; and

---

[1] [An old market, modeled on the one in Granada, which existed until 1860, one block west of the Cathedral (Spell, p. 188). –Tr.]

[2] [*Tlemolillo, tlemole* (Nahuatl, "fire sauce"): a stew of ground red chili, tomatoes, and spices. *Tostaditas*: toasted corn tortillas. –Tr.]

that's when they do well, because most of the time they return their winnings with interest.

As a consequence of being left without a nickel, I also was left without dinner, but the operator did me the great favor of letting me spend the night on a bench in the pool hall, where I was surrounded by the cozy feeling of rats and fleas jumping on me, bedbugs biting, the sweet music of my companions' off-key snoring, the pestilent fragrance of their badly digested food, the persistent fluttering and crowing of a damnable rooster that perched next to my head, the fluffy delight of a wooden plank for a bed, and all the discomforts that such provisional accommodations can offer.

At last, day broke and everyone arose to their customary breakfast of liquor, while I tried to imagine what I could do to get something into my mouth, because unfortunately I had a healthy stomach that was ready to digest stones if it came to that, but I had nothing to put in it.

Under these sorry circumstances, I remembered that I still had a rosary with a good silver medallion, and a nearly new pair of white linen underpants. I took it all off in a corner of the room, and since I always sold cheap when I was hungry, I let them go to the first fellow who offered me a peso for both things, quickly, before he could reconsider.

I went to a café, where I ordered a cup of coffee and a roll to go with it, and on the way back I passed by the cheap restaurant and left two and a half reales in advance to pay for dinner at midday; I bought a half-real's worth of cigarettes, and returned to the pool hall with a stake of four reales, but my stomach was soothed and it comforted me to think that I already had my dinner and cigarettes guaranteed for the day. The brothers of Birján gathered together, and when there were enough of them, they cheerfully began to gamble. I settled into the best seat, with my grand total of four reales, and the betting started.

I started by betting half a real or one real, in keeping with my treasury, and as I kept winning, the pot kept rising, with such good luck that before I knew it, I had won four pesos and recovered my medallion as well.

I didn't want to expose myself to going bust as quickly as I had the day before, so without even saying *there's the keys*, I went outside and headed off for lunch.

With that business concluded, I began wandering to and fro with no goal in mind, almost unconsciously, thinking only about what I might do or where I might go to keep a roof over my head and food on my plate.

So I spent the whole morning, until around two in the afternoon, when my stomach let me know that lunch was done and gone, and reinforcements were called for; so, not to slight its hints, I entered the tavern of an inn, where I ordered the four-real dish, which I ate, distrustful that I would have supper that night.

After I finished, I went into a pool hall to rest from my long and fruitless wanderings and to entertain myself by watching the pool sharks and billiards experts; but instead of playing pool, they were putting up a game of monte in a corner of the hall.

Since I never had a better time than when I was gambling on my luck, I squeezed into the circle, feeling a bit of shame, because the other gamblers were bumpkins with money, and none of them were as filthy or as shabby as I was.

Nevertheless, when they saw that my first bet was a whole peso, and that I won it, they made room for me, and I decided to bet bravely.

It turned out not to be a bad idea, for I had soon won some fifty pesos, a silk kerchief, a cloak, and a whole Our Lady of Guadalupe lottery ticket.[3] Seeing that I had won a good stake, I wanted to get up and leave, and I even made to get up on more than two occasions; but since I was having such good luck and had so much money, greed got the better of me, and I stayed right where I was until luck got tired of favoring me; the deck turned against me, and I began to make mistakes so quickly that, if I had won everything I had in twenty hands of monte, I lost it all in ten or twelve, since I was trying to use my money to force my luck.

So by four in the afternoon, I had lost the money, lost the cloak, lost the silk kerchief, and even lost my medallion. All I had left was the lottery ticket, which nobody wanted to buy from me, even when I offered it at one real off.

The game ended, everybody went on about their business, and I went outside with a real or two that they had given me as a tip.

I walked over to the Alcaicería, where I knew the pool hall operator, and after giving him a real to spend the night there, I went out to wander around the streets, because I didn't have anything else to do. At nine at night I ate a half-real's worth of supper and went back to go to bed. I spent a dog's night, just like the night before. The following day, I got up and stood in the pool hall door, warming myself in the sun until ten; then, seeing that no one was going to invite me for lunch, and that I had no way of getting into a game so I could play by my wits, since the most anyone would offer me was a little money for my shirt, which I didn't dare take off, I went for a walk, putting my faith in the saying that goes: a dog has to walk if it's going to find a bone.

I went up one street and down another, without any aim in mind, and without getting anything out of all my walking, until, passing by Tiburcio Street,[4] I saw a lot of people in the patio of a house, who were crowding around a raised platform with a canopy, chairs, and guards. Since they were all entering the patio, I entered, too, and asked what was going on. They told me that they were about to draw the lottery of Our Lady of Guadalupe. I immediately remembered my lottery ticket, and even though I had never placed any faith in such games of chance, I stayed in the patio, more to see the drawing ceremony than anything else.

The raffle began, and after ten or twelve balls, out came my number (which I remember was 7596), with a prize of 3,000 pesos. My ears stood up when I heard them call it out, and when they wrote it up on the board I even rubbed my eyes and looked at it again; but when I was sure that it was the same number I held, I don't know how I kept from going mad with delight, because I had never had so much money in my life.

---

[3] [A lottery to benefit the Sanctuary of Our Lady of Guadalupe was held regularly in Mexico, from 1794 to the mid-1800s (Spell, p. 188). As with most Spanish and Latin American lotteries, participants could buy an entire sheet (a "whole ticket") of a number, or just a fraction of the sheet, in which case a winner would receive the corresponding fraction of the prize. –Tr.]

[4] [Two blocks south of the Zócalo, today part of Uruguay Street. –Tr.]

I came out of there cheerier than Easter and headed straight back to the pool hall, because at the time, the only companions I had were the pool hall operator and the gamblers in there; for even though I kept running into people who used to call me their friend, sometimes in my shame I'd duck like the man who sets off the fireworks, so as not to see them, while other times—most times—they were the ones who pretended they didn't see me, either because they were ashamed of my appearance, or to avoid having me beg something from them.

So I went to my well-known apartment, where I found the circle of cardsharps already in full progress, and my friend the operator presiding with his moneybox, glue, cards, scissors, and the other tools of the art.

Since money imbues one with some strange sort of pride, as soon as I entered I greeted everyone, not bashfully as before, but with a jauntiness that seemed natural.

"How's it going, my operator friend? What's up, pals?" I asked.

They barely lifted their eyes to look at me, and answering me as coyly as the daintiest lady, they went back to the task at hand without a word of reply.

Then I put the spurs to the steed of my vanity, and since I was dying to let them all know about my good fortune, I said to them, "Hullo! So nobody greets me, eh? Well, don't bother. Thanks to God, I've got lots of money and I don't need any of you."

One of the gamblers at the gaming table that day knew me, for he had been my classmate in my first school and he remembered my nickname, so when he heard my bluster, he looked at me and mockingly said, "Oh, Periquillo, my dear! Is it you? My goodness! So you made lots of money, did you? Come here, brother, sit down next to me, because I think I deserve to get more of that money than the charity box will."

He made room for me, and I accepted the favor; but how cross the others got when they saw me let eight or ten hands of monte pass without betting a single real. Then my classmate said, "So where's the money, Periquillo?"

"In a payment draft."

"A payment draft?"

"And a very safe one, too; and it's not for four reales, but for 3,000 big, fat pesos." Saying this, I showed them my lottery ticket, and they all burst out laughing, not imagining I could be telling the truth, until by chance a lottery vendor walked in with a list of winning tickets, and I asked him to lend it to me so I could see if my ticket showed up.

Once the operator and the gamblers saw that what I was telling them was indeed true, the whole scene changed immediately. They stopped the game, everyone stood up, one of them embraced me, another gave me a kiss, another a bear hug, and each of them endeavored to outdo the others with his demonstration of affection.

The mere news that I was going to have money meant that, from that moment, I no longer went without, yet it didn't cost me a penny, because they laid out a grand lunch for me, gave me two or three boxes of fine cigarettes, offered to loan me money to gamble—and for that, the operator and the others would have pawned their own cloaks. Of course, I turned them down, thanking them with the air of a rich man, figuring that their favors were directed by their self-interest; so even before I had a single peso, my head was already full of air, and the friendship of those ragged beggars was beginning to weigh on me.

Nonetheless I still needed them, at least for that day, so I stayed with them, offering them all my protection, without intending to keep any of my promises, while they vied in fawning on me, in the faith that the 3,000 pesos would be divided among them all on a prorated basis, and I believe they even started calculating what they were going to spend it on.

In the end, I ate, drank, supped, and smoked all day long without spending a thing. That night the operator wouldn't allow me to sleep on the bare bench, as I had for the two previous nights, insisting instead that I take his bed while he slept on the pool table; and I barely had to hint that the rooster's crowing bothered me for them to throw the bird outside.

Lying on a mattress, which at least was soft, and with sheets and a blanket and pillow, I couldn't sleep; I spent the whole night coming up with plans. At four in the morning, I fell asleep; I voluntarily woke up around eight and noticed that they were all gambling but keeping quiet, a quiet such as is rarely heard among such people. Taking advantage of their civility, I pretended that I was still asleep, and heard that they were talking about me, though in an undertone.

One said: "I'm hoping I can redeem all my pledges with this lottery."

Another: "If I don't get a new cloak out of that money, I'm never gonna get me one."

Another: "I pray to God that when Señor Perico collects that money, we'll all get set up straight."

"You bet we will," said the operator; "the good thing is, he's a little dense; all you gotta do is keep buttering him up."

And so they all plotted against those poor 3,000 pesos; and I, who could hardly wait to go collect them, stretched and pretended to be waking up. I raised my head and hadn't even finished greeting them when I already had coffee, chocolate, liquor, and biscuits sitting in front of me, so that I could breakfast on whatever I pleased. I drank the coffee, thanked them for everything, and went to collect on my ticket.

Ten or twelve of those *léperos* tried tagging along with me; but I refused everyone's company except for that of my classmate, who was already calling me Pedrito, not Periquillo; and luckily for him I noticed he hadn't said a word that showed he had any interest in my money.

I went with him to the place where I should have collected on the lottery ticket; but not only did they not pay it out, when they saw how we were dressed they even questioned whether we hadn't stolen it, and, giving me the number and a receipt, they held it for me until I could find a guarantor.

Who would guarantee the payment for me in the shape I was in—and I don't mean for 3,000 pesos, but even for four reales? Nevertheless, I did not despair. I went to the inn where I had gambled and bought the ticket two days earlier, and as soon as I entered and the gamblers and the operator recognized me, they congratulated me on the good news and asked for their handouts in all earnestness, because the lottery vendor had told them that the number he sold there had won the 3,000-peso prize.

Seeing that everyone knew what I had come to tell them, I said, "Pals, I'm ready to give you all your hand-outs; but first I need you to get me the guarantor that the lottery's demanding from me; since I'm poor, they don't trust me, and they're even holding my ticket."

"Well, that's nothing to worry about," said the operator; "we all saw you buy the ticket, and the vendor who sold it to you wouldn't let us lie."

Just then the owner of the inn entered, and when he heard the story, he called for his carriage of his own free will and told me to get in with him; we then went back to the lottery, where he countersigned for me and they gave me the money.

When we were returning in the carriage, the gentleman who had done me this favor told me, "Friend, now that God has sent you so much aid through such an unlikely route, you should make sure to take advantage of the occasion and not do anything wild; because Fortune is very jealous, and wherever she finds herself unappreciated, she doesn't stay around."

He gave me this and other such advice, which I thanked him for, asking him to keep my money safe. He offered to do that for me, and in the meantime we arrived at the inn. The gentleman stored my bullion, leaving me the hundred pesos I had asked from him, of which I spent twenty on hand-outs for the good news that the operator and his companions had given me, and on a good meal for myself and my assistant and classmate, whose name was Roque.

That afternoon I went to the Parián, where I bought a shirt, pants, a jacket, a cape, a hat, and everything I could find that I needed; and I did all this with the help of my Roque, who did a very good job of flattering me. We went back to the inn, where I took a room, and even though I didn't have a bed, I had a good supper and slept grandly, waking up late like the rich folks do.

After breakfast, I wrote out a draft for 500 pesos and sent it to the gentleman who had my money in safekeeping, and who immediately remitted the money to me; I went out with one hundred pesos, and after a short walk found a house that rented for twenty-five pesos a month, which I took on the spot, because I liked the way it looked.

Then Roque took me to an auctioneer, with whom I settled on a payment of 200 pesos for furnishing the house, under the condition that he would have to have the whole house ready by the next day. We left him twenty pesos as a down payment and went to the shop of a good tailor, from whom I ordered two very decent suits of clothes and asked that he do me the favor of finding a good and accurate seamstress, which the tailor said he could do in his own house. I asked him to have her make me four sets of the best undergarments she knew how—cambric shirts, and the rest of equally good material; I gave the tailor eighty pesos to work with, and bid him farewell.

Roque told me that he could serve as my valet, my secretary, and anything else I wanted him to do, but that he was very shabby. I offered him my protection, and we returned to the inn.

We ate very well, slept the siesta, and at four in the afternoon I put another hundred pesos in my pocket and we went back to the Parián, where I outfitted Roque with some average clothes, and bought myself a watch that cost me I don't know how much; but in the end I had one peso left over, with which we had some refreshments; and when we returned to the inn, I took out more money and we went to see a comedy. Afterward we ate supper in the tavern, drank some wine, and went to bed.

So I spent four or five days, without doing anything more useful than going on strolls and happily spending money. At the end of that time, the tailor came to the inn and gave me two complete and well-made suits of elegant cloth, the four sets of undergarments just the way I wanted them, and the bill, which said that I owed him one hundred some-odd pesos. I didn't bother checking it, but simply paid him in cash and even gave him a tip. How true it is that money made without effort is spent profusely and with a false sense of liberality!

Soon after I concluded my business with the tailor, the auctioneer came to tell me that the house was ready; all it needed was bedclothes and servants, which he could provide for me if I wished, but for that he would need some money.

I told him, yes, I wanted sheets, a blanket, a bed cover, and new pillows, a good cook and a boy to run errands, and all of it in no time. I gave him the money he requested, and he left.

I spent the rest of that day in idleness, the same as the days before, and the next day the auctioneer returned to tell me that all the house needed now was my presence. Then I told Roque to get a carriage, and I went to the house of the gentleman who was keeping my money, looking so changed and so decent that he did not recognize me at first.

When he was convinced that it was me, he said, "I do not think there is anything wrong with your dressing decently, but it would be better if your clothes matched your quality, your profession, and your means.[5] As for your quality, I suppose that you are not unworthy of this suit, or even something more expensive; but as for the rest, that is, your lack of skills, I would think that you have passed beyond the limits of moderation, and that ten or twelve suits like this would be enough to finish off all your assets. To be sure, there is a popular saying that goes, *dress like your name*, so with a name like Don Pedro Sarmiento and the means to buy the clothes, you should dress like Don Pedro Sarmiento—that is, like a poor but decent man; but now your clothes make you look like a marquis, even though I know you're not a marquis and you do not have anything approaching the wealth of a marquis. Men's desires to pass rapidly from one rank to another, or at least to give the appearance of passing, have spelled the ruin of many families and even entire states. Don't think that there is any other reason for the great poverty one observes in populous cities than the disorderly luxury with which all people seek to rise above their own spheres. This is as true as it is natural, because if a man who makes, for example, 500 pesos a year through his job, commerce, trade, or industry, tries to uphold a luxurious way of life that costs 1,000, he will necessarily have to go into debt to pay the other 500, if he doesn't resort to even more illicit and shameful means. That is why an age-old saying goes, *a man who spends more than he earns shouldn't get angry when he's called a thief.*

"Women who lack judgment are not the least of the causes behind ruined houses, with their untimely vanities. It is generally among women that we see luxury exalted. The wife or daughter of a physician, a lawyer, or the like wants to have

---

[5] [Quality (*calidad*): in this context, the word refers roughly to what we now call "race and class." –Tr.]

a house, servants, and a level of decency that competes with or at least equals that of a rich marquise; to this end, the father or the husband agrees to everything that his reckless affection dictates, and over the short run or the long run, the creditors show up; they seize on the little they can find, his credit dries up, and the family perishes. I've seen one fellow's estate sold after his death, and the most remarkable thing was to see his tailor, his hairdresser, his shoemaker, and I think even his seamstress and his water carrier taking part in the auction, because he owed all of them. With wasps like those around, how much nectar could have been left for his poor children? None at all, surely. They all perished, as do others just like them. But what else could have happened, if their father could never earn enough to pay for the carriage, the box seats in the Coliseo,[6] the gifts to visitors, the big house, the fancy presents, and all the waste that goes along with that kind of big spending? The wound was concealed while he was alive; respect for his business stopped some of his creditors short of demanding that he pay them, and adulation stopped others; but when he died, both their fear and their self-interest disappeared at the same time, and so they descended upon the few items that he owned, leaving his widow and children to live on a woven reed mat. I am telling you this story so that you'll open your eyes and learn how to manage the little bit of money you have, not waste it all on costly clothes, because if you keep on this way, you'll be left with four rags that you'll hardly be able to sell, and not one peso left in your treasure chest.

"Besides, properly considered, it is madness for someone to try looking like something other than what he is, at the cost of his money, while exposing himself to the risk of appearing truly dishonorable. That's called becoming poor to seem rich. I have no doubt that your suit would fool anybody who doesn't know you, because anyone who sees you today in this set of fabulous clothes, and tomorrow in another, will never believe that your entire wealth amounts to 2,000 pesos and change; instead, he'll figure that you own mines or haciendas; and this world is full of flatterers and self-interested people who'll all surround you and offer you lots of humble adulation; but when you fall (as you inevitably will if you don't follow my advice) into the deepest poverty, and are no longer able to maintain your little shell, they'll realize that you weren't rich, just a vain good-for-nothing; and then your pleasures will turn to bitterness, and their deference into disdain.

"So, I've given you a friendly sermon with my words, and I could also give you a sermon with my example. I have 20,000 pesos saved up; I've been tempted to get a very nice house for my wife, and a little carriage; and as you can see, I could easily do it; but I still haven't made up my mind. But what else! Your appearance is indisputably better than mine. Perhaps you would classify my economy as miserly, but it isn't. I also have my bit of self-love and vanity, like every other mother's son, yet my vanity is what stops me. Would you believe it? Well, it's the truth. I'd like to have a carriage, but a carriage demands a great house; the house demands lots of servants, with good salaries so that they'll serve well; and those salaries require funds that won't dry up in four days. After that comes lots of good clothes, excellent furnishings, at least a half-set of silverware, a box in the Coliseo, another carriage for elegant

---

[6] [Coliseo: see Chapter 2, footnote 3. –Tr.]

occasions, two or three good, sprightly, well-maintained teams of mules, footmen, and everything that the rich keep effortlessly, and that I would keep for four days of deadly anxiety, at the end of which, since I do not have enough wealth, I'd lose the carriages, the servants, the mules, the clothes, and everything I once had, and I'd be forced to suffer the sacrifice of having owned and lost, apart from the disdain that the utterly indigent have to suffer.

"That is why I can't make up my mind, friend; and better a slow trot that you can maintain than a gallop that exhausts you. I don't pretend that what keeps me within my limits is economic virtue, just refined vanity; the effect, however, is wholesome, since I owe nothing to anyone; I don't lack any of the things a man needs; my family is decent and contented; I am not overwhelmed by the fear of suddenly going bust; and I enjoy the greatest satisfactions. If you were to tell me that you could have a carriage without needing all the other ostentation I just described, I'd say, that's the way other people think; but I'm not about to become one of those fellows who have carriages and owe their cooks at the end of the month, if it comes to that; that's why I would need more wealth than those other people; because, friend, it's so ridiculous to show off your luxuries on the one hand and display poverty on the other; to have a carriage, and drive around in it with mules so skinny you could count their ribs, or coachmen who look like children's stick figures; to have a grand house, but have the landlord breathing down your neck; to hold balls and go out strolling, yet to have creditors, dodges, and fistfuls of pawn tickets. No, friend, that doesn't suit me, and the worst part is that there is so much of this sort of ridiculousness in Mexico, and outside of Mexico, too. What do you want me to tell you about a manual craftsman or some other poor fellow, who, having saved up no more than some piddling amount through a tremendous amount of work, shows up on a Sunday wearing a frock coat and all the other clothes corresponding to a man of means, and on Monday is back in his worn-out old cloak? What should I say about someone who lives in a low, one-room house, who owes the landlord for a month or two of rent, whose wife doesn't have a petticoat, and whose children wear clothes that are more tattered than a scarecrow, while he spends eight or ten pesos on a day out or on a lunch, perhaps having to pawn something the next day to buy breakfast? I'd have to say that some are vain, some are conceited, and some are crazy; and I'd say the same of you if the case came to it. So, go do whatever you will, since I've said more than enough for your good."

I was enchanted by this man, who had given me so much disinterested advice; but I had no plans to accept his advice at the time; and so, mouthing my thanks to him, I promised to follow what he said exactly, and asked him for my money.

He gave it to me right away, asking for a receipt. I gave him twenty-five pesos as a gift for the good news. He refused to accept it many times; but I insisted so tenaciously that he finally took the pesos; however, in front of me, he picked up a hammer and a nail and started marking them one by one, and when he was finished he put them away in a drawer in his desk.

I asked him what that ceremony had been about, and he replied that he had no need for the money, so he was keeping it to give it as alms to some miserable beggar.

"But, since all our coins are worth the same," I said, "couldn't you give a beggar any pesos at all, and not the precise ones you just marked?"

"There's a great mystery behind this," he said, "and God grant you never find out what it is."

With that I took my leave of him, tired from our long conversation, and after I gave the money to Roque, the two of us got into the carriage with the auctioneer, who was getting tired of waiting for me.

We reached my house, which I found clean, well furnished, and tidy. I took possession of it, though I was not very pleased with the bill that was presented to me, which, not to wear myself out with the details, came to I don't know how much; the fact of the matter is that, between clothing, idle leisure, gifts, and the furnished house, in four days I had spent 1,200 pesos.

To my misfortune, the cook that the auctioneer had found for me was the same Luisa who had served as a chambermaid for Chanfaina and me.

I recognized her as soon as the auctioneer presented her to me, and she recognized me perfectly; but we both pretended not to. The auctioneer left after his house was paid; I sent Roque for some cigars, and I called Luisa, with whom I had a long and satisfying talk. She told me how, after I had left the notary's house and he had run after me, she had fled in the same way I had, and had gone seeking adventure to find me, for she loved me so tenderly that she didn't feel right without me; she had learned that when Chanfaina found her gone, he was so passionate for her that he had fallen ill with rage and had died a short time later; she had made her living as a servant in one house after another, until the auctioneer, whom she had also served, asked if she could come to work in my house; and, since customs change with conditions, and she had known me when I was poor, now that I was rich she would be content to serve me as my cook.

Since the girl was devilishly pretty, and I hadn't changed the roguish character that I professed, I told her that she wouldn't be my cook, because she was not fit to serve, but rather, she should be served.

Then Roque returned, and I told him that this girl was a cousin of mine, and I was duty-bound to protect her. Roque, who was quite a rogue himself, understood the ruse and supported my sentiments. He himself bought good clothes for her and hired a cook; and imagine me now, with Luisa as the lady of the house.

I was happy with Luisa, but I couldn't help feeling ashamed when I considered that, after all, she had arrived as a cook, and that no matter how much I tried to pretend to Roque that she was my cousin, he was far too quick to let himself be fooled, and far from believing me, he must have been muttering to himself about my vulgarity.

With this hanging over me, and hoping to hear my guilt forgiven in his own words, I said one day when we were alone, "What must you be thinking about that cousin of mine, Roque? Surely you don't believe that's what she really is, because we treat each other more familiarly than any cousins, and indeed, if you did think that's what she was, you were mistaken; but, friend, what else could I do? This poor girl was my chum from way back, and because of me she lost her cozy old position and got exposed to being beaten, or worse. See, it wouldn't have been honorable for me to abandon her, now that I have four reales; but still, I feel a little bit ashamed, because, after all, she was supposed to be my cook."

Roque, who understood my spirit, said, "That shouldn't make you feel ashamed, Pedrito: first, because she's white and pretty, and with the clothes she wears, nobody will take her for a cook, but rather for a marquis' daughter at the least; second, because she loves you very much, she's very faithful, and she is very good at running the house; and third, even if everybody knew that she had been your cook and that you had raised her up by making her the mistress of your affections, no one would think the worst of it, knowing how much merit the girl has. Besides, this isn't the first time we've seen such a thing in the world. How many women are passed off as seamstresses, chambermaids, and so forth, when they are nothing but other Luisas in the houses of their masters and lovers! So don't be so fastidious; have fun, and swagger while you have the cash, like everybody else does, because tomorrow old age or poverty will come and everything will come to an end before you've had a chance to enjoy life."

Clearly, the devil himself couldn't have given me more demented advice than Roque; but as you know, bad friends are like vice-devils, with their wicked examples and pernicious advice; they diligently fulfill the malignant spirit's functions to his fullest satisfaction; which is why the venerable Father Dutari says that we should flee, among other things, from the demons that do not frighten us: that is, from our bad friends.[7]

Such was poor Roque, on whose recommendation I became completely brazen, treating Luisa as if she were my wife, and living it up without a care in the world.

It was a rare day that there wasn't a dance, a gambling session, luncheons, banquets, and get-togethers at my house, all of which my best friends attended with the greatest punctuality. But what friends they were! The same scoundrels who, when I was poor, not only did not help me, but as I have said before, were even ashamed to greet me.

These were the first people who sought me out, the ones who celebrated my good luck, those who cajoled me at all times, and those who ate side by side with me. Could I have been so stupid and worthless that I didn't realize all their flattery came solely from their self-interest, without the slightest esteem for my person? Well, I was; and their cajolery so blinded me with vanity that I paid for their lies in gold.

It wasn't just my friends and my old acquaintances that wheedled me; even fortune itself seemed to be trying its best to flatter me. It was a rare event when I lost at gambling; most often I won, and the pots were large—300, 500, even 1,000 pesos. That gave me enough to keep spending freely, and since they all flattered me for my wonderful generosity, I worked to keep them from changing that opinion, and so I gave away and spent without rhyme or reason.

If Luisa had known how to take advantage of my madness, she would have saved something away for when times were hard; but she trusted to her beauty and the fact that I loved her, and so she also wasted money on showy baubles, not stopping to think that her good looks might not last, or my love might grow tired, and that she would then descend into the most miserable poverty; but the poor girl was a foolish coquette and thought the same way almost all her companions did.

---

[7] [See Chapter 16, footnote 5. –Tr.]

I paid no attention to anything. Flattery was my favorite dish, and since the leeches that surrounded me could tell how simple I was, and had learned by the book the art of cajoling and swindling, they cajoled and swindled me to their hearts' content.

I scarcely had to mention that my head hurt, and suddenly they were all physicians, each one of them prescribing a thousand cures for me; if I won at gambling, they never attributed it to chance, but to my great knowledge; if I threw a small banquet, they'd praise me as being more liberal than Alexander; if I drank more than usual and got tipsy, they'd say it was my natural cheerfulness; if I said forty nonsensical things in a row, they listened as closely to me as if I were an oracle, and they all celebrated me as one of those rare talents who only appear on earth once in a hundred years. In a word, whatever I did, whatever I said, whatever I bought, whatever I had in my house—including a scruffy little dog and an insipid, shrieking parakeet whose *caw, caw* would have been enough to wear the nerves of Job himself—were objects of admiration and praise among my dear (*very* dear!) friends.

But what else, if Luisa herself would laugh when she was alone with me, to see herself coddled excessively? And she was right to do so, for the auctioneer who set up my house soon became my friend, through coming over so often to sell me a number of pieces of furniture that I bought from him; and after he saw how I was treating Luisa, he himself forgot that he had been the one who brought her to my house as a cook, and he courted her, treated her like a hot dish, and repeatedly called her, in all seriousness, *the young lady.*

For four or five months I had fun, exulted, and wasted plenty of money, and then fortune began to be cruel to me—or, to speak as a Christian, Divine Providence began to dispose a righteous punishment for my waywardness, or a merciful restraint for the same.

Among the ladies or non-ladies who came to visit me, there was a good old woman who would come with her daughter, a girl of about sixteen, much prettier than Luisa, whom I obstinately fawned over and wooed behind Luisa's back, thinking that I would find it as easy to conquer her as any of the many other women I had known; but that turned out not to be the case: the girl was very quick, and although she didn't mind being loved, she didn't want to prostitute herself to my lust.

She would treat me in a bittersweet style, which day by day inflamed my desires and increased my passion. When she saw that I was intoxicated with love for her, she told me that I had a thousand talents and deserved to be matched with a princess, but all she had was her honor, which she valued above anything she could own in this life; she certainly admired me and was grateful for my kindnesses, so she was sorry that she could not give me the pleasure that I sought; yet she was determined that she would marry the first upright man she found, no matter how poor, before she would ever become some rich man's plaything.

This disappointment left me utterly desperate, and realizing that there was no other way I could have her than to marry her, I broached the subject then and there, and in a blink of an eye we were celebrating our future betrothal.

My new fiancée, whose name was Mariana, informed her mother about our agreement, and her mother approved it with delight. I tactfully and secretly notified a grave and virtuous friar, Mariana's uncle and protector, of our betrothal, and it wasn't hard for me to get his blessings for the union; but to put the plan into action, I still had to overcome one small difficulty, which was to see how I could get rid of Luisa, whom I feared, knowing how resolute she was and how little she had to lose.

While I was figuring out what means I could use to get that job done, I did not neglect all the other operations that were necessary to setting up the wedding. I needed to turn to my relatives so that they would provide me with my references.[8] As soon as they had heard from me on this occasion, and found out that I wasn't poor, they were attracted to my house like flies to honey. They all recognized me as their relative, and my rogue of an uncle, the lawyer, was even the first to visit me, coming over several times to fill his stomach at my expense.

With most of the preparations made, just two things remained: put together a trousseau for my bride-to-be, and throw Luisa out of the house. For the first of these, I didn't have enough money; for the second, I had too much fear; but with Roque's assistance, I managed everything, as you will see in the next chapter.

---

[8] [The partners in a marriage had to demonstrate to the presiding priest, with documents or testimony, that they were not already married and that they were of equal social standing. –Tr.]

CHAPTER 31

IN WHICH WE LEARN OF HOW PERIQUILLO THREW LUISA OUT
OF HIS HOUSE, AND HIS MARRIAGE TO YOUNG MARIANA

Once my fiancée and I had exchanged vows and presented our references, and once the banns had been published, all that I had left to do (as I just said) was to put together a trousseau for my sweetheart and throw Luisa out of the house. In both cases, I found the difficulties insuperable. I had already conveyed to Roque my scheme of getting married, and had entreated him to keep the secret; but I hadn't told him about the tight circumstances I was in, nor did he dare ask me the reason behind my delay; until, trusting in his cleverness, I told him about everything that was holding me back from realizing my plans.

As soon as he knew the truth, he said, "Why have you been patiently keeping me in the dark about all this nonsense that's got you so scared? You know I'm your servant, your classmate, and your friend, and experience has shown you that I've always served you with loyalty and affection. Come on, I find this hard to believe about you! But let's leave off the sentimentality; and you, get your spirits up, because you'll get over your troubles easily. As for the trousseau, I suppose you'll want a really good one, right?"

"That's right, exactly," I said. "You know that I've already spent a lot, and it's been days since I've done any good at cards. I couldn't have more than 300 pesos in the money-box, and that'll barely be enough for the wedding party. If I start spending it all on the trousseau, I won't have a penny left by the wedding day; if I reserve it for the wedding, I won't be able to give anything to my wife, which would be a terrible embarrassment, since even the poorest wretch makes sure he can give his bride a little something on his wedding day. So you see, this isn't an easy bar to jump over."

"Sure it is," Roque told me quite calmly. "What else do you have to do, than get some fabric on credit from a merchant, and buy a middling set of jewels from a silversmith's shop?"

"But who'd ever loan me the money I need, when I've never bothered getting to know anyone in the business world?"

"You're so silly, Pedrito! You could drown in a teaspoon of water. Tell me, isn't Licenciado Maceta, the lawyer, your uncle?"[1]

"Yes, he is."

"And isn't he well known for his wealth?"

"Yes, he's that, too," I replied, "very well known here in Mexico."

"Well, there you go," said Roque, "that's the solution to our problem. Put on your finest clothes, get a carriage, and I'll take you to a dry goods store and a jewelry shop where I know the owners; you just ask for the fabric you like the best, ask for as much as you need, have them draw up the bill and cut the cloth, and when it's all cut, you tell the storekeeper that you're expecting the money from your hacienda in two or three weeks, but since you are just about to get married and you need to make the clothes for your bride's hope chest or trousseau, you'll be very obliged to him if he

---

[1] [*Maceta:* literally a flowerpot, or a large mallet; colloquially, "dim-witted." –Tr.]

does you the favor of advancing the cloth to you, which you'll guarantee by leaving him a bond signed by your own hand. Naturally, the merchant will resist; he'll give you a few good excuses and allege a thousand obstacles, because he doesn't know you. Then you'll ask him whether he knows the lawyer Maceta, and whether he thinks he's a trustworthy man. He'll say yes; and right then, you'll say he's your guarantor. The merchant will want to move his merchandise, so when he sees that the payment's guaranteed, he'll agree without any problem. Then you go do the same thing with the silversmith, and there you have it: your tremendous problem is solved."

"Your plan doesn't seem bad to me," I said to Roque, "but what if my uncle refuses to guarantee my credit? I'd find that even more embarrassing."

"How could he refuse?" Roque said. "He thinks you're rich, he visits you all the time, and he loves you so well."

"All that is well and good," I replied, "but my uncle's as stingy as they come. If you only knew: one time when he saw another nephew about to be given 200 lashes in public, not only did he not help him, he even wrote him a very dry note in which he let this nephew know that, if he thought it would take money to get him out of that insulting situation, then he shouldn't count on him; instead, the nephew should bear with the punishment, since he had earned it. What would you say about that?"

"I'd say," Roque replied, "that he did that to a poor nephew; but I'd bet my ears that he'd never do it to a nephew like you. Look, Pedrito: a stingy man is normally very greedy, and his own self-interest makes him act generously when he least expects it; that's why there's a saying: *greed breaks the sack;* and another one: *the constipated man always dies of diarrhea.* Anyway, let's give it a go, because it doesn't cost anything to try. Tell him you barely have 2,000 pesos in the money-box; tell him you're thinking of taking out money on interest so you can do things right on this occasion; tell him that in two or three weeks, they'll be bringing you either money or cattle from your hacienda; tell him whatever lies you can think of, bring some pretty present for his wife, and invite the two of them to be godparents at your wedding; and when you've done all that, tell him that the shops are holding the fabric and the jewels until you can get a guarantor, and you proposed that he could do it for you, trusting in his friendship and feeling certain that he wouldn't slight you. You've got to do all this after dinner, and after refilling his cup five or six times; and you've got to have the carriage waiting for you at the door, and you can have my ear if it doesn't all go just like we're hoping."

Convinced by Roque's arguments, I decided to put his advice into action, and everything turned out to the letter as he had predicted, because the word *yes* was hardly out of my uncle's mouth when, without giving him time to reconsider, we went to the dry goods store and the bond was drawn up in my uncle's name, in the following terms:

"I, Licenciado Don Nicanor Maceta, declare: that by this bond, I do oblige myself in every way to make good to Don Nicasio Brundurín, of this commercial establishment, the quantity of 1,000 pesos, this being the value of the cloth that my nephew Don Pedro Sarmiento has taken on credit from his house for his wife's trousseau; and that I shall fulfill this obligation after one month has passed, if, by said time, my above-mentioned nephew should default on payment. Signed, etc."

Don Nicasio was very satisfied with his big sheet of paper, as I was with my fabric, which I loaded into the carriage; and off we went to the silversmith's, where the same scene was repeated, and they gave me a set of diamond jewels that cost 500 pesos and change.

I left the fabric at the tailor's, giving the tailor my fiancée's address and a work order to get her measurements, make the clothes for her, and leave her presents on my behalf.

This done, I returned home with my uncle, who told me from time to time as we drove along, "Be careful, Pedrito, for the love of God; let's not let them down, because I'm a very poor man."

I responded with the cheekiest sarcasm, "Don't worry—I'm an upright man, and I've got money."

Meanwhile we arrived at my house, we refreshed ourselves, and my uncle continued on to his house; we ate dinner, and after Luisa had gone to bed, I called Roque and said to him, "No doubt about it, friend, you've got a good fix for everything. I've got to thank you for the nice maneuver you showed me to get out of my first jam; but I still have to get out of the second, which is to see how to get Luisa to leave the house; because, you know, if you put two cats in the same bag, they'll fight. She can't stay in the house with Marianita and me, because she's too jealous; my wife will be the same; and we'll have a miniature hell here. Holy Scripture compares a jealous woman to a scorpion, and it is said that no anger is greater than a woman's anger, that it would be more pleasant to live with a lion and a dragon than with an angry woman,[2] so what could I say about living with two jealous and furious women? So, please, Roque, you can see that there is no way it would be good for me to be living with Luisa and my wife under the same roof; but even though I ought to prefer my wife, I don't know how I can wriggle free of the other woman, especially since she hasn't given me any motive; but she's got to leave my house somehow, I just don't know how."

"That's easy," said Roque. "Do you give me permission to woo her?"

"Do whatever you want," I replied.

"Well, then," he went on, "you can count it good as done. What woman is harder than stone? Yet a little water can carve a cleft in stone if it drips continuously. I promise you, I can make her fall in four days. I don't love her; but just to serve you, I'll seduce her as best I can, and when I gain her favors, I'll give you the critical date when you can find us in a suspicious position, and then, if you wish, you can beat her as if you had all the reason to do so, and throw her out of the house on the spot, and she won't have any way to argue that you're wrong."

I realized how treacherous and unjust Roque's plan was, but I agreed to it because I couldn't think of a better one; and so, letting him step in for me, I anxiously awaited the pressing moment when I could toss Luisa from my house.

Roque was not a bad-looking young man, and was quite a rogue to boot, and with the coins that I supplied to him for the job, he made use of every stratagem his spirit suggested to him for conquering the unsuspecting Luisa, which was not very

---

[2] [Ecclesiasticus 25:23 (25:15–16) and 26:10 (26:7). –Tr.]

hard to accomplish, since she wasn't used to resisting such assaults; so all it took was a few sorties by Roque before the fortress of her false fidelity fell, and the general informed me of the day, time, and place where the surrender would occur.

With the two of us in agreement, he gave me the pre-arranged signal, and when the poor girl was beside herself with pleasure in the arms of her new and treacherous lover, I entered, as if in surprise; then, feigning an implacable rage and jealousy, slapping her, and handing her the bundle of her clothes that I had prepared in advance, I put her outdoors in the street.

The wretched girl got down on her knees to beg me, wept, made promises, and did everything she could to satisfy me; but nothing could do that, since what I needed from her wasn't satisfaction, but her absence. The poor girl finally went away crying, while Roque and I stayed behind laughing and celebrating how easily we had dispelled the formidable phantom that had been holding up my wedding.

Eight days after she left, we celebrated the wedding with all the luxury possible, not forgetting the good banquet and the dance that usually take place at such events.

My relatives and friends were all at the dinner, along with plenty of interlopers whom I didn't know, but who used their skills of shameless flattery to crash the gate, and whom I could not throw out of my house without raising a fuss; but the fact is that they reduced the amount of food we were able to serve our legitimate guests, and because of them, the poor kitchen staff went hungry.

After dinner was concluded, we began the dance, which went on until three in the morning, and would have gone on until dawn, had it not been interrupted by an amusing and perilous incident.

What happened was that, when the drawing room was crowded with people, two decent men suddenly stood up from their chairs for some reason having to do with a woman, and after insulting each other in words, in an instant they came to blows; one of them grabbed his enemy by the hair, and found himself holding a toupee in his hands: his adversary appeared to be a layman in all his clothes, but he had a friar's tonsure.

At that moment, the enemy set aside his wrath; the woman who was the object of their argument disappeared from the dance; all the bystanders' fear of a brawl collapsed into laughter; and the friar looked as if he were trying to shrink down to the size of an ant so he could scurry under the rug and hide.

Under these ridiculous conditions, my wife's uncle, that good friar whom I have mentioned before, appeared in his full friar's robes; for on the occasion of his niece's wedding, he had yielded to our insistent pleas and had publicly attended the dinner, and had been enjoying the dance for a while from the privacy of the bedroom. As I was saying, he came out of the bedroom, filled with holy wrath, and confronting the friar-in-disguise, he told him:

"I don't know whether to speak to you as a friar or as a layman, because you seem like both to me at this instant; you're like the bat in the fable, who showed his wings when he found it convenient to pretend he was a bird, and when he wanted to be a mammal, tried to prove it by pointing to his teats. From the cut of your hair, you seem to be a friar, but by your body you seem secular; so I have to say once more that I don't know what to take you for, or how to address you, though simple logic indicates that you must be a friar, because it is easier to believe that a wayward friar would disguise himself in secular clothes to go to a dance, than that a layman would tonsure his hair before the party. But if you are a friar, don't you realize that by appearing at a dance dressed like this, you are indicating that you are ashamed to be seen in your habit, because friar's habits don't look good at dances? Aren't you trumpeting your laxity and committing a continuous apostasy? Don't you see that you are breaking your vows of obedience? Don't you stop to think that you will scandalize your brothers who find out what you're doing, and the laymen who recognize you, since it is a rare friar who isn't recognized by someone at a dance? Don't you care that you are unjustly damaging your prelates' honor, since the laymen who don't understand will think that it is your superiors' neglect or ignorance that produces this kind of disorderly license, when the truth is that those of us who are in charge of guiding our fellow friars cannot always control the rebellious ones, or penetrate the infernal stratagems they use to avoid our watchful vigilance? And if that is true about the simple act of going to a dance in layman's clothing, what about going out with women, and provoking quarrels and fights over them, perversely motivated by jealousy?

"I am not interested in knowing who you are, or what order you belong to; for me, it is enough to see that you are a friar, and to consider that I am one, too, to be ashamed of your excess. But, my dearest brother, how much farther will the most scandalous laymen go when they see that a man of the faith—a man who has professed virtue, who has sworn to separate himself from the world and to restrain his passions—is the first to scandalize everyone with his depraved example? What will the gentlemen who know you and who are here right now say? The more prudent among them will attribute this event to human fragility, from which no man is free, not merely in the cloisters, but even among the ranks of the apostles; yet the ungodly, the foolish, and the imprudent will not simply murmur about your lewdness: they will scoff at your whole order, saying that the friars from that monastery over there are lover-boys, dandies, braggarts, and rowdies, like so-and-so; and they will unjustly chalk up the personal scandal that you just gave them, with your bad example, to the dishonor of your holy order.

"Perhaps—and not even perhaps—on this account, there are certain particular orders that are the objects of private jeering on the part of imprudent libertines. . . . But why do I say *private?* The general public scoffing that almost all the religious orders have suffered is motivated by nothing other than the bad behavior of a few of their scandalous and cruel brothers.

"You shouldn't think, because of this, that I'm a friar who is scandalized over nothing, nor that I am pretending to be saintly. I'm a sinner—if only I weren't! I know that your slip here is neither the first, nor the most horrendous that the world has ever seen. I also know that there are occasions on which friars cannot avoid going to dances. But I know that, on such occasions, they can keep wearing their habits, which are far from unseemly when an individual of the faith wears them; I know that the mere presence of a friar at a dance, with the tacit or express permission of his prelate, is no sin; I know that the friar who goes to such an event is under no obligation to gamble, dance, fight, court women, or scandalize the laity; rather, he has a fine space at such dances and gatherings to edify them and to honor his order, without affectation or antics. I would say the same of priests, if it were my place. And how easy is this to achieve? Simply by showing no inclination to do such things, and indeed avoiding such an inclination; and by acting like friars when politeness or other circumstances oblige us to attend laymen's functions.

"In a word: to my mind, what's wrong isn't that a friar might attend these celebrations from time to time; it is that he frequents them, and doesn't attend as who he is, but as a scandalous layman.

"There is no quarrel between virtue and civilization. Jesus Christ, who came to show us the path to heaven with His life and His example, put His stamp of approval on this truth, both by attending the weddings and public parties to which He was invited, and by getting to know sinners such as the Samaritan and the Publican. But how did the Lord attend these events, why, and what results did He glean from going to them? He attended like holiness itself; He attended to edify the people with His example, to teach them His doctrine, and to favor men with His grace; and the fruit of His divine presence was the conversion of many wayward sinners. Oh, if the friars who went to secular functions and parties only attended them to edify the guests with their modest examples, how differently the laity would think of them, and how much crudity and sinful impudence could be avoided because of their respectable presence!

"Well, enough of my sermon! If I have gone beyond the limits of a brotherly rebuke, please understand that the aim was not to embarrass this friar, but to straighten him out and teach him a lesson; and I did it right here, because this was where he committed his offense, and he who sins in public should be corrected publicly; and finally, I said everything you have heard, gentlemen, so that you will all realize that, if there are a few dissolute friars who scandalize you, there are also many more who abhor such scandals and who seek to edify with their good example. Please continue your celebration, and may you all have a good night."

Having said this, my uncle entered the bedroom that had been set aside for him, leading the shame-faced friar in by the hand. Most of the dancers had already left, because the sermon didn't sit well with them; the musicians were sleeping, my godparents and I were ready to turn in, and so Roque paid the musicians what we owed them, everybody went home, and we went to bed.

The next day, my wife and I woke up late, after her uncle had already taken the young friar back to his monastery; though, as we later learned, he merely left the friar in his cell, accompanying him as a friend, without accusing him before his prelate as the young friar had feared he would.

I spent some fifteen delightful days in the company of my wife, whom I loved more every day, both because she was pretty and because she endeavored to win me over; but since no delights last forever in this world, and it is equally certain that sadness and tears always walk in the train of joy, it so happened that the payment date set by the dry-goods shopkeeper and the silversmith came around, and each of them began to demand that I pay them their money.

I was so far from being able to pay them that I had already gone flat broke, and was having to send things to the Parián and the pawn shop behind my wife's back so that she would not learn so quickly how thin my purse was.

When my creditors saw that I didn't pay them after the second notice, they descended upon the poor lawyer; and he, not wanting to pay for something that he hadn't enjoyed himself, pestered me with a swarm of notes and messages, which I answered with short, polite words meant to give him hope, and concluding that he should pay them, and I would repay him later; but that was exactly what he was trying to avoid.

My creditors could not abide any further delay, so they complained before a judge, showing him the bond that the lawyer had signed, promising to pay if I defaulted. The judge was no greenhorn; when he saw the bond, he smiled and told the petitioners that it was an illegal document, and that they should watch what they were doing, because they had lost their money, by virtue of a law that expressly states:

> And to remedy the imponderable abuse that occurs in these times because of such weddings: I declare that no merchants, goldsmiths and silversmiths, grocers, or any other sort of person may at any time request, demand, nor bring suit over the merchandise and goods that they might give on credit for such weddings, to any persons or any state, quality, or condition whatsoever.[3]

The poor creditors were chilled by this news; but instead of fainting, they appealed the case before the Audiencia. The lawyer, seeing himself under assault by two enemies in such a serious tribunal, tried to defend himself, and he found the law and cited it in his favor; but that did him no good, for the gentlemen of the Audiencia ruled that, by way of a fine, the lawyer should pay the amount for which he had been sued, since he had acted either maliciously or in ignorance, and in either case he owed the fine, whether for the bad faith with which he had operated by defrauding the plaintiffs, or for his crass ignorance of the law that prohibited what he had done, which was inexcusable for a lawyer.

With this, my miserable uncle sullenly spat out the cash, and continued the lawsuit against me; but I knew everything that had occurred and, still promising to pay up when my fortunes improved, I took advantage of the same law to free myself of the judgment, and it was declared that the lawyer's suit had no judicial standing.

That was the end of the matter, and my uncle lost the money, which I never repaid. Wrong on my part; but a just punishment for the lawyer's greed, flattery, and stinginess.

All these lawsuits took up about three months, during which time I was no longer able to hide my lack of funds from my wife, and was forced to begin selling and pawning all of our clothes and jewels to keep up the pretense of luxury to which I had become accustomed, so my friends would not miss the luncheons, dances, and entertainments that they were accustomed to enjoying.

---

[3] Auto 4, Título 12, Libro 7 of the *Recopilación*, in paragraph 26. Don Marcos Gutiérrez, in his revised edition of *Febrero*, in proof of this legal decision, refers to the suit that was tried between Don Antonio Zorraquín, merchant, and Don Eugenio Cachurro, his debtor, for more than 12,000 reales, which the merchant loaned to the debtor for his wedding. The merchant sued in 1760, demanding payment; the judge declared the bond document to be null, as it was written contrary to the express law; the Council upheld this sentence on appeal. *Febrero*, tomo 2, chapter 18, p. 1, paragraph 25.

My wife was the only one who was unhappy, as she saw her wardrobe growing empty. That was when she realized that I wasn't the rich young man she had thought me to be, but a vain, lazy, and useless pauper who would be reducing her to misery in no time; and since she had not given herself to me out of love, but out of self-interest, as soon as she had ascertained that there was no wealth to be had, her affection began to grow cold, and she no longer treated me with the same attention as before.

I likewise began to notice that I no longer loved her as tenderly as at first, and I even recalled poor Luisa with regret. You see, since I did not marry for love, either, but for other less honest ends, being dazzled by Mariana's beauty and roused by her denial of my appetite, as soon as my appetite was satisfied by possessing the object I desired, my love imperceptibly grew cooler and cooler, especially when I noticed that my wife no longer had the same striking appearance as she did before she married me; to say it once and for all, as soon as I had satisfied the first impetus of my lust, she didn't look half as good to me as she had at first. Once she understood that I was broke and that she couldn't enjoy the good life with me that had been promised her, she also looked at me differently, and we both went from viewing each other with indifference to treating each other with disdain, until we ended by detesting each other to death.

Around the time we had gotten to this last step, it so happened that I had come to owe four months' rent, and the landlord couldn't get a penny from me no matter how many times he dropped by. I could always count on one of my very good friends to tell him how poor I was and that he should keep a better eye on his money; of course, even if nobody had told him that, he could have seen my poverty in the way I dressed, which was no longer with the luxury that I had gotten used to; my visitors began to flee my house as fast as if I had the plague; my wife was only seen wearing the plainest dresses, because she had no fancy gowns left; our house furnishings amounted to some chairs, sofas, tables, desks, six lampshades, a pair of bell jars, four saints, my bed, and a few other trinkets of little value; and to top it all off, when my uncle and guarantor saw that I wasn't going to pay him, not only did he break off our friendship entirely, he became my most committed enemy, and after that there wasn't a single acquaintance of mine who hadn't heard how I had made him lose one and a half grand, for he told everybody the story, and added that he didn't have any hopes of ever seeing that money again, because I was a no-good low-life, a swaggering peacock, and a first-class rogue.

My uncle's base actions were those of the common sort of person who isn't content unless he announces to everyone who his debtors are, while at the same time, he makes sure that he collects what's owed him. That is why the discreet Bocángel says:

> Don't borrow from miserly men,
> For while you are owing them,
> They'll collect your reputation first,
> And then go after your money.[4]

---

[4] [From *El Cortesano* (1655). –Tr.]

With so many people trumpeting my poverty, the landlord was clearly anxious to get his money out of me. And he did try. When he saw that I was showing no signs of paying, that I was falling further behind in the rent, that my luck was going from bad to worse, and that his extrajudicial warnings had no effect, he complained before a judge who, after hearing my case, set a deadline of three days for me to pay up, threatening to attach and seize my estate otherwise.

To avoid any further arguments, I agreed to everything, and I went home with Roque, who advised me to sell all my furniture to the auctioneer who had sold it to me, since nobody would give me a better price for it; then, he said, I should take the money and rent a little house, but in some other neighborhood far away from where we were living, just keeping the bed, the pots and pans, and the most necessary furnishings; I should fire the cook and the maid right away, to do away with any witnesses, even if it meant eating in a tavern; and when all these things were done, on the night before the day they were threatening to seize my property, I should move out of the house, leaving the keys with the auctioneer.

Since I was always quick to do everything Roque advised me, with his help I did everything he had proposed, to the letter. He went to find a smaller house, which he secured for me, and over the next two days, I worked to move my bed and the most necessary furnishings there. On the third day, Roque called the auctioneer, who came right away, and I told him that I had to leave Mexico the next day on very urgent business; so, if he wanted to buy the furniture that I was leaving in the house, I would prefer to sell it all to him, because he knew better than anyone how much it cost, but if he didn't want it, that he should let me know so that I could find some buyers; but that I needed to complete the deal that very day, since I was leaving the next morning.

The auctioneer agreed to buy it immediately; but he began to point out a thousand defects that he had missed when he sold the furniture to me. "This piece is old," he said, "and this one is out of style; this one is broken and has been mended; this one's all moth-eaten; this is very plain wood; this piece has been soldered; there's a part missing here; another part here; this is tarnished; this is a run-of-the-mill painting"—and so he went on, pointing out the defects in each piece for me to see; until at last I angrily took 80 pesos from him for everything that he had sold me for 160; but we finally closed the deal, and he offered to come bring me the money at vespers that evening.

He was true to his word. He came promptly with the money; he gave it to me and asked for a receipt, in which I declared that I had sold him, for the stated amount, such-and-such furniture from my house, with a detailed description of each piece. What I most wanted was to get my hands on the coins and get out of there, so I gave him the receipt to his full satisfaction, together with the keys to the house, asking him to give them back to the landlord, and without any further ado, I took the money and got into the carriage (which Roque had waiting for me) along with my wife, bidding the auctioneer farewell, and I directed the coachman to the new house that Roque had indicated.

As soon as we arrived, my wife realized that the house was smaller and poorer than the one she had lived in before she married me, with fewer furnishings and not even a scullery maid on a salary of twelve reales. The unhappy woman grew sad and rashly revealed her feelings; I felt put out by her daintiness, and I threw in her face the fact that she hadn't brought any dowry to the marriage; we had the first fight in which we thoroughly unburdened our hearts, and from that moment on, our mutual loathing was declared. But let us leave our unhappy marriage in this state, and move on to see what happened the next day in my old house.

It sometimes seems that ill-fated accidents are determined by some wicked spirit that makes them happen during the most critical moments of misfortune; because, on the same day that the auctioneer came with the keys to take out the furniture I had sold him, and at that same hour, the landlord arrived with the notary, who brought with him the order to carry out the seizure of my belongings on the spot.

The auctioneer unlocked the door and entered with his porters to clear out the house, and the landlord arrived with the notary and his porters to do the same. Then it all started. As soon as they saw each other and conveyed to each other the reason why they had come to that house, they began to wrangle over who deserved preference. The landlord pointed to the judge's order, and the auctioneer showed my receipt. Both were right; both demanded justice; but only one of them could keep my furniture, which wasn't enough to satisfy both of them. The landlord would have agreed to split the baby and let each of them keep half; but the auctioneer, who had paid out his own money, wasn't about to fall for that.

In the end, after a thousand pointless arguments, they agreed to leave the furnishings in the house, inventoried and put under the watchful eye of the most trustworthy man in the neighborhood, until a decision was reached by a judge; the judge decreed that it all belonged to the auctioneer, since he had written proof that I had sold it to him, while the landlord was free to bring up the case against me, if he ever found me. I learned all this through Roque, who never neglected to find out every last detail about my affairs. When I heard the decree, I figured I was safe, since my insolvency meant that the landlord couldn't do me any harm; and so all I did was look for entertainment while ignoring my wife, as well as ignoring the obligations that marriage placed on me. With the same kind of erring behavior, I merrily enjoyed myself until the eighty pesos were gone. After that, my poor wife began to experience the hardships of destitution, and to know what it meant to be married to a man who had yoked himself to her like the horse that married the mule, neither of which has understanding. She naturally began to grow more and more tired of me, and to show me how much she detested me. I therefore loathed her more every second, and since I was a rogue, it didn't bother me in the least to keep her unclothed and dying of hunger.

Under these trying circumstances, my mother-in-law, moved by my wife's tales, mortified me to no end. Every day, she criticized and reprimanded me endlessly, not forgetting that famous line, "If only I had known who you were! You can be sure you never would have married my daughter, because she had plenty of better suitors." That just added fuel to the fire, because, far from loving my wife better, I loathed her all the more after these caustic reprimands.

It was my wicked nature, more than my wife's character or figure, that made me detest her, together with my mother-in-law's injudicious comments; proof of which was that I became devilishly jealous of a neighbor who lived across the street from us. I took it into my head that he was after my wife, and that she was responding to his overtures; and without any kind of positive evidence, I made her life a living hell, as do many married men who turn their good wives bad through their dunderheaded jealousies.

After the unhappy girl, who was all too faithful despite her yearning for luxury and ease, saw how badly I was treating her because of my jealous suspicions of that man, she decided to pay me back with the same coin; and so she pretended to go along with his advances, to give me something to regret and to make me think she was being unfaithful. That was foolish, but she did it because my imprudent jealousy provoked her. Husbands, I'd certainly advise you never to let that damnable passion overcome you, because it so often turns shadows into full bodies, and suspicions into realities!

If I watched over her and pestered her when there was nothing going on, how much more do you suppose I did when she was doing her best to make me feel sorry? It's easy to imagine; and yet I am not sure how I combined the loathing that I felt toward her with the jealousy that was eating me up, for if the common proverb is true, that *where there is no love, there can be no jealousy*, I certainly never would have felt jealous; unless it could be argued that jealousy is nothing but the fierce envy roused by our own self-love, in which case it would rise to a fever pitch whenever we knew, or assumed, that some rival of ours wanted to possess the object that belonged to us by some right; for in that case, clearly, we do not feel jealous because we are in love, but because we think we are being aggrieved: and there we find jealousy without love, and so may conclude that the vulgar saying is entirely false.

The first thing I did was to move my poor wife to a tiny, damp, and deplorable one-room house on the outskirts of the neighborhood of Santa Ana.[5]

Next, since I had nothing left to sell or pawn, I told Roque that he should seek better shelter, for I was in no condition to give him so much as a tortilla; he instantly took my advice, and from that time forth, my wife lacked even the trivial support he had given her by running her errands, by consoling her, and on a few occasions even by helping her out with half a real or two that he finagled. This makes me think that Roque was one of those people who are bad by necessity, rather than because they have an evil character, for the bad actions to which he stooped, and the wicked advice he gave me, can be attributed to his efforts to flatter me, due to his wretched state; but on the other hand, he was very loyal, polite, and considerate, and above all he had a sensitive heart and was always ready to forgive an insult and sympathize with others' misfortunes. In the course of my life I have observed that there are many Roques in this world; that is, many naturally good men who have been shoved, shall we say, by poverty to the threshold of crime. True, man should perish before committing a crime; but I would always leave room for pardoning someone who had transgressed when compelled by utter destitution; and I would increase the punishment for someone who had done so because of the depravity of his character.

---

[5] [A poor area around the Plaza Santa Ana, one mile north of the Cathedral. –Tr.]

In any case, Roque took leave of my house, and my poor wife began to experience the ill treatment of a roguish husband who loathed her; although, far from using her good judgment to tame me, she irritated me more and more with her proud and irascible temperament. As you can see, she did not love me, either.

Every day we had arguments, altercations, and quarrels, and she always got the worst of them, for I finished off my anger with kicks and punches, and in that way made up for my rage; she would be left crying and abused, while I would go out on the street to have a good time doing bad.

Sometimes I wouldn't show up again at home for eight or ten days after a fight, and then I'd start quarreling again over any trifle and accusing her out of my own jealousy; the basest thing about my reprimands was that I would make them even if I hadn't left her a penny for food; and in this, I was just like so many other shameless husbands, who only remember their wives to watch over them jealously or to use them like servants, but not to make sure they have enough to eat, as if they don't understand that a woman's honor is attached to cooking, and when no smoke rises from the kitchen hearth, the man has no right to shout;[6] because even if these miserable wives were more honorable than Lucretia, they don't have chameleons' stomachs, that they can live on air.

My unfortunate wife suffered her nakedness and troubles, despite the hatred she felt for me, without daring to go live with her mother—the only person who visited her, consoled her, and supported her (a mother, after all)—because both of them were very afraid of me, and I had threatened my wife with death if she ever abandoned the house. Not even her uncle the friar wanted to get mixed up in our business.

I have mentioned that, along with all my bad qualities, I had the good one of possessing a sensitive heart, and I believe that if, instead of irritating me from the beginning with her pride, and convincing me that she was being unfaithful, my wife had overwhelmed me with affection and sound judgment, I would never have been so cruel to her; but some women have a talent for spoiling the best of men.

Her illnesses and her bad life worsened my wife's position day by day. On top of this, she became pregnant, which not only left her thin, pale, and freckled, but tiresome, irate, and unbearable.

In this state, I detested her even more and spent even less time around the house. One night when I happened to be home, she began to complain of sharp pains and to beg me for the sake of God to call her mother, because she felt terrible. This submissive language, which I was not used to hearing from her, together with her pain-

---

[6] That is, when the hearth is cold because of the husband's laziness, uselessness, or wickedness, as in Perico's case; but when it is cold because of poverty, then the wife should always be faithful and even assist her husband; because when God created the first woman for the first man, He did not say: let Us make a mistress whom he shall serve, nor an idle creature whom he shall maintain, but rather a woman who shall be a help like unto himself. *Faciamus ei adjutorium simile sibi* [Genesis 2:20].

Also: The moral of the annotated passage and of the author's note is not pure. No matter how roguish and negligent one spouse might be in fulfilling his or her obligations, that fact does not excuse the other partner from fulfilling them; and thus, under no circumstances should a wife be unfaithful to her husband, nor he to his wife. –E.

ful moans, made a new impression on my heart, and looking at her with pity from that point, forgetting about her irascible and unloving temper, I ran to get her mother, who recognized as soon as she arrived that her exertions and her pains pointed to a bad labor, and that a midwife was indispensable.

Once I knew what her illness was and that she needed a professional, I asked a neighbor woman to go find the midwife while I tried to round up some money. She ran off, found the midwife, and brought her to the house; I pawned my cloak, which was the best thing I still owned and not in bad condition, and for it they loaned me four pesos, though I would have to pay five to redeem it. Typical graciousness of usurers, whose steadfast motto is: may the devil take you!

I was very happy when I got back home with my four pesos, at the same time that the exceedingly ignorant midwife had finished ripping out the fetus with her fingernails and another infernal apparatus,[7] scraping my wife's insides along the way and causing a flow of blood so copious that not even a good surgeon's expertise was able to contain it, depriving her of her life on the second day after the sacrifice, just after she had been given last rites.

Oh, Death! How many mysteries your fateful advent reveals to us! As soon as I saw unhappy Mariana laid out lifeless on her bed of torment, which amounted to a few rags on top of a woven reed mat, and heard the tender weeping of her mother, my sensitivity was awakened, for at every instant, her mother said: "Ay, my poor, unfortunate daughter! Ay, my sweet, sweet darling! Who would have thought that you would die in such poverty, just because you married a man who didn't deserve you, and who didn't treat you as a husband should, but as would an executioner and a tyrant?"

To these expressions she added others, even harder and more sensitive, which tore my heart to bits, so that I could no longer contain my emotions.

At that moment, I realized that I hadn't gotten married with the holy aims for which one should contract matrimony, but like the horse that married the mule, neither of which has understanding; I recognized that my wife was naturally faithful and good, and that I had turned her into an annoying woman by harassing her with my wicked behavior; I saw that she was beautiful, for even with her loss of blood, and deprived of the breath of life, her deceased face displayed her grace that shone through her unlucky youth; and I understood that I had been the author of this fatal tragedy.

And then . . . (so late!) I regretted my villainous conduct; I realized that my wife was neither ugly nor so bad-natured as I had judged her, for if she did not love me, it was for a thousand perfectly just reasons, because I myself had carved a devil out of material that could have been shaped into an angel;[8] and with all these passions of

---

[7] Some midwives are so ignorant that they think they can make a labor easier by using their fingernails, and others who substitute artificial fingernails made of silver or some other metal for the same purpose. Beware of midwives!

[8] There is no way around it: it is almost always men's fault that their wives are bad. Women, especially women who get married when they are very young, are normally disposed to become whatever their husbands want them to be.

grief and regret surging through my spirit, I poured it all out by hurling myself onto my deceased wife's cold corpse.

What a mournful and terrible moment for my exhausted imagination! How tightly I hugged her! How many kisses I planted on her purplish lips! How many sweet expressions I whispered to her! How many times I begged for forgiveness from a body that could no longer feel thanks for my blandishments nor pardon my offenses! . . . Oh, spirit of my unhappy spouse, do not denounce before God the many troubles I caused you so unjustly; rather, please accept in compensation for them the vows I have offered for you to the Lord of Mercy at his immaculate altars!

Finally, after a scene that I am incapable of painting in its true colors, I was forcibly removed from there, and my wife's body was given a proper burial, I do not know how, though I assume that the efforts and diligence of her uncle the friar played a large part in arranging it.

My mother-in-law, as soon as the funeral was over (and with it, the unfortunate fruit of her womb entombed), bid me farewell forever, thanking me for the fine way I had finished off her daughter; and that night, unable to endure the sentiments of Nature, I locked myself inside my little room to mourn my widowhood and loneliness.

Absorbed in the most sorrowful fancies, I could not sleep a wink all night long; scarcely would I close my eyes when I would wake up trembling, shaken by the dread of my conscience, which represented my wife to me with the greatest vividness: it seemed that I saw her standing in front of me, gazing at me with terrible eyes, and saying: "Cruel man! Why did you seduce me and take me away from the loving side of my mother? Why did you swear that you loved me, and tie yourself to me in the most tender and tightest of all yokes; why did you call yourself the father of this child, who was stillborn because of you, if in the end you were nothing but an executioner for your wife and your son?"

These were the sorts of charges that I seemed to hear from the cold lips of my unhappy spouse, and filled with fright and anguish, I waited for the sun to disperse the black shadows of the night so that I could leave that baneful room, which reminded me so starkly of my contemptible conduct.

At last day dawned and, since there was nothing worth a penny in the whole room, I went out and left the key with a neighbor woman, intending to withdraw once and for all from those lugubrious quarters.

CHAPTER 32

IN WHICH PERIQUILLO DESCRIBES LUISA'S FATE, A BLOODY ADVENTURE
HE HAD, AND OTHER DELIGHTFUL AND ENTERTAINING EVENTS

I did just what I had proposed, and set off to wander the streets with no destination in mind, filled with confusion, without a penny in my pocket or the means to get one, and quite hungry, since I hadn't eaten supper the night before, nor breakfast that morning. In this ghastly state I headed back toward my old hang-out, the pool hall on the Alcaicería, to see if I could find any of my old acquaintances there who might feel pity for my sorrows and perhaps aid me in some way—at least for the most pressing matter, which was my stomach.

I wasn't mistaken about the first part, because I found almost all the old crowd there at the pool hall; and as soon as they saw me, they all recognized me and questioned me about my deplorable condition; but rather than feel any sympathy for my luck, they merrily made fun of my misfortunes, saying, "Oh, Don Pedro, sir! We poor folk sure must stink like corpses! When you won your jackpot, you never stopped to think about us or the favors you owed us. If you met one of us in the street, you'd look the other way and pass by without saying hullo; if one of us talked to you, you'd pretend you didn't recognize us; if we ever got through to you, you'd send us off to talk to Roque, that barber of yours who's also going around in rags now; and finally, after you won that jackpot of yours, you showed as much disdain for us as you possibly could. Don Pedro, sir, money has the power to make some people forget their best friends, if their friends are poor. When you had money, you made sure you'd never rub shoulders with any of us, since we're poor; so now that you're broke, get along with you, off to your gentlemen friends with their capes and their cloaks, and don't set foot in here again until you can bring a peso to gamble, because we don't feel like hanging around with you, Your Honor."

In this way, each and every one of them insulted me as much as they could, and the only reply I could make was to scuttle off with my tail between my legs, as they say, reflecting that everything they had told me was true, and that I couldn't help but reap the fruits of my vanity and folly.

Since hunger was pressing me, I tried going to ask for help from the friends who had eaten well by my side and who had entertained themselves at my expense.

It wasn't hard for me to find them; but what anger and distress I felt when, after debasing myself before each of them by showing up in such an indecent state, and after relating all my troubles to them and trying to evoke their pity with all the energy that destitution brings on such occasions, all I heard were words of disdain, sarcasm, and mockery!

Some of them said: "It's all your fault that you're in this state; if you hadn't been a playboy, today you'd have food on your plate."

Others: "Friend, I barely have enough to feed my own family; you're still young and strong: go enlist in the army, because the king is the father of the poor."

Others, pretending to be shocked and amazed, said: "God help me! How did you go bust so soon?" I would tell them, and they'd reply: "With all your expenses and vanities, it couldn't have turned out any different."

Others: "Go complain to the rich, because they're the ones who should be handing out alms, not poor folks like me."

And so they all shut the door on me; the kindest among them made me feel that they felt sorry for my misfortunes, but that there was nothing they could do to help me. Thus, feeling sad, indignant, and hungry, I left all their houses without a single one of all those who had been so pleased to call themselves my friends offering me so much as a tiny mug of chocolate.

This was not the first time I had met such ingratitude; but I had never learned my lesson. I kept thinking that all the people who said they were my friends meant it in their persons, not just in their self-interest; however, at that time and thereafter, I have seen that there are many friends in this world, but little friendship.

The falsity of friends is a very old story in this world. In the holiest and truest of books, we read all these pronouncements: "For there is a friend for his own occasion, and he will not abide in the day of thy trouble. And there is a friend, a companion at the table, and he will not abide in the day of distress." In the same book it says: "Blessed is he that findeth a true friend. In the time of his trouble continue faithful to him. Keep fidelity with a friend in his poverty. I will not be ashamed to salute a friend, neither will I hide myself from his face: and if any evil happen to me by him, I will bear it." Speaking of good friends, it says: "A faithful friend is a strong defense: and he that hath found him, hath found a treasure"; and finally, it says: "Nothing can be compared to a faithful friend, and no weight of gold and silver is able to countervail the goodness of his fidelity." But who might this unselfish, this prudent, this faithful, this true friend be? "He that feareth God," the same book of Ecclesiasticus goes on to say, "shall likewise have good friendship."[1]

In those days I was far from knowing such things, and from taking advantage of the lessons that the world itself was offering me; and so, feeling nothing but the sorrows that afflicted me at the moment, seeing that the hopes I had placed in my friends had been dashed, that I had found no shelter or comfort anywhere, and that my hunger was growing minute by minute, I laid hands on my poor jacket to sell it, which I did, and went to have lunch, which left me with eight or ten reales to spare.

I spent the whole day trying to figure out where I could spend the night; but when night came, I felt the sky caving in on me, because I didn't have so much as a *jacal* to sleep in.[2]

Under these conditions, I decided to go to the house of the tailor who had made my clothes and beg him, for the sake of God, to put me up for the night.

With this decision in mind, I was walking along Mesones street when I saw Luisa in a low, one-room house, looking rather fine. She seemed prettier than ever to me; so, hoping to strike up my friendship with her again and make use of her to relieve

---

[1] Ecclesiasticus 6:8, 6:10; 26:12, 26:23 (22:29), 22:28, 22:31; 6:14, 6:15, 6:17.

[2] [*Jacal* (Nahuatl *xahcalli*): a hut or shack, used as a house by the poorest Indians in central Mexico. –Tr.]

my ills, I approached her door and said to her, in a very expressive voice, "Luisa, dear Luisa, do you remember me?"

No doubt she recalled my voice, but to be certain, she said, "No, sir, who are you?"

To which I replied, "I am Pedro Sarmiento, the same Pedro who loved you so well, and when I had some wealth, I maintained you at a level of decency and distinction to which you never would have attained on your own virtues."

"Ah, yes!" Luisa said sarcastically. "It's you, Periquillo Sarniento, sir, old Chanfaina's former servant boy, the one who slapped me around and kicked me out of his house. Now I remember, and I sure have lots to thank you for."

"Fair enough, Luisa," I replied; "but your unfaithfulness with Roque gave rise to that attack."

"What's done is done," said Luisa; "so, what do you want now?"

"What else could I want? To enjoy your caresses once more."

"Well, sir," she answered, "don't you see how foolish that is? Go away and stop trying to fool me, and don't get mixed up with unfaithful women. Go and may God be with you; I wouldn't want my husband to come home and find you here talking with me."

"What, darling, have you gotten married?"

"Yes, sir, I have indeed, to a boy who's a very upright man and loves me very much, and I love him. What, did you think I was going to miss you? No, sir; maybe you spat me out, but another fellow picked me up. Anyway, I don't want to talk with you."

Saying this, she went inside; and she would have slammed the door in my face, except that I, as impudent as I was incredulous about her married state, rushed in after her.

When I did that, poor Luisa got such a fright that she tried running outside; but she couldn't, because I had grabbed her arms, and with both of us struggling—she to leave and I to stop her—she fell down on the bed. She then raised her voice to defend herself, and almost in a scream told me, "Go away, Don Perico, or rather, Don Diablo; I'm a married woman, and I don't have any intention of offending my husband."

The door to the small house had been left ajar; I was blind and paid no attention to that, nor did I foresee that her screams, which came louder by the second, would arouse the curiosity of people walking down her street and expose me to embarrassment or worse. If only it had just gone that far! But heaven was preparing a punishment for me that better fit my crime. Instead of some Sancho or Martín, the man who walked in was Luisa's husband; she was trying desperately to escape my grip, while I was beside myself trying to make her yield once more to my impudent seductions, and so neither of us noticed that her husband, after shutting the door more firmly behind him, had been watching the scene long enough to be sure of his wife's innocence and my execrable intentions.

When he was satisfied on both counts, he fell on me like a crack of lightning from a cloudburst, and without saying anything other than these words: "Rogue, this is how you force a woman," he stuck a knife between my ribs with such fury that the only reason the handle didn't go in was that it didn't fit.

"Jesus help me!" I said as I fell to the ground, floundering in my own blood.

I had fallen on my back, and the furious husband, ready to finish the job he had started, raised his arm with the knife pointed at my heart. Then, full of fear, I said, "By Holy Mother Mary, please let me confess, even if you kill me later."

My cry, or Our Lady's intercession at my invocation of her sweet name, restrained the angry man, and throwing away the knife, he told me, "Her divine name has saved you, because I've always respected it."

By this time the small room had filled with people; the night watchmen had detained my attacker; poor Luisa had fainted with fright; and the confessor was at my side.

I more or less confessed, though I don't know how; because who knows how a man can confess, repent, or talk when he's in such a tight spot that it's all he can do to struggle with his painful wounds and his fear of death.

Once this ceremony was over (for that's all it was in my conscience, given my utter indisposition), once I had voiced forgiveness of my enemy, and once he and his wife had been taken unjustly to jail, all that I was told was that I would undoubtedly die, because I was bleeding too profusely and there was no one who could staunch the flow, or even cover the wound—not even a certain surgeon who happened to enter the room—because everyone said that the authorities had to intervene first in these urgent affairs.

The effusion of blood that I was suffering was copious, and I was growing weaker by the moment; a feeling of queasiness announced my imminent death; seeing my cadaverous face moved everyone's human nature to sorrow and a desire to help me; yet no one dared impart the assistance that their benevolence demanded, nor even to move me from where I lay, until, thanks to God, the judge ordered that I be brought on a stretcher to jail.

There they put me in the infirmary, and since it was already night, some time passed before the surgeon arrived; when he came, he had them turn me face-down, and introduced a probe into me, which hurt more than the knife blade; he stuck a candle into the wound to see if my lung had been punctured, and did who knows how many other maneuvers; and when he was finished, it occurred to him to staunch the flow of blood, which was easy to do, given how much I had already lost.

Then they gave me some atole or some such restorative, and declared that it was not a mortal wound.

I got through that night somehow or other, and the next day they brought me to the hospital, where I didn't miss the long-winded doctor or the care that the nursing staff showed me in the jail infirmary.

There, in bed, I made my declarations and gave my apologies, which, together with Luisa's statements, were enough to free her and her husband.

Twenty days later, the surgeon declared me better, and when the judges considered the depositions I had given and the time and suffering I had endured, they freed me, while warning me never to pass near Luisa's threshold; I promised to comply with their sentence with all my heart, since the scare I had been given called for at least that much.

Imagine me now, released from the hospital, out on the streets as always without a penny in my pocket; I don't know if it was the night watchmen, the jailhouse nurses, or the ones in the hospital who did me the favor of stealing the last few reales I had left from selling my jacket, but there's no doubt that it was one of them.

When I was out of the hospital, I kept looking for a job that would at least give me something to eat. By accident, I got it into my head to go to Mass in the parish church of San Miguel.[3]

I heard Mass with great devotion, and when I left, I met an old acquaintance at the door to the church and informed him of all my troubles. He told me that he was the sexton there, and needed an assistant, so that if I wanted, he could offer me a position.

"I'll take it," I said; "but first you have to give me some lunch, because I'm very hungry."

The poor man did so; I stayed there with him; so imagine me now, an apprentice sexton.

---

[3] [San Miguel Arcángel: a church seven blocks due south of the Cathedral. –Tr.]

CHAPTER 33

In which we learn how Periquillo became a sexton; his
adventure with a corpse; his entrance into the brotherhood
of beggars; and other things as true as they are interesting

If every man would present the public his life story written with as much simplicity and precision as mine, you would find a multitude of Periquillos in the world; their ups and downs, their favorable and adverse adventures are only hidden from our view because each of them endeavors to conceal his indiscretions.

The anecdotes of my life that I have told you, and those which I still have to write, are not at all unnatural, rare, or fabulous, my dear children; they are altogether normal, common, and true. Not only have they happened to me, but most of them have probably happened every day to the hidden and shamefaced Pericos. All I can do is repeat my plea to you, which is that you should not read my story as a mere pastime; rather, in between my erring ways, the ridiculous things that happened to me, my long digressions, and burlesque scenes, you should be sure to take advantage of the maxims of solid morality that I have sown, imitating virtue wherever you see it, fleeing from vice, and always learning your lessons from the wrongs for which others are punished. That would mean separating the wheat from the chaff, and by so doing, you would not only read this chapter and those that follow with pleasure, but with profit.

Fixed up with a job as a sub-sexton, with a minimal salary and the meager meals that my patron allowed me, I began to serve him in everything he asked of me.

It wasn't hard for me to please him, because one of his sons, a boy of twelve, not only trained me in all my obligations, but also showed me how to get my perks; and so I quickly learned how to hide the wax that dripped from the candles, and even whole candle-ends, to sell them; how to pilfer the fathers' wine; how to pester bridegrooms and godparents at baptisms to give me a tip; and how to do even bigger swindles and hustles, which didn't bother my conscience in the least.

In no time I was a master of the art, and then my boss stopped watching over me altogether. There were also one virtue and one defect that I brought to this job, both of which I dropped after a short time as an apprentice.

The virtue was the apparent respect that I still had for images and sacred things; the defect was the great fear I always felt for the dead; but all that came to an end. At first, when I passed by the sanctuary, I bent both knees to show my respect; and when I got up at night to trim the lamps, I trembled with fear, and my imagination turned my own shadow and the noise that the cats made into dead people rising from their tombs.[1] But later I became so irreverent that when I passed by the tabernacle, I was satisfied with making a little skip, like a dancing Indian, and in my sacrilegious daring I even went so far as to stand on top of the altar.

---

[1] [As noted above (Chapter 13, footnote 2), most people were buried under the floor of the church itself, until new laws mandated the creation of outdoor cemeteries in the early 19th century. –Tr.]

Just as I lost my respect for the venerable sacrament and the sacred images, chalices, and vestments after dealing with them, in the same way I lost my fear of the dead after I began handling them regularly to put them in their tombs.

My companion apprentice was very useful to me, because when I started the job, he was already well along in the trade, and so he helped me become daring and irreverent; of course, I repaid him by teaching him one or two ways of stealing that had escaped his notice. The first was to pocket a certain proportion of the money that was collected for Mass; the second was to strip the dead men and women that were going into the hole decently dressed.

One night, thanks to these pleasant tricks, I had an adventure that didn't cost me my life, but surely did cost me my job.

What happened was that, one afternoon when the sexton's boy and I were burying a rich woman who had died unexpectedly, as we placed her in the coffin I noticed something glittering on one of her hands, which was partly sticking out from the sleeve of her shroud. Immediately, pretending I had noticed nothing, I placed her inside and strewed the customary basketful of lime over her. While the accompanists warbled and the choir joined in the music, I had time to tell my companion, "Pal, don't tighten it too hard, because there'll be lots of loot tonight."

So he hit the nail once with the hammer, and the wood of the coffin a hundred times, and we enclosed the deceased in the tomb, likewise making sure not to pile too much dirt on top, to make the exhumation easier for us. The funeral came to its conclusion and the mourners and onlookers all went home believing that this cadaver was as thoroughly buried as any.

After I was left alone with the little sexton, I told him what I had observed on the dead woman's hand, which I said couldn't be anything but a fine diamond ring that had stayed there because of a gross oversight or some other unforeseen reason.

The boy seemed to doubt this, because he said to me, "Even if it isn't a diamond ring, the dead woman was rich, so she should at least have a rosary and good clothes; so we shouldn't lose this fortune that has come knocking on our door, especially since we've saved ourselves the work of unnailing the coffin, because the nails barely grazed the lid. Anyway, this is an opportunity we shouldn't miss."

Having decided on this course, we waited until the bells rang midnight, the hour when the principal sexton would be sunk in the deepest part of his sleep, and came down to the church, prepared with a lit candle.

We started work on the operation of shoveling out dirt until we had uncovered the coffin, which we took out and unnailed very cautiously.

When we had the lid open, we took out the body and stood it up; my companion leaned against the nearby altar and held the body against his chest with great difficulty, because there was no other way we could strip the body, given that it had become extraordinarily rigid or stiff.

At this, I went straight for the hands, which were what I was most interested in. I pulled out the right hand and saw that it did indeed have a very nice ring on it, which cost me many drops of sweat to remove, partly because of the old terror that always overtook me on such occasions, partly because of my exertions, both to help my companion hold her up and to pull off the ring, since her hand was closed pretty tight and her fingers were very swollen; but in any case, at last I had it in my hand.

We then went on to inspect the state of the rest of her clothes, and I observed that my companion had not been mistaken to think it would be good material: the blouse was very fine, as were the petticoats; the skirts were nearly new, made of fine Chinese material; a silk sash, a cambric kerchief, a rosary with a medal (I never found out what it was made of), and a good pair of silk stockings.

"All this stuff is as good as cash in our pockets," my pal said, "but how are we going to get her clothes off? Because the damn dead woman's as stiff as a stick."

"Don't you worry," I said, "just pick up her arms and hold them outstretched for her, and I'll untie the sash, which has got to be the first order of business."

My companion did this with a great deal of difficulty, because the sinews of her arms kept trying to return to the position they had held right after she died.

The dead woman was fairly old and had a respectable face; our audacity was worthy of punishment; the emptiness and darkness of that place filled us with terror; so we endeavored to pick up our slow pace as much as we could. For that reason, I put all my efforts into untying the sash, which was knotted behind her, but so tightly that I couldn't undo it. I told my companion that I would try holding her while he undid the knot, since it was on his side.

We both agreed to this plan. I grabbed her arms; my companion lifted the shroud and began trying to untie the knot; but he made no progress for the same reason that I wasn't able to. But while he was working on it, he leaned against the body, and I pressed against it because it was falling on top of me, and since I was standing below the dais, I had to bear the full weight of the body, which meant that the two of us were squeezing it like a press.

My companion worked so hard, and we squeezed the poor dead woman so tight, that we pressed out a little bit of air that must have stayed in her stomach; that is what I conjecture now that must have happened, but at that moment and in the middle of our tightest squeezes, all we knew was that the dead woman suddenly moaned and breathed such a nasty stench straight at my nose that, stunned by the breath and the frightening moan, I went all out of joint and let go of her arms, which went right back to their original position, crossing over my neck; while at the same time a damnable cat jumped up on the altar and knocked over the candle, leaving us to rely on the sad and lusterless light of the altar lamp.

It hardly needs to be said that, given all these accidents, and having the body fall on top of me, I became inexpressibly frightened and fainted away under her shrouded weight, by the very edge of her tomb.

When the worried assistant heard the dead woman moan and saw her wrap her hands around my neck and fall on me, and when he saw the ferocious cat jump next to him, he believed that the devils had come to take us in punishment for our audacity, and he lost the spirit to wait until the end of this scene, falling down senseless with me.

The fright was not so trivial that we were able to recover quickly. We remained there, stretched out unconscious next to the dead woman, until four in the morning, when the sexton woke up and, finding that we had left the room, supposed that we must be down in the sacristy getting the vestments ready for our early-rising priest to say Mass.

With this in mind, he headed down to the sacristy, and when he didn't find us there, he went to look for us in the church. But how surprised he was when he saw the tomb opened, the dead woman exhumed and thrown on the floor, along with the two of us, who showed no signs of life! All he could do was go notify the priest about what had happened; as soon as the priest saw us in the position just described, he ordered his serving lads to come down and bring us inside, proceeding at the same time to rebury the corpse.

Once all that was done, he worked to revive us with alkali salts, cupping glasses, bindings, burnt wool, and everything he conjectured might be useful for such a case. With all those efforts, we recovered from our fainting spells and each drank a mug of chocolate that the priest himself gave us; as soon as he saw that we were out of danger, the priest asked the cause behind what we had suffered, and what we had seen.

Realizing that there was no way to deny what had happened, I ingenuously confessed to it all and gave the ring to the priest, who found it hard to stop laughing after he heard the tale; but when he recalled that he was accountable for our mistakes, he handed my companion over to his father for punishment, while he told me that I would have to leave the church that very day, and that I should be very thankful that he wasn't sending us off to jail, where I would be sentenced in accordance with the laws against breaking into tombs, disinterring corpses, and stealing clothes, jewelry, and other things.

"Those laws," the priest said, "so that you'll know better than to commit such a great crime again, state that if the tombs are robbed by force of arms, the offenders will incur the death penalty; and if they are robbed clandestinely, without the use of arms, they will be condemned to hard labor on the king's business. Out of charity I would like to spare you this sentence, but I cannot keep you here in my curacy, because anyone who dares to steal a ring from a corpse today will easily dare to loot an image or an altar tomorrow. So please go, and never show your face in my parish again."

Saying this, the priest withdrew; my companion's father gave him a good tanning; and I left for the streets before anything else could happen.

I went back to my accustomed round in these adverse adventures. The pool halls, the street, the *pulque* stands, and the inns were my usual shelters, and I had no better friends and comrades than cardsharps, drunks, idlers, petty thieves, and *léperos* of every kind, for they tended to provide me a cold bite to eat, plenty to drink, and vile places to sleep.

I had spent four months working as a sexton and pulling off my little swindles, and that (more than my measly salary) gave me enough to afford one or two miserable pieces of clothing, which I completely wore out within two weeks of my expulsion.

I remember that one day when I had nothing to eat, I met a friend in front of the Cathedral, next to the Portal de las Flores, and when I asked him for half a real to get a bite of food, he said, "I don't have a penny; I'm in the same boat as you, and I was hoping you'd take me to lunch in the Alcaicería, because I've heard the old woman who runs the eatery say that she's holding all your savings there, two or three reales."

"You're right, that's true," I said, "but I had gotten so swept up with my jackpot that I forgot all about it. I'm amazed at the old woman's good conscience; if it had been anybody else, that money would have been lost."

With that, we went to eat as well as we could, and when dinner was done, my friend went his way and I went mine, to continue experiencing the same troubles as before.

I was looking like a wastrel—dirty, skinny, pale, and ill from the bad life I was living—when I made friends with another fellow as ragged as I was; and when I told him all my problems, adding that not even turning to the Church had done me any good, as if I were the most treacherous delinquent in the world, he told me that he had a move he could teach me, which might not make me rich, but which at least would give me enough to eat without working; he said it was easy and would cost me no trouble to learn, that some of his friends lived by doing it, and that if I wanted to try, I'd never regret it.

"Well, why not give it a try?" I asked. "I'm already howling with hunger, and the lice are eating me alive."

"Fine," said my tattered friend, "let's go home, because my pupils start showing up after nine, and after you eat supper, you'll hear the lessons I give them and you'll see how far my students have advanced."

That's what I did. We reached his tiny house around eight at night; it was a room in the house of some women who sell *atole* out around the neighborhood of Necatitlán:[2] indecent, dirty, and foul. All they had there was one of those little portable stoves made of clay, four or six reed sleeping mats rolled up and stacked against the wall, a wooden bench, an image of some saint or other on a rough-hewn wooden shelf on one of the walls, two or three earthenware pisspots, a cobbler's bench, lots of crutches in one corner, a few woven baskets and a number of clay pots in another, a shelf with sticking plasters, medicinal oils, and ointments, and other such junk.

As soon as I saw the house and its ghastly furnishings, I began to doubt how sure a thing the ragged man's proposal would be; guessing at my distrust from the face I was pulling, he said, "Perico, sir, I know what I'm selling you. This miserable dwelling, the mats and the furniture you see here, are not as contemptible and useless as they seem to you. All this helps our project, because. . . . "

Just then the tramps began arriving, one by one and two by two, until there were eight or nine of them, all shabby, covered with plasters, and dirty as devils; but what most amazed me was that as they came in, some of them propped their crutches in a corner and walked away perfectly well on their two feet; others pulled off the sticking plasters they were wearing, and their skin appeared clean and healthy; others took off their long, thick beards and the gray hairs that had made them look so old to me, and they appeared fairly young; others stood up straight and got rid of their humped backs when they entered; and all of them left their illnesses and diseases at the door to the room; and all the men who came in looked quite fit to pick up a rifle, and the one woman who entered looked fit to grind a bushel of corn on a grinding stone. Then, rightly filled with amazement, I asked my shabby friend, "What's all this? Are you some kind of saint, that your mere presence can work all the miracles I'm seeing? Because everyone comes here crippled, blind, maimed, lame, leprous,

---

2   [Necatitlán: two blocks farther south of San Miguel parish, this was a poor, mainly Indian neighborhood near the city slaughterhouses. –Tr.]

decrepit, and wounded, but they barely set foot inside this disgusting room, and they're restored to health and even made young again, a marvel that I've never heard preached about the most powerful of saints."

The shabby man laughed so heartily that each corner of his mouth seemed to touch his ears. His companions played backup with more laughter, and when they stopped to rest, the man said, "Friend, I'm no saint, and neither are my companions, and we haven't met any saints, either; and I don't think we'll even have to swear to that for you to believe it. The miracles that have astonished you aren't performed by us, but by the faithful Christians, whose charity we rely on to make us sick every morning and get better every night. If pious people weren't so charitable, we wouldn't find it so easy to get sick or to heal."

"Well, now I'm more in the dark than before, and I'm even more anxious to learn how you work so many wonders and how they can be produced by virtue of Christian piety; and I hope," I added, "that you will do me the favor of settling my doubts."

"Well, friend," the tattered man replied, "I can tell you're trustworthy and know how to keep a secret. None of us is blind or crippled or hunchbacked, the way we look out in the street. We're a bunch of poor beggars who spin stories, repeat thousands of prayers, cry about our misfortunes, and pester and bother everybody to get a crust of bread in the end. We eat, we drink (and it isn't water), we gamble, and some of us keep our *pichicuaracas*,[3] like Anita." (This Anita was the pudgy, raggedy, but not too ugly woman who had just entered with a baby in her arms; the mistress of the head beggar, who was the one that was talking to me). "The way we do it," the shabby man continued, "is to pretend we're blind, disabled, lame, leprous, and struck by every sort of disaster; to weep, beg, plead, tell tales, spout blasphemies and nonsense in public, and to badger whomever we meet by every means possible, in order to get our cut, which is what we always do. So there you have it: that's all the miracle behind our business, and that's the great project I was offering you if you don't want to die of hunger. The main thing is not to be foolish, because a fool is no good at doing anything, right or wrong. If you can figure out how to follow my advice, you'll eat, drink, and do everything you want, depending on your skill, since what you get paid depends on how well you work; but if you're foolish, embarrassed, or cowardly, you won't get anything. All the people you see here owe everything they've gotten to me; but they all know how to work hard. Now it's up to you."

After this, each of them came up to tell him, as if in conversation, how much they had made during the day, and they each showed their little pots and baskets full of hard crusts and the leftovers of other people's meals, along with the few reales they had gathered.

The last one to come up was Anita, who only presented five reales, saying, "This darn boy's so thick-skinned now that I've barely eaten today, and all I got was this little bit of money; but tomorrow he'll pay."

---

[3] *Pichicuaraca*: this word is used to designate the woman or girlfriend that a man lives with in illicit friendship. –E.

I was amazed to hear this accounting, and tried to find out exactly how her tender baby was supposed to contribute to the beggars' trade, and to my great sorrow I discovered that this unworthy mother, this pitiless woman, would pinch the poor innocent child when she was begging for alms, in order to move the faithful and arouse their charity with his loud cries.

I was more than a bit scandalized by her inhumanity; but since I saw how easy and well paid the trade was, I tried to pretend not to notice, and decided to enter as an apprentice right on the spot.

It was very funny to hear those scoundrels talk about the ploys they used to get pennies out of the most tightly closed money pouches. Some of them said that they pretended to be blind, others that they were injured, others that they were simple-minded, others that they had leprosy, and all of them that they were dying of hunger.

My friend, the head or maestro of the gang, said to me: "See? I'm the one who told each of these poor folks how they should make their living, and you can bet that not one of them has regretted following my advice; and I'm happy with whatever small amount they want to give me so I can live my own life, since I'm retired now and need to rest, because I worked so long in this career. If you want to follow it, tell me what your vocation is so that I can fit you out with what you need. If you want to be a cripple, we'll give you crutches; if you want to be lame or disabled, we'll give you a leather sack to drag yourself along; if it's wounded you want to be, we've got plasters and rags steeped in medicinal oil; if it's a decrepit old man, we've got your beard and gray hairs; if it's a simpleton, you know what you've got to do; and, to sum it all up, we've got the right tools for everything, including all the baskets, pots, rags, and canes or staffs you'll need. If you're going to try living with us, you can't be slow to beg, or quick to give up the first time they insult you; you have to keep in mind that men don't always give alms for the sake of God: they often give alms for their own sakes, and sometimes for the devil's. They do it for themselves when they want to get rid of a man who keeps pestering them for two blocks without being scared off by their excuses or their insults; and for the devil when they give alms to make a good impression and to come off looking liberal, especially in front of the ladies. I have grown old in this honest business, and I know by experience that there are men who never give a penny to a poor man except when they are in front of some girls they are trying to impress, whether it's so they'll appear generous, or so they can get rid of some inopportune witnesses who, because of their tenaciousness, might spoil their flirting or interrupt their seductive conversations. I'm telling this so that you won't give up the first time somebody says *Excuse me, sorry;* instead, you have to keep following and pestering and pestering anyone you can tell has money, and not let him go until he coughs up the dough. Learn how to badger: that's how you get the crust. Assail men who are out with women before you go after the ones who are alone. Don't beg from soldiers, friars, college boys, or tramps, because all those people are dedicated to holy poverty, even if they haven't taken any vows; and finally, don't lose sight of your companions' examples, because they'll show you what you ought to do and the formulas you ought to observe to beg from each person according to his class."

I thanked my new maestro for his lessons and told him that my vocation was to be blind, since I figured it wouldn't cost me too much trouble to feign the drop serene[4] and walk around with a stick as if I were groping my way along, and I had observed that no beggar is better at stirring people's pity than a blind man.

"That's good," my disheveled director replied, "but do you know any tales you can tell?"

"How could I," I responded, "if I've never tried my hand at this business before!"

"Well, friend," he went on, "you must know some, because a blind man with no tale is like a nobleman with no income, a poor man with no wit, or a body with no soul; so the first thing you have to do is learn a few, such as *The Speech of the Just Judge, Farewell to Body and Soul,* and a few of the myriad stories and exempla of blind men both real and fake, which your companions can tell to you so that you can pick the ones you want them to teach you. You'll also have to learn how to beg according to what season of the year and what day of the week it is: so on Mondays you'll beg by Divine Providence, by St. Cajetan, and by the blessed souls in Purgatory; on Tuesdays, by St. Anthony of Padua; on Wednesdays, by the Precious Blood; on Thursdays, by the Most Holy Sacrament; on Fridays, by the sorrows of the Blessed Virgin; on Saturdays, by the purity of the Virgin; and on Sundays, by all the saints in Heaven. Never forget to pray in the name of the saints that people have most devotion for, especially on their feast days, so you'll have to look in the almanac to find out when it'll be the saint's days of St. John Nepomucene, St. Joseph, St. Aloysius Gonzaga, St. Gertrude, and so forth; and you should also remember to beg by the season of the year. During Easter Week, you'll beg by the Passion of Our Lord; on the Day of the Dead, by the Blessed Souls; during the month of December, by Our Lady of Guadalupe, and so on: in every season you'll beg by the saints and festivities of the day; and if you can't remember whose day it is, just say you're begging by the saint whose day is today, like all your companions. These points may seem frivolous, but they're indispensable tricks of the trade, because when you beg by the right saint on the right day, you stir people's piety and devotion better, and then the charitable Christians will loosen their grip on their pennies."

At this, all those rascals began telling me 60 tales of chivalry and relating 200 exempla and apocryphal miracles, each one of which was larded with 200,000 bits of twaddle and bunkum, some of which could have passed for heresy, or at least for blasphemy.

Hearing so much drivel all at once left me bewildered, and I said to myself: How is it possible that nobody is in charge of restraining these abuses and gagging these madmen? How has it gone unnoticed that the audience surrounding them and paying attention to them is made up of the stupidest and most idiotic of all the commoners, the people who are most easily disposed to soaking up the nonsense that these fellows spread over their spirits, and to embracing every error that comes to their ears? How is it that no one considers that the ghosts and apocryphal miracles these fellows preach about can induce some of the foolish common folk to trust blindly in God's mercy,

---

[4] [Drop serene (*gota serena*): amaurosis, a progressive loss of sight without visible damage to the eye. –Tr.]

with the idea of getting them to give alms; others to place more faith in the power of the saints that they talk about than the Divine Power itself;[5] and to fill almost everybody's heads with lies, ghosts, miracles, and revelations? There is no doubt that all this merits attention and reform; it would be very useful if all the blind men who use their tales to beg would present their stories to the parish priests in the towns, and in the capital and other cities to a group of clerics dedicated to examining them, because no examiner would ever let them preach anything but the explication of Christian doctrine, anecdotes from Church and secular history, geographical descriptions of other kingdoms and cities, and similar things; but any such thing would have to be well done, put into fine verse, and better rehearsed; and they should absolutely not be allowed to broadcast all the fables that they try to sell us now as exempla.

My proposal seems trivial, yet if it were put into practice, time would tell how much the crude public would benefit from it, and how many errors it would stop from spreading.

I was entertaining myself with these reflections when they called me to supper, which did not bother me, since I was hungry.

We sat in a circle on a woven mat, without any tablecloth other than the reeds it was made from; Anita served us a big pot of chili with cheese, eggs, and two kinds of sausage; but it was all so well cooked and well seasoned that the aroma alone would have whetted the most recalcitrant appetite.

After we had passed the pot around, she brought out a large gourd or *guaje* full of rum liquor, a glass, and another pot of beans fried with lots of onions, cheese, chilies, and olives, together with all the bread that was called for.

We each filled our plates, and the gourd began making the rounds, and when we were all feeling merry, the chief of the beggars asked me, "What do you think about this life, pal? Could a count have it any better?"

"No way," I answered, "and it suits me just fine, and I give a thousand thanks to God that I've finally found what I've been looking so hard for ever since I was old enough to think for myself, which is a trade or a way of making a living without having to work; because, it's true, I've always eaten (if not, I would have died by now), but how much work has it cost me? How much shame have I been put through? How many imprudent patrons have I had to put up with? How many dangers have I been exposed to? How many times have I had to live by flattery, and how many frights and even beatings have I suffered? But now, gentlemen, I am so delighted! Who wouldn't envy my fortune now when they see me admitted into the right honorable guild of master beggars, in whose respectable corps one can eat and drink so well without working? You get dressed, you gamble, you go strolling without danger; you enjoy every possible comfort without any cost other than giving up a certain amount of shame, which will no doubt bother me for the first few days, but once I get over that difficulty, which I don't think I will find very hard, darned if I won't be as good as the rest of you, and hallelujah. Captain; gentlemen; my illustrious companions: I give you 1,000, 10,000 thanks, and I implore you take me under your

---

[5] Anyone who has had the patience to listen to very many beggars' tales will know that this is no misrepresentation.

mighty protection, and in just compensation I offer never to part from your eminent company so long as God gives me life, which I will place fully in the service of your munificent persons."

The whole troupe burst into laughter when I concluded my ridiculous sermon, and they offered me their friendship, advice, and training. The gourd was passed around one more time, and before long we could see the bottom of it, and of the pots as well.

We went to sleep on the reed mats, which certainly make for very uncomfortable beds, and worse when you consider how little cover we had. We slept very well, however, thanks to the liquor, which narcotized us or knocked us out as soon as we lay down.

The next day, Anita was the first one up; she left her unhappy baby asleep and went to bring us atole and *pambazos*[6] for our breakfast.

After the crude breakfast was done, we all went outside with our respective insignias. I wrapped my head in some rags, slung a basket and a small clay pot over my shoulder, picked up my stick and a well-trained guide dog, and went off in my own direction.

At first it cost me a little bit of trouble to beg, but bit by bit I got better at the trade, and soon became such a good journeyman that within two weeks, I was eating and drinking in grand style, and bringing home six or seven reales, and sometimes more, every night.

For some time I lived at the expense of the piety of the faithful, my beloved brothers and companions. I did very well at my business by day, but even better by night, because then I lost all sense of shame and pestered everyone with my sighs and my pitiful pleas, so that few escaped without paying me a few pennies in tribute.

One of those nights, when I was standing next to the holy image of Our Lady of Refuge[7] begging as piteously as I could, expounding on my great need and saying that I hadn't eaten all day (even though I had plenty of food and a few swigs of rum in my belly), a decent man passed by; I assaulted him with my usual moans and groans, and he stopped to listen to me, and then said, "Brother, I feel inclined to help you, but I don't have any money in my pocket. If you'd like, please come with me, and you won't be sorry."

"By the love of God," I said, "I will go with Your Honor to receive your blessed charity; but you must have a tiny bit of patience with me, because I cannot see, and I must hold onto your person."

"That's no trouble at all," said the gentleman; "I want to help you, brother, so it will not hurt me in the least to serve as your guide. Please come this way."

He took me by the hand and brought me to his house. As soon as we arrived, he let me into his study and sat me down facing him at his desk, where there was plenty of light.

---

[6] [*Pambazo*: a large loaf of the cheapest grade of bread, made from an inferior wheat and used by the poorest people in Mexico at the time. –Tr.]

[7] [Spell (p. 189) notes that this image, by the famous Mexican painter Miguel Cabrera, was on permanent outdoor display one block west of the southwest corner of the Zócalo. –Tr.]

How embarrassed I felt when I realized that this person was precisely the same man who had given me so much advice in the inn, and who had held my money in safekeeping! But since I was being a blind man, I pretended for the time being, and the man spoke to me as follows:

"Friend, I am happy that you cannot recognize me by sight, though I am very sorry that your terrible blindness has brought you to the unhappy state of begging for alms, which you were once in a position of giving. Don't imagine that I am trying to reproach you. I want to help you, but also to give you advice. If you are not very blind, you will recognize me just as easily as I recognized you, and you will remember that I am the same man who guarded your money at the inn. Yes, I'm sure you must remember, because not that much time has passed; and if I recognized you when it was nearly dark, in your disheveled clothes, and merely by your voice, how could you help but recognize me, now that you've had a good look at my face, thanks to this lovely flame that illuminates us both, while I am wearing the same clothes as before, and you are listening to the echo of my voice and remembering the signs that I have pointed out for you? I hope you don't think me so ingenuous as to believe that you are really blind in your bodily eyes, much as your rags indicate your spiritual blindness to me. I realize that your situation must have been unhappy enough that you felt obliged to adopt this indecent career so that you wouldn't have to resort to robbery; but, friend, you should know that you're nothing but an unpunished idler, a leech on the State, and a tolerated thief; indeed, a contemptible thief who deserves the severest punishment, since you are robbing the legitimate poor. Yes, sir, you and your odious companions are doing nothing but cheating those who really need aid. It's your fault that I, and others like me, never give a penny to any beggars, because we are convinced that the majority of those who beg for alms could work and be useful, and that if they don't, it's because they have found a safe haven in the mistaken piety of the faithful, who think that charity means giving indiscriminately. No, sir; charity should be well ordered; it is good to give alms, but only if you know beforehand who you are giving it to, how, when, for what, where, and how it will be used by those who receive it. Not all those who beg need to beg; not all those who say they are in the deepest poverty really are; and not all those who are given alms deserve to receive it. A thousand times we do harm when we try to do good, and the worst of it is that the harm we do is far-reaching for the State, for we are keeping some people idle and dissolute with the same money that we could be using to support the true poor, the ones who legitimately deserve public assistance. You don't have to take my word for it, either. Listen to this bit of what many wise men, who have thought deeply about good policy, have to say on this subject. One author[8] says:

> Habitual begging effaces shame and makes man an enemy of industriousness. . . . The truly poor are the disabled who cannot work. To allow an able man to beg for alms is to deprive that man and the national body of the

---

[8] Licenciado Don Francisco Peñaranda, in his *Resolución universal sobre el sistema económico y político más conveniente a España*. [Madrid, 1789; see Chapter 15, footnote 8 above. –Tr.]

products of his labor. When alms are wrongly directed into the hands of a voluntary beggar, charity—queen of virtues—degenerates into a protector of vices; the fact that many find a sure meal in charity is one of the greatest obstacles to hard work. The lack of employment among the people is the cause of vices, havoc, and ruin against the inclination to work among most, who become corrupt *(which is what I think has happened to you)*. Without study or exercise, men and their minds become dull. The most notably wealthy political power will become degraded to the rank of barbarity if it does not cultivate its talents.

"Don Melchor Rafael de Macanaz, speaking about beggars in his 'Petition to King Philip V on the Notorious Evils of Depopulation . . . and Other Harms Worthy of Notice, with General Advice for Their Universal Remedy,' says, 'Panhandling is not to be permitted, because at times those who seem crippled by day are able to rob by night. Also, they are not permitted in any cultured court.' Just above this statement, he says, 'If they go around asking for alms, they are not working, they happily give themselves over to profligacy, and . . . become depraved.'[9]

"But though these observations are very judicious, they cannot be more so than those that were made much earlier in the sacred scriptures. God cursed the first man by telling him he would eat by the sweat of his brow. Later, He said that the day laborer deserves to be paid for his labor; and elsewhere, that the ox that plows—this is the law that the Israelites observed—that the ox that plows or threshes wheat shall not be muzzled, which is a way of telling us that those who work should eat by their labor, just as he who serves at the altar should eat from the altar.[10]

"Finally, the apostle St. Paul, deserving as he was of the charitable contributions of the faithful, did not wish to bother them, but instead worked with his own hands to earn his living,[11] and so he wrote to the Thessalonians in his Second Epistle, Chapter 3: 'For yourselves know,' he tells them, 'neither did we eat any man's bread for nothing: but in labor and in toil we worked night and day, lest we should be chargeable to any of you;' and so 'if any man will not work, neither let him eat: *quoniam si quis non vult operari nec manducet.*'[12]

"In view of this, friend, what just excuse could any lazy man or woman have for trying to live at the expense of the mistaken piety of the faithful, while cheating those who legitimately deserve their assistance?

"If you were to tell me that many people cannot find jobs even if they want to work, I would reply: there might be a few such cases, due to lack of agriculture, commerce, shipping, industry, and so on; but not as many as are supposed. Otherwise, let's look at the crowds of vagrants who wander around meeting each other in the streets, or lying drunk on them; leaning on street corners; hanging out in pool halls, *pulque* stands, and taverns; both men and women; let's ask them, and we'll discover

---

[9] Volume VII of his *Semanario erudito* [Madrid, 1787–1791], pp. 199 and 203.

[10] [See Genesis 3:19; Leviticus 19:13; Deuteronomy 25:4; and the interpretation of the latter in 1 Corinthians 9:8–10. –Tr.]

[11] We must note that St. Paul was a noble Roman gentleman, yet he was not ashamed to work for his living.

[12] [2 Thessalonians 3:7–10. –Tr.]

that many of them know a trade, and others of those men and women are healthy and robust enough to serve. Let's leave them there, and go inquire around the city whether there are artisans who need journeymen, or houses where there is a need for serving men and women; and when we find that there are many with such needs, we will conclude that the abundance of vagrants and villains (a group that includes false beggars) is not so much due to the lack of work, as they suppose, but to the laziness that they have found so congenial.

"It would not be difficult for me to point out the means that are called for to wipe out begging, at least in this kingdom; but others will have done that elsewhere.[13] Besides, it is not my place to dictate general economic plans, but to give you good particular advice, as a friend.

"In virtue of this, if you find yourself ready to become an upright man, to work and to part from the contemptible career you have embraced, I have the desire to help you with a small trifle that you might find more useful, with the experience you now have, than the 3,000 pesos you won in the lottery."

Shamefaced and bewildered by the fistful of truths that this good man had just tossed in my face, I told him that, of course, I was ready to do everything he suggested, and I swore to this; but that I had no knowledge of how to find work.

The gentleman, who knew that my handwriting was fairly good, offered to speak with a friend of his who had just been appointed Subdelegado of Tixtla[14] so that he would take me with him as a clerk. I thanked him for the favor; then he took fifty pesos out of a chest and put them in my hands, saying, "Here you have twenty-five pesos that I am giving you, and another twenty-five that I'm returning: they are the same ones that I marked while you were standing here, for I was always certain that what has happened would come to pass: that in the end you would find yourself assailed by poverty and unable to find a job, and would come to beg me for aid sooner or later; but since this occasion was hastened by our chance encounter, please take these pesos and tell me how you ended up a beggar, for I am sure that someone led you into this."

I told him everything that had happened to me, point-by-point, without forgetting to mention the perverse Anita's infernal trick of pinching her innocent little boy to make him cry, and moving the gullible by telling them that he was crying from hunger.

The gentleman was kicking with rage when he heard about this inhumanity, and he couldn't help but ask me to go with him and point out the house, promising to conceal not only my face, but my name.

I couldn't refuse his pleas, for no matter how much pity I felt for my companions, those fifty pesos were an inescapable stimulation to agreeing with my generous benefactor; and so, putting on another set of rags and an old hooded cloak that he gave me, I left his house with him and we went straight to the house of a magistrate; when the judge was informed of all the details of the matter, he supplied my protector with

---

[13] Something was said on this subject in *El Pensador Mexicano* [*The Mexican Thinker*, Lizardi's first periodical, 1812–1814], volume 2, number 9.

[14] [Tixtla: a town 120 miles south of Mexico City; see Chapter 18, footnote 9. –Tr.]

a notary and twelve bailiffs, and without wasting any time, we all went straight to the sad cottage of the false beggars.

I stayed back, half-hidden among the constables, who caught the whole gang there red-handed. They tied them up and brought them to jail, along with the plasters, medicinal oils, crutches, and baskets, since the notary said it should all be taken in along with the prisoners, for it formed the material evidence for the crime.

They remained in jail, and I returned to my patron's house, where I freeloaded as a guest while the new subdelegado (who soon took me on as one of his clerks) prepared to make the journey.

The case of the beggars was concluded soon and summarily. Anita was sent to finish raising her son in the Women's Shelter at San Lucas, and the others to earn their keep in the fortress of San Juan de Ulúa.[15]

As for me, with my fifty pesos I bought the things I needed, and after I had won the affection of the new subdelegado while he was still in Mexico, the day arrived for our departure to Tixtla.

Then I bid farewell to my benefactor, giving him well-deserved thanks, and I left with my new master for my destination, where I made the progress that you will read about in the next chapter.

---

[15] [San Lucas, San Juan de Ulúa: see Chapter 22, footnote 3, and Chapter 29, footnote 16. –Tr.]

CHAPTER 34

IN WHICH PERIQUILLO RELATES HOW HE GOT ALONG WITH THE SUBDELEGADO; THE LATTER'S CHARACTER AND WICKED BEHAVIOR, AND THAT OF THE PARISH PRIEST; THE SETTLEMENT THAT THE SUBDELEGADO WAS FORCED TO ACCEPT; HOW PERICO DISCHARGED HIS DUTIES AS INTERIM MAGISTRATE; AND FINALLY, THE HONORABLE WAY IN WHICH THEY KICKED HIM OUT OF TOWN

If the schoolboys who nicknamed me the Mangy Parrot had called me the Jumpy Parrot instead, I can say now that they would certainly have foretold my adventures, because I found it so easy to jump from one job to another, and from an adverse fate to a more favorable one.

So look at me now, going from sexton to beggar, and from beggar to clerk for the subdelegado of Tixtla, with whom I hit it off so well from the day we met that he soon began to show a great deal of affection for me; and to crown my happiness, he had a falling-out not long thereafter with his managing secretary, who left his house and his town.

My master was one of those self-serving and penny-grubbing subdelegados; as he put it to me, he intended not only to recover the money he had laid out to get the position,[1] but to make a tidy profit from his subdelegation during the five-year term.

Given his proper and lawful intentions, he did not overlook any method of stuffing his pockets, no matter how wicked, illegal, and forbidden. He was a merchant, and he made his forced distributions of goods,[2] which meant that he would give out his goods on credit at a high price to the farmers, and would then make them pay him back with grain at a lower price than it fetched at harvest time; he would collect his debts punctually and strictly, but as long as his debtors paid him, he turned a blind eye to the justice that their other creditors demanded, so if those poor people wanted to collect, their only recourse was to cut my master in on a share of the debt.

Despite the abolition of the custom that subdelegados had of collecting a silver mark as a fine from those accused of the crime of debauchery, my master ignored that fact and kept a group of spies, through whose reports he was constantly informed of the lives and miracles of all the townspeople; not only did he get his silver mark from the debauchees, he squeezed them for exorbitant fines, in proportion to their wealth; and after they paid them, he let them go with a warning not to backslide, because in that case they would pay double. They'd leave the courthouse and go straight home. He'd let them rest for a few days, and then he'd suddenly fall on them again and squeeze them for more money. There was one poor farmer who lost

---

[1] [High colonial offices, such as that of subdelegado, were sometimes sold by the Crown as a means of raising money for the Royal Treasury. Since such officials represent the highest executive and judicial power in provincial towns, they had a virtually free hand in inventing ways to repay themselves for the cost of the office. –Tr.]

[2] [Forced distributions: known to colonial historians by such terms as *repartimientos de mercancías* and *reparto de efectos*, this form of monopolizing trade was one of the more common means that colonial officials had of milking their offices for money, even after it was outlawed in the late 1700s. –Tr.]

everything he had made in a year of good harvests through fines like these. Another lost his little farm by the same means; one shopkeeper went broke; and the truly poor lost their shirts.

My master had other clever tricks like these; but as skilled as he was at extorting his subjects, he was a real fool at running a courtroom, much less at defending himself from his enemies, of whom he had many, thanks to his fine behavior!

He found himself plunged into these troubles as soon as he lost his managing secretary (the one who had done everything for him), because he was nothing but a sponge living off of society, and a paper-pusher who signed whatever legal proceedings and official correspondence were put in front of him. The poor man couldn't figure out what to do: he didn't know how to draw up a brief, formalize a testament, or even reply to a letter.

Seeing that he hadn't finished a lick of his work and couldn't figure out how to move backward or forward, I offered to write up a case and reply to an official request; he liked my style and my skills so much that he hired me on the spot as his managing secretary and made me his personal confidant, and so I came to know every last ploy and intrigue of his, and helped him carry them all off with my crooked dodges.

We got along with the greatest familiarity, and since I knew all his rotten tricks, he had to overlook mine; the upshot of it was that, if he was a devil by himself, he and I together were two devils, and the sorry town had no way to fight us, because he did his own deviltry on his account, and I did all I could on mine.

Faced with this fine pair of scoundrels, one cloaked by the veil of regular authority and the other by the most brazen pretense, the unhappy Indians raged, the half-castes groaned, the whites complained, the wealthier townspeople damned their luck, and the whole town tolerated us perforce in public while heaping curses upon us in secret.

You would have to close your eyes and cover your ears if I were to describe here the atrocities we committed between the two of us in less than a year, so terrible and scandalous were they; I will recount the lesser ones, however, and tell them in passing, so that the readers will not be left utterly in doubt, and also so that they can calculate, based on these smaller crimes, what the more atrocious ones we committed must have been.

There are always a few poor beggars in every town who'll bootlick the subdelegados with all their might, endeavoring to curry their favor by stooping to the vilest crimes.

The subdelegado used to give money (by my hand) to one of these fellows, so that he could put up a game of monte—and tell us where it would be happening. This rascal would take the money, seduce as many gamblers as he could get to come gamble, and send word to us about where it was happening. With this information we'd get a patrol together, fall upon them, jail them, and rob them blind; and we'd repeat this contemptible procedure (and the scoundrel would repeat his vile ploy) as often as we liked.

Contravening every royal decree that favors the Indians, we'd make use of those wretches whenever we wished, forcing them to work for us on everything we wanted, and profiting from their labor.

We'd use any pretext to publish edicts with monetary fines that we'd ruthlessly demand from offenders. But what edicts they were, and how odd their topics! For example: that donkeys, pigs, and chickens not be allowed to wander out of the farmyards; that cats had to be on leashes; that no one could go to Mass barefoot; and so on.

I have said that we perpetrated and committed these foul deeds in common, because that was the truth of it; we'd do whatever we liked, aiding each other mutually. I recommended my deviltries, and the subdelegado authorized them, and by these means the people of the town suffered terribly, except for the three or four most powerful citizens of that place.

These solid citizens paid us hefty taxes, and the subdelegado let them get away with anything. They were usurers, monopolists, thieves, and bloodsuckers who lived off the poor people of the town; some were merchants, others were rich farmers. On top of that, they were incredibly arrogant. If any poor Indian asked one of them for his daily wage, or haggled with one of them, or tried to work for a master who was less cruel, they would beat and mistreat him more freely than if he were their slave.

These tolerated kinglets held sway over the subdelegado, over his managing secretary, over the court, and over the jail; and so they'd jail anybody in the blink of an eye.

Being so avaricious and so ill-loved by the people didn't keep these fellows from being scandalous as well. Two of them kept their girlfriends at home so shamelessly that they would even bring them along when they went to visit the subdelegado, who deemed these visits a great honor and offered to serve as the godfather to the child that one of their women was about to bring into the world, which he indeed went on to do.

These four rogues were the only people we respected; as for the rest, we squeezed them and mortified them every chance we got. True, a lawbreaker who had money, or a pretty sister, daughter, or wife, could be sure of going unpunished no matter what crime he had committed; because, since I was the subdelegado's scribe, his notary, his clerk, his managing secretary, and his pimp, I drew up the cases however I wished, and the prisoners suffered the fate that I appointed to them.

The mangled cases went to the assessor[3] in whatever slipshod way I formed them; he passed judgment on them according to what he read, since it had been authorized by the judge, and his sentences came out tied in devilish knots—not due to any ignorance on his part, nor because of any injustice of the judges, but because of the exorbitant malice of the subdelegado and his managing secretary.

The worst of it was that if the prisoners had cash or a skirt to protect them, they'd go free even if the aggrieved party begged for justice, without having to pay any more than what they had forked over, despite all their enemies; but if a prisoner was poor, or the women in his family were very honorable, that was his tough luck, because we'd punish him to the limit of the law; so if he was hardly a lawbreaker,

---

[3] [Assessor (*asesor*): a colonial official who read the judicial cases drawn up by a provincial magistrate, such as the subdelegado, and passed judgment or recommended a sentence (*dictaminar*). In important cases, the assessor's recommended sentence (*dictamen*) was then sent to the next level of bureaucracy, such as the Audiencia or the viceroy in Mexico City, for approval. –Tr.]

he'd have to put up with eight or ten months of prison, and even if he sent us pile after pile of petitions, we'd pay as much attention to them as to the lyrics for a lively dance tune.

Meanwhile, the parish priest took turns with us at mortifying the poor townspeople. I wish I could be silent about this cleric's bad qualities; but it is indispensable to say something about them, because they were connected to my leaving that town.

The priest was fairly well educated; a doctor in canon law, he avoided all scandalous behavior and was polite to a fault; but these fine qualities were tarnished by his sordid self-interest and his pronounced greed. As you can imagine, he had no sense of charity; and as everyone knows, where that solid foundation is lacking, the beautiful edifice of virtue can never be built.

And so it was with our priest. He was very energetic in the pulpit, conscientious in his ministry, sweet in his conversation, affable in his behavior, generous in his home, modest in the street, and he would have made an excellent man of the cloth if the world had never known coinage; but money was the touchstone that revealed the bogus gold of his moral and political virtues. He was very clever at making himself beloved and at hiding his condition, so long as no pennies were involved; but as soon as he got the idea that his purse was being cheated of the most miserly sum, it was good-bye friendship, good upbringing, sweet words, and amiability; all that came to an end, and then he showed a completely different personality than usual, because he would become utterly cruel, a man lacking the slightest urbanity or charity toward his parishioners. His heart hardened to anything other than getting his money; the misery of the poor left him unmoved, and the tears of the unfortunate widow or the sad orphan had no power to soften his heart.

But so that you can see that there's a little of everything in this world, I'm going to tell you one of many anecdotes that I saw with my own eyes.

On the occasion of a fiesta in Tixtla, our priest invited the priest of Chilapa, the reverend Don Benigno Franco, a man with a lovely character—virtuous without a trace of hypocrisy—who kept up with all society; the good priest came to the fiesta, and one afternoon, while they were getting ready to pass the time with a hand of ombre in our parish priest's house as they waited for the day's festivities to start, a poor woman entered, crying bitter tears, with a baby at her breast and leading another child of about three by the hand. Her tears demonstrated her innermost affliction, and her rags revealed her legitimate poverty.

"What do you want, child?" the priest of Tixtla asked her.

The poor woman, holding back her tears, replied, "Father, sir: the night before last, my husband died; he left me nothing but these children; I don't have anything to sell, or any cloth to shroud him with, or even any candles to put around his body; it was all I could do, begging for alms, to collect these twelve reales that I'm bringing for Your Honor; and as of now, I haven't had a bite to eat, and neither has my girl here; I'm begging Your Honor, by your mother's memory and by God, to do me the charity of burying him; I'll spin wool on my spinning wheel and give you two reales a week against what I owe you."

"My child," said the priest, "what was your husband's quality?"

"He was Spanish, sir."

"Spanish? Well, then, you're six pesos short for what his burial is going to cost you; that's what it says on the fee schedule—here, read it. . . . "[4]

Saying this, he put the fee schedule in her hands, and the unhappy widow, watering it with tears of grief, told him, "Ay, Father! What do I need this piece of paper for, if I don't know how to read? What I'm begging Your Honor to do is to bury my husband, for the sake of God."

"Well, my child," the priest replied sarcastically, "I understand what you're saying; but I can't do that kind of favor; I have to make a living and pay my assistant priest. Go on, try Don Blas or Don Agustín, or any of those gentlemen who have money, and beg them to advance you what you need against your work, and then I'll have the body buried."

"But Father," the poor woman said, "I've already been to see all those gentlemen, and none of them wants to help."

"Well, hire yourself out; become a servant."

"Who would hire me, sir, with these young children?"

"Well, get along with you; go see what you can do, and don't bother me about it," the priest said, growing angry. "They didn't give me this parish for me to go around handing out my emoluments on credit; the shopkeeper and the butcher don't give me anything on credit, and neither does anybody else."

"Sir," the unhappy woman insisted, "the body is beginning to rot, and the neighborhood can't bear it for long."

"Well, eat him, then, because if you don't bring me exactly the seven and a half pesos you owe me, don't think for a second that I'm going to bury him, no matter how you pester me with your tears. Who couldn't see through women like you— shameless cheats! You have plenty of money for your parties and your luncheons when your husbands are alive, for buying new shoes, new skirts, and other things; but you never have it when it's time to pay the poor priest. Get out and good riddance, and don't bother me any more."

The unfortunate woman went away bewildered, tormented, and filled with shame by her priest's harsh treatment of her; his hard-heartedness and lack of charity scandalized all of us who were present there; but shortly after the widow left, she hastily returned and, laying the seven and a half pesos on the table, said to the priest, "Here is the money, sir; please do me the favor of sending the assistant Father to bury my husband."

"What do you think about all this, friend?" our priest asked the priest from Chilapa, bringing him into the conversation. "Aren't my parishioners a bunch of rogues? See how this rascally woman had the money on her all the time, and just pretended to be suffering to see if I'd bury her husband for free? Wouldn't another priest, with less experience than I have, let her pull the wool over his eyes with all those fake tears?"

---

[4] [Fee schedule (*arancel*): a standardized list of the fees for various priestly services in a parish. Fees were higher for parishioners who were classified as Spanish than for Indians, who generally had less access to the cash economy. "The most common and persistent source of friction between parish priests and Indian parishioners in the late colonial period was the fees for spiritual services that curas treated as an indispensable part of their living," according to Taylor, who writes about "arancel disputes" in *Magistrates of the Sacred*, p. 424 ff. –Tr.]

Father Franco lowered his eyes and fell silent as if his prelate had been reprimanding him; the color in his face rose and fell, and every now and then he looked earnestly at the woman, as if he were trying to tell her something.

We were all watching this scene expectantly, unable to fathom the mystery behind Don Benigno's blushing; but the priest of Tixtla, confronting the woman severely and throwing her money in his purse, told her, "Fine, scoundrel; we'll bury your husband; but we'll do it tomorrow to punish you for your craftiness, you shameless cheat."

"I'm no cheat, Father, sir," the sad woman said in the greatest affliction; "I'm a miserable woman; I was given the money just now, in alms."

"Just now? That's another lie," the priest said. "Who gave it to you?"

Then the woman let go of the child she had been leading by the hand and, holding her baby at the breast with one arm, threw herself down at the feet of the priest from Chilapa, embraced him by the knees, rested her head on them, and burst into a flood of tears, unable to articulate a single word. Her little girl, the one who was walking, also cried when she saw her mother sobbing; our priest stood astonished; the priest of Chilapa leaned over, tears streaming down, and struggled to lift up the heartbroken woman; and all the rest of us were entranced by this amazing spectacle.

At last, the woman herself, after she calmed down her grief somewhat, broke the silence by telling her benefactor, "Father, please allow me to kiss your feet and wash them with my tears, as a sign of my gratitude."

And turning to face us, she went on, "Yes, gentlemen: this Father, who must be not merely a priest, but an angel from heaven, called out to me softly in the corridor, soon after I left the room, and, near tears, he told me, 'Here you go, dear child, pay for the burial and don't tell who assisted you.' But I would be the most ungrateful woman in the world if I didn't shout out loud who had done this great work of charity for me. Forgive me for telling, because besides wanting to thank you publicly for this favor, my heart was grieving to hear how my own priest mistreated me, calling me a cheat."

The two priests blushed mutually and did not dare glance at each other, both of them bewildered: the priest of Tixtla because he saw his greed reproached; the priest of Chilapa because he found his charity praised. The assistant priest very prudently took the pretext of having to go perform the burial right away, and he led the woman out of there; and the subdelegado made all the guests sit down and entertained us with the card game, which distracted everyone.

As I've said, I witnessed this whole scene, as well as the crooked schemes our priest came up with for keeping his moneybox stuffed. One of these was to tax the Indians by making them pay a certain amount during Holy Week for each image of Jesus Christ that they carried in what they called the Procession of the Christs; but this fee was not destined for alms or meant to support church functions, for they had to pay for those things separately: it was a fee for the priest, which he charged according to the size of the image: e.g., if the Christ image was two yards tall, he charged two pesos; if it was half a yard, twelve reales; if it was one foot tall, one peso; and so on, ranking the sizes down to half a real. I rubbed my eyes to see the fee schedule better, but I couldn't find these fees printed on it anywhere.

On Good Friday, they'd go on what they called the Procession of the Holy Burial; along the procession route, they had a number of small altars that they called waysides, and at each of these, the Indians would pay a load of coins, requesting a prayer for the dead each time to be said 'for the Lord's soul'; the blessed priest would keep their pennies, sing the prayer of the Holy Cross, and leave those poor people submerged in their ignorance and pious superstition. And what else? He knew that on the Day of the Dead, the Indians would bring their offerings and put them up in their houses, believing that the more fruit, tamales, atole, *mole*, and other food they offered, the more relief the souls of their dead relatives would find; and some Indians were even so ignorant that while they were in church, they would be stuffing pieces of fruit and other things through the holes in the tombs. I repeat that the priest was fully aware of the origin and the spirit behind these abuses, but he never preached against them or reprimanded them; and through his silence, he supported their superstitions, or rather, he authorized them, and those unhappy people remained blind because there was no one to lead them out of their errors. It is greatly to be wished that such abuses only occurred in Tixtla, and only at that time; but the pity is that even today, there are many Tixtlas. God grant that every town in the kingdom might be purged of these and other such nonsense, through the watchful eyes, the charity, and the effective work of the parish priests!

As is easy to imagine, with the subdelegado being such a penny-grubber and the parish priest being much the same, there was rarely any peace between the two of them; they were always at each other's throats, because it's the truth that you can't keep two cats quiet in one bag. Each of them tried to get his business done first, and to squeeze the townspeople for his own side. That meant they were constantly in competition, which gave rise to complaints and quarrels. For example: the priest would pursue the unmarried debauchees, even though that was not his mission, to see if he could get them to marry and pocket the wedding fees; the subdelegado pursued them so that he could collect his fines; the priest would capture some of them; the secular magistrate would demand to have them turned over; the cleric would refuse; and there you see a competition formed between their jurisdictions.

In all their competitions, the poor people were the victims, and they regularly had to pay the piper by going to jail or handing over their cash; and the miserable Indians were the weakest party which suffered the most from the selfishness of both dealers.

Apart from the four wealthy favorite sons, who bought impunity from their crimes with their money, nobody could stand either the priest or the subdelegado. A few of them had already petitioned against them in Mexico for personal grievances; but their complaints were easily eluded, since there were always witnesses who could testify against them and in favor of the defendants, making the plaintiffs look like a bunch of quarrelsome slanderers.

But crime cannot go unpunished for long, and so it happened that the principal Indians and their governor came to this capital, scourged by the ill treatment they were receiving from the magistrates; and without yet taking on the priest, they formally accused the subdelegado, presenting a terrible denunciation of him before the Royal Audiencia, laying on him such criminal charges as these:

THAT the Subdelegado trafficked in commerce and the forced distribution of goods;

THAT he forced the Indians of the town to buy from him on credit, and demanded that they repay him in grain at a price below the current market;

THAT he forced them to labor in his fields for a daily wage set by him, and that whosoever resisted or refused was given lashes and thrown in jail;

THAT he allowed public debauchery among all those who had the means to pay him off constantly;

THAT for 500 pesos he gave cover to a treacherous murderer and freed him from prison;

THAT he staged betting games through a third party, and then sacrificed everyone caught in his trap;

THAT he occupied the Indians in his domestic service without paying them anything;

THAT he made use of Indian serving girls, bringing three of them to his house every week as maids without pay, and that not even the daughters of the governor were exempt from this servitude;

THAT he demanded the Indians pay him the same fee for bringing petitions that he charged the Spaniards;

THAT on market days, he was the first seller to corner all the scarcest goods, having them brought to his store and then selling them to the poor at excessive prices;

FINALLY, THAT he trafficked in royal tributes.

These were the charges that they made in their petition, which concluded by asking that the subdelegado be called to the capital to answer them; that a commissioner be sent to Tixtla so that, together with an interim magistrate, he might proceed to ascertain the truth; and that, if the accusations be proved true, the subdelegado should be removed from office and obliged to make good the particular damages he had done to the sons of the town.

The Royal Audiencia issued a decree that agreed with everything the Indians requested, and sent out a commissioner.

While this whole tempest was brewing in Mexico, we knew nothing about it, nor did we infer anything from the absence of the Indians, because they had pretended that they were going there to order a religious image. Therefore my master was caught unawares when the commissioner broke the news to him one afternoon while he was relaxing in the cool air of the corridors in the government offices, telling him that he was to cease all his activities on the spot, name a deputy to take his place, leave the town within three days, and present himself in the capital within a week, to respond to the charges of which he had been accused.

This list of demands left my master chilled; yet there was nothing else he could do but hightail it helter-skelter out of there, leaving me in charge of justice in the town.

When I saw myself alone and invested in all the authority of a magistrate, I quickly got up to my old tricks, to my greatest satisfaction. To start off, I banished a pretty girl from the town because she lived in debauchery. That's what was said; but the true reason was that she refused to go along with my solicitations, despite my offering her all my interimly magistrational protection. After that, with the help of a tiny gift of 300 pesos, I incriminated a poor man whose only crime was to be married to a beautiful, dishonorable woman; and through my skill, he was packed off to a distant fortress prison, while his wife was left to live openly with her lover.

Next I hunted down and threatened all the other poor men who were guilty of the same crime, and they, fearful that I might banish their mistresses as I was wont to do, paid me whatever fines I demanded, and sent me gifts so that I wouldn't pester them too often.

Nor did I neglect to revoke the most properly drawn-up documents, rummage through the wills and testaments, misplace public instruments such as bonds and securities, and commit other dishonest acts of the same ilk. Finally, during the one month that I lasted as substitute magistrate, I did more deviltry than the subdelegado himself, and managed to incur the hatred of everyone in town.

To top it all off, I set up public gaming sessions in the government offices; and on the nights that they beat me, I'd go out patrolling to round up all the private gamblers, so that on some nights, the cardsharps would leave my house for their own homes at twelve midnight, and the poor beggars that I found gambling in the streets would enter the jail; and with the fines that I demanded from them, I'd pay myself back everything or nearly everything I had lost.

One night they took me for so much money that I didn't have a penny of my own left, so I unlocked the community chest[5] and gambled away all the money it held; but I didn't take many precautions when I did it, and some people who saw me doing it notified the priest and the Indian governor, who—being the ones responsible for that money, and knowing that I didn't have a leg to stand on—quickly informed the capital, sending personal testimonies along with their report, which they collected not only from all the honorable citizens in town, but from the commissioner himself; but they did this so secretly that I didn't get a whiff of what was up.

It was the priest who called the governor, drew up the report, collected the testimony, sent them to Mexico, and acted as the prime agent of my ruin, as I have said; and he did all this, not out of his love for the town or his zeal for charity, but because he had conceived the plan of keeping most of the money in the community chest himself, under the pretext of fixing the church, since he had already proposed that project to the Indians, and it seems that they were disposed to go along with it. So when he found out about my adventure and lost all hopes of swiping the money, he lost his temper and set about trying to destroy me, which he did.

To relieve my troubles, the subdelegado—who had no reply or any excuses he could make for the crimes that the Indians and other townspeople accused him of

---

[5] [Community chest (*cajas de comunidad*): a strongbox in which the people of an Indian community saved important documents and the money they collected for communal uses. –Tr.]

committing—resorted to the excuse of stupidity, and said that he was surprised to discover that these things were crimes; that he was a layman; that he had never been a judge, and didn't understand any of this; that he had relied on me, as his managing secretary; that I had suggested all those injustices to him; and therefore I should be held responsible for them all, since he had trusted me completely.

These excuses, prettied up by the pen of a clever lawyer, did not fail to find a place in the Audiencia's final judgment: not that they found the subdelegado innocent, but at least they reduced his proportion of guilt, for the honorable gentlemen determined (not unreasonably) that the greater share of guilt was mine, especially since, at the very time that they were issuing their judgment, they received the priest's report, in which they saw that I had committed even more atrocities than the subdelegado.

Therefore (and I would have thought the same) they turned upon me the full harshness of the law that had threatened my master; they exonerated him for the most part; they determined that he was a fool and unsuitable for serving as a magistrate; they removed him from office and made his bondsmen responsible for reimbursing the royal treasury, letting private plaintiffs reserve the right to renew their complaints against the subdelegado should his fortunes improve, for at the time, he was insolvent; and they sent seven soldiers to Tixtla to bring me back to Mexico on a mule outfitted with a horse-blanket saddle and Biscay shackles.

I was so unaware of what was about to befall me that on the afternoon when the soldiers arrived, I was playing a game of ombre with the priest and the commissioner at one real a hand. The only thing I was thinking about at the moment was how to win back the money I had lost in four tricks that they had taken one after another. They had just laid out a pretty hand for me, and I was set to take it, when the soldiers arrived and entered the drawing room; and since those folks know nothing about etiquette, they unceremoniously asked who was in charge of justice there. As soon as they found out that it was me, they informed me of my arrest and, without letting me finish my hand, took me away from the table, gave a piece of paper to the priest, and led me to jail.

The paper, I figure, would have contained the Audiencia's royal decree and the name of the person who was to continue governing the town. The fact is, I went to jail, where all the prisoners mocked me merrily and in a short time made up for the trouble I had given them all month long.

Bright and early the next morning, before I had a chance for breakfast, they stuck the fetters on me, sat me on the saddled mule, and led me to Mexico, where I was placed in the city jail.[6]

When I entered that sad prison, I recalled the damnable shower of urine that the other prisoners had splattered over me the first time I had the honor of visiting; the trusty's harsh treatment; my friend Don Antonio; El Aguilucho; and all the awful things that had happened to me there; and I consoled myself with the thought that I wouldn't have it so bad this time, both because I had six pesos in my pocket, and because Chanfaina had died and I couldn't fall into his hands.

---

[6] [See Chapter 19, footnote 2. –Tr.]

Nevertheless, the six pesos were soon spent, and I couldn't avoid the troubles that always go along with poverty, especially in a place like that.

Meanwhile, my case continued along the normal course; I had no excuses I could make; I found myself confessed and convicted, and the Royal Court of Justice sentenced me to the king's service for eight years in the Manila militia,[7] which was recruiting out of Mexico at the time.

Indeed, the day came when I was taken out, marched through the recruiting office, and led off to the barracks.

They draped me in my recruit's uniform, and here you have me: a soldier, whose sudden transformation served to make me hold the law in deeper respect out of fear, though my habits had not changed for the better.

Since I saw no way out of it, I tried to reconcile myself to my fate and pretend that I was utterly content with a military life and career.

I feigned my complaisance so well that in four days, I had mastered the drill; I could always be relied on to be on time at roll calls, reviews, guard duty, and every sort of toil; I endeavored to be clean and well pressed at all times, and to flatter the colonel whenever possible.

On his saint's day, I sent him some verses that were no better than could be expected of me; but I put a lot of elbow grease into writing them, and the colonel, who loved my handwriting and my talent (so he said), relieved me of all my duties and made me his adjutant.

Then I got more satisfaction, and I saw and observed many things among the troops, which you will learn about in the next chapter.

---

[7] [Manila: the capital and major Spanish city of the Philippines, the only Spanish colony in Asia (1565–1898). The trade route from Spain to Manila went through Mexico, and administratively, the Philippines was under the Viceroyalty of New Spain. –Tr.]

CHAPTER 35

WHEREIN PERIQUILLO DESCRIBES HIS GOOD FORTUNE IN BEING THE
COLONEL'S ADJUTANT; THE CHARACTER OF THE COLONEL; THEIR
EMBARKATION FOR MANILA; AND OTHER ENTERTAINING DETAILS

When men are not restrained by reason, their fear of punishment tends to restrain them. Such was the case with me during this period, when, fearful of suffering the punishments I had seen visited upon some of my companions, I tried to become an upright man by sheer force, or at least to pretend that's what I was; and by these means I managed to avoid the rigors of military discipline, and through my hypocrisy and flattery, I won the affection of the colonel, who, as I have mentioned, took me into his household and made me his adjutant.

If I had managed to gain the good graces of my previous bosses without any mentor, what couldn't I do once I saw the first fruits of my pretense in the colonel's appreciation of me? It is easy to imagine.

I wrote out in longhand whatever was needed, ran his household errands well and quickly, cut and combed his hair to his taste, served as his steward, and watched over his domestic expenses with punctuality, efficiency, and economy. In compensation, I got my board; the colonel's castoff clothes, which were in good condition and would have looked fine on an officer; a few pesos now and then; complete and absolute relief from soldier's duty, which was nothing to sneeze at in itself; a bit of freedom now and then to go out strolling; and the colonel's high esteem, which was what most tied me to him. After all, I had come from a good background, and was more moved by affection than by self-interest. The truth is that I came to love and respect the colonel like my father, and he came to return my feelings with my father's love for me.

Whether because of his esteem for me or because I was always at his service with my pen, I was rarely far from his desk, and he held me in such trust that he allowed me to be present at all his conversations. This gave me an opportunity to learn a few things that most enlisted men, and perhaps a few officers, never find out.

The colonel had a very considerate, affable, and circumspect character; he would have been about fifty years old; he was very well educated, because he was not only a good soldier but a good jurist; and for that reason, officers from other regiments frequented his house every day, either to consult with him about some matter or to engage him in entertaining conversation. I listened in on several private consultations (at least, that is what I took them to be), among which was the following:

One day, two officers entered his house together, a sergeant-major and a captain. After the customary greetings, the sergeant-major said, "Colonel, birds of a feather flock together. My buddy and I both need to pick your brains, so we flocked here to bother you together."

"I'll be pleased to serve you in any way I can," the colonel replied; "please tell me what's going on."

Then the sergeant-major said, "Let's not waste time on ceremony. A soldier is going to be court-martialed for having killed a man. He has what looks like a justification, which is that he killed him out of jealousy because he had gotten the idea that the man was going out with his wife. He didn't actually catch them in the act, but he had such strong suspicions and evidence of the illicit friendship between them that he will surely be exonerated. However, since I am the prosecutor for the case, I can't argue anything in his defense; instead, I have to accuse him and see to it that he gets the ultimate punishment. His defender will urge every exception he has going for him in order to save him, so you can imagine that my bill of indictment will be completely unsuccessful. That is why I'm coming to consult with you, so you can tell me how to couch my accusation in a way that the defense won't laugh my indictment out of court."

"There are many things to tell you about this matter," said the colonel. "First, the motive for the homicide appears to be adultery. Adultery means *violatio alterius thori*, the violation of another man's bridal bed, because the woman is considered to be her husband's bridal bed.

"In our legal code there are many laws imposing penalties on adulterers. Law 3 of Title 4, Book 3 of the *Fuero Juzgo* decrees that the adulterers should be turned over to the husband so that he might do with them as he wishes. Other laws agree with this punishment; but they add that the husband may not kill one and let the other live. Law 15, Title 17, Part 7 declares that the adulteress loses her rights to her wedding gifts and dowry and must enter a convent. Law 5, Title 20, Book 8 of the *Recopilación* declares that when the husband kills the adulterers on his own authority, he has no claim on his wife's property. This law seems aimed at reining in the husband's arbitrary power, which had been expanded by Law 13, Title 17, Part 7, and by Law 4, title 4, Book 3 of the *Fuero Juzgo*, which allow the husband to kill the adulterers.

"Although all this is true, the enlightenment of the times has modified these penalties, and surely you have never heard of a case in which the adulterers have been handed over to the husband so that he can do as he wishes with them; the most that is done in practice is to pardon the husband if he kills the adulterers, or better stated, to commute his sentence from capital punishment to exile, depending on the circumstances; though there could well be circumstances in which he would be freed entirely, after proving the fact that, without his having given his wife any motive whatsoever, the husband found her in the offensive act; but as for punishing the adulterers, the normal thing, according to Dr. Berni in his *Criminal Practice*,[1] is to cloister the woman and banish her accomplice, if they are from the middle sphere; and if they are plebeians, to jail the woman and send the man to a fortress prison. That is, of course, after the accusations have been filed and proven, which can only be done by the husband and by the father, brother, or uncle of the adulteress, as the case may be, and by no others. The woman cannot accuse her husband of adultery, because she is not dishonored by it, as expressed in Law 1, Title 17, Part 7. Nevertheless, the tribunals do admit a woman's complaints, and justice imposes penalties.

"An accusation of adultery cannot be levied against one adulterer alone; both must be accused.

---

[1] [Joseph Berni y Catalá, *Práctica criminal con nota de los delitos, sus penas, presunciones, y circunstancias que los agravan y disminuyen* (Valencia, 1746). –Tr.]

"The author cited says, quite correctly, on page 8, that 'since no one goes looking for witnesses when he commits adultery, the law allows for proof by conjecture; but the evidence must be strong and sufficient to give full knowledge of the crime . . . because in case of doubt, it is better to absolve than to condemn.' The suspicious circumstances that clearly denote adultery are: when witnesses worthy of faith and credit, even if they be from the house itself, declare that they have seen Pedro and Marcia in the same bed or suspicious place, either by themselves, or in a closed room, or naked, or kissing or hugging each other. Several interpreters of the law speak on this topic at length.

"The exceptional circumstances that favor the adulteress are: First, when the husband initiates a complaint of adultery and then abandons it with no intention of taking it up again. Second, when the husband states in front of the judge that he does not wish to accuse his wife because he is satisfied with her conduct, or words to that effect. Third, when the husband receives his wife in his marriage bed after learning that she is an adulteress. Fourth, whenever the husband knows what is happening and is complaisant. In that case, far from being able to take action against his wife, he is guilty of pandering. Fifth, when the woman is forced. Sixth, when she is deceived and commits adultery thinking that she is with her husband. And seventh, when the husband abjures the Catholic religion and embraces other diverse sects, becoming a Moor, a Jew, or a heretic. In those cases, the adulterous woman is freed from her husband's accusations, and is favored by Laws 7 and 8 of Title 17, Part 7, and by Laws 6, 7, and 8 of Title 9, Part 4.

"Here you see, in summary, what adultery is, what the penalties for it are, who can bring the charge, what exceptions favor the woman, and what is meant by strong suspicions or presumptions. In view of all this, being well informed of the case, you can decide how to formulate your accusation."

"The problem is that the man had very strong suspicions," said the sergeant-major, "because, on top of the fact that there are witnesses who have testified to seeing the murdered man with the soldier's wife, the soldier had already reproached the man and ordered him to stay away from his house; but in spite of that, he entered, and when the soldier killed him, he had found him alone with his wife, confident that the soldier was on guard duty; but his jealousy had led him to abandon his post, and he had found the door bolted and had broken it down. This leads me to believe that my accusation won't be strong enough."

"But what, are you hoping to have the prisoner executed even though he doesn't deserve it?" asked the colonel.

"No, sir," the sergeant-major replied, "I don't want him executed; but since I am the prosecutor, I ought to dispel his defenses, ignore his exceptions, and make his crime seem as bad as possible. That is my obligation."

"You are quite wrong, Major," said the colonel, "to think that it is your obligation to incriminate the prisoners. The prosecutor is no less than the upholder of the law, and to fulfill his duties, he does not have to seek to have the accused imprisoned."[2]

---

[2] Don Marcos Gutiérrez, in volume 2 of his *Práctica criminal de España* [Madrid, 1805], page 9, says: "The post of prosecutor is one of great responsibility in the court system, and the staff officers

"So, if that's true," the sergeant-major said, "I will be doing my duty if I explain the case at the court-marital just as it is, and ask that the prisoner be given a moderate sentence, or at most, the sentence decreed for abandoning the guard post."

"That is what I think you should do, and even that penalty should be modified for the sake of justice, giving heed to the violent passion of jealousy, without which he never would have left his post; and therefore his defense will be able to show that this military offense, which in any other case deserves the gauntlet or the ultimate sanction, depending on when it is committed, was not carried out with premeditation, and since penalties should be raised or lowered depending on the intention with which the crime is done, it undoubtedly follows that the court-martial will give this soldier a lighter sentence than the regulations decree, considering that, as King Don Alonso the Wise said in one of his Laws in the *Siete Partidas*, 'the prime movements that move the heart of man lie not in his power.' "[3]

"I am completely satisfied," said the sergeant-major, "and I thank you for the wealth of detail with which you have made me understand that prosecutors are not obliged to incriminate the accused or to have them found guilty at all cost, but simply to uphold the law; though it seems to me that you would make a better defense attorney than a prosecutor."

"We'll find out about that right now," said the captain, "because I am defending another soldier who treacherously killed a man, and I cannot see how to get him acquitted, since that is my first obligation."

"You, too, are mistaken," said the colonel, "because if your client is a murderer, and his treachery has been proven, he could have little hope for your defense, so long as you do it in accordance with your conscience; for *he who kills another man must die*, says God.[4] That is, except for when it is done in self-defense, in a raw and unpremeditated act, by accident, in just satisfaction of wounded honor (as in the case of adultery), or for some other such cause; but if the murder is committed with forethought, and none of those other exceptions mitigate the homicide, it is an act of treachery, and the murderer must die according to the country's laws, and not even

---

who play this role in courts-martial will not live up to this responsibility unless they endeavor to do so with rectitude, bringing their accusations in good faith, with all possible integrity, and as upholders of the law, without slandering or insulting anyone unjustly; therefore, they must aim for the truth, and not the glory of finding the innocent guilty through sophisms and unfounded accusations. Zeal for the public good has its limits, and when those are crossed, it becomes unreasonable and unjust, which is why it is a great mistake and barbarously foolish for some people to believe that the sergeant-major or adjutant must incriminate the prisoner and make his crime seem as bad as possible in his closing statement."

[3] This doctrine is consistent with the reason and spirit of our laws. Señor [Manuel] Lardizábal [y Uribe], in his *Discurso sobre las penas [contrahido a las leyes criminales de España para facilitar su reforma*, Madrid, 1782, p. 112], says: "Freedom can also be diminished by intrinsic factors; and this happens when the force of the passions is so great that it obfuscates the spirit, blinds the mind, and almost involuntarily brings about wrongdoing, as happens in the first movements of wrath, anger, grief, and other such passions, in which case the misdeeds committed should be punished less severely than when they are done in cold blood and utter premeditation."

[4] Genesis 9 [verse 6, "Whosoever shall shed man's blood, his blood shall be shed"].

the sanctuary of the church can protect him. So you can imagine what kind of defense you can come up with, if you admit that your client is treacherous."

"That is true," said the captain, "but he has a very powerful exception to defend him in his favor, which you have not mentioned. At least, I believe that he will escape the ultimate sanction, though I'd like to formulate his defense so that he gets off free, or at the most, that he'll be sentenced to serve his term in the militia over again. That is my endeavor, and that's why I have come to get your advice."

"And what is this exception that he has going for him?" asked the colonel; and the defender replied that he was drunk when he committed the murder.

The colonel laughed merrily, and said, "If he had been insane instead of drunk, you would certainly have been in a good position; but drunk! Drunk! . . . That man would be headed for the gallows even if Cicero defended him."

"How could that be?" asked the captain. "You said yourself that penalties should be raised or lowered depending on the intention with which the crime is done. Following that doctrine, and having proven that my client was drunk when he killed the man, it is clear that he committed the murder without full premeditation, and therefore does not deserve the death penalty."

"That is how it must look at first sight, but 'the laws,' says Señor Lardizábal, 'should make a distinction, when it comes to imposing penalties, between one who becomes intoxicated accidentally or for some extraordinary reason, and one who does so habitually and customarily. As for the former, if he commits a crime when deprived of his judgment, his penalty should be lowered and perhaps pardoned, depending on the circumstances; but the latter should be punished as if he had committed the crime in his full senses, and no attention should be paid to his intoxication, except perhaps to increase the penalty; for no legislator should be considered unjust were he to wish to revive the law of Pittacus, who imposed a double penalty on anyone who committed an offense while intoxicated: one for the crime, the other for the intoxication.'[5]

"This same author cites the words of Aristotle on the same subject, which are worth your learning. That pagan political thinker said, 'Whenever a crime is committed through ignorance, it is done involuntarily, and thus there is no injury. But if the person who commits the crime is the cause of the ignorance through which it was committed, then there is true injury and there is cause to accuse him, as in the case of drunken men, for if they cause damage while possessed by wine, they are committing an injury, insofar as they themselves were the cause of their ignorance, for they should not have drunk so much.' "[6]

"Then we're badly off," said the defender, "because the witnesses who declared that my client was drunk when he committed the murder also stated that he was

---

[5] These are the words of Señor Lardizábal, in his *Discurso sobre las penas*, cited above.

[6] [The Aristotle citation appears to be a paraphrase from *Nichomachean Ethics*, III.1, "An act done through ignorance is in every case not voluntary," and III.5, "Indeed the fact that an offence was committed in ignorance is itself made a ground for punishment, in cases where the offender is held to be responsible for his ignorance; for instance, the penalty is doubled if the offender was drunk, because the origin of the offence was in the man himself, as he might have avoided getting drunk, which was the cause of his not knowing what he was doing." –Tr.]

accustomed to getting drunk, and in that case, I realize that the exception does not favor him."

"Clearly not," said the colonel; "and less so when we consider that, in any case, a man who commits a crime while drunk is, in my opinion, guilty of it; because under no circumstances should anyone risk losing his sense of reason. Besides, if the matter is considered seriously, a drunk deserves indulgence only if he commits crimes that harm society very remotely and indirectly, such as the insults that a man might hurl when he is drunk, even if they touch on someone's honor, for two reasons: first, because a drunken man has a very loose tongue, and experience shows that there's never been a drunk yet who hasn't stammered out streams of balderdash; and second, for the same reason, there is hardly anyone who pays the slightest attention to such drunken drivel.

"Not so when action and other circumstances contribute to the crime, clearly denoting a fair amount of forethought and deliberation in what is done, as in the case of a homicide; for then the aggressor has a weapon at his disposal, looks for the object of his wrath, prepares the occasion for his revenge, and asserts the fatal blow with as much force and aim as the sanest man could muster. I would certainly never pardon the life of a man who had taken away another's under the pretext of drunkenness. Those who drink to excess lose only their shame, and there are many men who drink a little liquor and pretend to be drunker than they are, as a mask for committing a thousand infamies and ducking the penalty that they deserve; but such men have not earned any leniency, even when their reason is truly unhinged: indeed, they deserve less, because even though they suffer from a lack of reason, they do so by their own fault, and they deserve double punishment, as has been said.

"It is true that drunkenness is a passing insanity; but it is a voluntary insanity, as Seneca said; and just as a man who commits suicide is considered a criminal, even though he voluntarily takes his own life, the same should be said of someone who commits a crime while drunk, because he got drunk of his own will.

"Besides, according to my way of thinking, there is only one case in which a drunk is worthy of indulgence, and that is when he is in no state to be able to commit any crime or hurt anyone. And when would that be? When he is so knocked out and narcotized that he cannot move, nor hear, nor see, nor speak, or at least when he cannot get up; and if he speaks he does so with a stuttering tongue and without knowing what he says. That may be a paradox, but it will always be my way of thinking; because so long as a drunk can speak, walk, see, get angry, and manage to avoid dangers, it is wrong to say, as it is commonly said, that he has lost his senses. True, he uses them in an unhinged way for some things; but he's got them, and he uses them quite to his advantage. I, at least, have never seen a drunk throw himself off a rooftop, or try to wound someone with the handle of the knife, or hit Juan when he means to hit Pedro, or anything of the kind. They are crazy, true; but no madman tries to eat fire; and finally, if I were the judge, I'd judge the degree of a drunken man's deliberation according to the amount of order or disorder in his actions immediately before and after the moment when he committed the crime: thus, if he had to take a few steps before carrying it out, and if he took more afterward to flee because he feared the penalty he deserved, there can be no doubt that I would not be merciful toward him, for a man who can control his feet can also control his head. Given this information, you should know the particulars of your client's case, and you can form his defense as you deem best; but if you want to do it as God and the king would wish, I don't think you can defend this poor fellow."

"But," the captain said, "doesn't a good defender's skill consist in freeing his client from the penalty he deserves, no matter how murderous he might be? And don't the defender's obligations bind him to take advantage of every means at his disposal to do so?"

"No, sir," said the colonel; "the obligation of the defense is to examine whether the crime is justified; to examine the strength and the value of the evidence against the prisoner; to scrutinize the sort of witnesses and the form in which they testify; to fathom whether they understand what they have said; to see if they tally with each other in substantial matters of place, time, means, person, occasion, and number, or whether, on the other hand, they are in such close agreement in their statements that bribery can be surmised; if their declarations change or are unbelievable, and so on; thus, the obligation of the defense is to argue in his client's favor every exception that favors him in the eyes of the law, and to examine whether there is some hole in the case on which his defense might rest; but it is illicit to make use of malign and illegal means, such as corrupting witnesses, presenting false documents, censuring the prosecutor unjustly, and other methods like these, which are opposed to justice and morality."[7]

"Well, buddy," the sergeant-major told the captain, "if we hadn't come to consult with the colonel, we would have each been disappointed in our own way. You, for hoping to save a murderer, and me, for trying to incriminate somebody who's not a murderer, or at least not as much of one as I had supposed."

"That's why it's good," the defender said, "never to rely only on yourself, especially in cases where a man's life is at stake, or the common good of the Republic, rather than submitting to someone else's better judgment, as we have done. As for me, I give you a thousand thanks, Colonel, for your timely lesson."

"And the same goes for me, as far as I'm concerned," said the prosecutor.

After this they changed the subject, and after talking for a while about unimportant matters, they bid farewell.

I was present at several of these consultations, and I began to feel a certain desire to learn. The fact is, I got a bit of learning thanks to that wise man's conversations and his good library, which was small but select, and not meant as mere home decoration,

---

[7] This is the doctrine taught by the author just cited, who says in his *Práctica criminal* (published in Spain by the order of the Council and printed in Madrid in 1805) that the obsession and vanity of some defenders, who base their honor on getting their clients off the hook no matter what means they use to accomplish it, are utterly reprehensible, for their crass ignorance and misplaced sense of charity lead them to believe that it is licit to use every means at their disposal, even if they are as unjust as those mentioned.

The obsession of prosecutors in thinking that they must lead the prisoners to the scaffold, together with that of defenders in imagining that they must acquit them of all charges, contributes more than a little to the confusion and length of court cases, to the detriment of the administration of justice.

but for improving his mind. He was rarely without a book in hand, and he'd frequently tell me, "There's no quarrel between letters and arms, son. A man's a man, whatever class he finds himself in, and he has to nurture his reason with erudition and study. I've known some officers who'll only study their regulations and their Colón,[8] and who not only refuse to devote themselves to any kind of studying or reading, but who look down on all other books with a kind of indifference that almost seems like disdain, wrongly believing that a military man shouldn't know about anything but his profession, and doesn't need to know anything else. What they don't realize is that, as Saavedra says in his Sixth Maxim,[9] "A profession that has no notion of, and derives no embellishments from, other professions, is a form of ignorance." That is why I've also seen that these fellows have had to play the stone guest in conversations with educated people, standing there, as is commonly said, like fools with their mouths hanging open; and they're the ones who come off better than those who try putting in their two cents and moving beyond the small radius to which they have limited their education, for they barely start in on it before they break out into a thousand ineptitudes, thereby earning a reputation of being ignoramuses at best.

"If you should some day become an officer, Pedro, you should endeavor to enlighten your mind with books, and work hard so that you are ignorant about as little as possible.

"I'm not saying you should be omniscient, or that you should neglect your actual duties in favor of study; rather, that you should not disdain books or think that, just because you are a military man, you have license to spout nonsense in every conversation, because in that case, everybody who hears you will take you to be stupid, or pedantic, or perhaps lacking education due to your humble origins.

"On the other hand, a well-educated military man is respected everywhere, is counted among the society of the wise, and is a credit to his family, demonstrating its nobility without having to prove it with documents and coats of arms.

"I repeat, there's no quarrel between letters and arms; rather, in a thousand cases, letters have been an embellishment and an aid to arms. Don Alfonso, the king of Naples,[10] when asked whether he owed more to arms or to letters, replied: 'I have learned about arms in books, and about the law from arms.' There have been many military men who have become imbued with this understanding, have applied themselves as hard at letters as at arms, and have left us in their writings an eternal testimony to the fact that they could handle a pen as dexterously as a sword. These men are the Francisco Santoses, the Gerardo Lobos, the Ercillas,[11] and others.

---

[8] [Félix Colón de Larriátegui, *Juzgados militares de España y sus Indias* (Madrid, 1788–1789, 4 volumes). –Tr.]

[9] [Diego Saavedra Fajardo, *Idea de un Príncipe político Christiano representada en Cien Empresas* (also known as *Empresas políticas*; Munich, 1640; *The Royal Politician, Represented in One Hundred Emblems*, London, 1700), a widely read collection of political maxims. –Tr.]

[10] [Alfonso V of Aragon (1416–1458), who became Alfonso I of Naples after leading the conquest of that country in 1432. –Tr.]

[11] [Francisco Santos (1623–1700), a Spanish soldier and writer of picaresque stories; Gerardo Lobo (1679–1750), Spanish Baroque poet; Alonso de Ercilla y Zúñiga (1533–1594), author of the epic poem *La Araucana* on the conquest of Chile, in which he participated. –Tr.]

"As for your conduct in the case we are imagining, you should be no less careful. You should dress decently yet not effeminately, be frank yet not rude, valiant in battle, jovial and sweet in your personal relations with people, moderate in your words, and an upright man in all your actions. Never imitate the example of bad men; do not try to be more a son of Adonis than a friend of Mars; never be a grandstander or a braggart, and never adopt the military character, as some people misunderstand it, by being obscene in your words and gross in your actions: that does not show soldierliness, but a lack of education and too little shame. An officer is a gentleman, and a gentleman's character should be considerate, affable, courteous, and restrained at all times. Note that the king doesn't decorate you, or anyone, with an officer's badge in order to increase the number of pests, smart-alecks, recreants, spongers, or rogues; but rather to secure the defense of the Catholic religion, his crown, and the well-being and tranquility of his states, under the direction of a few men of honor.

"Think about the fact that, if an enlisted soldier deserves a double punishment for anything, an officer deserves fourfold punishment for the same thing, because the enlisted man is almost always a poor plebeian without high birth, without background, without education, and perhaps without the least talent, and therefore his errors are worthy of some indulgence; while on the other hand, the officer who thinks of himself as well born, well educated, and talented, should surely be held more culpable, since when he commits a wrong, he does so with full knowledge, and it is his obligation to avoid wrongdoing with double the effort of the common soldier.

"Finally, if you find yourself in this position some day—that is, if some day you are an officer, which is not impossible—and you unfortunately misbehave, I would advise you not to brag about your purity of blood, or publicly commemorate the hallowed ashes of your forefathers, for that kind of boasting will only serve to make you more hateful in the eyes of upright men, because the better you ancestors were, the worse your depravity, and you yourself will be letting everyone know how you are inclined toward wickedness, for you will have demonstrated that you had to work to become bad despite your good parents, which is a good that too few recognize and appreciate in this world."

This was the sort of advice that the colonel frequently gave me; he was, at one and the same time, my boss, my master, my father, my friend, and my benevolent teacher, for this good man performed in all these capacities for me.

However, as my virtue was not solid—or rather, was not virtue at all, but a cover-up for my malice—I didn't stop getting up to my old tricks now and then behind the colonel's back. I used to visit my friends, who were the enlisted soldiers then, for I didn't have anyone else who desired my friendship; I'd go to the barracks sometimes, and sometimes to the lunch stands, the taverns, and the pulque stands and brothels where my pals brought me; I'd play my little games of monte quite often, I'd woo the girls, and after I finished making these innocent rounds and learned that the boss was home, I'd retire inside to read, clean his frock coat, fuss with his boots, and keep up my hypocritical flattery.

My frequent dealings with the soldiers got me used to their manners. Around them, I was foul-mouthed, shameless, rude, brazen, and loutish to beat the band. A few times I recalled the colonel's good example and wholesome instructions; but how could I help but do what everyone else was doing? What would they have said of me if I had abstained from doing or saying some roguishness or obscenity in front of them, so as to observe my boss's advice? What gags would they have come up with at my expense if they had heard the words *God, conscience, death, eternity, divine rewards or punishments* from my lips? How would they have mocked me if I had let my guard down and had tried to correct them with my own advice or good example, supposing I were capable of it? Terribly, no doubt; and so, to keep from falling out with these fine friends, and so that they wouldn't call me *The Phony, The Hypocrite,* or *Mr. Holier-than-Thou,* I went along with all their mischief, and despite the fact that some of it revolted me, I managed to get a name for myself as the worst of the worst, riding roughshod over all considerations both human and divine in exchange for their esteem and the sweet-sounding and honorific epithets of *old hand, good old boy, regular guy, sad sack, trooper,* and other such titles that my friends bestowed upon me. The only thing I studied was how to keep news of my deviltries from getting back to my boss, both to keep from suffering the punishment I deserved and to keep from losing my comfortable position, which I knew from experience was incomparable.

In my conversations with the soldiers, I sometimes heard them grumbling merrily about the sergeants. They complained that some of them were cruel, and that others were thieves who took them for their money, purchasing shirts, shoes, and so on, for them at one price and selling them to them at another. Altogether, they told 1,001 stories about the poor sergeants: I figured that maybe they were lies and slander, but I didn't dare talk back to them, because I hadn't lived under the sergeants' rule for long enough, and so I couldn't speak with authority about the matter.

I spent several months in this way, until the day came when we were to depart for Acapulco, which we did, bringing with us all the recruits who were to embark for Manila.

Nothing noteworthy happened along the way; we arrived happily in the royal city, port, and fortress of San Diego de Acapulco.[12] I found the Royal Militia there nothing to wonder at; the city itself, with its humble buildings, bad climate, and terrible site, seemed smaller to me than many Indian villages I had seen; but alongside this disappointment, I had the surprising pleasure of seeing the sea, the castle, and the ships for the first time, and I imagined that all ships must look like the San Fernando Magallanes,[13] which lay at anchor in the bay. On top of this, I had fun with the brown women who live in that country, who, though they look unpleasant to someone coming from Mexico, are very open and attentive.

I also regaled my palate with fresh fish, which is very good and abundant there; and these fooleries helped me put up with the discomfort that I suffered from the heat and lack of society, since I had few friends. Besides being deprived of entertainment in that city, my fear of sailing—which assailed me as it can only assail

---

[12] [Though it was Mexico's only Pacific port, and a key point in the trade with the Philippines, the coastal town of Acapulco was a city in name only, depopulated for most of the year (except when the fleet came and went), due to then-prevalent tropical diseases. Many of the year-round residents of the coastal region were (as Periquillo implies below) of African descent. –Tr.]

[13] [The name of a Spanish navy frigate that was actually used on the Acapulco-Manila run. –Tr.]

someone who has never been aboard a ship, and who has to trust his life to the fury of the winds and the instability of the waves—did not fail to torment me from time to time.

The day came when we were to set sail. The galley convicts were handed over to the captain, we boarded the ship, the anchors were weighed, the cables were cut, and with a cry of *Buen viaje!* that went up from all the friends and onlookers on the pier, we headed out through the harbor mouth onto the open sea.

From that first day, the skies foretold an easy navigation, for soon after we left port a favorable wind picked up and, filling the sails that had been fully unfurled, swept us away with what seemed to me to be utter calm, because four hours out I could no longer see, even with a spyglass, the Tetas de Coyuca, which are the highest peaks in the South and the first signs of land for those coming in from the sea.

This saddened me somewhat, since I knew what a long voyage awaited me. Nor did I fail to get seasick and suffer from nausea and headaches, being a rookie at such trips; but after that torture was past, I continued merrily on my voyage.

CHAPTER 36

IN WHICH PERIQUILLO RECOUNTS THE EGOTIST'S DISASTROUS
ADVENTURE AND HIS UNTIMELY END AS A RESULT OF THE SHIP'S
RUNNING AGROUND; THE ADVICE THAT THE COLONEL GAVE HIM
ON THIS OCCASION; AND HIS HAPPY ARRIVAL IN MANILA

When I had recovered from my bout of nausea, I came up on deck and could no longer see any land at all: just sky, water, and the ship on which we were sailing, which had me good and scared, especially when I reflected in my heart on all the risks that surrounded me. First I'd picture a violent storm coming; then us becalmed or run aground and dying of hunger; then I'd think the boat was about to smash against a coral reef, so each of us would have to escape through our own portholes to become fodder for sharks and man-eaters; then I'd start fearing an encounter with pirates, and expecting the dreaded call to action stations; then I'd imagine how easy it would be to make a mistake with the galley stove, and I'd see the whole craft on fire, the tar melting, and everything being consumed by the voracious flames in spite of the ship's pumps, and I'd figure that when the flames lost their respect for St. Barbara,[1] we would all go up in smoke to wander around God's good sky, never to breathe again until the end of days.

I spent a little time each day contemplating these imagined disasters and reasonable fears until, seeing that a month had passed and nothing adverse had happened, I slowly began discarding them and getting my sea legs, as they say, to such an extent that I truly enjoyed sailing; for on moonlit nights you could see the moon reflected on all the waves, making them shine like a mirror; and this, along with the scudding sunset clouds that we observed along the horizon, entertained us nicely, especially when the winds blowing astern were all you could want for sailing quickly and without any risk of stormy northers, for then the sailors got a rest from the riggings and we could all enjoy conversing with the merchants, officials, and decent passengers who'd come up on deck to marvel at the lovely night; or listening to folks who'd play music and sing; or watching the peacefulness of nature as it revealed itself during those times.

I remember that on one of these nights, I got into a conversation with a merchant who had befriended me because he needed the colonel's protection in Manila, and he could see that I enjoyed his good esteem. In this conversation I told him about all the troubles I had suffered in the course of my life, exaggerating them for no particular reason.

He listened to everything I said with cold indifference, which rather scandalized me; and to see whether this was really his character or just a pretense, I said, "We mortals sure lead wretched lives: we're assailed by evils all around us from the cradle on, and we suffer so much, not just now and then, but from generation to generation!"

---

[1] [St. Barbara is the patron saint of those who pray not to die without last rites, so presumably everyone on a burning ship would be praying to her. –Tr.]

"And what do you care about that?" he said with a sarcastic smile. "Are you the one who suffers all those things?"

"No, I'm not," I said, "but I feel pity for my fellow men who suffer, because I think of them as my brothers, or rather, as parts of myself."

"Oh, come off it!" said the merchant. "You're just one of the many superstitious men in this world: I can see it now! You're just a poor soldier, and there's no reason to expect you to be educated."

I couldn't help feeling annoyed by this excuse, and so I told him, "Maybe I'm not as dull-witted as you imagine, and maybe I can make you see that not all soldiers come from common backgrounds and lack any education; but tell me, why do you figure that I'm superstitious? Because I told you that I pity my fellow man for the evils he suffers, as if he were my brother or a part of myself?"

"Yes, sir," he said, "because that belief is a foolish preconception. We are our own brothers, and we'd all do well to look out for ourselves without getting mixed up with other men's problems, unless we can get some particular benefit out of their friendship."

"If that's true," I said, "then we should only be friends with people who are useful to us, or who we think might be useful to us at some time."

"That is precisely how it should be," he replied, "and this is a good time to recall the proverb that goes, 'The friend who won't give, and the knife that won't cut: if you lose them both, it won't matter much.' And as you know, proverbs are like miniature gospels."

"As I understand it," I said, "not all of them are: some proverbs are false, the sort of nonsense that nobody should follow, and I'd count the one you just cited as one of those, because there must be lots of friends whose friendship is worthwhile even if they never give you anything but their good esteem, their advice, or the lessons they can teach you; and losing those things is surely a heavy loss, if you know how much they are worth."

"Balderdash," he replied; "advice, esteem, lessons, and anything else other than cash or something you can trade for cash are just pleasant fantasies—fine for entertaining kids, but without a drop of usefulness. As for me, I detest that sort of friend; no, I'd never put myself out to look for one, and if I got one without trying, I wouldn't worry about it if I lost him."

"So you'll only be friends with someone who can get you money?"

"Nobody else deserves my friendship," he answered me. "And if one of my friends had a misfortune, I'd feel sorry about it insofar as it affected me; and as for the rest, let every man scratch his own back."

Scandalized at hearing these ineffable maxims, I changed the topic of conversation and soon moved away from his side.

The next day, while I was combing the colonel's hair, I told him about my conversation, and he said, "Don't be surprised, Pedro, that you found this merchant to be so callous, and don't let his avarice and selfishness scandalize you. There are many people in this world who think and act as he does: he's a great egotist, and as such, he's ambitious, cruel, and fawning: common vices among those who think the world was made just for them; but in addition to being an egotist, this fellow has the misfortune of being stupid, because he's bragging about his own vices and displaying them openly, which is why you were scandalized; but you should know that this vice is so widespread in the world that out of every hundred men, I doubt you'd find one who isn't an egotist.

"As you know, being an egotist means loving yourself so immoderately that you trample on the most sacred conventions to make yourself happy or to satisfy your passions. It follows that egotism is not only a dreadful vice (because it has long been the cause of so many misfortunes that befall men every day), but the most loathsome of vices, for it is the root of every crime committed in the world; and thus, nobody is a criminal without first becoming an egotist. Everyone who sins does so to give himself pleasure and because he loves himself too much, which is the same as to say that everyone sins because he's an egotist, and consequently the more egotists there are, the more sinners. These truths are easy to prove, to wit: you'll admit that there are few people if any, in this world, who are not egotists; but there's this difference: some are tolerable egotists, and some are intolerable. Let me explain. Most men, almost all men, love themselves too much, and so they do good and refrain from doing evil only because it is in their own best interest, try as they might to gloss over this fact with fine-sounding words that make a big impression, but that only hold hot air. This type of egotist is sometimes harmful to society for this reason, and he is often useless; but insofar as he never neglects to consider his relation with other men, he is disposed to help them now and again, even if only for his own vain interest in benefiting from them; and that is why I call him a *tolerable egotist.*

"The other sort are the ones who each make themselves the center of the universe, loving themselves so inordinately that they disregard the most sacred conventions in favor of their self-interest. For them, the precepts of religion mean nothing, nor the closest ties of blood or society; they walk through everything as if they were on a safe bridge, and the calamities of men never affect them. This perverse quality means they are haughty, selfish, envious, and cruel, and for the same reason, they are *intolerable.* That's the sort of egotist that the merchant is who rightly scandalized you with his conversation just now; but by the very token that his way of thinking revolted you, you should make sure not to let it contaminate you, noting that self-love is very clever about diminishing our defects in our own eyes and even making us think of them as virtues. Everybody loathes egotism, and nobody thinks he's an egotist, despite how widespread the vice is. To be sure that you're not one, the measure to take is whether you feel moved to benefit your fellow man, and whether you indeed can subordinate your own interests to those of your brothers; and when you've made this maxim second nature, you can live satisfied that you're not an egotist."

This is the way my good mentor always instructed me, and he never lost a good occasion to do so, though unfortunately he was sowing on hard ground at the time; however, as I've returned from my erring ways, I have found his sound advice very profitable.

I was sailing along contentedly by now, thinking that the whole forest was oregano and the whole ocean was pacific, when I was shaken from this ingenuous error by one of those sea accidents that are beyond the control of the best navigators.

One night when the first mate was sick, he left a second mate in charge of the compass; though the sailor was skilled in steering the helm, he was a mortal, and when sleep overcame him, he dozed off on the bench and nobody noticed, for all of us passengers had done the same, lulled by the calm weather we were having.

With the navigator asleep, the ship was left to wander as free as a horse with no one holding the reins, and so it went in whatever direction the wind took it; and in the deepest part of our sleep we were awakened by the rasping sound of the keel grating against sand.

The first to notice the misfortune was the good first mate, who hadn't been able to sleep due to his aches and pains. From his cot, he immediately cried out, "Luff, luff, port the helm! We're grounding! . . . Shallows, shallows!"

The whole crew, the boatswain, the passengers, and everybody woke up and got to work at the riggings, but not in time to avert damage by following the first mate's practical warnings; the best they could do was to lash the helm and haul in the sails, to keep the craft from becoming any more mired in the sands.

Anyone who has found himself in similar straits during a voyage will understand how dismayed we were, especially since, immediately after the disaster was known, an order went out to cut everyone's rations of food and drink, which greatly saddened all of us, and me most of all, because I ate enough for seven. All of us displayed our dejected spirits in the sorrowful expressions on our faces. From that moment, no one could sleep; all we felt was fright, and the only topic of our sad conversations was baneful terror that we might die of hunger and thirst while stuck on that sandy spit.

The mates and officers of the ship held a solemn council in which they decided to attempt every possible method to free us from the risk that threatened us, and in virtue of this resolution, they put all the boats and launches to sea, using them to pull the ship with cables; but this effort was entirely in vain, and consequently they decided to move on to the final possibility, which was to lighten the ship by throwing overboard enough things to make it float.

As everyone knows, when frigates on the China run are returning from Acapulco, they carry no cargo other than food for the voyage and silver; given that the food should not be thrown overboard, the decree therefore fell upon the silver. The king's share[2] was set aside, and the sailors began to cast out chests and trunks full of money, just as they found them, without making any distinctions.

My boss and maestro opened his trunks, took out his papers and two changes of clothes, and he himself, with my help, hurled the trunks into the sea; his example served as a powerful stimulus to almost all the other officers and merchants to do the same—not merrily, because nobody is happy to make that kind of sacrifice, but at least in resigned agreement, because they had no other hopes of freeing their lives.

My colonel encouraged them all with prudence and joviality. After the ship began to move and lighten, he had them suspend the maneuvers for a short while, which he dedicated to having the people eat a bite and drink a sip of liquor; this done, they continued the chore in the same high spirits as before.

---

[2] [The text adds, "which they call *situado* [situated]," referring to the silver destined to pay for the defense of Spanish port cities—in this case, the defense of Manila. –Tr.]

My boss had nothing left to lose, for he had even thrown his wrought-iron cot into the blue, and so his exhortations built upon his example, and therefore bore better fruit.

"There are plenty of mines, friends," he'd say in the fervor of toil; "a man doesn't need much to live; your credit is safe in a case like this, and you're all free of any responsibility; the only thing you're losing is your profit; but by making this sacrifice, we'll purchase our whole future existence. We'll buy our lives with this money, and we'll see then that life is the best gift man has and the first thing he should try to conserve; while money, pesos, ounces of gold are nothing but glorified pieces of rock, without which man can live quite happily. Come on, then, let's be generous, since we've got nothing to lose; let's buy our lives, and the lives of all the poor folk here with us: it'll just cost us a little of this white and yellow dirt that you call gold and silver, because we don't want to die with our arms round our treasures, like miserly Croesus."

With these and other such exhortations, my beloved colonel plucked up the flagging spirits of those who saw the profits of their work and their sweat being buried in the depths of the sea; and so, with each of them putting their elbow to the wheel, as it is said, they worked to destroy themselves and save themselves at the same time, each of them hurling his own treasure into the sea and marking the spot with buoys; but they had hardly touched the trunks of the egotist (who was sitting on them, coolly observing the scene), when he swore, cursed, blasphemed, offered substantial rewards, and did everything he could to save his wealth, but to no avail; the sailors—poor people who, in cases like this, respect neither king nor cur—elbowed him aside and heaved his trunks and chests overboard.

They must have been the heaviest ones on the whole ship, because as soon as they were gone, it began to float, and warping the vessel from the stern with the sheet-anchor and the capstan, we headed out to open sea and were free of the sand bank in a trice.

It is impossible to imagine how all our hearts filled with rejoicing when we saw ourselves free of a danger from which few ships escape, especially since many of us were already resigned to dying of hunger. Only the sleepy pilot and the wretched egotist were overwhelmed by the deepest melancholy, which, in the latter, progressed into dreadful desperation, for when he had worn himself out with crying, swearing, cursing, and pulling out fistfuls of his hair, he saw that the ship was slipping away from the spot where he had left his treasure and, filled with fury and greed, he said, "Why should I want to live without money?"

No sooner said than done: he jumped overboard before any of us who were standing near him had a chance to stop him.

Throwing a life preserver into the sea proved a pointless task, because he didn't know how to swim, and as soon as he hit the water, he sank like a stone and disappeared from our sight, leaving us filled with compassion and alarm.

The first mate never let go of the sounding lead, and when he saw that we were out of the sand banks and in an adequate depth, he stopped the ship and had it secured with the anchors; the sails were taken in, the helm was lashed to, and all the skiffs, boats, and launches we had were put to sea and, manned by the most skilled sailors and a few good divers, were taken out to attempt the recovery of the treasure, which was so successfully accomplished, with the help of the calm weather we were having, that within twenty-four hours every trunk and chest that had been thrown overboard was back on the ship—even those of the unhappy and miserly egotist, whose body had less luck than his money; and who knows whether his soul did not meet an even more unfortunate end.

With all the treasures back aboard and claimed by the owners according to their respective marks, a general vow was made to the Blessed Virgin Mary in a very proper act of gratitude for the great good we had been shown, and after a list had been made of the chests and trunks belonging to the egotist, they were turned over to the colonel for safekeeping, so that he could hand them over to his unfortunate family, who best deserved to receive them.

Fifteen or twenty days after this event came the feast day of the Immaculate Conception of the Queen of Angels, Patroness of the Spains,[3] and on this occasion the ship was dressed, and all day long there was a constant and solemn artillery salvo, which came as an agreeable surprise to me, as it would to anyone who saw a vessel for the first time bedecked with pennants and flags of diverse colors and shapes, denoting those of every nation, as well as the particular signals that are used at sea. On top of this, seeing them raised and lowered almost at the same time caused me a good deal of amazement, though I tried not to show it, because the colonel had taught me that passionately displaying our amazement at anything was as much a sign of foolishness as was looking at the rarest things with stone-like indifference.

That man, whose memory lives on in my own, never lost an occasion to instruct me, as I have said, and continuing with this laudable system, which I will never be able to thank enough, one day when I was combing his hair, he recalled the unfortunate end of the egotist and told me, "Do you remember poor old Don Anselmo, son? Poor man! He threw himself overboard and lost his life, and perhaps his soul, because he missed his money. Ah, money! Dismal motive for the worldly and eternal ruin of men! Many years ago, a certain pagan described the hunger for gold as foolishly sacred (rather, he should have said 'accursed'), and exclaimed, 'What would it not compel mortals to do?'[4] Son, never let silver and gold be the mainsprings of your heart; never let personal greed be the axis upon which your will revolves. Seek money as an incidental means, not the only or the necessary means, for living your life. God's liberal wisdom when He created man provided him with everything he needed to live, and He did not give a single thought to money; I hope that this way of putting it is legitimate, so that you'll understand me: God created everything man needs in Nature, except for coins struck in any mint, proof that money is not necessary for man's survival. As long as man was happy tending to his needs with the help of Nature alone, he never missed money; but after he began to indulge in luxuries, he found he had to avail himself of money to acquire easily the things he could not get in any other way. I do not condemn the use of cash; I recognize the advantages it

---

[3] [The feast day of the Immaculate Conception is December 8. "The Spains" (*las Españas*) is the formula used in the liberal 1812 Spanish Constitution of Cádiz to refer (on a hypothetically equal level) to both Spain and its overseas empire, particularly Mexico, or "New Spain." –Tr.]

[4] [Virgil, *Aeneid*, III: 56–57. –Tr.]

affords us; but I appreciate the thinking of those who have shown that wealth does not consist of silver, but of the products of the earth, of the industry and labor of its inhabitants; and I think it is imprudent for us to search for wealth deep inside the earth while not deigning to pick it up on the earth's surface, where it abounds so liberally. If happiness and abundance do not come from the countryside, as a wise Englishman has said, it would be vain to expect them to come from anywhere else.[5]

"Many nations become wealthy without having any mines of gold or silver, and through their industry and labor they are able to gather up the precious metals that are mined in the Americas. England, Holland, and Asia are proof enough of this truth; and it is just as obvious that the Americas themselves, having emptied their treasuries into Europe, Asia, and Africa, are in a deplorable state.

"Possessing these beautiful metals without any labor other than removing them from the craggy peaks that conceal them is, in my understanding, one of the worst plagues that can befall a kingdom; because this wealth, which, for the common inhabitants of the country, is a pleasant illusion, awakens the greed of foreigners while enervating the industry and laboriousness of the natives.

"These are not metaphysical speculations; rather, they rely on hard evidence. As soon as a rich mine or two are discovered in a place, that town is said to have hit a bonanza, and that is precisely when it becomes worse off. The second the lode of ore appears, everything becomes more expensive; luxury mounts; the town fills with strangers, perhaps the most vice-ridden sorts of people; those strangers corrupt the natives; in short, the mining town is transformed into a scandalous theater of crime; gambling, drunkenness, quarrels, woundings, robberies, murders, and disorder of all sorts abound everywhere. The most diligent actions of the authorities cannot contain this evil, even at the beginning. Everyone knows that mining people are generally depraved, provocative, arrogant, and wasteful. But it will be said that these defects belong to the unskilled mine workers. Since this is clear as daylight and cannot be denied, it proves my point.

"Besides, when a mining town hits a bonanza, it loses all its artisans, or if any are still to be found, they charge exorbitantly for their labor. The number of farmers decreases, either because they go into the mining business or because they cannot find enough day laborers to keep working their land; and there you see how the town is shortly faced with a precarious supply of food and becomes dependent on its neighbors.

"Poor boys, who make up the majority, and who will some day become men, do not devote themselves and are not devoted by their parents to learning any trade, but are content with learning how to cart metal or comb through the earth, which is as good as learning how to be idlers.

"This is the portrait of a boom town; its much vaunted wealth is monopolized by two or three mine owners, and the rest of the town barely survives on their crumbs. I have seen families perishing on the outskirts of the richest mining towns.

---

[5] [According to Spell (p. 166), Lizardi may have read this statement in a translated extract of Jeremy Bentham's *Manual of Political Economy* (itself a restatement of Adam Smith's work), published in a Mexican journal of the early 1800s. –Tr.]

"This means that, in proportion to what occurs in a mining town, the same and worse occur in a kingdom abounding in gold and silver, such as the Indies.[6] For twenty or thirty powerful people that live in the Indies, there are 4 or 5 million people scarcely scraping by, and among them there are many families in poverty.

"If I'm not mistaken, proportional relationships operate the same between kingdoms as between towns; and if we descend from the town level to compare particular cases, we should be able to see the same effects produced by the same causes. Let's hypothesize two boys under our absolute control, and call one of them *Poor* and the other *Rich;* and let's educate the latter in the midst of abundance, and the former in the midst of need.

"It is clear that Rich needs nothing, and therefore devotes himself to nothing and learns nothing; on the contrary, Poor has no comforts to delight him, while on the other hand his need forces him to seek out the means of making his life less difficult, and so he endeavors to find them, which he manages to do by the sweat of his brow. Under these conditions, let's imagine that our boy Rich is hit by one of those disasters that can strip a moneyed fellow of the moniker we've given him, and he finds himself reduced to utter destitution. In this case, which is not uncommon, a peculiar thing happens, which seems to be a paradox: Rich becomes poor, and Poor becomes rich, because the boy who had been rich is poorer than our boy Poor, and the boy who was born poor is richer than the one born rich, since he doesn't make his living by sponging off an accidental fortune, but by the labor of his own hands.

"I would make this same comparison between a kingdom that abides by its mines and another that subsists on industry, agriculture, and commerce. The latter will always flourish, while the former will rush headlong into ruin.

"Not only the kingdom of the Indies, but Spain itself is certain proof of this truth. Many political thinkers attribute the decadence of its industry, agriculture, character,[7] population, and commerce to no other cause than the wealth it received from its colonies. And if that is true, as I believe, I can guarantee that the Americas will be happy the day when no lode of silver or gold ore remains to be found in their mining towns. Then their inhabitants will resort to agriculture, and you won't see (as you do today) so many hundreds of leagues of land lying fallow in spite of their enormous fertility; blessed poverty will keep from our shores the foreign ships that come in search of gold, to sell us the same things that we have at home; and we natives, pressed by need, will boost our industry in every branch known to life's luxuries or comfort; this will suffice to increase the numbers of farmers and artisans, and their growing numbers will lead to infinite weddings, which are avoided by the idlers and loafers of today; this multitude of marriages will naturally produce a numerous population, which will expand to fill this vast and fertile continent and give rise to estimable men in every class for the State; the precious goods that Nature has offered in abundance almost exclusively to the Americas, such as cochineal, cotton, sugar,

---

[6] [The Indies (*las Indias*): the Spanish term for Spain's American colonies, now commonly known as Latin America, though it is clear that Lizardi is referring in particular to Mexico. –Tr.]

[7] Referring to its ancient vigor and disdain for luxuries unknown to the Goths, the Visigoths, and so on.

cacao, and so forth, will take their place among the many rich lines of goods that will invite all the nations to undertake a profitable and active commerce with us; and finally, an endless number of circumstances that will necessarily link tightly with each other, the description of which I omit so as not to make my digression too prolix, will make the kingdom and its metropolis richer, happier, and more respected among their rivals than they have been since the days of Cortés and Pizarro.

"Do not think that I have wandered far from the main point at which I am driving in my conversation. I have just told you this so that you will realize that an abundance of gold and silver is so far from making mortals truly happy, that it more readily becomes the reason for their moral ruin, just as it causes the political decadence of states, and therefore we should neither ill use money, nor chase after it so avidly, nor guard it so jealously, that its loss would cause us irreparable grief, which might perhaps lead us to our utter ruin, as it did to foolish Don Anselmo.

"That poor wretch thought his whole happiness depended on his possession of a few shining shards of earth; he believed he had lost them; black sorrow overwhelmed his avaricious heart, and, unable to resist it, he hurled himself into the sea in an excess of desperation, losing all at once his honor and his life, and God grant he did not lose his soul.

"You were a witness to this fatal event, and you will never recall it without remarking that gold does not make us happy, that avarice is a great evil, and that we should avoid it with all our might.

"Don't think that I am preaching a disdain for wealth with the kind of art that so many philosophers from pagan times showed, when they spoke badly of wealth in revenge for how little of it they possessed. Much less would I think of praising poverty to the sky, when I myself, thanks to God, do not suffer from it. I'm no hypocrite; let's leave it to Seneca to say, in the heart of plenty, that 'no man is poor but he who believes he is'; that 'Nature is satisfied with bread and water, and no one who obtains those is poor'; that 'poverty is no trouble except for him who refuses it,' and other things along these lines that were no more than lip service, as they say; for in reality, at the time that he was writing this, he enjoyed the good graces of Nero, he was loved by his wife, he was earning enormous rents, he resided in magnificent palaces, and he relaxed in delicious gardens.[8]

"How sweet it must be (says one author) to moralize and preach virtue in the middle of such delights! To pretend that a man passing through this mortal life and surrounded by passions might be entirely perfect, is a chimera. It is easier to praise virtue than to practice it, and these authors depict man not as he is, but as he ought to be; that is why so few of the people we deal with in the world could pass as the originals for the portraits we find in books. Seneca himself, grasping the significance of this truth, went so far as to say that it would be impossible to find among men one as completely virtuous as he would wish, and that 'the best of men is he who has the fewest defects.' *Pro optimo est minime malus.*[9] Thus I am not demanding of you that you utterly disdain the goods of fortune, much less am I exhorting you to

---

[8] [A paraphrase of statements in Seneca, *Epistles*, ch. 25, as excerpted in Jamin, *Frutos.* –Tr.]

[9] [Seneca, *On Tranquility of Mind*, 7. –Tr.]

embrace an idle poverty.[10] If a dazzling state of luxury puts a man in risk of becoming wicked because he finds it too easy to satisfy his passions, a miserable state of poverty may reduce him to committing the foulest crimes.

"Far be it from me to tell you that poverty makes men wise and virtuous, as Horace said to Florus;[11] even less would I tell you that the poorest man is the happiest, since he lives a freer and more independent life, as I have heard from many who claim to envy the fate of the poor street porter; I recall the clever definition that Juvenal gave in his Satire III of the much vaunted liberty of the poor man, and I do not envy him. That witty genius said, 'This is the poor man's liberty: to beg for pardon from the man who has harmed him, and to kiss the hand of the man who has beaten him, hoping to escape with a few teeth left in his mouth.' Those are the great privileges that this class of poor folk enjoys! And to this we could add their absolute lack of shame and their stone-like resignation to suffering life's discomforts; this type of poverty you should avoid.

"What I do advise you is never to base your happiness on wealth; never to covet it or chase after it longingly; and if you do have wealth, not to worship it or make yourself its slave; but I also advise you to work for your living, and finally, to crave moderation, and to be content with it, for that is the most appropriate state for living a tranquil life.

"This advice is wise, and decreed by God Himself in Proverbs 30, verse 9, through the mouth of the sage who said, 'Give me neither poverty nor riches; give me only the necessaries of life: lest perhaps being filled, I should be tempted to deny, and say: Who is the Lord? or being compelled by poverty, I should steal, and forswear the name of my God. . . . '"

This was as far as the colonel had gotten when his conversation was interrupted by the clapping and shouting of the cabin boys and seamen, who were jumping up and down and yelling on deck, "Land! Land!"

At the gratifying sound of these cries, everyone abandoned what they were doing and came up on deck, some with spyglasses and others without, to assure themselves with their own eyes or with their neighbor's whether what the boys' shouts had announced was really true.

The closer the ship came to the coast, the more they were all convinced it was real—motive enough for the captain to order that the crew be given a good drink and double rations that day, which they accepted even more heartily after the first mate (who had recovered from his illness) assured them that, with the aid of God and the favorable winds we were having, we would disembark the following day in Cavite, the bay of Manila.

That night and the rest of the appointed day were spent in song, games, and pleasant conversations, and around five in the afternoon we anchored in the long-awaited port.

---

[10] The colonel used this expression to signify that he was not referring to evangelical poverty, which is always commendable but is not for everyone, for not all of us have the disposition of spirit that it demands.

[11] [Horace, *Epistle* I, III: 25–29. –Tr.]

The staff officers set about disembarking at once, and I, too, got to put ashore early with my boss. The next day, they continued unloading everything else, and when it was all done, everyone saw about getting to Manila, which was their place of residence; and we were among the first to go, since the colonel had no commercial ties to slow him down.

We reached the city, my colonel delivered the galley convicts to the governor, handed the egotist's goods over to his family, discreetly concealing the sad manner of his death, and we went to the colonel's house, where I served him and accompanied him for eight years, the full length of my sentence, and during that time, I amassed a fair amount of money while serving him.

Copy of the documents that demonstrate the arbitrary nature of the Spanish government in this America, as relates to this fourth volume, for which reason its prompt publication was hindered at the time, and it has not seen the light of the public until the present. The original documents are in my possession.[1]

Most Excellent Sir: I, Don Joaquín Fernández de Lizardi, appear before you with all due respect and declare: that the gentleman who preceded you in office gave me his permission to print a small book that I have composed under the title of *The Mangy Parrot*, pending the approval of the honorable judge Don Felipe Martínez.

With this condition and permission, the first three volumes of this little book have been published. The fourth is finished and has been approved by the ecclesiastical judge, as Your Excellency may see by the original document that I append; and, given that the license of Your Excellency is needed for its publication, I beg you to grant it to me, and to decree whether it should pass to the censor's office of Sr. Martínez like the three previous volumes, or to some other person more to Your Excellency's liking.

God keep Your Excellency many years. Mexico, 3 October, 1816. *Joaquín Fernández de Lizardi.*

Mexico, 6 October, 1816. Send it to the censor's office of the criminal court judge Don Felipe Martínez. (A signature.)

Most Excellent Sir: I have seen and inspected the fourth volume of *The Mangy Parrot:* everything that is marked in the margin in the fourth chapter, speaking about the blacks, appears to me very repetitious, inopportune, harmful under the circumstances, and impolitic, for it is directed against a trade that the king has permitted; similarly, the words marked in the margin and underlined in the sixth chapter should be suppressed; as for the rest, I find nothing opposed to the royal prerogatives of His Majesty; and if Your Excellency pleases, you may grant your license for its printing. Mexico, 19 October, 1816. *Martínez.*

Mexico, 29 November, 1816. There being no reason to publish this paper, archive the original, and notify the author that no permission is granted for the publication he has requested. (A signature.)

Done. (A signature.)

---

[1] [These documents were published at this point in the text in the 3rd edition of 1830–1831, which, as noted here, was the first time that the last sixteen chapters of the book were published. The 4th and 6th chapters of volume 4 mentioned in the documents correspond to Chapters 37 and 39 in the present translation. –Tr.]

CHAPTER 37

PERIQUILLO DESCRIBES HIS GOOD BEHAVIOR IN MANILA,
THE DUEL BETWEEN AN ENGLISHMAN AND A BLACK,
AND A LITTLE ARGUMENT THAT IS NOT TO BE MISSED

We men undergo deep moral changes within ourselves from time to time, the origins of which we might not even be able to guess at, in much the same way that, in the physical world, we feel many effects of Nature and do not know what cause produced them, as is still the case with the attractive power of the magnet or the power of electricity; this is why the poet sang: happy is he who can know the cause of things.[1]

But, just as we make use of physical phenomena without investigating them, I profited in Manila from the results of my moral phenomenon without bothering at the time to analyze its origins.

It may have been because I had ended up so far from my homeland, or because I wanted to free myself from the discomforts of having to spend the eight years of my sentence in military service, or because of the splendid treatment that the colonel showed me (which is the most likely reason), but the fact of the matter is that I endeavored to repay him for his trust, and in Manila I became a full-fledged upright man.

Each day I earned more of the colonel's love and more of his trust, and I came to gain so much of each that at last I was the one who controlled all his interests, which I dealt with as I pleased; but I figured out how to manage things so well that, far from frittering away his fortune (as might have been expected from me), I increased it considerably by making as many commercial deals as I safely could.

My colonel knew about my trading; but since he saw that I wasn't taking anything for myself—indeed, I kept a book on the desk that I myself had drawn up and titled *Economic Notebook Detailing the State of My Master's Properties*—he was satisfied with it, and crowed about the honesty of "his son," which is what that good man called me.

Since the prominent citizens of Manila saw the way the colonel treated me, the trust he placed in me, and the affection that he showered on me, everyone who appreciated his friendship held me in special regard and greater esteem than they would have given a simple assistant, and the appreciation that the decent people gave me served to restrain me and keep me from doing things that might be talked about in that city. So you see that, when properly ordered, self-love is no vice, but a principle of virtue.

Since I lived a proper life during those eight years, I did not have any perilous adventures worth mentioning. I have already told you that honest men have few misfortunes to recount. Nevertheless, I witnessed a few incidents that were out of the ordinary. One of them was the following:

One year, after a few foreigners had landed at the port and entered the city on business, one rich, but black, merchant was walking down the street. He must have

---

[1] [Virgil, *Georgics*, II: 40. –Tr.]

been on some very important business, because he was coming down the street very quickly and distractedly, and in his headlong rush he couldn't stop before running straight into an English officer who was busy courting a young lady from one of the prominent local families; but the crash or collision was so hard that if the Manila girl hadn't supported him, he would have hit the ground in a very unpleasant way. Even so, this street corner encounter knocked his hat off and mussed his hair.

The young officer's vanity couldn't bear this tremendous loss, so he immediately ran to where the black man stood, drawing his sword. The poor black man was caught unprepared, because he carried no sword, and he may well have believed that the end of his days had come. The young lady and others accompanying the officer restrained him, though he never ceased to issue blustery threats along with a thousand promises to vindicate his honor, which had been wounded by a black man.

He denigrated and reviled the guiltless colored man so much that the latter told him, in English, "Sir, let us be quiet; tomorrow I will wait for you to give you satisfaction with a pistol in the park."

The officer agreed, and the matter was smoothed over, or so it seemed.

I witnessed the encounter and, since I half understood a little English, I knew the time and place that had been agreed upon for the duel, and I showed up there punctually to see how the affair would end.

Indeed, both arrived at the appointed time, each with a friend whom he had named as his second. After they met, the black man took out two pistols and, presenting them to the officer, said, "Sir, I did not intend to offend your honor yesterday; running into you was an unforeseen accident; you wore yourself out cursing me, and even tried to wound or kill me; I had no weapon to defend myself at the moment of your rage, so I summoned you to a duel, knowing that it would be the quickest way to stop you and give you time to calm down; and now I have come to give you satisfaction with a pistol, just as I promised."

"Fine, then," said the Englishman, "let us begin; for, even though it is neither legitimate nor decent for me to measure my valor against a black man, I am nevertheless sure to punish a bold villain, and so I have accepted your challenge. Let us choose pistols."

"Very well," said the black man; "but you should know that I did not intend to offend you yesterday, and neither have I come here today with that plan in mind. It seems to me not honorable, but capricious for a man of your class to endeavor to kill or be killed over such a meaningless trifle, just as it undoubtedly is to feel insulted by an unforeseen accident; but if the satisfaction I have given you means nothing, and you will only be satisfied by killing or dying, I do not want to be guilty of murder, nor to expose myself to dying though innocent, which is what would happen if you hit me or I hit you with the pistols. So, without refusing the challenge, may the best man win, and may fate decide in favor of the one who has justice on his side. Please take both pistols; one is loaded with two bullets and the other is empty; shuffle them around, give me whichever one you prefer, and let the advantage fall as it may."

This proposal caught the officer by surprise; the witnesses said that this was not the proper order of the duel, that they should both fight with equal arms, and other things that did not convince our black man, for he insisted that they had to carry out the duel this way so that he could console himself with the thought that, if he killed his opponent, it would be because heaven had so ordered things or had specially favored him; and that if he died, it would not be because of his guilt, but by the disposition of chance, just as he might die in a shipwreck. To this he added that, since neither of them would have the advantage, refusing the challenge could only be attributed to cowardice.

As soon as the hot-blooded youth heard this word, he disregarded the witnesses' arguments, shuffled the pistols, and took the one that he felt was right, giving the other one to the black man.

They turned back to back, walked a short distance, and wheeled around to face each other; the officer fired at the black man, but to no avail, because he had picked the empty pistol. This turn of events stunned him and, together with the witnesses, he believed that he would become the defenseless victim of the black man's wrath; but the latter said, with the greatest generosity, "Sir, we have both come off well; the duel is over; you have had no choice but to accept it, and I could have done nothing else myself. Firing or not firing depends on my choice; but since I never meant to offend you, how could I wish to do so now, seeing you disarmed? Let us be friends, if you are satisfied; but if only my blood will satisfy you, please take the loaded pistol and fire both bullets at my chest."

Saying this, he offered the horrendous weapon to the officer, who, moved by this show of generosity, took the pistol, fired it into the air, and threw his outstretched arms around the black man, telling him with the greatest tenderness, "Yes, sir, we are friends, and shall be friends forever; please forgive my vanity and my madness. I never believed that black men were capable of having such great souls."

"That is a prejudice that many sectarians still maintain," said the black man, as he embraced the officer effusively.

All of us who were present at this affair were interested in seeing this new friendship sealed, and I, though the least known among them, was not embarrassed to offer myself as their friend, begging them to receive me as the third member of their party and to accept my offer of taking them for a cup of *ponche* or *sangría* in the nearest café.

They both thanked me for my offer, and we went to the café, where I ordered a good refreshment. We merrily ate and drank as much as we liked; and I, wishing to hear the black man explain himself, said to them, "Dear gentlemen, the last statement you made was an enigma to me, when you, sir, said that you never believed that black men were capable of having generous souls, and you, sir, responded by saying that this way of thinking was a prejudice; to be sure, up until today I have thought the same as the captain here, and I would appreciate learning from your own mouth the fundamental reasons you have for asserting that such a thought is a prejudice."

"I feel myself," said the judicious black man, "caught between respect and gratitude. As you know, any conversation that makes comparisons is hateful. In order to answer you clearly, I would have to draw comparisons, and then perhaps my good friend the officer would be upset, in which case I would be doing badly by him. But if I do not satisfy your wish, I would fall short of the gratitude that I owe you for your friendship; and so. . . . "

"No, no, sir," said the officer; "I wish to please you and make you see not only that, if I have prejudices, I am not headstrong about them, but that I would like to get rid of as many of them as I can; and I should also like that these gentlemen have the pleasure of hearing you speak on the subject, and I am especially grateful to have a mediator in our dispute who has aired this question for me."

"Well, in that case," said the black man, turning to face me, "I'd like you to know that thinking a black man is less than a white man is a prejudice that is generally opposed to the principles of reason, humanity, and moral virtue. I could not tell you right now whether it is considered acceptable by any particular religions, or whether it is sustained by commerce, ambition, vanity, or despotism.

"But I should like it if one of you, whoever knows the most arguments to the contrary, would argue against me and try to persuade me, were that possible.

"I know and have read a bit of the many things that wise and sensitive writers have written in this century in favor of my opinion; but I also know that these doctrines have remained mere theories, because in practice I find no difference between what the Europeans did to blacks in the 17th century and what they do today. At that time, greed brought their vessels to the shores of my countrymen, and they filled their ships with those men, either through bribes or through force; they then disgorged them onto their docks, and they trafficked contemptibly in human blood.

"During these voyages, how did they treat us? In the rudest, most inhumane way. I do not wish to cite to you the histories written by your own compatriots, guided as they were by truth, because I assume that you know them, and also because I do not want to disturb your sensibilities; for who would not grieve on hearing that on one occasion, when the child of an unhappy black woman was crying on board and its cries disturbed the captain's sleep, he ordered that unfortunate infant tossed into the sea, and that this scandal to Nature was carried out?

"As for the service that my countrymen (and your fellow men) performed for the gentlemen who bought them, how did it go for them? Just as cruelly. Let the island of Haiti, today known as Santo Domingo, tell us; let the island of Cuba or Havana tell us: there they would provide the slaves with a cab to hire or a supply of sweets to sell, and obliged them to pay their masters a fixed amount of tribute every day, in repayment, as it were, for the money their masters had spent to buy them. And if the black men did not manage to get enough fares for their cabs, what did they suffer? The lash. And what did the black women have to do if they couldn't sell all their sweets? Prostitute themselves. Caves of Havana, avenues of Guanabacoa, speak for me!

"And if those black women gave birth to the fruits of their lewdness or need in their masters' homes, what was done to them? Nothing; the results of the crime were received with glee, for in them the masters enjoyed one more little slave.

"The worst of it is that, when it comes to it, what happened in Havana happened in the same way everywhere, and to this day I have found no difference in the matter between that century and this. Cruelties, contemptible acts, and outrages against humanity were committed then; and outrages, contemptible acts, and cruelties are being committed today, still against humanity, under the same pretexts.

"Humanity, says the celebrated Buffon, 'cries out against these odious practices, which were introduced by greed, and which would perhaps be revived any day, if our laws did not restrain the brutality of the slave masters by taking measures to mitigate somewhat the misery of their slaves; they are forced to work very hard and they are given very little to eat, even of the most common types of food, with the excuse that blacks tolerate hunger easily, that the amount of food that a European needs for one meal will sustain one of them for three days, and that no matter how little they eat and sleep, they are always just as robust and have just as much strength to work. But how can men with any last trace of human feeling adopt such cruel maxims, elevate them into prejudices, and attempt to use them to justify the horrible excesses to which they have been led by their hunger for gold? Let us turn away from such bar-barous men. . . . '[2]

"It is true that the cultured governments have repudiated this illicit and shameless trade, and without trying to flatter Spain, your government has been one of the most opposed. You," the black man said to me, "you, as a Spaniard, must be well aware of the restrictions that your kings have placed on this traffic, and you must know of the decrees that Charles III issued regulating the treatment of slaves; but all that has not been enough to stay such an impure trade. I am not surprised; that is one of the con-sequences of greed. What will man not do, what crime will he not commit, when it comes to satisfying that passion? What does amaze and scandalize me is to see this trade tolerated and these evil practices permitted in those nations where they say that peace and religion reign, and in those where individuals are recommended to love their fellow man as they love themselves. I wish, gentlemen, that you could help me decipher this enigma. How can I properly fulfill the precepts of the religion that obliges me to love my neighbor as myself, and to do nothing to anyone else that I would not have done to me, by buying a poor black man for my vile self-interest, forcing him to pay tribute to me as his tyrannical master, paying no attention to his happiness and perhaps not even his sustenance, and treating him at times as little more than a beast? I do not understand, I repeat, how I could fulfill those holy obli-gations in the midst of such iniquities. If either of you knows how those things can be reconciled, I would appreciate it if you could teach me, just in case I wanted to become a Christian some day and buy black men as if they were horses. The worst of it is that I have heard it stated as a fact that Christians are normally not permitted to speak with this much clarity, for what they call reasons of State or who knows what; if this is indeed true, I could never join such a religion; but I think that this is slander spread by those who do not like Christianity.

"Given all this, I have to conclude that the mistreatment, the harshness, and the disdain that have been shown to blacks result from no other origin than the haughti-ness of whites, which consists in believing that blacks are naturally inferior, which, as I have said, is an old and irrational prejudice.

"All you Europeans recognize one man as the beginning and origin of all men; at least, the Christians recognize no other progenitor than Adam, from whom, as from the trunk of a robust tree, all other offspring in the universe descend or derive. If that is so, and if you believe it and confess it in good faith, then you will

---

[2] [Georges Louis Leclerc, Comte de Buffon, *Histoire naturelle de l'homme* (1749; *Natural History, General and Particular*, Edinburgh, 1780). –Tr.]

have to be accused of stupidity for making distinctions among his offspring simply because they vary in color, when that variation is an effect of the climate or of nutrition, or if you prefer, of some property that the blood has acquired and has transmitted to this posterity or that through inheritance. When you read that the blacks disdain the whites for being white, you don't hesitate to judge them stupid; but you never judge yourselves with the same severity when you think in the same way as they do.

"If you think less of blacks because of what you call their barbaric customs, their wild educations, and their lack of European civilization, you should realize that every nation finds the customs of others barbarous and uncivilized. A refined European would be a barbarian in Senegal, the Congo, Cape Verde, and so on, for he would be ignorant of their religious rites, their civil laws, their provincial customs, and finally, their languages. Transport in your mind a wise Parisian courtesan to any one of these countries, and you will see him turned into a blockhead who can barely manage, with a thousand gestures, to get across the idea that he is hungry. Therefore, if every religion has its rites, every nation its laws, and every province its customs, it is a very crass mistake to label as stupid or savage those who do not coincide with our way of thinking, even if ours might be the one that is in closest agreement with Nature, for if other people are innocently ignorant of these prerequisites, we should not blame it on them.

"I understand that man has had the seeds of vice and virtue alike planted deep inside himself; his heart is a fertile field in which either one may bear fruit, depending on his inclination or his education. His inclination is influenced by climate, food, and his individual organization; and his education, by religion, government, local usages, and the degree of care his parents give him. So there is nothing to be surprised at if nations vary greatly in their customs, given how diverse their rites, usages, and governments are.

"Therefore it is an error to label as barbaric the individuals of this people or that, who do not subscribe to our usages, whether because they are unfamiliar with them or because they reject them. The most sacred customs of one nation are held to be abuses in another, and even the most cultured and civilized peoples of Europe, over the course of time, have discarded as rubbish a thousand worn-out customs that they once revered as civic dogmas.

"From what I have said, we can deduce: that disdaining blacks for their color and for the difference in their religions and customs is an error; that mistreating them for these reasons is cruelty; and that being convinced that they are not capable of having great souls that cultivate the moral virtues is an extremely crass prejudice, as I have told the officer, and a prejudice that experience should have disproved for you, for wise blacks and brave blacks have flourished among you; just, unselfish, sensitive, grateful, and even admirably heroic blacks."

The black man finished speaking, and we, having nothing to respond, sat quiet as well, until the officer said, "I am convinced of these truths, more by your example than by your arguments, and from this day forth I will believe that blacks are every bit as much men as whites, just as susceptible to vices and virtues as we are, and with no other distinction than the accidental one of color, by which alone we must not, in all justice, label the inner nature of a thinking being, much less judge him highly or cut him down."

The conversation was about to break up when I, still desiring to listen to the black man, refilled our glasses, proposed a toast to our fellow men, the blacks, and after this pleasant ceremony, said to our black man, "*Mister*, it is true that all men descend, beyond our first Maker, from a first creation, call him Adam or however you wish; it likewise follows from this natural principle that we are all intimately linked by a certain undeniable connection or kinship, so that the Emperor of Germany, like it or not, is related to the foulest thief, and the king of France is kin to the lowest ragman in my country, much as he'd like to deny it; the fact is, all of us men are each other's kin, for our ancestor's blood circulates in all our veins; and therefore it is a prejudice, as you say, or a quixotic notion, to disdain a black man for being black; an act of cruelty to buy and sell him; and an intolerable act of tyranny to mistreat him.

"I agree enthusiastically with all this, for such treatment is repugnant to any rational man; but if we restrict what you call disdain to a certain air of lordship, such as that with which a king looks at his vassals, a boss at his subordinates, a prelate at his subjects, a master at his servants, and a noble at the plebeians, it seems to me that there is a right and proper place for it in the economic order of the world; for if, because we are all sons of the same father and all part of the same big family, we were to treat each other all in the same way, the ideas of submission, inferiority, and obedience would surely be lost, and the universe would descend into the sort of chaos in which all men would expect to be superiors: all kings, judges, nobles, and magistrates; and then who would obey? Who would make the laws? Who would restrain the depraved man by threats of punishment? And who would guarantee the individual citizen's security? Everything would become confused, and the terms *equality* and *liberty* would become synonymous with anarchy and allowing every passion to run riot. Each man would feel himself free to raise himself up to lord it over the rest; natural pride would make each man think his own atrocities were justified; and in this case, no one would feel himself subject to any religion, any government, or any law, for everyone would want to be the universal legislator and pontiff; and as you can see, in this sad hypothesis there would be nothing but murders, robberies, rapes, sacrileges, and crimes.

"But fortunately for us, man has seen from the beginning that such a brutal state of liberty would be far too harmful to him, and so he has subjected himself willingly and uncoerced; he has accepted religions and governments, sworn fealty to their laws, and bowed his neck under the yoke of their kings or the heads of their republics. This subjection, born of a well-ordered egotism, has given rise to the differences between superiors and inferiors that we find in every kind of State, and in virtue of this alternative argument, it does not seem to me that it is unnatural for masters to treat their servants with authority, nor for servants to recognize their masters with submission; and since black slaves are a certain kind of servant, acquired with particular rights by virtue of the money they cost, it is easy to see that they should live with more subjection and obedience to their masters, and that their masters have twice the authority to give them orders."

I finished speaking, and the black man answered, "Spaniard, flattery is not my custom; please forgive me if my sincerity discomfits you; but you have stated a number of truths that I have not denied, yet from them you have tried to deduce a conclusion that I will never concede. It is indisputable that the hierarchical order is well established in the world, and among the blacks whom you call savages, there is a certain kind of society that, even if it and their religions alike are riddled with a thousand errors, proves that in their state of barbarity, those men have some idea of the Divinity and of the necessity of living in dependency, which is what you Europeans call living in society. It follows that they must necessarily recognize superiors and subject themselves to some laws. Nature and Fortune themselves decree that some men must accept certain kinds of subordination, while conferring a certain authority on other men; and so, is there any nation, no matter how barbaric, that does not recognize the father's authority to command his son, or the son's obligation to obey his father? I have never heard of a single nation that is set apart from these innate sentiments. The same holds for the man in regard to his wife, and the wife toward her husband; the master in regard to his servant; the lord in regard to his vassals; the vassals toward their lords; and so on. And is there any nation or people among those called savage, I ask again, in which men fail to be tied to each other by some of these connections? There is not, because in every one of them there are men and women, parents and children, old men and young lads. Thinking that there is some people in the world among whom men live in absolute independence and enjoy such a brutal liberty that each man does as he wishes without any respect for or subordination to any other man, is thus a mere fantasy, for not only has there never been such a nation, despite all the lies that travelers might tell: there never could be one, because man is always haughty and would always aspire to satisfy his passions at any cost; and with every man hoping to do the same, each would try to raise himself up as a tyrant over the others, and this tumultuous disorder would inescapably result in the ruin of every individual. Up to this point, you and I are in agreement. Nor do I think it unreasonable that masters and every class of superior should behave with a certain circumspection toward their subjects. That is in order, because if everyone were treated with equality, the subjects would lose their respect for the masters, and this loss would be followed by insubordination, which would lead to insults, and then to the general upheaval of the State. But I cannot agree that this kind of gravity or seriousness should lead the masters to scowling in pride and arrogance. I am sure that, just as behaving seriously will make them beloved, behaving arrogantly will make them detestable. It is a prejudice to think that seriousness is opposed to affability, when both work together to make a superior beloved and respected. It would be ridiculous for a superior to expose himself to losing the respect of his inferiors by making himself one of them; but it is also abominable to have to deal with a superior who is constantly looking down on his subjects with a stiff neck, growling a few scant words, screwing up his eyes, and wrinkling his nose like a bulldog. Far from being a virtue, this is vice; not a serious, but a quixotic notion. No one buys the hearts of men more cheaply than a superior, and the less it costs him, the greater his superiority. A gentle glance, a soft reply, a courteous gesture: these things cost little, but are worth much for gaining someone's good will; but unfortunately, affability is scarcely known among the great. They use it, true; but they use it with the people they need, not with those who need them.

"I have traveled through a few provinces of Europe, and in each of them I have observed this kind of conduct not only among the great superiors, but among every rich . . . why did I say rich? A drudge, an office flunky, a steward in a great house, a grocer's boy, a nobody who enjoys any degree of protection from his master or head boss, will behave more arrogantly and rudely toward anyone who is forced to deal with him than perhaps even the man on whose favor his haughtiness depends. Poor wretches! They do not realize that the ones who suffer their snubs are the first to denounce their uncivil behavior and their high and mighty personalities in the cafés, on the streets, and at social gatherings, not neglecting to look into their family background and the possibly shameful ways in which they managed to raise themselves up.

"I have gone on for too long, gentlemen; but you should reflect on the fact that I have learned to reconcile the seriousness appropriate to a master—that is, to any superior—with the affability and humane treatment that all men deserve; and you, Spaniard, should note that the laws of society are one thing, and the prejudices of pride are another; but as for the masters of blacks having 'twice the authority,' as you have said, to give them orders, I will say nothing, because I think you said it merely to pass the time, for you cannot be unaware that no law, human or divine, can justifying trafficking in the blood of men."

Saying this, our black man rose and, without demanding a reply to a statement that had none, he toasted us for the last time and, after we all embraced and offered each other our reciprocal service and friendship, we each retired to our homes.

A few days later, I had the satisfaction of meeting now and again with my two friends, the officer and the black man, and bringing them to the house of the colonel, who gave them a royal welcome; but this satisfaction was short-lived, because a month after the event that I have just related, the pair set sail for London.

CHAPTER 38

During the eight years that I lived with the colonel, I behaved honorably and responded honorably to his trust; this afforded me a few reasonable advantages, for my boss loved me, and he had money, so he generously granted me as much as I requested to buy several packets of goods each year, which I sent through him to a few merchants to sell for me in Acapulco. As everyone knows, goods from China—especially in those days, when things were done in the shadow of what they called the permit offices[1]—yielded a profit of a hundred percent or more. It's easy to imagine, therefore, that from a beginning sum of 1,000 pesos, after my eight years in Manila and four successful voyages that I managed to have my agents make, I was worth some 8,000, all easily acquired and just as easily saved, since I had nothing to spend my pesos on and no friends to squander them for me.

On the day that I completed the eight years of my sentence (counting from the day that I enlisted in Mexico), the colonel called me and said, "You have now served by my side the length of time that you were to serve in the militia as your punishment, according to the sentence you were handed down in Mexico for your waywardness. In my company you have behaved with honor, and I have truly loved you, as I have shown you in my actions. Banished to a foreign land, you have acquired a tidy sum that you were never able to amass in your homeland; you should attribute this not to good luck, but to your reformed habits, which ought to teach you that a man can have no better fortune than his own reformed conduct, and no better homeland than the place where he devotes himself to working as an upright man. Up until today you have been merely my adjutant in name, though not in the way you have been treated; but you are henceforth relieved of that office; you are free: here, take your discharge papers; you know that I am holding 8,000 pesos for you, and so, if you want to return to your homeland, get your things ready for when the ship departs."

"Sir," I said, touched by his generosity, "I do not know how to tell you how grateful I am to Your Honor for the all the many favors I owe you, and Your Honor's proposal saddens me greatly, for even though I celebrate being freed from the militia, I certainly would not like to leave this house, but rather to stay here even though it be to serve as your lowest servant; for I recognize full well that by detaching myself from Your Honor, I would be losing not my boss or my master, but my benefactor, my best friend, and my father."

"Come on, stop that," said the colonel; "I didn't tell you those things because I'm unhappy with you or because I want to kick you out of my house (which you should think of as your own), but to put you in full possession of your liberty; for even though you have served me like a son, you came to me as a prisoner, and whether

---

[1] [Permit offices (*cajas de permiso*): customs offices that issued permits for the strictly regulated and monopolized official trade with the Philippines until the late 1700s. –Tr.]

you liked it or not, you would have had to stay in Manila all this time. Besides, I feel that even though love for one's homeland is a prejudice, it is one of those prejudices that are not only innocent in themselves, but that can serve as the basis for certain civic and moral virtues. I have told you before, and you have read, that man should be a cosmopolitan in this world, a fellow countryman to all his fellow men, and that the philosopher's homeland is the world; but not all men are philosophers, so we must agree or at least pretend to agree with the outdated ideas of most men, because it would be an arduous, if not impossible, task to reduce them all to the focal point of reason; and the prejudice of setting apart the place of our birth with a certain particular love is very ancient, very deeply rooted, and very hallowed by the mass of men. You will remember reading how Ovid howled in Pontus, not so much for the stormy climate or his fear of the Getae—a barbaric, warlike, and cruel nation—as for his missing Rome, his homeland; you've read his letters, and in them you've seen the efforts he made to come at least a bit closer to home in his exile, no matter how much flattery he had to lavish, going so far as to deify Caesar Augustus, the man who had banished him. But why waste time citing that example of love for country, when you yourself have seen how an Indian from the village of Ixtacalco wouldn't trade his shack for the viceroy's palace in Mexico? Indeed, call it prejudice or what you will, this love for the land where we were born is somehow so forceful that we would have to be great philosophers indeed to free ourselves from it, and the worst of it is that we couldn't repudiate this particular obligation without bringing down upon ourselves an ugly reputation as ingrates, villains, and traitors. That is why I wanted to inform you, Pedrillo, of the freedom you now enjoy, and also because I thought that your greatest satisfaction would be to restore yourself to your homeland and to the bosom of your friends and family."

"That is all very well, sir," I said; "it would be proper to love one's homeland because one was born there, or because of the links that tie men to one another; but we will have to leave that to those who consider themselves the sons of their homeland, and for those whom their country has served as a mother; not for me, however, for with me she has played a stepmother. Among my friends, I have observed the most sordid interest for private gain, so that whenever I had one peso, I could count on having endless numbers of friends; but as soon as they saw that I was broke, they'd do a swift about-face and leave me to my destitution, and even act embarrassed to speak with me; among my family, I've known the worst kind of rejection, and the greatest ingratitude among my fellow countrymen. Could I possibly love a land like that on account of her people? No, sir; it is easier to recognize her as a mother on account of her houses and avenues, her Orilla, Ixtacalco, and Santa Anita, her San Agustín de las Cuevas, San Ángel, and Tacubaya, and things like that. Indeed I assure Your Honor that I have no other reason to miss her. There isn't a soul there who's worth a single thought of mine, even while I'm dreaming about the fiesta of Santiago and the lunch stands of Las Cañitas and Nana Rosa."[2]

---

[2] [The places that Periquillo remembers were all pleasure spots to the south of the city (and now swallowed up by its expansion), where the well-off of Mexico City went to relax on weekends and holidays. The editor of the 4th edition comments on the last two:]

The first *almuercería* [lunch stand] was famous in olden times for the delicious enchiladas

"No, don't put yourself out trying to convince me of your way of thinking," said the colonel; "but you should know that you're being very childish and very unjust. It is true that for many people, not just for you, the country is a stepmother; but beyond political reasons that would hinder an equality of fortunes anywhere, you must realize that, for many people with thick skulls, it's their own fault that they languish in their homelands, no matter how charitable their fellow countrymen are; because who would want to loan his money or offer his house to a dissolute, vice-ridden young fellow? Nobody. And if that's the case, should those rogues complain about their country, or rather about their own disorderly conduct? You yourself are irrefutable testimony to this truth; you've told me about your former life: examine it, and you'll see that all the troubles you went through in Mexico, including being thrown into jail as a thief and finally being banished as a prisoner, weren't the fault of your country or of your fellow countrymen's bad character, but of your own follies and your depraved friends."

While the colonel was making this sound speech, I looked back through the annals of my life, and I saw only too clearly that all was just as he was telling me, and I silently confirmed his assertions, remembering both the bad friends who had led me astray, such as Januario, Martín Pelayo, El Aguilucho, and more, and other good friends who had tried to restrain me with their advice, and had even helped me with their money, such as Don Antonio, the owner of the inn, the man in rags, and the like; and so, convinced deep down, I told my boss, "Sir, there is no doubt that it is just as you have told me; I realize that I am still very rough-edged, and I need many more blows of your sound doctrine to get the polish I need; and because of that, I would rather not leave your house."

"No need for all that," said the colonel; "so long as you keep behaving as you have up to now, this will always be your house, and I will be your father."

I gave him a hearty embrace for the favor he had shown me, and after this serious session I remained in his company, with the same trust and enjoying the same satisfactions as ever; but the end date to my happiness was drawing near, and soon it was over.

One day about two months after my return to civilian life, after dinner, my master suffered an attack of apoplexy that was so sudden and grave that he scarcely had a long enough respite to receive the sacrament of absolution, and by twilight he passed away in my arms, leaving me in the deepest grief and despair.

The best society of Manila immediately gathered at the house; they arranged to give the body a military funeral, and to do everything that was necessary at that hour, because I was not capable of doing anything.

---

and delicacies it served, in back of the Regina church in a shack constructed of canes, from which it derived the name of *Las Cañitas*. In later days, a tavern with the same name was built next to the church itself, but it never acquired the same reputation, and it is now gone as well.

On the banks of the irrigation canal on the Paseo de la Viga, there was a little garden park where Nana Rosa, who lived to be nearly a hundred, attracted the people of Mexico, with her affability and pleasantries, to enjoy merry country outings in her house, charging them stiffly for the good luncheon spreads she prepared; and even today, the *envueltos de Nana Rosa* still figure in the cookbooks. –E.

Since self-interest is the devil, there was of course someone who then tried to get the authorities to confiscate the late colonel's estate, asserting that he had died intestate; but the colonel's confessor quickly set about revealing the fraud, asking me for the key to his private desk.

I gave it to him, and the authorities removed the sealed testament that my master had made some days earlier; the testament was read, and we learned that he had named as his executor his *compadre* the Count of San Tirso, a very virtuous gentleman who loved him dearly.

The testament declared that upon his death, all his remaining debts should be paid by his estate, and that whatever remained should be divided into three parts, one to be given to a niece he had in Spain, in the city of Burgos; one to me, if I were still in his company; and the third to the poor people of Manila, or wherever he was living when he died; and in case I was no longer at his side, the portion he had willed to me should be awarded to the poor.

That ended the underhanded hopes of those who had alleged the intestate death, and the funeral could go forth.

The next day, hardly had the news of the colonel's death hit the city when the house filled up with people; but what kind of people? Poor young women, destitute widows, defenseless orphans, and other such unfortunates, whom my master had aided in utter silence, and who depended on his charity for their livelihood.

The body was in the coffin in the center of the drawing room, surrounded by all those unhappy families, who wept bitterly at the orphanhood they faced with the death of their benefactor, whose hands they held with the greatest tenderness, kissing them and wetting them with their tears, while crying, "He is dead—our patron, our father, our best friend. . . . Who will console us now? Who can take his place?"

Neither the public funeral nor the grand gentlemen who, as always, solemnized the proceedings with their ceremonious presence, were enough to restrain all the poor people who felt themselves bereft and subject now to the hard yoke of destitution. They all wept, moaned, and sighed, and even when they could halt their crying, they gave public testimony to their benefactor's generosity in the sad expressions on their faces.

They did not leave the body until the earth had covered it. The funeral music harmonized sweetly with the sorrowing moans of the poor folk who were the legitimate mourners of the deceased, and the vaults of the sacred temple echoed with the final exertions of their deepest sentiments.

At the conclusion of this religious ceremony, I returned home filled with such grief that I was not capable of receiving the visitors who came with their condolences during the nine days of mourning.

After that period was past, the executor inventoried the colonel's estate; everything was done properly, his will and testament was carried out, they set aside the portion that belonged to me—3,000 some-odd pesos, which I received with great affliction because of the way that they had come to me.

After about three months, I was feeling calmer, and I no longer recalled my father and patron so constantly; as you can see, his memory lived on in me much longer than my memories of others, for as I have noted, the children, wives, and friends of the dead—even those who pride themselves on being well loved—tend to forget them more quickly and to begin to enjoy themselves as coolly as if they didn't know them at all, despite the black mourning clothes they wear to remind them of the deceased during this time.

Since I now had more than 11,000 pesos of my own, and was well thought of in Manila, I endeavored not to stray from the way of life I had led while the colonel was alive, despite the shady advice and provocations of false friends, who never fail to show up around unencumbered men with money; I did this to keep from squandering my money, but also to keep from losing the reputation that I had acquired as an upright man. How true it is that the love of money and our own self-love, though not virtues, can restrain us and cause us not to stoop to vice!

This obvious principle leads to a necessary consequence: the less a man has to lose, the bigger a rogue he is, or if not, the more likely he is to become one. That is why the poorest and dirtiest men in a republic are the most depraved and dissolute, because they have no honor or wealth to lose; and by the same token, they are more prone to commit any crime and undertake any act, no matter how base and loathsome; likewise, reason decrees that their superiors should make the greatest efforts to insure that they not grow up to be useless idlers.

But, leaving these reflections to those who have the position of ruling others, and returning to myself, let me say: when I found myself alone in Manila and with this much money, a desire came over me to return to my homeland, both so that my fellow countrymen could see how I had reformed my behavior, and so that I could show off in Mexico and enjoy my wealth, as I felt I could now call it, according to my calculations.

To do this, I put my coins to timely use, buying very low, and when it was time for the ship to sail to Acapulco, I bid farewell to all my friends and the friends of my master, to whose memory, above all, I ordered a solemn novena of Masses said, which I found very appropriate; and when they were done, I left for Cavite and set sail with all my possessions.

CHAPTER 39

IN WHICH OUR AUTHOR DESCRIBES HOW HE SET SAIL FOR
ACAPULCO; HIS SHIPWRECK; THE WARM WELCOME HE WAS GIVEN IN
THE ISLAND WHERE HE LANDED; AND OTHER CURIOUS MATTERS

How delightful are those gardens of fantasy in which we like to stroll at the mercy of our desires! How easy it is to count our eggs before they hatch; that is, without taking into account the things that can go wrong, or better yet, without reckoning that Providence may well have disposed things very differently from the way we have imagined them!

That's how I was reckoning things in Manila when I set sail with my packet of goods for Acapulco. Eleven thousand pesos invested by buying low, I told myself, after selling high in Mexico, would yield me twenty-eight or thirty thousand; those, reinvested in commerce in Veracruz, would, in a couple of years, turn into fifty or sixty thousand pesos. With a fortune like that, and me being no fool and none too ugly, why shouldn't I dream of marrying a girl with an equal amount for her dowry? And with that kind of capital, why shouldn't I be able to pile up, in another couple of years, figuring on the low side and after expenses, another forty or fifty thousand? And with that, why shouldn't I be able to acquire a title of count or marquis from Madrid? I certainly know that other people have gotten one for less. Very well; but once I'm a count or a marquis, it won't do for me to continue as a shopkeeper with a public store: they'd call me the Marquis of Paintbucket or the Count of Muslin; but what of it? Haven't lots of people gotten titles and climbed to the top by the same stairs? But still, I'd have to look into some other way to make a living, if only to keep all the envious backbiters from pestering me too much. What should it be? I've got it: the countryside; what could be more proper and honorable for a marquis than a country estate? I'll buy me a couple of the best haciendas; I'll staff them with faithful and intelligent administrators; and, generally counting on the fertility of my country, I'll bring in abundant harvests, hoard up piles of doubloons, become a presentable person in Mexico, be held in high regard by everyone, and my wife (who will doubtless be very beautiful and witty) will attract everyone's attention; why not the attention of the viceroy's wife, the virreina, as well? Of course she will; the virreina will love her—for her bearing, for her discretion, and because I'll promote their friendship with little gifts, which, as we know, can wear down rocky cliffs. Once the virreina is ready and has become my wife's intimate friend, why not make use of her patronage? That's what I'll do; I'll become very close friends with the viceroy; and when I've done that, it won't take me much money to outfit a regiment; I'll be a colonel, and here we see Periquillo from one day to the next wearing three stripes and fancy title, puffed up bigger than a house.

Will it stop there? No, sir; my haciendas will increase their production; my money chests will overflow with doubloons; and then my friend the viceroy will retire to Spain, and I'll accompany him. He'll be well loved by the king and, on the other hand, burdened by all the favors I've done him, so he'll do everything he can for me in the Ministry of Justice, Department of the Indies; I won't forget to win the favor of the secretary of state, and after a few attempts, within two years, tops, I'll get assigned to be the next viceroy of Mexico. This cat's in the bag, it'll get done easy as that, and then. . . . Ah! How my heart will rejoice the day that I take up the post of viceroy in my own land!

Oh! And how everyone I know will flatter me! How many relatives and friends will come out of the woodwork, and how they'll fear my indignation if they've looked down on me in the past!

Apart from that, what happy days I'll have governing that vast and expansive kingdom! How much money I'll amass by every means possible, be those what they may! What entertainments I'll enjoy! What a crowd of flatterers will surround me, praising my vices as if they were the highest virtues, even if they forget all about me when it's time for the judicial inquiry at the end of my term, and perhaps even become my worst enemies! But after all, I will at least have spent those years wallowing in delights; and I won't neglect to hoard lots of silver, which will come in handy for silencing my enemies and buying off my friends, so that the latter will laud my good behavior and the former will keep quiet about my defects; and if all this comes to pass, here you have me: a Periquillo, an hidalgo as they say, a man with a middling fortune, and, if you will, a first-class scoundrel, improved in the eyes of the king and good men, much as his wicked deeds might cry out for vengeance from the aggrieved parties.

This was all I was thinking during those first days of sailing back to my country, and if God had carried forth my wicked desires to the full, who knows if there wouldn't be countless destitute families today, with my own family dishonored and myself beheaded on a gibbet.

We were seven days out at sea, and during that time, my head was brimming with a thousand delirious visions of my viceroyalty. Decrees, embroidered uniforms, Your Excellencies, gifts, submissiveness, banquets, fine china, parades, coaches, lackeys, liveries, and palaces were the puppets dancing without a rest in my mad brain and entertaining my foolish imagination.

This idiocy had me so overexcited that I hadn't even laid the first foundation stone for this vain edifice when I was already putting on haughty airs, acting as if I already deserved the perks of being viceroy while I was nothing yet but a sorry little Periquillo; and in virtue of this, I spoke but few words, in very measured tones, with only the most illustrious people onboard, and less or not at all with my peers, while treating my inferiors with the most ridiculous air of majesty.

Everyone immediately noticed the change that had come over me, because they had known me to be jovial and affectionate, but within four days I had become finicky, arrogant, and unsociable; as a result, some ridiculed me, others snubbed and rebuffed me, and everyone rightly loathed me.

I noticed how little I was loved, but I said to myself, "So what if this riffraff detests me? Why should a viceroy need them? The day I take office, these fellows who are keeping their distance from me today will be the first to bend over backward to flatter me." That's how the new Quixote went off on in his chivalrous madness, which increased so much from day to day and moment to moment that if God had not allowed the winds to shift, by now I would be taking office in a cage in San Hipólito.

As things turned out, on the night of our seventh day out, the heavens grew overcast, and the sky darkened with thick, black clouds; the northeast wind blew hard against us; within a few hours, the threatening clouds closed in on us, obscuring the horizon; sheets of rain began to fall, and multitudes of lightning bolts crisscrossed the atmosphere, terrorizing the eyes of those who saw them.

After six hours of these troubles, a furious southwest wind picked up; the sea was rising moment by moment, and such huge waves were swelling that each one seemed likely to bury the ship. Between the hurricane winds and the ceaseless rolling of the ship, not one lamp remained lit; the sailors worked gropingly to handle the rigging; and the fearsome flashes of lightning served to terrorize us even further, for in each other's pallid faces we seemed to see the image of death, which we expected to come at any moment.

In this state, one sea surge broke the rudder; another broke the bowsprit; and a furious blast of wind smashed the foresail topmast. The timbers and the rigging creaked, but no one was able to take down the tattered sails because they couldn't stand on the yardarms.

The winds kept shifting and the rudderless ship drifted wherever the waves took it; battening down the hatches did nothing to keep water from flooding in with each sea surge, nor could we pump the water out fast enough.

In this deplorable situation, you can imagine how dismayed we were, how frightened, and how many vows and promises we made.

Under these critical and perilous circumstances, the fatal moment of sacrifice arrived for the sailing victims. The ship was bouncing back and forth like a ball, and in one of its bounces it hit a coral reef so hard that it smashed against it, opening up like a pomegranate from helm to waist and taking on so much water that we had no remaining hopes but to commend our souls to God and repeat our acts of contrition.

The ship's chaplain absolved us en masse, and everyone resigned himself to his fate, since there was nothing else to do.

As for me, when I noticed that the ship was sinking, I climbed on all fours up onto the deck, where Divine Providence had a plank waiting for me; I held onto it with all my strength, because I had heard it said that a plank was a good thing to have in a shipwreck; but I had hardly grabbed onto it when I found myself floating, and by the wan light of a lightning bolt, I saw the whole ship founder and sink before my eyes.

Then I was overcome by the innermost terror, reflecting on how all my companions had perished and I could not help suffering the same baneful fate.

Nevertheless, the love of life, and that tenacious hope that stays with us so long as life lasts, picked up my flagging spirits, and with a tight grip on the plank and millions of vows and invocations to the Mother of God, Our Lady of Guadalupe, I struggled to keep my head above water while the waves and winds tossed me about at their discretion.

Sometimes the weight of the waves sank me; other times, the air contained in the pores of the plank held me up on the water's surface.

I must have battled these mortal fears for about an hour and a half, without any human hope of salvation, when the clouds scattered, the sea calmed down, the winds grew quiet, and dawn broke, looking more lovely to me from that vantage point than it could have seemed to the most peaceful monarch in the world. The sun soon showed its beautiful and resplendent face. I was almost naked, and I could see the ocean spreading around me; but my spirit had been daunted by the recent accident, and I still feared losing my life in the deep, so I could not entirely enjoy watching the delights of Nature.

Holding onto my plank and trying only to float, in constant fear of being surprised by some meat-eating fish, I suddenly heard human voices close by me. I lifted my head, looked out, and observed that the people shouting at me were a bunch of fishermen piloting a boat. I watched them attentively and saw that they were drawing near. I cannot express the joy in my heart when I saw those good men rushing to my aid, especially when their boat pulled up alongside my plank and they held out their arms to lift me aboard.

By then I was entirely naked and almost unconscious. They placed me face down in that state and made me bring up a quantity of saltwater that I had swallowed. Then they gave me a general rubdown with some wool rags and comforted me with spirit of deer horn,[1] which one of them was carrying for just such a case, after which they wrapped me up and brought me to the dock of an island that lay nearby.

As I was brought ashore, I recovered from the fainting spell or convulsion that had overcome me, and I saw and noticed the following:

They placed me under a shady tree that stood by the dock, and a group of people soon gathered around me, among whom I recognized a number as Europeans. They all looked at me and asked me thousands of questions out of mere curiosity; but none of them bothered to help me. The only thing one of them did was to give me a coin worth half a real in our money. The rest of them sympathized with me in words alone, and withdrew saying, "What a pity!," "Poor thing!," "So young!," and other empty phrases like these, and having given this timely aid, they were satisfied and left.

The poor islanders looked at me and were moved to pity; they gave me nothing, but they did not pester me with questions, either because they knew we would not understand each other or because they were more judicious.

Despite these people's poverty, one of them brought me a cup of tea and a piece of bread, and another gave me a torn cloak, which I thanked him for with a thousand courtesies, putting it on very happily, because I was naked and freezing to death. That was the miserable state of the future viceroy of New Spain: content to wear the clothes of a poor Chinese trader,[2] which is what I took him to be. Of course, by then I wasn't thinking about viceregal palaces or liveries, and I wasn't scowling and refusing to speak with my inferiors, either; rather, I was trying to make myself look as pleasant as I could to everybody, and, more timid than a dog in a strange neighborhood, I affected an air of the most charming humility. How true it

---

[1] [Spirit of deer horn (*espíritu de cuerno de ciervo*): Ruiz Barrionuevo notes (p. 749) that this potion was considered effective against apoplexy, asthma, and other illnesses, according to one of the pharmacologies cited by Lizardi in an Chapter 25. –Tr.]

[2] [Chinese trader: *sangley,* referring specifically to a member of the Chinese merchant community resident in the Philippines. –Tr.]

is that some of us become arrogant with money, when without it we might be more human and sociable!

I must have been lying in the shade of that stout tree for three or four hours, with no idea of where I might go or what I might do in a land that seemed so foreign to me, when a man came up to me: by his clothes I figured he was an islander, and a rich one, seeing how costly they were, for he was dressed in a blue satin tunic or robe embroidered in gold with loops of sable plush, tied with a scarlet silk crepe sash that was also embroidered in gold; the tunic fell almost to his feet, which barely peeked out, shod in gold-colored velvet sandals. In one hand he carried a gold-handled bamboo cane, and in the other a gold pipe. His head was uncovered, and he had little hair; but on the crown of his head, or a little farther back, he had it tied up in what looked like a chignon like the ones our ladies use, and he decorated it with a band of diamonds and an insignia whose meaning I did not yet understand.

With him came four servants who bowed and scraped before him, one of whom was carrying a *payo*, as they say, or *umbrella*, as we call it, made of crimson satin with a golden fringe; and another servant with him seemed by his clothing to be a European to me, as indeed he was: no less than his Spanish interpreter.

He drew close and looked down at me with a pitying gaze, which was enough to show a mile off that my misfortunes interested him, and through the interpreter he told me, "Do not worry, unhappy castaway, for the gods of the sea have not carried you to the Islands of Sails,[3] where they enslave those who are spared by the sea. Come with me to my house."

Saying this, he ordered his servants to pick me up and carry me. A murmur instantly went up among the onlookers, ending in a chorus of cheers and exclamations.

I immediately realized that this was a distinguished person, because everyone bowed and curtseyed as he passed.

I was not mistaken, for as soon as I reached his house, I saw that it was a palace, but a palace at the top of the hierarchy. He set me up in a decent room; he provided me with food and clothes—in his style, but good quality—and let me rest for the next four days.

After four days, when he was informed that I had completely recovered from the broken health I had suffered in the shipwreck, he entered my room with the interpreter and said, "Well, Spaniard, is my house better than the sea? Are you comfortable here? Are you content?"

"Sir," I said, "the contrast that you are offering me is remarkable; your house is a palace: it is the shelter that has freed me from destitution, and the safest port that I could have found after my shipwreck; how could I help but be content here and recognize your liberality and generosity?"

After that, the islander treated me with the greatest affection. He visited me every day and he assigned me instructors to teach me his language, which I soon learned imperfectly, just as he knew Spanish, English, and French, because he understood a little of each, though he frequently mangled and mixed them with his own language.

---

[3] These islands are also known as the Ladrones [or Marianas].

Nevertheless, I spoke his language better than he spoke mine, because I was in his country and I had to speak and deal with its people. As you can see, there is no quicker or more effective method of learning a language than being forced to deal with those who speak it naturally.

After two or three months, I knew enough to understand the islander without an interpreter, and then he told me that he was the brother of the *tután*, or viceroy, of that province, whose capital was this island, called Saucheofú; that he was the tután's second assistant, and his name was Limahotón.[4] I then informed him of my name and the reason for my voyage through those seas, and also of my homeland. I fully satisfied his curiosity, and he showed that he felt sorry for my fate, while also marveling at some of the things I told him about New Spain.

The day after this conversation, he brought me to meet his brother, whom I greeted with the bows and ceremonies in which I had been instructed; the tután paid close attention to me, but for all his affection, he said, "And you, what do you know how to do? Because even though it is the custom in this province to show hospitality to all strangers, poor or not, who show up on our shores, nevertheless we are not so indulgent with those who attempt to remain in our cities after a certain amount of time, unless they can tell us about their skills and trades so that we can put them to work in what they know how to do, or learn from them what we do not know. The fact is that, here, nobody eats our rice or our delicious beef or fish without earning it by the work of their hands. So if someone has no trade or skill, we will teach him, and within a year or two he will be in a condition to begin slowly paying back what the king's treasury spent to foster him. In virtue of all this, tell me what trade you know, so that my brother can recommend you to a workshop where you can earn your keep."

This news caught me by surprise, because I didn't know how to do anything useful with my hands, and so I answered the tután, "Sir, I am a noble in my own land, and therefore I do not know any trades, because it is considered beneath a gentleman to do manual labor."

The dignified mandarin lost his grave demeanor when he heard my excuse, and he began to laugh uproariously, holding his belly and leaning against one and then another of the cushions that surrounded him; and when he had had his fill of laughing, he said to me, "So in your land it is considered beneath your dignity to work with your hands? Every noble in your land must be a tután or a potentate, and so all your nobles must be very rich."

"No, sir," I said, "all our nobles aren't princes, and they aren't all rich; in fact, countless numbers of them are extremely poor, so much so that in their poverty they get confused with the scum of the people."

"Well, then," said the tután, "if there are so many examples of this, it must be supposed that all the people in your land are chivalrous madmen, for they can see

---

[4] [Lizardi got the names and some of the details that he used for Periquillo's voyage to this entirely imaginary island from the Jesuit P. Juan González de Mendoza's *Historia de las cosas más notables, ritos y costumbres del gran reino de la China* (Rome, 1585; *The Historie of the Great and Mightie Kingdome of China, and the Situation Thereof*, London, 1588). –Tr.]

every day how little good nobility does the poor, and they know how easy it is for a rich man to become poor and find himself humbled even though he is a noble, yet they still raise their sons to be lazy idlers, exposing them through this madness to the likelihood that they will perish one day in the grip of destitution. Besides, if the nobles in your land don't know how to use their hands to seek their food, they must not know how to use the hands of others, so tell me: what good for your land are the nobles or the rich (because it seems to me that you consider them to be the same thing)? What good is one of them, I mean, to the rest of their fellow citizens? Surely a rich man or a noble must be a very heavy burden on the republic."

"No, sir," I replied; "the nobles and the rich are steered by their parents into the two illustrious careers we have, which are arms and letters, and in either of them they are very useful to society."

"That seems very good to me," said the viceroy. "So all the usefulness that can be expected from your nobles is limited to arms or letters? But I don't understand those terms. Tell me, what kind of trades are arms and letters?"

"Sir," I answered, "they are not trades, but professions, and if they were to be called trades, they would be considered base and nobody would want to devote himself to them. The career of arms is the one in which illustrious young men devote themselves to learning the art of war, with the help of the study of mathematics, which teaches them how to elaborate designs for fortification, how to undermine a fortress, how to direct squadrons symmetrically, how to bombard a city, how to prepare for a naval battle, and other such things; and through this science the best students become prepared to be good generals and serve their homeland, defending it from enemy incursions."

"That science is noble in itself, and very useful to the citizens," said the Chinese, "because each individual's desire for self-preservation compels him to appreciate those who devote themselves to defending him. The soldier's career is very noble and reputable; but tell me: why are the soldiers in your land so exquisite? What, aren't all your citizens soldiers? Because every citizen here is. You yourself, so long as you live in our company, will be a soldier and will be obliged to shoulder arms along with everybody else, in case the island comes under enemy assault."

"Sir," I said, "that is not how things are in my land. There are groups of men devoted to serving at arms, and paid by the king, which are called armies or regiments; and that class of people is obliged to face the enemy alone, without demanding that the others (whom they call civilians) do anything more than contribute money to support them, and even that they only do in the gravest emergencies."

"Terrible are the usages of your land," said the tután. "Poor king! Poor soldiers, and poor citizens! What an expense it must be for the king! How vulnerable must the soldiers be, and how poorly defended the citizens by those hired hands! Would it not be better if, in case of war, all persons and all interests were to join in a single point of defense? How much harder they would fight if that were the case, and how their general union would strike fear into the enemy! A million men that a king might put on the field at the expense of endless troubles and payments could not equal a fifth of the force that a nation could field if it were composed of all the 5 million able-bodied men who make up that nation. In that case, there would be more soldiers, more bravery, more resoluteness, more union, more interest, and less expense. At least that is our practice here, and we are invincible before the Tartars, the Persians, the Africans, and the Europeans. But this is mere conversation. I am not an expert on your king's politics, nor those of any king of Europe, much less do I know the character of its nations; and since they are the most interested parties and they have arranged things in this way, they must be right, although this system will always amaze me. But, given that you are a noble, tell me, are you a soldier?"

"No, sir," I said; "I made my career in letters."

"Fine," said the Asian. "And what have you learned through letters, or science, which I suppose is what you mean?"

Thinking that this man was a fool, since I had heard it said that anyone who cannot speak Spanish is a fool, I replied that I was theologian.

"And what is a theologian?" asked the tután.

"Sir," I replied, "he is a man who studies the divine science—that is, what belongs to God."

"Hullo!" said the tután. "Such a man must be worthy of eternal worship! So you understand the essence of your God, at least? You know what his attributes and perfections are, and you have the talent and the ability to reveal his arcane secrets? From this moment on, I will consider you the mortal most worthy of reverence. Sit by my side, and please deign to be my advisor."

Again I was surprised by his ironic wit, and I told him, "Sir, the theologians of my land do not know who God is, nor are they capable of understanding Him, much less of probing the infinite depths of His attributes, nor of discovering His arcane secrets. They are just men who can explain the properties of the Deity and the mysteries of religion better than other men."

"That is," the Chinese answered, "in your country, theologians are what you call the holy men, wise men, or priests, who in our land have the deepest awareness of the essence of our gods, our religion, or our dogmas; but just knowing those things and teaching them to the rest does not spare them from being useful and working with their hands; so being a theologian from your land will not do you any good."

Finding myself under this sustained attack, and hoping to escape the attack through lies, since I still believed that the man I was speaking with was stupid like me, I told him that I was a physician.

"Oh!" said the viceroy. "That is a great science, if you prefer not to call it a trade. A physician! That is a fine thing. A man who lengthens the lives of others and saves them from the grasp of pain is a treasure wherever he lives. The king's treasury is open here for good physicians who invent new medicines unknown to the ancients. In our land, this is not a science but a liberal trade, and one to which only the wisest and most experienced men devote themselves. Perhaps you may be one of them, and you will find your fortune in your skill; but we shall see."

Saying this, he ordered that they bring him an herb from flowerpot number ten in his garden. They brought it and, placing it in my hand, the tután said, "Which illness does this counteract?"

The question stumped me, for I understood as much about botany as I did about comets when I raved about them in Tlalnepantla; but remembering my foolish pride,

I took the herb, looked at it, smelled it, tried it, and feeling very self-satisfied, I said, "This herb is similar to one we have in my land that is called either *tianguispepetla* or pellitory; I don't remember which this would be, but both are febrifuges."

"And what is a febrifuge?" asked the tután, to whom I replied that it was something especially effective against fever.

"Then I think," the tután went on, "that you are as much a physician as you are a theologian or a soldier; because this herb, far from curing a fever, is actually very good for bringing one on: so much so that anyone who drinks an infusion of five or six of these little leaves in half a pint of water will break into a terrible fever."

With my ignorance so shamefully exposed, I had no other escape than to say, "Sir, the physicians in my land are not obliged to remember the particular characteristics of herbs, nor to know how to deduce the powers of each one from general principles. All they have to do is memorize the names of 500 or 600 herbs, with a knowledge of the powers attributed to them by medical authors, so that they can make use of this tradition by the patient's bedside; and they can easily look up these things with the help of the pharmacopeias."

"Well, you will not find it so easy to convince me," said the mandarin, "that the physicians in your land are so generally ignorant of the uses of herbs, as you say. When it comes to physicians like you, I won't deny it; but those who deserve to be called physicians surely are not mired in such gross stupidity, which, apart from dishonoring their profession, would result in countless disasters in their society."

"That should not shock you, sir," I said, "because in my land, medicine is the least protected of all sciences. We have schools where they teach Latin, philosophy, theology, and both civil and ecclesiastic law; there are those where they teach many good classes on chemistry and experimental physics, on mineralogy or the art of recognizing rocks that contain silver, and on other subjects; but nowhere do we teach medicine. True, there are three professorships at the university—the *prima*, the *vísperas*, and the *methodo medendi* chairs—where they teach a little bit, but that is just for a short time during the morning, and not even every morning; because, apart from Thursdays and holidays, there are many days that they give the students off; and, being young men, students are usually happier going off on strolls than studying. For this reason among others, physicians who truly deserve the name are rare in my land, and if there are a few who have reached that rank, they did so at the expense of lots of hard work and sleepless nights, and by getting close to some skillful professor or other so as to profit from his intelligence.

"To this you can add that, in my land, medicine is divided into many branches. The people who cure exterior illnesses, such as sores, fractures, and wounds, are called *surgeons*, and they cannot cure other illnesses without incurring the wrath of physicians, or getting them to look aside. Those who cure illnesses such as fever, pleurisy, dropsy, and so forth, are called *physicians*; they are more respected because they work more by guesswork than do surgeons, and their knowledge is honored with honorary degrees and titles, such as bachelor and doctor. The men who perform both kinds of medicine, internal and external, employ their assistants, who do bleedings and cuppings, apply and heal caustics, and employ leeches and other cures, not including medicines that are taken by mouth; these assistants are called barbers and bleeders. And there are yet others who prepare and dispense medicines, and who have recently begun to be well educated in chemistry and botany, which is what you call the science of herbs. These people do know their plants; they can distinguish them by sex and speak handily about calyces, stamens, and pistils, and they boast of knowing their generic properties and powers. These men are called *apothecaries*, and they are the physicians' assistants."

"I could abide by the latter," said the tután, "because at least they take pains to consult Nature to learn something as essential to medicine as what the classes and powers of herbs might be. Indeed, there must be apothecaries in your land who can heal people more successfully than many physicians. Everything you have said has amazed me, because it lets me see how many differences there are between the usages of one nation and those of another. In mine, we only call men physicians and allow them to follow that trade if they have a very profound knowledge of the structure of the human body, the causes of the illnesses it suffers, and how the medicines they prescribe work; in addition, medicine is not divided as you say it is in your land. Here, every healer is physician, surgeon, barber, apothecary, and assistant. When the patient is entrusted to his care, he must cure him of whatever illnesses ails him, internal or external; he must prescribe the medicines, make them, and administer them; and he must practice whatever he considers opportune to alleviate him. If the patient is cured, he gets paid; if not, he gets kicked out with a curse. But every nation has its usages. What is certain is that you are no physician, nor could you even serve as an apprentice to one here; so tell me what else you know how to do to earn your living."

Stunned by the way the Chinese kept pinning me down at every step, I told him that perhaps I would be good with an attorneyship.

"Attorneyship?" he said. "What's that? The art of turning ships at sea?"

"No, sir," I told him. "Attorneyship is the profession that many men study in order to learn their nation's laws and plead their clients' rights before their judges."

Hearing this, the tután leaned over the table, placing his hands on his eyes and keeping silent for a long time, until at last he raised his head and asked me, "So, in your land, attorneys are what they call those men who learn the laws of the kingdom, which they use to defend those who hire them, clarifying their rights before the tutáns or magistrates?"

"That is it, sir, precisely."

"*Tien* help me!" said the Chinese. "Is it possible that the people of your land are so ignorant that they do not know their own rights, or which laws favor them or condemn them? I had never thought so lowly of Europeans."

"Sir," I told him, "it is not easy for everyone to learn all the laws, because there are so many, much less the interpretations of the laws, which only attorneys can do, because they have a license to do it, which is why we call them *licenciados*. . . . "

"Wait, what was that about interpretations?" asked the Asian. "Can't the laws be understood by following the letter of what the legislator wrote? Are they still subject to the interpreter's sophisms? If that's the case, I pity your fellow natives, and I loathe the learning of your attorneys. But, be that as it may, if all you know is what you've told me, you don't know anything; you are useless, and we will have to make you useful so that you won't live idly in my country. Limahotón, set this foreigner to learning how to card silk, how to dye it, how to spin it, and how to embroider with it, and when he hands me a tapestry made by his own hand, I will find him a position that will make him rich. In a word, teach him something useful for making a living in his land and in foreign lands."

This said, he withdrew, and I went off with my protector feeling very shamed and wondering how I, at my age, could learn a trade in a land that makes no allowances for useless and idle Periquillos.

CHAPTER 40

IN WHICH OUR PERICO TELLS HOW HE PRETENDED TO BE A COUNT
ON THE ISLAND; HOW WELL IT WENT FOR HIM; WHAT HE SAW
THERE; AND THE CONVERSATIONS HE HAD WITH THE FOREIGNERS
AT DINNER, WHICH ARE NOT ENTIRELY TO BE SNIFFED AT

You will recall that I had been supported since my early youth or puberty by my naïve mother's indulgence, so I had resisted learning a trade; and, loathing all forms of labor, I had given myself over to idleness. You will have noted that this was the cause of my humiliations, which was why I struck up friendships with the most obscene characters, who not only presented examples that gave me over to vice, but who made me pay dearly for the liberties they took with me, so that I was constantly finding myself detested by my relatives, abandoned by my friends, beaten by both beasts and men, slandered as a thief, left with no honor, no money, and no esteem, and always leading a tiresome and miserable life; and when you consider that, at the age of more than thirty, after escaping naked from a shipwreck and having the good luck to find such a warm welcome on the island, they were proposing to teach me some art by which I might not only make my living but even become rich, you will say: of course, this is where our father opened his eyes and, recognizing here the original reason for all his past misfortunes, he must have gladly embraced the opportunity to learn how to earn his bread on his own, without depending any further on the help of others, as the only way to avoid the misfortunes that might await him in the future.

That's what you might think, if you are following sound reasoning; and that's what I should have done; but that isn't what happened. I had a terrible aversion to work in any form whatsoever; I always loved the idle life, and living off of unwary and good men; and if I ever half submitted to some sort of work, it was either because I was assailed by hunger, such as when I worked for Chanfaina and the sexton, or because I was pleased by a pampered life in which I worked very little and had hopes of prospering greatly, such as when I worked for the apothecary, the physician, and the colonel.

When all is said and done, I had found myself, through an unexpected accident, in a Jauja[1] with the late colonel; but such Jaujas aren't for everyone, and they aren't found every day of the week. I should have taken that into account on the island, and should have worked hard at becoming useful to myself and to all other men, with whom I would have to live no matter where I went; but far from doing that, running away from work instead and falling back on my old rackets, when I saw that

---

[1] Jauja: An imaginary city that some people, giving credence to fraudulent travelers' tales, searched for futilely in Spanish America, carried away by the magnificent descriptions and long-winded praise of its richness, fertility, and beauty. Today its name is used only as a synonym of the Garden of Earthly Delights, to exaggerate the abundance of some city or country where the land produces everything man needs without need for cultivation, and where one need not work in order to eat. –E.

Limahotón was determined to teach me a trade and make me work, I told him that I didn't want to learn anything, because I wasn't planning to stay very long in his land, for I wanted to return to my own, where I would have no need to work, since I was a count.

"You are a count?" the Asian asked in amazement.

"Yes, I'm a count."

"And what's a count?"

"A count," I said, "is a rich nobleman who was given his title by the king for his services or those of his ancestors."

"So in your land," the Chinese asked me, "you don't have to serve the king personally; it is enough for your forefathers to have served him, to be generously honored by your monarchs?"

The question provoked me, and I told him, "The generosity of my kings does not stop with awarding honors to those who actually serve them; they extend their favor to the sons of those men. Thus, I was the son of a valiant general to whom the king granted many favors, and since I was born his son, I grew up with money, an entailed estate, and the possibility of becoming a count, which I am today, because of my father's merit."

"It follows, then, that you are also a general," said Limahotón.

"I'm not a general," I said, "but I am a count."

"I don't understand this," said the Chinese. "So: your father battered down castles, captured cities, overthrew armies, and in a word, kept the crowns on his lords' heads, at the risk of losing his life in one of those frays; while you, just because you were the son of that brave and loyal gentleman, found that you had become a rich count from one day to the next, without ever tasting the hardships of the battlefield, and without knowing anything about the tasks of government? Nobles must truly be more common in your land than in mine. But tell me—these men who are born and not made nobles: what work do they do in your country? Given that they don't serve in the army or in your princes' governments, that they're useless both for peace and for war, and that they don't know how to work with the pen or the sword, what, then, do they do? How do they keep themselves busy? What is their occupation? What good does the king or the republic get out of them?"

"What else could they do?" I said, imbued with my lazy ideas. "They try to have fun, go out strolling, and at most, they work at something that won't diminish their wealth. If you could just see the houses of some of the counts and noblemen in my land, if you could sit at their tables, if you could observe their luxury, the number of servants they have, how magnificent their bearing is, how ostentatious their coaches, how grand their livery, and how costly and exquisite their retinues, you would be filled with amazement."

"Oh Tien almighty!" said the Chinese. "It must be so much better to be a count or nobleman in your land than a royal official in mine! I'm a nobleman, true; and in your land, I'd be a count; but how much it has cost me to acquire this title and the income I enjoy! Hardship and risk in battle, and endless discomforts in peace. I am an assistant, second to the tután or head official of the province; I have honors and a good income; but I am a faithful servant of the king and a slave of his vassals.

Without even reckoning the personal services I did to obtain this position, now that I have it, how many sleepless nights and how much suffering have I had to put up with to keep it and not lose my reputation! No doubt about it, friend, I would rather be a count in your land than a *loitia*[2] in my own. But after all, don't you want to return to Mexico, your homeland?"

"Yes, sir," I said, "and I am longing for an occasion to go."

"Well, don't lose hope," Limahotón said; "there's a good chance you'll get what you want. In one of our coves, there is a sunken foreign ship that arrived here nearly destroyed in a shipwreck that occurred in our seas a few days before your accident. That ship is almost finished being rebuilt, and the passengers who came in it are staying in the city, waiting for it to be done and for the weather to settle. Once both things are ready, which will be about three moons from now, we'll set sail; for I wish to see more of the world than my homeland; my brother has approved my desire; I am rich, and I can carry it out; but please keep this to yourself. I have two friends among the passengers who love me dearly, so they say, and who come to eat with me every day. I haven't shown you to them because I figured you to be a poor plebeian, but since you're a rich nobleman like them, from today on I will seat you with them at my table."

The Chinese finished our conversation, and at the dinner hour, he brought me into a large hall where the meal would be served.

There were several characters there, among whom I recognized two Europeans, the ones that Limahotón had mentioned to me. As soon as I entered the hall, he said, "Here, gentlemen, is a count from your lands who was tossed naked by the sea onto our shores, and who wishes to return to his country."

"We will gladly bring Your Honor with us," said one of the foreigners, who was Spanish.

I displayed my gratitude, and we sat down to eat.

The other foreigner was English, a very merry and rakish youth. There was a great deal of chatting about the details of my shipwreck. Afterward, the Spaniard asked me about my homeland; I told him what it was, and we began to weave a conversation about matters pertaining to the kingdom.

The Chinese was amazed and content to hear so many things that he found surprising, and I was just as amazed to see that I was winning his affection; but the Spaniard's curiosity almost spoiled my pleasure when he asked me, "So, what is your title in Mexico? Because I know them all."

The question embarrassed me deeply, and I didn't know what name I could use to baptize my countdom; but I remembered how important it is not to flush and show your embarrassment in a tight spot like this, so I told him my title was the *Conde de Ruidera*, the Count of Louder.

"Do tell!" said the Spaniard. "Well, it couldn't be more than three years since I was last in Mexico, and since I was rich and served as consul in that capital city, I had many connections and I knew all the titled nobles; but I don't remember your title, loud as it is."

---

[2] A gentleman's title.

"That's not surprising," I said, "since it's just been a year since I was made count."

"So, it's a new title?"

"Yes, sir."

"And what motive did you have for claiming such an extravagant title?"

"My main motive," I answered, "was that I figured, a count makes a pretty noisy splash in the city where he lives, because of the money he spends, so the title of Louder fits me to a tee."

The Spaniard laughed and told me, "That's a witty one; but if it's true, you must have lots of money to make so much noise, and I bet not every count in the world would dare to adopt a title as loud as yours. In fact, I have heard it said that:

> In the house of a count, the scuttlebutt's
> That's there's lots of noise but very few nuts.[3]

"Well, sir, in my house, so far we have always had more nuts than noise, as I trust in God that you will see with your own eyes some day."

"I will welcome the chance," said the Spaniard; and with a change of topic, that act concluded, the tables were cleared, they all bid me an affectionate good afternoon, and we went our separate ways.

That night a servant came on behalf of the Spanish merchant, bringing me a trunk full of underclothes and top clothes, all new and cut in our own style. The servant handed it over to me with a note that said, "My lord: May it please Your Excellency to make use of these clothes, which will fit you better than the little robes of this land. Forgive the poor quality of this gift, which is owing to the lack of time. Your humble servant, Ordóñez."

I accepted the trunk, penned a grandiose reply on the same piece of paper, and then it was time for supper and bed.

The next day, I got up dressed in the European style. At dinner there was plenty to laugh about and criticize with the young Englishman, who was a bit rakish, as I have said; spoke Spanish like the Devil; and, on top of that, had the bad judgment to praise everything in his land in preference to the products of the country where he was staying, and to do this right in front of Limahotón, who took affront at these comparisons; but on this occasion, when the Englishman grumbled about the bread he was eating, the Chinese couldn't bear it and, growing more peeved than I would have expected from someone with his character, he said, "*Mister*, for many days I have honored you at my table, and for many days I have observed your rudeness in my presence, as you snipe at the goods and even the inventions of my homeland, to praise those of your own. I do not blame you for finding our country, usages, religion, government, or food strange; that is unavoidable, and the same would be true of me in your London. Much less do I blame you for lauding your laws and customs or the products of your land. It is proper for each man to love and prefer the country of his birth, and to find its customs, climes, and foods congenial, preferring them to

---

[3] [Lots of noise but very few nuts: *mucho ruido y pocas nueces* is the evocative Spanish translation of "much ado about nothing." –Tr.]

those anywhere else in the world; but it is not right for you to praise them by belittling the land where you are living, right in front of the man who has invited you to his table. If you talk about religion, you inveigh against mine and extol Anglicanism; if about legislators, you stupefy me with talk of your Houses; if about population, you tell me about your capital and the million men who live there; if about temples, you repeat your descriptions of the Cathedral of St. Paul and Westminster Abbey; if about places to stroll, I always hear you praising your Park of St. James and your Green Park. . . . Altogether, you have given me a map of London on the brain. If, instead of wearing yourself out praising the things of your land while scorning or sniping at those of mine, you would be content with simply relating what you are asked and what is to the point, and leave the praising and the comparisons to your listeners, you would certainly be well thought of; but speaking badly of the bread of my land, and saying that your country's is better, when it is this bread, not yours, that is nourishing you, is a discourtesy that does not please me, nor could it please anyone who hears you. Rather, your boastfulness bores everyone, and they must all be wondering who asked you to come to this land and, if you don't like it, why you don't take the first fast ship home; and that is what I am saying to you right now."

Having spoken, Limahotón stood up without finishing his dinner and, without taking anyone's leave, he withdrew in a great huff.

We all sat there embarrassed, most of all the Spaniard, who carefully explained to the Englishman everything the Asian had said, and added, "He shamed us, but he was right, mate. You've overstepped the bounds of urbanity. In a foreign land, especially when we are being shown favors by the patricians, we must abide by their usages and everything else, and if we cannot stand them, we should leave; but we should never snipe at them or praise everything about our own lands above those of theirs. The loitia was correct. Even if the bread in London, or Madrid, or Mexico is better than the bread here, this bread is more useful for us and better than any other, because this is what we are eating; and it is very low to refuse to give thanks for the favors we are shown, trying to belittle them in front of the man who's doing us the favors. What would our Count of Louder here think if I were to start praising the wine of San Lúcar while speaking badly of the regional drink of his land, which is called pulque? What would he say if I were to extol the Escorial, the cathedral of Seville, or other things pertaining to Spain, while grumbling in the same measure about the Alameda, the Viceregal Palace, and other things of the Indies, and if I were to do all this in Mexico itself, right into the ears and whiskers of the Mexicans, and perhaps in his very house and at the very time that he was lavishing attention on me? Wouldn't he be doing me a great favor if he merely took me for a rude and low-born fool? Well, that's the impression you have given of yourself to Limahotón, and as an upright man, I give my word that he is absolutely right."

If the Englishman had been shamed by the Chinese's reproach, he blushed all the more when the Spaniard drove it home; but even though he was a rakish youth, he was gentle and understanding; and so, convinced of his error, he tried, with the Spaniard's help, to make it up to the Japanese,[4] which they quickly managed to do;

---

[4] [Japanese (*el Japón*): Lizardi evidently thought this term was synonymous with "Chinese." –Tr.]

they begged him to come back out, and he, being a true gentleman, declared himself satisfied, and we all remained as close friends as ever; and the Englishman took care never to say anything demeaning about the country where he was living.

We remained in the city for many more days, very contented, and I most of all, because I found myself held in high esteem and lavished with attention thanks to my feigned title; and deep down I congratulated myself for concocting this fraud, for in its protective shade I was well dressed and well treated, and was beginning to put on the airs of a rich nobleman, and almost got to the point of believing that's what I actually was. That was how much affection, attention, and respect they paid me, especially the Spaniard and the Chinese, who were convinced that I would be useful to them in Mexico. The fact is, I had a fine time on land and on sea, which I wouldn't have managed to do if they had known that my true title was the Mangy Parrot; but most of the time, the world values men not by their real titles, but by the titles they claim to have.

I am not saying that I approve of pretending, no matter how useful it might be to the pretender; pimps and cardsharps also find their ploys and hustles useful, yet they are not legitimate. What I want you to get out of this story is an understanding of how we are always exposed to clever rogues who fool us by depicting us as giants of nobility, talent, wealth, and influence. We believe their blandishments, or what they call *the soft soap*; they con us if they can; they always fool us; and by the time we discover the hoax, it's too late to do anything about it. In every case, my children, study the man, observe him, penetrate his soul; see how he operates, looking past the outer appearance of his clothes, titles, and income; and if you ever find someone who always tells the truth and doesn't stick to his self-interest like steel to a magnet, trust him and say: this is an upright man who won't fool me or bring any harm to me; but to find a man like that, you'll have to ask Diogenes to borrow his lantern.

Returning to my little tale, let me tell you that when the Asian took me to be a noble, he did not shy away from letting me accompany him in public; rather, on many days, he invited me to stroll by his side, showing me the finest parts of the city.

On the first day I went out with him, my curiosity was seized by a man who was copying very slowly on a piece of paper some characters that were engraved on a marble monument that stood on a street corner.

I asked my friend what this meant, and he replied that the man was copying down one of his country's laws that he no doubt found interesting.

"What," I asked him, "are your country's laws written on the street corners in your land?"

"Yes," he told me; "all our laws are posted in our city so that the citizens can teach themselves about them. That is why my brother was so amazed when you told him about the lawyers of your land."

"True, he was right," I said, "because we certainly should all learn about the laws that govern us, so that we can deduce our rights when we face our judges, without having to use the services of any third party to do that job for us. Our litigants would surely come off better in general under this method, both because they would defend themselves more carefully and because they would save the countless expenses that are now wasted on agents, prosecutors, attorneys, and court reporters.

I rather like this custom of your land, and I don't think this is the first time it has been heard of or practiced in the world, for I remember reading that Plautus said, speaking about how useless or at least how disrespected laws are in a land where customs have become lax, that:

> *Eae miserae etiam ad parietam sunt fixae clavis ferreis, ubi*
> *Malos mores adfigi nimis fuerat aequius.*[5]

The Chinese frowned as he listened to me, and said, "Count, I understand Spanish badly, and English worse, but I understand the language you just spoke least of all, because I didn't catch a single word."

"Oh, my friend!" I said, "that language is the speech of the learned. It is Latin; and what I said means, 'How unhappy are the laws to be posted on the walls with iron nails, when it would be more fitting to have our bad customs nailed up there.' Which proves that in Rome they used to post the laws publicly on the walls, just as you do in this city."

"So that is what the verse you said to me in Latin means?" Limahotón asked.

"Yes, that's what it means."

"Well, if you know what it means, and you can say it in your own language, why did you tell it to me in a language that I don't understand?"

"Didn't I say that it's the language of the learned?" I replied. "How would you know that I understood Latin or that I knew that florid snippet of erudition from Plautus, if I hadn't named him and cited his words in Latin, and then translated them? If there's a sure way of passing ourselves off as learned in our countries, it's by spouting off Latin catch phrases every now and then."

"That must be the case," said the Chinese, "when the learned talk among themselves, because, according to you, it's the language of the learned and they must understand it; but it couldn't be the custom to speak that language to people who don't understand it."

"How little you know of the world, Limahotón," I told him. "It is in front of those who know no Latin that you have to pepper your conversation with Latin words, so that they'll take you for an educated man; because in front of those who do understand it, you'd be too liable to be caught with a barbarism, a false citation, an anachronism, a short vowel where there should be a long one, and other such tidbits; but among men who only speak the vernacular, and among women, your erudition and your *latinorum* are totally safe. In my land, I've heard plenty of fellows who've sat in a ladies' drawing room, talking about legal codes and digests; about the systems of Ptolemy, of Descartes, and of Newton; about the electric fluid, the prime matter, vortices, attraction, repulsion, meteors, ignis fatuus, aurora borealis, and a thousand things like that, all the time citing whole sections of the authorities in Latin; so that the poor girls, who haven't understood a word of it all, just sit there with their mouths hanging open and saying, 'Will you look at that!'"

"That's what's happened to me," said the Chinese, "hearing you spout this nonsense in your own language and in that foreign tongue; but the fact that I can't

---

5 [Plautus, *Trinummus*, Act IV, Scene III, lines 1039–40. –Tr.]

understand you would never make me mistake you for a learned man; rather, I should think that you have a long way to go first, for the grace and skill of the learned man consist in making himself understood by everybody who hears him; and if I were to hear, in your land, one of those conversations that you just described, I would come out of it thinking that the speakers were a bunch of conceited ignoramuses, and that their listeners were a bunch of genuine idiots for pretending to enjoy and marvel at something they didn't understand."

Seeing how my pedantry displeased the Chinese, I began to blush; but I concealed it, and tried to flatter him by applauding the customs of his country, and so I told him, "In any case, I am delighted with the lovely provision of posting the laws in the city's most public places. I'd bet that nobody here can plead ignorance of the law that favors or condemns him. Boys must be learning the legal code of their land from when they are babies; not like in my land, where laws seem like arcane secrets whose discovery is reserved for jurists, and where bad attorneys like to take advantage of this ignorance to confuse, ensnare, and fleece the poor litigants. And don't think that their ignorance of the laws is due to the legislators' whims; rather, it comes from the people's indolence and from the mob of authorities who've set out to interpret the laws, some of them so tiresomely that to explain (or obfuscate) the decisions that have been taken on a given topic, e.g., divorce, they've written ten huge folio books—as big as this, my friend, as big as this—so that just seeing them there staring down at you takes away your desire to open them."

"So, if that's true," said the Chinese, "among those gentlemen there must also be those who are trying to seem learned by using irrelevant words and arguments?"

"There certainly are," I answered, "and besides, there's no science that doesn't have its charlatans. If you could only see what I read about this in a little book owned by a friend of mine, a colonel who died recently in Manila, it would make you laugh out loud."

"Yes? What did it say?"

"What didn't it! The little book is titled *Tirades against the Charlatanism of the Erudite*,[6] and the author lays into charlatan grammarians, philosophers, antiquarians, historians, poets, physicians—in a word, into everybody who practices charlatanism in the name of science; and in the part where he speaks of bad lawyers and pettifoggers, the least of what he says is this:

> "'No better than these are the muddled citers of texts, a large and abundant family among men of law, for if pedants abound in every profession, in jurisprudence some stroke of ill luck has always produced them in excessive numbers. Whether they are giving an opinion or swearing an oath, they mix in as many authorities as they can get their hands on; they pile up a whole forest of citations, cramming the margins of their huge sheets of paper and thinking they deserve to be awarded grandly for their skill in copying useless and irrelevant things from a hundred authors. . . .

---

6 [Mencke, *Declamaciones* (see author's Prologue, footnote 1). The textual citations that follow are from pages 164–67. –Tr.]

"We should also say something here about the practitioners of pettifoggery, or what Aristotle called the Art of Lying. When we see them acting like brute necessity—that is, doing without laws; when we see them trying to make a name for themselves among the ignorant by resorting to ridiculous subtleties, indecent sophistries, uproarious clauses, and the other arts of the most pestilent charlatanism; when, making perfidious, loathsome use of the tricks allowed by versatile formulas and legal interpretations, and deducing articles from other articles, new excuses from old ones, they prolong their law suits, conceal their knowledge from the judges, twist and entangle the ends of justice, switch and alter the appearances of things to confuse those who have to decide; and when they do all this for base personal gain, for sordid self-interest, and sometimes for wicked obstinacy and obsession; when we see them, I repeat. . . .' "

"Enough of that," said Limahotón, "for that is too much talk, and grumbling does not please my ears."

"No, Loitia," I said, "this isn't grumbling; it is the author's judicious critique. A grumbler or detractor deserves to be punished, because he reveals the defects of others with the damnable objective of damaging his neighbor's honor, which is why he always names the person he is accusing. A critic, whether a moralist or a satirist, never thinks about any particular person when he is writing; he only reproaches or ridicules vices in general, with the laudable hope that we will come to loathe them; and so Johann Burkhard Menke, the author whose words you have just heard, did not speak badly of lawyers, but rather of the vices that he observed in many but not all of them, for he does not deal with good and learned ones."

"There are also good and learned lawyers, then?" asked the Chinese.

I replied, "There certainly are excellent ones, both in their moral conduct and in their solid education. Many of them are Solons in justice and Demosthenes in eloquence; and these lawyers, far from deserving the satire I have mentioned, are worthy of our esteem and respect."

"Despite all that," said the Chinese, "if you and that author were to fall into the hands of those bad and fraudulent lawyers, you would find yourselves in a nasty quarrel."

"If that is the only reason for your feeling sore," I replied, "you are adding unfairness to foolishness, because neither the author nor I has named Pedro, Sancho, or Martín; and so a lawyer couldn't do worse than to complain about us, for then he would be accusing himself, against our innocent wishes."

"Be that as it may," said the Asian, "I am content with my country's custom, for here we need no lawyers, because every man is his own lawyer when he needs one, at least in ordinary cases. Nobody has authority to interpret the laws, and nobody can get away with ignoring a law under the pretext of not knowing it. When the sovereign repeals or in any way changes a law, the posting is immediately changed to show how it must be followed in the future, and the old law does not remain posted where it had been. Finally, all parents are obliged, under the threat of serious penalties, to teach their children to read and write and to present them, already educated, to the territorial judges before the age of ten, so that no one will have a justifiable motive for ignoring the laws of his country."

"Those provisions strike me as quite lovely," I told him, "and not only very useful, but very easy to carry out. I think the people in many cities of Europe would be amazed at this politic stroke of legislation, which can only give rise to many good things for your citizens, whether it frees them from inopportune litigation or does no more than deliver them from the crafty tricks of agents, attorneys, and other pen-pushing officials, from whom there is no escape as things stand. But as I said, this evil, this ignorance of the law that the people suffer, both in my country and in Europe, does not stem from the kings; for they are as interested in their subjects' happiness as they are in making them obey their wishes, and so they not only want everyone to know the laws, but they even have them published and posted in the streets as soon as they are ratified; what happens, though, is that they do not post them inscribed in marble like here, but printed on sheets of paper, a material too fragile for one to expect it to last long. The soldiers are read the ordinances, their penal code, so that they cannot allege ignorance; and, finally, in the Spanish code, we see clearly expressed that this is the monarchs' will, for among all the many laws it contains, we can read the following words: 'Yea we hold that all those under our lordship should know these our laws.[7] And the law should be manifest, that all men might understand it, and none be deceived through it.'[8] All of which proves that, if the people live in ignorance of their rights and have to beg for guidance, when they need it, from those who devote themselves to the law, that is not because of the will of the kings, but because of their neglect, because of the lawyers' license, and most of all, because of their own inveterate customs, against which it is not easy to struggle."

"You amaze me, Count," said the Chinese. "You are truly odd; sometimes you explain yourself far too flippantly, and other times very judiciously, as you've done now. I don't understand you."

Just then we reached the palace, and our conversation came to an end.

---

[7] Law 31, Title 14, Part 5.
[8] Law I, Title 2, Book 2 of the *Recopilación.*

CHAPTER 41

IN WHICH PERIQUILLO DESCRIBES HOW HE WITNESSED SOME
EXECUTIONS IN THAT CITY; HE TELLS WHO THE PRISONERS WERE;
AND HE RELATES A CURIOUS CONVERSATION ABOUT PENAL CODES
THAT TOOK PLACE BETWEEN THE CHINESE AND THE SPANIARD

The next day, we went out on our accustomed stroll, and having walked past the most public places, I observed to Limahotón that I was amazed at finding no beggars in the entire city. He replied, "There are no beggars here even though there are poor people, because even among the poor, most people have trades by which they make their living; and if they do not, the government forces them to learn one."

"And how does the government know," I asked, "who has a trade and who doesn't?"

"It's easy," he told me. "Haven't you noticed that every person we've seen is wearing a particular emblem on his headdress or on the tip of his hat?"

I realized that what the Chinese said was true, and I told him, "Yes, it's just as you say, though I hadn't noticed it; but what do those emblems signify?"

"I'll tell you," he answered.

Just then we were approaching a large crowd that had gathered for some reason in a plaza, and there my friend told me, "Look: that fellow who is wearing a wide, pearl-colored silk ribbon on his head is a judge; that one with the yellow ribbon is a physician; the other with a white one is a priest; the one wearing the blue ribbon is a fortune-teller; the one over there, with the green one, is a merchant, this one with the purple ribbon is an astrologer; the fellow with the black one is a musician; and if they're wearing wide silk ribbons embroidered with yarn or with one metal or another, we can tell that they are practitioners of the main arts and sciences.

"High-ranking employees of the political and military government (for the two are not separated here) and of the religion are distinguished by jeweled bands in their hair, and the kind of jewels and the form of the band show their grades.

"My brother, who, as you have seen, is the viceroy, or the second after the king, has a diamond band set on the crown of his headdress, at the very top of his head. I am the chaen, or inspector general, in his name, so I also have a diamond band, but a smaller one that I wear farther back; that man there with the band of rubies is a magistrate; that one with the emeralds is the high priest; the one with the topazes is an ambassador; and in the same way, we can distinguish all the rest.

"The nobles are the ones who wear silk tunics or robes, and if they have distinguished themselves in war, they wear their robes embroidered in gold. The plebeians wear worsted or cotton robes.

"The artisans wear colored emblems, but theirs are short and made of wool. Those fellows that you see with the white ribbons are weavers of white muslin and linen cloth; the ones with the blue ribbons weave all varieties of silk; the ones with the green are embroiderers; the ones with the red are tailors; the ones with yellow are shoemakers; the ones with black are carpenters, and so on. The executioners wear no ribbons or headdresses at all; they keep their heads shaved and wear a noose tied to their waist, from which a knife dangles.

"The ones you see, both men and women, who are wearing white bands in addition to these tokens, are unmarried; the men wearing red bands have one or more wives, depending on their income; and those with the black bands are widows and widowers.

"In addition to these markings, there are a few other peculiar ones that you might observe easily, such as those that are used by people from other kingdoms and provinces, and from our own in certain cases; for example, on wedding days, during mourning, on feast days, and others. But what I have shown is enough for you to see how easy it is for the government to know the status and trade of every person just by looking at him, and without giving anyone room to pretend, because any auxiliary judge (and there are lots of them) is authorized to examine anyone he finds suspicious in the trade that he claims to have, and he carries out this examination through the trivial expedient of calling the person over and ordering him to make some artifact of the trade he says is his. If he can do it, he goes in peace and is paid for what he made; if he cannot do it, he is led to prison and, after suffering a severe punishment, is forced to learn the trade within that same prison, from which he cannot leave until the master tradesmen certify that he is fit to work for the public.

"The judges aren't the only ones who can do these examinations; the masters of the various trades are also authorized to reprimand and examine anyone they suspect does not know the trade whose emblem he wears; and in this manner, it is very difficult for anyone in our land to be completely idle or useless."

"I cannot help," I said, "but praise your country's economy. If all the provisions that are in force here are as good and commendable as the ones you have shown me, your land must surely be the happiest of all lands, and here you must have realized the ideas imagined by Aristotle, Plato, and other political thinkers, in the way your very well ordered republic is governed."

"I don't know whether it's the happiest of all lands," said the Chinese, "because I haven't seen any others; and it would be a mistake to think that we have no criminals, who exist everywhere in the world, because our citizens are men, just as they are everywhere. What happens is that we try to prevent crimes with our laws, and offenders are punished severely. Tomorrow will be execution day, and you will see whether our punishments are terrible."

With that, we retired to his house, and nothing else of note happened that day; but at dawn on the following day, I was awakened early by the noise of artillery, because all the guns positioned on the walls of the city were being fired.

I got out of bed in fright and looked out the windows of my room, and saw lots of people running about to and fro as if rioting. I asked a servant if their movement signified some kind of popular disturbance or some invasion by external enemies. The servant told me not to be afraid; the uproar was because it was execution day, and since that only came from time to time, countless people flowed into the provincial capital from other provinces, which was why there were so many people in the streets; and also because on these days, they closed the city gates and did not let anyone in or out, nor were the shops allowed to open, nor was anyone allowed to work at any trade until after the executions. I was astonished to hear about all these preparations, and expected to see things that I would undoubtedly find extraordinary.

Indeed, a few hours later, three cannon blasts signaled that it was time for the judges to gather. Then the chaen called for me, and after he had greeted me courteously, we both went to the main city plaza where the punishments were to be carried out.

All the judges were gathered on a large stage, accompanied by the decent foreigners, who were allowed to join them as a courtesy; three more cannon blasts sounded, and about seventy prisoners were paraded out of the prison between the executioners and the ministers of justice.

Then the judges again reviewed the trial records to see if any of those unfortunates had some slight excuse that might reduce his sentence, and finding none, they signaled for the execution to proceed; it began, and all of us foreigners were filled with horror at the harshness of the punishments; for some were impaled, others were hanged, others were whipped cruelly on the calves with wet lashes, and so each prisoner was assigned his own punishment.

But what shocked us was to see that some were marked on their faces with red-hot irons, and then had their right hands cut off.

As you can imagine, those poor people all felt the pain of their torments and screamed to high heaven; in the meanwhile, the judges on the stage passed the time by smoking, chatting, having refreshments, and playing checkers, distracting themselves as best they could so as not to hear the groans of those miserable victims.

This dreadful spectacle ended at three in the afternoon, and then we went to dinner.

The dinner table conversation was all about penal laws, and everyone spoke sensibly on the matter, I thought, especially the Spaniard, who said, "Truly, gentlemen, it is a hard thing to be a judge, and more so in these lands, where custom declares that the judges must be present when the prisoners' sentences are carried out, and their sensitive souls must be tormented by the groans of the victims of justice. It offends our human nature to see one of our fellow men turned over to the fierce executioners, who ruthlessly torment them, and often deprive them of life, adding ignominy on top of their pain.

"One of these poor wretches, whether he is condemned to a villain's death on the gallows, to suffering the pain and public shaming of the lash, or even to being banished from his country and to languishing in a fortress prison, is a tormenting sight for a kind soul. He will not just consider the material affliction that the man feels in his body; he will also realize how his spirit will suffer from the idea of his disgrace, and from the fact that he has no hopes of escape—none of those hopes, I mean, to which we hold on like a life preserver in the common travails of life.

"These reflections are grievous enough in themselves, but a sensitive man does not limit his consideration to them; he is too tender-hearted to forget the particular sentiments that must assail the individual in society.

" 'What anguish this poor prisoner must feel!' he will say to himself or to his friends; 'what anguish, seeing that justice has wrested him from the loving arms of his wife, knowing that he will never again kiss his tender young children or enjoy the conversation of his best friends, but that they will all abandon him forever, and he will be forced to leave them! And how does he leave them? Oh, grief! His wife: a widow, poor, alone, downtrodden; his sons: orphans, unhappy and viewed with scorn; his friends: scandalized and perhaps regretting the friendship they had once professed.'

"Will this humane soul end his reflections here? No: he will go on to embrace those miserable families. He will seek them out in his thoughts; he will find them with ideas; his mind will penetrate the walls of their shelters and, seeing them submerged in grief, disgrace, and helplessness, his spirit will not be able to do less than feel moved by the deepest affliction, to such a degree that if he could, he would rip the victim from the executioner's hands and, thinking to do a great good, would restore him, unharmed, to the bosom of his adoring family.

"But how unfortunate for all of us if such a misconceived humanity were to guide the minds and pens of magistrates! No crime would be punished; the laws would languish in idleness; every man would act on his desires; and the citizens, unable to depend on any personal security, would fall victim to the fury, strength, and daring of others.

"In that sad case, the dams of religion could do nothing to restrain the depraved; it would be mere fantasy to try establishing any kind of government; justice would be unknown, reason would be abused; and the deity would be disobeyed entirely. And what would happen to men without religion, without government, without reason, without justice, and without God? It is easy to see that the world, if it still existed, would be a chaos of crimes and abominations. Each man would be a tyrant over his neighbor whenever he was able. Fathers would not care for sons, sons would not respect their fathers, husbands would not love their wives, wives would not be faithful to their husbands, and on top of these evils, all the affection and reciprocal gratitude of society would be destroyed, and then the strongest would be the executioner of the weakest, against whom he would satisfy his passions by taking away his possessions, his wife, his sons, his liberty, or perhaps his life.

"Such is the appalling vision of despotism that the world would see if justice lacked severity, or better said, if it lacked the restraint of the law to hold back the indomitable and safeguard the way for the well-ordered man of good conduct.

"I will concede without any reluctance that, despite this reasoning, a sensitive soul cannot watch in indifference as the most murderous criminal is beheaded. I will go further: the very judges who sentence the prisoner wet their pens with their tears before they have a chance to dip them in ink for signing the death decree. Such cold and bloody acts are repugnant to them, as they would be to any man brought up amid gentle customs; but they are not the arbiters of the law; they must submit to its sanctions, and they cannot allow justice to be evaded through their indulgence of the prisoners, much as their hearts resist, as they inevitably will. Proof of this is the fact that in my land, judges never attend these funereal events.

"But if these catastrophes afflict our sensibilities, is it possible that reason might deny that they are just, useful, and necessary to the citizen's common good? By no means whatsoever. It is true that a tender soul does not see a criminal perishing on the gibbet, but a fellow man, a human being; and then he ceases to think of the justice of his suffering, and considers only his suffering; but this is not the same thing as bringing our passions in line with reason.

"It has happened to me, on occasions such as this, that I have spilled tears of compassion in favor of a hapless prisoner being led to the gallows, before stopping to reflect on the gravity of his crimes; but when I have carefully considered them, and when I have remembered that this man who is suffering today is the same one who, to satisfy cold vengeance or perhaps to steal some trifle, treacherously murdered some upright man who had worked long and hard to support a large family, which, because of the criminal, was delivered into the cruel grasp of destitution, and that the unfortunate innocent may have perished forever for lack of the spiritual relief prescribed by our religion (I am speaking of the Catholic religion, gentlemen); then I have no doubt that I would willingly subscribe to his sentence of death, certain that in this I would be doing society a great good, proportionate to what the skilled surgeon does when he cuts the rotting hand from his patient to save his entire body.

"So it goes with every sensible man who recognizes that these painful sacrifices are determined by justice for the security of the State and of the citizens.

"If men would submit to the laws of equity, if everyone would act on the inducements of righteous reason, then punishments would be unknown; but unfortunately, men let themselves be ruled by their passions, they cast reason aside, and since they are too inclined by their own weakness to trample over reason to satisfy those passions, in order to restrain the fury of their disordered impulses we must resort to the terror brought about by their fear of losing their possessions, their reputations, their freedom, or their lives.

"Here we have readily discovered the origin of penal laws—just, necessary, and blessed laws. If man were left to act according to his inclinations, he would act more fiercely than wild beasts. Surely no animal could outdo man in ferocity when he loses the reins of reason. There is no dog that isn't grateful to anyone who feeds it bread; there is no horse that does not submit to the rein; there is no hen that refuses to raise its own chicks by itself; and so on.

"Finally, on what occasion have we seen even the most bloodthirsty wild beasts join in a pack to take the life of another member of their own species, even those unfamiliar to them? And man—how often does he ignore loyalty, gratitude, filial love, and all the moral virtues, and join with others to destroy as many of his species as he can?

"A horse will obey a spur, and a burro will carry a burden if threatened with a stick; but when man abandons reason, he is more indomitable than any burro or horse, and in consequence, he necessarily needs harder incentives to restrain him. Such is the fear of losing what he values most, such as his life.

"Justice, or rather the judges who distribute justice in accordance with good laws, do not deprive a prisoner of his liberty or his life out of vengeance, but out of necessity. They do not take away Juan's life solely because he killed Pedro, but also because, when he atones for his crime on the gallows, the people will become confident that the State is watching out for their security and will know that, just as it punished this man, it will punish any men who commit the same crime, which is the same as imposing a general object lesson through the death of a particular offender.

"All nations were imbued with these principles when they adopted criminal laws, laws as ancient as the world itself. God created man, knowing that man would disobey His precepts; but, before man could do so, God informed him of the penalty to which he would be condemned. 'Thou shalt not eat,' He said, 'of the fruit of this tree, for if thou shalt eat of it, thou shalt die.' Here you have the highest authorization for obliging man to obey the law through fear of punishment.

"But for punishments to produce the healthy effects for which they were invented, it is necessary 'that they be derived from the nature of the crime; that they be proportionate to the crime; that they be public, prompt, uncommutable, and necessary; that they be as lenient as possible under the circumstances; and finally, that they be dictated by the law itself.'[1]

"The punishments we have just seen, I believe, followed all of these conditions, with the exception of moderation, for I truly found them to be too cruel, especially the punishment of branding so many wretches with a hot iron and then cutting off their right hands.

"That penalty, in my judgment, is far too cruel, for after punishing the offender with pain, they leave him marked forever with an indelible note of infamy, making him unhappy and useless to society because of the obstacle that cutting off his hand will put in the way of his working.

"These harsh penalties do not shock me as something new. I have read that in Persia they break the teeth of usurers with blows of a hammer, and that fraudulent bakers are thrown into a hot oven. In Turkey they beat them with sticks and fine them for the first and second offense, and for the third they hang the man in the door of his house, leaving the body to hang there for three days. In Moscow they whip those who defraud the tobacco tax until their bones show. In our own penal code, we have laws that prescribe capital punishment for someone who fraudulently declares bankruptcy, and for a house burglar when the quantity stolen amounts to more than fifty pesos; other laws that mandate cutting off the hand of a notary who falsifies documents, and similar laws that are no longer in use because of changing times and the softening of customs.

"Señor Lardizábal, speaking about this topic, says that 'it is not the cruelty of the penalty that is the best curb for restraining crime, but the infallibility of the punishment.' After noting the harshness of some countries, he also says that 'the malefactors, however, continue as always, as if they had not been punished so harshly,' and he adds: 'So it must be, for a very natural reason. As the cruelty of punishments increases, men's spirits harden at the same rate; they become familiar with the punishments, which, after some time, cease to make a large enough impression to restrain their impulses and the ever-burning force of their passions.'

"I have said all this, Loitia, to convince you to intercede with the tután, so that he will do the same with the king, and see if this punishment might be commuted to something less cruel. I would not like any offender to go unpunished; but I would prefer that he not be punished so harshly."

Having said this, the Spaniard fell silent, and the Asian, taking the floor, answered, "One can see, foreigner, that you are very kind-hearted and that you have

---

[1] Señor Lardizábal [see Chapter 35, footnote 3] expresses himself in these same terms in his discourse on criminal penalties [on pp. 65, 66, and 69].

had some education; but remember that 'since the first and foremost aim of any society is the security of its citizens and the health of the republic, it follows as a necessary consequence that this is also the first and general aim of criminal penalties. The health of the republic is the highest law.'

"Remember, too, that 'in addition to this general aim, there are other particular aims subordinate to it, though equally necessary, without which the general aim could not be achieved. These include the correction of the offender to make him a better person, if possible, and to keep him from harming society again; giving a lesson and setting an example so that those who have not sinned will abstain from doing so; the security of the citizens' persons and goods; and the repayment or redress of the harm caused to the public order or to individuals.'[2]

"No doubt you remember all these principles, and in virtue of this, note that the punishments you find excessive are in accord with them. Those who have died have purged the homicides that they committed, and have died with more or fewer torments, depending on the aggravating circumstances of their treachery; because, if punishments are always to fit the crime, it is reasonable for someone who killed another with poison, by drowning, or some other cruel method, should suffer a harsher death than one who deprived another of his life with a simple stab, because the latter made his victim suffer less. The fact is, here anyone who kills another man treacherously will die, without any doubt.

"Those whom you saw being whipped were thieves who were being punished for the first or second time, and those who were branded and mutilated were the incorrigible thieves. No injustice was done to them, because even if their hands were cut off, that only makes them unfit to continue stealing, since they are already unfit for anything else. Society loathes the one skill they have; it would prefer that every thief be unfit to harm it, and therefore it is content to see that justice will leave them in this state and mark them with the hot brand so that they can be recognized and guarded against, even though they are missing the one hand, so that they cannot harm people with the hand they have left.

"In Europe, I am told, a hardened thief will be hanged; in my land, he is branded and mutilated, and I think that the results are better. First, the offender is punished and forcibly reformed, while being allowed to enjoy the best of all possessions, which is life. The citizens are protected from him, and the example set is long-lasting and effective.

"In London, Paris, or elsewhere, one of these thieves would be hanged, and I ask you: does everyone find out? Do they see it? Do they know that they've hanged such-and-such a man, and why? I don't believe so; a few people will see it, fewer individuals will know what the crime was, and the great majority will never find out that a thief has died.

"Not so here: these hapless wretches, who are left with no means of supporting themselves other than begging from door to door (the only ones allowed to beg), are like heralds of the righteousness of justice, and walking testimony to the unhappy state to which man is reduced if he obstinately persists in his crimes.

---

[2] It seems that the Chinese must have read Señor Lardizábal, because the words quoted are his.

"The thief who is hanged in Europe remains exposed to public view for only a short time, and consequently public fears are short-lived. As soon as the baneful sight is removed from view, the idea of his punishment is also erased in the mind of the depraved, who is left without the slightest restraint to dissuade him from his crimes.

"In Europe, such object lessons are isolated (if they serve as warnings to anyone at all) to the city where the executions take place; and on top of that, children, whose delicate brains are more easily impressed by what they see than by what they hear, never see thieves perish, but only hear them spoken of with hatred, and so the most they learn is to hate them, much as they might hate rabid dogs; but they do not conceive all the horror of stealing that is to be desired.

"Here quite the opposite occurs. The offender remains among the people, good and bad, and by the same token his example remains, not isolated in a single city or town, but spreading wherever the wretch might go; and children are imbued with the terror of committing robbery and the fear of punishment, because they get the most eloquent lesson possible through their eyes.

"Compare now whether it is more useful to hang a thief than to brand and mutilate him; and if you still persist, after all that I have said, in thinking it better to hang him, I will not oppose your way of thought, because I know that every kingdom has its own particular laws and customs, and it not easy to abolish them, just as it is not easy to introduce new ones; and with this proviso, let us leave it to the legislators to correct laws that may seem defective with the changing times, and content ourselves with obeying those laws that govern us, so that these punishments never touch us."

We all applauded the Chinese, the table was cleared, and we each retired to our houses.

CHAPTER 42

In which Perico describes how he earned the Chinese's trust;
how he came with him to Mexico; and the happy days he spent
at his side, spending money grandly and passing as a count

I was contented and amazed at my life with my new friend. Contented because of how well he treated me; and amazed to hear him speak so forthrightly every day about matters that he seemed to understand deeply. In truth, his style was not like the way I write, but very sublime, filled with phrases that regaled our ears; his locution was very natural, however, adding unwonted grace to his speeches.

While I was enjoying the good life, I didn't forget to do a little business under the shadow of the friendship that the chaen granted me; so I would put in a few words, insinuate my requests, and make my moves on anyone who came to me without empty hands, and in this way, my skimmings soon filled up a trunk with valuable little gifts.

I did all this, you understand, behind my patron's back, for he was so righteous that if he had seen through my wicked arts, I might not have left that city, since he himself would have condemned me to a fortress prison; but it isn't easy for a superior to distinguish between someone who is advising him and someone who is flattering and deluding him, especially if he is prejudiced in that person's favor, and it follows that villains will continue behaving like rogues, and that superiors will be helpless to see through their deceptions.

Being well aware of these secrets, I always endeavored to speak to the loitia with the greatest discretion, declaring myself to be a tenacious partisan of justice; showing myself to be compassionate and scrupulously disinterested, keen for the public welfare, and in every way an adherent of his way of thinking, all of which flattered his taste exceedingly.

The Chinese was wise, judicious, and good in every way; but I was already accustomed to taking advantage of men's goodness to defraud them for all they were worth, so I didn't find it hard to delude him. I strove to understand his character; I realized that he was just, kind, and unselfish; I always attacked him on these flanks, and rarely failed to obtain my objective.

In the middle of this lucky streak, I couldn't help feeling sorry that my viceroyalty had gone to pot, and many times my pretended countdom wasn't enough to console me—though I didn't mind the way they regaled my ears with the title, since every day the foreigners who visited the chaen would say to me, *Please hear me out, Count; Count, please see here; Count, this is for Your Honor,* and Count this, and Count that, until they were *Counting* me all up and down. Even the poor Chinese called me Count, following everyone's example, and since he saw that they all treated me with respect and affection, he believed that a count was at least as high as a tután in his land, or a vizier in Turkey. On top of this mistaken concept, he formed an idea that I was an important person in Mexico; and so he endeavored to secure my protection, showing his friendliness to me in every way he could; and the foreigners who needed his protection, seeing how well he liked me, strove to flatter him by expressing their esteem for me; and so, each deluding the other, they unwittingly conspired to make me lose the little good judgment I had, for they *Counted* me and *Your-Honored* me so much; they flattered me so much; and they showed me so much affection and obsequiousness, that I was at the point of believing I had been born a count and just hadn't noticed it.

"What a lark," I'd say to myself when I was alone, "what a lark if I were a count and didn't know it! True, I just gave myself the title; but if you're going to be a count, what difference does it make if you give the title to yourself or the king gives it to you? So long as you've got the title, it all comes out in the wash. Now, what's to stop me from being the best count in the universe? Nobility? I've got that. Age? I'm old enough. Knowledge? I don't need any of that; and as for desire, I have plenty. The only thing I don't have is money and merit; but that's just a trifle. You think all counts have lots of money and merit? How many of them lack both? So hang in there, Perico, one more garbanzo won't burst the pot. I was born to be a count, given my character, and I am a count, and I'll be a count come what may, and I'll do whatever deviltries it takes to remain a count, and I bet I won't be the first man who became a count by being a rascal."

I used to entertain myself with this sort of nonsensical soliloquy from time to time, and I'd get so absorbed in it that I'd often lock myself into my room, and the chaen would have to send for me, telling me that he and his retinue were waiting for me to have dinner. Then I'd come to, as if recovering from a bout of lethargy, and exclaim, "Lord God, do not allow these fantastical ideas to take root in my mind and make me go more crazy than I already am!"

Divine Providence must have heard my prayers, and ordained that I not end up a count in San Hipólito, since I had already lost all hope of entering there as viceroy, just as many madmen enter it for going off on a foolish bent that is difficult, if not impossible, to undo.

A few days later, they notified the foreigners that the ship was ready and that they were just waiting for the tután's permission to sail. His brother easily obtained that; and as soon as everything was prepared for us to embark, he revealed his designs for sailing to America with the king's permission, a very distinguished favor in Asia.

All the passengers celebrated his intentions at a banquet, with plenty of cheers, vying with each other in their offers to serve him in whatever capacity they could. After all, they were well-born people, and they knew that they were bound by the laws of gratitude.

The day arrived when we were to set sail, and when we were all on board and waiting for the chaen's luggage to be loaded, we saw in amazement that it amounted to no more than one cot, one servant, one trunk, and one suitcase.

When the Chinese came on board, the Spanish merchant asked if the trunk were filled with ounces of gold.

"No, it isn't," said the Chinese; "not more than about 200 ounces."

"Well, that's not much money," the merchant replied, "for the kind of voyage you are planning to undertake."

The Chinese smiled and said, "I have plenty of money for seeing Mexico and traveling through Europe."

"You must know what you're doing," said the Spaniard, "but I repeat that this is very little money."

"It is more than enough," said the Chinese. "I am counting on your money, on the money of your countrymen who are accompanying us, and on what the rich people of your land keep in their coffers. I will withdraw their money legally, and I'll have more than enough for everything."

"Please," the Spaniard replied, "do me the favor of deciphering this enigma. If you mean out of friendship, of course you may count on my money and that of my companions; but if you mean through commerce, I don't know what you might have that you could trade for a single peso."

"Bits of stone and animal diseases," said the Chinese, "and don't ask me any further, because when we are in Mexico I will decipher the enigma for you."

That left us all perplexed; but then they lifted anchor and we headed out to sea, and by God's will our journey was so happy that three months later, we were sailing with the wind at our back into the port and miserable city of Acapulco, which, despite being so decrepit, looked so lovely to me when I kissed her sands that it rivaled the capital of Mexico. A natural feeling of delight for someone who sees once more, after suffering many hardships, the hills and hovels of his homeland.

We disembarked very contentedly, rested for eight days, and arranged to make the journey to Mexico in litters.

On the way, I kept wondering how I would part ways with the Chinese and my other pals, leaving them with the belief that I was a count without being taken for a fraud or a rude ingrate; but much as I brooded over it, I couldn't find a way around the obstacles I kept bumping up against.

Meanwhile, we advanced several leagues each day, until we reached this city and all took rooms at the inn of La Herradura.[1]

Since the Chinese knew none of the customs of my country, he would stop for everything and bewilder me with questions, because it was all new to him, and he begged me not to leave his side until he was somewhat educated; I promised him I would do so, and we came to an agreement; but the foreigners constantly pestered me about my countdom, particularly the Spaniard, who would say to me, "Count, we have been in Mexico for days, and not a sight of Your Honor's servants and coaches to take you to your house. Now, of course, it's true that you're a count, but . . . please don't be upset, but I think that you're some kind of count-in-waiting, in the same way that there are gentlemen-in-waiting."

When he told me this, I got upset and said, "Whether or not you believe I'm a count doesn't make any difference to me. My house is in Guadalajara; it will take quite some time before they get here for me; and meanwhile, I cannot perform the role that you are expecting of me; but someday we'll both know who's who."

After that he left me alone and didn't say another word about the countdom to me. The Chinese meanwhile revealed the enigma that he had spoken about when we were setting sail; he took out a small case full of exquisite diamonds, and a small box,

---

[1] [The *mesón de la Herradura* was near the Zócalo, in the same neighborhood as the *mesón del Ángel* where Don Antonio had lived with his wife (Spell, p. 192). –Tr.]

the size of a snuffbox, packed with lovely pearls, and he said, "Spaniard, I have fifteen of these little cases, and forty of these boxes; what do you think,[2] will I get enough money with these?"

The merchant, amazed by so much wealth, couldn't stop thinking about how many carats the diamonds had and how large, round, and white the pearls were, and so, in the midst of his engrossment, he said, "If all your diamonds and pearls are like these, and if there are this many of them, you could easily get 2 million pesos for them. Oh, what richness! What beauty! What loveliness!"

"I would say," the Chinese replied, "what foolishness, what insanity, and what stupidity for men to pay so much for a few stones and a few hardened oyster humors, which might well be diseases, like the stones that men grow in their urinary bladders and kidneys! Friend, men value difficulty more than beauty. One of these diamonds is beautiful, true, and harder than flint; but there are plenty of stones that equal it in brilliance and that reflect as much light into our eyes as these, tinged with all the colors of the rainbow, which is all that the diamond gives us, nothing more. A piece of cut glass shines as brightly, and a string of glass beads is more colorful than a string of pearls; but diamonds are uncommon, and pearls hide at the bottom of the sea, and there you have the real reasons why they are so highly esteemed. If men were saner, they would lower their opinions of many things that gain a high value only through men's madness. In one of the books that your companions loaned me on the trip, I was shocked to read that a certain Cleopatra gave her beloved Mark Anthony a glass of wine with a pearl dissolved in vinegar, but a pearl so large and exquisite that they say it was worth a city. Nobody can doubt that this was an outrageous act of madness on Cleopatra's part, and stupidly vain; but I don't blame her much. True, it was the extravagance of a woman who was passionate for a man and who thought she might win him over by giving him that priceless pearl, as a sign that she was ready to give him the richest thing she had; but there is nothing about it that is peculiar to a woman in love. I would think that the health, freedom, and honor of women are worth more to them than Cleopatra's pearl, yet every day some woman sacrifices her health, her freedom, and her honor to her passion for a man who may not even love her. What scandalizes me is not Cleopatra's liberality, but the value of that pearl; yet, as you can see, this proves that men have always been willing to pay for what is rare. As for me, what interests me now is to take advantage of their prejudices so that I can have enough money."

"Well, you will get that easily enough," said the Spaniard, "because so long as there are men, there will always be some who'll pay for diamonds and pearls; and so long as there are women, there will be plenty of people who will make men sacrifice themselves to buy them for them. This afternoon I'll come with a jeweler, and I'll invest ten or twelve thousand pesos in you."

It was then time for dinner, and after the meal the merchant went out into the street, soon returning with the expert; he settled on a few diamonds and four strings of pearls with three lovely, long teardrop pearls, paying for it in cash.

---

2 [At this point, Limahotón switches from *vos* to *usted* to mean "you"; Lizardi comments in a footnote:] During the voyage, the Chinese had learned our ways of speaking and address.

Three days later, he parted company with us, leaving us with the Chinese, myself, his servant, and another serving lad from Mexico whom I had hired to do his errands.

My friend still believed that I was a count, and he constantly asked me, "Count, when are they going to come from your land for you?"

I would give him whatever answer popped into my head, and he would be completely satisfied, but not the Mexican servant, who thought I looked decent enough but didn't see any of the luxury that a count would boast; so much so that it began to bother him, for one day he asked me, "Pardon me, Your Honor, sir, but are you a real count, or you jis' call yourself one?"

"I call myself one," I answered, and I got that curious blockhead off my back.

And so I went along, having a great time as a no-count count with my Chinese, winning more and more of his affection every day, and acting as the guardian of his trust and his money—so liberally that I myself, afraid that the gambling bug would bite me and that I might get up to one of my old tricks, kept trying to hand him the keys to the trunk and the suitcase, asking him to keep them and just give me the spending money. He would never take them, until one day when I insisted on it, he grew serious and said to me with his customary ingenuousness, "Count, for days now you have persistently argued that I should watch my own money; but I want you to watch it, if you wish, for I do not mistrust you, because you are a noble and nobles should never be mistrusted, since anyone who is noble will make sure that his actions match his principles; this obligation weighs on every nobleman, even if he is poor; how much more will it weigh on a distinguished noble who is as visible in society as a count? So keep the keys, and feel free to spend the money on everything you find necessary for my comfort and decency; for let me tell you that I am very displeased with this house, which is too small, uncomfortable, dirty, and badly staffed, the worst of it being the dinner service; please do me the favor, then, of finding me a better house, and if all the houses in your land are no better than this, let me know so that I can resign myself to it once and for all."

I thanked him for his trust and told him that if he wished to live in the style of the gentleman he was, he had the money, and I undertook to do it for him, telling him not to worry because I would have it all ready in a week.

Just then the servant who was my fellow countryman came in, leading the barber, who opened up his arms and embraced me as soon as he saw me; he squeezed me so hard that I thought I'd choke, and he told me, "Blessed be God, master, for letting me see you again, and looking plenty handsome! Where've you been? Because after those damnable Indians ran you out of Tula, I never heard another peep about you. All I could find out was, a friend of mine told me they'd sent you off to some fortress as a soldier because of something or other you did in Tixtla; but that was the last news I had of you. So tell me, sir, how're things?"

Having said this, he let me go, and I recognized that my great friend who had just made me look so bad was young master Andrés, the one who had helped me to shave dogs, flay Indians, break old women's jaws, and administer enemas. I can't deny that I was glad to see him, because the poor fellow was a good lad; but I don't know what I would have given to make him less effusive and blockheaded than he was, causing me to blush and bringing my countdom crashing to the ground with his simple-minded questions right in front of the Chinese lord, who, being anything but slow-witted, realized that my countdom and my wealth were just a racket; but he pretended not to notice, and waited until after he had been shaved, and when that was done, I paid Andrés a peso for the job, for it is easy to be generous with someone else's money.

Andrés embraced me again and invited me to visit him at his barbershop in La Merced next to La Casa del Pueblo,[3] for he had many things to tell me. With that he left, and the Chinese, whom I should now call my master, said to me with the greatest judiciousness, "I have just discovered that you are neither rich nor a count, and I believe that you used that ruse to live well by my side. I am not shocked in the least, nor do I think badly of you for arranging a better life for yourself through an innocent lie. Nor should you think that I have lowered my opinion of you because you are poor and have no countdom; I judged you to be an upright man, and that is why I liked you. As long as you remain one, you will retain your place in my esteem, because for me no one can be more noble than an upright man, whosoever he may be; and no rogue could convince me of his nobility, even if he were a count. So go on, don't be ashamed, keep serving me as you have up until now, and set yourself a salary, since I don't know how much servants like yourself earn in your land."

Although I did feel a bit ashamed at seeing myself drop instantly in my master's opinion from count to servant, his affection did not displease me, much less his generosity in letting me set my own salary and pay myself by my own hand; and so, endeavoring to cast aside that bit of shame like a wicked thought, I strove to enjoy the good life, beginning with winning my master over and pleasing him.

With this thought in mind, I went out to find a new house, and I found a handsome one with every comfort one might desire, and inexpensive and on a good street to boot, the street called Don Juan Manuel.[4]

Next, since I already knew how this was done, I dickered with an auctioneer, who furnished the house quickly and in a very decent style. Then I hired a good cook and a doorman, and finally I bought a splendid carriage with two teams of mules; I took on a coachman and a footman; I sent them to have liveries made according to my specifications, and when everything was ready, I brought my master to take possession of the house.

We should note that I hadn't let on about anything I had been doing, nor did I tell him that this was his house; I just asked him what he thought of the house, its furnishings, carriage, and all. When he replied that it was not bad indeed, unlike that hovel where he was living, I gave him the relief of letting him know that it was his. He thanked me, asked me for the bill so that he could note it down in his expense log, and was very happy to stay there.

I was no less content, of course: who wouldn't be pleased with as plush a deal as I had found? I had a good house, good board, decent clothes, lots of gold at my disposal, freedom, a carriage to get around in, and very little work to do, if you can even call it work to order servants around and give them money to spend.

---

[3] [La Casa del Pueblo ("the house of the people"): possibly referring to the Ayuntamiento (city hall) of Mexico City. –Tr.]

[4] [On the street now known as Uruguay, two blocks south of the Zócalo. –Tr.]

Altogether, I had hit the jackpot with my new master, who, apart from being very rich, liberal, and good, loved me more each day because I made a study of flattering him. I acted very circumspect in his presence, and so thrifty that I would chew out the servants over a candle-end that had been left burning or a bit of hay that had been spilled in the patio; and so my master trusted that I was looking out for his interests; but he didn't know that when I went out by myself, my pockets weren't empty, and that I would merrily spend his gold and silver with my friends and their girlfriends.

They were all amazed at my luck, and they were drawn to me like flies to honey. The girls made a bigger fuss over me than a hungry dog would over a tasty bone, and my good luck made me conceited.

One day when I was riding alone in the carriage, on my way to a lunch in Jamaica[5] to which I had been invited, I said to myself:

"How wrong my father was when he used to preach to me that I should learn a trade or devote myself to learning something useful for making a living, because if I didn't work, I wouldn't eat! Maybe that was true in his time, back when Perico was a pup; way back when everybody used to work and men were ashamed to be useless and lazy; back when rich people and even kings and queens made a big deal out of working with their hands now and then; back when men wore wide breeches and broke their backs working for a few pennies. The Iron Age! The Dark Ages! The age of stupidity!

"Thank God that those years were followed by the Golden Age and the Age of Enlightenment that we're living in now, when nobles aren't confused with plebeians or rich with poor! Leave work, the arts and sciences, agriculture and poverty, to the poor, because we do our cities plenty of honor with our carriages, party dresses, and liveries.

"If the plebeians cultivate our fields and serve us with their handicrafts, we certainly compensate them for their trouble—we pay them any old thing for their work and their goods, and we lavish our riches by the fistful on the heart of society, through our gaming, dancing, strolling, and all the luxuries that keep us entertained.

"For me to spend money the way I spend it, what kind of science or trade did I have to learn so that I could acquire it the way I acquired it? What skill did I need, beyond a little gab and some good luck? I'm no count, but I'm getting away with a marquis' life. There might even be counts and marquises who can't spend a peso as freely as I can, because it cost them so much trouble to earn it, and it must cost them just as much to keep it.

"No doubt about it: if you were born to be rich, you'll be rich even if you don't work, even if you're a lazy beast; maybe that's why they say, *if God wants to give you something, walls won't stop Him;* just like, if you were born to be poor, then even if you're wise as Solomon, even if you're the most upright man ever and you work night and day, you'll never have a peso, and if you manage to get one, you still won't be able to show off—everything will turn into salt and water for you, and you'll die in the darkest obscurity, even if you own a candle shop."

---

5 [Jamaica: then a small town and popular hangout of the well-to-do (today a neighborhood of Mexico City), near Ixtacalco and Santa Anita, about four miles southwest of the city center. –Tr.]

That was the crazy way I talked to myself when I got drunk with freedom and with the opportunities I had to give into pleasures, without noticing that I was not rich and that the money I was spending wasn't my own, and that even if it had been, Providence had hardly provided it to me so that I could act arrogantly or disparage my fellow man; nor had I been given wealth so that I could squander it on gambling and excess, but so that I could put it to use in moderation and be useful and beneficial to my brothers, the poor.

I didn't think about any of this at the time; rather, I believed that having money was like having a license to do whatever you wanted with impunity, no matter how bad it was, without having the slightest obligation to be useful to other men at all. I formed this false and wicked opinion not only because of my own depraved inclinations, but with the help of the bad examples set for me by a few dissipated, useless, and immoral rich men; and their examples not only supported my long-standing laziness, but made me cruel despite the seeds of sensitivity that my heart sheltered.

Spoiled by my free control over my master's gold; conceited about the good clothes, house, and carriage that I enjoyed for free; stunned by the way I was always being buttered up by countless flatterers, who themselves were more than a bit well off, and who constantly praised my talent, my nobility, my elegance, and my liberality (praises that I paid for dearly); and, worst of all for me, duped by my belief that I had been born to be rich, to be the viceroy or at least a count, I looked down on my equals with disdain, on my inferiors with contempt, and on the ill, tattered, and unfortunate poor with disgust, and with what seems to me a criminal hatred, merely because they were poor.

It goes without saying that I never helped the destitute, since I could hardly be made to talk with a poor man, and in the rare cases when I was forced to speak with them, my phrases seemed as if they had been passed through a sieve: *fine, we'll see, another day, all right, well, yes, no, come back,* and other such laconic phrases were all I ever used with them when I couldn't get away with saying nothing, unless I got upset and treated them even more haughtily, stepping all over them and even threatening to kick them downstairs.

And don't think that this is what I'd do with the ones who begged for alms from me, because I never let anyone get in to see me for that annoying purpose; I would carry on in this proud way with the porter, the tailor, the hairdresser, the shoemaker, the laundry woman, and other unhappy artisans and servants who justly asked to be paid for their work; to the point that my master finally had to pay more than 2,000 pesos for debts that I had made him take on for such things, all the while that I spent money profusely on outings, picnics, seats at the Coliseo, and parties.

There was never a function that I missed in Santiago, Santa Ana, Ixtacalco, Ixtapalapa, and other points, together with my friends and girlfriends, gallantly squandering the gold on them. There was no famous lunch stand where I didn't pay for everybody's meals some day, and there was never a wedding, saint's day party, high mass, or any other hustle-and-bustle to which I wasn't invited—and they always cost me more than I had expected.

In other words, I was a puppy at every party, duping the poor Chinese to my heart's content, and I was a sweetheart to my flatterers and wormwood to the poor.

Once when I was getting out of the carriage, a man rushed up to talk to me; his clothes were poor, but he seemed to be decently born. He told me about the miserable state he was in: sick, out of work, unprotected, with three little children and a wife who was also sick in bed, whom he had no food to give at that hour, which was two in the afternoon.

"May God help you," I replied as dryly as could be; and then, kneeling in front of me as I stood at the bottom of the steps, he told me with tears in his eyes, "Don Pedro, sir, please help me out with two bits, for the sake of God, because my family is dying of hunger; I am poor, but too ashamed to go about begging from house to house, so I made up my mind to ask you, trusting that you will help me out with this little trifle, if only because I am asking you by the soul of my brother Don Manuel Sarmiento, whom you should remember; and if not, let me tell you that I am speaking of your father, the husband of Doña Inés de Tagle, who lived for many years in Calle del Águila, where you were born, and who died in Calle de Tiburcio, after serving as reporter to the Royal Audiencia; and. . . . "

"Enough," I told him; "those details prove that you knew my father, but not that you're my relative, because I have no poor kin; go, and may God be with you."

Saying this, I ran upstairs, cutting him off in midsentence, and leaving him unaided and so exasperated with the bad welcome I had given him that he could only avenge himself by hurling curses at me, calling me cruel, ungrateful, arrogant, and unappreciative. The servants who heard him swearing at me tried to flatter me by beating him and kicking him out, and I witnessed the whole scene from the corridor, laughing uproariously.

I ate dinner and slept a good siesta, and that evening I went to a party where I lost fifteen ounces of gold in a game of monte, and I returned home feeling quite serene, without a trace of regret; but I didn't have two bits to help my unlucky uncle. I am told that there are many rich men who behave today the same way I did then; if that is true, I find it hard to believe.

I spent two or three months like this, until God said: "Enough."

CHAPTER 43

In which Perico tells of the wicked way he left the
house of the Chinese, and other pretty little details;
but you will have to read them to know them

Since no man is so bad that he doesn't know a few good tricks, I retained a few seeds of sensitivity in the middle of my erring ways and dissipation, though they were stunted by my arrogance; and I also kept a bit of respect and love for my religion, which was why—hoping to win my master over so that he would become a Christian—I would take him to the splendid feast-day celebrations that were put on in some temples, whose magnificence surprised him; and I would watch, with pleasure and edification, the great respect and devotion with which he attended these fiestas, not only imitating what he saw the faithful do, but serving as an exemplar of modesty to the irreverent, for not only did he remain kneeling throughout the sacrifice of the Mass, he never raised his eyes, never turned his head, never chatted, never did any of the other irreverent acts that many Christians do at such times, to the detriment of the place and the divine service.

I noticed that he would move his lips as if he were praying, and since I knew that he had never learned our prayers and I had no reason to think that he believed in our religion, this fact struck me; so one day, to settle my doubts, I asked him what he was saying to God when he prayed in the temple. To this he answered, "I do not know whether your God exists or does not exist in the beautiful shrine that you've shown me; but you say He does, and all Christians believe it, so you must have solid reasons, proofs, and experiences that have convinced you. On top of this, I deem that if it is true, then the God you adore can be no other than the Highest God, or God of Gods, to whom all other gods are subject and subordinated; surely you adore Laocon Izautey,[1] who is the governor of Heaven, and in this belief I say to him, 'Great God, whom I worship in this temple, have pity on me, and make all those who know you love you, so that they may be happy.' I repeat this prayer many times."

The Chinese astonished me with his answer, and, stirred by it, I tried to make him love our religion more and more, and to learn about it; but I discovered that I wasn't up to this enterprise, so I proposed to him that it would be very appropriate to a man of his decency and demeanor to employ a chaplain in his house.

"What is a chaplain?" he asked me, and I said that chaplains were the ministers of the Catholic religion who lived with great gentlemen such as himself, to say Mass for them, confess them, and administer the holy sacraments in their houses, subject to the bishop's and the parish priest's approval.

"That is well and good," he said, "for you Christians, who are instructed in your religion, which compels you, and who obey its precepts with exactitude; but not for me, a foreigner who doesn't know any of your rites, and who therefore cannot carry them out."

---

[1] [Laocon Izautey: another name taken from González de Mendoza's *Historia* (see Chapter 39, footnote 4). –Tr.]

"No, sir," I said; "it isn't true that everyone who employs a chaplain obeys the precepts of our religion exactly. Some have chaplains as a matter of form, and might not confess with them in ten years, or hear Mass once in twenty months."

"Well, then, what good are they?" asked the Chinese.

"Lots of good," I replied; "they can say Mass inside the house so that the servants won't have to go out to church and fall behind in their chores; they can serve as adornments for the house, for showing off its luxury, for helping the ladies climb in and out of carriages, for carrying on dinnertime conversation; and on occasion, for carrying a letter to the post, for cashing a bill of payment, for playing a hand of ombre, and things like that."

"That is to say," the Chinese retorted, "that in your land, rich men keep ministers of religion in their houses more out of luxury and vanity than devotion, and these ministers serve more to flatter than to correct the vices of their masters, patrons, or whatever you call them."

"No, I didn't say all that," I replied; "they don't act the same way in every house. There are some houses where they do just what I said, and there are some servile chaplains who ignore the decorum that is appropriate to their character and who stoop to flattering the gentlemen and ladies of their houses as if they were errand runners or footmen; but there are other houses where they keep chaplains out of devotion, not just for show, and give them the high regard that their dignity deserves; and as you can imagine, such chaplains aren't ecclesiastical toothpick-holders, laymen in soutanes, fools wrapped in taffeta and black cloth, nor in short are they immoral ignoramuses who, to the scandal of the people and their own humiliation, lead their patrons by the hand and shorten their path to Hell by disgracefully appeasing them in the confessional, or by allowing them to get into voluntary proximate occasions of sin,[2] or by absolving them for usury, or by relieving their consciences with lax and shaky opinions, or by supporting their most reprehensible misconduct, or, finally, by confirming their errors not only with their maxims, but with their own detestable examples. Because, what will a libertine family do if it sees that its chaplain—who is, or should be, an apostle, a minister of the sanctuary, a guard dog barking incessantly against sin without the slightest regard for a person's rank, a living standard by which the faithful should be able to measure their own actions, an expert in the law, an angel, a sure guide, a clear light, and a tutelary god of the house in which he lives— what, I say, will the family who gives itself over to his protection do if it sees that the chaplain is the first to dress up in luxurious clothes, to attend every ball and gaming session, to hang out by the girls' sitting room and affect the bowing and scraping, the sweet-talking, and the antics of the cheekiest fops, and so on, and so forth? What will it do, I repeat, but canonize its vices and think itself saintly, or even imitate everything the chaplain does? I realize, sir, that you will say it is impossible for any chaplain to be so immoral, or for any patron to be stupid enough to keep such a chaplain in his house; but what I say is, if only it were impossible! In that case, I never would have met the originals whose portraits I have painted; but alongside these there are also saintly houses, as I have hinted, and there are wise and virtuous chaplains whose

---

[2] [Voluntary proximate occasion of sin: see Chapter 14, footnote 4. –Tr.]

presence, modesty, and composure alone can restrain not only the servants and employees, but even the patrons themselves, even if they are counts or marquises. I have known some chaplains whose conduct was so well ordered and who were so zealous in their love of God that they have not hesitated to tell their patrons the unvarnished truth, seriously reproaching them for their vices, encouraging them to practice virtue through their persuasion and examples, and leaving their houses when they find stiff opposition to reason."

"A chaplain like that would suit me," the Chinese said, "and of course you may hire one for the house; but I warn you, he should be wise and virtuous, because I don't want him as a decoration or a piece of furniture. If possible, find me an old one, because if gray hairs do not prove knowledge or virtue, at least they show experience."

With this decree I marched off, happy as could be, in search of a chaplain to hire, believing I had done something good, and telling myself, "Lord help me, what a pack of home truths I told my master, all in an instant! No doubt about it, I can pull my own weight as a missionary when I feel like it. I could grab me a pulpit and wander around this God's green earth, preaching pretty sermons, as Sancho said to Don Quixote.[3]

"But what does it mean that, knowing the truth so clearly, knowing how to preach it, and praising virtue while disparaging vice, as I sometimes do so reasonably in favor of others, I personally hold it in so little account that I've never preached a sermon to myself in my life?

"And what does it mean that I'm such an Argus for seeing my fellow men's sins, and such a Cyclops for ignoring my own? Why can I see the mote in my neighbor's eye so clearly, but not the beam sticking out of mine? Why, if I want to be the world's reformer, don't I start by fixing up my own shabbiness, since I've got so much to fix? And finally, why do I love to give good advice so much, but I don't take the advice of others when they offer it? I'm surely a priceless devil of a preacher.

"But of course, why should it surprise me if I speak clear truths at times, or praise virtue, or condemn vice, perhaps to the benefit of those who hear me, when I am not the one doing these things, but God, the source of all good? Indeed, God was making use of me to bring a good minister to this Chinese, perhaps so that he would embrace the Catholic religion; and since He made use of me, couldn't He have made use of a different instrument, better or worse than me? Who could doubt it?

"Yet Divine Providence does not do things haphazardly, but rather in an ordered way, for our good; therefore, why shouldn't I think that God has put all this in my head not only so that the Chinese will get baptized, but so that I will convert and change my life around?

"That must be it; and I'm ready to keep this opportunity from slipping away, and grab hold of it right now. But what a devil I am! So long as I'm not hanging around my friends and my darlings, I can think straight; but as soon as I'm with the boys and girls, I forget every good resolution I make, and back I go on my adventures.

---

[3] [Actually, Don Quixote said this about Sancho; *Don Quixote*, Part II, chapters XX and XXII. –Tr.]

"These aren't the first resolutions I've made, and this isn't the first sermon I've preached to myself; I've done this several times, and each time I've ended up as much a Periquillo as ever—just like Balaam's ass, who admonished the wicked man and then went back to being the same ass it was before.[4] But must I always be so stubborn? Might I not be tamed sometime by the soft counsel of my conscience; not respond someday to the calls of God? Why shouldn't I? Hey, Señor Perico, it's a new life! Let's remember that we're incorrigible from cradle to grave, that we're mortal, that hell exists, that eternity exists, and that death will come like a thief in the night and will catch us unawares, and then all the devils will carry us off in the blink of an eye.

"But no; they're tolling those bells for repentance, Periquillo; repent, and curb that dog, because the things of this life are here today and gone tomorrow. I'll look for a chaplain, and I'll hire one with learning, prudence, and experience; I'll confess with him; I'll stay away from tempting situations: so, good-bye social gatherings; good-bye outings, Alameda, Coliseo, and visits; good-bye lunches at Nana Rosa's; good-bye billiard games and monte; good-bye friends; good-bye Pepitas, Tulitas, and Mariquitas; good-bye fancy party clothes; good-bye dissipation; good-bye world; I'm going to be a saint from here on out, a saint.

"But what will my villainous friends and my female admirers say? Won't they say that I'm a holier-than-thou hypocrite, that I've turned to living a righteous life because I'm tired of spending, and other things that'll leave a bad taste in my mouth? Well, so what? Let them say what they will, because they aren't going to come and get me out of Hell."

With these good though superficial thoughts, I entered the house of Don Prudencio, a friend of mine and an upright man, who was holding a gathering at his house. I told him who I was trying to hire, and he told me, "I know exactly what you're looking for. My uncle, Dr. Don Eugenio Bonifacio, is an old cleric; he has led a very orderly life, and he's a fount of learning, according to those who know. He's very poor right now, because his chaplaincies have been declared insolvent, and he is so good that he hasn't wanted to get mixed up in lawsuits, because he says that the tranquility of his spirit is worth more than all the gold in the world. I'll suggest this job to him, and I believe he'll accept it gladly. I'm going to send for him right now, because there's no point in mourning until the dead man's present."

This said, Don Prudencio left; they brought out some chocolate for me, and while I drank it, the bells rang for vespers and my fellow party-goers began to arrive.

The party got going, with men and women, and the mandolins were waking up people's flagging spirits and putting their feet in motion.

By seven in the evening, things were pretty hot, and I was standing there trying not to dance, remembering my good resolutions; my sudden prudishness was the news of the hour, because nobody could get me to dance, even after wasting lots of saliva trying to talk me into it.

I sure wanted to dance: these little parties were my weakest flank; my feet were itching to go; but I wanted to practice keeping steadfast in the midst of temptation and staying unharmed in the fiery flames, so I said to myself, "No, Perico, watch it;

---

[4] [Numbers 22:28–30. –Tr.]

no reason to faint; nobody wins the crown unless he fights to the end; cheer up and stick it out; sit tight."

I entertained myself with these interior monologues, convinced that my resolutions were holding firm, for I had managed to keep from dancing for two hours and had found the strength to resist not only the pleas and persuasions of my friends, but also the insistent demands of various young ladies, who never tired of badgering me to dance, both because I was good at shaking my hooves and because I had money: a most powerful reason for being loved by the ladies.

Nevertheless I snubbed all the nagging girls, and I would have snubbed Prester John himself, because I didn't want to break my promises.

But at half past seven, who comes walking in but Anita la Blanda, a girl who was pretty like no other, rowdier than anyone, and my favorite little flirt. I had enjoyed conversations with her at social gatherings; she was my inseparable partner at the contra dances; and all I had to do for her to single me out above all others was to take her to her house after wining and dining her in a tavern, leave her six or eight pesos the next morning, and show her a little tenderness. All of this was done very honorably, because she was always accompanied by her Aunt . . . well . . . by her aunt, who was a good old woman.

So as I was saying, that night my Anita walked in, dressed in a snowy blue taffeta shift with white trim, a white knit shawl, shoes of the same color, lace stockings, and hair done up in the latest style. Her dress was very simple; but if I always liked the way she looked, this night she looked like a goddess to me in the dress she was wearing, because the subdued colors brought out the gold in her tresses, the blackness of her eyes, the pink of her cheeks, the scarlet of her lips, and the whiteness of her breasts.

After she had taken her place in the ladies sitting room, my eyes were fixed on her; but I pretended otherwise, chatting with a friend and making not to notice her; she noticed my pretense, though, and she had heard that I hadn't wanted to dance, and fearing that I might be sulking on account of something she had done (because she gave me reasons to sulk all the time), she came over to me and said in a voice as soft as butter, "Pedrillo, didn't you see me here? They tell me that you haven't wanted to dance, and that you've been sad all night; what's wrong?"

"Nothing, ma'am," I said with the greatest circumspection.

"But what is it? Are you sick?"

"Yes, I am. I am suffering."

"Suffering?" she said. "But no, my darling, you shouldn't have to suffer; Don Prudencio thinks highly of me; come to the bedroom, and I'll have them boil a little chamomile tea or anise for you to drink. You must be suffering from gas."

"No, it isn't gas that makes me suffer," I said; "it is something more solid, and this suffering is beneficial for me. Please, go dance."

I spoke about suffering from my sins; but the girl understood that I was suffering bodily, so she continued to insist with a thousand tender gestures, until she saw how recalcitrant and aloof I was being, and then she got angry and left me, allowing some other little fop, who had always been my rival and who kept an eye out for the moment I abandoned her, to take my place at her side.

As soon as she gave him half a chance, he sat down with her and started wooing her with heart and soul. My good fortune was that he was poor; otherwise he would have dethroned me in four or five minutes, because he was a more handsome lad than me.

Noticing her disdain and my rival's fervent determination, I was so inflamed by jealousy that I tossed out all my considerations and wished my resolutions to the devil.

I jumped up like a raging lion; I went over to lambaste the other poor fellow in the most impolite and provocative terms. The girl, who acted flighty but was actually more prudent than I was, endeavored to deny what she had done; she calmed down the quarrel with many caresses, and we remained as close friends as ever.

After tossing out my conversion, I danced, drank, frolicked, and challenged Anita to give me satisfaction, body to body, for the attack of jealousy she had caused me. She excused herself, saying that dueling was prohibited, especially between such unequal opponents.

My merrymaking was reaching its most ardent pitch when Don Prudencio informed me that his uncle, the doctor of theology, had arrived, and that I should go converse with him in his study, so that he could hear the proposal I had to make from my own mouth.

I wasn't in any mood to converse with theologians, so, stealing half of a quarter of an hour, I entered the study and finished up my business as quick as I could, arranging to meet the father at eight the following morning and bring him to the house.

The poor priest was hoping that I would inform him at length about everything his nephew had mentioned; but I didn't yield to his desires, telling him that we'd see each other the next day and that I would answer all the questions he wanted to ask me then. With that, I bid him farewell, giving that good cleric an opinion of me as a spoiled libertine.

As soon as I had given him the slip, I went back to Anita, and at nine—the hour when I always went home, out of respect for my master, and even that at the cost of a thousand lies I'd drop on him—I brought her to her house, as honorable as ever, and went home to my own.

When I arrived, the Chinese was already sleeping, so I had a fine supper and went to bed myself.

The next day, I went at the appointed hour to get the distinguished father, who was already waiting for me at Don Prudencio's house; I had him get into the carriage and brought him to meet my master.

The respectable cleric was tall, white, and thin, with well-proportioned features; his eyes were black and lively, his expression serious yet affable, and his hair was snowflake-white. When he entered the drawing room where my master was waiting, I said, "Sir, this is the father I hired to be chaplain here, after our talk yesterday."

As soon as the Chinese saw him, he rose from his armchair and walked up to the father with open arms, and, embracing him in the most affectionate sign of respect, he said, "I congratulate myself that you have come to honor this house, which you may consider your own from this moment forth; and if your conduct and wisdom match the whiteness of your hair, I will surely be your best of friends. I have brought you to my house because Pedro tells me that the gentlemen of your land have the custom of keeping chaplains in their houses. I knew, even before I left my own land, that it is very prudent to conform to the customs of the place where one lives, especially when those customs are not harmful, and so you may remain here from this moment, your job being to make sacrifices to your God for my health, and to insure that all my servants live in accordance with your religion, because it seems to me that they are beginning to stray. You will also instruct me in your beliefs and dogmas, for I should learn them, if only out of curiosity; and finally, you will be my teacher and will teach me everything you consider a foreigner should know about your land, which he has come to visit only because he wants to see this part of the world; and as for the salary that you will enjoy, you may set your own at whatever level you see fit."

The chaplain listened attentively to everything my master said, and so he answered that he would do everything in his power to see that his family led orderly lives; that he would gladly instruct him not only about the principles of the Catholic religion, but about everything he asked and wanted to know about the kingdom; that as for his honorarium, if he had clothes and board, a little bit of money would be more than enough to cover all his necessities; but if he was to take charge of the family, it was also imperative that he be given some authority over it, so that he might correct the unruly and expel the incorrigible if necessary, for only thus would he be respected and the master's good desires be achieved.

This struck my master as a very good plan, and he told him that he would give him all the authority he had in the house to reform whatever he thought necessary. The chaplain went to fetch his bed, trunk, and books, and to seek permission for establishing a private oratory.

The first task was done that very day, and the second was not difficult to achieve, so within two weeks he was already saying Mass in the house.

Day by day, my master's trust in the chaplain grew, along with the affection he had begun to feel for him. Most of the servants tried to live as fast and loose under the chaplain's rule as they had under me, but they didn't get away with it; he quickly threw them out and replaced them with good servants. The house was converted into a little monastery. They held Mass every day, they prayed the rosary every night, they had Communion once a month, there were no more nightly strolls or outings, and I was forced along with all the rest to observe these religious mandates.

You can imagine how this life made me feel: desperate, no more, no less, to think that I had hired the crow who was trying to scratch out my eyes;[5] nevertheless, I grinned and bore it, since that was all I could do, if only to keep from losing my control over the purse-strings, the respect I commanded in the street, and my use of the carriage from time to time.

I wished I could make the chaplain look bad and get him out of my hair; but I couldn't make up my mind to do it, because I could see how much my master loved him. Ever since he arrived at the house, he frequently took my master out strolling in

---

5 [Crow . . . scratch out my eyes: an allusion to the Spanish proverb about ungrateful children, *Cría cuervos y te sacarán los ojos* ("Raise crows and they will scratch out your eyes"). *Cuervo*, crow, is also a slang term for a black-frocked priest. –Tr.]

the carriage and on foot, taking him not only to temples, as I had done, but on outings, to social gatherings, on visits, to the Coliseo, and wherever there were crowds, so that within a short time, my master had met several Mexican gentlemen who visited him and offered him their friendship, leaving me feeling snubbed in his house, for they considered me nothing but an overpaid butler.

No sooner would they return from one of these outings than my master and the chaplain would hole themselves up to talk, and so in a short time, the chaplain taught him to speak and write Spanish perfectly, and my master took to this skill with such zest and verve that he would write long passages every day, though I didn't know what he was writing about, and he would read all the books that the chaplain gave him, to great profit, because he had a remarkable memory.

As a result of these lessons and instructions, one day my master asked me for the accounts of his wealth in great detail, since he knew arithmetic perfectly and was familiar with the value of all the coins of the realm. I gave him some overblown figures, and it turned out that in two or three months, I had spent 8,000 pesos. The Chinese had the carriage, clothing, and household goods appraised; he added the total for the housing expenses, food, and servants, and he figured out that I had wasted 3,000 pesos.

Nevertheless, he was so prudent that he merely pointed this out to me, and asked me for the keys to the moneyboxes, which he handed over to the chaplain, putting him in charge of the expenses of the house.

For me, this was the mortal blow, not so much because I felt any shame at losing control of the keys, as because I needed them so badly.

From the moment the chaplain met me, he had formed the opinion of me that I deserved—that is, that I was a rogue; and I think that he made my master see this, for on top of taking the keys away from me, the Chinese began to look at me not only with a frown, but with a certain disdain, which I saw as a precursor to my expulsion from that Jauja.

With this fear, I put every effort into buttering up my master as much as I could; and one day when I was at work on this estimable aim, because the chaplain was not at home and I thought my master looked sad, I asked him what was wrong, and the Chinese told me simply, "Tell me, is it against the customs of your land for foreigners to have women in their houses?"

"No, sir," I replied; "those who want them, have them."

"Then bring me two or three beautiful ones to serve me and entertain me, because I will pay them well, and if I like them, I'll marry them."

Here I found the perfect way to make the chaplain look bad, unjust though it might be; so I told him that the chaplain didn't want women in the house, and that was the only obstacle I saw, because there were plenty of women in Mexico, very pretty and not very expensive.

"Well, bring them," said the Chinese, "because the chaplain cannot deprive me of a satisfaction that Nature and my religion permit me."

"All the same, sir," I remarked, "that chaplain is a devil; he can't stand the sight of women, ever since one beat him on account of another woman on a stroll, and since he is so puffed up with the favors you've shown him, he'll want to take his revenge on any girls that I bring here, and he'll even kick them outdoors, now matter how lovely they are or how much you like them."

The Chinese was enraged to think that the chaplain might deny him his pleasure, and in his fury he said, "What does he mean by kicking out a woman that I like? I'll kick him out if he dares to try it. Go on, bring me the most beautiful women you can find."

I happily went out to find the madams I had been ordered to bring, thinking that after the seed I had planted, the chaplain would be forced to leave the house and I would regain the confidence of the Chinese.

I didn't much like the job of pimp, nor had I ever tested my skills in this area; it shamed me to go out on such an errand among the flirts, because I wasn't old or wearing rags; so I was afraid of the vulgar jokes they'd make; and above all, I trembled to think how quick the girls themselves would be to take away my respect; nevertheless, my desire to handle the money and to free myself from the chaplain made me trample over the tiny scrap of honor I still retained, and I made up my mind to carry out the plan. I came, I saw, and I conquered more easily than Caesar. Looking for the little tarts, finding them, and convincing them to come with me to serve the Chinese was the work of a minute.

I came strutting into the study of the Chinese with my three courtesans at the very moment when he was talking with the chaplain, who took one look at their modest clothing and realized what they were, and with knitted brows, he asked them what they wanted.

They were surprised by the question—which had been asked, moreover, by a priest known for his virtue; and so, unable to speak clearly, they said that I had brought them there, but they didn't know why.

"Well, daughters," the chaplain told them, "get along, and may God go with you, because there's no business for you here."

Those girls left, blushing with embarrassment and swearing to take their revenge on me. The chaplain turned to face me, and said, "Without wasting an instant of time, take your cot and your trunks and get out of here, you slanderer, you knave, you villain. Isn't it enough for you to be a rogue without having to become a contemptible pimp? Aren't you content with everything you've swindled out of this poor man without wanting to let these madwomen swindle him, too? Finally, aren't you satisfied with damning yourself without trying to damn others as well? Eh! Get out of here, and God go with you, before I call the constables and have them put you where you belong!"

You can imagine how I left that house: my ears were burning red. There were two porters standing in front of the courtyard; I called them over, they hoisted my trunks and my cot on their backs, and I left without saying good-bye.

I was walking with my frock coat and my cane behind the porters, feeling ashamed of myself, thinking that every insult I had heard him say was well deserved and a natural result of my bad conduct.

I was turning a corner, thinking I should go to the house of one of my friends, when who do I find there, to my great misfortune, but the three young ladies who had just been run out of the house because of me; and no sooner had they recognized me than one grabbed me by the hair and another by the hem of my shirt, and between the three of them, they scratched me and squeezed me and gave me such a thorough working-over that in the blink of an eye, they had yanked out my hair, covered my face with scratches, and reduced my clothes to ribbons, all the while competing to see who could give me the worst tongue-lashing, incessantly repeating the sonorous title of pimp.

Through the efforts of a few decent men who showed up to witness my last rites, they finally left me in the state I have just mentioned, and the worst of it was that the porters, seeing how busy I was, ran off with all my things, and I could never catch them because I didn't know where they had gone.

So it was that, beaten to a pulp, smashed to bits, and without a penny in my pocket, I found myself around vespers in front of the Plaza del Volador,[6] an object of ridicule for everyone who saw me.

I sat down in an entrance way, and at eight I stood up with the intention of hanging myself.

---

[6] [Plaza del Volador: immediately south of the National Palace, the spot where the current Supreme Court building was constructed in 1940. –Tr.]

CHAPTER 44

IN WHICH OUR PERICO TELLS OF HOW HE TRIED TO HANG HIMSELF;
THE REASON WHY HE DID NOT DO IT; THE UNGRATEFULNESS HE
EXPERIENCED FROM A FRIEND; THE SCARE HE SUFFERED AT A WAKE;
HIS ESCAPE FROM THIS CAPITAL, AND OTHER LITTLE THINGS

It is true that God often puts his own people to the test in the crucible of tribulation; but more often, it is the irreverent who suffer because they want to. How many times do men complain about the troubles they suffer, and how often do they claim that misfortune pursues them, never realizing that they deserve what they get, and that they bring it on with their tumultuous behavior!

That is what I told myself the night I found myself in the sorry state I have just described; and feeling desperate, or tired of existence, I tried to hang myself. To carry out my plan, I sold my watch in a store for the first price they named; I downed a pint of liquor to get up my courage and lose my judgment—or, what amounts to the same thing, to keep from feeling it when the Devil carried me off. That's the kind of courage that liquor brings.

With that amount of spirits now sitting in my stomach, I bought a length of rope for half a real, rolled it up, tucked it under my arm, and took it and my damnable design to the avenue that they call La Orilla.[1]

I arrived half drunk around ten at night. The darkness, the isolation of that spot, the sturdy trees that abound there, the hopelessness I felt, and the vapors of the valiant liquor all invited me to carry out my wicked intentions.

At last I made up my mind, knotted the rope, found a stone that I tied around my waist with considerable trouble to give myself more weight, and climbed up on a wooden bench that stood next to a tree so that I might swing from it more easily; then, having accomplished all these important tasks, I tried to tie the rope to the tree; but that I would have to do by looping the rope over the branch that would support my hanging body.

I began fervently throwing the rope over the sturdiest branch of the tree so I could make the loop, but I couldn't manage to do it, because the liquor unbalanced my head more and more, making my feet unsteady and destroying my aim; I was unable to accomplish what I wanted to do. I kept falling to the ground, armed with my rope and my desperation, bursting into a thousand blasphemies and calling all the demons of hell to help me in this very profitable business proposition.

I spent two hours in these labors, until, exhausted by the stone around my waist, the work I was doing, and the beating I had sustained, and realizing that it was getting very hard for me even to keep on my feet, while fearing that day would break and somebody would find me occupied in this criminal enterprise, I was forced to

---

[1] [Paseo de la Orilla: now known as Calzada de la Viga, this avenue headed southeast out of the city from the church and Colegio of San Pablo (mentioned below, half a mile southeast of the city center), flanking what was then the Viga Canal; according to Spell (p. 191), it was "one of the most popular pleasure resorts of the capital." –Tr.]

desist against my will; so I untied the stone from my waist, threw the rope into the canal, and looked for a place to rest; and, after heaving all the contents of my stomach, I lay down on the naked ground and slept as soundly as I could have done in the fluffiest bed.

A drunken sleep is very heavy, so heavy that I wouldn't have noticed it if oxcarts had ridden right over me; so I didn't notice the people who did me the favor of undressing me and taking all my clothes, even though the damnable tarts had left them looking so unattractive.

When the spirits of the vine that filled my brain had dissipated, I woke up around seven in the morning and found myself wearing only my shirt, which they had left me out of pity.

Imagine me in this state, at this hour, in this place. All the Indians who passed by there saw me and laughed; but for me their innocent laughter was a terrible insult, filling me with so much anger that I regretted over and over again that I hadn't been able to hang myself.

At this baneful moment, a poor old Indian woman came over to me, moved to pity by my misfortune, and asked me what had happened. I told her that I had been robbed during the night; and the unhappy woman, full of compassion, brought me to her sad *jacal*, gave me atole to drink and hot tortillas with a bit of brown sugar to eat, and dressed me in her son's cast-offs: a pair of unlined leather breeches, a very old poncho of coarse, striped homespun, a straw hat, and a pair of sandals. That is to say, she dressed me in the clothes of an unhappy Indian; but after all, she did dress me, she covered my flesh, she sheltered me, she helped me, she did everything she could in my favor. Every time I remember this kind Indian woman, my heart grows tender and I judge her a heroine of charity of her class, for she gave me all she could, without any interest other than being generous to me without any merit on my part. Even today I wish I knew who she was so that I could repay her kindness. It is so true that in every class of the State, there are kind souls, and that to be kind, one needs heart more than money!

In the end, moved by the gifts that my poor old Indian woman found me worthy of receiving, I thanked her many times, embraced her tenderly, kissed her wrinkled face, and went out into the street.

I was heading into the city; but when I saw my bedeviled appearance, and reflected that the day before I had ridden in a carriage and been dressed in gentleman's clothes, I stopped walking for some time, for every step I took seemed like moving a tower of lead.

I spent about two hours wandering around the little plaza of San Pablo and all the boondocks out there, unable to make up my mind to enter the city. During one of these postponements, I stopped in an entranceway on the street they call Manito,[2] and stood there like a sentinel until one in the afternoon, when I began to be haunted by hunger, though I had no idea where I could satisfy it; just then, one of my best friends walked into that house, a man whom I had invited to lunch just the day before with his girl and her brothers.

---

[2] [Today the block of Misioneros that lies one block north of the Colegio de San Pablo. –Tr.]

As soon as he saw me, he drew up short; he stared closely at me, and, satisfied that he recognized me, he tried to pretend that he hadn't, and to get inside his house without speaking with me; but I had a notion to get some sort of aid from him, so I wouldn't let him; instead, disregarding the shame that my Indianized clothes filled me with, I took him by the arm and said, "It's me, Anselmo, don't act like you don't know me; I'm Pedro Sarmiento, your friend, the one who has always helped you in every way he could. Don't turn away from me or pretend you don't recognize me; I've told you who I am; just yesterday we went out together on a stroll and you swore you'd be my friend forever; you said you were proud of my friendship, and that you wished you'd have a chance to repay me for all the favors I'd shown you. Well, your chance has come, Anselmo. Your unhappy friend Sarmiento has shown up unwittingly at the door of your house, left helpless by the worst sort of misfortunes, without anyone to turn to, without a *jacal* to shelter him or a tortilla to eat, wearing an Indian's poncho and an indecent pair of leather breeches that a poor old woman gave him out of charity; which, though they cover his flesh, are so indecent that they keep him from showing his face in Mexico to beg his other friends for their favor. You've been my friend, and you've often honored me by calling me your friend; act like a friend, then, and help me out with a few old clothes and a few crumbs from your table."

"What do you think, rogue," this cruel friend told me, "what do you think, that I'm a brute like you? That you can fool me with a couple of lies? Don Pedro Sarmiento, who looks a little bit like you, is indeed my friend; but he is a fine man, an upright man, and a man of wealth; not a scoundrel, a vagrant, and a bum. Get out and may God go with you."

Without waiting for a reply, he entered the courtyard of his house, slamming the door in my face.

How this snub made me feel must remain unsaid, left up to the reader's imagination, for some misfortunes of this world are so great that no words suffice to explain them with the force they deserve, and silence alone is their best interpreter.

Between anger and desperation, sadness and regret, I stood there in the entranceway, brooding over what had just taken place. I wanted to run away from that neighborhood; I wanted to wait for Anselmo and tear him limb from limb with my own hands; but my fury subsided when I remembered that he had spoken well of me, and that he hadn't recognized me.

"No doubt about it," I said, "he's my friend, and he loves me; these clothes, and the bad time I had of it last night, disfigured me so much that he couldn't recognize me; I'll wait for him right here, and if he still pretends he doesn't know me after I prove that I'm Pedro Sarmiento, I'll run from his sight as I would from any monster; I'll detest his friendship and loathe his name, and wander wherever God wills me to go."

So I stood there, wavering in my imagination, until vespers, when Anselmo came out with a naked saber and said to me, "It seems that you have turned to stone here in my house; get out, because I am going to shut the door."

"When I spoke with you on the first occasion," I said, "I did so thinking that you recognized me and that you were my friend, and availing myself of that sacred title, I dared to beg your favor. I do not beg you for anything now; I only want to tell you that I am not a rogue, as you said, nor am I stealing Don Pedro Sarmiento's name;

rather, I am he, and in proof of this fact, recall that you and your beloved Manuelita went with me yesterday, along with her two brothers and a maid, to the Orilla lunch stand, where I bought lunches all around, consisting of *envueltos*,[3] chicken stew, *adobo*, and pulque flavored with prickly pears and pineapple. Recall that the lunch cost eight pesos, and that I paid for it with gold. Remember that when I washed my hand, I took off a diamond ring, which captured your lady's fancy; she praised it highly, placed it on her finger, and I gave it to her; you thanked me greatly for my generosity and praised my liberality. Recall that when you and I strolled alone around one of those open shelters, you told me that your wife had sniffed out the rotten wench (those were your words), giving rise to frequent arguments, and that you were thinking of leaving her and taking Manuelita to Querétaro, where you had a job waiting for you. Recall that I told you not to do any such thing, for that would be to add injustice to injury; that you should put up with your wife and endeavor to deny everything she had found out, giving her no cause for suspicions, showing affection for her and behaving prudently, for after all, she is your wife and the mother of your children. Finally, recall that when we parted, I helped Manuelita into the carriage, and that she caught the hem of her percale dress on the running board and tore it. These are plenty of proofs, and they are too private for you to doubt that I am telling the truth. If my face is disfigured and my clothes do not match who I am, that is because of the adversity of my fortunes and the vicissitudes of men, from which you are not safe yourself, and perhaps you will find yourself in an even more deplorable situation than I am in tomorrow. Denying that you know me would be a contemptible sign of stubbornness after all the proofs I've given you and after you've listened to all I have to say, because even if a face is disfigured, the voice has the same tone, and it is very hard not to recognize someone by his voice after knowing him so long."

"All your babbling," said Anselmo, "proves only that you are a first-rate rascal, and that you've been running around spying so that you could pull a fast one on me, looking into my private life, maybe taking advantage of some scheme with my friend Sarmiento to find out my secrets from him; but you're barking up the wrong path. Now you have less reason than ever to expect a penny from me; I'd sooner run away from you, perfect rogue that you are. . . . "

"Kill me with your saber," I said, cutting him off: "kill me, before your tongue wounds me with such insults—insults hurled by a friend, moreover. Is this how you show your affection, Anselmo? Is this how you repay me? Are these your own words? What separates you from the dirtiest rabble—you, who pride yourself on being so noble—when you act so contemptibly that you not only refuse to return favors, but you obstinately pretend not to recognize the person to whom you owe them? Anselmo, friend: now that you refuse to have pity on me as someone whom you once counted as your own friend, at least you could have pity on a poor wretch who has taken shelter in your doorway. You know full well that our religion obliges all Christians to exercise charity with friends and enemies alike, with our own people

---

[3] [*Envueltos*: corn tortillas with tomato sauce and a filling such as scrambled eggs, rolled up and covered with a sauce of tomatoes, green chilies, onion, cheese, and so on. –Tr.]

and with strangers; so if you can't consider me a friend, consider me a poor wretch, and for the sake of God. . . . "

"For the sake of God," that tiger replied, "get out of here, because it's late, and I'm starting to find your gabbing and foot-dragging suspicious. Yes, I'm starting to think you must be a thief, and that you're stalling for time until all your companions can get together and attack my house. Get out and be damned with you, before I call for the guards to come from their barracks."

"What do you mean, a thief?" I said, filled with wrath. "You're the thief, the rogue, the villain, you low-born, ungrateful swine."

Anselmo didn't dare use his saber as I had feared, but he did use his tongue. He started shouting "Help! Help! Thieves! Thieves!" and his shouts intimidated me more than his saber; so, fearing that people would come see and that I would end up in jail on account of this miscreant, I left his house, cursing his friendship and all the friends in the world who are anything like the odious Anselmo.

Around eight, wrapped in the gloom of night, I headed into the city, dying of hunger and of anger at my false and unfaithful friend.

"Ah!" I said, "if only I still had the diamond that I gave to his pig of a girlfriend yesterday, I'd have something I could sell or pawn to relieve my hunger; but what can I pawn or make use of now? I don't have anything that's worth a dime, except for my shirt. But could I really sell the shirt off my back? There's no way out; it's all I've got; I'll have to take it off."

While performing this soliloquy, I took it off, and since it was clean and nearly new I had little trouble getting eight reales for it; with that, I was able to wolf down supper with a ravenous appetite and buy some cigarettes.

Between the pawning and the supping, the time slipped by without my noticing it, so that when I left the tavern the bells were ringing ten, and at that late hour I couldn't find any *arrastraderitos* still open.

Disconsolate at not being able to rely on my old haunts for shelter, I made up my mind to spend the whole night wandering the streets, aimlessly and in fear of falling into the hands of the night watch at every turn, until I fortunately found a tiny, one-room house in the Santa Ana neighborhood that was open for a wake.

I ducked in without waiting to be invited, and there I saw a dead man laid out with his four candles, six or eight *léperos* in mourning, and an old woman who had fallen asleep next to the hearth with the fan in her hand.

I politely greeted the living, and gave half a real to support the funeral for the dead.

My sympathy brought out more of the same among my fellow men there, and, accepting their thanks, I stayed with them in peace and good company.

When I arrived, they were telling tales; at twelve midnight they recited a rosary in between yawns, they sang a hymn rather badly, and they each swigged a cup of *champurrado*[4] very well; and I did not just stand and watch them.

Around one in the morning, the old woman went to bed and snored like a dog, and to keep the rest of us from doing the same, one charitable soul brought out a

---

4 [*Champurrado*: a drink of atole (thin corn gruel) mixed with hot chocolate. –Tr.]

deck of cards, and we all sat down in a corner to play a few hands in honor of the dead man's soul.

I went bust in no time, since my bet was very weak and my luck had turned against me. Nevertheless, I kept dealing for the bank to see if I could get back in by my wits; but our little candle burned out, and there was nothing we could do but borrow a candle-end from the deceased gentleman.

They had already shut the door to the house in the fear that the night watch might pass by on their rounds and find us gambling. Who knows who shut it, or who had the key; the room was tiny, with just the one door and a window that opened onto an incredibly filthy drainage ditch; the framing of the house was in devilishly bad shape, and they had unwittingly laid out the dead man on top of a floor beam that was unsupported on one end; therefore, when one of the sorely grieving mourners went to get the candle-end so that we could keep gambling, he stepped on the floor beam where the cadaver was lying at the point where it had no support, and his weight made the floor dip down, and the floor beam rise up, which also made the deceased sit up; which, when my pals and I saw it, filled us with such horror (thinking that the dead man was rising up to punish us) that we all jumped up at the same time, trampling over each other in our eagerness to get out of there, and each of us shouting every prayer he knew.

As you can easily imagine, we immediately plunged into darkness, stepping over and even bumping flat into the dead man and the fellow who had sunk into the floor, who kept screaming incessantly that the Devil had come to take him; the unhappy old woman had no better time of it, because we each fell all over her every time we came near her; each time one of us ran into another, he thought he was bumping into the dead man; our affliction grew moment by moment because the key refused to appear; until someone thought of opening the window and getting out that way. We all followed his example, without giving a thought in the world to the drainage ditch. So we let ourselves fall into it one after another, and we crawled out of it filthy with mud and something worse than mud; but we did get out, in the end, without paying the slightest attention to the poor old woman, who had to stay and accompany the deceased. Each man went home to his own house, and I went off with the most raggedy beggar of them all, who showed a little pity for me.

As soon as we arrived, he woke up his wife and gave her a formal report of our scare, telling her how the dead man had risen and beaten us all. The woman didn't want to believe him, and the dispute over whether or not it had happened took up what was left of the night, but by the light of the new day the woman had to believe the ghost story, seeing how pale our faces had gone; as for our fall into the mire, there had never been any doubt, for her nostrils had told her what happened as soon as we walked in, and even without light she believed as firmly as if she had seen us that we were shellacked with muck.

In the end, the poor woman washed her husband's clothes, and threw in mine while she was at it; the two of us sat wrapped in an old blanket while our things dried.

Even though mine amounted to two items, to wit: the poncho and the breeches (because the hat and sandals had been left on the battlefield), they took the longest time to dry, so that my friend was soon dressed, while I couldn't move from where I sat.

The poor woman gave me a little atole and two tortillas; I drank the atole more out of obligation than anything, and then, to while away my sorrows, I sharpened a piece of charcoal into a point, and on the back of a print that was lying near me, I wrote the following verses:

> *Men, learn when you look at me*
> *What happens from night to day:*
> *Yesterday, viceroy and grandee;*
> *Not even a ragman today.*

> No one should fall in the snare
> Of believing that their good fate
> Will never change nor abate,
> For luck does not always stay fair.
> All men should live full of care;
> Let each man keep an eye out to see;
> For fortune is always flighty
> And changes again and again;
> I am an example to men:
> *Men, learn when you look at me.*

> I know that fortune and fame
> Are mere passing fancies and dreams,
> But for me, or so it seems,
> My "happy days" once really came.
> If only I had known how to claim
> Use of that time, then today
> I would not be in this woeful state;
> But I neglected my happiness,
> Am now mired in wretchedness:
> *What happens from night to day!*

> Yesterday all my riches
> Gave my noble bearing a boost;
> But today you see me reduced
> To wearing leather britches.
> Yes, yesterday I had riches,
> Today not a maravedí;
> I'm crying—oh, woe is me!
> Lamenting my past presumption;
> I was, in my imagination,
> *Yesterday viceroy and grandee.*

> In this world fickle and contrary,
> A doctor I was, and a barber,
> A subdelegado, a soldier,

A sexton and an apothecary.
I was a friar and secretary;
Though I am poor now, sad to say,
I was a merchant down Philippines way;
And before, a university man.
But that, dear me! was back then:
Not even a ragman today![5]

As soon as I finished writing my ditties, I memorized them and pasted the sheet of paper to the door of the house with a dab of atole.

By now my poncho was dry, but the leather breeches were still soaking wet, and I was desperate to go out in search of new adventures and didn't have the patience to wait for the sun to dry them, so I grabbed them and lay them out to dry next to the *tlecuile*,[6] or open fire, where the woman was making tortillas; however, I went out to relieve myself, and on my return I found them dry but shriveled up like crisp bacon.

I do not have the words to express my grief when I found all my gear unusable. When my friend was informed of my misfortune, he gave me a bit of tallow and advised me to massage it into the leather to soften it up a bit.

I took his advice, and the breeches became more flexible but not much more use to me, because in the places where the fire had really penetrated them, there was nothing that could be done; the scorched pieces fell off, and more holes opened up than were really necessary, which hardly pleased me since I had no underpants. I put them on in any case, and since they were blackened with soot and full of holes, the whiteness of my skin stood out, making me look like a spotted jaguar.

Realizing how ridiculous I looked, and in the hopes of fixing it, I took a bit of soot and mixed it with another dab of tallow, creating a dye that I used to paint my skin and make it look a little more passable.

The owners of the house sympathized with me, though they laughed at what I was doing, and when they learned that my intention was to leave Mexico then and there to seek my fortune, they told me I should go to Puebla,[7] because I might find a job there. At the same time, they gave me some frijoles for lunch, and the woman prepared me an *itacate*[8] of tortillas with a piece of roast meat and two or three chilies, all wrapped up in a dirty rag, which I tied to my waist.

---

[5] [The poem takes off on Luis de Góngora's poem *La brevedad de las cosas humanas* (1621), which Lizardi has already imitated in Chapter 29. –Tr.]

[6] [*Tlecuile* (Nahuatl *tlecuilli*): the traditional hearth of central Mexico, consisting of three stones arranged around an open fire, on which a cooking pot (such as the flat *comal* for cooking tortillas) can be placed. –Tr.]

[7] [Puebla: an important Spanish city about seventy-five miles east of Mexico City, on the road to Veracruz. On the way to Puebla, Periquillo will pass out of the capital through the *garita de San Lázaro* (see Chapter 21, footnote 4) at the city's eastern entrance; go through the small town of Ayotla, eighteen miles from the city center; and get to Río Frío, a small town halfway between Mexico and Puebla, set in "a wooded, mountainous region [that] was for many years infested with bandits who preyed upon merchants and travelers" (Spell, p. 194). –Tr.]

[8] [*Itacate* (Nahuatl *ihtacatl*): a bundle of food to bring on a trip. –Tr.]

So, after eating lunch and thanking them, I looked for a stick to use as a walking staff, picked up an old straw hat that someone had thrown away on a dungheap and put it on, said good-bye to my kind hosts, and set out for the San Lázaro checkpoint.

I reached the town of Ayotla, where I spent the night without anything of notice to report other than finishing off all my supplies for supper.

The next day, I got up early and continued on the road to Puebla, living off of alms until I reached Río Frío, where I had the adventures that you will read about in the following chapter.

CHAPTER 45

There is nothing fabulous about the story you have just heard, my dearest children; it is all true, it is all natural, it all happened to me, and much of all this, or even more, has happened and will continue to happen to everyone who lives as I did: sunken in licentiousness and trying to support themselves and show off in the world at the expense of others, with no trade, no job, and without trying to work or be useful to the rest of our brothers.

If all men had the courage and the sincerity to write about the troubles they suffered, candidly moralizing and confessing their conduct, there is no doubt that you would discover a whole gang of Periquillos who are cloaked and disguised now by shame or hypocrisy; and you would gain a deeper understanding of what I have been telling you: that is, that the man who is vice-ridden, lazy, and dissipated suffers more in this life that the man who leads a good and orderly life. Of course, we all suffer in this sad life; but the wicked suffer disproportionately more, in every type of republic, whether because of the natural order of things or the punishments of Divine Providence, which endeavors to execute justice even in this miserable life.

Since I was one of those lost souls, of necessity I also mourned my misfortunes, which inevitably mounted at the same rate as my evil deeds, in keeping with the principles we have established.

When I left off my story, I was telling you that I was walking to Puebla, naked, hungry, tired, dishonored among all who had learned about my misconduct, despised by my friends, and abandoned by everyone.

So, filled with a profound melancholy and an inner remorse that tore at my heart by bringing to mind a thousand misdeeds, I arrived at nightfall one day at an inn near Río Frío, where I begged them for the sake of God to give me shelter. This they granted me; for after all, God punishes His sons but does not destroy them, however ungrateful to Him they may be. I ate what they gave me for supper and slept in a hayloft, thinking I had hit the jackpot by finding something so soft to sleep on, since I had spent the past few nights sleeping on the hard ground.

The next day I was up at dawn, and the innkeeper, knowing where my path lay, told me to be very careful, for there was a band of thieves on that road. I thanked him for the warning, but I didn't desist from my intentions, for I was sure that, since I had nothing they could steal, I could walk calmly right past the thieves, as Juvenal has written.

Absorbed in a thousand baneful thoughts, I was walking along with my head sunk against my chest, holding my stick in my hand, when nearby I heard the galloping of horses; I lifted my face and saw four men, mounted and well armed, who surrounded me and, taking me for an Indian, asked me, "Where did you set out from today, and where are you from?"

"Gentlemen," I said, "I set out from the last inn on this road; and I am from Mexico, and am at your service."

Then they realized that I was not an Indian; and one of them, whom I had an inkling of having seen once before, stared at me, and then jumped down from his horse and embraced me affectionately, saying, "Aren't you Periquillo, brother? Aren't you Periquillo? Yes, there's no doubt about it; you have the same features; I never forget my friends' faces. Don't you remember me? Don't you remember your old friend El Aguilucho, who did you so many favors when we were living together in jail?"

Then I recognized him perfectly, and, trying to take advantage of the favorable opportunity that the occasion had presented me, I squeezed him so tightly in my arms that poor Aguilucho told me in a pinched voice, "Enough of that, Perico, brother, enough; for God's sake, don't hang me before my time."

"Yes!" I said, full of hope and enthusiasm, "yes! Now all my troubles are over, since I've had the good fortune of finding my best friend, who did me so many favors, and who I hope will help me out of the bitter situation I'm in now."

"So, what's happened in your life, my dear boy?" he asked me. "What kind of luck have you had? What misadventures have happened to you, for me to find you looking so bad and wearing such awful clothes?"

"What do you think has happened?" I answered. "Just that I'm the unluckiest man ever born! Since the day I left my friend Juan Largo, who (no offense to those present) was as much of an upright man and as good a friend as you, I've had a thousand adventures, both good and bad; though, if truth be told, more bad than good."

"Well, that sounds like a long story," the little mulatto said, interrupting me; "climb up behind me here on my horse and we'll head up that hill over there, and then we can talk at our leisure; because if we stay on the highway, we'll scare off the game."

"I don't get what you mean by scaring off game," I said, "because I've never heard of hunting on a highway, only in forests and places where people don't crisscross all the time."

"That just shows how bone-headed you are," El Aguilucho told me; "but after you learn that we aren't hunting rabbits or jaguars, but men, you won't be surprised by what I'm telling you. For now, the only thing you should worry about is getting up on this horse."

Obeying his imperious demand, I climbed up, and we all headed toward a small hill not far from the road.

As soon as we got there, we dismounted, they hid the horses behind the crest of the hill, and we sat down in some scrub, from which we could easily look out without being seen by anyone passing along the highway.

When we were all settled, El Aguilucho reached into a burlap bag and pulled out a very good cheese, two loaves of bread, and a bottle of liquor.

He pulled a knife from his leggings and cut the bread and the cheese, and we all began passing them around.

After our dinner, he poured us each a swig of liquor with his own hand, but so little that mine was barely enough to reach the back of my throat. My eyes kept following the bottle, as did everyone's, but he put it away, saying, "There's nothing crazier that a man can do than give in to drink. Nobody should ever get drunk, least of all those who follow our trade, because we follow a very risky one."

"What trade is that, then?" I asked in amazement; he smiled and told me, "We're *hunters*, and as you can imagine, a drunken hunter has lousy aim."

"But in that event," I replied, "the worst that could happen would be that the hunting party would come back without any game. I don't see any risk there."

"Yet there is," he said; "the game might hunt us, and do such a good job of it that we wouldn't get out of our chains until we died."

"Don't speak to me in riddles," I said, "on your life; explain what you're talking about."

"You'll find out soon enough," he said; "but first, tell us about your adventures."

"Well, let me tell you," I said; "when I was sent to the jail where I had the honor of meeting you, it was on account of a handful of friends, because my dear Juan Largo was planning to hit a widow's house, and he could easily have gotten caught by the soldiers and watchmen that night, but he had the good fortune to escape in time, along with another friend of his—a skillful and brave fellow named Nicky the Gobbler, as fine a boy as they come, who Januario told me had learned the craft of thieving backward and forward. . . . "

"Bless you and keep you," laughingly said a tall black man with a snub nose and a pair of tiny, lively eyes. "That's me," he went on; "I'm the Gobbler, though I'm no turkey, and I remember you, and remember the night when I saw you with the night watchman while I was running away. So whatever happened to you? How did you end up in the pokey instead of us?"

Then I told them all my adventures, which they praised mightily. They told me that Januario was a captain of a gang of man-hunters, and was hanging out not far from where we were; they practiced the same art that he did, along with three other companions, who had gotten separated from them a few days earlier, and whom they were expecting any hour with a good haul of plunder; Señor Aguilucho was their boss; it was a well-paying line of work; it tended to have its hazards; but, in the end, it was a good way to spend your life and have some fabulous times; and, "finally, friend," the Gobbler told me, "if you want to enlist under our flag, experience this life, and bid your troubles good-bye, you can do it, given your friendship with our captain and your gentle disposition; and since you've been a soldier, you won't be shocked by the hardships of battle, the assaults, the advances, the retreats, or any of the stuff we always have to deal with."

"Friend," I said, "I value your invitation and your desire to do me this favor; but you're mistaken if you think that I'll be any use to you, because for a campaign like this, my disposition isn't just gentle or gentile, it's heretical and Jewish,[1] because it's totally useless. I've always been afraid of getting a beating, and I've steered clear of

---

[1] [Gentle, heretical, Jewish: a fairly innocuous (though bad) pun in Lizardi's day, this play on words reflects the religious prejudices of his time and class. *Gentil* means both "gentle, polite" and "gentile, pagan," and was used most commonly to refer to unconverted Indians. *Hereje*, "heretical," was the usual epithet for Protestants. In the religious struggles of the time, unconverted (but potentially convertible) pagans were "better" than apostate Protestants and Jews. –Tr.]

such opportunities, and even so I haven't always managed to avoid it. There was one time when an old woman smashed me on the jaw with a shoe; another when a bumpkin beat me to a bloody pulp; another when I was walloped by the prisoners in jail, together with your captain El Aguilucho, who wouldn't let me lie; another when I got stuck with a knife, and I'm lucky to be here to tell the tale; another when the Indians of Tula pelted me with stones; another when a wild Indian smashed seventy clay pots over my head; another when a bunch of tarts yanked my hair out by the roots; and finally, there was once when a dead man beat me up at his own wake. So you all tell me if I'm not unlucky and if I don't have good reason to feel cowed."

"Come on," said El Aguilucho, "don't be so squeamish about details like those; men should never be cowards, especially not because of a little child's play. In all those fights of yours, my cowardly Periquillo, have you ever lost a yard of your intestines? Have you ever had to replace your skull with a gourd? How many ribs have you lost? How many feet and hands are you missing? None of that's happened to you; you're whole and bona fide, without any traces or scars that anybody'd notice. So we're either dealing with a piece of shameless cowardice or a bad case of coziness, because I think your problem is more that you love to be cozy than that you're a coward, and you'd like to live the easy life without putting yourself at any risk; but, my boy, that's a pretty green way of thinking about things, because you can't cross the sea without getting your feet wet, and troubles were made for men."

"Brother," I said, "it isn't just coziness, it's that I'm fearful by nature, and I naturally lack the stomach for getting beaten up. It's true that they haven't ripped out my guts on any of my adventures, or torn off an arm or a leg, like you said; but it's also true that, except in my fight with the Indian, I've gotten whomped without asking for it and without doing anything to provoke anybody. That's what made me such a coward; because, if I fared so badly when I wasn't trying to act bravely, when I was even going out of the way to avoid risky situations, what would have happened to me if I had been a braggart, a bully, and a thug? I'm sure I'd already have been hauled off to hell, at best, after being made into minced meat. So no, brother, no, I'd be no good as a hunter. If you'd like, I could serve as your scribe in your old age, or your kitchen boy or ranch hand, your butler, your valet, your accountant, your stableman, your physician and surgeon, since I know a little about that business, your advisor, your barber, or anything of the kind; but as for going into battle and fighting with travelers, don't even think of it. If it were a matter of finding them all tied up and fast asleep, well, maybe I'd pitch in and help, so long as I was with all of you; but as for coming after them in hand-to-hand combat, and having them come back at us, with their hands untied and holding sabers or pistols or shotguns, Jesus save me! Don't even think of it, pals, don't even think of it. I've already told you that I'm afraid, so watch out, because for a man to say he's afraid is the greatest sacrifice he can make to truth; because, if you stop to think about it, you'll see that hardly any man will brag about being good-looking, or wise, or rich, or anything of the sort; in fact, most men don't have any problem with thinking they're less handsome, less talented, less rich, or less skillful than others; but when you question their bravery, body of Christ!, nobody's a coward—at least not so as they'd admit it; they all turn into Scipios and Hannibals; nobody's afraid of anybody else, and they all think they're capable of facing up to Fierabras himself.[2] This proves that even if all men aren't brave, at least they all want to seem brave when the time comes, and they are so far from recognizing and confessing their cowardice that the most timid among them tends to talk the biggest when his enemies aren't around. So, if I'm an exception to the rule, and I come here confessing that I'm afraid, that proves that I'm a truly upright man, since I cannot tell a lie—another quality that is as fine as it is rare among men."

"Look at all the words you spoke just now, brother," El Aguilucho told me; "there's a good reason why they call you the Parrot. But tell me, man: if you're such a coward, how did you ever get to be a soldier? Because that job doesn't mix with fear any more than light does with shadow."

"That shouldn't surprise you," I answered; "first, as a soldier I was as soft as butter, since I never got past being a lazy and pampered adjutant, and I never even felt the hardship of service, much less battle. Second, not all soldiers are brave. How many of them go into battle because they are forced to, and would never go if the generals published an edict like Gideon's when the enemy was approaching, saying that whoever felt weak of spirit should go home?[3] I bet there wouldn't be more than 300 brave men in the biggest, most splendid army—unless they were good and stewed, or tempted by their greed for plunder. Third and last, not everyone who says he's brave knows what bravery is. M. de la Rochefoucauld says that 'for a simple soldier, bravery is a risky vow that he takes to save his life.' He explains the different kinds of bravery, and concludes by saying that 'perfect bravery consists in doing unwitnessed what you would be able to do in front of everyone.'[4] So you can see that being a soldier is no proof of being brave."

"Goodness gracious, Periquillo, how much you know!" El Aguilucho said ironically. "But for all your knowledge, you're still naked; we know a few more things than you do. So let's get the horses, you'll go see our house, and if you feel comfortable, you can stay with us; but don't think you can eat for free, because you'll have to do whatever work you can."

While he was talking, they went to get the horses and tightened their saddle straps; I climbed up behind El Aguilucho on his splendid horse, and we took off.

On the way, I quietly flattered myself on the skill I had shown in fooling the thieves by exaggerating my cowardice, which wasn't as bad as I had depicted it; but I didn't feel like going out to rob people on the highway and risking my life, either.

"If the way these fellows robbed," I said to my poncho, "wasn't so dangerous, damned if I wouldn't join them, since being a thief is about the only thing I haven't tried; but the likelihood that they'd catch me or shoot me—that's a devil of a problem. How lucky are the thieves who can rob peacefully in their own houses, without any risk to themselves! If only I were one of them!"

---

[2] [Scipio and Hannibal were Roman and Carthaginian generals in the ancient Punic Wars; Fierabras was a legendary bellicose giant who figured in several medieval romances set in the time of Charlemagne. –Tr.]

[3] [Judges 7:3. –Tr.]

[4] [François duc de la Rochefoucauld, *Réflexions ou sentences et maximes morales* (Paris, 1665; *Moral Maxims and Reflections*, London, 1694). Lizardi quotes from the 1781 Spanish translation. –Tr.]

While my thoughts were busy spinning this nonsense, we kept climbing hills, descending into valleys, and rounding a thousand curves, until we reached the entrance to a very deep ravine.

Soon after we entered, some wooden houses came into view; we were very happy when we reached them and dismounted; but three other hunters were even more glad to come out and greet us: these were the ones that El Aguilucho told me had gotten separated from him a few days earlier.

As soon as they saw El Aguilucho, they gave him many hugs, which he returned with great dignity. We entered the cave and they showed him two money boxes, a trunk of fine clothes, and a bundle of more ordinary clothes, along with a good pack mule and two excellent horses.

"All this," said one of them, "is the fruit of the business that we have accomplished in the seven days we've been away from your side."

"I expected no less from villains like you," said El Aguilucho. "Come on, let's have a look at it and split it up like brothers."

This said, they began dividing the clothes among everyone, and they dumped all the money into some chests that stood there, while their captain said, "You all know that we don't divide the money; so each of you can take as much as you want, so long as you let me know, for whatever you need. This poor lad," he went on, pointing at me, "needs each of you to help him out, because he's my old friend; he's depending on us here, and even if he's a little bit scared, he'll get over it in time; he's got the best thing you can have: he's no fool; there's hope for him."

Scarcely had these good neighbors heard his recommendation than they began vying with each other to make me feel welcome. One gave me two cambric shirts in very good condition; another gave me a first-rate blue cloth jacket decorated with gold braids and fringes; another gave me a pair of black velvet breeches with new silver buttons, and no defects other than that the lining was stained with blood; another fitted me out with socks, underpants, and a belt; another presented me with leggings, shoes, and gaiters; another gave me a chocolate-colored wide-brimmed hat of rich wool, with gold braiding around the edges and a splendid trim; and the last one gave me a good cloak made of scarlet cloth, with a collar of black velvet, adorned with silver braiding and fringes.

After they had all supplied me with what they wished, El Aguilucho gave me his own horse, which was a very worthy, dapple-gray steed, and he gave it to me without taking off its saddle, chaps, bridle, or any other gear. To this gallantry he added the fine detail of making me a present of his good spurs and as many pesos as he could pick up in six fistfuls, and they sent me off to get dressed right away.

That business concluded, they signaled with a whistle, and four big, fine-looking, well-dressed girls came out and greeted us very affably, and then they served us a better meal than I ever would have expected to find in such hidden ravines, so far from human commerce.

After dinner, they told me that these ladies were dedicated to serving all of them in common, and that the girls behaved with each other just as the men did among themselves, like sisters and brothers, without standing on etiquette, and without a whisper of the damnable passion of jealousy in that happy Arcadia.

These innocent conversations came to an end; El Aguilucho and the Gobbler ordered their horses saddled; and they all galloped off to see if they could hunt some game, leaving me alone with the women and telling me to keep busy by examining and cleaning their firearms.

I had never cleaned a shotgun; but the women showed me how, and they stopped to help me; and to make the work easier to bear, they asked me about my life and miracles, and I entertained them by telling them a thousand lies, which they believed as if they were the articles of the faith; and in payment for my tale, they related all their adventures to me, which amounted to telling me that they had strayed from the straight and narrow and had ended up with those heartless men— one, because her mother had scolded her; another, because her husband was jealous; this one, because the Gobbler tricked her; and the last one, because the devil tempted her.

In this way, each of them tried to cover up her lewdness and pass herself off as a saint; but I was a pretty old dog to be fed that line; I was too familiar with the mass of women, and I knew that most women who went astray did so because they couldn't accept being subordinated to their fathers, husbands, masters, or patrons.

Nevertheless, I pretended to be a merry fool, and in this way I discovered all the hidden secrets of my invincible companions; they told me they were thieves and that they made fabulous raids; that they were all very brave; that they rarely returned without lots of booty; and that they were already rich.

In proof of this, they showed me a room full of clothes, jewels, chests full of money, all sorts of arms, saddles, bridles, spurs, and a thousand other things, which was enough to show me that they really were wholesale robbers; but when I expressed my surprise that they hadn't left this life (which couldn't be very good or very safe) now that they had plenty to live on—if not without inner anxieties, at least without the constant fear of the authorities and the risks posed by the people they robbed— the women told me that it was impossible for them to leave this life: first, because they couldn't show their faces without exposing themselves to being recognized; and second, because robbing was a vice, just like drinking, gambling, and smoking; and so, trying to separate these gentlemen from their highway robberies would be like trying to separate cardsharps from their cards, or drunks from their cups.

This is what we were talking about when, at nightfall, the brave gang came back home; they dismounted and, after playing cards and making merry for three or four hours, we all ate supper very happily together, and then we went to bed, for which they gave me plenty of blankets and a tanned buffalo hide.

I noticed that four of them were keeping watch at the entrance to the ravine, like soldiers pulling sentinel duty, so I lay down and slept as peacefully as if I were in the company of apostolic saints; but around three in the morning, my sleep was interrupted by the ear-splitting shouts that they all cried out, some calling for their carbines, others for their horses, and all of them for quits, as people say.[5]

---

[5] [Calling for quits: *pedir cacao*, literally "asking for cocoa," on which the editor of the 4th edition comments:] *Pedir cacao* is a familiar phrase that means to admit defeat or to surrender unconditionally. –E.

The men's alarm, the women's shouts and screams, the sound of several gunshots that were heard at the entrance to the ravine, and the general hubbub all left me stunned. All I did was sit up stock-still on my bed, waiting for this terrible adventure to end, until a woman came in and went over to my corner, where she tripped over me and saw who I was; infuriated by my impassiveness, she rapped me so sharply on the neck that I quickly jumped up.

"Get out there, yellow-belly," she said, "weakling, pansy, sissy; the law's down on us and everybody's out there defending us, and here's the big lummox lying around like the shameless pig he is. Go on, get out there, you conniving sneak, and pick up that saber behind the door, or I'll empty this pistol into your gut."

This whole party took place in the dark, but as soon as I heard the bit about emptying pistols, I ran out of there like lightning, because that's not the kind of banter I enjoy.

Since I ran out in my shirtsleeves and holding the saber that the woman gave me, my companions didn't recognize me, so they figured I was a wandering constable, and they rained down so many blows with the flats of their swords on me that they came this close to killing me, which they easily could have done, since one of them was shouting, "Hit him with the sharp edge, get him, get him"; but just then, God granted that the woman came out with a burning torch, and in the light they recognized me and, feeling sorry for the deed they had done, took me back and lay me back in my bed.

Soon afterward, the uproar quieted down, followed by a profound silence among the men and a ceaseless wailing among the women. I was feeling somewhat recovered from my blows, so when I heard the wailing, I feared it might signal another scare that would bring some damnable disorderly woman to my bed, and I got up in anticipation, threw on some clothes, went into the other room, and found all the men and women standing around a corpse.

This baneful spectacle gave me a terrible surprise, and I couldn't rest until they had told me everything that had happened, which was: that the sentinels who had been keeping watch had seen a pack of wolves pass by them, going in the direction of the ravine, and, thinking they were constables, they fired their carbines at them; the noise aroused the guards posted farther down, who climbed up the hill, and, thinking that the two companions who were coming down to warn them were constables, they fired on them with such good aim that they broke the leg of one and killed the other outright.

When I heard about these tragedies, I had to feel better that I hadn't suffered anything worse than a few blows with the flats of their blades, and I even think my pain lessened a bit. As you can see, when a man compares his fate with that of someone else who has done better, he feels unlucky; but when he compares it with that of someone more wretched than he is, then he consoles himself and stops whining so much about his troubles. The pity is that we usually don't compare ourselves with those who are more wretched, but rather with those who are luckier than we are, and our troubles therefore come to seem unbearable.

In the end, dawn broke, and with its arrival they concluded the wake and buried the dead man. El Aguilucho told me, "You told me you knew about being a physician;

take a look at this wounded companion and tell me what medicines we need from Puebla, and they'll have to go get them, because all the innkeepers are our friends and *compadres*, and they'll do us the favor."

This demand stunned me, because I understood surgery about as well as I did medicine; I had no idea what to do, and I told myself: if I say that I'm a physician, not a surgeon, I'll look bad, since I told him that I knew how to do everything; if I make the patient worse and send him off to Purgatory, I'm afraid I'll have a worse time of it than I did in Tula, because these villains could kill me without thinking twice about it. Sweet Mother of God! What should I do? Enlighten me. . . . Blessed Souls, help me. . . . St. John Nepomucene, give discretion to my tongue. . . ."[6]

I was making all these petitions to myself, without replying, while pretending that I was inspecting the wound, until El Aguilucho got angry at my sluggishness and said, "So when are you planning to order the medicine? What do you need?"

I couldn't keep covering up, so I told him, "Look, this leg can't be set, because the bone has been turned to splinters" (which was true). "It will have to be cut off above the broken tibia, but that would take instruments that I don't have."

"So, what instruments will it take?" asked El Aguilucho.

"A curved knife," I replied, "and an English saw to cut through the bone and remove the jagged ends."

"Fine," said El Aguilucho, and they left.

That night, they came back with a shoemaker's heel-knife and a butcher's saw. Without wasting any time, we started the operation. God help me, how I made that poor man suffer! I don't want to remember that sacrificial scene. I cut his leg off like I was getting ready to make jerked meat from a piece of deboned mutton. The wretch screamed and wept bitterly, but to no avail, since everybody was holding him down. I then went on to saw off the jagged edges of the bone, as I had said, and in this operation he fainted, both because of the unbearable pain and because of all the blood he had lost; and I couldn't find any way to stop the flow of blood, until I tied his veins with a piece of pita fiber and took advantage of his unconsciousness to cauterize his flesh with a hot iron. Then he came to, and screamed more loudly than ever; but the hemorrhage was somewhat staunched.

In the end, none of the remedies I tried did any good—not the fir resin, not the sugar and powdered rosemary, not the horse dung, nor any of the others I put on his wound; the bandages kept coming off, and the blood streamed out. That, together with the rest of the bad job of healing, made the debilitated patient turn gangrenous quickly, and he kicked the bucket within two days.

Everyone was upset with me, attributing his death to my ineptness, and for very good reason; but I was able to gab my way into blaming it on the lack of tools at hand, so that they ended up believing me and burying the dead man, and we remained friends. How much baneful damage men do because they get into things they don't understand!

After this I spent about two months there without anything new to report, writing

---

[6] [St. John Nepomucene (*San Juan Nepomuceno* in Spanish) is the patron saint against indiscretion and slander. —Tr.]

whatever notes they wanted, shaving them, and staying home during the day to keep watch over the seraglio of my masters, friends, and companions. One night, of the five who had gone out, four returned, very perturbed, because one of them had been killed on some campaign of theirs; but they didn't lose their spirit; rather, they swore that they'd get their revenge another day.

"There's three of them," they said, "three serving lads."

"They're worthless, so the next match is ours."

"They'll pay, by my mother's bones. Tomorrow they'll be passing through Río Frío; that's where we'll meet them."

When they were done making threats, they ate dinner and went to bed. I did the same, though not very happily, for I was thinking about the way the company was falling apart, and I told myself that I should soak my beard, since I could see my neighbors shaving theirs so frequently.[7]

I was planning to desert, but I didn't dare do it because I didn't know the way out of that enchanted labyrinth; nor did I have the nerve to communicate my secret to the women, fearing that they would give me up.

I spent the night making these calculations, and very early the next day they got me out of bed and made me get dressed. I did so right away. Then they saddled my horse, stuck two pistols in my belt, and gave me a cartridge belt and a saber to wear; they put a broad knife in my boot, and a carbine in my hand.

"Why so many weapons?" I asked, frightened.

"Why do you think, brute?" said El Aguilucho. "So you can attack them and defend yourself."

"Well, I'm sure I won't do anything," I said, "because I'm not brave enough to attack, and I'm not skillful enough to defend myself. When the going gets tough, I count on my heels, because I can run faster than a jackrabbit, so for me all this is unnecessary."

My cowardice made El Aguilucho angry, so he drew his saber and told me in a fury, "As God lives, you lazy coward, if you don't get on that horse and come with us, the demons are going to carry you off right here."

Seeing him this angry, I plucked up my courage, pretending that my cowardice had just been a joke and that I was up to attacking the devil himself if he were to come dressed as a traveler with money; they decided they were satisfied, and we went on our way with the plan of falling upon the traveling merchants, robbing them, and killing them; but things did not turn out as they expected.

---

[7] [Soak my beard . . . : alluding to the Spanish proverb, *Cuando la barba de tu vecino vieres pelar, echa la tuya a remojar,* "When you see your neighbor shaving his beard, it's time to soak your own," meaning that you should watch out for what your neighbors do, so that you can take the necessary precautions. –Tr.]

CHAPTER 46

IN WHICH OUR AUTHOR TELLS THE ADVENTURES HE HAD IN THE
GANG OF THIEVES; THE SAD SPECTACLE PRESENTED BY THE CADAVER
OF A HANGED MAN; AND THE BEGINNINGS OF HIS CONVERSION

Though God often allows the wicked to achieve their intentions, whether to test the righteous or to punish the depraved, He does not always permit their designs to go forward. His Providence, which keeps watch over the conservation of His creatures, constantly hinders or destroys their iniquitous plans, that the righteous might not become fodder for the ferocity of the wicked.

So it happened with El Aguilucho and his companions, the morning that we came out to surprise the traveling merchants.

It was about six in the morning when, from the crest of a hill, we spied them coming down the highway. Three men went in front, with their shotguns in hand; then came four horses with empty saddles, which is to say, without riders; after them came four mules loaded down with trunks, cots, and bedrolls—we could see what the cargo was from far off, even though it was all covered with blue cloaks; and finally the three serving lads were in the rearguard.

As soon as El Aguilucho saw them, he vowed to take his revenge and a large booty, so he made us hide behind a steep slope at the foot of the hill, and he told us, "Now it's time, companions, to show our bravery and take advantage of a lucky situation, because there's no doubt that they're merchants on their way to Veracruz, and their cargo's bound to be made up of cash and fine clothes. The important thing is not to hold back, but attack them boldly, knowing that the advantage is ours, since we're five and they're just three; because the serving lads are hired hands and cowardly folk who have no reason to give us pause. They'll take off running at the first shots; so you, Perico, and me and the Gobbler will jump out in front of them as soon as they come within a good distance, I mean, within a gunshot; and Lefty and Snubnose will take the rearguard so they'll know they're surrounded. If they give up right away, all we'll have to do is take away their weapons, tie them up, and bring them here to this hill, where we'll let them go after night falls; but if they resist and fire on us, don't give them quarter: they all die."

Between the sight of our enemies, who were coming closer second by second, and thinking about the dangers that threatened me, I was trembling like a hatter, unable to hide my fear, to the point that my terror became noticeable, because my legs were trembling so hard that the little chains on my spurs were jangling perceptibly against the stirrups; this attracted El Aguilucho's attention, and, noting my fear and glaring at me, he said, "What are you trembling about, you shameless pansy? Do you think you're going to go fight against an army of lions? Haven't you noticed, you chicken, that they're men like you, and they're just three against five? Don't you see that you're not going in alone, but with four men—four real men—who are going to be exposed to the same danger, and who'll defend you like the apple of their eyes? You think it's so likely that you'll perish and not one of us? And finally, let's say they hit you with a bullet and kill you: what's so new or unheard of about that? Are you planning to die in childbirth, you spineless lout, or are you expecting to stick around in this world to witness the coming of the Antichrist? What, do you expect to have money, eat well, dress well, and ride good horses if you're a lazy bum, closed up in a shop and never taking any risks? Well, that's too green, brother; you've got to take some risks to pay the rent. If you tell me, as you have, that you've known thieves who rob and stroll down the street without the slightest danger, I'll tell you that's true; but not everybody can rob that way. Some people rob in a military way—I mean, out in the open, risking their necks; others rob in a courteous way, that is, in the cities, living it up and never running the risk of losing their lives; but not everybody can manage to do it that way, though most would like to. So, watch your spinelessness, because I'll shoot you myself before you have a chance to turn your horse around."

I was frightened by his harsh rebuke and fearsome threats, so I told him I wasn't afraid, and that if I was trembling, it was just because of the cold; so we should get on with the attack, and then he'd see how brave I was.

"God grant that will happen," El Aguilucho said, "though I doubt it very much."

Meanwhile the travelers had reached the point prescribed by El Aguilucho. Snubnose and Lefty broke off from our group and took on the rearguard, while at the same time, the Gobbler, El Aguilucho, and I came out in front of them pointing our shotguns and shouting: "Everybody stop, if you don't want to die at our hands."

At our shouts, four armed men jumped up out of the packed cargo, immediately mounted the four empty horses, and went after Lefty and Snubnose, who opened fire on them with their carbines, killing one before fleeing like jackrabbits.

The three traveling merchants attacked us, killing our Gobbler in the first volley. I fired my shotgun, aiming to kill, but only managed to get a horse, which bit the dust.

When El Aguilucho saw that he was all alone (because he didn't count me at all), he told me, "This isn't an even match any more; one of us is dead, two ran away, there's nine against us: let's get out of here."

As he said this, he tried to turn his horse and run, but he couldn't, because it shied on him; so in spite of the fact that we were loading and firing as fast as we could, we weren't doing any damage, while bullets kept whizzing by us; and we were afraid they'd catch us with their swords, for the three merchants were galloping toward us full speed, unafraid of our shotguns.

The El Aguilucho jumped down, killing his horse with a blow from his rifle butt to the head, and while he was leaping onto my horse behind me, they fired a shot at him that was so well aimed it went right through his temples and he fell down dead.

The bullet came close to going through my body, too, for it nipped off a piece of my poncho. The blood of the unhappy Aguilucho spattered my clothes. I had no time to do more than tell him, "Jesus bless you," and, finding myself alone with so many enemies on top of me, I spurred on my horse and fled down that highway faster than an arrow. Fortunately it was an excellent horse, and it galloped as quickly as I could have hoped. In fact, a quarter of an hour later, I couldn't even see my pursuers' dust.

I took roundabout side paths, and although I thought of going to give the sad news to the madams of the house, I couldn't make up my mind to do it, both because I didn't know the way and because, even if I had, I was too afraid to return to that unlucky hideout.

Tired, filled with fear, and riding an exhausted horse, I found myself around noon in an empty and pleasant little wood.

There I got out of the saddle; I loosened the horse's straps, took off his bridle, gave him water in a stream, and let him pasture on the green grass; I sat down under a cool, shady tree, and gave myself over to the most serious considerations.

"No doubt about it," I said; "laziness, licentiousness, and vice cannot be the surest means of achieving our true happiness. True happiness in this life can never consist of anything other than having a tranquil spirit, whatever one's fortunes; and that's something a criminal can never have, no matter how merry a time he has of it when he's satisfying his passions; his ephemeral merriment is succeeded by an unbearable languor, many hours of boredom, and incessant remorse, so that in the end he pays a long and costly tribute for his miserable bit of pleasure, which he perhaps bought at the expense of a thousand crimes, frights, and hazards.

"These truths are recognized by anyone who seriously thinks about them. My father had warned me about them since I was very young; the colonel never ceased to recite them to me; I've read them in books, and perhaps have heard them preached from pulpits; but what else? The world, my friends, my experience have been constant teachers that have never ceased to remind me of these lessons in the course of my life, despite the ingratitude with which I have ignored their warnings.

"The world," I said; "yes, the world, my bad friends, the baneful events of my life: they have all unanimously conspired to rid me of my illusions, though from different directions; because a deceptive and fanciful world, a depraved and flattering friend, a misfortune brought on by our dissolute behavior, and all of life's ills are teachers telling us to put our actions in order and to better our way of life. It is true that bad teachers can give good lessons. A friend's unfaithfulness, a woman's treachery, the tricks pulled on us by a flatterer, the blows we suffer from someone we've wronged, the imprisonment to which justice sentences us for our own guilt, the illnesses we suffer because of our excesses, and other such things are truly unwelcome to our spirits and our bodies; yet our experience of these things should bring us sweet fruit from their bitter roots.

"And what better fruit could we get from these grievous experiences than the object lesson that we need to control ourselves in the future? Then we would restrain ourselves from making friends indiscriminately or without recognizing the traits of a true friend; we would know to distrust women and not give our hearts to just anyone; we would flee from flatterers as we would from tame but treacherous beasts; we would endeavor to harm no one, not to expose ourselves to the blows of vengeance; we would take care to behave honorably, not to suffer the hardships of prison; we would restrain our sensual appetites, not to struggle with diseases; and finally, we would try to live according to divine and human laws, not to keep experiencing these troubles, and to attain true happiness, which, as I have said, is the fruit of a good conscience.

"We would achieve all this if we knew how to make use of experience; but the pity is that we never learn, no matter how frequent our lessons.

"Let me tell it. How many troubles, how many snubs, how many embarrassments, how many blows, imprisonments, frights, sorrows, and setbacks have I experienced? How many risks have I been exposed to, and what deplorable situation am I in now? I've been whipped and reproached by my teachers; bruised by bulls and horses; hit with shoes, showered with boiling water, threatened, and shamed by old women; I've suffered disloyalty, mockery, and disdain from bad friends; I've been beaten by bumpkins, snubbed by courtiers, disowned by relatives, loathed by strangers, thrown out by masters, harassed by scoundrels, imprisoned by justice, hit with pots by Indians, justly wounded by married men whom I had aggrieved, worked over by hospitals, scratched by tarts, frightened by dead men, robbed by rogues, and I've suffered 300,000 misadventures, which, far from serving to teach me a lesson, seem only to have stimulated me to go from bad to worse.

"What do I have left to lose? The luster of my noble birth has already been darkened by my shameful misconduct; my health has been ruined by my excesses; my material fortune has been squandered by my constant dissipation; I have no good friends; and my bad friends despise and abandon me. My conscience is troubled by remorse for my crimes; I cannot rest calmly; and the happiness that I am always pursuing seems to be a phantom made of air, which dissolves in my hands when I try to grasp it.

"Thus I have lost everything. I have nothing left to care for but my life and my soul. Those are all I have, but they are also the most precious things one can have.

"God is concerned that I not be lost for all eternity. How many times might I have lost my life—at the hands of men, in the power of beasts, in the midst of the sea, and even by my own hands! Too many to count. Today could have been the last of my days. The Gobbler fell to one side of me, El Aguilucho to the other, and the bullets crackled one after the other in the air next to my ears; bullets that were no doubt aimed at me personally, bullets that brought death before my eyes.

"Just as those two died, couldn't I have died? Since there were bullets aimed directly at them, couldn't there have been one for me? Did I escape them because of my virtue and agility? Of course not. An invisible and Almighty Hand was what turned them aside from my body, with the pious end that I not be lost forever. And what merit have I amassed to deserve such care? Oh, God, how it shames me to recall that my whole life has been an uninterrupted chain of crimes! I have run through childhood and youth like a raving lunatic, trampling on the most sacred considerations, and now I have reached manhood, older and with more crimes on my conscience than in my puberty and adolescence.

"I have had thirty some-odd years of life, and a sinful, immoral life it has been. However, it is not too late; I still have time to truly convert and change my conduct. If it saddens me to think how long my life has been immoral, let it console me to know that the Great Father of all families is most liberal and kind, and He pays as much to the man who enters His vineyards in the morning as to the man who begins to work there late in the day. What is done is done; let us reform ourselves."

Saying this, full of terror and compunction, I readied the horse, mounted it, and headed toward the town or inn of San Martín.[1]

I arrived at nearly seven at night; I asked for supper and told them to unsaddle and care for my horse, relying on pure bluster, since I didn't have a penny.

After supper, I went out to take the fresh air in the little porch of the inn, where another traveler was doing the same.

We greeted each other politely and became engaged in conversation, to the point that we got familiar with each other, the principal topic being the events that had happened that day with the thieves. He told me that he had left Puebla and was traveling to Calpulalpan, and that he would have to spend a short time in Apam.

I told him that I was going to that same town, and from there I was to go on to Mexico, so we could travel there together, because the thieves made me very apprehensive.

"As you should be," the traveler replied, "though with the frights they've suffered over the past week, we can expect that they won't be so quick to form new gangs. In the last few days, they've caught six and hanged one, and four have been left dead in the field. So you can see, their count is down by eleven, and at this rate, the days are breezing by."

Since I hadn't seen anyone captured, I knew of only two dead, and I was sure that there were only five of us, I said to him with a hint of doubt, "That might be possible, but I'm afraid that someone has misled you, because that's a long list of thieves taken out."

"No, nobody misled me," he said; "I know it very well: not only am I a lieutenant in the Acordada,[2] I have all their descriptions; I know their names, the areas where they robbed, the damage they've done, and who has fallen up to today; so tell me whether I know it or not."

I felt a chill when I heard that he was a lieutenant, though it consoled me when I realized that I hadn't gone on more than one campaign, so it was impossible that anyone would recognize me as a thief.

Then I believed him fully, and asked him where the others had been caught. He told me it was between Otumba and Teotihuacán.

We chatted about other things for a long time, and at the end I told him that I had good reason to fear thieves, since I had been pursued by them.

"For you see," I said, very formally, "I was not attacked by those thieves, but last night my own serving lad ran off with the mule that carried the sleeping rolls, and he left me penniless, as he took the 200 pesos that were all I carried in my chest."

"What villainy!" the lieutenant said very sympathetically. "That rogue must be with them by now. What is his name? What features does he have?"

---

[1] [San Martín Texmelucan, a town fifteen miles east of Río Frío, heading away from Mexico City and toward Puebla. From here, Periquillo will turn north to Calpulalpan (twenty-five miles north of San Martín, in the state of Tlaxcala) and Apam (another twelve miles north, in Hidalgo), before turning west to Otumba and Teotihuacán on his way back to Mexico City. –Tr.]

[2] [The Acordada: a special tribunal with its own constabulary, established in 18th-century Mexico to deal with the endemic problem of highway robbery. –Tr.]

I told him whatever came into my head, and he wrote it down very efficiently in a small memo book; and when he finished, we went inside to go to bed.

He invited me to stay in his room; I agreed and went to sleep there. As soon as he saw my pistols he fell in love with them, and tried to buy them from me. With a prayer on my lips I sold them to him, fearing that their owner might show up some day. In any case, I got rid of them and took his money without worrying about it.

We went to bed, and we set out on our way very early the next day, on which nothing particular happened. We reached Apam, where I pretended to go off to look for a friend, and the following day we parted and I continued my journey to Mexico.

That night I slept in Teotihuacán, where I learned that the thieves had been defeated the previous week, and their ringleader had been captured and hanged at the entrance to the town.

Filled with fear by this news, I managed to sleep, and the next day at six in the morning, I saddled my horse, commended myself wholeheartedly to God, and continued on my way.

I had gone a league or a bit farther when I saw, tied to a tree and held up by a stake, the cadaver of a hanged man, with his white sackcloth, his tall hat adorned with a cross made of red cloth, which had fallen forward to cover his forehead, and his hands tied.

I came closer to look at him carefully; but how did I react when I saw and recognized that misshapen corpse as my old unhappy friend Januario? My hairs stood on end; my blood froze in my veins; my heart raced; my tongue became a knot in my throat; my forehead was covered with a deadly sweat; and, having lost the elasticity of my sinews, I was about to fall from my horse due to the distress of my soul.

But God wished to aid my faltering spirit, and, with an extraordinary effort to keep brave on my part, I managed to recover slowly from the turmoil that oppressed me.

At that moment, I recalled his misdeeds, his corrupt advice, his infernal examples and maxims; I greatly mourned his misfortune; I cried for him, for after all he was my friend and we had grown up together; but I also gave hearty thanks to God for separating me from his friendship, since, between that and my evil disposition, I would certainly have become a thief like him, and perhaps at that hour I would have been hanging from the next tree.

I confirmed more and more my resolutions to change my life, endeavoring to take advantage thenceforth of the world's lessons, and to profit from the wickedness and adversities of men; and, imbued with these righteous thoughts, I took out my short knife and carved the following verse in the bark of the tree from which Januario was hanging:

SONNET[3]

Are crimes then punished in the end?
Will felony no longer lift its head

---

[3] [Two somewhat different versions of this sonnet exist, that of the 3rd edition and that of the 4th, whose editor notes:]

In the manuscript that was reviewed for this edition, whose authenticity cannot be proved,

Up high in pride? Januario, lifeless now,
Proclaims thus to the public from this mast.

Oh, ill-starred friend! How long these regions have
Endured your robberies, your homicides;
But now your death—so hateful, so deserved—
Has cut the wicked thread of your excess.

You taught me many maxims that mislead,
Which I too often followed, to my grief;
Yet hanged from this noose now, you dispel
All misconceptions. Here, your rigid corpse
Does preach an end to lies, and I will learn
The truthful lessons you give now in death.

My sonnet complete, I went on my way, commending his soul very fervently to God.

I managed to enter Mexico by night, stopping at the Santo Tomás inn,[4] where I had supper and, while strolling in the corridor, heard the sound of women weeping in one of the rooms.

Curiosity or pity drew me to the door of the room, and listening in on them, I heard an old man saying, "Come on, my dears, stop your crying, there's no help for it; what can we do? Justice had its job to do; the boy turned ornery when he was little; my warnings, my threats, my punishments didn't do him any good; he decided he was going to go bad, and he finally did it."

"But I mourn him," said a poor old woman; "after all, he was my nephew."

"I mourn him, too," the elderly man said; "and the proof is all the work I've done and the money I've spent to get him off; but I couldn't do it. God help poor Januario! Come on, my dear, don't cry; look, nobody knows he was our kinsman; everyone thinks he was an orphan we took in. This incident will make poor Poncianita feel so ashamed! But after all, the girl is a nun now, and even if they found out how she was related to him, she'd remain a nun; commend his soul to God, and let's go to bed so we can leave early tomorrow."

---

though there are reasons to believe it to be that of the Thinker [Lizardi], the sonnet has been corrected in the form published here. Other corrections have been taken from the same manuscript, which will be noted if this edition is compared with earlier ones. –E.

[Many of the other poems that appear from this point to the end of the book also have variant versions. The version of this sonnet from the 3rd edition reads, in a fairly literal translation, as follows: "So, are his offenses paid for at last, / And his odious and corrupt conduct? / So it is, Perico, so it is; and albeit lifeless, / Januario shouts this clearly to me. / You were a highwayman in these regions, / Oh sad friend! Yes, you were a murderer; / Yet an odious and well-deserved death / Put an end to your countless excesses. / You fed me misleading maxims, / Which I sometimes followed mistakenly; / But now, from the pole on which you rest, / You advise me to mend my ways; and I realize / That I should listen to you, for you are making amends / By preaching well to me after your death." –Tr.]

[4] [Near the Zócalo. –Tr.]

My neighbors finished talking, and I was left without any doubt that they were Don Martín and his wife. I turned in, and the next day I got up at dawn to speak with them, which I managed to do furtively, so that I recognized who they were without giving myself away to them. I found out that they had left the hacienda and that they were going to settle in the interior. I bid farewell to those good people, whom I never heard from again. No doubt they have died, for grief, illness, and long years can bring nothing but death.

I went to Mass very early, came back for breakfast, and did not go out again all day, busying myself with making the most serious reflections on my past life, and with affirming the resolutions I had made to reform my life in the future.

One of the things by which I recognized that this was a firm resolution, unlike my earlier ones, was the fact that I could have made some money off of the horse, cloak, saber, and spurs, for they were all good and valuable, yet I did not make up my mind to do so, not only because I feared someone would recognize one of the pieces (as they had once recognized Dr. Purgante's cape), but because I rightly demurred, for these things were not mine, and by the same token I could not and should not dispose of them.

I resolved, therefore, to keep these articles until I could hand them over to a confessor, with the intention of paying for the pistols I had sold, if God ever gave me the means to do so and I learned who their owner had been.

With this determination, I went out around nightfall to take a walk around the streets with no particular destination. I passed by the temple of La Profesa,[5] which was open; I entered with the intention of praying the Stations of the Cross and leaving.

They were in fact reading the points of meditation right then; I commended myself to God during that time as best I could, and I heard the sermon that was preached by a very wise priest. His topic was the unhappiness of those who disdain last rites, and the uncertainty we have of knowing which rites might be our last. The preacher concluded by proving that spiritual aid is never far away, and that we should take advantage of it, fearing that any one of those rites could be our last, and that if we were to disdain them, God might stop us in our tracks and put an end to the measure of our crimes, or our hearts might harden and we might fall into final impenitence.

But what spirit and energy the preacher put into expounding these truths!

"The worst calamity," he said, filled with holy zeal, "the worst calamity that can befall a man in this life is final impenitence. In this unhappy state, Heaven and Hell would be objects of the coldest indifference for the impenitent. His stony heart would not be susceptible to the love of God, nor to the fear of eternity, and though certain that enduring awards and punishments are to come, he would neither aspire to the first, nor endeavor to free himself from the latter. The plagues rained down on Pharaoh and on Egypt; the punishments were frequent, yet Pharaoh persisted in his blind obstinacy, because 'his heart was hardened,' as the holy scriptures tell us: *induratum*

---

5 [La Profesa: a church and monastery at the corner of the streets known today as Madero and Isabel la Católica, two blocks west of the Zócalo. Formerly Jesuit, the monastery passed to the order of St. Philip Neri in 1767, when the Spanish crown expelled the Jesuits for suspicions of working against royal interests. –Tr.]

est cor Faraonis.[6] Therefore, dear listeners, 'if one of you has heard His voice today, harden not your hearts'; if you feel inspired by any rite, you should not disdain it, nor delay your conversion until tomorrow, for you may not know whether, having spurned that rite, there might never be another, and your heart might be hardened. *Hodie si vocem ejus audierites, nolite obdurare corda vestra,* the sainted prophet-king tells us.[7] Today, then, this very instant, we must open up our hearts if the Lord's grace touches them; we must respond today to His voice if He calls us, not waiting for tomorrow, for we do not know if tomorrow we will live, nor if, when we try to implore God's mercy, His Majesty might disown us as He did the foolish virgins, making our efforts fruitless and bringing down upon our heads the terrible anathema with which the Lord Himself threatened obstinate sinners. 'I called you,' He tells them, 'and you refused to hear me; I touched your hearts and you did not yield them to me; I also will laugh in the hour of your death, and will mock your pleas.' "[8]

This was the style of the sermon I heard, which filled me with such terror that as soon as the father stepped down from the pulpit, I went in after him and begged him to hear two words of penitence from me.

The good priest consented to my entreaty with the greatest sweetness and charity; and after he had heard about my life in brief and was satisfied that my resolve was true, he summoned me to come the next day at half past five in the morning, when he would be finishing Prime, the early morning Mass, adding that I should meet him in that same spot, a dark corner of the sacristy. We agreed on it, and I went back to the inn, somewhat consoled.

The next day I woke up early; I heard him say Mass and waited for him where he had told me.

He didn't let me confess just yet, because he told me I would have to make a general confession; there would be a beautiful occasion that I could take advantage of if I wished, for that afternoon they were beginning a program of spiritual exercises at a retreat that he would be leading, and I had a chance to enter it if I wished.[9]

"I surely do wish to, Father," I said, "since that's what I aspire to do—to have a good confession."

"Fine, then," he replied, "prepare your things and come back this afternoon; tell the father doorkeeper your name, and ask no more questions."

This said, he rose, and I went back, feeling even more content than the night before, though I couldn't help wondering at what the confessor had told me—that I should give my name at the entrance door—since he hadn't asked me what it was.

Nevertheless, I made no attempt to clear it up.

I arrived at the inn, ate dinner at the usual hour, paid what I owed, left my horse in their care, giving them money for its feed, and at three in the afternoon, I went to La Profesa.

---

[6] [Exodus 7:13. –Tr.]

[7] [Psalms 94:8 (95:8). –Tr.]

[8] [A paraphrase of Proverbs 1:24 and 1:26. –Tr.]

[9] [Spiritual exercises are a set program for prayer, reflection, and spiritual renewal, usually practiced in a group retreat. –Tr.]

CHAPTER 47

IN WHICH PERIQUILLO DESCRIBES HOW HE ENTERED THE
RETREAT IN LA PROFESA; HIS ENCOUNTER WITH ROQUE; WHO
HIS CONFESSOR WAS; AND THE FAVORS HE OWED HIM, NOT
THE LEAST OF WHICH WAS FINDING HIM A JOB IN A SHOP

The moment I arrived at the door of La Profesa, I delivered the message from the father who was going to lead the retreat. The doorkeeper asked me my name; I told him; then he looked at a piece of paper and told me, "Fine, have them bring in your bed."

"It's here already," I said; "I'm carrying it on my back."

"Please come in, then."

I entered with him, and he took me to a room where another man sat, telling me, "This room is for you and this gentleman, your companion."

This said, he left; and as soon as I turned to talk to my companion, I recognized him as poor Roque, my old classmate, friend, and assistant. He also recognized me, and after we had embraced each other with all the tenderness imaginable, we asked about each other, and found out each other's adventures.

Roque was amazed to discover my experiences. I was not so amazed by his, for he had not been as wayward as I had, and therefore hadn't suffered as much, so his minor adventures were nothing out of the ordinary.

In the end, I told him, "I'm so glad that we have found each other in this holy cloister, and that the two of us, who once ran together down the path of wickedness, should now meet again here, moved by the same sentiments to beg for grace."

"I'm just as happy," Roque told me; "and to that I can add the satisfaction of being able to beg your pardon (which I do now) for the bad advice I gave you; for even though I gave it in order to flatter you and to win your protection, being beset by poverty, that's no excuse; rather, I should have advised you well, even if it meant losing your house and friendship, instead of leading you into evil."

"I didn't need much leading," I said; "don't worry about that. You can believe that I would have behaved as badly without your persuasions as I did with them."

"But are you seriously trying to change your life now?" Roque asked.

"That's my intention, no doubt," I answered, "and with that plan in mind, I've come to cloister myself here for these eight days."

"I'm so glad," Roque went on. "But, man, what if your thoughts aren't inspired by the Virgin? We're grown up now, and you've seen the wolf—not just his ears but his whole body[1]—so you should think this through very seriously."

"Your passion doesn't offend me," I said; "no doubt you'd make a good friar, and I'd bet missionary work would suit you."

"I'm not planning to be a preacher," he replied, "because I figure I'm not educated enough, and I don't have the right spirit for it; but I do plan to become a friar, and that's why I've come to these spiritual exercises. I've already been admitted to

---

[1] ["To see the wolf's ears" means to find oneself in great danger. –Tr.]

San Francisco,[2] and if God helps me and it is His will, I'm planning to leave here and enter the novitiate right away."

"I'm glad, Roque, I'm glad. You've thought it out sensibly, though the proverb says that when the wolf gets tired of flesh, he becomes a friar."

"That's one of the many vulgar, foolish proverbs we have," said Roque. "Even if you mean to tell me that I've given the prime of my youth to the world, and that, now that I have one foot in old age, I expect to submit to the cloister and live subject to obedience, you wouldn't be wrong; but, just because we were bad boys and bad youths, do we necessarily have to be bad old men, too? No, Perico; you have to start thinking sensibly sometime; it's never too late for conversion; and there's another proverb that says: better late than never."

"No, don't get angry, Roquillo," I said, "you're quite right; that was just a stupid joke—you know my character, which is naturally jolly, especially with friends who are as close as you; but you're quite right to think the way you do, and I'll try to benefit from your anger."

"Anger, fiddlesticks!" said Roque. "I knew you were joking; but I was just explaining the situation to you."

Then they rang the bell and we went to the opening sermon.

After the exercises that night, the doorkeeper entered my room and gave me a message from my confessor: that after hearing Prime in the chapel, I should wait for him in the sacristy. Roque and I read the good books that were on the table until time for supper, and afterward we retired for the night, Roque giving me a sheet and a pillow.

The following day I rose early, heard Prime, waited for the father, and began my general confession. I was more taken every day with the confessor's prudence and gentleness.

On the seventh day, I concluded my confession to my confessor's satisfaction, and to the great consolation of my spirit. The father told me that the next day, there would be a general communion, and that I should take communion, and not go to my room for breakfast, but to his room, which was the seventh one on the right as you come out of the chapel. I promised to do so, and we parted.

It will be hard for anyone who has no experience of these things to believe how well and how calmly I slept that night. I felt that an enormous weight had been lifted from me, or that a thick fog stifling my heart had lifted; and so it truly was.

The next day we got up, washed, and went to the chapel, where, after the usual exercises, a thanksgiving Mass was said with the greatest solemnity, and after the priest had communion, we all took communion from his hand, filled with the sweetest, most inexpressible joy.

When Mass had concluded and we had given thanks, everyone else went to have breakfast in the *chocolatero*,[3] and after bidding a very affectionate farewell to Roque, I went to do the same with my confessor, who was waiting for me in his room.

---

[2] [San Francisco: a huge Franciscan monastery that occupied what are now the four city blocks between Lázaro Cárdenas, Bolívar, Madero, and Carranza. –Tr.]

[3] [*Chocolatero*: according to Santamaría, *Diccionario de mejicanismos* (p. 413), this was a small dining room in schools "in the old days" where the students were served hot chocolate. –Tr.]

But how surprised I was when, after assuming that he was some father whom I had only known for those past eight days, I saw that my confessor was none other than Martín Pelayo, my old friend who had given me such excellent advice!

When I realized that he was no longer plain old Martín Pelayo, nor a dancing and scatterbrained boy, but a wise, exemplary, and circumspect priest, and that I had been telling all my delightful stories to him and not to some stranger, I couldn't help but blush; at least, the father must have seen the blush on my face, for he tried to cheer me up by saying, "What, don't you remember me, Pedrito? Won't you give me a hug? Come on, give me one, but good and tight. I wanted so much to see you and hear about your adventures! Fitting adventures for a boy without experience or authority."

Then we hugged each other tightly, and afterward he made me sit and drink my chocolate, while he continued telling me, "You'll get over any shame you feel for having confessed with me, when you learn that I was worse than you, so much worse that I was your teacher in the ways of dissipation. Perhaps my bad advice contributed to your own dissipation, for which I am very sorry; but God has seen fit to give me the pleasure of being your spiritual director and replacing the perverse advice I once gave you with maxims of solid morality. To keep your spirit from being cowed by shame, I was always careful to confess you in darkness, and to cover my face with my handkerchief; but after I was able to absolve you, I wanted to show you that I am your friend. Nothing that you told me came as a shock. I would have committed every crime that you did; I am an offender in the eyes of God; if I have not found myself in as much trouble, and if I submitted myself to authority somewhat sooner, that was a special result of His mercy. So don't stand there in front of me feeling ashamed. In the confessional I am your father, here I'm your brother; there I serve as a judge, here I play the role of friend, for I have always been your friend, and now with twice the motive. In view of all this, you should treat me here as you do here, and there as you do there."

As you can easily imagine, this gentle and prudent style raised my spirits tremendously, and I began to lose my shame, especially since he wouldn't let me call him *usted,* just *tú,* as I always had.

During the conversation, I told him, "Brother, since I owe you so much that I could never repay you, and you've told me that I should return the horse, the cloak, the saber, and all the rest to their owners, let me tell you: that's what I want to do most of all, because I feel like I'm wearing a badge of shame, and I'm afraid that this might lead me into some cruel joke even worse than what happened to me with Dr. Purgante's cape. True, I didn't steal these things; but be that as it may, they're stolen goods, and I shouldn't keep them in my possession for a second. I'd like to get rid of them as quickly as I can, and hand them over to you so that you can tell the Acordada about them, or announce them in the *Gaceta,*[4] or however you want to do it, whether it all gets back to their owners as soon as possible or not; the thing is, I want to be rid of this burden, because, if it's true that the Devil carries off everything you earn, you can imagine what'll happen to what you get by stealing."

---

[4] [*Gaceta del gobierno de México,* the official tri-weekly publication of the colonial government in Mexico City, was published from 1784 to 1822. –Tr.]

"That's all well and good," Pelayo told me, "but do you have any other clothes to wear?"

"What could I have!" I said. "Just these clothes, and six pesos that I have left from selling the pistols."

"Well, there you go," said Martín; "for now, you can't get rid of everything, since you find yourself in extreme and legitimate need to cover your flesh, even if it be with stolen clothes. Nevertheless, we'll see what we can do. But tell me: what do you plan to do now? What kind of work do you want to do? Because, to live you have to eat, and to put food on the table it is necessary to work, and for you that is so essential that if you don't support yourself with some sort of job, you're very likely to give up on your good desires, forget your recent resolutions, and go back to your old life."

"God forbid," I said very sadly; "but, dear brother, what can I do, since there's no one I can turn to in this city, and nobody who could help me find a job or a place where I can serve, even if it's just as a doorman? My relatives reject me because I'm poor; my friends ignore me for the same reason; and everyone has abandoned me, whether because I'm a cad or because I don't have a penny—which is more likely, since if I had money I'd have plenty of friends and relatives, even if I were the devil, just as I've had plenty in the past when I was rich; because what they're looking for is money, not good behavior, and as long as you have something for them to swindle you for, they don't bother with checking up on how you got it. Wherever it comes from, the thing is to have something for them to skim, and even if the guy they're skimming from is more vile than Satan, with Gestas[5] and Judas mixed in, they don't care; those flatterers and butter-uppers will burn incense for whatever idol favors them, no matter how criminal he is, and they'll shamelessly praise his vices as if they were the most heroic virtues. I'm sorry, brother, but I know all this from continuous experience. These roguish friends, who led me astray and who lead so many others astray in this world, know the damnable art of dressing up vices as virtues. They call dissipation, liberality; they call gaming, honest entertainment, even though it's an entertainment that squanders fortunes; they call lewdness, good etiquette; they call drunkenness, pleasure; they call arrogance, authority; they call vanity, circumspection; they call rudeness, being frank; they call vulgar jokes, good wit; they call stupidity, prudence; they call hypocrisy, virtue; they call provocation, bravery; they call cowardice, caution; they call garrulousness, eloquence; they call dullness, humility; they call simple-mindedness, simplicity; they call . . . but what is the point of boring you, since you know what the world is better than I do, and what these sorts of friends are? In virtue of this, I don't know what to do or who to turn to."

"Don't worry about it," Father Pelayo told me, "I'll do whatever I can for you. Trust to Divine Providence; but don't let your guard down, because in this sad world we always have to 'pray to God but put our shoulders to the wheel.' "

"And may God repay you for your advice and consolation," I said; "but, brother, I wish you'd intervene with your friends to see if I could get some kind of job, whatever it might be, and you can be sure I won't make you look bad."

---

5 [Gestas: the traditional name of the "bad thief" crucified on the left of Jesus (see Chapter 11, footnote 4). –Tr.]

"Something just occurred to me right now," he said; "wait for me here."

Saying this, he went out into the street, and I stayed there reading until noon, when my friend returned.

As soon as he entered, he said, "Great news, Pedro, you've got a job. This afternoon I'm taking you to sign on with the man who'll be your patron, to whom I've recommended you very highly. He's a friend of mine, and my spiritual son; therefore I know him and I am certain of his fine circumstances. Well, I'd say you should give a thousand thanks to God for this new favor, and be on your best behavior around him, because it's time to start thinking sensibly now. Always keep the misfortunes you've suffered in mind, and reflect on the wages of the world and of having bad friends. Let's go eat."

I gave him the thanks he deserved, the table was set, we ate, and afterward we prayed an Our Father to the soul of our unhappy friend Januario. We slept the siesta, and at four, after drinking chocolate, I rode in a coach with Father Pelayo to the house of the man who was to be my master.

As soon as he saw me, it seems that I hit it off with him, because he treated me with a lot of politeness and affection. That was how well our confessor and friend must have spoken to him about me.

The man was a widower and childless, rich and liberal: qualities that should have made him a good master, which indeed he was.

My job was to work as the administrator of the inn of the town called San Agustín de las Cuevas,[6] which, as you know, lies four leagues from the capital, and to operate a good shop that he had in that town, splitting the revenue that both businesses produced with my master, half and half.

It goes without saying that I accepted immediately, showering Pelayo with my gratitude; and having come to an agreement and set the date for my taking the position, my friend Martín and I went back to La Profesa.

That night we chatted about various matters, and Pelayo wound up the conversation by charging me with behaving honorably and not letting him look bad. I promised to do that, and we went to bed.

The next day, my friend left me in his room, and he shortly returned laden with fabric and with a tailor in tow; he had the tailor measure me for a suit and cape, and having paid him I don't know how much, he bid him farewell.

As you can easily imagine, I was amazed by Father Pelayo's generosity, and couldn't find the words to express my gratitude. He told me, "I gave you this money and did these things for you for three reasons: so you won't keep wearing out the clothes you have on, which aren't yours; so those clothes don't leave you exposed to some embarrassing situation; and so your master will treat you as a refined and civilized man, not like a wild bumpkin. The way a person dresses is very relevant in this world, and even though we shouldn't dress with excessive pomp, we should dress decently and in accordance with our origins and our ends."

---

[6] [San Agustín de las Cuevas: thirteen miles south of central Mexico City, this village was a popular weekend spot for the well-heeled of the city, and one of the favorite residences of the viceroys; today it is a southern suburb of the city and is known as Tlalpan. –Tr.]

Three days later, the tailor returned with the clothes; I got dolled up with a long cloak and a short jacket, but that's what was in style in Mexico. Pelayo went with me to the inn, where I handed the horse and its trappings over to him; we returned to La Profesa, where I made a list of everything I was putting in his hands; and the next day, Martín handed all those things over to the captain of the Acordada so that he could seek out their owners or decide what to do with them.

There was nothing left to be done with this matter, so when the day came that I was to take over the shop and the inn, we left for San Agustín de las Cuevas; I took possession of everything satisfactorily; my master and the father returned to Mexico, and I remained there in the town, where my conduct was exemplary, while Heaven rewarded me with an increase in my wealth and with a string of temporal happiness.

CHAPTER 48

IN WHICH PERIQUILLO DESCRIBES HIS CONDUCT IN SAN AGUSTÍN
DE LAS CUEVAS, THE ADVENTURE OF HIS FRIEND ANSELMO, AND
OTHER EPISODES THAT ARE NOT UNPLEASANT IN THE LEAST

It is said that the wise man can overcome his fate; it would be even more true to say that the upright man, through his consistently orderly conduct, can almost always dominate his fortune, however disastrous it might be.

I myself had this experience of dominating my fate, even when I was behaving honorably out of hypocrisy; of course, as soon as I stumbled and brazenly returned to vice, my unlucky adventures rained back down on me.

This sudden and painful observation made me see things as they were, and I tried to think seriously, considering that I was over thirty-seven years old, more than old enough to start thinking sensibly. I endeavored to behave with honor and to give rise to no gossip in that town.

One Sunday a month, I'd go to Mexico, confess with my friend Pelayo, and then go with him to spend the rest of the day in my master's house and in his company, and my master displayed more confidence in me and more affection for me every time. In the afternoon, I would go out strolling in the Alameda or elsewhere.

How many times did Pelayo say to me:

"Go out, take it easy, have fun. There's no contradiction between virtue and being merry or having an honest good time. The beauty of the countryside—as a recreation for the senses and for reciprocal communication among men, for explaining their opinions and unburdening their souls—is blessed by God Himself; for His Divine Majesty created the beauty, the aromas, the flavors, the virtues, and hues of the plants, flowers, and fruits, as well as the liveliness, wit, insight, and sublimity of men's minds; and He made, created, and destined all these things for man's use and recreation; otherwise, why would He have made His subordinate creations beautiful, while giving the rational ones the spirit to perceive beauty, unless it is legitimate for us to exercise our talent and our senses on them? That would amount to a pointless creation on the one hand, and on the other a kind of tyranny that would degrade the Deity, for it would show that He had created delightful objects to see and taste, and had endowed us with appetites, while forbidding us to use our appetites or to enjoy those objects. The gentiles imagined that this kind of denial served as the infernal punishment for cruel and avaricious men such as Tantalus, who was condemned to gaze at apples and running water right in front of his mouth, while never being allowed to sate his thirst or his hunger.

"As you can see, this would be an absurd thing to think, yet even if they do so without malice, that's the poor opinion of the Divinity that is formed by those who believe He is offended by our innocent pastimes.

"What is forbidden isn't use, but abuse, even in matters of virtue. I hold this opinion to be very sure, and therefore I advise you: *never sin, and have all the fun you want;* for God wants saints, not mannequins, fools, wet blankets, or sad sacks. Leave that to the hypocrites, because the righteous—in the words of holy King David—

should rejoice and be glad in the Lord, and they do well to sing and dance with His blessings to the sound of the harp, the lyre, and the psaltery.[1]

"These are phrases that the Holy King uses to explain that God doesn't want kill-joys or bores. The yoke of the Lord's law is soft and His burden very light. Any Christian may enjoy all the entertainments that aren't sinful or dangerous. No entertainment can help but be sinful and dangerous—not even attending church—if your heart is corrupt and disposed to evil; while none will be sinful—not even a dance or a wedding feast—if we go to it with righteous intentions and in the spirit of avoiding transgression. A proximate occasion of sin is a risky situation that we should flee when we know from experience that we're weak. So go ahead and have fun within the limits of your prudent observation."

Relying on this and many similar pieces of advice, I would go out to stroll about freely; and although I met many of the little rascals I had once called my friends, I did my best to pretend I didn't see them; and if I couldn't avoid them, I freed myself of them by telling them that I was working outside of Mexico and was leaving that night, at which they would lose hope of swindling me and seducing me.

On one of these innocent strolls, a little boy whispered to me; he was wearing ragged clothes, but he had a pretty face, and he begged me by the love of God for a bit of charity for his poor mother, who was sick in bed and had nothing to eat.

Since his words were accompanied by copious tears and the simplicity natural to a six-year-old boy, I believed him, and, moved to pity by the unhappy condition he had painted for me, I told him to bring me to his house.

As soon as I entered the house, I saw that everything he had told me was true, because in one room (which was the whole house) there lay a lady of about twenty-five years upon an indecent plank bed with no mattress, covers, or pillow other than a reed mat, an old blanket, and a bundle of rags at the headboard. On a corner of the bed sprawled a baby of about one year, frail and emaciated, who strained from time to time at the dry breasts of his weakened mother, squeezing from them what little sustenance he could.

Around the dirty little one-room house wandered a little fair-haired girl of three years—a pretty girl, to tell the truth, but dressed in tatters and showing in her color-less face the hunger that had stolen the life from her cheeks.

There was no fire in the hearth, not even an ember to light a cigarette, and all the furnishings of the house were on the same level of misery.

Such an unhappy scene couldn't help but stir my sensibility; so, sitting down at the sick woman's side, on her very bed, I said to her:

"Ma'am, this boy told me your story, which moved me to pity, so I decided to return with him to see its truth for myself, and indeed the original is more unhappy than the portrait of it that this child had painted. Now that I am satisfied, however, I don't intend that my coming to see you should be entirely unfruitful to you. Please tell me who you are, why you suffer, and how you've reached this deplorable situation, for even if you attain nothing through telling this story but to dissipate the sadness that seems to weigh you down, that would not be a bad thing to achieve; for as

---

[1] [Psalms 31:11–32:2 (32:11–33:2). –Tr.]

you know, our sorrows are lessened when we can communicate them confidentially."

"Sir," said the poor sick woman, in a listless and exceedingly sad voice, "sir, my sorrows are of such a nature that I think telling them will hardly serve to console me, but rather will reopen the wounds that pain my heart; nevertheless, it would be impolite and ungrateful of me if I were to refuse to satisfy your curiosity. . . . "

"No, ma'am," I said, "God forbid I should demand any such sacrifice from you. I believed that telling your misfortunes might bring you surcease in their midst; yet if that is not so, please do not let it worry you. Please take this small amount that I have in my pocket and suffer your troubles in resignation, offering them up to the Lord and trusting in His ample Providence; for He will never forsake you, being a loving Father Who rewards us and grants us merit when He tests us, and Who punishes us tenderly, and even so His hand is afflicted. I will make sure that a priest, who is a friend of mine, comes to see you and give you whatever spiritual and temporal assistance he can. Farewell, then."

Saying this, I lay four pesos on the bed and stood up to leave; but the lady did not allow me to go; rather, sitting up as best she could in her sad berth, she told me, with tearful eyes:

"Please don't leave so soon, and don't deprive me of the consolation that your words bring me. I beg you to sit down; I want to tell you my misfortunes, and I believe that it will indeed be a relief to communicate them to someone who, without any merit of mine, has shown such interest in my wretched luck.

"My name is María Guadalupe Rosana; my parents were honorable nobles, and though they were not rich, they had enough to raise me in comfort. I lacked for nothing in my home; I was loved as a daughter and indulged as an only child. I lived in this way to the age of fifteen, when it pleased God to take my father; my mother was unable to bear this blow, and she followed him to the grave within two months.

"It would be too long a story to tell you of the troubles I suffered and the risks to which my honor was exposed during my orphanhood. One day I lived in this house, the next day in that; here they snubbed me, there they tried to seduce me; and nowhere did I find a safe haven or a trustworthy protector.

"For three years, I wandered here and there, experiencing God only knows what, until—tired of this life, fearing my perdition, and desiring to ensure my honor and my sustenance—I gave in to the insistent amorous pleas of the father of these children. I finally married, and for four or five years, my husband never gave me cause for repentance. Every day I was happier with my state; but a bit more than a year ago, my husband neglected his obligations and became captivated by a fine woman who, like so many women, knew the art of turning him into a bad husband and a bad father, and since then he has given me a very unhappy life, making me suffer hunger, poverty, nakedness, illness, and a thousand other troubles, which, even so, are not enough to pay for my sins. My husband's dissipation has brought its natural fruits to us all: the utter misery in which you find me, and in which he finds himself.

"When he was an upright man, he supported his house decently, because he had a well-stocked booth in the Parián, and he carried goods and effects from all the merchants, in virtue of the good opinion they had of him because of his good conduct; but when he began to stray in the company of his bad friends, and when he took to his other lady, everything was lost in a few moments. His booth lost its reputation with his absence; the cashier did whatever he wanted, sure that my husband wouldn't be around, because he only went to the Parián to take out money and for nothing else; our house was completely neglected, the children were abandoned, I was looked down on, the servants were discontented, and everything was going downhill.

"True, when he was renting me a house for ten pesos and had me reduced to two dresses and six reales for spending money, he had enough to rent his mistress a house for twenty, hire two servants, and buy her lots of clothes, and plenty of outings and entertainments; but that's how it turned out.

"The expenses were mounting, and his business was being damaged at the same rate. He soon ruined his booth, and when the lady saw that he was poor, she abandoned him and took up with someone else. Then my husband sold the few clothes and furnishings he had left, and the landlord took the mattress, the trunk, and the little money he had set aside, throwing us into the street; and then we had nothing left to do but to take shelter in this damp, indecent, and comfortless room.

"But when troubles assail men, they come in throngs; and so it happened that when my husband's creditors learned that he was unable to cover his debts, and were convinced that he had squandered their loans on gambling and sprees, they showed up and had him thrown in prison, where they will keep him until he can present them with a guarantor for the 6,000 pesos he owes them. That is impossible, since he doesn't have anyone who will even lend him six reales—not even his friends, though he told me he had many, and some of them very wealthy; yet as everyone knows, in times of tribulation, all your friends disappear.

"Our misery, the dampness of this comfortless room, and the torment that my spirit suffers, have laid me flat in this bed with who knows what illness, for I don't know what ails me; what I am sure of is that I believe my death is coming soon, and that this unhappy child will expire even sooner from hunger, since my withered breast cannot nourish him; these two other children will be exposed to the most sorrowful orphanhood; my husband will remain in the cruel hands of his creditors; and everything will undergo the sad end that awaits.

"This, sir, is my hapless tale. See whether I wasn't right to say that mine are the sort of sorrows that cannot be relieved by telling them. Ay, my dear husband! Ay, Anselmo, what a piteous state your disorderly actions have brought us to . . . !"

"Pardon me, ma'am," I said. "Who is this Anselmo of whom you complain?"

"Who else, sir? He is my poor husband, whom I cannot stop loving, no matter how thankless he once was to me."

"That is a noble trait," I said.

I then inquired and fully satisfied myself that her husband was my friend Anselmo, who had not recognized me, or who hadn't wanted to recognize me, when I begged him for charity at my lowest point; but at this time I wasn't mindful of his ingratitude, only of his misfortune and of that which his sad and innocent family suffered, and I endeavored to do whatever I could to relieve them.

Again I consoled the poor sick woman; I sent for an old neighbor woman who loved her well and who usually brought her a bite to eat at midday, and, as I offered her a good salary, she happily stayed there to serve her.

I left the house, saw my master, told him what had happened, borrowed money against my account, had him get into a carriage, and brought him to witness for himself the miserable fortune of those innocent victims of indigence.

My master was a very sensitive and compassionate man, and as soon as he saw that sad group of unhappy people, he displayed his generosity and took an interest in helping them.

The first thing he did was to send for a physician and a wet nurse to care for the ill woman and the baby. That same night, he sent over from his house a mattress, sheets, pillows, and other things that the woman urgently needed.

He did not let me leave for San Agustín just yet, and the next day he sent me to seek better living quarters for them. I eagerly found one, and as soon as I could, I moved the lady and her family there.

With the money I had borrowed, I bought clothes for the children, and with nothing left to do for the moment, I took my leave of the lady, who incessantly showered me with blessings and thanks by the thousands. Every few moments, she asked me my name and where I lived. I didn't want to answer, because it wasn't necessary; instead, I told her that it was my master who deserved her gratitude, since he was the one who had come to her aid, and that I was nothing but a feeble instrument whom God had used for that purpose.

"All the same," said the poor woman, quite moved, "even though that gentleman might have spent more money than you in our favor, you were the cause of it all. Yes: you spoke to him, you brought him here, and through you we have received all these favors. He is a kind man, I have no doubt, nor am I capable of thanking him or repaying him for the good he has done for me and my children; but you are not merely kind, you are generous, for you have spent your money liberally though you are an employee, and so. . . . "

"There now, ma'am, there now," I said; "try to recover, because that's our main concern, and good-bye until Sunday."

"Are you coming on Sunday to see me and the children, who are your children now?"

"Yes, ma'am, I am."

I bought fruit for the little ones, hugged them, and bid them farewell, not without tears in my eyes for the tenderness I felt at hearing those innocent babes call me Papá; they knew no other way to show me their gratitude than by holding onto my knees with their tiny arms while they cried and begged me not to leave. It was very hard for me to release myself from those thankful children; but at last I went off to my job, entrusting them once more to my master and to Pelayo.

The following Sunday, I made sure to come. My master was not home, so as soon as I dropped off the horse, I went to see how the sick woman and her children were doing; but how happy I was to find her fully recovered and neatly washed, playing in the sitting room with her children! She was so occupied by this innocent entertainment that she did not see me until I said to her, "I am very glad, ma'am, very glad."

She raised her eyes, saw me, and recognizing me she got up and, filled with an inexpressible enthusiasm and a delight that bubbled out of her, she began shouting,

"Anselmo, Anselmo, come quick; come meet the man you were hoping to see. Hurry up, come; here's our benefactor and our father."

The children surrounded me and, pulling me by the cape, led me into the sitting room just when Anselmo came in from the bedroom.

He was surprised to see me, and stared at me until he was sure that I was the same Pedro he had snubbed and tried to slander as a thief; torn between gratitude and shame, he wanted yet didn't want to speak to me; more than once he set out to throw his arms around my neck, and twice he was at the point of returning to his bedroom.

Finally, looking at me with tenderness and a blushing face, he said, "Sir . . . I thank you . . . "—and, unable to pronounce another word, he lowered his eyes.

I recognized the contrasting passions that were struggling in his poor heart, and I endeavored to raise his spirits as much as possible; and so, taking my friend by the arm and wrapping my own arms around him, I said, "What's with 'sir'? No need for thanks! Don't you recognize me, Anselmo? Don't you recognize your old friend, Pedro Sarmiento? Why act like such a stranger and so ashamed of yourself with someone who has loved you so long? Come on, wipe off that blush, get rid of those tears, and admit once and for all that I'm your friend."

Then Anselmo, who had been listening to me with his head resting on my left shoulder, was cheered up by my words; he raised his face and, turning to his wife, said, "Do you know, my darling, who this kind man is, who has done us so many favors?"

"No, I haven't had the pleasure of learning his name," said the lady; "I only recognize that he is an exceptional benefactor, and that we all owe him our lives, our sustenance, and our honor."

"Well, let me tell you, my dearest, that this gentleman is Don Pedro Sarmiento, my old friend, whom I owed a thousand favors, and whom I repaid with the most terrible villainy when he was in critical circumstances and needed my help the most."

He then kneeled down and, embracing me tenderly, said, "Pardon me, dear Pedro; I'm a villain and an ingrate, yet you are a gentleman and the only man who deserves the sweet title of friend. From this day on, I will recognize you as my father, as my liberator, and as the man who came to the aid of my wife and children, whom I let down with my excesses. Forget my ingratitude; don't pay these innocents what I alone deserve. . . . We'll be your slaves. . . . Our happiness will be to serve you . . . and. . . . "

"For the sake of God, Anselmo, that's enough," I said, lifting him up and pressing him to my breast. "Enough; I'm your friend, and that's what I'll always be, so long as you honor me with your friendship. Compose yourself, and let's talk about something else. Caress your children, who are crying because they see you cry. Console this lady, who is caught between grief and surprise, listening to you. I have done nothing but carry out, to some small degree, the natural sentiments of my heart. When I did what I could for your family, it was out of sympathy for your unhappy situation; and I did it knowing that the family was none other than yours—a circumstance that should have been enough in itself to make me lavish all the attention

I could on you, in order to fulfill the duties of friendship. But in the end, it was God who wished to help you; give your thanks to His Divine Majesty, and let bygones be bygones, by the lives of your children."

I wanted to take my leave, but the lady wouldn't hear of it; she had prepared a lunch, and she kept me there to eat it.

We sat together very pleasantly, and at the table they informed me that Pelayo and my master had carried out my request so well that, not content with helping the sick woman and her family, they had called on Anselmo's creditors, and though they found some of them to be hard-hearted, they had begged them so much and with such persistence that at last they got them to defer his debt until his fortunes improved; and so that Anselmo could sustain his family, my master had hired him as the foreman of one of his haciendas, where he was to go as soon as his wife had fully recovered.

This news filled me with joy, to consider that God had made use of me to make this poor family happy; I congratulated them and then bid them all farewell amid a thousand embraces, tears, and expressions of affection.

I also gave many thanks to my master and to Pelayo for what they had done, and that afternoon I returned to my job, feeling who knows what sweet satisfaction in my heart for the great good that had come to that sad family through me.

"I saw them looking so different just a week later from the way I had first found them! She," I said to myself, "was trapped in destitution. The father was delivered over, without honor or hope, to the voraciousness of his creditors, and was mixed with the scum of the people in a gloomy prison cell; his wife, her spirit tormented and fainting with hunger, lived in an indecent basement apartment; their little ones were naked, emaciated, and likely to die or to be lost; and now everything has changed. Anselmo is free now; his wife has her health and her husband back; the children have their father; and all of them have their greatest consolation in each other. Blessed be the infinite Providence of God, Who shows such concern for His creatures! And blessed be the charity of my master and Pelayo, who saved this hapless family from the cruel grasp of poverty and returned them to the bosom of happiness, where they are today! How the Almighty will remember this deed and repay them for it in the inevitable hour of their deaths! How indelibly the book of life must have recorded the steps and expenses that both of them have undertaken to give these things! How happy are the rich who put their money to such holy use, and who save it in the moneybags that time will never rot! And what sweet pleasures people deprive themselves of when they don't know how to do good to their fellow men! Because the pleasure felt by a sensitive heart when one does a kindness, helps someone in misery, or in any way wipes the tears from the afflicted, is beyond expression, and only one who has experienced it can, not depict it as it deserves, but at least sketch it with some hint of coloring.

"There are no two ways about it; the sweet rapture that the soul feels when it has just done a kind deed should be in itself a powerful stimulus to make all men kind, even without the hope of an eternal reward. I don't know how misers could exist; I don't know how there could be men so cruel that, having chests full of pesos, they could watch so coolly while their luckless fellow men perish. They view, dry-eyed, the sallowness that hunger and illness paint on the faces of so many miserable people; they hear the sighs and groans of the widow and the orphaned child as if they were soft music; their hands do not soften even when they are washed with the tears of the orphan and the oppressed. . . . In a word, their hearts and their senses are made of bronze: hard, impenetrable, and unbending to grief, to man's sorrow, and to the purest sensations of Nature.

"True, there are false beggars, and poor people to whom we should not give alms; but it is also true that there are many people with legitimate needs, especially among all the decent families who are too ashamed to beg openly, but who moan in silence and suffer their misery in hiding. These are the ones who should be sought out to be given assistance, but they are the ones who generally receive the least attention."

Entertained by these serious reflections, I reached San Agustín de las Cuevas.

In that town I endeavored to behave in an orderly way, doing whatever good I could for all those who had dealings with me, and in this way winning everyone's good will.

Just as I felt inclined to do good, I did not forget to make up for the bad I had caused. I repaid everything I owed to my old landlords and to my uncle, the lawyer; however, I did not accept his friendship again, nor that of other ungrateful, selfish, and egotistical friends.

I had the satisfaction of seeing my master always content and relying on my good behavior, and I was witness to Anselmo's reform and his family's happiness, for I had been given the hacienda where he was working to administer.

The poor man in rags was the only one I was unable to find, try as I might, to repay him for his generous hospitality; all I was able to discover was that his name was Tadeo.

Nor did I find Nana Felipa, my mother's faithful servant, nor others who had once done me favors. Some, I was told, had died; with others, no one knew where they had moved; but I performed my investigations to find them.

I continued serving my master, and serving myself, in my sad town, very happy with the help I found in a faithful cashier I had hired, a very upright man and widower who, he told me, had a daughter of about fourteen years in the Colegio de las Niñas.[2]

I relied entirely on his good conduct, and I endeavored to reward him for his usefulness to me. He was called Don Hilario, and he looked so much like the man in rags that more than once I was on the point of thinking that they were one and the same, and to settle my uncertainty I asked him a thousand questions, which he answered ambiguously or in the negative, so that I was always left with my doubts, until an unexpected accident allowed me to discover who this fellow really was.

---

[2] [Colegio de las Niñas (School for Girls): "A school for poor girls of Spanish blood, located in the same block as the Franciscan monastery" (Spell, p. 196). –Tr.]

CHAPTER 49

IN WHICH PERICO TELLS THE ADVENTURE OF THE MISANTHROPE,
HIS LIFE STORY, AND THE DISCOVERY OF THE WHEREABOUTS OF
THE MAN IN RAGS, WHICH IS NOT TO BE SCORNED

Though my cashier was, as I have said, a very upright man, very exact in the fulfillment of his obligation, and little fond of outings, on the Sundays when I didn't go to
the city, I would close the shop in the afternoon, take up my shotgun, and have him
bring his own, and we would go out to amuse ourselves on the outskirts of the town.

This display of friendship and affability on my part was very satisfying to my
good employee, and I did it studiously, for not only did he deserve it, but I figured
that, without losing anything, I gained a lot, since he would look at the money in
the cashier's boxes as belonging to a friend rather than a master, and so would work
with all the more zeal. I was never mistaken in thinking this, nor would anyone be
making a mistake if they were to make distinctions among their employees, treating
the upright men with love and particular confidence in the safe knowledge that they
would be making them better men.

One of these Sunday afternoons when we were out hunting rabbits, we saw a
runaway horse galloping toward us, but in such a headlong rush that, try as we
might, we were unable to stop it; indeed, if we hadn't jumped aside, it would have
pitched us to the ground against our will.

We felt pity for the poor horseman, who struggled to no avail to rein in the horse.
We thought the beast's blind fury would soon be the death of him, especially when
we saw the steed sheer from the highway and head straight down a narrow path;
meeting the stone wall around an Indian's garden, it tried to jump over it but was
unable, and it fell to the earth, catching the horseman's leg under its body.

The blow that the horse sustained was so great that we thought it had killed itself
and the horseman with it, for neither of them stirred.

Moved to pity by this misfortune, we ran to help the man; but hardly had he seen
us approaching him when he managed to sit halfway up and, pulling a pistol from
his saddle, he aimed it at us, and shouted in a hoarse and irascible voice, "Damnable
enemies of humankind, kill me if that is what you are coming to do, snatch this
wretched life from me. . . . What are you doing, villains? Why have you stopped,
cruel men? This brute was unable to relieve me of the life that I detest; no brute is
capable of doing me such wrong. Only you, ferocious beasts, only you are able to
destroy your fellow men."

While that man insulted us with these and other such affronts, I watched him
fearfully and attentively, and indeed his figure inspired terror and pity. His black and
tattered clothing, which revealed his white skin in places; his pallid face, covered
with a thick beard; his sunken, sad, and furious eyes; his unkempt hair; his hoarse
voice; his desperate attitude; and his whole being manifested the piteous state of his
fortunes and his spirit.

My cashier said, "Let's go, let's leave this ingrate here; we don't want to lose our
lives by trying to save this monster."

"No, friend," I said, "God, who sees our sound intentions, will keep us safe. This wretched man is no ingrate, as you imagine. Perhaps he figures us for thieves because he sees us holding shotguns, or he might be some poor man who has lost his wits, or is about to lose them, because of some serious cause; but however that may be, it would not be right at all to leave him in this state. Humanity and religion demand that we help him. Let's do it."

As we talked about these things, we pretended that we weren't watching him and that we were planning to withdraw, and all the while he never stopped insulting us as badly as he could; but, seeing that we were paying no attention to him and that we had turned our backs, he endeavored to pull his leg out by lashing the horse with the whip to get it to stand up; it couldn't, however, and the man, hoping to requite his anger, tried to fire his pistol at his own head, but in vain, because it didn't go off.

Then he checked the priming pan and found it empty of gunpowder; he was trying to prime it when, taking advantage of this favorable interval, we rushed him and, holding him by the arms, my cashier took away his pistols; I roused the horse by pulling on its tail, and in this way we got the sad, tattered man out from under it; but more infuriated by our sudden action than grateful for the kindness we had done him, he redoubled his curses, telling us, "You're wasting your effort, you insolent, impertinent thieves. If you want the horse and these rags, take them, and take my life, as I told you before, and you can be sure that you'll be doing me a great favor."

"We aren't thieves, sir," I said; "we are men of honor who were just walking by when we saw your accident and, obliged by humanity and religion, we have tried to assist you; so please, don't repay this proof of the true friendship we offer you with insults."

"Barbarians!" the man, standing now, replied. "Barbarians! Do you still have the nerve to profane the sacred words of honor, friendship, and religion with your impure lips? Cruel villains! Those words have no place in the unworthy mouths of the enemies of God and men."

"No doubt this man is a lunatic, as you thought," my cashier told me.

Then the tattered man confronted him and said, "No, I'm no lunatic, you scoundrel; would to God that I had never had my wits, for then I wouldn't have so much to feel sorry for on account of you two."

"On account of us?" my cashier asked in amazement.

"Yes, you cruel monster, on account of you and all your kind."

"But who are we?"

"Who are you?" said the tattered man. "You're a bunch of heartless, cruel thieves, ingrates, murderers, sacrilegious flatterers, schemers, misers, liars, wicked evildoers, and every bad thing there is in the world. I know you all too well, villains. You are men, and you can't help being all that I said, because that's what all men are. Yes, I know you, vile men; I detest you, I loathe you; stand back from me or kill me, because your presence is more irksome to me than death itself; but go, knowing that I am not insane except when I look at men and recall their infernal machinations, their damnable actions, their double-dealing, their wickedness, and all that they have made me suffer. Go on, go away."

Far from getting cross with this wretched man, I sympathized with him with all my heart, recognizing that if he was not insane, he was not far from it; and I sympathized all the more when I heard from his words that he was a refined man who showed considerable talent, and if he loathed humankind, his awful misanthropy had not arisen from any malice in his heart, but from the resentments that violently shook his spirit when he recalled injuries he had suffered from some of the many wicked mortals who live in the world.

At the same time that I was making these considerations, I reflected that, if you want to calm a demented man, it is never a good idea to oppose his ideas, however extravagant they might be; and so, taking advantage of this recollection, I said to the cashier, "This gentleman is quite right. Men in general are depraved, hateful, and malignant. That's what I was telling you a few days ago, Don Hilario, and you thought I was being unfair, but thanks be to God, we've found another man who thinks right, as I do."

"That's the experience I've had of them," said the misanthrope, "and those are the evil sorts of deeds they've done to me."

"If we're going to start recalling injuries," I said, "and loathing men for the harm they've done us, nobody has more motive than I do to hate them all, because there's nobody they've hurt more than me."

"That can't be," said the misanthrope; "nobody has suffered greater harm or cruelty from damnable men than this wretch you see before you. If you only knew my life story . . . !"

"If you were to hear my adventures," I answered, "you would loathe the evil mortals even more, and you would have to admit that no one under the sun has endured more than I have."

"Fine, then," he said; "tell me the motives you have for loathing and complaining about them, and I will recount mine; then we'll see which one of us is more right to complain."

This was exactly where I was trying to lead him, so I said, "I agree to your proposal, but to carry it out, we'll have to go to my house. Please come there, and we will sit and talk."

"That's all right with me," said the misanthrope; "let's go."

He fell down with the first step he took, because one of his feet was badly injured. We picked him up between us, and he supported himself on both of us as we led him to the house.

Into the town we walked, making the most ridiculous scene, because the man in the tattered mourning suit was hobbling between the two of us, while we supported him and carried our shotguns on our other shoulders, at the same time pulling along the horse, which had also been left lame by the crash.

This spectacle soon attracted the curiosity of the novelty-seeking mob, and, since many people were in town on the occasion of the feast days for the town's patron saint, they surrounded us in a flash.

These witnesses rather annoyed the misanthrope, and more so when one of the onlookers said out loud, "That fellow must be some big robber, and those gentlemen tackled him and are taking him hobbling off to jail."

Then, glaring wildly, he said to me, "See what men are like? See how easy it is for them to think the worst of their fellow men? The second they see me, they take me for a thief. Why can't they think I might be sick or disabled? Why can't they think you're helping me, showing me charity? But instead, they have to think of justice and punishment. Oh, damn all men!"

"Who pays any attention," I said, "to the common mob, when we know that it's a many-headed monster, with little or no mind? The mob is composed of the stupidest part of the people, the ones who never tend to think, and who, when they think at all, almost always think the worst; for, not knowing the laws of criticism, they base their ideas on the surface appearances that material objects present to them, and since the things they say are not aligned with true reason, most of the time they are pure nonsense, and they frame them in the same ignorance as the insane; but just as we should not take offence at the insults of a madman, since he doesn't know what he's saying, neither should we pay attention to the taunts and perverse opinions of the mob, for they are like a madman who doesn't know what he is thinking, nor what he is saying."

Just then we reached the house; I had the horse unsaddled and arranged to have it treated with the greatest care. The veterinarians came, inspected the horse, and treated it; I had it put in its own stable, groomed, and fed plenty of corn and barley, and I assigned a serving lad to take solicitous care of it. All of this took place in front of the misanthrope, who, amazed by the care I was taking of his horse, told me, "You must value horses very highly."

"I have even higher esteem for men," I said.

"How can that be," he said, "when you assured me not more than twenty minutes ago that you loathed them?"

"This is how it is," I answered: "I loathe bad men, or rather, the bad things that men do; but as for good men such as you, I love them dearly, I want to serve them in any way I can, and the more unhappy they are, the more I love them and the more interested I am in assisting them."

When he heard these words, which I pronounced with all the enthusiasm I could, I noticed some kind of agreeable transformation in the misanthrope's face, and without stopping to reflect, we went into my parlor, where we had chocolate, sweets, and water.

After this frugal refreshment, he asked me about my misfortunes; I begged him to tell me his, and he, acting very courteously, made up his mind to please me; but just then a serving lad came in to say that someone was looking for Don Hilario. He left, and in the meanwhile the misanthrope told me, "My story is too long to tell it as briefly as I would like; but you should know that, far from owing any kindness to men, I have received nothing but a thousand evil deeds from everyone I have dealt with. There are some mortals who count their parents among their first benefactors, rightly boasting about them and considering their favors both just and necessary; but poor me! I cannot delight my memory by recalling paternal caresses, as everyone does, nor did I even know who my worthless mother was. Please don't be scandalized by my harsh expressions until you learn the motives I have for uttering them."

At this point, my cashier walked back in, very content, and although I hoped he would reveal the motive for his joy, I could not get him to do so, for he told me that he would finish listening to the misanthrope and then would give me some news that wouldn't fail to please me.

Now my curiosity was roused for two reasons. First, I wanted to know the misanthrope's adventure; and second, I wanted to find out about my employee's good news; but since he wanted the other to continue, I begged him to do so, and he went on as follows:

"I was saying, sir," the misanthrope proceeded, "that I have good reason to loathe my father and mother above all other people. That is how unpleasant and thankless they were to me! My father was the Marquis of Baltimore, a fellow known everywhere for his title and his wealth. This villain had me with Doña Clisterna Camões, a native of Portugal.[1] She was the daughter of very noble, yet poor and virtuous parents. The wicked marquis courted Clisterna to satisfy his appetites, and she let herself be swayed, more as a flight of folly than because she believed the marquis would really marry her; since he was rich and titled, such a union would not have been easy for him, because, as everyone knows, the rich very rarely marry the poor, and much less when the former are titled noblemen. Ordinarily, the marriages of the rich amount to nothing but shameful pacts, which would be better celebrated in the commercial tribunals because of the great amount of commerce in them, rather than in the ecclesiastical court because of the little bit of sacrament they have. They consult their money-boxes before they look at the wishes and qualities[2] of the bride and groom. It is not surprising, given this system, to see so many matrimonial lawsuits originating from unions that are made by self-interest and not by the inclinations of those being married.

"Since the marquis did not court Clisterna for the holy ends that matrimony demands, but to satisfy his ravenous passion, after he had assuaged it and she told him that she was with child, he sought one of those pretexts for abandoning women that men find so easily, and he never again saw her or remembered the son he had left deposited in her womb. Could I possibly love this cruel man, or call him by the tender name of father?

"This woman Clisterna proved very skilled at hiding her swelling womb, passing off her nausea and her attacks as another infirmity of her sex with the help of a physician and a maid who abetted her affair. She did not neglect to take every stimulant she could to provoke a miscarriage, but Heaven did not allow her to attain her wicked goal. The natural time arrived for me to see the light of the world. The birth

---

[1] [This is clearly a fantastic story. Lizardi has taken the name of Baltimore from the English Catholic baron (not marquis); the last Lord Baltimore (1731–1771) had a scandalous number of illegitimate children and no legitimate heirs. The name Clisterna comes from a character (a Catholic from Scotland) in a short novel by Cervantes, *La inglesa española*; it is a humorously ugly name, apparently a hybrid of *cisterna* "cistern" and *clíster* "clyster, enema." –Tr.]

[2] [Qualities (*calidades*): in this context, the word refers to what we would call "race and class," a prime concern for those arranging proper marriages in accordance with the moral thinking of the time. In the case being described here, the Marquis and Clisterna were both white (European) and noble, and therefore suitable marriage partners despite the disparity in their wealth. –Tr.]

was a happy one, because Clisterna hardly suffered, and she quickly found herself free of me and free of the risk that, for the time being, her easiness would be discovered. She immediately wrapped me in a few rags, put a note on me saying that I was the son of good parents and was not baptized, and handed me to her trusty maid to get me out of the house. Could this cruel woman deserve the tender name of mother? Could she be worthy of my love and gratitude? Oh, heartless woman! To the scandal of wild beasts and the horror of nature, you had barely given birth to me against your will when you hurled me from your house. You were ashamed to be seen as a mother, yet you set all blushing aside to become one. You had no scruples to restrain you from prostituting yourself and conceiving me; but when it came to giving birth to me, how many you had! When it came to raising me at your breast, how insurmountable they were! I have no reason to thank you, wicked woman, and many reasons to hate you so long as I live this life, which I have so often desired to end with some potion. . . . But let us avert our gazes from this monster, who unfortunately has so many equals in this world.

"The dishonest maid, as cruel as her mistress, took me outside around ten that night and discarded me on the threshold of the first little one-room house she found.

"There I was truly likely to die of hunger or to serve as fodder for a hungry pack of dogs. My desire to suckle or the inclemency of the weather naturally forced me to cry, and the impetuosity of my cries woke up the owners of the house. They could tell by my voice that I was a newborn; they got up, opened the door, saw me, took me in with the greatest charity, and my father (so I have called him all my life), giving me many kisses, left me in my mother's lap, and went out at once to find me a wet nurse.

"He found one with great difficulty, but he was very happy when he returned with her. The next day, they strove to baptize me, my godparents being the same couple who had adopted me as their son. These fine people were very poor, but very well born, pious, and Christian.

"Humbling themselves, borrowing money, going into debt, selling and pawning the little they owned, they managed to raise me, educate me, give me my studies, and make me a man; and I had the sweet satisfaction, after I had gotten a position with a regular salary in an office, of supporting them, indulging them, aiding them in their illness, and closing the eyes of them both with the true affection of a son.

"They told me all that I have recounted to you about the cruel marquis and heartless Clisterna, after they had learned it, some time later, from the mouth of the maid herself, in whom Clisterna had confided so blindly. When they told me this story, they held me tight in their arms; whenever they saw me happy, they were gladdened; if I was sad, they felt sorry and tried everything they could to cheer me up; if I was sick, they treated me with the greatest care; and they never called me by anything but the loving epithet of son; nor could I call them anything but my parents, and I loved them as such. . . . Ay, gentlemen! And wasn't I right to do so? Out of their charity, they carried out the obligations that Nature had imposed on my legitimate parents. My father took the place of the Marquis of Baltimore, a man unworthy not only of the title of marquis, but of being counted among the ranks of upright men. His wife excelled at the job that should have been done by Clisterna, a tyrannical woman to whom I will never give the loving and tender name of mother.

"When I outlived the shelter and protection of my loving godparents, I recognized how much I loved them and that they deserved more love than I was able to give them. Ever since, I have never met or dealt with any other mortals more sincere, more innocent, kinder, or more worthy of being loved. Everyone I have dealt with has been ungrateful, hateful, and malignant—even a woman in whom I was so weak as to confide all my feelings, giving my heart to her.

"This woman was the daughter of a rich man; she was a cruel beauty, with whom I had celebrated a contract of betrothal. A thousand times she offered me her heart and her hand; she assured me as many more times that she loved me and that her faith would last forever; but from one day to the next, she entered a convent, and the worthless perjurer offered to God a soul that she had sworn was mine. She wrote me a letter laced with insults that my love did not deserve; she misled her father, attributing crimes to me that I never committed, so that he would declare himself my eternal and powerful enemy (which he did); and finally, not content with being ungrateful and perjuring herself, she obliged everyone she could to turn against me, to pursue me and harm me; and one of these was a certain Don Tadeo, her brother, who, pretending to hold me in the most tender friendship, had told me that he would be very happy to call himself my brother-in-law. Oh, cruel people!"

While the misanthrope was telling his life story, I noticed that my cashier was listening to him very attentively, and from the time he touched on the matter of his unrequited love, the color in the cashier's face changed from moment to moment, until, unable to bear it any longer, he broke in and said, "Pardon me, sir; what was the name of lady about whom you have so many complaints?"

"Isabel."

"And your name?"

"I am Jacobo, at your service."

Then the cashier stood up and, enfolding him in his arms, said with the greatest tenderness, "Good Jacobo, unlucky friend, I am your friend Tadeo: yes, I am the brother of unhappy Isabel, your loving fiancée. You should have no complaints about me or about her. She died loving you, or rather, she died from the great love she had for you; I did everything I could to inform you of her fate, her death, and her constancy; but I could find no trace of you, no matter how hard I tried. Everything that you, my sister, and I suffered was occasioned by my father's selfish interests, for in order to uphold my brother Damián's mayorazgo, he obstructed Isabel's marriage, forced Antonio to enter the clergy, and left me to perish alongside my unhappy mother, may God have pity on her. So don't complain about poor Isabel, nor your good friend Tadeo; perhaps it was Divine Providence that allowed me this rare encounter so that I might set things right for you, relieve your grief, and repay your virtue to whatever extent I can."

The misanthrope heard all this as if in a trance; while I, remembering the story of the man in rags and hearing that the cashier's name was not Hilario but Tadeo, and that everything he had just said matched what the man in rags had told me, said to him, "Don Hilario, or Don Tadeo, or whatever your name is, please tell me, on your life and with your customary frankness, have you ever been slandered as a thief? Have you ever lived in a low, one-room apartment? Have you ever had any other children than the daughter you have mentioned? And finally, is your real name Tadeo or Hilario?"

"Sir," he told me, "I have been slandered as a thief, I have lived in a one-room apartment, I have had two children apart from Rosalía, both dead, and indeed my name is Tadeo, not Hilario."

"Please tell me, then, about that slander."

"One afternoon I was standing," he said, "in an entrance way near El Factor, dressed in the most despicable clothes, when a strapping young lad passed by with some soldiers and claimed that I had been the one who had sold him a cape with a ruffled collar, which turned out to be stolen; and it seems that some books, a wig, and who knows what else had been stolen along with it. The soldiers brought me before the judge; fortunately, the judge knew me and my whole family; he knew what my conduct was, and the reason for my misfortune, and he did not hesitate to assert that I was innocent, and he promised to prove it if the man who had slandered me were to appear; but that couldn't happen, because the soldiers had already let him go; and so they set me free."

"And what did you do, Don Tadeo?" I asked. "Did you get to see the fellow who slandered you? Did you find out who he was? And if you saw him, what did you do to him in revenge? Normally, you would have had him thrown in jail."

"No, sir," he said; "that very afternoon he passed by my house. I recognized him, I dragged him inside, and when I had convinced him that I was an upright man, I let him spend the night in my house; my mother treated him for some slight head wounds he had, and I let him go in peace."

"And what was the name of the rogue who had slandered you?" I asked.

Don Tadeo told me that he didn't know it and hadn't wanted to ask. Then, filled with a joy that is beyond my powers to explain, I embraced Don Tadeo; and the misanthrope, satisfied with his friend's good behavior and thinking that I must be somewhat good, embraced us both, and we linked our arms in a knot that expressed our mutual affection and trust; our tears displayed our feelings of gratitude, reconciliation, and friendship, and an emphatic silence eloquently stated the noble passions of our souls.

I was the first to interrupt this mysterious rapture, and I told Don Tadeo: "I, noble friend, am the self-same person who, when I was utterly debased, insulted you by charging you with a robbery you had not committed; I am the one you benefited with your extreme charity; the one who knows all your misfortunes; the one who has kept you here as my servant; and finally, I am the one who will henceforth consider it as a great honor if you would count me as your friend."

My sincere confession did nothing but confirm to them both that I was a full-fledged upright man; and so, after we had recounted our adventures more calmly, we confirmed our friendship and swore to maintain it forever.

The misanthrope, now entirely transformed, said, "Gentlemen, I certainly have a good reason to thank my horse, since it brought me to a town where I hadn't planned to come . . . but what am I saying? It is Heaven, Providence, the God of all goodness, that I should thank for this unanticipated good fortune. Through one of those labored designs of the Deity that we foolish men call coincidences, my horse bolted just in time for you two to see me, and you insisted on bringing me to your house, where I have watched the denouement of my misfortunes with unexpected happiness; for it gladdens me to find proof, late as it is, of the constant faithfulness of my beloved and of my good friend Tadeo. I realize now that it is ridiculous to loathe all humankind because of the ungratefulness of many of its individuals, and that, no matter how many wicked men there are, there remain a few who are worthy, grateful, refined, loyal, sensitive, virtuous, and upright men in every sense. We must do justice to the good men, however many bad men there are. I recognize you both, and in proof of this, I ask you to excuse me from the insane notion you must have had of me."

"Stop," said Tadeo; "I have been, am, and will be your friend as long as I live. I am convinced that your own natural goodness, your simplicity, and your virtue made you believe that all men would behave the way they should, following the orders of reason; and, having learned from experience that this was not so, you fell into another gross error, believing that there were no good men in the world, or at most that they were all too rare, and given that mistake, your misanthropy does not surprise me; but now you see that things are not the way you thought, and that, susceptible to this error, you believed that Isabel and I were cruel to you when in fact she died of her love for you, while I have spared no effort to find you and confirm my friendship with you. I also thought that men who had given in to vice could never entirely transform their conduct; I believed that they would hold onto the bad habits of their licentiousness and find it very difficult to submit to reason and be kind, yet today I am very pleased to see that my friend Don Pedro has set me straight, for his conduct over the time that I have served him has edified me with its orderly. . . . "

"Quiet, please, Don Tadeo, sir," I said; "don't shame me by reminding me of my erring ways and praising me for acting as I should. And please, do not call me your master, but rather your friend, a title I hold dear. I hired you to serve me, not knowing who you were, and I have plenty to thank you for during the time that you've been with me. I have had nothing but happiness all this time, and the final happiness has been your happy meeting with this gentleman, Don Jacobo."

"This isn't the last bit of joyous news that you will hear today," my cashier said; "there is still one more, which it will please you both to hear. Listen to this letter that I have just received. It says:

> Señor Tadeo Mayoli.
> Mexico, 10 October, etc.
>
> Dear Friend:
>   Sir, your brother, Don Damián, has passed away; and, as you are the next in line to receive the mayorazgo that he possessed (for he had no heir), the Royal Audiencia has declared you the legitimate heir of this entailment; therefore, after congratulating you in due form, I request that it please you to come as soon as possible to the capital, so that I

may inform you of the contents of your brother's will and testament, and hand over to you the possession of your estate, in fulfillment of the royal order to this effect, which resides in my power.

I am glad for this occasion to put myself at your disposition, as your affectionate friend and devoted servant.

> Most sincerely,
> Fermín Gutiérrez.

"This fellow is the notary who executed the testament. In virtue of this letter, I must set out for Mexico as soon as possible. Don Pedro, sir, my friend, my master, and my patron, I thank you for the good things you have done me, and for your good treatment of me in your house; I offer you my few belongings, and I beg you not to forget that, whatever Fortune might bring, I am and always will be your friend; and you, dear Jacobo: I offer you my possessions with equal sincerity, and to appease you for the harm that my father did by denying you my sister because you were poor, I put my belongings at your disposition, together with my daughter's hand, if you will take it. She is a tender girl, well brought up, and not ugly in the least. If you will, marry her; she isn't Isabel, but Rosalía, yet I mean to tell you that she is a branch of the same trunk."

The misanthrope, or Don Jacobo, couldn't find the words to thank Tadeo; but it shamed him to think that he was poor and that he might not please his daughter; however, Tadeo lifted his spirits, telling him, "Poverty is no defect in my mind, when it comes with so many noble qualities; you are not old yet, and I think that my daughter will love you as soon as I tell her who you are."

Following these affectionate conversations, we set about dressing Jacobo in decent clothes. The next day, Tadeo sent for a coach, and they rode in it to Mexico, leaving me quite sad at the absence of such fine friends.

A few days later, they wrote to me that Jacobo and Rosalía had gotten married and were living in the midst of pleasure and tranquility.

Soon afterward, the administrator of the hacienda where Anselmo worked died, and my master wrote to me, telling me to go take his position.

With this occasion, I went to the hacienda and had the agreeable satisfaction of seeing my friend and his family, who received me with great affection and expressiveness.

From that day, Anselmo was my employee, and I was witness to his good conduct. When men of refined education and understanding resolve to be upright men, they almost always achieve that flattering title.

I returned to San Agustín and lived there tranquilly for many years.

CHAPTER 50

I was not very contented after Don Tadeo left; I missed him more each day, because it wasn't easy for me to find a good employee for a long time. I had several, but I had problems with each one of them, for if he wasn't a drunk, he was a gambler; if he wasn't a gambler, he courted the ladies; if he didn't court the ladies, he was lazy; if he didn't have that defect, he was inept; and if he had some skill, he tended to be too casual with the money-box.

It was then that I realized how difficult it is to find entirely good employees, and how much they should be appreciated when they are found.

Despite my loneliness, I didn't stop going to Mexico frequently on my business. I visited my master, who showed me more signs of trust and friendship every day; and I didn't stop seeing Pelayo, sometimes in the church and sometimes in his house, and I always found him to be a true father and friend.

One day I happened to run into the chaplain of my master the Chinese in my friend Pelayo's room. This chaplain had a very retentive mind—that is, he conserved the ideas he had learned very vividly; and since he enjoyed his job on account of me, while he had been the cause of my leaving his patron's house, he retained my features very well in his imagination, so the second he saw me, he recognized me; seeing that Father Pelayo held me in high regard, he spoke to me with the same; and, convinced by his questions, by my sensible conversation, and by Pelayo's report that I had transformed my habits, he revealed himself to me, praised my reform, endeavored to strengthen it with his good advice, thanked me for my influence in obtaining his position, assured me of his friendship, and brought me to the Asian's house in spite of my resistance, because I felt very ashamed.

When we entered, the chaplain said to him, "Here you see your old friend and employee Don Pedro Sarmiento, whom we have recalled so often. He is worthy now of your friendship, because he is not a depraved or reckless youth, but a man of sound judgment who conducts himself according to the laws of honor and religion."

Then my master rose from his armchair, hugged me tightly, and said, "I am very pleased to see you again and to know that you have mended your ways at last, and have learned to make use of the mind that Heaven gave you. Sit down; today you'll eat with me, and you can believe that I will serve you in every way I can so long as you're an upright man, because I loved you since I first met you, and by the same token I missed you, wanted to see you, and today that I have done so, I am very pleased and contented."

I gave him a thousand thanks for his favor. We ate, I informed him of my situation and where I was living, I offered him my meager belongings, I begged him to honor my house with his presence from time to time; and, after I had received his most tender demonstrations of affection, I left for my San Agustín de las Cuevas; yet the reciprocal friendship among the Asian, the chaplain, and me did not dissolve, because I visited them in Mexico, I lavished attention on them in my house when they visited me, we gave each other presents, and we came to treat each other with the greatest affability and affection.

On another one of the days when I came to Mexico, I also found poor Andresillo, looking very ragged and shabby. He spoke to me with great respect and esteem, then took me almost by force to his house, where his good wife gave me lunch, and the poor man didn't know what to do with himself to demonstrate his gratitude to me.

I sympathized with his situation, and I asked him why he was so down in the mouth—whether it was because he was no good at his trade, or because he gambled, or because his wife was very spendthrift.

"None of those things, sir," Andrés told me; "I never see a deck of cards, I'm not so lazy at my trade, and my wife is the best there could be—beyond thrifty, she's downright stingy. But this Mexico, sir, is in a sorry state. For every ten people who need a shave, there're 10,000 barbers; as you know, sir, there's plenty of everything and more in a big city, so I think there're more barbers than beards in Mexico. It's just on Sundays and feast days that I get fifteen or twenty haircuts to do at half a real apiece, but during the week I don't even get six. I barely even get to try the other stuff—bleedings, cuppings, leeches, curing with caustics, and all that; so I don't make enough to support myself, because in this city you spend double what you do in the towns, and since eating comes first, you know, I eat up the little money I make, and I don't have anything left for clothes or for paying the rent."

Moved to pity by Andrés' simple narration, I proposed that if he wanted to come to my house, I'd hire him as my cashier and give him the opportunity to look for whatever business he could find in his own trade.

The poor fellow saw my proposal as a break in the storm clouds; he accepted immediately, and put his affairs in order right away so that he could leave with me that very day.

He was coarse, but not stupid. He easily learned the mechanics of running a shop, and he turned out to be such an upright man for me that, when it came to serving customers and being trustworthy, I no longer missed my good friend Don Tadeo, whom I also continued to visit, nor his son-in-law Don Jacobo, whom I visited frequently at his house, having the pleasure of seeing him married and contented with the young lady Doña Rosalía, whom I had first seen as a very young girl when I met her as the daughter of the man in rags.

These were the friendships I had and kept up when I was an upright man, and I never had any reason to regret them: clear proof that good and true friendship is not as rare a thing as it would seem; yet it is only to be found among good men, not among rogues, flatterers, and villains.

For some four years, I lived contentedly as a widower in San Agustín de las Cuevas, increasing my master's wealth, calmly and quietly amassing 6,000 or 8,000 pesos of my own, paying very pleasant visits to my master, the Chinese, Roque, Pelayo, Jacobo, and Tadeo, and sleeping with the tranquility afforded by a conscience free of remorse.

One afternoon, as I strolled beneath the covered porch of the shop, I saw a poor woman arrive at the inn, which stood next door, leading a donkey that bore a pitiful old man. The donkey couldn't walk any farther, and if it took a few steps, it was because of a young girl who was also coming with it, whipping its haunches with a rod.

They entered the inn, and soon the girl came to see me; she was about fourteen years old, very white, ragged, barefoot, very pretty, and in great distress; stuttering and spilling abundant tears, she told me, "Sir, I know that you are the innkeeper; my father is dying, and my mother is too. For the sake of God, give us a room to stay in, though we don't have a penny to pay you, because we were robbed on the way here."

I have mentioned that God blessed me with a sensitive soul, and that I sympathized with my fellow men's problems even in the midst of my madness and misconduct. It is therefore easy to imagine that in this moment, I immediately concerned myself with the fortune of these unhappy people. Indeed, sending them to the inn for shelter seemed too little to me, so I replied to the messenger, "Girl, don't cry; go tell your father and your mother to come to my house, and tell them to stop worrying."

The girl ran off very happy and, a few minutes later, returned with her aged parents. I had them come into my house, and ordered that they be given a clean room and attended with great care.

In keeping with my orders, Andrés arranged beds to be made for them and had a good supper set out, not sparing any expense needed for their relief.

I was very glad to see how liberal he was in a case like this, in which extreme need demanded liberality; and at ten that night, desiring to learn who my guests were, I entered their room and found the poor old man lying on a straw mattress; his wife— a woman of forty, more or less—was by the headboard, and the girl was sitting at the foot of the same bed.

As soon as they saw me, the lady and the girl stood up, and the old man tried to do the same, but I would not permit it; instead, I asked the poor women to sit back down, and I found a place for myself next to the sick man.

I asked him where he was from, what ailed him, and when or how they had been robbed.

The sad old man, displaying the anguish of his spirit, sighed and told me, "Sir, most of the events of my life have been piteous; you seem to be a very sympathetic fellow, and for sensitive hearts it is no kindness to be told tales of woe."

"It is true, friend," I replied, "that for those who love their fellow men as they ought, it is unpleasant to hear the stories of their destitution; but it might also bring them the experience of a certain inner sweetness, especially when they can do something to help. That is my case here, and so I want to hear your misadventures, not out of sheer curiosity, but to see if I can be useful to you in any way."

"Well, sir," the poor old man continued, "if that is your merciful plan, I will tell you my misfortunes in brief. My parents were noble and rich, and I would have enjoyed the inheritance they left me if the executor of their estate had been an upright man; but he squandered my property, and I was reduced to poverty. In that state, I served a rich gentleman who loved me like a father and left me all he owned when he passed away. I took to commerce, but as the result of some smuggled contraband, I lost all my wealth from one day to the next. When I began to recover, at the cost of a lot of hard work, I wanted to get married, and I did wed this poor lady, whose life I have ruined. She was beautiful; I brought her to Mexico; a marquis saw her, fell passionately for her, found that my wife resisted him honorably, and set about taking his revenge in the vilest way; he accused me of a crime that I didn't commit, and had me thrown in prison. At last, in the hour of his death, God touched him, and he returned my honor and the money I had lost on account of him. I left prison, and. . . . "

"Pardon me, sir," I broke in, "what is your name?"

"Antonio."

"Antonio!"

"Yes, sir."

"Did you have a certain friend in jail whom you helped during the last days you were held?"

"Yes, I did," he said; "a poor lad known as Periquillo Sarniento, a well-born boy with a fine education, talents that were above the ordinary, and a good heart, who could well have become an upright man; but unfortunately for him, he had befriended a bunch of rogues, they had led him astray, and on account of them, he had ended up in that jail. Recognizing his moral virtues, I loved him, did whatever good I could for him, and even told him to write to me in Orizaba and tell me where he was living. I asked the same of his notary, a fellow named Chanfaina, to whom I left a hundred pesos to speed up the young man's legal proceedings and to make sure he was fed as long as he stayed in jail; but neither of them ever wrote to me. I don't feel sorry about not hearing from the notary, and maybe he just took my money for himself; but I always regretted Periquillo's ingratitude."

"And rightly so, sir," I said; "he was an ingrate; he should have held onto the friendship of a man as kind and liberal as you. Who knows what might have happened to him; but if you were to meet him now, would you still love him as before?"

"Yes, I would, friend," he said; "I would love him as much as ever."

"Even if he were a rogue?"

"Even so. With men, we should loathe their vices, not their persons. From the moment I met that lad, I was convinced that his crimes arose from imitating his bad friends rather than from the wickedness of his own character. But it should be noted that, just as virtue has degrees of goodness, so does vice have degrees of wickedness. The same good act can be more or less good, and the same bad act can be more or less bad, depending on the conditions that applied when it was carried out. Giving charity is always good; but giving it on certain occasions and to certain people, or for instance if a poor man who had nothing to spare were to give it, would be better, whether because it is done in a more orderly fashion or because the poor man is making a bigger sacrifice when he gives alms than is a rich man, and therefore what he does has more merit. I would say the same about bad actions. We all know that it is wrong to steal; but a robbery committed by a poor man assailed by need is less wrong, or has less wickedness in it, than a robbery or a fraud committed by a rich man who has no need of anything; and worst of all is when he robs or defrauds the poor. So we should always examine the circumstances in which men commit their acts, whatever those might be, so that we can justly determine their merits or lack thereof. I realized that this boy Periquillo was bad because of the influence of his bad friends, rather than the wickedness in his heart, and so I was always convinced that, if he could be removed from those provocative enemies, he in himself would be rather inclined toward good."

"But, friend," I said, "if you were to see him now, and if he were in no condition to give you any help at all, would you still love him?"

"You insult me by doubting it," he replied; "what, do you think that I have ever in my life loved and valued men because of the good they can do me? That is an error. A man should be loved on account of his own particular virtues, not because of what we can get out of him. A good man deserves our friendship, even if he doesn't have a penny to his name; and a man whose heart is not corrupt and malign deserves our sympathy no matter how many crimes he commits, for he might be transgressing out of need or out of ignorance, as I believe was the case with my Periquillo, whom I would embrace if I were to see him now."

"Well, worthy friend," I said, throwing myself into his arms, "here is your wish, granted. I am Pedro Sarmiento, the same Periquillo whom you helped so much in jail; I am that wayward youth; I am the ingrate or fool who never wrote back to you; and I am the one who, seeing the truth about the world, has changed my conduct and now has the inexpressible satisfaction of hugging you here in my arms."

The good old man cried tenderly when he heard these things. I left him and went to embrace and console his wife, who was also crying to see her husband's tender feelings; the innocent young girl spilled her little tears, hardly knowing the reason why, and I also embraced and caressed her. After this first rapture, Don Antonio finished telling me his troubles, which were these: as they were on their way to Mexico to place his daughter in a convent, with the plan of living here in the capital, after having sold everything he owned in Acapulco, a gang of thieves assaulted them on the highway, robbed them, and killed their old servant Domingo, who had always served them most faithfully. In this deplorable situation, they availed themselves of a gold locket, which his daughter had hidden or the thieves had overlooked; they sold this and bought the beast of burden on which Don Antonio had arrived at my house, very ill with dysentery, for the three of them had been forced to travel some thirty leagues without a penny, living off of charity until they reached my house.

When my friend Don Antonio concluded his story, I told him, "Your worries are over. This house, and everything I have, belongs to you and your whole family. I love them with all my heart, for they are yours, and from this day on, you are the master of this house."

Then and there, I made them move into my own bedroom and gave them good mattresses; we ate supper together and went to bed.

The next day, I took fabric from my shop and ordered new clothes made for them. I sent to Mexico for a physician to care for Don Antonio and his wife, who was also sick, and with his assistance they recovered shortly.

Now that they were relieved, recovering, and dressed in good clothes, Don Antonio told me, "I feel sorry, my good friend, for having bothered you so many days; I have no words to express my gratitude, and nothing to give you that might pay for the favors you have done; but I would be an impolite fool to stay here and be a burden on you any longer, so I am leaving on my donkey as soon as I can, begging you that, if God should see fit to change my fortune, you will treat what is mine as your own."

"Hush, please, sir," I said. "How could I possibly let you leave my house, trusting to whatever fate might bring? You once protected me; I was your poor man, and today I am your friend, and if you are willing, I will be your son, and we will all be a family together. I have been watching and observing the good attributes of young Margarita; she is old enough; I love her passionately; she is innocent and appreciative. If my honest desire is compatible with your will and your wife's, I would be very happy with such a union, and would display my love for her and my high regard for you and your wife in every way possible."

The good old man seemed somewhat astonished as he listened to me, but after three moments of suspense he said: "Don Pedro, we would gain much if such a marriage were to take place. In truth, considering it in relation to our unhappy situation, we could not hope for more. The girl is nearly fifteen, and is rather pretty; I am old and infirm, and will not last much longer; her poor mother is not healthy, nor can she count on any protection to support her after my time is past. As a rule, if the girl does not get married while I am alive, she will be fodder for the wolves, and will become a ruined young woman. This is a thought that gives me many sleepless nights. In other words, friend, I do want to marry off my daughter as soon as can be; but, being her father after all, I would like her to marry, not a rich man or a marquis, but an upright man who has some experience of the world, and who I would know was marrying her for her virtue and not her passing beauty. These qualities and many more shine in you and, in my opinion, make you worthy of a woman of better attributes than I think Margarita possesses. Yet it is necessary to consider the fact that you must be nearly forty, judging by your appearance; and, supposing that you are thirty-six or thirty-seven, that is old enough to be the father of the bride, which could be enough to prevent her from loving you.

"I know two very common things. First, if a man exceeds his wife slightly in age, that is far from being a defect; indeed, it should be seen as a prerequisite for contracting matrimony, for when men are as young as their brides when they marry, the marriage usually ends up badly, because—given that the feminine sex is weaker than the masculine and has to suffer more disadvantages in the marital state than at any other time—after two or three childbirths, the woman gets ugly; and since (in the case of which we are speaking) when young men arrange a marriage, they generally don't look at anything other than acquiring a beautiful object, it also usually happens that when the wife's beauty goes, so does the man's love: for when he is thirty or thirty-six years old, his wife looks like she's fifty already; she becomes an object of disdain, and he loathes her unjustly. This should be the most powerful reason, among others, why men should not get married very young, and that girls should not wed boys; but it is an arduous endeavor to subdue the inclinations of both sexes to reason, at an age when Nature dominates men so imperiously. The truth is, matrimonies celebrated by old folks are ridiculous, and those undertaken by children are most often ill-fated.

"This means that I approve, and it seems good to me that you should marry my daughter; but I do not know whether she wants to marry you. It is true—and this is the other thing that I know—it is true that she is very docile and very innocent, that she loves me very much and will do what I tell her; yet I would never force her to get married if she is not inclined to do so; nor, should she choose matrimony, would I force her to wed someone she does not love. In virtue of this, you must realize that your union with my daughter does not depend on my doing. It is up to her; I will give her complete freedom, and will not force her decision in any way; and if she should choose to marry you, for me that would be most pleasant."

Don Antonio finished his lecture, and I said to him, "Sir, if these are the only objections that you have, they have all been smoothed out in my favor, and my happiness will be assured if you and your dear wife give your blessings; because, before speaking with you about this particular, I examined your girl's character, and I was amazed to find in a girl of such tender years a very solid sense of virtue, and very wise sentiments. These qualities have captivated me more than her beauty, for the latter may be terminated by age or diminished by illness and disease, which have no respect for beautiful women. Straight away, I declared my wholesome intentions to your girl, and she answered me with these words, which I will always preserve in my memory:

" 'Sir,' she said to me, 'my father says that you are a man of honor, and at other times he has said that he would prefer an upright man for me, even if he were not rich. I always believe my father, because he never lies, and I have loved you very much ever since you came to his aid; it seems to me that by marrying you, I would assure my poor parents' repose; and so, both to keep them from suffering ever again, and because I love you for what you have done for them and because you are an upright man, as my father has said, I would marry you very willingly; but I do not know whether my father and mother will wish for me to do so, and I am ashamed to ask them.'

"This was your girl's simple reply, all the more eloquent for being stripped of artifice. In her I have discovered great reserves of sincerity, innocence, gratitude, filial love, obedience, and respect for her parents and benefactors. I was wondering how to indicate my desire to you, yet when you declared that you would be leaving my house, I was forced to reveal my hopes. On the part of the betrothed, everything is ready; all that remains is to get the consent of yourself and of her mamá, which I beg you to give me."

Don Antonio was serious yet affable; and so, after hearing me out, he smiled, and, slapping me on the shoulder, said, "Oh, friend! If you two were already done with your scheming, we've just been wasting our saliva. Come on; there's no such thing as a foolish girl when it comes to looking out for her own interests. I approve her choice; everything is set as far as we are concerned; but, if you've thought this through, you should pick up the pace; because, if two people love each other, even if they have legitimate aims, it isn't very safe for them to live unmarried under the same roof for long."

I understood my father-in-law's well-founded and Christian scruple, and, asking him to watch over the shop and the inn, I ordered my horse saddled then and there, and I left for Mexico.

As soon as I arrived, I told the whole story to my master, informing him of my plans, which he approved so willingly that he offered to be my godfather at the wedding. I also informed Pelayo, as my confessor and as my friend, of my intentions, and in proof of his approval, he intervened with his contacts, and within a week he had my marriage license approved by the ecclesiastical court.

During this time, I visited my old master the Chinese and his chaplain, and Don Tadeo and Don Jacobo, inviting them all to my wedding. Likewise I sent to Anselmo to invite him and his family; I bought the trousseau, which I gave to my bride; and, since I had money, from here in Mexico I arranged everything that would be needed for preparing the festivities.

A convoy of coaches left with me for San Agustín de las Cuevas on the day that I had set for my marriage. Anselmo was already at my house with his family, and his wife, whom I had chosen as godmother, had dressed and adorned Margarita in the best taste, though not in the most current fashion, because she was discerning and knew that the wedding banquet was being held in the countryside, and that in it I wanted innocence and abundance to be on display, rather than pomp and luxury. Following this plan, and employing my ample means, Anselmo arranged my reception and the festivities as he saw fit, not sparing any expense. I arrived in San Agustín around half past six in the morning, and in the parlor of my house I met my bride, dressed in a simple dress and a black veil,[1] accompanied by her parents; then Anselmo with his wife and family; then Andrés with his, and all the usual servants.

After going through the preliminary greetings that etiquette prescribes, Anselmo sent for the parish priest, who immediately came to the house with his assistant priests, the altar boys, and everything that would be necessary for us to give each other our hands. We were read the private marriage banns, we were confirmed in our declarations, and this part of the ceremony was concluded to everyone's fullest satisfaction.

We immediately went on to the church to receive our nuptial blessings and to swear our constant love once more at the foot of the altar.

After this august sacrifice, we returned and waited for the parish priest and his assistants. My wife took off the dress she had worn, and while the godmother helped her into her wedding dress, I entered the kitchen to see how Anselmo had arranged things; but he had done it all in such a way that I, though the host of this function, was taken aback by its eccentricities.

One of them was that there was no fire burning in the hearth. I went outside to look for Anselmo, feeling very embarrassed, and I told him, "For God's sake, man, what have you done? So many people here that I hold in high regard, and you still haven't bothered to even get some lunch prepared? Didn't I write you that you weren't to think about money, just spend as much as you needed? I swear! You're really going to embarrass me, Anselmo! If I'd have known, I never would have counted on you, for sure."

"Well, what else, my boy! What's done is done," he replied phlegmatically. "But don't you worry, I've got a family here in town who like me, so we can all go there for lunch, after the priest and his assistants get here."

"That's even more foolish, and it's the most impolite thing I can think of," I said. "Have you stopped to think how more than twenty of us are suddenly going to show up and try to squeeze into a house, where they might not have any idea of what's going on? And then have lunch there, without telling them about it first!"

---

[1] [Black was the traditional color of the bride's clothes in Spanish custom. –Tr.]

"That's the sort of indiscretion you see every day in the world," said Anselmo. "In an emergency, you have to be a little shameless if you want to have a good time."

I was cursing Anselmo and his phlegm when they called out to tell us that the priests were already at the house.

I was very peeved when I went out to greet them, and I found my wife transformed from a lady of the court into a shepherdess of Arcadia, because our godmother had dressed her in a gown of the finest muslin with gold brocade; she was wearing shoes of gold lamé, and across the dress she wore a ribbon of sky-blue silk with golden fringes. Her hair lay loose on her shoulders, and was gathered at the top with an embroidered headband, and covered by a small blue satin hat with a spray of white feathers.

This simple dress also surprised me, and I calmed down a bit from my anger at Anselmo's carelessness; because, since my bride was lovely and so young, to me that dress made her look like one of the nymphs that the poets describe. Everyone else thought the same, and they vied with each other to praise her.

When Anselmo saw that I was a bit more serene, he said, "Let's go, ladies and gentlemen, for it is getting late."

They all left, and I went with them by my wife's side, wondering what piffle this smirking Anselmo would come up with next; but how happy I was when we came to a great country house, which belonged to a rich count, and I saw what I had never expected!

Anselmo wouldn't let us dally to look at the house, but led us straight into the orchard, which was lovely and well cultivated.

The moment we entered, a number of very graceful young girls of twelve or thirteen years came out to receive us; dressed with simplicity and elegance, each holding a bouquet of flowers in her hand, they performed a set of colorful contra dances to the rhythm of the splendid beat of the wind and string music that had been arranged for the occasion.

This merry retinue led us to the center of the orchard, where many decent chairs had been placed with skillful symmetry, and the ground was likewise carpeted with rugs.

We enjoyed the fresh air without being bothered in the least by the sun's rays, because several canopies of crimson, yellow, and white damask had been hung from the trees, giving shade and beauty to that place, where we breathed the purest, most innocent delights.

After a short while, a number of well-groomed serving lads and maids entered from one side of the garden and spread tablecloths over the rugs; we sat down in a circle and were served a clean, abundant, and flavorful lunch, during which we were entertained by the cadences of the music and by the sweetness of the girls' voices, as they sang many discreet nuptial songs for my wife.

After lunch, we went for a stroll through the orchard until it was time for dinner, which was also held there, to everyone's delight.

At seven in the evening, we were served a good refreshment; there was dancing until twelve, when we had supper; and afterward we all went home content.

The next day, our honored guests took their leave with many expressions of their affection, putting themselves at my disposal and my wife's. My godfather, who, as you know, was my master, learned that Anselmo had kept track of all the expenses for the function, and he asked him for the bill with the intention of paying it, for he wished to give me a large gift; but he was quite amazed when, instead of a bill for 600 pesos or more, which is what he had expected, given the abundance and magnificence of the fiesta, he found that it had amounted to less than 200 pesos.

He scarcely believed it, but Anselmo assured him that it came to no more than that, and he added, "Sir, festivities aren't more magnificent when they cost more money, but when they are arranged in a more orderly way; and since the finest order is not incompatible with the greatest economy, a very impressive function can clearly be held without any waste, which is what nobody pays attention to, and what makes a function more costly without making it more splendid."

"That is quite true," said my master; "and if the expense was so small, let my godson pay it, and I will wait for a better opportunity to give a good present to my little goddaughter."

Saying this, he left for Mexico; Anselmo returned to his job; and I went back to my shop.

I lived with the greatest consolation and satisfaction in my new state, in the company of my beloved wife and her parents, whom I loved more each day, and who returned my love with their own.

My wife had already given birth to you, my dear children, and you were the center of our love, the delights of your grandparents, and the worthy objects of my attention; you, Juanita, were two years old, and you, Carlos, were one, when your grandparents paid the tribute that nature demands, only a few months apart from each other.

They both died with the kind of resignation and tranquility with which the righteous die. I gave them burial services and honored their funerals to the extent of my means. Your mother was inconsolable with this loss, and had to take advantage of all the considerations with which the Catholic religion alleviates us in such situations, for it can minister sound comforts to the truly bereaved.

Since that cruel winter, everything has been springtime, with your mother, I, and yourselves living together and enjoying peace and innocent pleasures in our modest but honorable circumstances, which, while not furnishing me with the means for superfluous luxuries, has given me everything I need, so that I have never envied the fate of rich men and potentates.

Your godfather was my master, who loved you very much as long as he lived; and in his death he proved his affection for you with an extraordinary action, which you will learn about in the next chapter.

CHAPTER 51

IN WHICH PERIQUILLO RECOUNTS HIS MASTER'S DEATH, THE DEPARTURE
OF THE CHINESE, AND HIS LAST ILLNESS; AND THE EDITOR CONTINUES
TELLING THE REST OF HIS STORY, UP TO THE DEATH OF OUR HERO

Let us skip the circumlocutions and go straight to the heart of the matter. My beloved master, godfather, compadre, and protector died; he died without children or legally entitled heirs; and, in ultimate proof of the affection he had declared for me, he made me the sole heir of his estate, which included the hacienda that I administered together with Anselmo, under the conditions that he expressed in his will and testament, which I fulfilled as his friend and protégé, and as an upright man, which is the title we should be proudest to hold.

If I grieved at the death of this good man, I have no reason to praise myself, because I would have had to have been dumber than an ox not to have loved him as was proper.

I read the testament he had made out in my favor, and when I reached the clause in which he said that, because of how well I had served him, how satisfied he was with my honest conduct, and his desire to come through with the large present he had promised to his goddaughter (my wife), he left his entire estate to me, and so forth, I couldn't help dampening those paragraphs with my tears of love and gratitude.

I attended his funeral; I wore mourning clothes, together with my whole family, not out of ceremony, but to display my true sorrow; I fulfilled all his requests to the letter; and, having come into possession of my inheritance, I enjoyed it with the blessings of God and my master.

I didn't forget myself just because I now had a little capital of my own, as I had done on earlier occasions, nor did I forget my good friends. I treated them just as I always had, and served them in every way I could, especially those who had ever favored me in any way.

Chief among these in my esteem was my old master, the Chinese, to whom I repaid a good 3,000 pesos that I had squandered when I lived in his house; but he didn't want to accept them; instead, he wrote to me that he was very wealthy in his own land, and lacked for nothing in mine, so he considered my debt settled, and he sent me back the pesos for my children. He concluded his letter by telling me that he was preparing to return to his country and that he had no desire to see other cities or kingdoms in America, for three reasons: first, because his health was broken; second, because the world couldn't help but be the same everywhere, with little difference from place to place, because men were men everywhere; and, third and last, because the war, which at first he believed would be nothing but a popular uprising that would quickly be suppressed, was spreading and blazing everywhere.[1]

---

[1] [The war: this is the first reference in the novel, since the author's preface, to the Mexican wars of independence, which began in November 1810. By 1813, the rebels held most of the territory surrounding Mexico City, but a counteroffensive by royalist forces was apparently successful; large-scale military operations had ended and Spanish rule seemed assured in 1816, when Lizardi

I accepted his favor and gave him all due thanks for his generosity; and on a day when I least expected him, he arrived at my house in a traveling coach, preceded by servants and mules carrying his luggage.

He had them halt the coach at the door to the shop, and he tried to say good-bye from there and continue on his way. I wouldn't allow it; rather, relying on the soft insistence that usually characterizes friendships, I forced him to come down from his coach and unload his mules. The mules, the servants, and the coachmen were given lodging in the inn, and my master stayed in my house, where my wife gave him a hearty welcome.

We had much to talk about that day, and among the many things we said, I asked him: "What was all that you were writing when I lived in your house?"

"If you were to see it," he said, "it might upset you, because I was writing some critical notes about the abuses I've noticed in your country, and I expanded on them with the information and explanations I heard from the chaplain, to whom I later gave the notebooks so that he could correct them."

"And what happened to those notebooks, sir? Are you taking them with you?"

"No, I'm not," he said; "two years ago I sent them to my brother, the tután, with a few characteristic items from your land."

"Well, far from being upset by your notes, sir, I would greatly appreciate being able to read them. Who has the first draft of them?"

"The chaplain kept them himself," he replied; "but I don't know why he has held on to them so tightly that he hasn't wanted to lend them to anyone."

I promised myself that I would spare no effort that seemed opportune for getting my hands on those notebooks. Dinnertime came, and I ate with my family in the company of that good gentleman.

Later in the afternoon, we went to the countryside to entertain ourselves with our shotguns, and when we passed by the place where the horse had thrown the misanthrope, I told him about that man's adventure, to which the Asian listened with great pleasure.

In the evening, we returned to the house; we passed the time in good conversation among ourselves, the parish priest, and other gentlemen who favored me with their visits, and when it was time for supper, we ate and then retired.

The next day, we were up at dawn, and I accompanied my dear master as far as Cuernavaca,[2] from which I returned home after bidding him farewell with the most tender expressions of love and gratitude.

I couldn't forget about the notebooks he had written, and I soon began to plead with all my might to see them, through my good friend and confessor Martín Pelayo, since I knew that he was a friend of Dr. Emilio, the former chaplain of my master, the Chinese, and the commentator or semi-author of those papers.

---

wrote these pages. Guerrilla operations, however, continued until changing conditions in Spain sparked a second outbreak of all-out war in 1820. Independence was won in 1821, five years after the novel was published. –Tr.]

[2] [Cuernavaca: a city on the road to Acapulco, about thirty-five miles south of San Agustín de las Cuevas. –Tr.]

He hasn't clearly discouraged me from asking for them, but so far I haven't yet seen them in my hands, because the chaplain says that he is making a fair copy of them and that he will loan them to me as soon as he is done. He is an upright man, and I believe that he will be true to his word.

I lived in peace for some two more years in that town, visiting my friends now and then and receiving their visits in return, given over to fulfilling my domestic obligations—the only ones I have put up with; for although they wanted to make me a judge in the town, I never acceded to their pleas, nor did it occur to me to seek any other position, mindful of my inappropriateness and of the fact that a government post often spreads an air of a kind of vanity that could ruin the man who fills it and destroy even the most constant virtue.

As I have said, my only concerns have been to educate you, to ensure your sustenance without harming anyone else, and to do what little good I can in atonement for the scandal and harm that I caused with my waywardness; my pleasures and diversions have been pure and innocent, for they have concentrated on my love for my wife, my children, and my good friends. Finally, I give infinite thanks to Heaven, because at least I didn't grow old in the career of vice and self-debasement; rather, late as it was, I recognized my errors, loathed them, and avoided falling into the abyss where my passions were leading me.

Though it really is never too late for repentance, and so long as a man lives, it is always the right time for him to set himself on the righteous path, we shouldn't place trust in this fact, for it could happen that, in punishment for our persistence and rebellion, we will not find the right opportunity when we hope to.

I have written you about my life without disguises; I have put my errors and the motives for them on display without covering them up; and finally, I have revealed in my own life the rewards that a man finds when he subjects himself to living in accordance with true reason and the wise precepts of wholesome morality.

God forbid that, after my days are done, you should give yourselves over to vice and take only your father's bad example, perhaps with the foolish hope of mending your ways, as he did, halfway through your lives; and do not tell yourselves, in the recesses of your hearts, "Let's follow our father in his erring ways, and later we'll change our conduct, because maybe his worst fears won't come to pass." My dear children, consecrate your early years to God, for then you will be able to enjoy the sweet fruits of virtue early on, honoring the memory of your parents, saving yourselves from the misfortunes that accompany crime, being useful to the State and to yourselves, and passing from the temporal happiness you will enjoy to a greater joy that will never cease.

I have broken the thread of my story; but perhaps you will not find my final digressions completely useless.

For two more years after the departure of my master the Chinese, as I was saying, I lived in San Agustín de las Cuevas, until I found myself forced to liquidate my estate and move to this city, both to see whether I could recover here my health (which was weakened by age and assailed by anasarca or generalized dropsy), and to protect my wealth from the results of the insurrection that arose in the kingdom in the year 1810. A truly fatal and disastrous time for New Spain! An era of crime, blood, and desolation!

How many reflections I could have made for you about the origins, progress, and probable outcomes of this war! It would be very easy for me to sketch the history of America, and leave the field of speculation open for you to decide who among the contenders has right on their side—whether it is the Spanish government, or the Americans trying to make themselves independent of Spain; but it is too dangerous to write about this in Mexico in the year 1813. I do not wish to compromise your safety by teaching you about political matters that you are in no state to understand. For now, it is enough for you to know that war is the greatest of all evils for any nation or kingdom; but incomparably more harmful are the bloody disturbances within a single country, for wrath, vengeance, and cruelty—inseparable from any war—feed off the citizens themselves, who arm themselves for their mutual destruction.

The Romans were well aware of this truth, experienced as they were in these civil calamities. Horace and Lucan, among others, are worthy of note. The former, scolding his maddened fellow citizens, tells them: "Where are you going, villains? Why are you taking up arms? Have the fields and seas been perchance too little stained by Roman blood? Neither wolves nor lions have ever been in the habit, as you are, of exercising their rancor on any wild beasts but those that differ from them in kind. And when they do fight, is their fury perchance more blind than yours? Is their anger more bitter? Are they as guilty? Reply! But what could you reply? Hush; your faces are clouded over with a horrid sallowness, and your souls are filled with terror, convinced of your crimes."[3]

That is how the sensitive Horace put it; and Lucan gives a vivid description of the damage done by a civil war in some verses that I will translate freely into Spanish. In popular uprisings, he says:

> Nobles and plebeians perish together,
> And the cruel sword wanders hither and yon;
> No breast is safe from the bite of its blade.
> Red blood stains all, even the sacred walls
> Of the holiest temples; no one finds
> Defense in his age; gray-haired elders
> See their days cut short, and the sad infant
> Dies before his thankless life begins.
> But for what crime must the poor old man
> Give up his life, or the child who does no wrong?
> Oh! just to live in times like these
> Is a great crime—yes! That is cause enough.[4]

Erasmus was more resolute in depicting all the horrors of war, and he went all out when he spoke of civil wars. "Fighting," he says, "is a common thing; one nation tears itself to bits with another nation, one kingdom with another kingdom, prince against prince, people against people; and what even the gentiles held to be impious:

---

[3] [Horace, *Epodes*, VII, lines 1–4 and 11–16. –Tr.]
[4] [Lucan, *Pharsalia*, II, lines 101–108. –Tr.]

kindred against kindred, brother against brother, son against father; and finally, what seems to me even more atrocious: Christian against man; and what about (I say this as the worst of all atrocities) Christian against Christian? But, oh the blindness of our minds! That, instead of abhorring this, there should be those who applaud it, who praise it, who—the most abominable thing in the world!—call war holy, and who inflame the anger of their princes, throwing fuel on the fire until the flames rise to high Heaven!"[5]

Virgil recognized that there was nothing good about war, and that we should all beg God to make peace endure. That is why he wrote: *Nulla salus bello, pacem te poscimus omnes.*[6]

From all this, you should infer what a great evil war is, how just the reasons are that militate against it, and that a citizen should only take up arms when the common good of the country is at issue. Only in that case should he grab the sword and shoulder the buckler, and in no other, no matter how pleasant the ends that the commoners propose; for such ends are very contingent and unpredictable, while the misfortunes that follow upon the origins and the means are always certain, baneful, and generally pernicious. . . . But let us set our pen aside from this subject, so hateful by its nature, and refuse to stain the pages of my life story with the recollections of an era stained with American blood.

After liquidating my estate and settling in Mexico, I tried to have my illness treated, but the physicians said that it was incurable. They all concurred in the same opinion, and there was at least one pedant who tried to disabuse me of any hope by bringing up an aphorism about old age and telling me in Latin that the accumulation of the years is a very serious disease: *Senectus ipsa est morbus.*

I, who knew well that I was mortal and that I had lived through a lot, was ready to believe it. Like it or not, I resigned myself to the physicians' sentence, realizing that sometimes one has to resign oneself to being trapped by the legitimate will of God, for whether we like it or not, there is no escaping it; I made a virtue out of necessity, as people like to say, and tried only to preserve the little health I had through palliatives, but without any hopes of making a full recovery.

During this time, my friends would come to visit me, and by chance I acquired a new friend, a fellow named Lizardi, who was godfather to Carlos for his confirmation, a writer without any luck in your homeland, and known to the public by the epithet under which he distinguished himself when he wrote during these bitter times, which was the *Mexican Thinker.*[7]

During the time that I have known him and been friendly with him, I have noted that he has little education, less talent, and finally no merit at all (speaking now with

---

[5] [Erasmus, *Adages*, IV, i, 1. This is an essay on Pindar's adage *Dulce bellum inexpertis*, "War is Sweet to Those Who Do Not Know It," written with particular reference to the religious wars of Europe in the early 1500s. –Tr.]

[6] ["No war is wholesome; we all implore you for peace." Virgil, *Aeneid*, XI: 362. –Tr.]

[7] [*Mexican Thinker (Pensador Mexicano)*: the title of Lizardi's first newspaper, and the pseudonym under which he published it; he put out forty-five issues between October 1812 and the end of 1814, when it was suppressed by the re-established absolutist Spanish government in Mexico City. –Tr.]

my customary frankness); but in exchange for these faults, I know that he is not a swindler, a cheat, a flatterer, or a hypocrite. I can state that he doesn't pretend to be wise nor virtuous; he recognizes his faults, he sees them, confesses them, and detests them. Though he is a man, he knows that's what he is: that he has a thousand defects, that he is full of ignorance and self-love, that he overlooks his ignorance far too often because his self-love blinds him; and finally, when wise men have praised his productions in his presence and in mine, I have heard him say a thousand times, "Gentlemen, don't fool yourselves; I am not wise, educated, nor erudite; I know how much it takes to wear those titles; my productions have dazzled you on a first reading, but they're nothing but brightly glittering tinsel. Myself, I'm ashamed to see errors in print that I didn't notice when I was writing them. The ease with which I write does not prove me correct. Too often, I am writing in the midst of the distractions of my family and my friends; but that doesn't justify my errors, for I should be writing in calm and taking the time to polish my writing, or not write at all, following the example of Virgil or the advice of Horace; but after writing in this fashion, and after realizing that by my natural inclination, I don't have the patience to read much, write, erase, correct, nor consult my own writings at a slow pace, I admit that I don't do it as I should, and I firmly believe that the wise will forgive me, attributing the reprehensible haste of my pen to my overheated imagination. I mention the opinion of the wise, because I pay no attention to that of the foolish."

Hearing such expressions from the Thinker, I made him my friend; and—recognizing that he was an upright man and that, if he made mistakes now and then, it was because his mind was befuddled, not because his will was depraved—I counted him among my true friends, and he gained my affection to the point that I confided my most hidden thoughts to him, and we have loved each other so well that I could even say that I am one with the Thinker, and he with me.

One of these days recently, now that I am so ill that I can barely write the events of my life, he came to visit me; my wife was sitting on the edge of my bed, and you children were sitting around her; I realized how exhausted I was from my ailments, and saw that I could not keep writing, so I told him, "Take these notebooks, so that my children might benefit from them after my days are done."

At that moment I left all my notes to the Thinker, along with these notebooks, so that he could correct and annotate them, for I am very ill. . . .

Notes of the Thinker

Everything up to here was written by my good friend Don Pedro Sarmiento, whom I loved as I do myself, and whom I attended in his illness with the greatest affection, until his death.

He sent for a notary, and he made out his last will and testament with all the formalities. In it he declared that he had 50,000 pesos in cash, invested at a guaranteed interest rate with the Count of San Telmo, according to a notarized document, which he displayed and which should be sewed together with the original testament; and he continued:

"Furthermore: I declare it to be my will that, having paid for vows and funeral expenses from the fifth of my estate,[8] the rest of the fifth should be distributed in favor of decent poor people who are upright men and married, in this fashion: if 9,000 some-odd pesos are left, they will be used to help nine poor men, each of whom must show the executor (named above) a certificate from his parish priest, stating that he is a man of orderly conduct, legitimately poor, with a poor family to support, with some trade or skill, not foolish or inept, and, on top of this, that he has a guarantor, a man of means who will pledge to answer for the 1,000 pesos which he will be given to invest so that he can find a way to make a living with them; it being understood that the guarantor will be responsible for this amount if it should ever be proved that his client has embezzled it; but if it is lost through commerce, robbery, fire, or something of the sort, the guarantor and the grantee alike shall be free.

"I declare: that although I could use 9,000 pesos to give alms to twenty, thirty, a hundred, or a thousand poor men, giving a trifle to each of them, which is what is usually done, I have decided not to do so, because I deem that this does not give them true assistance; but my proposed way does; for it is my will that, after the grantees have done business and ensured their livelihood, they should return the 1,000 pesos so that other poor men might be assisted.

"I also declare: that although I could give alms to widows and maidens, I do not do so, because most rich men tend to leave them money, yet they are not the neediest; rather, poor upright men are, though testaments rarely mention them, believing (wrongly) that simply because they are men, they have plenty of resources for supporting their families."

This was the tenor of the stipulations in his will. When he had finished, it was time for him to take the holy sacraments of the Eucharist and extreme unction. He received the viaticum from his true friend, the very helpful Father Pelayo. His friends Don Tadeo, Don Jacobo, Anselmo, Andrés, myself, and many others attended the ceremony. The music and solemnity that accompanied this religious act spread a sense of respectful rejoicing over all those in attendance, which increased when we saw the tenderness and devotion with which my friend received the sacramental Body of the Lord. The way he begged us all to pardon him for his scandals and erring ways, the way he exhorted us, and the unction that he poured into his words, brought tears to our eyes and left us filled with edification and solace.

After this sweet rapture of his soul, he retired, thanking everyone, and two hours later he called his wife and children into his bedroom.

I was sitting at the headboard, and his family surrounded his bed, when he told them with the greatest calm:

"Dear wife, dear children, you would never doubt that I have always loved you, and that my hard work has constantly been consecrated to your true happiness. Now it is time for me to depart from you, not to meet again until the end of time. The

---

[8] ["The fifth of my estate": that is, the portion that he could legally dispose of according to his own will, after four-fifths had been distributed to his legitimate heirs; see Chapter 13, footnote 10 and Chapter 29, footnote 11. –Tr.]

Author of Nature is calling at the door of my life; He gave that life to me when He wished, and when He wishes, Nature will fulfill its end. I am not the arbiter of my existence; I know that my death is approaching, and I am dying very content and resigned to the divine will. Set aside the excess of your sorrow. Much as you mourn my passing from your sight, for you've always been my darlings, you should moderate your grief, considering that I am mortal and that sooner or later my spirit must leave the corruptible mass of my body.

"Note that my Lord and the Lord of my life is the one who takes it from me, because Nature is immutable in fulfilling the demands of its Author. Console yourselves with this true consideration, and say: 'The Lord gave me a husband; the Lord gave us a father; He is taking him away; blessed then be the name of the Lord.' Humble Job consoled himself with such resignation in the extremes of his bitter travail.

"These thoughts do not inspire sorrow or sadness, but rather steadfast solace and joy, based on no less than the word of God and the maxims of the sacred religion we profess. Leave hopelessness to the ungodly, and let the unbeliever doubt in our future existence, while the repentant and well-disposed Catholic trusts with good reason that God will fulfill His word and forgive him his sins; and his kinsmen, with the same sureness, will piously believe that he has not died, but has passed on to a better life.

"So do not cry, my darlings, do not cry. God is still here to comfort you and aid you, and if you fulfill His divine precepts and trust in His high Providence, you may be sure that you will never lack for anything, anything at all, to make you happy in this life and the next.

"Do be sure to behave in this life with honor and good sense, whatever state you might embrace. If you, Margarita, decide to remarry (for I would not forbid it), try to learn your spouse's character before he becomes your husband, for there are many Periquillos in the world, although not all of them recognize and detest their vices as I do. Once you know that he is an upright man who has met with the approval of my friends, go ahead and join him in marriage with my blessings; but always endeavor to gain his love by praising his virtues and ignoring his defects. Never disdainfully oppose his tastes, especially not in things that he rightly orders you; do not waste what I am leaving you to live on with fashions, outings, or extravagances; do not take vain, proud, and mad women as models for your conduct; imitate prudent and virtuous women. Although my children are big now, if you should have others, do not have any favorites among them; treat them all equally, for they are all your children, and in this way, you will teach your husband to behave well with the ones you had with me; make them all brothers and sisters, and you will avoid the feelings of envy that arise in cases of favoritism; be thrifty, and do not waste on sprees what I leave you, nor what your husband earns; understand that it is harder to earn 1,000 pesos than to say 'I had 1,000 pesos'; but to say 'I had money' when you are living in poverty is exceedingly painful; finally, my dear girl, try not to forget the maxims I've taught you; stay away from the damnable passion of jealousy, which, far from being useful, is harmful to poor women and is the final cause of their total ruin; even if your husband should unfortunately stray, ignore it, and then show him more affection and appreciation, for I assure you that he will recognize that your merit surpasses that of the prostitutes he adores, and in the end he will be tamed, he will ask you to forgive him, and he will love you with twice the solicitude.

"And you, my precious children, what could I say to you? That you should be humble, thoughtful, friendly, kind, courteous, honorable, truthful, simple, sensible, and upright men in every way. I am leaving my life story written for you, so that you can see where reckless youths usually crash; so that you will learn where the precipices lie, and thus avoid them; and so that, recognizing what virtue is and how many sweet fruits it promises, you will devote yourselves to it and follow it from your earliest youth.

"Therefore: love and honor God and observe His precepts; endeavor to be useful to your fellow men; obey the government, whatever it may be; live in subordination to the authorities it sends to you in its name; do no harm to anyone, and don't hesitate to do whatever good you can. Refrain from having too many friends. That is a piece of advice that I especially recommend to you; I speak from experience. One man alone, no matter how bad he might be, if he stays alone, without friends, will be the only one who knows what his crimes are; they won't scandalize anyone in particular, for no one will witness them; but on the other hand, a sharper and a rogue who has many friends will have many people to teach his bad example, and many witnesses to his ill deeds.

"Besides, as you will see in my life story, there are lots of friends, but few friendships. Friends swarm like flies when the weather's nice, but few remain when it turns bad. Be careful with your friends, and test them. When you find one who's unselfish, true, and a completely upright man, love him and keep him forever; but when you notice self-interest, double-dealing, or misconduct in your friend, rebuke him and never trust his friendship.

"Finally: observe the maxims that my father wrote down for me in his final hour, when I was in the novitiate, and which you will find written in Chapter 12 of the first volume of my life story. If you carry them out to the letter, I assure you that you will be happier than your father was."

After these and other similar talks, Don Pedro embraced his children and his wife, gave them many kisses, and bid them farewell, making me weep bitterly, for the extreme emotions of the lady and the children gave the lie to any philosophy of preventive reasoning. Their wailing, tears, and displays of emotion were as great as if the sick man hadn't said a word.

Finally they left the patient alone, and he told me, "It's time now for me to let go of the world and to think only about how I have offended God, and that I hope to offer Him the pain and anguish I am suffering as a sacrifice for my wickedness. Send for my confessor, Father Pelayo."

Since this cleric was a good friend, he was never absent from his own friends' sides when their hour of tribulation came. He had scarcely taken off his vestments when he returned to the house to console his spiritual son. Before I had left the room, he entered and asked Don Pedro how he felt.

"I'm fading fast," said the sick man; "it's time for you stay constantly by my bedside, I earnestly beg you; not because I'm afraid of the devils, visions, or ghosts that they say appear to the dying at this hour. I know that it's a vulgar superstition to think that everyone who dies sees those specters, because God doesn't need to use such ethereal puppets to punish or terrorize a sinner. The sinner's own bad conscience, and the remorse it brings at this hour, are the only demons and bogeymen his soul can see, confounded by the memory of his bad life, his lack of repentance, and his servile dread of an exasperated and righteous God; all the rest are the gullible notions of the foolish mob. The reason why I want you by my side is so that you can impart the solace I need at this hour, and ease my heart with the sweet balm of your admonitions and your consoling words. Don't leave me until I expire; I wouldn't want some devout man or woman to come in here and start Jesusing me with the *Ramillete* or some collection like that,[9] battering my heart with their cold singsong voices and giving me a headache with their ear-splitting yells. I don't mean that I don't want them to talk about Jesus—God forbid I would say such a thing. I'm well aware that His sweet name is above all other names; that when He is invoked, Heaven rejoices, the earth is humbled, and Hell trembles; what I don't want, though, is for some good man to plant himself by my bedside with one of those pamphlets I mentioned, trying to read it out letter by letter, and when he finds he can't, to pick up the usual chant—*Jesus help you, Jesus aid you, Jesus favor you*—not leaving off for anything, and then, recognizing his own coldness, to attempt to inspire fervor in me by yelling, which is what I've observed at other men's deathbeds. For God's sake, friend, don't allow one of those fellows near my side; far from helping me die well, they would only help me die more quickly. You know that the important thing in these moments is to move the ill man to contrition and faith in divine mercy; to have him recite in his heart the acts of faith, hope, and charity; to raise his spirits with the recollection of divine goodness, reminding him that Jesus Christ spilled His blood for his sake, and that He is his intercessor; and finally, to drill him in the acts of love of God, and to inflame his desire to see His Divine Majesty in His glory.

"That is what it rightly means to help a man to die well, but not everybody can do it, and those who have the education and grace for it do not stoop to shouting and yelling like those fools who, far from aiding the dying man, frighten and pester him.

"I also beg you not to allow the old ladies to finish me off with their good intentions, by forcing a hearty soup or a potion of palate water down my throat when I'm in the throes of death. Let them know that this is a superstitious prejudice that will shorten the ill man's life and make him die with twice the anguish. Tell them that we have two tubes in our throats, called the esophagus and the larynx. Through one of them, air passes to our lungs; through the other, food goes to our stomachs; but you must let them know that the tube through which air passes comes before the one through which food passes. In a state of health, when we swallow, we cover up the air tube with a little valve called the glottis, and when it is covered, the food can pass over it to the stomach tube, as if it were crossing over a bridge. We accomplish this by pressing the tongue against the palate in the act of swallowing, so that nobody

---

[9] [*Ramillete*, "Bouquet," was a popular title for collections of prayers, devotions, and dirges, such as Bernardo de Sierra, *Ramillete de divinas flores escojidas en el delicioso jardin de la Yglesia para recreo de el christiano lector* (Madrid, 1710; literally, "Bouquet of Divine Flowers Picked in the Delightful Garden of the Church for the Entertainment of the Christian Reader"). –Tr.]

could swallow a little saliva without pressing his tongue and covering the air tube; and when, by some chance, we neglect to do this, and something goes down the wrong way, as we say, even if it's as little as a drop of water, our lungs, which will not allow anything other than air, immediately reject that foreign object, sometimes so forcefully that they expel it through our nostrils, if it's a liquid. When the water, e.g., that gets into the lungs weighs more than the air the lungs hold, then the patient drowns; and if it is just a little water, he expels it, as I've said.

"After you explain these things to the old women, let them know that a dying man does not have the strength, perhaps not even the consciousness, to press his tongue; therefore, when they force liquid down his throat, it goes straight to his lungs, and if he doesn't cough it up, it's either because that organ is already damaged, or because he doesn't have the strength to cough, and so the ill man dies more quickly. Tell them all this, and tell them that the safest thing is to moisten his mouth with a damp cloth; though such efforts do more to comfort the visitors than to relieve the patient.

"Finally, Pelayo, by your life, have them hold a wake for my body for two days, and don't let them bury it until they are very sure that I am really dead, because I don't want to end up dying in the graveyard like so many others, especially women in childbirth who, suffering nothing more than a prolonged fainting spell, have died before their time, buried alive by the rash haste of their mourning families."

Don Pedro finished talking to the father confessor about these things, and he said to me, "Compadre, I feel very weak now; I think my parting hour has come; send for my neighbor, Don Agapito" (who was an excellent musician) "and tell him that it is time for what I planned with him."

As soon as the musician got the message, he ran out, and soon came back with three young boys and six musicians with flutes, violins, and clavichord, and he entered the bedroom with them.

We were all surprised by this unexpected scene, and more so when the boys began to raise their sweet voices, accompanied by the musicians, in a hymn composed for this hour by Don Pedro himself.

We were quite touched, as well as amazed, by our friend's skill in making this baneful passage less bitter. Father Pelayo said, "See here how my friend has learned the art of helping himself to die well. No matter how little consciousness remains in him, how could these sweet voices and this harmonious music help but awaken in him the tender effects that his devotion has consecrated to the Supreme Being?"

Indeed, they sang the following

HYMN TO THE SUPREME BEING

Eternal God, immense and
Almighty, righteous, wise, and holy,
Give Your benign protection
To us who were created by Your hands:
     With gratitude, I render
The homage that Your majesty deserves,

For when I was afflicted,
You were my shield, my staff, and my support.
        And when I had sunken in
The deepest swamps, and when I looked in vain
For someone who would help me,
My eyes were stiff with tears and swollen shut;
        You then held out, to help me,
Your generous and compassionate hand,
Which freed me from all danger
And brought me safely home, without a scratch.
        You, oh Lord, have ever since
Robustly guided me, though I still walk
With wavering, wayward steps,
Along the narrow path of righteousness.
        My vices have abashed me;
My offenses I detest; with this, my cry,
May my record be erased,
My Lord, from the writing in the Judgment Book.
        And at this critical hour,
Do not recall, oh Lord, all of my sins,
Into which I had been led
By the inexperience of my young years.
        Please remember only that,
Although depraved, a sinner, and a wretch,
I am Your son, Your creature;
I am the work of Your almighty hands.
        If I have greatly wronged You,
Then I am greatly grieved, and greatly love
You, my Father, Whom I've wronged
And Who has yet forgiven all my crimes.
        Trusting in Your promises,
I invoke Your mercy, and *to Your hands*
my spirit I do commend.
Receive it, Lord, and keep it evermore.[10]

Twice they recited this tender hymn, and on the second recital, when they reached
the verse that reads *To Your hands my spirit I do commend*, our Pedro gave up his
spirit into the hands of the Lord, leaving us filled with tenderness, devotion, and
solace.

   At the news of his death, which fell at the end of that same year of 1813, grief
spread throughout the house, and was displayed in the tears not only of his family,

---

[10] [The translation of this hymn follows the text of the 4th edition, taken from the manuscript of
the novel, and differs significantly in words (though not much in meaning) from the text of the
3rd edition. There are similar emendations in the Latin epitaph and the first two poems of the
next chapter. –Tr.]

but of his friends, his servants, and his protégés, who had come to be witnesses to his death.

His wake was held, as he had asked, for two days, and throughout that time the house was never empty of his friends and those he had helped, all of whom wept bitterly to lose such a good father, friend, and benefactor.

At last the time came to bury him.

CHAPTER 52

IN WHICH "THE THINKER" RECOUNTS THE BURIAL OF
PERICO, AND OTHER MATTERS THAT LEAD THE READER BY
THE HAND TO THE END OF THIS VERY TRUTHFUL HISTORY

After two days, his funeral rites proceeded and he was given solemn honors; afterward, his body was brought to the graveyard and buried according to the special request he had made me.

The tomb was sealed with a gravestone of *tecal*,[1] a kind of marble that his confessor bought for this purpose, first ordering two epitaphs carved in it that the deceased himself had composed before his final illness. One was in Latin, and the other in Spanish; I will include them here, in case they please the readers. The Latin epitaph said:

> HIC YACET
> PETRUS SARMIENTO
> (VULGO)
> PERIQUILLO SARNIENTO
> PECCATOR VITA
> NIHIL MORTE.
> QVISQVIS ADES
> DEVM ORA
> VT
> IN AETERNUM VALEAT

Which means, in Spanish:

> HERE LIES
> PEDRO SARMIENTO,
> COMMONLY KNOWN AS
> PERIQUILLO SARNIENTO.
> IN LIFE HE WAS BUT A SINNER:
> NOTHING IN HIS DEATH.
> PASSERBY,
> WHOEVER YOU BE,
> PRAY THAT GOD GRANT HIM
> ETERNAL REST

The Spanish epitaph was a *décima*,[2] which said:

---

[1] [*Tecal* (better, *tecali*): onyx from the Tecali region of Puebla. —Tr.]
[2] [*Décima*: in Spanish poetry, a stanza of ten lines, with metric and rhyme schemes that I have tried to follow; the *quintilla* below is likewise a five-line verse. —Tr.]

> Look, consider, contemplate,
> If you are living without a care,
> That a wastrel is buried here
> Who died in a blessed state.
>   Not everyone meets his fate;
> Think, before your passing bell,
> That if one lives a life pell-mell,
> Just so he usually dies:
> So surely you should realize
> It is safest to live well.

These creations of the deceased pleased all his friends with their propriety and simplicity. Father Pelayo picked up a piece of charcoal from the censer, and on the white wall of the graveyard, he improvised the following

SONNET

> Here lies Periquillo, who half his life
> Was wicked, and the other half was good;
> When he from virtue at a distance stood,
> He even once attempted suicide.
> God touched him, and he welcomed grace inside
> His tender breast; within him, God's grace strewed
> The flowers of virtue. He was imbued
> With charity's pure flame before he died.
>   When it comes to wickedness, dear friend,
> How many are the men who mimic you!
> But not so many will, like you, amend.
> We clamor after vice and its milieu
> In myriad crowds; but should a man repent,
> How many imitate him? Very few.

Rightly or wrongly, we all praised Father Pelayo's sonnet, some out of politeness and others out of affection or inclination for the poet.

Imitating him, his friend Anselmo wrote the following:

DÉCIMA[3]

> Standing by these stiff remains,
> I am ashamed of acting hateful;
> Although his friend, I was ungrateful,
> Yet in his death he now retains

---

[3] Unfortunately, the final pages of the manuscript are missing, and thus these verses could not be corrected as might have been wished, and the best that could be done was to leave them just as they were in the earlier edition. –E.

My gratitude. No doubt remains:
My very best of friends was he.
His virtue witnessed was by me;
And God forgives him, I believe;
In helping me, he did relieve
And did forgive his enemy.

Since we all have a bit of the poetaster at least about us, we continued inscribing on that humble wall whatever lines of doggerel came to our imaginations and to our hands. When his friend Don Jacobo had read the décima above, he took the piece of charcoal and wrote this:

OCTAVE

I owe to this cadaver—which we, here today,
Entomb in the cold earth beneath this slab—my life;
I bless the happy day when chance brought me his way;
He freed me from opprobrium and from deadly strife.
They tell me he was bad, but that I could not say:
I only knew him good, which makes me realize
That one who could withdraw from vice and unbelief
Is finally worthy of our mourning and our grief.

Don Tadeo took the charcoal away from Jacobo and wrote the following:

QUINTILLA

Here lies my good friend—yes, my best;
He slandered me once, recklessly;
I was witness to his noblesse;
He came to aid me mercifully,
And now his memory I bless.

Tears were streaming down the face of maestro Andrés as he read these tributes to his master, and Father Pelayo, knowing how much he must have loved him, and wanting to see what he would come up with, gave him the piece of charcoal; and, much as he refused to take it, we all surrounded him and insisted that he write something or other. It took a lot of work for us to convince him, but at last, harassed by our pleas, he grabbed the crude pencil and wrote this:

DÉCIMA

My master taught me to yank molars
From the mouths of cussed hags;
He taught me 'bout shaving dogs,
And four hundred thousand errors.

> But I doubt the dead man drags
> The clanking chains of sins so hoary,
> 'Cause I can swear that, sure enough,
> He also taught me some good stuff,
> And he'll receive his palms of glory
> When he gets out of Purgatory.

We rightly celebrated good Andrés' décima, and I was about to write my own ditty, but before I could begin, the cleric said to me, "You've got to write a sonnet; but not in blank verse—you have to write it in proper meter, and make it rhyme."[4]

"That is a lot to ask of me, Father," I said. "I'm a real bungler at this business of writing verses, and I admit it, so how do you expect me to write a sonnet? And on top of that, to make it rhyme! Even without that, composing a sonnet is the punishment that Apollo sent to poets, as Boileau has said;[5] so what will become of me, with all the requirements you're putting on me? Besides, the whole system of acrostics, meter, rhyme, labyrinths of double meanings, plays on words, and those sorts of things have gone out of fashion for a thousand good reasons, and they just remain as examples of the barbarous babbling of past centuries."

"All that is quite true, and it's just as you say," the priest replied; "but since you're going to write it among friends, and in a graveyard, not to show off in some academy, you're authorized to do the best you can and try to please us. We've got to be doing something while we're waiting for them to place the lid on the tomb."

I felt it would be impolite to refuse, and so, against my will, I picked up the charcoal and wrote this devilishly convoluted:

SONNET

> As great a criminal as a man might be,
> Although from virtue he might be distant,
> Although his sins might be extravagant,
> He should not give up hope so foolishly.
>   If he converts to virtue truthfully—
> His faith in following God is adamant,
> His virtue is not false or hesitant—
> Then God will pardon him unfailingly.
>   Our late friend therefore died without complaint,

---

[4] [What the priest literally says is: "You've got to write a sonnet, but not blank verse; rather, end the lines with the syllables *–ente, –ante, –unto,* and *–anto.*" In effect, the priest is challenging Lizardi to an improvised rhyming contest known as *pie forzado,* which is still practiced in parts of Latin America. Lizardi responds by including *pie forzado* among his list of things that have "gone out of fashion" in Mexico, but he ultimately comes up with a sonnet that answers the challenge. –Tr.]

[5] [Nicolas Boileau–Despréaux, *L'art poétique* (1672; *The Art of Poetry,* London, 1683), Chant 11, lines 82–84. Spell notes (p. 170) that two Spanish translations of Boileau existed, one of which was advertised in Mexico in 1808. –Tr.]

For though he often sinned in early years,
He later proved a model of restraint.
He sinned too much, 'tis true; but with his tears,
He scrubbed his sins and did not leave a taint;
In life a sinner, but he died a saint.

They all praised my verse as much as they had the others; for you know, can anything be so bad that there won't be anyone to admire it? Just by saying that they praised Andrés' verse, and the following ditty by the Indian Fiscal of San Agustín de las Cuevas,[6] who came to Mexico to attend his friend's funeral as soon as he heard of his death, I've said it all.

As for the fiscal's ditty, we made many comments on it because the abominable handwriting made it all but unintelligible, and in the end we decided that it said:

I'll just say this, and I'll be done:
Señor Don Pegros[7] here is gone.
A thousand favors for us he done,
Not one of us'll forgit you, sir, not one.

Nobody else wanted to write anything, after they had all heard our praises for the Indian's ditty; and so we passed the time by copying down the verses with the help of a pencil that Don Tadeo chanced to find in his pocket.

I never expected that a muddled hodgepodge like this would find as much acceptance as it has. Passing from hand to hand, the number of copies has grown so fast that today there are doubtless more than 300 copies in Mexico and beyond.[8]

They finished placing the gravestone, and after Father Pelayo and the other invited priests said the final responsory for the dead over his tomb, we got into our coaches and went to express our condolences and pay our respects to his widow.

All nine days, the house of mourning was filled with the closest friends of the deceased, and among them there were many poor and downtrodden but decent men, whom he had aided in silence.

We hadn't known before then that he had given so much charity, and had distributed it so well. In his testament, he left a bequest of 2,000 pesos for me to distribute among these poor men as I saw fit, and in accord with the specifics he left me in the corresponding section of the will, which contained a list of their names, addresses, families, and marital statuses.

---

[6] [Fiscal: in a colonial Indian town, the parish priest's lay assistant. In most towns, the fiscal headed the ecclesiastic government of the town (under the supervision, real or theoretical, of the Spanish priest), much as the governor headed its civil administration (under the supervision of the Spanish subdelegado and his lieutenants). –Tr.]

[7] [Pegros: there is no sound corresponding to "d" in Nahuatl, so a Nahuatl speaker would be likely to make such an error in spelling Pedro's name. –Tr.]

[8] It may be supposed that the Thinker is speaking of the copies of this volume [i.e., the censored 4th volume of the book], of which he ordered 300 copies printed for the 1st edition. –E.

I carried out this assignment with exactitude, as I did with all his requests; I continued visiting his widow and doing what I could to serve her, and I always noticed and was even amazed by her good sense, her good conduct, her thrift, and the order in which she kept the house; and so she has educated her children so wisely that they will certainly honor the memory of their father and be their mother's comfort.

After some time had passed, when the lady was more serene, I asked her for the notebooks that my friend had written, so that I could correct and annotate them, as he had requested I do in the corresponding section of his will.

The lady gave them to me, and it cost me more than a little trouble to put them in order and correct them, they were so jumbled and badly written; but in the end I did what I could, and then I brought them back and asked her permission to put them into print.

"God forbid," the lady said, quite scandalized; "how could I possibly let my husband's amusing, witty tales be publicly aired, and allow every carping critic out there to have a field day at his expense, feasting on his respectable bones?"

"Nothing of the sort is going to happen," I replied. "Your late husband's tales truly are amusing, and his witticisms are worthy of being published and read. They are amusing, but in a very rare way: both edifying and enjoyable. Do you think it shows little wit, or a common mind, for someone in this day and age to recognize, confess, and repudiate his errors with as much humility and simplicity as my compadre showed? No, ma'am; something like that is marvelous and, I dare say, inimitable. Today, the most anyone does is recognize his faults, but no one would think of confessing them; and even recognizing them is a rare occurrence; the most common thing is for us to be blinded by our self-love and obstinately cover up our vices, conceal them with hypocrisy, and perhaps try to pass them off as virtues.

"It is true that Don Pedro wrote his notebooks with the plan that only his children would read them; but fortunately they are the last ones who need to do so, because, on top of the good and solid foundation that my compadre built for constructing the edifice of their political and Christian education, they have a mother who is capable of shaping their spirits in a good way, and there is no doubt that you will do so.

"In Mexico, ma'am, and throughout the world, there are crowds of Periquillos who could surely use this book for the sound doctrine and moral teachings it contains.

"My compadre displays his crimes openly; but he does not boast about them: rather, he reproaches himself for having committed them. He depicts the crime, but he always shows the punishment as well, so that it can serve as an object lesson.

"In the same way, he relates many good actions, praising them in order to arouse the imitation of their virtues. When he relates the good things he did himself, he does so in passing, without affecting either humbleness or pride.

"He wrote his life story in a style that is neither low-down nor stuck-up; he avoids pretending to be wise; he uses a familiar, homely style, the one we all commonly use to understand each other and to get our points across most easily.

"In this study, he hasn't left out the common sayings and proverbs of the mob, because his aim was to write for everyone. In the same way, he likes to stick in some tomfoolery here and there, so that his work will not be too serious and therefore boring.

"Your husband really understood men's characters; he knew that being too serious tires them, and that no matter how good a serious book might be, if it is dealing with moral subjects, it will normally have very few readers, while on the other hand something written in his style will have plenty.

"A book like this will be happily handled by a mischievous boy, a dissipated youth, a fashionable young lady, and even a shameless rogue and scoundrel. When those individuals read it, the last thing they're thinking about is getting some good out of their reading. They'll open the book out of curiosity, and they'll read it with pleasure, thinking that they're only going to entertain themselves with sayings and light stories, and that those were the author's only objectives in writing the book; but when they least expect it, they've already imbibed a good amount of moral maxims that they never would have read if the book had been written in a serious and sententious style. Books such as this are like the pills that are coated with sugar so that the wholesome antidote they contain will go down more easily.

"Since nobody thinks that such books are speaking specifically about him, he eagerly reads the spiciest satires, and even fits real faces to the characters whom the author never had in mind; but after he recovers from the delicious rapture of entertainment and reflects seriously that he is also implicated in the critique, far from being annoyed, he endeavors to keep the lesson in mind, and sometimes it does him some good.

"Books of morals teach us things, true, but only by the ear, and that is why their lessons are so easily forgotten. These books teach by the ear and by the eye. They depict man as he is, and they depict the ravages of vice and the rewards of virtue through events that really happen every day. When we read these things, it seems like we are watching them, we retain them in our memories, we tell them to our friends, we mention the subject whenever it seems appropriate, we recall this character or that from the story when we see someone who looks like them, and therefore we can profit from the instruction that the anecdote administered to us. So you tell me, ma'am, if it would be right to leave your husband's labor sunk in oblivion, when it might be doing some good.

"I am not lauding the work because of its style or method. I'm talking about what it might do, not what it necessarily will do. Much less am I saying this to flatter you. I know that your husband was a man, and as such, he couldn't have done anything with absolute perfection. That would be a miracle.

"This little book must have lots of defects, but those can't take away the merit of the moral maxims that it includes, because the truth is the truth, no matter who utters it, and no matter what style he uses to tell it; much less could your husband's righteous intentions be stigmatized, for they were to create an antidote out of the venom of his erring ways, which could be useful to his children and to anyone else who read his life story, by showing them the harm that could be expected from vice, and the inner peace, even temporal happiness, that derives from virtue."

"Well," his widow said to me, "if you think this little book might be useful, go ahead and publish it, and do with it what you will."

My desires were satisfied when she gave me this permission, and I set to getting it published without wasting a moment. May its success repay its author's laudable intentions!